Frank Moorhouse was born in the coastal town of Nowra. He worked as an editor of small-town newspapers and as an administrator but in the 1970s became a full-time writer. He has written twelve books of fiction and one non-fiction book.

He has won a number of literary prizes including the Australian Literature Society's Gold Medal for 1989. *Forty-Seventeen* was given a laudatory full-page review by Angela Carter in the *New York Times* and was named Book of the Year by the *Age* and 'moral winner' of the Booker prize by the London magazine *Blitz*. *Grand Days*, the first of the Palais des Nations novels, won the SA Premier's Award for Fiction.

In recent years, Moorhouse has lived in Australia, France, Geneva and the UK, travelling in Europe and the Middle East where he has pursued a preoccupation with peace-keeping and with international relations. 'I am writing about the League of Nations because it is a trunk in the attic of history which has not been properly opened. It contains haunted, bitter and embarrassing stories for the world, but was also a human experiment of immense grandeur. They are stories which I have wanted to know and write since my school days.'

BY THE SAME AUTHOR

FICTION
Futility and Other Animals
The Americans, Baby
The Electrical Experience
Tales of Mystery and Romance
Conference-ville
The Everlasting Secret Family and Other Secrets
Forty-Seventeen
Dark Palace

OTHER BOOKS
Room Service
Lateshows
Loose Living

NON-FICTION
Days of Wine and Rage

BOOKS EDITED BY THE AUTHOR
Coast to Coast 1973
State of the Art
Fictions 88
A Steele Rudd Selection
Prime Ministers of Australia

COLLECTED WORKS
Selected Stories (also published as The Coca-Cola Kid)

FILM AND TELEVISION SCRIPTS
Between Wars (feature film)
Coca-Cola Kid (feature film)
Everlasting Secret Family (feature film)
Conference-ville (telemovie)
Time's Raging (with Sophia Turkiewicz, telemovie)
The Disappearance of Azaria Chamberlain (docudrama)

Grand Days

THE COMPANION NOVEL TO *DARK PALACE*

FRANK MOORHOUSE

V

VINTAGE

A Vintage Book
Published by
Random House Australia Pty Ltd
20 Alfred Street, Milsons Point, NSW 2061
http://www.randomhouse.com.au

Sydney   New York   Toronto
London   Auckland   Johannesburg

Originally published 1993 by Pan Macmillan Publishers
This Vintage edition first published 2000

National Library of Australia
Cataloguing-in-Publication Entry

Moorhouse, Frank, 1938- .
Grand days: the companion novel to Dark palace.

New ed.
ISBN 1 74051 037 2 (pbk.)

1. League of Nations - History - fiction. 2. Man-woman
relationships - Fiction. 3. Women diplomats - Fiction.
4. Historical fiction. I. Title

A823.3

Cover painting by J W Waterhouse
Cover design by Greendot Design
Printed and bound by Griffin Press, Netley, South Australia

10 9 8 7 6 5 4 3

I thank the Australian people, who, through the Creative Fellowship program and other agencies, made this book possible.

In particular, I thank the then Chairman of the Australian Council, Donald Horne, who with the then Australian Treasurer, Paul Keating, had the vision and will to set up the Creative Fellowship program.

'The League of Nations (1920–1946) . . . mankind's first effort at permanent, organised, world-wide international cooperation to prevent war and promote human well-being.'

DR HANS AUFRICHT

'The League of Nations . . . was a failure too bitter . . . it is as if it had been swept under the rug and that all its grandeur has no power to sway us now, and all its misery cannot serve to teach us.'

EMERY KELEN, *Peace in Their Time*

CONTENTS

How Edith Campbell Berry Ate Six Courses and
Practised the Seven Ways in the Dining Car on the
Train from Paris to Geneva 1

Presenting One's Credentials 31

International Civil Cowgirl 71

Entrée à la Haute Direction 119

The Accepting of Gifts: Miss Dickinson's Chair 147

International Language: Scat Singing, its Ramifications,
Magnitude, and Consequences 181

The Question of Germany 207

The Economics of Self 245

The Receiving of Envoys: George McDowell Comes
to Town 277

Public Life (1): Cry Me a River 307

Public Life (2): Return to the Molly 339

Confidence and the Giving of Confidences 359

Pact of Peace 393

Holding the Fort: The Night Sacco and Vanzetti Died 427

The Tenets of Civilisation and Various Wonders Not
to Be Talked Of 451

The Nature of Spies   479

The Weight of the Stone   537

The Key to All Predicaments   557

The Dance of Negotiation   587

Tramcar terminus Palais des Nations   631

The Years Which Followed   675

Postscript   677

Historical Notes

Rationalism   679

Eugenics   679

Union for Democratic Control   680

The World Population Conference   680

Under Secretaries-General   680

How a Registry Works – an overview   681

The Importance of the Duplicating Machine   685

The Covenant of the League of Nations – with
commentary   687

Structure of the League   689

Assembly   690

Council   690

Permanent Secretariat   692

Secretary-General   692

equally to men and women   692

diplomatic privileges   692

reduction of national armaments   693

manufacture by private enterprise of munitions and implements of war   693

external aggression   694

arbitration   695

Court of International Justice   696

severance of all trade or financial relations   698

Members of the League shall severally contribute to the armed forces to be used to protect the covenants of the League   699

Every treaty or international engagement entered into hereafter by any Member of the League shall be forthwith registered   700

Monroe Doctrine   701

peoples not yet able to stand by themselves   702

mandate   702

fair and humane conditions of labour   703

traffic in women   703

traffic in opium and other dangerous drugs   703

freedom of communications and of transit   704

prevention and control of disease   704

Red Cross   704

Original Members of the League of Nations   705

Who is Who in the Book   707

Acknowledgements   713

GENEVA
IN THE NINETEEN-TWENTIES

This book is, in part, based on the dramatic reconstruction of real people, identified by their actual names, and on fictional characters who sometimes embody features of people who existed at the time, but who are essentially fictional (see 'Who is Who in the Book'). Where people who actually existed say anything substantial, their words are taken from documentary sources.

All the historical and politically substantial events depicted (and quite a few of the insubstantial events) are inspired by documentary sources.

But the book is, above all, a work of the imagination.

ORGANISATIONAL CHART OF THE LEAGUE OF NATIONS, 1930

SECRETARY-GENERAL (British)

DEPUTY SECRETARY-GENERAL (French)

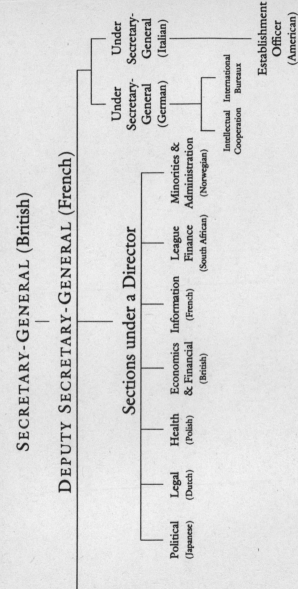

Sections under a Chief of Section

| Political (Japanese) | Legal (Dutch) | Health (Polish) | Economics & Financial (British) | Information (French) | League Finance (South African) | Minorities & Administration (Norwegian) |

Sections under a Director

Under Secretary-General (German)

Intellectual Cooperation   International Bureaux

Under Secretary-General (Italian)

Establishment Officer (American)

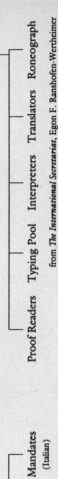

Social (British)   Disarmament (Spanish)   Transit (Belgian)   Mandates (Italian)

Proof Readers   Typing Pool   Interpreters   Translators   Roneograph

from *The International Secretariat*, Egon F. Ranshofen-Wertheimer

GRAND DAYS

How Edith Campbell Berry Ate Six Courses
and Practised the Seven Ways in the
Dining Car on the Train from
Paris to Geneva

On the train from Paris to Geneva, Edith Campbell Berry, at twenty-six, having heard the gong, made her way to the first sitting and her first lunch in a railway dining car.

She moved, in what she felt was a gathered-together way, along to the dining car, having remembered not to leave anything of value back at her seat, even if it were a first-class seat, and yet not having things in her hands — something she had a phobia about, having too many things in her hands. To have free hands allowed her to ward and hold, which she considered important in the technique of travelling. It could be considered as one of her Ways of Going. She also quickly noted to herself that, in life, she wanted to be a holding person and not always a warding person, and would describe herself as a holding person in all its meanings, which she would one day list. Fear in foreign places made one a permanent sentry, and more of a warding person than one would be in a familiar place. However, as she moved along the swaying train, trying not to need to use her hands or to lose her balance, Edith considered that she conducted her body well. In travel and in life. So far.

Her Ways of Going were mostly what she had thought about during the early part of the journey after the train had left the Gare de Lyon, especially as they applied to conversation. She had developed most of the Ways on the voyage over from Australia but they now needed refinement and further practice.

On the train from Paris to Geneva, Edith Campbell Berry, at twenty-six, made her way to her first lunch in a railway dining

3

car, in first class, at the first sitting, conducting herself well.

To keep her hands free she had a sensible, leather shoulder bag with outside pockets and a glove loop, a travelling bag which had belonged to her mother and, though far from new, was well-cared for, and had a remote odour of coachaline and polish. A bag which she privately considered to have a well-bred look and although she was an egalitarian through and through, she did not mind the well-bred look or what she took to be a well-bred look. She was, after all, well-bred. The bag was an Object of Ancestry.

She stood inside the door of the dining car and read the notice, *Reclami, reclamations, complaints*, more times than was necessary for comprehension, until the waiter showed her to her table.

At her table was a man in his late thirties. The waiter said something in French about whether she minded sharing a table with a gentleman. Edith said something in French about not minding the sharing of the table with a gentleman. The gentleman half-stood, half-bowed, holding his napkin to his lap with one hand, and smiled.

As the waiter seated her, the man spoke in English.

'I was about . . .' he said, the half-sentence hovering between them. Edith watched. Edith already knew the Way of Circumspection, and she waited to see how long he would allow the sentence to hover, she holding herself ready, of course, to save things, as always. He looked away and then said, '. . . to order a sherry. Would you care to join me in a sherry?' The sentence, having finished hovering, landed like a friendly bird.

'Why, yes, I will join you in a sherry,' she said strongly, and her joining him in the drinking of a sherry magically changed the bird into a warm cloud. The small green-shaded table lamp also now included them in its unnecessary daytime illumination, as the situation changed from what it had been — a nervous seating of two strangers at lunch in a railway dining car — into, indeed, lunch for two.

'The railway catering services . . .' he said incompletely, the half-sentence no longer birdlike, but now a sentence wanting to be joined, desiring the company of another part, to be overlapped by words to be given by her, the overlapping of his words with her words in the manner of sociability, a touching of a kind, not as intimate as a hand on another hand, but reflecting the nature of two strangers dining amiably. Edith joined him not with some words but with an amiable smile, which allowed him to be sure that she was within the conversation.

'I have been told — ' Edith said, finding a thought forming.

But his words nervously ran into hers. 'Oh, but, well, let me put it this way — '

This time she saw his words as a shawl which he was placing around her shoulder to make sure that she was, indeed, comfortably in, maybe forgetting what it was he had begun to say, or maybe it was an English way.

From incompleteness he leapt to mock assertion. 'I do firmly believe one thing,' he said, firmly. He believed that, as an aperitif, sherry was coming back and that the cocktail would go, but he believed with all his heart, and thankfully, that the serving of olives with drinks would not go, and that the serving of wine biscuits would not come back now that sherry was. Then he trailed off into silence, making courteous space for her in the conversation, to let her well and truly in, and, she could tell, also trying to avoid going from half-statements to overtalking which was caused, she appraised, by his pleasure at her joining with him in conversational lunch, and maybe from his taking pleasure at the way she looked and also pleasure from her having granted him the special bond which was taken to exist between those who took alcoholic drinks together, a bond she could not analyse just now, but which had to do with sharing a heightened openness — maybe the willingness to take a small subtle risk?

'Yes,' Edith said simply, having nothing much to say in favour of wine biscuits and having eaten olives only once, and with difficulty.

'What I really meant was — no, please — first you say what you intended to say earlier.'

'I'd rather you went on . . .'

'All right, then. I was going to say that the railway catering service is an institution which has few to praise it and very few indeed to love it.' The sentence seemed quite long, given the slow start to the conversation.

'I know,' Edith hastened to say, not knowing at all, conscious that she'd agreed too quickly because of her own enthusiasm for the conversation. 'Please, go on.'

'I have never met anyone who would praise or admit to love . . .' he said, then as if looking down at his words and seeing that he needed a few more, '. . . to love of the railway dining car as an institution.'

'I was told never to order soup on trains,' she said, happily finding something to say, hoping that it was, in fact, something to say. 'And Lord Curzon says that only the middle classes have soup for luncheon.' She felt that she would like to add a touch to this sentence, and so said, 'And that is all I know of soup and of railway dining cars as an institution.' Pleased with her humorous use of the Way of Companionable Confession. If only a confession of unsophistication of the minor order.

'As for the first proposition,' he said, his words slowing as he relaxed, 'I have recently performed the train soup splash-and-spill test on the Paris Nord . . .' he paused, showing on his face an effort of recollection, '. . . and on the London, Midland and

Scottish,' a further effort of recollection, '. . . and the Great Northern and, whether due to slower trains, or to twelve-wheeled bogies, or to smaller portions, I have not splashed or spilled.' He didn't smile when he told her this; he could very well have been correcting her. She wasn't sure. He went on, 'Turning now to your second proposition, did you know Lord Curzon?'

'Oh no,' she said. 'A fellow countryman, John Latham, reported that to me.'

'I have heard of Latham,' he said. 'As it happens, I worked with Lord Curzon. Went to his funeral last month. Stood there at the service saying to myself, "My name is George Nathaniel Curzon, I am a most superior person." And then, at the grave-side, changing it to, "was a most superior person". Lord Curzon never spoke to me of soup, but he did speak to me of inkstands.'

'Inkstands?'

'I was in the Foreign Office when he was Secretary of State and he called me in and pointed at the inkstand on the table and said, "A Secretary of State must have an inkstand of crystal and silver, not of brass and glass." '

Edith was interested to surmise that this man could be on his way to Geneva to do business with the League but she felt that on the matter of Lord Curzon she had nothing more to say. On the matter of crystal and silver inkstands and on the matter of brass and glass inkstands, she could, once started, have too much to say. She had, perhaps, a disproportionate interest in the things that went on tables, and in the decoration and design of things. To put it more precisely, she had an abiding passion for *l'art de la table*. Only yesterday in Paris, she had again visited the *Exposition des Arts Décoratifs*. For her to begin to speak at this point on such matters would bring about an avalanche of attitude from her, and she restrained herself. Instead she examined his gambit-in-response, and felt that he had not fully understood about the eating of soup on trains, or had not been listening closely; that he was, in part, pretending to understand what she'd said about soup and trains and that the theme of his answer had been more to display his travelled life than to exchange wisdom about soup and dining cars.

She would not let it pass. Otherwise they might stray further and further from mutual understanding. She always feared that in some unforeseeable way small early confusions led later to giant embarrassments.

'It is not to do so much with the soup in the plate, I am told, but more to do with the soup in the spoon on its way to the mouth. That is where the difficulty lies. It is not a problem of portions small or large in the plate. Or bogies. Further, I am told that it has to do with the unexpected stopping of the train — that's the incontestable danger point. It jerks. The train jerks.' She wanted him to understand, to get this soup business, at least, clear. 'I am, of course, only told this, this being my first meal on a train.' Throwing him another confession of unsophistication when she had not meant to. She felt the conversation stumble from her having talked too long and too intensely. It was almost lost, she thought, the easiness of the conversation, almost lost. She noticed also how much deceptive pose there was in her pedantic prattle about soup which hid her happy, inner anticipation of her first meal on a train, on the train from Paris to Geneva, with a strange man, a man she liked the look of, all of which she feared showing because her artless exhilaration would make her appear unworldly.

'I see, of course.' He tried then to fortify his statement. 'But the size of portions and the shape of the plate can matter when the train sways at high speeds.'

Edith felt he was on lost ground and left him there. He

would, on reflection at some future time, understand her clarification on the matter of soups and trains.

'I am not,' Edith said, courageously and wilfully deciding to save the conversation as she looked at the menu, 'overly accustomed to six courses.'

'When on a train, I would advise, but advise only . . .'

Edith watched him trying to regain his leadership in the conversation's slipping stream, a struggling British bird trying to gain altitude. He would advise her, would he?

'. . . I would advise you to order the full obligatory six courses, for one reason only.'

'Which is?'

'The killing of time.'

'I shall, then,' she said, 'join you in the killing of time.' She warmed to his tone.

'Together, then, we shall wage utter war on time,' he said, in a frolicking voice. She laughed. They settled now, both chuckling, perhaps more loudly than the exchange merited, but making it serve as a relaxing truce, allowing them to sit back in their chairs to read the menu and to order. She felt almost equal with him. That surprised and heartened her.

'I have an idea. Why don't each of us tell a food or wine story, with each course, an anecdote, one of us or the other,' he said boyishly, 'if we can, not as a task, only if we can come up with one easily, either you or I? Only if it's fun.'

'That suits me,' said Edith, already feeling it as a pressing task, losing the relaxation gained only a second before, wondering if this was an illustration of the British liking for games about which John Latham had told her, along with his advice on soup and other matters of the world. He said the British loved games but chose only those at which they had the skills and where they knew the rules.

9

After they'd ordered, both taking the *menu à prix fixe*, with him choosing the wine, he introduced himself as Major Ambrose Westwood. She introduced herself as Edith Berry, failing to put in her middle name, Campbell, forgetting momentarily that she now intended to use this middle name. They vigorously shook hands across the table.

She said, 'You were in the War?'

'Oh, I like being called the Major. I was in the War, but only as a doctor soldier, I'm afraid,' he said with a grimace, showing the customary diffidence she'd seen before in soldiers. She had trouble reconciling his being a doctor and yet being in the Foreign Office. She guessed that it would be eventually explained.

The soup Julienne arrived and he whisked it with his fork and laughed. 'Observe the bubbles — that's soap — we can be assured that the plates were washed.'

'I dare say we have eaten soap in one form or another all our lives and not suffered from it, but it doesn't stimulate the appetite. Does the talk of soap count as an anecdote about soup Julienne?'

'My apologies for having drawn attention to it. Childish. That doesn't count. You did the soup anecdote marvellously, antedate, as it were, and I have nothing to top that. Have you dined much in Paris?'

'A little.' Were three or four times sufficient to be described as having dined a little in Paris?

'This is my anecdote. Last night I dined at the Club des Cent. It was founded about ten years ago by some men who, besides a love of good food and good wine, love also the open road and motoring. They explore the food and hotels of France and, apart from lunching every Thursday in Paris, they put on feasts in other parts of France. The club has its own rooms and library and bar in the Faubourg St Honoré. Do you know the thing that surprised me at my visit to the club?'

'I do not accept the demand of the question,' she said, meaning it, because she hated those sorts of questions, but smiling to take away any edge of impatience. 'Given that I have no way of knowing what surprised you in the Club des Cent.'

'Objection accepted. What surprised me was this: the way they served the salmon — which, I have to say, was *première classe*. They placed the salmon on thick slices of crustless bread. Chunks of salmon on chunks of bread. At White's — in London — we serve it delicately, ever so thin slices on ever so thin biscuits.' He laughed as a prelude to what he was about to say. 'You see, we, the English, think of our way of serving salmon as being the French way. We think of the French gourmets as finicky, and so my surprise at the robustness of the servings.' He closed the anecdote in laughter, perhaps laughing to safeguard it from any chance of it failing to meet the tests of amusement. 'There was much discussion.'

'Much discussion?'

'You know how it is with food and wine enthusiasts.'

'I don't, really, you see we don't make much of a fuss about food back in Australia. Which is not to say that we shouldn't care more. In all things.'

'I'm sure that's not true — which city do you come from?'

What wasn't true? How would he know?

She realised she was being prickly, and should stop it.

'Sydney and Melbourne, but before that I came from a small town on the coast of New South Wales, the south coast of New South Wales.'

And she was, at twenty-six, having her first lunch in a railway dining car, at the first sitting, holding her own with an English gentleman to whom she didn't object, and she was disregarding the advice of both Lord Curzon and John Latham by having soup.

'I am a member of a dining club — the Saintsbury. Vyvyan Holland is a member of the Saintsbury.'

She observed that this was a conversational move which was not simple, maybe was not wholly kind, had something hiding within it. It was not only that she did not know the name Vyvyan Holland, and it was not that he was perhaps important and she should know — what was, perhaps, unkind was that this Major Westwood had said it with a teasing voice. As the conversation was running, she didn't have time to detect his secret theme. Was it, again, to give himself altitude, through displaying glamorous, worldly information about himself?

'Vyvyan with two *y*s,' he said, in the same teasing voice.

'Vyvyan with two *y*s,' she repeated, but she didn't make this a question; she wouldn't ask for his help. Not yet. As she said the name, she wrote it in her mind's eye, seeing the word with its two *y*s.

To ask, 'Who is Vyvyan Holland?' would lead her into the ambush of his tease. He knew that she did not know. She decided then to use the Way of the Silent Void, which she'd devised to overcome such conversational teasing and to hide her disadvantage. In her experience, the Way of the Silent Void usually forced the other person to explain themselves, and deflated the teasing.

As she allowed a silence to form in the conversation, it appeared to her, though, that he might be a Master of the Silent Void because he, too, looked at her without speaking, his mouth holding a small smile.

She continued to hold her silence, also bringing a small smile to her mouth. She steered another spoonful of soup to her mouth.

The silence was long enough and the void wide enough for

them to both hear the clack of the train over the track, and the conversation and laughter of the other diners.

She thought she heard a church bell somewhere out in the countryside of France.

She heard another diner say, in English, 'Buy Ford.'

At last he spoke, going into the void she had created. She quietly congratulated herself. However it did not release her from the tease or from her ignorance, because he said, 'In London, our club, the Saintsbury, meets twice yearly — on Shakespeare's birthday and on the birthday of Professor George Saintsbury. The club is devoted to wine and books.'

He was years older than she, at least, and from the FO, although as she examined his face, she felt uncertain of his age. He was boyish, but there was an exhaustion which dragged at his face. But he would have his Ways for All Occasions by now. Or maybe some people did not have Ways?

He was being inexplicable, being a dodger, trying to detour around her void.

But he was falling into the void, because he spoke again just as she was preparing to throw herself on the mercy of the conversation. This time he seemed to be presenting a clue but it didn't assist her.

'In Paris, at the Club des Cent, we ate,' he looked meaningfully at her, 'ortolans des Landes wrapped in Sicilian vine leaves.' He used his glance to prance the tease even further. She did not know what an ortolan was. She decided she could no longer either play with his tease or widen the void. She decided to Tip It All Up.

'You are teasing me. I don't know who Vyvyan Holland with two ys is and I do not understand your other references and I am not sure that I want to know what your tease is about.' She wrapped her Tip-Up in a simulation of gleeful laughter, to make

13

it pleasant. She felt she was correct in using Tip It All Up to stop him treating her like a girl. She laughed gleefully again to make sure that she was not spoiling things entirely and for all time.

He now dabbed at his mouth with his napkin, and he seemed uncomfortable, but put on a smile to show he was not too uncomfortable. She could see that he had embarked on the tease without foreseeing its end, and without knowing what it was he hoped to whet in her by teasing her. She looked across at him as the waiter served the oxtail Florentine. He was still uncomfortable. He had moved into his tease and now found himself without pleasure and without a way of gracefully concluding. Not very good for a man from the FO. Teasing could arouse unpleasant things in the person teased but usually, in her experience, it had to do with flirtation. Was he drawing back from the flirtation? Teasing was verbal tickling and, like tickling, could be bullying. She ruled out bullying. The thrill of flirtation, then, was what he hoped to achieve. She'd spotted the true shadow thrown by this anecdote. She'd Tipped It All Up when perhaps she shouldn't have been so impatient or insecure. Perhaps she should have allowed him to continue to tickle her into confusion and submission. She did not know how to revive the flirt.

In the silence the sound of the train seemed loud.

'It's really very silly of me,' he said.

'How is it silly of you?'

'There is no reason why you should have read *De Profundis*.' He was letting her off, but not immediately — not before making this not-so-enigmatic reference to *De Profundis*. She knew what *De Profundis* was. He was trying to go on with the flirtatious tease. Good. She let him finish a mouthful of food while waiting for the elucidation she needed. He was not being nasty; he wanted to pleasure her by teasing her so that she would not be in full control of herself, which was perhaps permissible for this kind of luncheon. 'Oscar Wilde. The manuscript itself is in the British Museum but no one has ever had access to it — some of it came out in the court case in 1913. And there's the disputed Methuen edition.'

He then delivered what she took to be his principal item. 'I have seen it — Vyvyan Holland's copy.'

She laughed, relaxing at the end of the tease, relieved by the smallness of the item. She was not overwhelmed at all.

He responded to her laugh by saying, 'I am being rather superior. Sorry.' He was now flustered. Having gained a little superiority he found it an encumbrance. He was not good with his Ways at all. There was nothing she could do to relieve him from his bother because the conversation had become unneat, they were both in confusion and it was of his making.

Ah. The name Oscar Wilde was what it was all about. That was the secret of his gambit. It was a name he believed could titillate her as a woman. It was a name about which hung sniggers and taboos. Although she was a modern woman and had talked about that subject — of men loving men — she couldn't lightly do so with a strange man on a train. But she sensed that the titillation he wanted to cause in her was to make her display something of her nature, to find out something about her responsiveness. Again, she quickly saw that it was not a nasty embarrassment he wished upon her. She decided to try her most difficult way, the Way of All Doors, which required her to try to be adept at talking of all things with all people. It would be the grandest way of all if she could ever confidently install it.

But he spoke. 'I'll begin again.' He was not teasing now and was going back to comradeship. 'You see, Vyvyan Holland, who is a member of the Saintsbury Club, is Oscar Wilde's son.'

'Oscar Wilde's *son?*' There was still more to the anecdote. The play was not finished.

'The mother adopted her family name because of the scandal.'

'I know of the scandal of Oscar Wilde,' she said firmly, testing her footing along the ledge of the Way of All Doors. 'Even in Australia we have heard of the scandal of Oscar Wilde.' As she said it she was disappointed with herself. She'd sworn never to apologise for her nationality.

'Of course you have. Anyhow, Oscar Wilde's son is a member of my club and, in *De Profundis*, Oscar Wilde recalls a meal he had with Lord Alfred Douglas.'

'His lover,' she said. 'Oscar Wilde's boyfriend.' She strengthened it with spice. 'His concubine.' Again firmly using the Way of All Doors and finding that she could go that Way with poise.

He seemed eased by her frankness. 'Yes, his lover. Wilde describes a meal of ortolans eaten at the Savoy with Lord Alfred, and there I was, eating these with Vyvyan Wilde-Holland just last night at the Club des Cent. So, you see — that is my anecdote.'

The warmth of shared purpose returned to the lunch for two, in the railway dining car, at the first sitting, on the train from Paris to Geneva.

As she looked over his anecdote she forgave him for his playing with her, and appreciated it as a rather breathtaking anecdote. Rather fine. The teasing had been more like gentle tickling. But the anecdote had, still, a question mark hooked into it, which she hadn't time to unhook.

She said to him, 'That was a fine anecdote.'

'Thank you. I'm glad it pleased you. Finally.'

'I have not eaten ortolans,' she said cautiously, his conversation having not told her what ortolans were.

'I was shown how to eat them only last night by Monsieur Massenat,' he said, and she noted that by his confession of a minor ignorance he was either admitting their equality or pretending to an equality, or appealing for an equality, careful now not to play with her or to try to overwhelm her. 'Monsieur Massenat took the bird by the head and put its body into his mouth. Thus.' He mimed this.

Conversationally, the waiting, at least, had worked. She now knew something of what an ortolan was.

'Biting through the neck, you chew gently, rejecting any tough morsels. The tiny bones will break. I felt like a cat. So small are the birds that three make only a moderate size course. We accompanied it with a burgundy from 1919, Clos de Tart.'

'We have had to travel some distance to reach the conclusion of this anecdote,' she laughed, 'which I now observe — checking back over the conversation — makes no reference to oxtail Florentine.' They both laughed.

'I apologise. I talk in riddles.'

It was no riddle, it was a tease, but she had wriggled out of it and Tipped him Up, even enjoyed the tickling a little, and they were back together in the conversation. She had wriggled out of it affectionately and had not recoiled. She had granted him, she hoped, some of the pleasure of his tease, and she hoped she had not gone out of the reach of his flirting.

She laughed, and executed the Way of Companionable Directness. 'It was a tease — you were trying to tease me, if not to embarrass me, for your own fun, and to flirt.' They laughed as he agreed, and they moved into a closer understanding. She said, 'At my school, new girls were not to be encouraged. But nor were they to be teased or baited.'

'You're very good,' he said sincerely. 'Edith Berry — Edith.' Using her name for the first time.

17

'Really, it's Edith Campbell Berry.' Wanting him to know her full and proper name, and then being quietly abashed at hearing how pretentious it sounded now, at least between them. Though she was absolutely sure, and her friends back home had agreed, that she needed a spirited name if she was to make her way here on the Continent. Anyhow, her visiting cards said Edith Campbell Berry. She would, at some point, get one out and give it to him.

He asked her whether she was bound for Geneva. She said yes, to take up a posting with the League of Nations. She enjoyed a tremor of importance as she said it.

'How remarkable! I'm with the League myself. Which section?'

'Internal Administration, division 1 class B.' She laughed, enjoying the sound of it and enjoying her feeling of self-importance.

'It's a shambles. Whereabouts in Internal?'

'In the Under Secretary's bureau. To start with, at least.'

'We'll be seeing a lot of each other, but I'm a notch or two above you, I'm afraid — I'm in with Tony Buxton, helping Sir Eric — in the *haute direction*,' he told her, also laughing at the pomp of the language. 'I'm dogsbody to the *haute direction*. Buxton's a great chap — one of the old gang — came over to Geneva with us at the start.'

She was pleasantly surprised that he'd be working there too. She tried to be mature and not show how pleased she was to meet someone else from the League. 'Tell me,' she asked, 'will they — we — admit Germany?'

'You'll find the Secretariat pretty much all for Germany. As for my countrymen, "unwise and premature" were Chamberlain's words.'

'If Germany could be admitted she would then cease to be a leper nation, could be taught the ways of civilisation, perhaps, through membership of the League.' Edith felt that what she'd contributed wasn't quite up to scratch. She tried to improve it by adding, 'Butler thinks it should happen.' Hoping that sounded authoritative, hoping that he respected Butler's book, which she'd studied on the voyage over.

'Brazil is the problem.'

'Brazil?' Edith feared she'd been caught way off the point.

'Brazil wants a permanent seat on the Council. Top secret. Only myself and Sir Eric know. And you.' He laughed. 'And Jules the messenger. The Germans want a seat on the Council but not at the same time as Brazil. Feel it lowers their status to that of Brazil. Which is exactly where I would put it. I'm inclined to keep Germany a prisoner, twenty years' hard labour, repay and repent, and certainly unarmed.' He held up a hand. 'We mustn't talk shop — in Geneva nothing else is talked. On the train from Paris to Geneva we can at least talk of frivolous matters. And, of course, as international civil servants, we have no opinions.'

It wasn't a rebuke. He seemed not to want to talk about Germany, as if it were exhausted as a subject for him. Maybe it had to do with having been in the War. Did international civil servants have no opinions?

'At least your government has conceded that the Germans didn't boil down corpses of soldiers to make grease for their machinery,' she said, finishing the topic in her own way and in her own time, thinking, then, that she had no right to talk that way, given that he'd been in the War. She watched to see if the criticism of his country had hurt him. He did not let on.

'Someone at Intelligence got it wrong, it seems, misread

some German document during the War.' Ambrose appeared uncomfortable with this confession of British error, or perhaps with talk of the War.

'It's taken seven years for your intelligence section to improve its German.' Edith bit her tongue, feeling that again she was perhaps pushing it too far and too hard, and backed quickly away. 'This is my first posting. I have not been to Geneva,' she said, taking a subordinate place in the conversation as a slap to herself for being a bit hard on the British.

He didn't let it go. 'They did tie people to the locomotives.'

'Oh, I'm sure they did things that were bad.' She looked out the window at the snowy fields of France, hugging the landscape to her.

He said, 'You'll dine well, and you'll talk nothing but League. You will even enjoy yourself. There are young people on the staff. The *esprit d'équipe* is fine.'

The waiter served the roast pheasant, Parmentier potatoes, and fresh beans.

To her pleasure, Edith found an anecdote rising to her mind without any effort. 'Chestnuts go well with pheasant. Do you know why that is?'

She waited to see if he had the answer. He did not.

'Because chestnuts are the favourite food of the pheasant. It isn't one of life's great stories, but it's an anecdote of sorts.'

'It is indeed. And I had not made that connection between pheasants and chestnuts. Oh yes, that definitely counts as an anecdote.'

'I also know that peasants, as distinct from pheasants, did not like chestnuts and would not eat them in France, even during times of great hunger.'

'Very good — two anecdotes for the price of one.' He chuckled and then said, 'Should lamb, then, be served with grass?'

She smiled. 'That, I think, annuls my anecdote. Must I pay a forfeit?'

'No, not at all, but my little joke must count as an anecdote.'

'Agreed.'

Edith let herself become aware that her curiosity about Vyvyan with two *y*s had been stifled earlier by apprehension and she had not, in fact, been fully true to the Way of All Doors.

She had been frightened, she was ashamed to note, to ask her way on into the hidden depths of his anecdote.

As they ate the roast pheasant, she concentrated herself to ask, and when ready, said as a preliminary, 'I do like one thing Oscar Wilde said — he said that he couldn't understand why we talk of red and white wine, when wine is in fact yellow. We should speak of red and yellow wine.'

Ambrose savoured this with a loud chuckle, which pleased her. 'The good thing about Wilde — now that he is quotable again — is that he said so many good things that one forgets them, so when they come up again they seem really quite new.'

He told her that on the PLM line she was entitled to second helpings if she wanted. She did not want second helpings.

She pushed herself back towards the perturbing gist of the earlier conversation. 'This Vyvyan with the two *y*s — is he as his father?'

'Is he "as his father"?' Ambrose repeated her expression as a way of grasping it. 'You mean, of the Greek inclination?' Edith supposed that was another way of saying it, his euphemism being a show of propriety.

She again reprimanded herself for not being true to the Way of All Doors. Euphemisms did not belong to the Way of All Doors.

'Does he take men as lovers, is what I mean,' she said explicitly.

21

She listened closely to her voice as the words came out. It sounded firm, not nervously firm, and not impatient. Just fine.

'I would say, no.' He then added, 'He is as his father, I suppose, in enjoying the good things of life.'

'Was Vyvyan aware of the reference in *De Profundis* to ortolans, as you ate them? Together.'

'No mention was made of that, no.'

She wanted now to ask if Ambrose was, whether he, Ambrose, was of the way of Oscar Wilde, but saw that she could not ask — not by any of the rules of casual conversation, nor by any of her private Ways — although she felt sure now that Ambrose had moved the conversation in this direction. Was that the confession loitering in his remarks? She knew that some conversations contained such latent confessions, especially perhaps with a stranger on a train, but they'd moved significantly from being strangers. Indeed, they were now colleagues. New rules now applied.

She considered again whether the Way of All Doors could be used to satisfy her inquisitiveness.

No, she could not ask.

Edith stared out the window of the train and said to herself, Edith Campbell Berry, at twenty-six, sits in the first-class dining car of the train from Paris to Geneva, eating six courses with a strange gentleman, a friend of Oscar Wilde's son, and disregarding the advice of Lord Curzon and John Latham about eating soup, and realises that she has no conversational way of finding out whether her male companion, whom she finds exceedingly attractive, is of 'the Greek inclination'.

She had, in disregard of another of John Latham's rules for a young diplomat, also lost track of how much wine she'd drunk.

The sorbet arrived and they agreed not to treat that as a course requiring an anecdote.

She then had a decisive realisation. It would be revealed. At some time it would be made clear whether or not her companion was of the Greek inclination. That was the Way of Compulsive Revelation, which was not a Way, strictly speaking, because it didn't have to be taken — it occurred; in fact, it was the Way which asked that no efforts be made, only that it be given space, time and implicit invitation to allow the compulsive revelation, timidly and appropriately, to appear at its rightful time. It could not be hurried. Though, she joked to herself, it must occur before the wedding night. If he were of that inclination, the earlier teasing took on a different character; might, in fact, have been meant as a warning. Or he himself may not know what revelation was trying to find its way out into his conversation. Surely not?

Picking up the conversation, he said, 'In places where there is dancing and dim lights, the label on a bottle of wine may not have any relationship to its contents. Geneva is a place where much dancing is done, some say only dancing.'

She grasped his meaning about the nature of the international diplomacy in Geneva and then again wondered if he were talking also of himself.

'Better banquets than bullets,' she said, feeling that it was a worldly thing to say, even if it lacked originality and was something of a *non sequitur*. It filled a space.

At the appearance of the cheese, she was quick to remember that the French had it before dessert. She also came up with an anecdote. 'I am told, although I have not been to Italy, that the Italians refer to the aroma of the cheese shop as "the feet of God".'

Ambrose thought that this was very good. 'Having begun this silly game, I seem to be the one always without an anecdote.'

'You told a rather complicated one to start things rolling. It could count as at least two.' And, nor, she thought, has it finished all its resoundings.

The bananas glacé chantilly arrived, with vanilla wafers and a glass of Tokay. Her first Tokay.

The swaying of the train and the wines now made Edith oblivious to any separation between her body and her social manoeuvres or, for that matter, of any separation between the train and her body. The wine and the train gave her a happy awareness of her body as she moved against the leather seat, of both the flesh of her buttocks and her loins, and of her fashionable new Parisian corset and elegant underwear. She was drawn to Ambrose and if she were to advance this attraction, it was best she determine whether he was the way of Oscar Wilde, who if she recalled correctly had said that going to a whore was like eating chewed mutton, a description she found objectionable. Maybe she could venture a Lure and see what reaction it caused. But Ploys and Lures could go off all over the place. Could go off in one's face. Not that she always resisted the unforeseeable. Knowing what was going on in a conversation was part of her training as an international civil servant, and also, was a way of becoming a woman to whom nice things happened.

There was no reason, she argued, why one couldn't nudge Compulsive Revelation along by using a Lure. Edith Campbell Berry plunged on.

'Oscar Wilde did, however, go with women — I remember reading somewhere that he said going with a whore in Paris was like eating chewed mutton. And he fathered Vyvyan with two *y*s and two *v*s.'

She felt that Ambrose could either find this amusing, or find it appalling that a woman should tell such an anecdote, or find the idea of a carnal experience with a woman beyond his knowledge or unimportant to his experience or he could find it objectionable as a way for Wilde to speak about a woman, about a forlorn person. Or he could pretend to any one of these positions.

Ambrose said nothing, but nodded.

That was not revealing. The Lure had flopped.

She struggled on. 'I find it rather appalling, that a man of alleged high sensibility should speak that way of another human being, a forlorn person, that he should speak that way of a human encounter . . .'

Say it, Edith, say it.

'. . . that he should speak that way of a carnal encounter.' That was the best she could do.

Ambrose's face became alert. 'Why, yes, that's my response exactly. I'm so glad, I'm so glad that you didn't find it amusing. The way you told it seemed to suggest that you found it amusing. It's not amusing at all.'

Which established that Ambrose was a person of fine sensibility but did not establish whether he was the way of Oscar Wilde. Why was it that she could not tell from the conversational clues? Was it his diplomatic training or was it that she had trouble understanding the British? Sometimes the nature of a man was revealed by the gesture and line of his talk, although she and her friends back home now agreed that one could *only sometimes tell.*

'How do you account for him having gone with a whore in Paris when he was so definitely the other way?' She felt this question would cause him to jump in one direction or another. Into her life or out of her life.

'Oh, I suspect that he was just revisiting, going back to that way to see if it was as unacceptable as he recalled it, or not the right way for him.'

'It would be distasteful for a man such as Wilde? Distasteful to go with a woman?'

He looked directly across at her. Perhaps he was now aware that he was being investigated. 'I imagine so.'

Was that it then? Was the use of the word 'imagine' a way of saying that he had no personal knowledge or feelings which could be brought to bear on this matter?

She pushed on. 'It is a line that cannot be crossed, do you think? Not happily?'

His face had become unrelaxed. He stared out of the window into the snowy fields. Ambrose was not at ease with this Probe.

She was tempted to talk away from the subject now, and go to lighter things, but she held back, feeling that because of his earlier flirting that she was justified in being curious, and in using the Way of the Silent Void to see what it might now elicit. She refused to relieve him from his subject, kept looking at him for a response.

He turned his eyes to hers.

'Oh, there are men who can cross the line back and forth, so to speak.' He tried to say this lightly, but it came out unsteadily.

Edith was unsure whether he was speaking of himself but he was revealing something about the practices of carnal love which she had not met before. This crossing of the borders. She was nonplussed. That was the trouble with the Way of All Doors — it sometimes plopped you down in the thistles. This was not an idea she had confronted before, that men might love both men and women. She felt she should leave it for now. Quickly. But she could not move the conversation fast enough and Ambrose went on. 'And there are those who live damned near the border but just to one side of it. There is another devilish zone there.' He said this with force, with the full effort of honesty, implying that it was not a serene place to dwell. 'The free city of Danzig,' he laughed, making a semi-private joke. She took his reference, a city belonging to no country, and maybe also the private meaning he was giving it. And, now, now, he was talking of himself.

Edith took fright and the Way of Cowardly Flight.

They were, thankfully, confronted by the fruit plate and she found herself again with something to say.

He had fallen into a careworn silence and she felt that it was her fault. That she had better carry things for a while. 'Orange, apple, and banana,' she said brightly, examining the fruit plate with more attention than it deserved. 'The three musketeers of the English winter.' She smiled at him, relieving him of the investigation not only because of her perturbation but also from tenderness. 'I count that as my anecdote on the matter of fruit.'

Edith was still in silent disarray from her efforts to use conversation detectively. Maybe she'd been successful by her code, had dared to go to a new place in ideas. She'd been fearfully close to a blunder, and a blunder could not be claimed as a manoeuvre. But a conversation couldn't be fully managed all the way. Not on trains. Part of the confusion was that it had begun as a conversation with a stranger on a train and had changed to a conversation with a colleague. It had at some point changed again to being flirtation, although she felt she wasn't always good at knowing flirtation from friendliness. She even suspected the flirtation had been moving towards seduction.

The meal was over. Ambrose told her not to pay the bill unless it was written out in her presence and never to make payment on a French train without a bill. 'Just good practice,' he told her. 'Keep the bill for the dreadful people in Finance.'

They returned to her compartment, which she had to herself, and he sat beside her and they sipped Singleton's, which Ambrose described as a single malt Scotch whisky, from Ambrose's well-worn and dented hip flask, in the small silver cups which went with the hip flask, embossed with Ambrose's corps insignia, and they talked of their childhoods and other things through the few remaining hours of the darkening winter's afternoon.

She'd drunk Scotch with her father back in Australia and it reminded her of those conversations where the presence of the Scotch decanter had marked his recognition of her maturity. She relaxed into the motion of the train with its sensation of velocity, the play of the light and dusk at the window, enjoying the landscape blurred by speed, winter snow, the feeling of rushing through time, the alcohol and its rug of carefree warmth, the steam-heating of the train, and the faint smell of burning coal from the engine. If she let her eyes become lazy, the window view became an abstraction of light and shapes. It was a winter dark when the train stopped at Bellegarde. Ambrose told her it was the border. They'd already showed their League *lettre de mission* and other papers to the customs officers who'd moved through the train earlier.

Standing together in the dim corridor after the train moved out on its last few miles to Geneva, looking out of the window, she admitted to him that she was rather elated at the idea of arriving in Geneva and with working for the League and she hoped that, when there, he might guide her in her work and watch over her a little.

'So you should be elated,' he said, 'Geneva's the place to be. And I should be proudly happy to be your guide, dear Edith, and to watch over you.'

Having, by her youthful admission, delivered herself into his care, she then let the train rock their bodies together, and she realised that the body also asked questions, and Ambrose kissed her, and as she played with his kiss, and gave herself to the kiss, she could not tell whether there was a difference to the kiss of a man who inhabited a place at or near the border, knowing more about conversation than she did about kissing. If, indeed, he did. As she looked over his shoulder, she wondered what a lady should do to give pleasure to a gentleman who inhabited this border place. And did she not believe in the ending of national borders? She returned then to the mild swoon of another kiss and, just before she entered the delight of the kiss, his body against hers, the swelling of his groin gave her the message that he belonged to the domain of men and women, definitely in that domain.

Presenting One's Credentials

On her first day, Edith set out for the Palais Wilson at 7.45 a.m. She was not dressed in her new yellow wool suit with the belt. She wore her familiar, but dapper, fine grey wool suit with black braid trim from her Melbourne days. She wanted not to have to worry about the feel and sensation of unacquainted clothing, especially the colour yellow, and, even though it sounded schoolgirlish, she did not want to appear 'all new'. Dress so as to pass unobserved. She had, though, heightened her make-up because of the grey.

She carried a parcel of personal things for her office.

Walking along the quai Woodrow Wilson to the Palais, she let a rush of exhilaration pass through her as she looked across Lac Léman but she did not linger and nor did she reveal her exhilaration to the passing Genevans.

She arrived at what she took to be the front door of the Palais, the entrance facing Lac Léman, but was directed to go around to the other side of the Palais by a man inside the building, gesticulating from behind the glass door.

That is, she thought, one incontrovertible error of the League. The front door should be where people expect a front door to be, facing a natural scenic attraction. Maybe the League of Nations had a higher order of priorities which could not acknowledge natural scenic attractions. Perhaps they had not beheld the lake. She believed in the Aesthetic of the Outside of the Inside. That the Outside determined the Inside, was part of the Inside. She wondered whether that should go on to her list of suggestions for improving the League which she felt a good officer with initiative and drive would be expected to have upon joining. She then thought that her saying, 'The front door should be where people expect a front door to be,' sounded like something Alice might have said to the Queen. And what would the Queen have replied? 'Sometimes in this world,' the Queen would have said, 'it is better to look both ways — hence to have two fronts and no back.'

Edith passed two dogs playing at the 'front door'. On the steps, she had a momentary but elusive and extraneous thought about carnal love, something from a joke she remembered from the non-members' bar at Parliament House in Melbourne about the 'two-backed beast', which she had, embarrassedly, asked John Latham to explain. He had not, though, made fun of her in his explanation.

She found herself standing, at last, in the foyer of the Palais Wilson, in the foyer of the League of Nations, in Geneva. Here, in the foyer of the League of Nations, Edith Campbell Berry stands.

This, she thought, is the very centre of the political universe. 'But only if you think the world is made up of a centre with all else being periphery,' the Queen commented. True, there are various systems of spherical co-ordinates, she told the Queen, and I have studied celestial mechanics.

Edith saw that the foyer area ran all the way through the building from 'front' to the 'back', to the door at which she had first arrived. She looked up, up the huge central stairwell rising from the foyer and around which the building was constructed, up the five floors to the skylight. She saw four clocks, one on each landing, all saying 8.29.

She breathed the odour of the building's life and savoured it.

In French, she asked the concierge to direct her to the office of a Mr Cooper, who was, she understood, her immediate superior. She hesitated about giving the concierge her card, confused about the protocol of such an action.

'This way, madam.'

She was disappointed that he had reverted to English, as if he assumed she would have difficulty in French.

The concierge had a St Bernard dog which she knelt and patted, glad to be able to touch an animal.

As she rose, she said, 'Oh, is that the Glass-house?' and pointed to the large hall off the foyer.

' "Glass-room". The Council room. Yes, madam.'

' "Glass-room". Of course. Would you show it to me?'

'Of course, madam.'

He led her into the room saying, 'It was formerly the ballroom, madam, when the Palais was the Hotel National.'

She gazed at the room, allowing its authority to ripple through her.

'Two wars have been stopped in this room,' the concierge added, with a knowing pride.

She looked around at him and smiled. She liked people who loved their work. 'Were you here when it was the Hôtel National?'

'Some of us from the hotel were taken on by the *Société des Nations*. Do you begin work here, madam?'

'This is my first day.'

'May I welcome madam. You will be working in Internal Services?'

'In the office of Under Secretary Monnet. For a time, anyhow. Until they find something to do with me. Or send me home.'

'You will be one of my chiefs,' he said.

'In a manner of speaking, I suppose,' she said smiling, unwilling just yet to claim any command.

She again breathed deeply, savouring the dignified, wax-polished aroma of the council room.

'From which nation does madam come?'

'Australia. All the way from Australia. And you? Are you Swiss?'

'Austrian. Viennese.'

'Then you are the first Austrian I have spoken to.' She smiled and held out her hand. They shook hands and introduced themselves.

'I will escort you,' he said, and they went towards the lift but she said she would rather take the stairs.

'If you wouldn't mind.' He pointed at his leg. 'It is the third floor.' He entered the lift and the lift boy closed the clanking grill.

Before going up the stairs, she gazed at the board which showed the location of the sections and services:

POLITICAL

LEGAL

INFORMATION

MANDATES

DISARMAMENT

INTELLECTUAL COOPERATION

ECONOMIC

COMMUNICATIONS AND TRANSIT

HEALTH

SOCIAL QUESTIONS

REFUGEES

TREASURY

INTERPRETING AND TRANSLATING
PUBLICATIONS AND PRINTING
PRÉCIS-WRITING
REGISTRY
PERSONNEL
LIBRARY

To her they seemed like the names of hallowed battlefields.

She trailed her hand on the banister, thinking to herself that her three heroes, Briand, Benes and Lord Cecil, had touched the same banister.

Or maybe they took the lift?

On the third floor, the concierge was waiting for her. He asked for her name, apologising for not remembering it.

'Edith Berry,' she said, 'Edith Campbell Berry, to be precise.'

He knocked on the door which said *Chief of Section* and they were admitted. The concierge announced her and withdrew, giving her an encouraging smile. Did she look as though she needed the supporting smile of a concierge?

She saw a file with her name on it on Mr Cooper's desk. She removed her gloves and took her card from her handbag and offered it to him but he waved it away. 'I know who you are. We expected you today.' He smiled and shook her hand. They looked at each other but for Edith it was a blur of unfocused smiles.

'It's no good me trying to explain how everything works,' he said, 'the *rouages*. I think you should just plunge in. When you need to know something, ask someone. Think that's best.'

'Yes, I think so.' And she understood the French word *rouages*.

He said that she would be 'on loan', as it were, from the Under Secretary's office to Internal Services. He would see that

37

she was given experience throughout the internal administration. 'Do you know anyone here?'

'I know Major Westwood.' To give the association a certain firmness, she restrained herself from saying they'd just met on the train coming down from Paris. And had kissed.

Twice.

'Good. At least you're not completely orphaned. I'll introduce you around at lunch. Now I'll take you to see Under Secretary Monnet and then I'll show you your office.' He stood up and came around to where she was standing.

Outside Under Secretary Monnet's office she asked Cooper whether she would be expected to proffer her hand to M. Monnet. She couldn't remember what Theodosia Ada Wallace said about the etiquette of that.

'Proffer your hand?'

'To be kissed. In the French way.'

'Oh no. Only married women. A handshake will be enough.'

At the office of the Under Secretary Monnet she was introduced. She spoke nervously in her best French and she was duly welcomed. M. Monnet asked two questions about the animals of Australia and then she and Mr Cooper withdrew.

In the corridors, the building had come alive with people going around and about her on the business of the world. She glanced at their faces, trying to determine what manner of people they were. She looked at the smart way the women were dressed but did not feel dowdy. They seemed so much in command of themselves.

Cooper took her to a small office, opened the door of the office and she stepped in.

It was small but grand. It had a window overlooking the lake. She went over and looked out. A window box of dead soil awaited a spring planting. Her first window box. She touched the soil — her first touch of European soil, or was it international soil?

She turned, elated, and looked around the room. Her desk had a blotter and pen and inkstand. Glass and Bakelite. A fireplace and also a steam-heater.

'Are officers permitted to put things on the walls? I mean, etchings and so forth?' she asked, trying to sound in command of herself.

'Forge ahead. We in Internal Services decide those sorts of things. We are the Masters. Masters of the floors and walls, at least.'

She rushed to smile at his joke.

There was another door in the office which she tried. It opened on to a second door. Both doors were padded for soundproofing. She turned to him, puzzled.

'They are the connecting doors to the other office. It's from the days when this was a hotel and people took connecting rooms. You can lock your side if you wish.'

'Oh.' She closed the connecting door. She wasn't familiar with hotels with connecting rooms.

'I suggest you spend the morning finding your way about the building. Have a look round. Good luck.' He again shook her hand and left her.

She looked at the documents in the incoming tray which were only Roneoed notices to staff about remembering to lock doors and drawers and such things. There was a water flask and glass on her desk. She thought she would look for a fine cut-glass water flask and glass for her desk. And a new pen and inkstand, perhaps of polished wood. And a vase. There were three newly sharpened pencils which she noted were from Germany, and which she smelled. She imagined that she was smelling the Black Forest but then the sawmill at Tomerong back home wished to be remembered. There was a notepad and other stationery with a letterhead which she touched with her finger, drawing authority from it.

She took off her coat and hung it on the door hook. She undid her blouse cuffs and turned them back. She stood staring out the window.

The telephone rang. She picked it up, wondering whether to speak in French or English. '*Oui*. Yes.' Then she added, 'Berry speaking.'

'*Bienvenue*. Welcome. Welcome on board, Berry.' It was Ambrose Westwood.

'Thank you, Ambrose — Westwood — Major Westwood.'

She heard him chuckle. 'In the office "Major" will suffice. I'll pick you up for lunch. Unless, of course, you've made arrangements?'

She told him that, yes, in fact, she had.

'Quick work. I'll have to be swift if I want to see more of you.'

'Maybe after we finish for the day?'

'Right. Drinks at the end of the day. Fine. What is the number of your office?'

'I don't know.'

'It's on the door.'

She put down the telephone and went to the corridor and looked at the door.

It was 366. The number of her parents' telephone back in Australia. Since beginning her travels, she'd had a couple of such coincidences. She told Ambrose the number and the coincidence.

'Oh, travellers' coincidences. Happen all the time when you move about the world. Think nothing of it. We look for connections, I suspect. I will call for you at 6.36.'

'6.36?'

'6.36 at 366. Just playing around.'

She worried about the pension which had its meal rather early. She could call them on the telephone and say that she would not be in for dinner, if that were permitted.

And she was presuming, presuming that she would eat with Ambrose Westwood. She could hardly go to a café and eat alone.

'Will we dine together?' she asked in a hesitant voice, hoping she was not too forward. 'I ask only because of the pension.'

'Good idea. Yes, let's dine together.' He hung up.

Part of her wanted to go to the pension after work and sit in her rooms until they melded with her — and to move the furniture perhaps. She had to make her house. But she also wanted to make her way.

To make romance, even, and with an older man.

What did two meals together in three days and two impetuous kisses on a train mean in Europe? Impetuous kisses had happened on the ship coming over but that was something else — the shipboard romance. When the boat docked the romance was assumed to have ended.

Perhaps this evening she would find out about romances begun on trains with older men. Perhaps kisses on trains and meals taken together counted for nothing in Europe.

Or had she already begun a romance? Surely she should know whether she had. She put that aside, sat at her desk and assumed a serious posture.

She unpacked her personal office belongings: her hand towel, her soap, her tooth cleaning things, a desk photograph of her parents and brother, her poor lost brother, and a photograph of herself and John Latham on the steps outside the Parliament in Melbourne — she thought to herself that her clothing in the photograph looked so out-of-fashion, although it had been taken only a year ago.

She took out a framed *Punch* cartoon, showing a hotel named 'League of Nations' whose advertisement read, 'The League of Nations Hotel. Healing Air. A Peaceful Outlook from every Window. No Hot Water.' It had been given to her by John Latham and the others in the office when she had left. She briefly considered whether to put this up or whether it was, perhaps, a joke against the spirit of the League. She tried it on the wall in a couple of places and made a note to get someone to fix it in position. She had her framed bachelor's degree in science which she would also hang. She put her four reference books — Karl Pearson's *The Grammar of Science* and Butler's *Handbook to the League*, and an Oxford English Dictionary and her dictionary of French and English — in the small bookcase against one of the walls. She had one desk ornament, an antique brass microscope from the late eighteenth century which her mother had bought for her as a graduation present, and she had a silver envelope knife which her father had given her when she first went to work with John Latham and a fruit knife he'd given her when she had left for Europe. She smiled. Had both gifts been his way of arming her for life?

After trying it in different places on the desk, she decided that the microscope looked outlandish and she put it in the cupboard to be taken back to the pension.

The telephone rang again. It was Claude Cooper. He told her that he was plunging her straight in. That afternoon she was to take minutes at a committee meeting. Had she taken minutes? She said she had sat on committees and taken minutes since she was eleven years old. He said, 'Fine,' and told her she was to minute a committee meeting on future League accommodation.

'You can fight for your office,' he said, chuckling.

Indeed she would, if that were required.

She spent the rest of the morning prowling about the building, from the restaurant in the cellar to the maintenance platform on the roof. She stood atop the building and gazed around Geneva.

She then sat for a time in the library, reading minutes, reading the background of the sub-committee for which she was to take the minutes, and reading League publications. At lunch she met people from Internal Services and then at two o'clock Cooper took her to committee room B. She was pleased to see Ambrose there.

'Major Westwood from the Secretary-General's office, whom I believe you know,' said Cooper.

Ambrose rose and winked at her. 'Yes, Berry and I know each other well.'

Well?

'Berry will take minutes,' Cooper said to Ambrose.

Cooper introduced her to the representatives on the accommodation sub-committee, one from each section and service — too many, she thought, for a sub-committee. She went around the table shaking hands with people as she was introduced. There were two women, one from Social Questions and one from Information.

It was as if the directory in the lobby had sprung to life as a playlet. Or at least a junior version of it, because those at the meeting were obviously not senior staff.

Edith drew a map of the table and the seating. She put the date and name of the committee at the top of the page, then drew a margin and wrote in it 'Present', listing the names of those at the meeting, and putting herself first. Her first official League of Nations duty. 'Present: Edith Campbell Berry (minutes secretary).'

She asked each person to spell their name for her.

The man from Legal thought it a great joke. 'S-m-i-t-h.'

She said to him, lightly enough, that there were three ways of spelling Smith.

He said, 'Oh — I suppose there are.'

Back in Australia, she'd liked astonishing people by saying that she revelled in a good committee meeting. She thought of committees as parlour games where each person's contribution was their throw of the dice from which followed certain moves around the board. For her, committees were the Great Basic Unit. When you understood the workings of a committee, John Latham said, you understood the workings of an empire. Of course, there should be a place in administration for dashing individualism and for grand leadership, but in her experience it was never a bad thing for lofty plans to be brushed down and combed by the committee. And she had known the committee itself, at times, to be an initiatory engine.

Bad committees, she admitted, were the intellectual drudgery of democracy. It was said that some national temperaments were not suited to it. Tolstoy had said the Russians, for instance, couldn't endure the drudgery of democracy.

'I'll be in the chair,' Ambrose said.

'Mr Chair,' she said, 'do you want full minutes?'

'Put down everything of importance. Sir E. would like to see what people feel about the issue.'

Ambrose outlined the business. He said that the Secretary-General had authorised the renting of sixty more rooms in a building which would be known, imaginatively, as 'the Annex', so as to ease the pressure on accommodation in the Palais.

The problem was, which section or sections should move from the Palais? He grimaced at them. 'Sir Eric suggested Health or Economic might like to move.' He raised his eyebrows and looked at Health and Economic.

There were shuffles of resistance from Health and Economic.

'Sir Eric wants to make it clear that any move shouldn't be taken as derogatory. That is, whoever goes is not being kicked out into the cold.'

'Only into the damp,' someone said. There were chuckles.

At this point a latecomer entered the room. Ambrose introduced him. 'Liverright, I would like you to meet Berry. A new arrival from Australia. Our first Australian.'

The young, but worn man shook her hand. He spoke English with only the slightest accent. 'Nice to meet you. Fine cricketers, the Australians. Don't play cricket, do you?'

She smiled. 'I played vigaro.'

'Too bad.'

'What's your section?' she asked.

'My section?'

'For the minutes.'

'I'm from the Commission Inquiring into the Admission of Zembla.'

She wrote this down. 'Zembla? Z-e-m-b-l-a?'

'Up there north of Bulgaria, up that way. A principality, Monaco style of thing, about the size of Parma.'

She felt herself facing her first embarrassment. She could not place Zembla. She knew there were a few of these principalities and kingdoms dotted about, untidily left over from history. She could bluff.

'Oh yes,' she was about to say, but realised immediately that was not the right move. Her mind hovered, trying to alight on a safe perch, to defend itself against pitfall. She could not find a Way. She would take the route of embarrassed ignorance. 'No. As a matter of fact, I don't remember it at all,' she confessed, colouring, knowing that in their eyes she would for ever be a dummy.

'Then you haven't been to Zembla, by any chance?'

'No.'

'Could help us in our report if you have.'

'I think I would know if I'd been to Zembla,' she said grittily, glad of his silly question as a way of clambering some distance back from her embarrassment.

'Lovely postage stamps. Triangles with pictures of their national casino. You must have seen their stamps?'

She did remember triangular stamps but thought they were from Mozambique. 'I know triangular stamps from Mozambique.'

A long way off in the haze of her first day, a foghorn of warning sounded about this Liverright and she became uneasy.

Liverright chattered on, 'Historically, Zembla is a natural ally of Rumania. Has a sizeable industrial region. I spent every summer there during Cambridge vac. Learned the language, all that. Charming. Has no word for "war". Twenty-five different words for "drunk on wine".'

'All right,' said Ambrose, 'enough is enough.' He turned to her. 'Liverright's from Translating and he's pulling your leg, Berry.'

She blushed. There was some gentle laughter.

But she didn't know about what he was pulling her leg — the language of Zembla or the existence of any such place?

Liverright from Translating smiled at her and said, 'I was beginning to believe it myself. Sorry, Berry, welcome. Just wanted to show you we aren't all earnest-minded officials here, like this bunch around the table. If you want fun, come along to Translating. Once again — sorry.'

'A new girl is fair game,' she said. 'Although at my school, while new girls were not to be encouraged, nor were they to be teased or baited.' She wondered how many times she would have to use that. Ambrose gave a small smile to her.

'Well said,' called Figgis from Social Questions.

'Let's get on with it,' Ambrose said, after glancing to her to see that she was all right. She was still burning from the leg-pulling.

The meeting moved on without elucidation of the question of Zembla, and, if she could in any way avoid it, she was not going to ask.

The woman from Information started the discussion. 'It's obviously out of the question to move Information away from the Palais. We have to be where people can find us and we can find them.'

'What happened to the plan to build an extension on the tennis court?' Political asked.

'Not the tennis court!' said Dr Joshi, jovially. He was Indian, and from Health. 'Save the courts. I would rather doss three to a room than lose the courts.'

'This is not a sporting club, Doctor,' said Liverright. 'Although sometimes I am confused.'

Edith began to feel at home. She knew about committee wits and their butts.

'Building on the tennis court was looked at and found to be too expensive,' said Lloyd from the Building Committee.

'Economic would have to stay here,' said Economic. 'We consult the library far more frequently than, say, Refugees.'

Joshi from Health pointed out that their section had moved twice already. 'And may I be sentimental?'

'You may be sentimental,' said Ambrose. 'Continue in a sentimental vein, Doctor.'

'Our chaps are spending a good deal of time away on

47

missions in foreign countries, out in the deserts and jungles, so to speak, and when they return, well, they feel like being back in the thick of things and catching up. Corridor chats and so on. Cups of tea. So we would like to stay here in the Palais and feel that it was our home.'

'Very moving,' said Liverright.

Political said, 'I take it that the rule will prevail that a member of section is entitled to an office of his own?'

Ambrose said the Secretary-General was committed to that rule, hence the new accommodation.

Figgis from Social Questions said the rule also seemed to apply more to the men than to the women members of section. In Social Questions sometimes three members of section worked in one office.

'Women are more accustomed to working in coteries,' Liverright said. 'Sewing circles, that sort of thing. And covens.'

Everyone laughed and Edith was pulled along by the laughter and the camaraderie, glad to be seen laughing along with them although as a general rule she believed minutes secretaries should not serve as audience to committee members.

Figgis said, 'I would have thought men were more used to working together — in secret cabals and smoke-filled rooms.'

'What is the collective noun for a flock of women in Social Questions?' said Political.

'A Concern of Social Questions. They are known as a "concern". As in a "going concern",' said Liverright from Translating. 'As in "going to the Annex".'

More laughter.

'Come on, chaps, down to business,' Ambrose said.

'There are the loners — people working on projects who are not really part of a section team,' said Political. 'They could perhaps be moved away from the Palais.'

'Wouldn't think there could be sixty of such,' said Ambrose, 'but we could follow up on that.' He half-turned to Edith to make sure she'd noted it.

Mandates asked if he could have the floor. Ambrose nodded.

Mandates said that he had been authorised by his Director to say that the moving of the Mandate section to the Annex would be firmly opposed.

Edith felt a tension enter the sub-committee. Back in Australia, she and John Latham had taken an interest in the Mandates section because Australia held New Guinea as a League Mandate. Members of this Section had been a little too enthusiastic in collecting evidence on the performance of the governing country from sources other than officials of the country, causing some unease among the mandate powers.

'On what grounds, then, does Mandates so strenuously oppose going to the Annex?' Ambrose asked, nodding in her direction, as if to say, get this down in full.

Mandates ran through a list of objections. 'For instance, the question of the mandate of Iraq will be coming up at the next Assembly and we need to be situated close to the Council during that debate.'

'The chaps who ride camels,' said Political, 'and who eat dust and flies.'

'And in the case of Syria,' said Liverright, 'we have the chaps who eat snails and frogs watching over the chaps who eat dust and flies.'

Edith enjoyed the irreverence while not smiling herself.

Mandates went on, 'May I continue, Major?'

'Settle down, everyone,' said Ambrose.

'Finally, there is something I wish to say that doesn't have to go in the minutes.' Mandates glanced at Edith.

Edith bridled. She did not like people instructing her on

what should or should not go in minutes. Minutes were a legal record.

She glanced at Ambrose who gave no indication that he saw the contention, so she spoke. 'I feel that anything of substance said at this meeting should be in the legal record.'

Mandates pulled a face of surprise. 'For God's sake, Madam Minutes Secretary, this is simply a sub-committee talking about the allocation of rooms.'

Edith swallowed, gripped her pencil, and said, looking straight at him, 'My name is Edith Campbell Berry.' She then turned making a silent appeal to Ambrose.

He said, 'I rule that anything of substance goes into the minutes.'

She did not say it, but it was also her experience that only the minutes truly remembered. Committees had faulty memories. 'One more thing, if I may, Mr Chairman?' Edith said, relishing speaking out, feeling the relaxation which always came to her once she had managed to speak.

'Speak, Madam Secretary, speak.'

'This meeting may only be about the allocation of rooms, but how we set ourselves up in buildings is a portrait of ourselves. More than that, even, it is an assertion of the gravity and spirit of the covenant.' She then said quietly, so that it didn't sound pretentious, 'The physicals incorporate the philosophical.'

'Nicely put,' someone said.

'We could adjourn and talk among ourselves,' Mandates said, persisting, 'or does Madam Minutes Secretary, Edith Campbell Berry, have objections to that also?'

Ambrose laughed loudly, perhaps to break the tension. 'I have ruled that everything said is for the record.'

Mandates continued on, unhappily, 'We fear that to move Mandates out of the Palais could be understood by the delegates as being a punishment of Mandates. In a sense, it will be seen as being thrown out of the Palais. Downgraded.'

'We won't sack you,' Joshi said. 'Someone has to stop those black chaps eating each other.'

Edith suppressed her smile. She was curious that Joshi didn't see himself as black. And she also noted to herself that she had never seen a black man on a committee before in her life.

Ambrose said, 'At the start of the meeting I told you that Sir Eric is adamant that moving to the Annex should not be seen as derogatory.'

'It's the way it will be seen. I have one other thing to say. Most of us here have heard that the Annex is damp and is not a particularly wholesome environment.'

Lloyd broke in to say that maintenance work would be done to correct those problems.

'Be that as it may, two of our ladies have been seriously ill in the last two months. Mademoiselle Bonna is convalescing. Miss Elwood, whose health is never strong, is completely run down at present and has been under great nervous strain. She is threatened by breakdown. I must add that the rumours about the future of the Mandates Section have contributed to her condition. It would be a calamity for these two ladies to be housed in anything but satisfactory accommodation.'

Edith bridled again. She suspected the men in Mandates were hiding behind a sickly women argument.

This time she must have allowed an expression of irritation and incredulity to pass across her face.

'Does Edith Campbell Berry have a comment?' Mandates said testily. 'Perhaps Australian women are made of more rugged stuff?'

'I know nothing of the personnel problems of Mandates,'

Edith came back, 'and I know of no medical data supporting the argument that women necessarily suffer more than men from damp.'

She would let the covert slight against the femininity of Australian women pass. For now.

She saw Liverright pull a so-take-that face at Mandates. But she also began to fall apart inside. I am here less than a day and I have already made an enemy of Mandates, my favourite section. And I have behaved improperly as a minutes secretary by grimacing, and I have been made to look a fool about Zembla. Top day. First-rate beginning.

Ambrose stepped in. 'Berry is a member of section and she is entitled to an opinion and to courtesy.'

'Hear, hear,' said Figgis.

'No,' she said, gathering herself, 'if I could add something, Major Westwood? I may be entitled to an opinion but I do apologise to Mandates. As minutes secretary, it is not my place to display unspoken snide reactions to what's being said. I apologise to Mandates.'

'Apology accepted,' Mandates said, 'and apology extended.'

'Both of you, stand in the corner for five minutes,' said Liverright.

Ambrose tried to pull the meeting together. He asked around the table for the attitudes of the sections and services which had not spoken.

Joshi leaned over to Liverright who seemed to be dozing off. 'Wake up, Liverright. Suffering from the sleeping sickness?' He winked at the others.

Without opening his eyelids, Liverright replied, 'It is not I who am suffering from sleeping sickness, Doctor. It is the rest of you who appear to suffer from insomnia.'

He again won some laughter.

'I have the funny feeling,' said Ambrose, 'that no one wants to go to our new Annex. I'll ask for volunteers. Who'd like to take over a fine new building and live happily ever after?'

He looked around the committee. They either looked down at their notes, or shook their heads as his gaze reached them.

'No one?'

As they all sat in adamant silence, Edith looked around at them. I can handle this crew, she thought, I am not fazed by these people. But it had not been a smooth beginning.

'We could draw lots,' Dr Joshi said.

'Coward's castle,' said Ambrose. 'I'll report back to Sir Eric that his Papal commission having thoroughly investigated all evidence, rules that the souls of the blessed saints do come face to face with the Divine Essence at the moment of sainthood.'

There were chuckles as people sat happily slumped in the impasse, as if it were an achievement.

Edith thought that given that no section wanted to go to the Annex, which must have been pretty much known before the meeting, there was, in fact, no decision that this committee could have reached — unless some sections ganged up on one section and threw it out of the Palais. For this committee the problem was insoluble. It was the wrong committee for the problem.

She put down her pencil. It clattered and the committee looked to her, as did Ambrose.

'Our minutes secretary has spoken,' said Ambrose. 'This meeting is closed.'

People gathered their papers and began to leave. But most of them came over to welcome her personally.

The two women came to her and told her not to take too much notice of Liverright's joking or Mandate's irritability. 'Liverright's a smart aleck,' Figgis said. They both said that they would contact her and invite her to tea.

As the two women stood there talking to her, she was aware that Liverright was also waiting back.

When they'd gone, he came over to her. 'Hope you weren't offended.'

'I can take a joshing.'

'Good.' He said lamely, 'I hope I see you about the place.' He then said, 'Do call in,' with a charm which changed it from a courtesy to a personal proposition. He shambled off.

Her first day and her first approach of that sort from a young man. She was conscious that Ambrose was eavesdropping.

Ambrose and she were left in the room. She liked the aftermath of committee meetings, the sudden relaxing into informality as the gathering was reduced to those who were allies, or to those who were linked together as officials of the situation. Now she was left with her new friend who at the same time was an allied functionary — the chairman and the minutes secretary.

'Somewhat of a flop,' he said. 'Hope you don't judge the Secretariat by this meeting.'

'I was somewhat of a flop as well. Sorry.'

'You weren't! Not at all. I thought you were precisely correct. Handled it all well.'

She needed to believe him but couldn't decently seek any further assurance. She said, 'It was not the right committee for the sort of decision we had to make,' hoping to repair her position by saying something of merit.

'Who should make it?'

'You and I should've made it,' she joked.

'Shall we?'

'Make a recommendation? On what authority?'

'Oh, we could say that following the impasse of the meeting

the secretary and chairman make the following recommendation, blah blah.'

'Could you and I agree?'

'Let's try. Who would you send to the Annex?'

'On the evidence of this one meeting?'

'Yes.'

'And bring down on my head the wrath of whatever section we send to Siberia?'

He laughed. 'And upon my head as well.'

'Translating can go for a start. As punishment for japing me.'

Ambrose pursed his lips. 'A very good idea indeed.'

It was too soon to admit it as a fully certain idea, but Edith already sensed romantic competition for her between Ambrose and Liverright. She said, 'After all, Translating is not dealing directly with delegates, only with documents,' trying to make it sound a rational suggestion.

'Fine, we send Translating to the Annex,' said Ambrose. 'Write it down. Bundle off Liverright and his gang.'

She laughed. 'I suppose I could punish Mandates as well. But that would be unfair.'

'You would have the death of two fine ladies on your conscience. We will send Translating. We shall wage utter war on Translating,' Ambrose said, looking to her as he echoed their time on the train.

She smiled at him and gathered her things.

After the meeting she went to the library and surreptitiously looked up Zembla in the atlas and encyclopedia and could not find it. Zembla was, then, a fictitious country.

She sat there staring at the encyclopedia in painful consternation. What if she had claimed to know Zembla in the meeting? As, in fact, she nearly had. She would have been a laughing stock. She would have been the laughing stock of the League of Nations. It would have dogged her days for ever. She may well have been laughed out of the Secretariat. She saw it now as a particularly cruel jape. Maybe this man Liverright had not fore-seen its potential consequences or maybe it had been a test. Perhaps they'd all planned it before the meeting. Was Ambrose part of it? While she was filled with relief at having somehow escaped, she was, at the same time, alive to the terror which came from having been so close to professional disaster. She also felt wary and isolated. She felt slightly queasy. She wiped perspiration from the palms of her hands with her handkerchief. She had nearly ruined her career. She would be very careful of this man Liverright — more wisely, she should befriend him. But she would not forgive him for having placed her at such perilous risk. She would also determine if it had been preplanned and whether Ambrose was part of it all.

After sitting for a minute, she took a deep breath and went on with her work. She took down the staff lists and counted the staff in Translating and Précis-writing and saw that they would fit neatly into the Annex. The Way of Numbers.

Back in her office, she laboriously rewrote the minutes of the meeting into a new notebook, this time deleting the word Zembla which she had written down beside Liverright's name, redrawing her map of the meeting, in case anyone should ever, at any time in history, look into her notebook and find the word Zembla there. She put the first notebook in her handbag to be disposed of somewhere far from the Palais. Or maybe she would keep it as a memento of her first day. She would see.

At 6.36 Ambrose collected her from her office and together they walked across the lake to the Bavaria Brasserie where he said most of the younger set and quite a few journalists gathered in the evenings. Delegates also dropped in during Assembly, he said.

She wanted to blurt out her question about whether the jape had been preplanned by them all but held back, waiting for the time to be right.

Ambrose said hello to people and introduced her to some, but it was all a blur. Through her mind kept going the phrases, here I am in Geneva, at the League. Here I am in the famous Bavaria. Here I am. But the jape had spoiled something of her arrival by making her feel guarded towards all the new faces. It was spoiling her feelings about Ambrose.

They settled down at a table on their own.

He asked her what she liked to drink.

'What should I be expected to drink?' She looked around her at what others were drinking.

'What should you drink now you are a lady of Geneva?'

'Yes.' She wondered if she would become a woman who drank cocktails.

'What would you have drunk back in Australia?'

'Sherry usually.'

'Quite acceptable here in Geneva.'

'But what would the French order? It is, after all, part of the French civilisation.'

'Oh, the French? They aren't like us. The Frenchman would order a port as an *apéritif*. They drink other vile things made from artichokes and meadow weeds. Stick to sherry and you'll come through all right.'

She was about to take his advice but instead when the waiter came she remembered Dubonnet which she had never tasted, and she asked Ambrose to order her a Dubonnet.

Ambrose raised his eyebrows.

'I have to explore my new world,' she said. 'All my life I've seen advertisements for Dubonnet in French magazines. I always dreamed of trying it.'

She sipped her Dubonnet and to her surprise, could not tell whether she liked it or not. The glamour of it and her new surroundings overwhelmed her taste.

'How is it?' he asked.

'I really can't say.' She gave a helpless laugh.

'You don't know whether you like it or not?'

'No.'

He laughed with her. Raising his Scotch, Ambrose proposed a toast. 'To your career as an international diplomat. To your first day.' They clinked glasses. 'And your first Dubonnet.' He made it rhyme.

'Thank you. But I still feel something of a fool on this my first day.' She would edge into the matter now.

'You handled yourself very well. Liverright's awfully plausible — when sober — but you fielded it well. I would've stopped it sooner but he slipped it through. You don't know the story of Zembla?'

She shook her head. By implication he had attributed the jape all to Liverright.

'It's rather an old joke. Vare, an Italian diplomat, started it. An Italian of the old school.' Ambrose made a regretful face.

'As distinct from the new school of Italians in black shirts?'

'Correct. Back in the early days, Vare and some others invented this mythical state of Zembla and put a nameplate on an empty desk at the Assembly. Some of the Italian delegation sat at this desk and made a contribution to the debate — as delegates of the mythical state of Zembla. I believe Zembla can be found in the minutes of the second or third Assembly. I haven't looked. Ever since then, people around here have fantasies about Zembla. It's cited as the perfect member state. Never makes trouble. Pays up its dues on time. Doesn't expect us to find hotel rooms or "companions of the night" for delegates. Doesn't leave unpaid bills around Geneva. That sort of thing. Zembla is the only perfectly well-behaved nation state.'

'What a charming idea.' She would write to John about that. 'I suppose it is.'

'But you were all in on the jape this morning?'

'Well, we all knew about Zembla, yes.'

'Is it used as a test for all newcomers?'

'Test?'

'Do you always put newcomers through the Zembla game?'

'I don't.'

'But you knew that Liverright would be testing me?'

'Heavens, no. That was his idea. Spur of the moment. Thought of it as he came in the door, I would imagine.'

She looked at him. She decided to trust him. She relaxed and felt warm towards all those around her in the café. 'You talk about the "early days" of the League. It's only a matter of a few years.'

'I suppose it is. Seems a long time ago.'

She again glimpsed an immense tiredness in Ambrose which he quickly wiped away with his smile.

Relaxing into the atmosphere and to the taste of Dubonnet, Edith decided she liked being the friend of someone who knew the ropes. Though, she thought, it would be nice also to have a friend who was just beginning. At Parliament House she'd had a first-day twin who'd begun on the same day as herself.

Ambrose said, 'I thought we made a good team.'

'We did.'

'You colonials are so good at cutting through to the issue.'

'Oh? We think of you British and Europeans as the supreme schemers. I suppose we are always fearful that something is "going on" behind our backs.'

'That's why we'll make a good team. You can see through the scheming for me and I can teach you how to scheme.'

'Agreed.' He seemed genuine about wanting her companionship.

'How's the Pension Levant?'

'I haven't seen much of it yet!'

'Your trunk arrive safely?'

'It was there waiting for me. No breakages. One room looks out on a courtyard.'

'It was an acceptable lunch we had on the train, wasn't it?'

'I thought it marvellous.'

He seemed already to be moving their couple of shared experiences into an album of memories. That was fine by her. She was sure now that he was wooing her. But she was more nervous about handling a romance on the Continent than she would be back home. She imagined that the rules of the game were vastly different.

After they had finished their apéritif, he suggested they dine at the Hôtel des Bergues to celebrate her arrival.

'But,' she looked down at herself, 'I'm not dressed for that kind of dinner.' She looked at him. 'We aren't dressed.'

'You'll pass muster. I like your outfit — for something in grey,' he said. 'As for me, I see lounge suits at dinner these days. They'll admit me with a frown.'

'I would prefer to go home and change.'

'Won't hear of it. We'll simply go. The French stay at the Bergues when they come to Geneva.'

She wasn't at all sure about it. 'The chef must be good.'

'Knowing the French, I would imagine they'd bring their own chef.'

Oh, was that so? 'Can we sit at the table where Aristide Briand sits when in Geneva?'

Without answering, Ambrose got up, went to another table and came back with a cigarette. He then put the cigarette in the corner of his mouth, drooped the corners of his mouth, mussed his hair, stooped forward and said in French, 'Madame, may I have the pleasure — Aristide Briand.' He gave a French half-bow.

She laughed.

Still impersonating Briand, he said, 'They say those who believe in peace are goats.' He paused, doing a Briand imperson-ation with the cigarette. 'If that is so, *Baaaaah*. I am a goat. *Baaaaah*.'

She laughed and clapped him.

As they left the Bavaria she noticed that it had two entrances. 'I see that the Bavaria, like the Palais, has two entrances.'

'It's the answer to the dreadful wind here. The Bise. You'll see why when the Bise hits. They close one entrance and open the other.'

She laughed. 'The Queen would like that.'

'The Queen?'

'The Queen from *Alice in Wonderland* would say that in a nasty world it is better that you have two fronts and no back.'

'Indeed she would,' he said.

They walked from the Bavaria back across the lake to the dining room of the Hôtel des Bergues. At the hotel it became clear that sometime during the day Ambrose had reserved a table for dinner. She liked that.

Ambrose took the head waiter aside and spoke to him in fast French.

The head waiter then took them to a corner table saying,

'In my opinion, Briand is France's finest statesman.' As he pulled back the chairs for them he said, 'Monsieur, Madame, the table of Monsieur Briand.'

Her first day at the League and here she was, seated at Briand's table. She leaned over and put her hand on Ambrose's. 'Thank you.'

Ambrose said, 'We will not, I repeat *not*, tell anecdotes concerning each course of the meal.'

'That was fun,' she said. 'But yes, no encore.'

'We are now in Geneva. In Geneva we make gossip.'

She was about to ask for gossip about Liverright but, given what she sensed was Liverright's flirtatious interest, she thought it tactful to refrain.

But Ambrose and she were thinking on the same track. Perhaps Ambrose wanted to eliminate Liverright immediately and absolutely.

'Don't worry about Liverright. He's part of the flotsam and jetsam of Europe.'

'Which?'

'How do you mean?'

'Flotsam or jetsam?'

'Oh, you're out to test me. See whether I went to a good school?'

'One person is rarely both flotsam and jetsam.'

'He's jetsam — I believe he was flung out of Austria. When he was talking of the desert chaps eating flies I thought of the Austrians eating rats, eating their zoo after the War. Until the League pulled them out of trouble. Put them back on their feet.'

Returning to the business of the afternoon, she asked Ambrose why the committee meeting had been called when it must have been obvious that it could not reach any decision.

'Consultation sometimes must be seen to have been done,' he said.

She didn't like that approach. 'I think that wastes everyone's time.'

'Oh?' He stared at her. 'How would you have done it?'

'Perhaps we could have looked more closely at which sections really need to be close to the Council room and to the day-to-day business of the Secretariat — statistically.'

'You would consult the crystal ball of numbers?'

She coloured a little. She'd been teased about this back in Australia.

'Government by numbers?' he persisted.

'For some questions I think they're the only escape from the guess and the false claim.'

'What about political intuition and the wise insight?'

'In the absence of those rare capacities, I opt for statistics.' She felt then that she'd asserted enough for one day. She thought she'd better shrink back to being more charming and womanly, as befitted a young woman new to the Continent spending the evening with a debonair older Englishman at the Hôtel des Bergues in Geneva, seated at Briand's table. She said, in a soft voice, 'I'm here to learn. I am a bemused and lost colonial lass.'

He looked across at her. 'Not so bemused it seems to me. Not so lost.'

She could see that she had soothed him somewhat. But she couldn't resist another remark about the meeting. 'It might have helped if we'd changed the name of the Annex. Called it the Petit Palais. Something like that.'

He smiled widely. 'I do believe you're right,' he nodded with regard, 'and that is not a statistical solution.'

They had what was perhaps the finest dinner that Edith had eaten in her life. It was not the sort of dinner that a chap bought for a girl if he were not seriously establishing something.

In his company, her conversation seemed much funnier than it usually was, and she found that her knowledge of the affairs of the world, while still limited, flowed readily to her mind. As good manners were a means of putting people at ease, he practised good conversation which was the skill of making others perform well at conversation.

After dinner they had a cognac in the lounge and listened to piano music. He walked her to her pension and, still standing, they kissed quite passionately in the empty parlour and held each other in a full embrace, their breathing rapid.

But they kissed only once and he then drew back, as if observing some sort of courtesy, and began to take his leave in an awkward way, as if the passionate kiss were enough to handle just now, or as if he were uncertain about travelling further in the direction that other kisses might go.

She wondered whether the rules of romance on the Continent might require her to be more forward than she would be usually, back home, or even according to her nature. As she understood her nature.

As he made noises rather than words and pulled on his gloves and coat and took up his hat, it occurred to her that he was also unable to conclude the evening in such a way as to set up a momentum which would lead to happy developments in the weeks to follow. It was not shyness that she felt in him. It was an incapacity to take the romantic leadership. She could see that he would be able to propose drinks and dinners where the rules were unequivocal, but that he was nervously reluctant to initiate any more intricate intimacy. She decided that she wanted things to unfold. She wanted to hold on to him. She also wanted to leap into the experience of being on the Continent. She wanted it all to happen to her. She wanted to be experienced as a woman, fully and finally, and this man would help her do that, just nicely.

As she was about to let him out of the pension, she followed her grandmother's advice that one should begin as one intended to continue, and this being her first day, she began as she, at least, *hoped* to continue. 'Perhaps we could do something together at the week-end?' she suggested, crossing her fingers, hoping that she had not committed a social gaffe, seeing that it was a breathtaking proposal that she'd made. She had spoken in a worldly voice, which she hoped didn't sound more worldly than she could eventually carry off.

'I'd like that,' he rushed to say.

She pushed on. 'We could perhaps hire a motor-car. We shan't need a driver. I can drive. If motor-cars can be hired.'

'You can drive? Excellent. We could go touring. Motor-cars can be hired. Leave that part to me.'

She immediately regretted her boast as unwomanly, but moved quickly to undercut it, 'However, I have never driven in snow. If it should snow we would have to abandon the idea.'

'I am sure you could drive in snow, or through anything.'

'Thank you for your expression of confidence. Perhaps we could stay at a village inn in the Alps? Or is that a cliché for you?'

'Not a cliché at all, on the contrary, an enchanting proposal. Excellent. Take in the Alpine air.'

She realised that it was now some months since she'd driven and that the rules of the road were different — indeed, here they drove on the other side of the road. She said this as they stood there at the door, her hand in his.

'Oh, not much traffic around the countryside. As a foreigner, you'll be forgiven if you hit a cow. Show them your *carte de légitimation*; they'll salute and tell you to drive on.'

The hand-holding then became a shaking of hands, they said good night, and this time they kissed lightly and he ducked out of the door and away into the cold night.

In her rooms, brushing her hair at the dressing table, she imagined the Alpine village inn, and imagined Ambrose, in a very Continental way, creeping to her room after they'd retired for the night. Or would she have to do the creeping? In a very Continental way? She sang, ' "Your love belongs to me, At night when you are asleep, Into your tent I'll creep".'

On their first night in the Alps, after eating fondue, drinking kirsch — for her, another First Time — and after two or three glasses of champagne beside the fire in the parlour with the only other two guests, they retired up the stairs hand in hand.

Although she did not want another drink, on the landing she said she would come to his room for a nightcap from his regimental hip flask but would first go to her room.

'Splendid,' he whispered on the stairs.

In her room she examined her make-up, decided not to remove it, brushed her hair, poured water from the jug into the hand basin and washed her hands. She opened the window and the shutters and breathed deeply of the freezing Alpine air, cooling her face. She found it curious that she had no qualms about what she was now intending to happen. She wondered whether to take her nightgown with her to his room and decided that was too brazen.

She closed the window and the shutters and gave the fire a poke and then she crept to his room along the corridors of the chilly, dark chalet.

In his room she also opened the shutters so they could look out at the Alpine landscape, the room lit by the glow of the fire

66

and the moon. They held hands, heads touching, and fell into a shy, tentative but arousing embrace and kissing.

The embracing led them to lie still fully clothed on the large Swiss bed where they confided that it was not the first time for either of them. But she emphasised, a little breathlessly and shyly, but firmly, that nor was it by any means a customary thing for her. They talked of a close affinity between them, that it seemed 'right' for them to sleep together in the bed.

'It does feel quite correct, doesn't it? For you too?' she said, needing that assurance.

'Dear Edith, it feels very correct, very much the natural thing to do.'

'Good,' she said, 'but I have no nightgown. I could go back and get it.'

He thought that a good idea. He would warm the bed.

Back in her room, she changed into her nightgown and robe and slippers, hung and folded her clothing, quickly removed her make-up, but refreshed her lipstick, and again crept back to his room. He had removed his clothing and was 'warming the bed'. She could see his pyjama top.

She took off her robe and slid into bed beside him and they turned to each other, taking each other's hands, looking at each other in the moon- and fire-lit room. He had on his pyjama trousers but she divined that the flies were rather gaping, and felt that anyhow, it suited that their night clothing held them a little apart at this first eternity, allowing them to come gradually to feel and be accustomed to each other's body. Maybe the clothing allowed her to momentarily pretend nothing momentous was about to happen. She was aware that he had splashed cologne on his face while she had been in her room.

The eternity of this clothed preliminary innocence then passed, and their bodies entwined, their hands went inside the clothing and they lost themselves in kissing. As their passion overtook them, he muttered to her that there was 'no need to worry about anything', but the champagne and the quivering of her body and the blood racing through her had already banished any qualms, social or biological, from her mind. With a slight happy nervousness they found their carnal way and although this was not her first time, it was very nearly her first time, and it felt unique in a physical way. He was not a man made trembling and strenuous by his nervousness, as she had experienced in younger men who embarked on carnal enterprise, but was made careful by his nervousness and sensitive to her hand's tentative guidance. She attributed this to his being older and not, she surmised, to being, as far as she could tell in such matters, any more experienced. Their slow, unfrenzied copulation was more an introduction to each other's body than anything like a passionate enraptured whole, but she was also aware of the physical fit of their bodies being hugely pleasant, and of her disappointment when she felt him withdraw from her.

As they fell towards sleep, holding each other, she felt an immense, pleasurable comfort from being with him in the bed, and their bodies remained touching, one way or another, during the night. She didn't mind their mingled wetness that came from her to the sheets during the night although she worried briefly what odours her body would give off in the morning but could not see that they should be offensive to either of them.

They were awoken by the breakfast gong and looked at each other with some curiosity, seeing each other in this other private way, the way of the bed and the morning, smiling with a rather guilty smugness.

Ambrose made the joke that it was the gong which the Swiss used to remind guests to return to their rooms.

She was able to say that she'd heard that joke made of

guesthouses in the Blue Mountains behind Sydney, adding that she wasn't an habitué of such guesthouses. She had gone there in weekend parties, usually chaperoned, at least conjecturally chaperoned.

Warm in bed, she waited for a time to see if he would take her again, then when it seemed that he wouldn't, she contemplated taking him, but decided that what had happened already constituted enough for both of them to handle, so she held back her desire for further carnality.

As she crept from the bed into the chilly room, she was aware that he was watching her body as it was revealed by the clinging fall of her silk nightdress, but he watched surreptitiously, without seeming to look. Pulling on her robe, she returned to the bed and bending over, kissed him, then went to the door, opened it, and looked out along the corridor. Turning once more to wave and to blow a kiss, she dashed for her room.

She was in the room only a matter of minutes before the maid knocked with hot water. Before she let in the maid she pulled back the bedding and made the bed seem slept in.

As she sponged herself with the hot water, face first, and then her private parts, detecting no unpleasant odour, only the smell of a slept-in body, she announced to herself that in only one week on the Continent she had already begun a romance.

And even if it were not a torrid romance, she was, she appraised, now the mistress of an older man.

She had spent her first full night in the bed of a gentleman. Although she had heard it said on the ship coming over that spending a night with a woman did not constitute an introduction, she felt that she and Ambrose were now well and happily introduced.

She had presented her credentials.

International Civil Cowgirl

The first time she realised that she truly belonged was when she gave directions to a visitor at the Gare de Cornavin.

She had been about to say that she herself was new to Geneva, but then realised that she knew the answer to the question asked of her, and gave her reply in French, pointing in the direction of the Paquis.

The second change which she noted was that now when she saw the word Australia, while it still caused a movement of her heart, she no longer had an urge to bring it to someone else's attention. Words which reminded her of home still caught her eye. But I am no longer a visitor, she said to herself, I am now a resident.

Now I am a resident of Geneva, venturing to the old city for coffee on a clean spring afternoon. She savoured it by saying it quietly to herself and by holding herself conscious of it for as long as she could. And my French is becoming acceptably good.

She went to the old city for coffee because she felt it was as far from the busyness of the League as Geneva could offer her. She felt it was refreshing for her work to be able to cut off from it, and turn away for an hour. It didn't mean that she was in any way fed up.

What would happen to the old city when Geneva really became the world capital? Would the new world capital require vice? Or would the League stamp it out? Not that much vice still remained in the old city. It now was mostly on the French border, or so she was told. Geneva's *ceinture de chasteté*.

She'd attended Professor Zimmern's lecture that week on International Man and had no doubts that was what she was becoming. She was an international man or, at least, an international woman in training.

She believed that she and the others at the League were a new breed dawning. She did not think that being in her mid-twenties was too late to refashion oneself, while still keeping a grip of political realism.

Sitting at the outdoor café in the old city, on a spring afternoon in Geneva, wondering if she would be mistaken for a woman from a *maison close*, Edith tested herself to see if she indeed felt international, in any bodily way or perhaps, and this was not so silly, whether she was different in style of movement from, say, those at the other table. She moved her mouth to an expression of resolution, cleared her mind of self-consciousness, and when her mind had settled to blankness, she let it pounce on herself. She then looked to the paws of her mind to see whether any signs of transformation had been caught by the pounce. She found nothing in the paws of her mind. Though surely such a change in the national sense of oneself and the detaching of oneself would mean a difference in the way she carried herself. Didn't ministers of religion move in ways different to laymen? Didn't royalty move differently? Didn't sporting people? Surely, then, an international civil servant also comported differently.

For instance, if one were skilful enough, strangers could be detected by the way they comported themselves in an unaccustomed environment. An internationalist would never be a stranger, would belong everywhere, and yet would neither be a person attached to the soil of the country upon which they walked. They would never, then, walk like a peasant walked on the soil of their village. But never would an internationalist walk like a tourist. Maybe one would move more like a diplomat. She would study the movement of diplomats while at the League, although diplomats represented their own country while living in another. They were a walking and talking piece of their own country. She thought that internationalism might feel like patriotism but it would be different in its compass.

She took out her non-work book to read — more Balzac in the French — to make it clear to anyone who might be watching that she was not an 'available woman'. She opened the book but today her eyes would not stay with the page.

She was one of a new breed, as they all were at the League — well, at least those in the Secretariat. Maybe not the messengers or Roneo operators, but she hoped that they, too, were part of the new breed, because if they could not be made or won to the new breed of internationalism, then what hope was there for the League? Or did they come next after seeing the Secretariat setting a mighty fine example?

She thought about the messengers and Roneo operators that she knew, and decided that, yes, they probably came next. Though some of them were refugees and had education. Jules the messenger, for instance.

She would have to begin setting a mighty fine example. When she'd got 'being international' right, that is.

Yet drinking Italian-style coffee outdoors in the old city on a clean spring afternoon was more cosmopolitan than international. That was another transformation. She would also like to be seen as cosmopolitan. She questioned herself about having sugar in the coffee and whether it was cosmopolitan to have it or not to have it. She would have to observe what cosmopolitan ladies did about sugar.

She sat at the outdoor table in the old city and drank coffee and felt that she was at peace, and in place. Not at home, but in place. The right place at the right time in history.

Or was that a feeling of being 'European', as a style, that she was having? Cosmopolitan or European? She also made herself conscious then that she had a 'lover' in the Continental sense, and that helped to make her cosmopolitan. Although Ambrose and she were unpledged as lovers they had an established love affair with a carnal side to it, albeit a polite carnality. Somehow, it seemed quite acceptable here in Geneva, especially in League circles, as long as one didn't flaunt it. She was very far from flaunting it and still felt a little furtive about it all, even though it seemed that it was only at the week-end that she spent nights with him and even then told Madame Didier at the Pension Levant that she would be spending the week-end away.

But yes, she had a lover, and that was a very cosmopolitan thing to have, although somewhere she thought that it would lead perhaps to a proposal of marriage.

Maybe she could never be European. If there was indeed such a state of personality as European, which M. Briand claimed. One, she imagined, could not 'become' European the way one could become an internationalist, or the way one could, eventually, after exposure to enough strong influences, become cosmopolitan. Although in the sense of her lineage, through England and through invasions long ago, through a family of Saxon warriors and wheat-threshing women, she was by blood joined to Europe. Howard Liverright had told her that one could become Viennese, that the Viennese had all come from somewhere else. Being Viennese also had to do with being part of the intellectual life of the city, rather than from having been born there, and that to be part of that intellectual life was to be a reborn in some way.

There was something about the age-old feel of Europe and the way that this entered her very marrow, giving her a sense of return. As though she had come, if not home, had come back to her historic quintessence, had passed through the photographic postcard and walked back into the scene. She felt slightly ashamed about this filling of her very marrow with ancient sensations, about admitting to herself that this had been missing back home, ashamed about feeling that maybe she needed this ancient texture about her. She even wished that the buildings of Geneva were older.

Back home, she'd grown up in a brand-new house. Her parents had grown up in a brand-new house, and so had her grandparents. No one had ever lived in old houses. There were no old houses. She yearned to live in a house where people had lived for 'generations'. She wanted ruins which spoke of former habitation, of the sense of habitation built upon habitation over centuries, and lost worlds around her and under her feet. The building beneath the building. Musty cellars of wine. Attics of old things. Home had been without cellars and attics. Her life had lacked the Gothic and the sublime. She had to confess to herself that the aged world of Europe consummated her in some way and that at the same time she couldn't bathe in this feeling yet — she had to fight off pangs of disloyalty to Australia when she felt this way.

As Mary Colum had said to her in London, Europeans were used to places where for centuries people lived and died and were buried, where a long exchange had taken place between man and the earth.

She ordered a second coffee. As for reconnecting with Europe, she thought, I will eat and drink myself into being European with wine and coffee and *galettes St Michel*. That surely was a truth, as well, that one could be changed by the cuisine.

Yet there was another paradox in her thinking. She wished the League had its own new building. A new building would emphasise the newness of their breed. She'd heard the argument for taking over an historic building, to make the lineage of the League to The Hague. But, in truth, there was nothing before the League with which it could be linked. The League was the newest thing in the politics of mankind. True, they were dealing with age-old predicaments.

She luxuriated then for a while in the old city of Geneva around her, and with appearing — if she could but stand opposite and look at herself — very cosmopolitan. Just 'appearing' cosmopolitan was enough, for now. She allowed herself to bathe in that.

I am not confused, she said, I am transmuting. Coming forth. That in itself may be an odd feeling, but it is not the feeling called discord. She also consciously felt that her inner self was immensely empowered by her status as a League official. She enjoyed the knowledge that in her handbag she had her *carte de légitimation*.

Regardless of the book in front of her, she became aware that a man was gazing at her — thinking maybe that she was available, part of the Traffic in Women. Or thinking that she was perhaps a Bohemian artist. She moved her eyes far from his. She blushed and the blush became intense. Perhaps she should experience that, the going with a man for money. Once. Before it was stamped out by the League. She laughed inwardly. She must tell Ambrose of her inclination towards infamy. She confessed infamous thoughts to him because he claimed to be hopelessly depraved, in a private way. 'I become depraved after dinner,' he said, although she had never seen anything particularly depraved about him and he was very good at his work at the League. She was able to relax with him but she did not know if it was 'love', or even if it felt romantic. Maybe more adventurous than romantic.

The man's gaze having moved from her, she returned to

contemplating the life of the old city, and was surprised to see a military-style vehicle stop and park. It had no gun but it was, she supposed, a former military vehicle. Incongruously, a conventional chauffeur got out of it, and opened the door for two men. She supposed they were wearing something resembling a uniform but they were not from any national military that she recognised. They looked about. They looked at her looking at them. She looked away, just before their gazes linked, while remaining aware of them, and knowing now that they were approaching her. All the people at the café had looked at the vehicle and at the men as they got out. Why pick on her? Was it to do with the way she was sitting? She straightened up her posture.

'Ma'am?' an American accent said. Edith turned to them, shading her eyes from the sun.

'Ma'am — may we have a moment of your time?'

Edith felt she should perhaps tell them straight out that she was not that sort of old-city woman. How to say that.

'Ma'am.' One of the men was imposing and the other was obviously a subordinate.

'I am afraid you have the wrong person,' said Edith. 'I am afraid you have the wrong kind of person,' she said, aware that she was not saying exactly what she meant. 'I am not that kind of woman,' she added, 'I'm afraid. Sorry.' She tried again. 'I'm afraid you have the wrong woman.' She thought briefly that she might be speaking the wrong language, and should be speaking in French. She thought of telling them to go across the border to Annecy. She remembered someone mentioning Annecy in conversations about this topic. But it was no doubt improper for her to advise men on this subject. On a number of counts.

'Ma'am?' The American appeared puzzled.

'The kind of woman you are probably seeking — I am not

that kind of woman.' This time she was almost impatient with them standing there forcing her to keep on saying it.

'Ma'am, I think you mistake me. We are looking for a woman to help us in a very special mission. We are hiring. What we are about is legitimate business.'

Oh. In a military motor-car? She was losing her hold on the situation. 'Help you? Well, maybe then I am that kind of woman — a woman who helps.' She smiled at them. They asked if they could sit. She gestured at the empty chairs, wishing that they would not.

'My name is Captain Strongbow and this is my associate, Mr Kennedy. Strongbow by name and Strongbow by nature.'

She turned the name over to find his meaning. Oh yes. A silly sort of name. Or maybe his family went back to Agincourt.

'We are supporters of the League of Nations, of which you may have heard.' They paused for her to confirm this.

She looked at them with a renewed focus. 'Indeed I have.'

Captain Strongbow went on to explain his concern. 'We have come to Geneva to aid the League. There are people out there,' he waved, gesturing Out There, 'who do not want the League of Nations to succeed, who would indeed stand to lose billions of dollars if peace came to this earth. Billions of dollars. I speak not only of the armaments manufacturers.'

Edith nodded. A nod, she hoped, of an international civil servant, an internationalist, and what else? The nod, also, of a cosmopolitan. 'I should stop you before you proceed too far,' Edith said to them. 'I am an officer of the League of Nations.'

Her voice did sound different to her as she said it. She felt that she should warn them of what she was, sensing that there should be or would be a rule requiring her to announce herself.

'You are? Well, that's grand.' Captain Strongbow turned to his associate, Mr Kennedy, and said, pointing at her, 'Isn't that grand? We have here an officer of the League of Nations.'

He turned back to her. 'Ma'am, this is pure luck. You don't know how hard it has been to get to talk to the officials of your organisation when I have so much to give which would be of benefit to that organisation.'

'I have to warn you,' she said, 'that I cannot commit the League in any way and that my opinions are not to be quoted.' Was she being now officious?

'Naturally. All we ask is that you help us get the attention of the Big Guys in there,' gesturing In There. Meaning, she supposed, in the Palais Wilson. 'And, say, you could help us get the attention of the world as well.' He gestured to The World.

'You can make a submission,' she said, trying to think how an American could make a submission given that they didn't yet belong to the League, 'to the Secretary-General.'

'Oh, I've done all that. I ain't so good with words on paper. I am a words-on-ears person.'

'Tell me again the nature of your business,' she said correctly.

'You League people need protection. You need to be surrounded day and night by a protective shield.'

'You need protection,' Mr Kennedy echoed.

It crossed her mind that they could be 'gangsters', but what they were doing in Geneva she couldn't imagine.

Captain Strongbow went on, 'You do not realise how hated and feared you are by the powerful. The munitions people are out to get you.'

Edith did not like the idea of the League being hated and feared. She stared at Captain Strongbow and Mr Kennedy, realising that there was political truth in what they said. How much truth? She looked at what she imagined was the tepid, Genevan vice in the people and buildings about her but felt no threat. Still, this was Europe, the place of assassinations, of plots, and thrown bombs. Even here in Switzerland a Russian diplomat had been assassinated at the Preparatory Commission in Lausanne, just before she'd arrived. That had been done by a fanatic, not by an armaments manufacturer.

She imagined men in long leather overcoats filled with menace and she saw, wide-eyed, for the first time, Europe with all its political menace. 'Do you intend to protect us?' she asked them. She looked back to Captain Strongbow and Mr Kennedy.

'Indeed we do.'

The League did have opponents but they were seen as political enemies, or 'those people yet to be convinced'. 'You think there are people who would try to harm us?' She was attentive now.

'I know they will. They will try to *kill* you. At least to assassinate those at the top, and maybe all sorts of violence will be brought to bear upon you.' Captain Strongbow said this with much emphasis.

'Your building may be exploded, for one thing,' Mr Kennedy put in.

'Hence I have plans. I have plans for an international police army. Empowered by our President Coolidge . . .'

'By President Coolidge?'

'President Coolidge. President Coolidge said that an international police force was now needed. I have designed a uniform. I have an insignia.'

To her attentiveness Edith now added caution. She had reservations about people who designed uniforms and flags, unasked. That reservation was perhaps unreasonable, but the League had encountered a number of people who designed flags unasked and they were rarely, somehow — well, on the right track. Though this was the first person she'd met in the flesh who designed uniforms and flags, unasked, for an international police army.

With a charming insistence, and some conviction, he went on. 'We plan also, a people's ballot. Mr Kennedy has the details. Mr Kennedy?' Mr Kennedy nodded strongly, and patted his satchel. Captain Strongbow continued, 'Your bosses must be made to listen. I am organising a convoy of ten automobiles to tour Geneva and then to tour the world, growing ever larger, to convey the message of a world court backed with a world force. On the way round the world we will conduct a ballot. We have ballot papers — the first people's ballot for the setting up of the world government at the League of Nations — the people of the world will vote together. You could join the team of one of our vehicles, Miss — ?'

Captain Strongbow's speech had a rush to it now. She sensed that for Captain Strongbow that last idea or last word was suggesting the next. There was a line, however, and on one side of the line was fertile thinking, and on the other, downright conversational fraud. The ballot idea was new. On World Federation she had not made up her mind, although she was, of course, for World Co-operation.

'My name is Edith Campbell Berry, of Internal Administration.' She took her professional card from her handbag. The third that she'd had a chance to present. She had stopped calling it a visiting card.

Captain Strongbow studied the card and said, 'Excellent. Pleased to make your acquaintance, Edith Campbell Berry.' He shook her hand and passed the card to Mr Kennedy who likewise read it, and shook her hand, and then carefully placed the card in his satchel.

She liked the idea of the people's ballot. Why hadn't

someone at the League come up with that? Why, with a people's ballot, you could override national boundaries. There were difficulties, of course.

Mr Kennedy said, 'It would give the League a direct mandate — an empowering more direct than any mandate which any government of a nation state could ever have.'

'A power greater than the sun. Our President Coolidge said that . . .' Strongbow took a note from his pocket and read from it. 'He said that: "Disaster will surely be the penalty if the world fails to devise methods of preventing war. It is for the generation which saw and survived to devise those methods of protection." '

She had not read President Coolidge's words. 'What became of your submission to the League?' she asked them.

Captain Strongbow said that he had made something of a submission with illustrations and drawings, but no reply had come forth. 'I have sent designs, I have sent in the colour chart showing how, by combining all colours — including, I add, the colour red from the red flag — I do not judge the Russians and their revolution, as many of my countrymen have — by the mixing of all the colours of the world, you achieve a result which is olive drab or khaki which is also the colour of the uniform which I am wearing, and Mr Kennedy is wearing, and which many brave boys wore not so long ago in the dreadful war of slaughter.'

Although intrigued, Edith was put off by the talk of mixing of colours and uniforms. She was perplexed about where reasonableness began and ended in the conversation of Captain Strongbow.

She looked at her watch to signal the conclusion of the unsolicited interview. She stood up, took money from her purse and went to put it on the table, but Captain Strongbow intercepted her hand, firmly preventing her, gesturing to Mr Kennedy to pay the coffee bill.

'I cannot accept that,' she said, feeling it would compromise her as a civil servant.

'I insist, as an officer and as a gentleman.'

'I cannot accept,' said Edith, equally firmly, placing the money in the saucer. 'If we are to quote presidents, I seem to recall that your President George Washington said that the President of the United States could never be "any man's guest" — it is the same at the League.' She then flushed because it sounded pompous. She tried to retrieve her composure by giving a small laugh to show that she recognised a distance between herself and George Washington.

Mr Kennedy was stalled, and stood with his money in his hand, looking to her and to Captain Strongbow.

'I accept the ruling of George Washington,' Captain Strongbow said, and turning to Mr Kennedy, he said, 'Brochure.' Mr Kennedy put away his money and took out a brochure from his satchel and handed it to the Captain.

Captain Strongbow gave her the copy. Taking it, she smiled at them, shook their hands and left.

Next day at the office, she sharpened her pencils with a knife her father had given her as a fruit knife. Maybe sharpening the pencils was the nearest to 'working with her hands' that she got these days. 'Writing with pencil: working with wood.' She laughed. Not very close.

She might write a poem about it titled 'Working with Wood'. She had learned only recently that Dame Rachel Crowdy, head of Social Questions section, wrote poems.

Jules the messenger knocked and entered, handing her a

memorandum from Cooper asking her to see him 'not urgently' — then why the messenger? — about a Captain Strongbow. She mentally kicked herself. She recalled now that yesterday some small voice in her head had caused her to hesitate about giving him her card. She had sensed there in the old city that he was a man who would use whatever he could to further his business but she had overridden her judgement there in the old city in the spring sun. Damn, damn, damn.

She had better get the seeing of Cooper over with or it would fret away at her during the day. She hadn't made an official record of her 'interview' with Strongbow, if that was what she was supposed to do. 'Encounter' was probably the precise word.

Cooper was all smiles. 'This Captain Strongbow . . .' He lifted, rather than held, a document she recognised as a telegram, together with Strongbow's prospectus, now all in a file. 'That couldn't be his real name, surely? Is he a friend?'

'Strongbow?' She affected an act of recall. 'Oh yes. Not a friend, no,' she said, as lightly as she could.

'He quotes your name in this telegram. The telegram, by the way, was addressed to the Secretary-General. It has now come on to my desk. It is not the sort of thing I want on my desk.' Cooper smiled.

'He approached me in the street.'

'In the street?'

'In the old city.'

'In the old city?'

Without showing it, she winced.

Cooper looked at her. She sat there. He looked back at the document from Strongbow.

He looked back to her. 'You say he came up to you in the street. In the old city?'

'He was driving a rather impressive motor-car.'

'You were impressed by his motor-car?' Cooper made it sound as if she were a dizzy woman.

She explained it to him but he seemed to be unwilling to make the effort to visualise for himself how it might have happened. 'I admit I should not have given out my name and connection to the League — but sometimes you have to give out your name. It would be discourteous not to give your name and business.'

'To strangers in the street?'

'He was an American.'

'How does that change the nature of things?'

She chafed under his authority because she believed that he was the sort of person whose judgement was distorted by having authority. Everything alerted and worried him. He worried that anything that passed into the section might be important but he could never be sure, so his attention itself exaggerated all business into its wrong size.

Struggling to be fair to Cooper, she admitted that she didn't know whether Captain Strongbow was important, wrong-headed, crazy or sinister.

Typically though, Cooper was concentrating on her having given out her name, which certainly was not the item of greatest importance in the matter on his desk.

Though, face up to it, she was defensive because diplomatically she had made a false move. Cooper was now aware of it and that deflated her.

'The man is obviously crazy,' he said, wanting, however, confirmation of this assessment.

'There might be truth in what Strongbow says,' she said. 'It might be that there are people threatening us.'

She should have stopped here but instead threw in, 'He may

be the wrong person to propose the idea but the international police army could be what we need. And the people's ballot could become a popular idea. There is that party which has been formed in Germany to bring about world unification. Could be a big thing. A turning point in world opinions. Sir Geoffrey Butler says that it's particularly encouraging to realise that community discussion in international affairs at last seems realised.'

Cooper looked up at her momentarily, and then back to the file. Cooper, she could see, was now perplexed by possibilities. Surrounded by them. 'Nonsense. Look at this. The motor-cars, the uniforms, the flags — the man is mad. Or it's a travelling circus. One or the other.'

That was right; Strongbow was a circus man, but more than that, he had combined his circus with international politics. That was new. 'I accept that he's a showman. It is a political circus. It could be made into a turning point.' She was beginning to make it up as she went, and to convince herself at the same time. 'We need a police army of our own.'

Cooper stared at her trying to decide whether she was dizzy or perspicacious.

If he thought she was dizzy, her career was probably ruined. Ruined by a chance encounter. As ruined as a woman from a *maison close*.

'We already have diplomatic jurisdiction over this building,' she added, lamely, but warming to the idea, feeling that she had to make it sound sensible or she would for ever be seen as dizzy. 'Why not create a force to protect visiting statesmen, for instance, and to stamp out opium or the traffic in women?' That was too big a leap — she calmed the idea down. 'We could run a small League police army — to protect the building and those who come here.'

She refrained from mentioning the French idea of a League of Nations army which had not got very far.

Cooper was further perplexed, probably now worrying that he would have to wear a uniform and hold parades of this police army.

'You're not suggesting we take this man seriously? You've met the man — what is it that you are advising?'

Cooper had played the right move. She was now on the spot. She had now to make her move. She paused, thinking about it.

He pushed at her. 'Are you suggesting that we arrange a meeting with Sir Eric?'

She wasn't suggesting that.

'Or what?' he said impatiently.

She wanted the mess off his desk and to get her hands on the telegram with her name in it, and the whole caboodle, so as to somehow save herself. She'd simply burn the file.

'You could dump it on to Political section, or you could make it my responsibility to investigate it and report,' she said, and before he could make a decision, she leaned over and took the file off the desk. 'I'll sort it out,' she said.

'I don't want us looking ill-advised,' Cooper said, 'or to seem to be a section which is always passing things on. And I don't want to let Political in on it — if it is in any way a going thing, that is.'

She suspected that Cooper was one of those people who often compulsively spoke the description of themselves that they most deeply dreaded. He was forever saying that he did not want to appear ill-advised, and yet that was just how his actions so often appeared to her. As she walked along the corridor, she looked at the file and saw that in the telegram Strongbow mentioned her as a 'wise counsellor'. That annoyed her but it could have been worse.

Back at her desk, she found that a box had been delivered to her. Addressed personally. From what Strongbow had told her, she thought immediately of bombs. She pushed the box with a pencil. Not a gift box but a serious-looking parcel the size of a shoebox. She wondered whether she should call one of the military chaps on the staff. She decided that she was being panicky and gingerly opened the box. Inside it was a card. The card was from Strongbow and it said that the box contained a gift for her, sent in the spirit of internationalism.

The Strongbow mess was spreading. With sickening apprehension, she looked into the box.

Inside was a jewellery box. She could not imagine how she would explain an expensive gift to Cooper — maybe she would even have to explain it to Sir Eric, to Tony Buxton, to the lot of them. Yikes. She opened the hinged jewel case and oh, it was velveteen-lined but it was no jewel case. Inside, in a recessed compartment was a small silver-plated revolver. A booklet of instruction said it was a Ladies' Handbag Pistol. There were five shining bullets in their velveteen recesses. She closed the presentation case and got up and locked the door to her office.

She looked at the revolver again. She took it out carefully. She had seen revolvers only in motion pictures and museums. She gripped it and awkwardly pointed it. She liked it. But she would have to think about the protocol, so she put the revolver back in the case and into her drawer. She could return it to Strongbow and not mention it. She would have to think.

If it had been diamonds, she would have given it in to Cooper or no, she would have given it to Under Secretary Bartou who handled these things until they had a *Chef du Protocole*. Under Secretary Bartou might be the person to see about the whole matter. That would keep it well out of Internal Services and anyhow, she felt intimidated by Under Secretary Monnet, her real boss who she rarely saw.

Part of her, though, was coldly certain that she intended to keep the revolver and to keep it a secret. It seemed to her that it was what she needed here in Europe. She had not realised it until this very moment, but she needed an instrument of personal safety. She thought that maybe Strongbow was correct about enemies of the League, not that they would go for someone at her level. At some point, she might need to defend others.

That evening she took the revolver home with her and exulted in the possession of it and the exultation pushed away any sense of dishonesty.

The next weekend when she went to stay with Ambrose at his apartment, she showed it to him, and asked him to teach her to shoot.

'Where did you get it?'

She told him.

'Send it back.'

'No.'

'It's against rules.'

'I consider it a personal gift — from a man to a woman. A gift of admiration.'

'From an admirer?'

She could tell that he had changed his approach and tone. 'From a would-be admirer. Will you teach me to shoot it?'

'I was a medical officer. Not very good at shooting.'

'Teach me the way it works.'

'What sort of captain is he, this Captain Strongbow?'

'I don't know what sort of captain he is. You were an officer. You must have had to shoot.'

They argued about her accepting the pistol and then he grudgingly agreed to show her how to shoot, 'For the sake of public safety,' and then he allowed himself to be interested in the pistol.

He was partly pacified when she said she would talk unofficially to Under Secretary Bartou. She would discuss the matter of Captain Strongbow with Under Secretary Bartou but would not discuss the pistol.

They argued.

She said, 'There is a distinction between a gift from an admirer and an intended bribe.' The pistol was a gift from an admirer.

They agreed to disagree.

That Saturday, they bought a packet of bullets and drove out to the Bois de Veyrier. Ambrose stood behind her and held her arms for her and guided her with instruction.

She felt the little spurt of power that firing the pistol gave to her. She loved it. She liked the explosive smell.

She fired off the whole box, but kept the original five bullets that had come with the gun.

She went to the tree and examined her target and the effect of the bullets on the tree. 'Will the tree die?' she asked.

'Oh no — trees are sturdier than we,' Ambrose said.

Back at his apartment, under guidance from Ambrose, and still warm with excitement, she washed the barrel and oiled the pistol.

On the Monday, she called on Under Secretary Bartou who had been a Swiss diplomat of the old school.

He welcomed her to the League and said the usual things about the expense of living in Geneva.

'I've been here five months now,' she told him, in case he thought she was green.

She explained the problem of Captain Strongbow. He seized the problem immediately. 'What we have with this Captain Strongbow is someone desperate to have a relationship with the League which can then be used by him elsewhere as a credential. If he can, he will use it on his letterhead, will mention some sort of relationship with the League of Nations. You understand?'

Edith nodded.

'The thing to understand in dealing with such a communication,' Under Secretary Bartou went on, 'is that we must avoid confirming any of his claims. An unscrupulous person will write calling himself, say, the Commissioner of the World Police, and if we reply addressing him as the "Commissioner of World Police", he will twist this into an acknowledgement by us of his status. You have been entrapped perhaps?' Under Secretary Bartou asked how she had communicated with this Captain Strongbow.

'In a street. At least, in a café conversation. I said for him to make a submission to the League, yes, I suppose.' She was colouring with embarrassment, more strongly felt in front of Under Secretary Bartou than in front of Cooper, an embarrassment not only of diplomatic naïvety.

'You may find that he now talks of "having been invited to make a submission to the League of Nations". I wouldn't worry,' he said, perceiving her embarrassment, 'we are all subjected to it. The best protection is to minute these encounters. Treat them as a letter not answered.'

In her favour, though, she had sensed back in the café that she was being used. Her instincts had been right. Damnation.

Under Secretary Bartou said, 'You must now minute your meeting and have nothing more to do with him. To reply or not to reply, by letter or by the telephone, is always a diplomatic act.'

He stood up and she stood up, and they shook hands. She thanked him for his advice.

Later she realised that she hadn't liked the tone in Bartou's advice. For all her respect, she resisted a little. It sounded like instruction, not advice. But then, he was trained in the diplomacy of the old school. She was of the new school of diplomacy — open diplomacy. She fiercely believed that the obscure issues from which international quarrels arise had to be dragged out into the light of day and the creation of a public opinion made possible. Diplomats and politicians had to learn to face the public and make themselves understood by the public on matters of foreign policy. No more secret treaties. But she had to keep back her irritation because she was, if not green, still a New Girl about the place.

She saw that Under Secretary Bartou and maybe even Cooper were worried about minor infractions to the dignity of the League and were, in that sense, hobbled in the most limiting way. They ought, she thought, to develop the philosophies and procedures of the League in a more enterprising way if they wished to escape from diplomatic restraint. Even if there were risks, the League had to take them. There was something she badly wanted to learn: she wanted to learn what made an idea tenable and what made an idea untenable. Politically. Diplomatically. She wanted to know about the assessing of ideas which were 'unprecedented'. Under Secretary Bartou and Cooper wanted to follow only precedented ideas. Golly, the League itself was unprecedented. She recalled something that Balfour had said, that in foreign affairs it was always politically safer to do an absurd thing with precedent than to make oneself responsible for an unprecedented act of wisdom. She couldn't remember, though, which position Balfour approved, the unprecedented or the precedented. But she was interested in Ideas Ahead of Their Time and Ideas Whose Time Had Arrived, as well as Seizing the Moment.

Overnight she decided that she had to make a name for herself at the League and contribute to the development of this new temper. Henceforth, as a rule of personal behaviour, she would do the opposite to that which she imagined Cooper doing. Or, for that matter, the way her dear friend Ambrose would act, he being another old style, British Foreign Office person. She put Under Secretary Bartou to one side because he was a different fish to them both.

At work next day she opened the file and looked at Strongbow's telegram and saw that it had been sent from the Hôtel Richemond. Taking a deep, deep breath, Edith had herself put through, by telephone, to the Hôtel Richemond and to 'Captain' Strongbow. Following Under Secretary Bartou's advice on this point at least, she pondered how to address him without granting him his title. She reached not Strongbow, but an eager-voiced Mr Kennedy, and she made an appointment to see Strongbow.

She wanted to see Strongbow and establish for herself, by her own tests, whether his ideas were tenable, regardless of the soundness of the man. If Captain Strongbow's ideas were honourable and valid, she wanted to advance those ideas. She wanted to find a way that would allow her to go into the jungle of the world Out There and mix with its animals and still keep unimpaired her analytical self-respect, and the loftiness of the League. She wanted to be a person who could arbitrate and respond to a vital idea of the times.

Her nerve deserted her for a second and she considered that maybe she was not destined for diplomacy: maybe she was someone who should work in the field. She sometimes yearned to be able to 'do something' — to bandage, to ladle soup, to fight malaria, to install wind pumps in Africa, even to fight in just combat.

But her nerve returned and she resumed her course of action. Further, she wanted to rebuke Strongbow for misusing her.

At the Richemond she told the desk clerk that she was there for an appointment with Mr Strongbow. The desk clerk said a porter would take her up to his rooms. She would rather have met with him in the lobby.

In his rooms she was pleased to see a woman, who was introduced as his wife Athena. Athena was dressed in a leather flying outfit with calf boots. Used, Edith guessed, as a motoring outfit. Why wear it in a hotel room? Did she not have any other clothing? They were drinking champagne. It did not feel like diplomatic intercourse, at all.

She refused the offer of a glass of champagne. In what she thought was a formal voice, she raised the matter of the use of her name in a communication to the Secretary-General. Strongbow apologised. She hunted around for a form of rebuke, but none came to mind and she felt she had to leave it at that.

She wanted now to somehow test his ideas and find if there was reason or evidence behind any of them. She had devised three ways. The first was the Way of Numbers: is there a statistic? Butler had said that a reliable supply of facts and statistics will in itself be a powerful aid to peace. They were the only escape from the guess, the national lie, the false claim, the delusion, and the wish. Statistics had no nationality.

The second was the Way of Recognition: did he have any

status in the eyes of anyone or any organisations which she respected?

The third was more difficult to use and she was uncertain of it. She called it the Way of Aura: was there an aura about this man Strongbow or his organisation which she could detect and which would substitute for the absence of the above?

Before she could apply her ways, Strongbow called for tea and said that before they talked about anything else, he had a proposition to announce.

Because it was difficult to talk seriously while waiting for tea, she thanked him for the pistol and made a half-hearted gesture of returning it as an extravagant gift from one stranger to another. But the mention of the pistol and her primly thanking him for it, seemed to make for a fanciful atmosphere and anyhow she'd already fired it. The unreality of the situation was taken further when Athena showed Edith her pistol, what she called a 'point two-five calibre'. She said it was a purse pistol. Edith took it and handled it. It had an engraved handle inlaid with silver and ivory. Every girl should have a pistol of silver and ivory.

'It's truly beautiful,' she said.

Talk about pistols took over for a time.

Edith lied and told them that her pistol would go into the League of Nation's armoury. Maybe, in a sense, it was the first weapon in the armoury. They engaged in small talk about her background, kangaroos, the condition of the roads of Australia, and she was told about the team's planned trip across Europe and Asia with the motor-cars.

The tea arrived and Strongbow said he would now make his proposition.

He outlined a parade through Geneva to launch the people's

ballot. 'We want you to ride with us because we want a woman in every vehicle.'

'That is out of the question.'

'Don't rush to say no. I swear that you will not be advertised as a representative of the League. You will simply represent Womanhood and add, may I say, a refinement and loveliness to the occasion.'

Edith shrugged off the flattery along with the preposterous idea of the parade.

Athena said she was recruiting women to be representatives of Womanhood in each vehicle.

'I am afraid,' Edith said, in her official voice, 'that it is out of the question.'

But she was brought face-to-face with a persuasive line. 'We must all come up with trail-blazing ideas for untried times,' said Strongbow. He raised a hand for a pause in the discussion. 'Before you make up your mind, Ambassador Berry, there is a warning. This could be a dangerous mission. We will probably draw their fire.'

'Draw fire? I don't follow. And I am not an ambassador.'

'In my eyes and in the eyes of the world, you are one of the New Ambassadors, an ambassador of the planet. This is no easy thing we do — if the cavalcade attracts the notice of dangerous elements and brings them into the open, we could expect that they may truly try disruption or worse.'

Edith saw herself being brave. The voice of her old head-mistress said, 'We choose the way of peril because it offers the possibility of glory. And if we fail we will be remembered as having behaved well.'

Strongbow boomed on, 'However if that be so, then, so be it. We will have exposed them and they will, we hope, be caught. Better the bombs, if they be thrown, be thrown at us in our motor-cars than at the vulnerable League Secretariat.'

Edith mustered herself and tried to apply her new ways. 'How many people are there against the League and what is the name of their organisation?' she asked, using the Way of Numbers. 'Round figures will do.' She had been waiting for places in the conversation to apply the tests, feeling a growing apprehension that she would not be able to find convincing answers which would allow her behaviour to proceed with prudent certainty. Maybe behaviour could only proceed with confidence, never certainty. Maybe behaviour proceeded on the footing of something even less than confidence. She saw now why people needed doctrines and dogma and effrontery to propel them into action. Maybe the will to action went by hunch and by lurch more than by the Way of Numbers.

'Can we take your silence as meaning assent?' asked Strongbow. 'Or at least serious consideration?'

She looked up and out from her thoughts. The man had not answered her. What did one do now?

'Oh, no,' she said. 'It is truly out of the question. As an officer of the League there is no way. And you have not answered my enquiry.'

Instead of answering, Strongbow asked her to promise him one thing.

'What is that, Captain Strongbow?' Oh damn. She'd been trying to get through the conversation without granting him his title. She told herself she was granting it only as an honorific.

'I want you to promise not to make up your mind. Not to give a decision now. Go away and do not give an answer until twenty-four hours have lapsed.'

'I would like the evidence,' she asked again, 'of this collusion against the League, in round numbers.' She ploughed on with her enquiry. 'Maybe you could supply me with references — someone who knows of your organisation?'

'Evidence is for juries,' he said, rising to his feet. He went to stand at the window with his back to them, booted feet apart, hands behind his back. 'We are at the visionary stage of mankind. I am a vision maker.'

She stared at him, trying to decide whether he had aura. He obviously had no statistics.

It was more swagger than aura.

'Not for twenty-four hours — no decision,' he said, turning from the window and standing before her. 'Agreed?'

'I will consider the matter further.'

'Grand,' he said. 'Grand. I sense that I am talking to a visionary.'

'I am first and foremost an officer of the League.'

'And we salute that,' he said, 'we salute that.' And he did, quite solemnly.

She stood and he led her to the door. She found herself then in the lobby, saying goodbye to Athena, who had accompanied her down in the lift.

'I know,' Athena said, 'that you will dare to be.'

Edith then found herself walking towards the Palais Wilson.

She thought that the language of the group was excessive, but she put it down to their American manner. She was disappointed in herself, for she had found out nothing which would allow her to assess them. Were they a circus, and was that bad? Were they charlatans? They stayed at the Richemond in a suite of rooms — that was something. They drank champagne during the day. What did that mean? Did Captain Strongbow have aura?

But wasn't that what made her different from the others? Strongbow had an American flair and that was something else. She could join with the American flair more readily than she could join with the diplomacy of the old world.

She turned and walked back to the Hôtel Richemond. The League may be against secret diplomacy but it was not against confidentiality in action. This was her confidential mission of sorts. Cooper had implied that she should investigate this man and his proposals. I must dare, Edith said to herself. The way to investigate was to go into the field.

She asked the desk clerk to call Captain Strongbow and to tell him to meet her down in the lounge.

Nor would she be told by Captain Strongbow how long to wait before making a decision. She was not one of those people who took twenty-four hours to make up her mind. She would make it now. She would make her decisions, however, on the neutral ground of the lobby.

The Captain, Athena, and Mr Kennedy, all came down the stairs.

She told Captain Strongbow that she would ride in the motor-car.

'Grand,' said Strongbow.

'Why, that's terrific,' said Athena.

'Welcome aboard,' said Mr Kennedy.

'You are a visionary, but more — you are a dauntless visionary,' said Captain Strongbow. He looked at his watch. 'And you made a decision in twenty-four minutes, not twenty-four hours.' He looked to Athena and to Mr Kennedy and said, 'This is a woman who acts with alacrity.'

'Indeed,' said Mr Kennedy. 'Indeed she does. With dispatch.'

Captain Strongbow turned to her and said, 'I will leave you with Athena to talk details. Thank you for the vote of confidence.' Captain Strongbow and Mr Kennedy both shook her hand strongly.

Athena and she sat in the lounge, and Athena told her

that the plan was for each woman in the cavalcade to wear a national costume.

'National costume?' Edith felt sick. She did not like fancy dress at any time. 'Australia has no national costume.'

'You can be a cowgirl from the golden west. I know that Australia has cowboys. They must, then, have cowgirls.'

'A cowgirl?'

'A cowgirl. I myself am dressing as a Hawaiian. In a grass skirt.'

A grass skirt.

Edith's spirit shied. She had seen it more as, well, a sober parade of serious concern. 'I cannot see myself dressed up. Dressed up as a cowgirl.' Saying that made her feel staid.

Athena said that they had to put on a show. These were show business times. She said that Captain Strongbow often said the League of Nations was the 'biggest show in town'.

Edith didn't quite see the League or the world ballot as a 'show'.

Athena explained that there was a time for attracting attention to an idea and that anything that served that purpose was right. 'I would take off my clothes for this idea,' Athena said.

Edith privately thought that Athena would take off her clothes for just about any persuasive reason. Athena had something of the chorus girl about her.

Edith was about to get up and go, once again, and once again she was filled with exasperation, disappointed with her reserve. 'Is there any other costume? Apart from cowgirl?'

'We really only have cowgirl left. I could swap with you. You could be Hawaiian.'

'Oh no,' she said, aghast, 'I'll be the cowgirl. But Athena . . . ?'

'Yes, Edith, what is it?'

'Could I be disguised? Could I wear, say a hairpiece or something which would disguise me?'

'No one will recognise you, I promise. I will make you up. I will get a wig from the costume wardrobe and you will be another person. I promise you, Edith. I am so thrilled you are joining us.'

Edith was not feeling 'glad' or 'thrilled' about anything. She was feeling trepidation. She had made decisions which were breathtaking. She prayed that the disguise would work, though should a bullet strike her breast, or if a bomb should take her life, she would be revealed as Edith Campbell Berry of Internal Administration, League of Nations Secretariat. Heroine. Or Nincompoop?

Back at the Palais Wilson, amid the scent of magnolias from the garden, she pondered her decision and tried to write an amusing minute on the encounter but it sounded more like a confession, or a will and testament, and she decided not to file it, just yet. If she died, Cooper would at least find it and see that she had done her work according to procedure. However, she did not mark it 'to be opened in case of death'. The magnolias reminded her of a funeral parlour. Usually she considered magnolias somehow 'blowzy'.

She told herself that she had until the next day to change her mind, but she knew that if she did change her mind she would feel that she had betrayed herself and the quest for a new diplomacy. If she did not do this, did not go out into the field and test the situation one more step, she would never know whether the ideas were tenable or not.

She had also to honour her audacious self, the country girl. She did not want to lose that part of herself. Not yet. There was betrayal enough in her desire to be disguised, but the wilder self was satisfied with that.

103

Of one thing I am certain, she said to herself: that this is an historically unprecedented action — an officer of the League dressed as a cowgirl sitting on the back of an open touring motor-car in the interests of the ballot for world government.

She told no one about her plans, not even her new friend Florence Travers, and certainly not Ambrose. Maybe when it was all over.

On the day, she first worried about what lingerie she should wear under a leather cowgirl outfit.

She went to the Richemond, still shivering with trepidation but resolved to go through with it. She loaded her new pistol and put it in her leather travelling handbag, saying to herself, If I am to need a pistol, it will probably be this very day. It gave her fortitude. She also thought that Captain Strongbow would expect it of her.

At the Richemond, Athena led her into a room of the suite which contained, it seemed, many costumes. Three other women — of the showgirl kind, to put it generously — were dressing in national costumes although which nations they represented was far from obvious to Edith.

Athena handed her a glass of champagne. She was thankful for that, drinking it in three gulps.

She was introduced to Simone and Nicole but not to the others.

Athena whispered, too loudly for Edith's comfort, that they were from an artists' model agency.

As she dressed in the outfit, the sweaty smell of its leather brought memories of childhood riding and she resolved to arrange to go riding regularly, there in Geneva, when all this was over — if she came through. As she shed her corset and other unneeded underwear she felt as she hadn't for a long time, like a young country girl, running free.

Nervously she put on the cowgirl suit with Athena's help, accepting, also nervously, Athena's praise of her underwear, her panties and brassière, and Athena's fondling of her brassière. The first woman, apart from her mother, to touch her body intimately. She put on the long blue denim trousers, Mexican boots with hand-tooled designs, leather chaps which tied behind the legs, an embroidered satin shirt with pearl buttons, a leather waistcoat and a bandanna. Edith tried to assure herself that there were times when one had to live at a high pitch. Though she was suddenly appreciative, also, of the place in life for times that passed in a quiet and ordinary way.

Edith did not like the way that Captain Strongbow, in his uniform of a captain but now with badges and medals that she could not identify, walked in and out of the 'dressing room', though she thought that it was probably acceptable in show business, that sort of thing. Athena kept her promise and fitted a blonde wig over Edith's red hair and changed her make-up quite dramatically, though not in a direction that a genteel woman would normally go with make-up. Still, Edith reminded herself, it was all show business. The wig and the make-up brought both a sense of hiding to Edith and oddly, a sense of becoming some other 'Edith'. But then Edith felt she became 'different' every time she had her hair styled by a hairdresser.

The final touch for the cowgirl costume was a coiled stock-whip which she was to carry over her shoulder.

'All set are we?' were Captain Strongbow's words. He looked them over as though he was — what? Inspecting the troops? Or a buyer of slave girls? He wore a revolver in a polished holster on his belt.

'I must congratulate you all on your bravery,' he said. 'And before we set off on this historic mission, I wish to address you.'

There were the six Representatives of Womanhood, and the four drivers of the other motor-cars. Edith had imagined a larger cavalcade.

Mr Kennedy, who was also in a uniform that Edith could not identify, brought a chair forward and Captain Strongbow, instead of sitting on it, stood on it. He held his hands together in a tidy speaker's clasp and he made a speech on the importance of the people's ballot. He quoted President Coolidge, again reading the words from his card. He concluded by saying, 'May God be with us, on this fateful day.'

He jumped briskly from the chair and led the way out.

The troupe received much ogling as they filed through the foyer of the Hôtel Richemond and out to the street where the motor-cars waited.

The convoy of five motor-cars — not the ten as originally stated by Captain Strongbow — was gaily decorated, and a battery-powered loudspeaker had been placed on the military motor-car.

The military motor-car led the cavalcade which moved slowly through the streets, and through its loudspeaker, Captain Strongbow propounded their mission.

Mr Kennedy also travelled in the military motor-car, and made a motion picture of it all with a camera on a tripod on the back seat.

Edith wondered briefly about Captain Strongbow and Mr Kennedy choosing to travel in the military motor-car while the others were in the open motor-cars, exposed to anything that might happen.

As instructed, the Representatives of Womanhood leaned out of the motor-cars and beckoned people to come and take the leaflets and the ballot paper. Some did, although the citizenry of Geneva seemed reluctant to accept anything offered by a stranger, especially colourfully dressed Representatives of Womanhood.

Athena and the other women took to getting out of the cars and going over to the people who gathered to watch, thrusting the leaflets at them. Despite urgings from Athena, Edith remained in her car and did the best she could from there.

After a while, and as the champagne relaxed her, she began to wave timidly and to blow kisses as well. There is something of the showgirl in me, she thought as she waved from the back of the motor-car, yes indeed. Of that I am glad. Occasionally people on the footpaths waved and sometimes cheered and clapped. Most stared.

It was warm and sunny and Edith, because of her coloration and complexion, was glad of the wide-brimmed hat.

She saw no one she knew in the streets, although some of the League staff were at the windows of the Palais Wilson. At this point she looked towards the lake and away from the Palais, pulling her hat further over her face. At the Palais the procession stopped and Captain Strongbow stood up in the military motor-car and solemnly saluted the Palais Wilson, the other hand on his chest, over his heart. Mr Kennedy set up his tripod and camera on the footpaths and made film of it.

The cavalcade took about two hours to travel along the busiest streets both on the left and right bank of the lake.

No shots were fired. No bombs or eggs were thrown, no unseemliness occurred. As for the idea of a people's ballot, Edith saw now that it would require more system and execution than the handing out of ballot forms from open touring motor-cars. She personally doubted that many people would fill them out and post them to the League. She could see that the cavalcade was not reaching a cross-section of the 'people'. She wondered who would handle any ballot forms which did end up at the League. Would it be her job? She vaguely imagined the organisation which would be needed to receive the ballot forms, verify their authenticity, count them, and so on, and felt tired.

She at least established for herself something about the feasibility of it all. That had been the value and success of her audacity.

They wound their way back to the Hôtel Richemond and dismounted, this time receiving some clapping from the staff of the hotel.

In the Strongbow suite, everyone was very talkative, sunburnt, and rather elated. Corks popped, champagne foamed onto the carpet, glasses were again handed around and filled to overflowing. Edith had never seen people so careless with champagne. They all stayed in costume while Strongbow made another speech on their bravery and the historic spirit of the occasion, world government, the Anglo-Saxon race, the importance of the automobile, the science of colour, and whatever else came to his mind.

Edith noticed that Mr Kennedy handed white envelopes to Nicole, Simone and the other two girls, and then put his arm around Nicole's waist, confidently but not naturally.

After the speech there was animated talk and laughter as they recalled funny things they had seen or that people had said. It became something of a party, with the assistant manager of the hotel and the hotel's *chef de securité* — a rotund cigar-smoking man — and a couple of Nicole's and Simone's friends coming to join in the festivity.

Strongbow stood with Edith and at some point asked her in a whisper if she would go to his room with him, and she said to him — for the second time in her life, recalling their meeting at the café terrasse in the old city, 'Captain Strongbow, I am not that kind of woman.' He kissed her on the cheek, and patted her just above her bottom, and said, 'I kinda knew that.'

She also turned down profuse invitations from Athena, Mr Kennedy and Captain Strongbow to join the troupe and carry the message around the world. The invitations were not without appeal in some fanciful way.

'Tomorrow we drive to India,' Captain Strongbow said.

'My work is here, I'm afraid,' Edith said. Wondering if she could find it in herself to impulsively say yes, and to become a showgirl from that day forth and drive with them 'to India', but it did not seem to her that joining the troupe was to be her destiny. Both Nicole and Simone seemed to have decided to go with the troupe.

The party was becoming a little risqué for her and she was feeling slightly tipsy, from the champagne and maybe from the sun. She changed out of her costume and back into Edith Campbell Berry of Internal Administration and said goodbye, feeling very close to them all, the showgirls, the drivers and Captain Strongbow. Impulsively she asked Athena if she could borrow the cowgirl costume, and the wig, overnight, seeing herself surprising Ambrose and having a laugh. Athena agreed happily and gave her a wink that she didn't quite understand. Edith winked back from comradeship although she was not practised at winking.

As she walked to Ambrose's apartment she felt tipsy but pleased with herself and full of good feeling for the world.

She let herself in to the apartment and, still singing with the champagne, again dressed in the cowgirl costume and read while she waited.

When he arrived home, he was delighted to be welcomed by a cowgirl. 'But what is the occasion? Is it a costume party, a *bal costumé*?'

'Well, yes, a costume party for two.'

'I'm flabbergasted,' he said, 'and impressed. You make a fine cowgirl.'

'I thought we should brighten up dull Geneva.'

'Quite right.'

He was really taken by it as she suspected he would be. She told him she'd hired it from the costume place in rue de Berne 'for fun'. She supposed that eventually she'd tell him the truth or that it would come out.

She urged him to open some champagne, which he did, and she put on some music. He took off his suit and put on his smoking jacket.

As she danced by herself to the music in her cowgirl outfit, he joined her and she coiled the whip around them both, binding them in its woven leather. As they danced she sensed that he wasn't only reacting from a sense of fun. She became aware of something about her being in costume and the wig which was not simple 'fun'. Not only a lark.

He grasped the whip end and pulled her tightly to him with it and they embraced.

Her body felt his arousal and responded. The fun of the costume had turned now to something entirely different. She didn't quite understand it but nor did she care, it was love play, she knew that, as they moved then to the bedroom, embraced.

She'd thought that dressing up as a cowgirl would be a lark but she had not really thought it through. But it wasn't only Ambrose who had been stimulated; she was feeling different and enlivened by the costume.

He undressed as she sat cross-legged on the bed and played with him and with the whip, drinking her champagne.

What she was doing was what should happen, she'd never felt so unthinkingly confident. She seemed to know exactly what to do. He made a noise of acceptance and pleasure, going then to his knees and kissing her cowgirl riding boots, smelling and seeming to enjoy the sweaty leather of the cowgirl outfit, smelling her around the groin, and under her arms, the leather made sweaty not only from the cavalcade but also from other times past, in other playlets performed by the troupe in its travels. She unbuttoned the satin shirt and exposed her breasts to him, framed now by the leather waistcoat.

As he kissed her breasts and her costume, she trailed the whip over and around his naked body.

Then he said to her in a tentative whisper, 'May I dress up too?'

She thought: in what would he dress? The cowgirl outfit? She asked, 'In what?'

'In your clothes.'

She at first chose to believe it was to do with her being in costume and that he was making a joke, but his tone of voice made it clear that it was not a joking game that he was proposing.

'In my clothes?'

Sheepishly, he said, 'Yes, your underwear.'

She realised that the champagne glass in her hand had gone to her lips, and was resting on her lip, but that she was not drinking.

'You'd like to wear my underwear?' she said, over the rim of the glass.

'Yes.'

Edith poured herself another glass. She took too big a mouthful, and it caught her throat, and some dribbled down her chin. She wiped it, hoping that Ambrose did not see her slight, although pleasant, nervousness.

Again, he looked at her and said coyly, 'Yes, your knickers, your corset. And so on. I'd love to.'

'Of course,' she said, more from not having any ready reply

than from consent, or from any clear understanding of the enchantment which was in play in his mind. 'Yes, of course,' she said, softly, this time her voice giving full consent to him.

She took a drink of champagne and said, now slightly enchanted by the idea herself, 'I'd love to see you dressed in my underclothes.' She guessed that given his slimness they would fit.

He left the bed, still aroused, and went to the wardrobe room where she kept some clothing for their week-ends together. When he returned, and she saw him dressed in her underclothes and observed the arousal of his body, she was certain then that this was not comedy and nor was it just *bal costumé*. It was outside anything that had happened in her admittedly limited experience with men in these matters, although now she thought about it, she'd occasionally read of it, and heard jokes about it. She supposed that in putting on the cowgirl costume, she had 'started it', but it had gone in these other directions, they were changing their roles for each other and she was falling so easily into it, effortlessly, as if she knew her part.

'You look delightful,' she said, and indeed he looked sensual. She saw now that his body had always carried some effeminacy, which was glamorised by the silk underclothing.

'You really think so?' He looked at himself in the mirror, posing for himself and for her.

He remained rather preoccupied with himself in the brassière, panties, camisole, stays and stockings. She turned off one of the lights so that the room was dim.

The imagery began to fascinate her and move through her, running its own course, taking over, and she lay back in her cowgirl outfit sipping champagne and watched him moving with confidence, with no self-consciousness at all. The clothing fitted him well, and he looked attractive and quite decadent.

He took her make-up from her handbag and applied it to

his face at the mirror. She saw the exhaustion creases from the War disappear, the make-up made him, once again, youthful, and at the same time, became a mask which unbridled him.

She removed the denim trousers and her panties, leaving on her silk stockings and her lace suspender belt, and putting on the leather chaps. She pulled on the cowgirl boots and spurs, and lay back on the bed, her breasts nicely exposed by the satin shirt and leather waistcoat.

He then came to her as a woman, as a man and a woman, for he was fully aroused in the masculine way, without any doubt. She remembered something that Nicole had said that afternoon and Edith repeated it, her voice husky, 'There is a law in Geneva against wearing masks. I think I see why.'

'Give a person a mask and they will tell you the truth,' he said softly in a new more effeminate voice.

'You have dressed up before?' she asked or observed, she too speaking in a voice she hardly recognised.

'Only in private,' he said, also in a voice she hardly recognised. 'This is the first time I've been able to do this with another woman, that is. With a woman, I should say. You don't mind?'

'It all seems very Weimar,' she managed to say. 'I'm sure it is an everyday thing there, a very natural thing in Munich.' She also felt intensely that she was on the Continent and all unthinkable and arcane things were possible. And were they also permissible?

'Yes — very Weimar.' Ambrose was relieved and grateful for her approval.

In further answer, she kissed him and they embraced and enclosed and joined. She found his newly released effeminacy softened their coupling, and she felt freed from expectations by the collapse of all decorum and at the same time she gained a sureness in her touch and movement. She surrendered to the release which flowed from their costumes, from the surging perversity of the atmosphere and the image of them both, which she kept glimpsing as she opened and closed her eyes. She kept glimpsing the attractive man in silk and lace and her silk-stockinged legs in the leather chaps and spurs. There was also an embrace of herself by herself, her embrace of Ambrose in her underwear which suggested her image back to her. With her legs wide around him, she brought the spurs to his buttocks and rolled them lightly into his flesh, giving a small calculated pain which caused him to hold her and to cry in a soft voice, 'Oh yes.' Much merging and confusing of selves and identities overtook them and pleasured them both as they lost themselves in a moaning and discharging which seemed out of time, and way, way outside of their orthodox world and the world she had known.

During the night, clothing was shed, and by morning they awoke as normal, except for traces of make-up on Ambrose's face. They smiled a wordless knowing and accepting.

She busied herself as if to make sure things were back to normal. She had to hurry to the Richemond to return the costume and to say goodbye. She was sure the costume, while having been a happy thing, did not belong in her life. She could find no aesthetic which would admit it. It did not come out of her ancestry. Or did it? From a time when there were fewer rules maybe? Whatever, she felt no compulsion to keep it even by the Aesthetic of Memento or Trophy.

It was quite a tearful farewell, and part of her still wanted to jump in with them and just go 'to India'.

'Come with us, Edith,' Athena said, holding both her hands.

'Plenty of room,' said Mr Kennedy.

Captain Strongbow however said, 'No, she has to carry our mission here — diplomatically. This is Edith's world.' He gestured to Her World.

She stood outside the garage and waved them off, watching until they were out of sight. She wiped her eyes.

Although it was Saturday, she went to the Palais and, in the library, she read the *Journal de Genève* and a small report of the cavalcade. The women in national costume were mentioned. The 'demure' cowgirl, she was gratified to see, was singled out for mention.

Captain Strongbow was quoted as saying he had 'permit and authority from the World Court and the League of Nations to carry out his mission'.

She snorted. That could never be controlled, that sort of thing, not with all the rules that could be devised. Not even by a world organisation with all its powers. At least she had that in perspective now.

She went to her small, safe office to sit for a while and think about her and Ambrose's behaviour the night before. She supposed his inclination to wear her underclothing was one of those impulses which a man might give in to, or which might pass through a man's mind to do once. To try out things like that. Although she had never wanted to wear her brother's clothing when she had been growing up. For Ambrose, though, it had been more than a trying-out. She had asked him that morning if he still wanted her 'to stay' at the week-ends. He'd answered, 'More than ever.' She took this as meaning that he wanted to be with her but as a woman — at least, at times. She saw very vaguely that it connected with things he'd tried to say, or implied, on the train on the way to Geneva. But she could not truthfully say that she understood.

Edith was pleased that she had been able to follow her wilder self in the parade, for a short time, and although it wasn't altogether related, to have been able to go also into her darker self that night, to those places of human behaviour about which she'd heard only whispers and jokes.

She felt she had learned two things. The first thing concerned the nature of innovation in public policy: that good ideas did not always have the proper and most appropriate of exponents and did not always come from the expected direction — she believed the international police army was a good idea. Good ideas were sometimes propounded by people who were not always personally sound and not always decorous.

The second thing Edith thought she had learned was the course of official inaction, of inoffensive passivity, together with discreet investigation. Simultaneous courses of incompatible action. Captain Strongbow's ideas were new and, as Athena said, they were at a stage where 'show business could be used to attract attention to them'. Good ideas would find their ways into the League policy through other doors. Sometimes what was required, she thought, laughing to herself nervously, was official inaction in combination with unofficial action. This action had to be what Ambrose would call a 'detached command'. Action unseen, unminuted. She had also learned something of fast-talking showmen, if nothing about aura.

She supposed, though, that she had to remember in which area she belonged, to knuckle down now and learn the ways of serious diplomacy.

With that reasoning, and before Cooper could call her and raise the matter again, she took the file on Captain Strongbow and wrote in it with a flourish the words, 'Recommendation: no action. ECB.' She also wrote 'Put Away' in the action box, knowing thankfully that it would never again be referred to. She then called for Jules and sent it to Cooper.

She admitted, in retrospect, that she was wrong in her argument that the pistol could be seen as a 'gift from an admirer' but it was too late to do anything about it now. It may have been a bribe but it had 'come into her possession' and there it would remain.

And what would she put in the other report, the intimate report to herself, about the ways of some men and their arousal, their wish to wear the clothing of women? The least she could say was that she had learned something about the power of costume.

And what had she to report to herself about her own carnality and its arousal in such steamy and bizarre circumstances?

Entrée à la Haute Direction

As Under Secretary Monnet was away, and as Cooper was ill, and given that she was, according to Ambrose, seen as 'pushy' by the others, she decided to let their view of her personality work for her rather than to be forever trying to correct it, and consequently she'd suggested to the others in the bureau that she 'go along and take notes' at the weekly Directors' meeting. She'd been the only one to realise that the section would have no one there. The others had agreed that she go as a rapporteur for the bureau but not, of course, as acting acting director or anything like that. Of course not. While deep in her heart she still believed she wasn't pushy, Edith did sometimes see herself as an unwilling leader, in a Girl Guide way. She wasn't sure that she had what was called leadership potential, but at times There Was No One Else and she had to step in, although she wasn't sure that was necessarily true leadership. She thought she was perhaps best as second-in-command, a good lieutenant. A leader was someone who needed followers to fulfil their existence. She was not like that. She needed a prescribed commitment.

'Of course, I will not be there pretending that I am acting acting head of section,' Edith said to Florence, her Canadian friend from Finance, who was pushy and proud of it.

'Of course not,' Florence said, laughingly, there again implying that putting herself forward was exactly what Edith would do. Florence thought it an excellent move for Edith to get to a Directors' meeting and be seen and, perhaps, even heard.

Florence was teaching her how to manoeuvre herself although, again, Edith was very unsure about whether one should ever 'manoeuvre' oneself. She could initiate and as in the Captain Strongbow incident, memory of which now caused her to flinch, she was even capable of taking the unorthodox path of action. That was not manoeuvring. Which was not to say that she wasn't a feminist either, but not an acute feminist. All right, yes, Edith admitted to Florence that she wanted desperately to go to a weekly Directors' meeting and she thought it would be good for her career to be seen at the Directors' meeting and, yes, she intended, if possible, to have something to say. She did not see this as pushy, she saw this as being a functioning part of the League crew, as being a trainee in international diplomacy.

She supposed she could be described as having 'drive'.

There'd been gossip at the Bavaria that the Directors' meeting was now running the Secretary-General. Some went further and suggested that it was getting control of both the Council and the Assembly agendas and she thought, privately, never expressing it to anyone, that this was perfectly acceptable, that the Secretariat should have a big say in setting agendas.

She did not challenge that you needed a masterful Secretary-General in the League. Whether Sir Eric was this sort of man was debated endlessly at the Bavaria. She always defended him. It was her aide-de-camp disposition, even though he was not her immediate superior. It was the tendency she had observed in herself and in the private secretaries and even among the stenographers — to have devoted loyalty to the person they were attached to professionally. She could see why it was efficacious for this to be so. You couldn't be working closely with a person and be unsupportive — although she believed it should be a 'considered' loyalty which involved speaking your mind. A 'seeing loyalty' rather than a blind loyalty. A devotion to seeing meant that you worked to provide your superior with the right particulars, so that he made the desirable decision, and a good aide-de-camp emotionally strengthened her superior when a decision had been made and had to be fought through. Provided supportiveness, too, at times of defeat. She didn't see anything demeaning about this. She wished she had someone to whom she could make this commitment. Cooper was not right for her, nor Monnet.

With Ambrose it was not like that either. They had something of a snug liaison. Ambrose was of superior rank to her, although not in her section, and he was more a mentor, although also at times needed support, which she was able to give. How would she describe this liaison? They saw each other nearly every week-end, and Ambrose, although he earned more than she, seemed to borrow money from her.

She told Florence that she felt tense at the idea of being there with the heads of section and other senior people. Even though she saw most of them daily, they were still fairly intimidating for her. Florence said some nervousness could be to one's advantage, a configuration of electrical energy which produced a higher alertness. Edith doubted this.

She made sure a memorandum went to Wilson as secretary of the Directors' meeting, saying that she would be there. Florence insisted on helping her with the wording, wanting to make it sound grander, and they settled on saying that she was 'representing the absent head of section' in the first paragraph and then, giggling, Florence had her sign it 'Head of section (rep)' and then made her type it again with (rep) in small, almost unreadable, handwriting next to the typed words HEAD OF SECTION. Florence looked at the memorandum and then said, 'I know. You must add an initial to your name. You must make them remember you.'

'But I'm already using my second name.'

'Go the whole hog,' said Florence.

Edith resisted and said that it would be excessive.

'Then change Edith to an E — and sign yourself "E. Campbell Berry".'

Edith tried it out a few times and had to agree that it looked good. She signed the memorandum E. Campbell Berry.

She would say something at the meeting but only if she could naturally find something to say.

On the day of the meeting the messenger, Jules, a limping refugee from Russia, complimented her on her dress and presented her with a yellow rose. He asked her to mention his family's lost estate, but she knew he wasn't serious. She wondered how he knew so much about her, but she guessed that there was talk about her going to the meeting. He probably read everything he carried.

It had been obvious to the others that she had dressed 'up' for the meeting, not excessively — it was a pale blue crepe suit with a pleated front panel, not even eye-catching — but it confirmed that she belonged there at the meeting and that she was of their standard. She knew there'd be only two women at the meeting, she and Dame Rachel, head of Social Questions. She wanted to be singular but not stand out.

At the door of the meeting, Under Secretary Bartou said to her in a comradely way, 'Remember, Berry, that a meeting is a diplomatic activity: pursue your interests: exercise comity.' He made a seat for her at his side. It would be good to be seen to have Under Secretary Bartou as an ally. However she thanked him and said that she'd sit with her friend Major Westwood. As she moved over to Ambrose, Dame Rachel indicated that she should sit next to her and Edith realised that the two women probably should sit together and went over to Dame Rachel.

Dame Rachel was head of her section but they had not yet given her the full status of Director.

'You'll find it a little like a football scrum,' Dame Rachel said, and Edith smiled at her, not quite understanding, worrying that Under Secretary Bartou would be wondering why she was sitting with Dame Rachel when she had said she would sit with Ambrose, thinking maybe that she had simply refused a seat beside him for no good reason. Oh well, it was one of those things that would go into history unexplained.

She glanced down the agenda:

Germany's entry to League
Filming in the Assembly
Behaviour of Journalists
Esperanto
Purchase of Furniture
Emergency Procedures
Complaint from NZ
Calendar Reform
Lighting of Coasts Committee Meeting in Stockholm

'Berry?'

Edith raised her head.

'Sir Eric?'

'Miss — Campbell?' Sir Eric paused and looked down at his notes, 'Miss E. Campbell Berry, I wish to welcome you to our meeting — our first Australian.' She hated the new form of her name and wanted to put her hand up like a schoolgirl and say, 'Please call me Edith.'

He went on, 'And to welcome you also to the League Secretariat. Unfortunately I now rarely have a chance personally to meet all our newcomers. Although I should as a gentleman go out of my way to meet young ladies who join us.'

The others chuckled.

Still glancing in her direction, but with a change of tone, he said, 'I hardly need to remind you, Berry, that you will hear discussed today things which are confidential to the Directors. I assume you will use judgement in conversation and, if in doubt, consult Under Secretary Monnet when he returns or Major Buxton or Major Westwood. Understood?'

'Of course, Sir Eric.'

Edith blushed. She wondered if Sir Eric knew of her connection with Ambrose. How many knew? They went out together but they did not, for instance, go to tea parties or dinner parties as a duo, although in League social life they were generally both there in their own right. She never took his arm in public. Ambrose and she looked across at each other correctly, without a flicker of anything improper. To think that they were sitting in the Directors' meeting, the *haute direction* of the League, all of the men in their pinstripe trousers and dark jackets, blue or grey shirts and white Eton collars, all dressed fairly much in the same fashion as Sir Eric, when last week she had seen Ambrose dressed in her knickers and corset and stockings. My, the world had been composed of many wonders since she'd met Ambrose on the train trip from Paris to Geneva. He had taken her into a realm of experience the import of which she could not yet discern. He had, she suspected, inducted her into the tempo and morality of the Modern Times. Oh dear, she thought, Mother, I'm a long, long way from home.

Sir Eric then led off about work hours, which wasn't on the agenda. She thought to herself that it was bad meeting practice to introduce matters that were not on the agenda. He wouldn't get away with that back home. He said that he had received a staff petition from Internal Services arguing for a change in the winter hours. Edith was surprised; she hadn't seen this petition.

The change in winter work hours was opposed by Comert from Information, who pointed out that if staff of the League began leaving at 5.30 p.m. when the rest of Geneva stopped at 6 p.m, it would create an unfortunate impression that the League staff led a privileged life. He also argued that in winter, 5.30 p.m in Geneva was still only 4.30 p.m. in London and Paris and it would look very bad if people called up the League on the telephone from London and Paris and got no answer.

Huston, who was from Internal Services, which came under her bureau, reminded the meeting that nearly all the members of section lived in pensions and had to observe the rather early pension hours for meals. When they left at 6 p.m. there was no time left for shopping.

Edith decided to test herself and decide what action she would take if she were Secretary-General — apart, that is, from not introducing substantial items not on the agenda. On this matter she agreed with Comert and was for having the same hours as the rest of Geneva. In fact, she thought the League should work longer hours because their work was so urgent.

Sir Eric ruled that because the petition for change had been unanimous he would give it a trial until December and then review the matter.

She felt like shouting out that it wasn't really unanimous — she, for one, hadn't signed it. The matter of the petition offended her but she felt that to raise it now would be to make too big a thing of it. Still, within the League, those sorts of tactics were out of place. Maybe she'd been out of the office or away. Or perhaps the trades-union-minded members were being dishonest and using tactics. She'd find out.

If she had been Secretary-General, though, she would have acted differently from Sir Eric. She would have checked on the real support for the petition. The other sections worked all hours and so would she.

They moved on to Germany's admission to the League and to a place on the League Council.

Sir Eric began by stressing the highly confidential nature of what he was about to say about Germany's entry. He started by stating that at last Germany would be admitted to the League and to a seat on the Council.

'There has been much private discussion about enlarging the Council,' Sir Eric said seriously. 'Brazil also wishes to be changed from a temporary member to a permanent member of Council to represent the Americas at the same time that Germany is given her seat. Brazil at present has a veto, and there was talk that she'd use it against Germany if she does not get a permanent seat as well as Germany. She's also talking of withdrawal from the League, becoming the first nation to do so since the League was set up. Our first serious loss, our first defeat.'

Someone said, 'Costa Rica.' Sir Eric said, 'Yes, there was Costa Rica.'

Edith exchanged glances with Ambrose. She again admired him. He had been the first to point out to her that Brazil would be uppity. Costa Rica wasn't important. It had found that it couldn't afford membership of the League. She thought too of the Argentine which hadn't pulled out but was sulking and wouldn't come to Assembly meetings.

Sir Eric went on to explain. 'However, everything has been ironed out. In Berlin, I talked with Herr Stresemann.' Sir Eric paused for effect. 'The problem had been that Germany wants to be admitted on its own, as an equal to the great powers and without any diminution of status, which she thinks would happen if she were admitted at the same time as a lesser power such as Brazil or Poland.'

He said that, consequently, there was loose speculative talk of enlarging the Council, if necessary, to permit everything to happen. To make Germany a permanent member and to create a new class of member — a 'semi-permanent' Council member — to allow seats to Spain, Brazil, and Poland. 'However, it won't come to that. Germany will go straight in.'

Ambrose said, in an aside to the meeting, that semi-permanent could be likened to the semi-virgin. There was general laughter.

'Quite so,' Sir Eric said, without looking up from his notes, as if he had heard that joke before. When he did look up, Sir Eric avoided her eyes or Dame Rachel's eyes, fearing, she supposed, that he'd permitted a joke which might be seen as blue.

As a connoisseur of conversation, especially the conversation of men, Edith thought that the point of Sir Eric's remarks were that he'd had private conversations with Herr Stresemann in Berlin and that this was a sign that Sir Eric was on equal footings with the powers of Europe, albeit Germany was a crippled power.

Ambrose carried the joke a little further, saying that the Spanish delegate had said that it was a pity that Adam had not considered the apple a semi-apple and thereby, Ambrose said, clearing his throat, 'committing only a semi-sin'.

Sir Eric frowned and moved his papers to show that he was continuing with important business, that Ambrose had maybe over-stretched the levity. Of course, being Catholic, Sir Eric was known not to encourage jokes with a theological flavour.

Under Secretary Bartou said that the protocol of seating had to be considered. Should the German delegates be seated last, given that, by date of entry to the League, Germany would be the lowest on the protocol list of precedence?

'Ah, but which list are you using?' Sir Eric asked. Sir Eric said that because diplomatic precedent among envoys *of the same rank* was established by date of appointment, he questioned whether it might be best to treat Germany and the other permanent Council members — and this was only an idea — as of a *senior diplomatic rank* to the other types of membership, and therefore Germany could be seated before the lesser nations.

Comert said that it was important that it should not appear that any radical change in the sitting order of the Council had been introduced simply to save the *amour propre* of Germany. 'It would,' he said turning to some of the anti-German faction, 'inflate the importance of Germany's entry.'

There were smiles of agreement at this. She realised that some felt that Germany 'had not changed'. Ambrose had told her that some of the officers, including himself, were uneasy about the arrival of Germans into the Secretariat after its admission. Secretariat positions had been promised.

Sir Eric said that seating arrangements and protocol were the prerogative of the Council.

They were all looking to the next item on the agenda when Sir Eric, after a canny pause, went on, 'However.' Everyone looked up. He then said, with a verbal wink in his voice, and looking straight at her, 'Maybe the appropriate people could see that a horseshoe table is purchased for Council before the admission meeting?'

Smiles crossed the faces of those there who seemed to see in the words of Sir Eric something which Edith did not see, although it was certainly her section which would do the purchasing.

Edith was uncertain about the political implications of the horseshoe table. She could see that it was considered a great move and that it restored good humour to the Directors' meeting.

Sir Eric said that the Council would then not have to worry

itself about the seating arrangement. At present the Council sat in a row with the permanent members sitting to the right and left of the President in descending order of seniority which would place Germany at the bottom of the table but a horseshoe table would give no clear indication of precedent without diminishing the status of the Presidency which a round table might.

Mantoux from Political said that the documents in original German would be circulated along with translations.

Colban from Translations protested. No German language documents had ever been included in League documents before.

Under Secretary Bartou also opposed this. He said that to reproduce the German text would encourage other countries to communicate in their own language and expect the League to circulate documents in that language, breaching not only the agreed practice of the League but creating administrative head-aches in the translation department. He felt it best to stay with French and English.

Edith would have ruled that way too, because although she was for Germany's entry she was dead against too many concessions to the Germans. Maybe Ambrose's influence.

Sir Eric said that the German documents circulated should be in French and English but a note included with them saying that the documents were available in their original language in the archives of the Secretariat for anyone who wanted to read them in German.

Edith liked Sir Eric's ability to find a third way.

'Finally, Mantoux, I want it to be known by the admission sub-committee — by a quiet word in the appropriate ears — that when Germany comes before the sub-committee formally for the admission, that Germany must not be expected to say anything on the question of her war guilt. If war guilt comes up she will withdraw.'

131

More grunts of both irritation at Germany's sensitivity and of understanding of the politics of the situation.

Dufour-Feronce from Intellectual Cooperation reported that he had been in Prague for the Esperanto Congress and that it had been a thoroughly lively affair.

'Congress?' Ambrose interposed. 'Not conference?'

'They called it a congress,' Dufour-Feronce said shortly. 'At the congress, encouraging evidence of the spread — '

'A conference, I should think,' Ambrose broke in again. 'There are yet, surely, no sovereign heads of Esperanto states.' Ambrose said this poker-faced. 'Or have I missed some recent political changes in the map of Europe?' The meeting laughed.

'They called it a congress, Westwood. I simply use their description,' Dufour-Feronce said, miffed by this diplomatic correction and by Ambrose's frivolous treatment of Esperanto.

Edith bit back an urge to correct Ambrose's correction of Dufour-Feronce and state that Satow, the expert on diplomatic usage, did not think that there was any longer a difference between a congress and a conference. It would be a Thing For Her To Say. She was torn with the urge to speak. But it was not to the point. It would make her sound like a know-all. She shut up. She would tease Ambrose later.

Dufour-Feronce went on with his dreary report. 'The French and German delegates fraternised completely — all conversing in Esperanto. I am not a complete convert but the movement is gaining ground. They are looking at the possibility that Esperanto might replace Latin for use in technical terminology.'

Ponderously, he turned to Sir Eric and said, 'I would like, if I may, Sir Eric, to make a personal statement to this Directors' meeting?' Sir Eric nodded assent. 'It was reported in the press that I made an opening speech and declared that the League would shortly take to using Esperanto. This is, of course, not true and I was not reported correctly. I want that to be recorded.'

Edith again groaned inwardly at all the efforts which needed to be made to correct all the wrong things which appeared in the newspapers about the League. They had to realise that corrections were futile.

He said it was appreciated by the Esperanto people that the League had a representative at the 'congress'. He went on, 'I suspect that Monsieur Benes or Monsieur Lafontaine might raise the question of the League's use of Esperanto at the next Assembly.'

Edith still hadn't spoken. She had nothing new to say about Esperanto. If there was to be an international auxiliary language, she supposed it might as well be one that already existed, that had some culture behind it. If everyone was to bother learning another language, why not a real one? The subject bored her.

Lloyd, from the Building Committee, said he was in a quandary because the tenders for new furniture showed that a Swiss company and an Austrian company had bid identically. 'Identical quotes exactly. I have never seen it before.'

Edith found herself a little breathless. Coming from a business family, she knew exactly what to do. She waited to see if Sir Eric would speak but he too, seemed to be unable to come up with an answer.

He simply said, 'Extraordinary,' and the meeting sat stalled.

In a voice which was nervously uneven, she asked if she might offer a solution.

The men turned to her. Ambrose raised an eyebrow of encouragement.

'Of course,' Sir Eric said, surprised. 'Go ahead, Berry.'

Her voice came out a little breathlessly and she deepened it and tried to speak slowly. 'Identical tenders are always to the buyer's advantage,' she said, 'that is the first thing to realise.'

She heard Dame Rachel whisper, 'Take it slowly.'

She made herself pause, although her breathing was broken. She counted to five. 'We should now go to the two companies which have given identical bids and explain to them the situation.'

She paused for the count of three. 'We then ask the two companies to re-tender.'

Pause, Edith, pause.

'Well, thank you, Berry, for your solution.'

Edith wasn't finished. She'd paused too long. 'I'm sorry, Sir Eric, that was not the end of my submission — there's more.'

'My apologies. Go ahead. Fire away.'

'Naturally we suggest to both companies that they re-tender at a lower price.'

Pause. They were looking at her with interest. Ambrose mimed a silent clap.

'They will both drop their bids — and we get an even lower price. That is how identical bids are always to the buyer's advantage.'

'What if they come in at the same price again?' Lloyd asked. He seemed put out by being told how to do his job by a newcomer and a woman.

Edith consciously spoke not to Lloyd but to Sir Eric. 'In the highly unlikely situation described by Lloyd, Sir Eric, you divide the order between the two companies.'

'Well done!' Sir Eric said. 'We need some business acumen in the League.'

Dame Rachel touched her arm and said, 'Well done, Berry.'

She didn't suggest that you could always ask the two lowest tenderers to re-tender on the pretext that they were identical. That would be unethical for the League but back home she knew people who had done it — however, she believed fiercely in the tender system as the bedrock of scrupulous administration. She was pleased with herself but wished that her contribution had been on something more diplomatic or political. She did not want to be known as some sort of horse-trader and she didn't want to end up buying furniture.

'Ingenious,' Under Secretary Bartou said.

Sir Eric said, 'Lloyd, will you see to that — following Berry's suggestion?'

Lloyd wrote something down in his notebook, far from happy.

Comert said that for 2,000 Swiss francs lighting arrangements could be made for the taking of cinema films at the next Assembly. Should the League admit cinema companies free or charge a fee?

Edith tested herself on this. If you charge, you are then under an obligation to the motion picture companies to provide all sorts of things. They will ask for more of this and more of that. You opened yourself to pestering but, anyhow, collecting fees for attendance at Assembly was petty. Cinema film was, after all, a new way of spreading the word about the League.

Sir Eric made the ruling that it was essential that the Secretariat not be under any obligation to the cinematographic firms which would be the case if the fee was charged. Comert must retain control of the situation. 'When cinema films are taken, and for how long, must be your decision, Comert.' Sir Eric added that if the cameras or whatever else they used were too noisy, they would have to go.

Edith felt pleased that she and Sir Eric had arrived at the same decision.

Under Secretary Professor Attolico of Transit informed the meeting that the President of the Association of Journalists at the League had displayed in the pressroom a copy of a letter which he had sent to Lord Cecil. The letter complimented Lord Cecil on his insistence that committee meetings be held in public. However, the letter, by supporting Lord Cecil, reflected unfavourably on the contrary attitude taken by Signor Scialoja, who had argued that the meetings be closed to the public. The letter, also, as it turned out, misrepresented the attitude of Signor Schialoja. The displaying of the letter placed him, Professor Attolico, in the position of having publicly supported one delegate against another.

Sir Eric said he was against political use of the noticeboard of the pressroom.

Comert said that notices of meetings and so on were posted on the pressroom noticeboard by journalists. He agreed that the room should not be used politically but thought any official reprimand about this would be the wrong approach. The journalists had to feel they weren't being supervised.

Sir Eric half-heartedly agreed. 'Before we move on, there is another thing which worries me,' Sir Eric said, tentatively, 'and I will be advised by you all on this — I was walking by the pressroom and glanced in. They seem to have taken to posting up caricatures of delegates and of the Secretariat. Comert, might not something be done to stop this? For these caricatures to be displayed takes away from the dignity of the League. In my opinion, that is.'

Comert thought that he should handle that informally, too.

Surreptitious glances of amusement were exchanged. Edith felt she should avoid them, being a newcomer and susceptible to giggling. Everyone had seen Emery Kelen's caricature of Sir Eric in the pressroom and anyhow, everyone, well, nearly everyone, did impersonations of Sir Eric.

'As you think best,' said Sir Eric; obviously, he would have liked a stronger stand.

Had she been Secretary-General, Edith did not know quite how she would have handled that. She would have been as sensitive as Sir Eric but she would not have raised it at a Directors' meeting — that gave further fuel to the joking. She would have handled it privately somehow. She wanted Sir Eric to be bigger than that. She looked at him curiously because of his raising it. It showed excessive self-pride. Or vulnerability. Or perhaps these things could be found together.

Major Buxton presented a short dissertation on the amount of reading that committee members had to do. He said, 'We in the Secretariat should be the world experts at presenting material so that people can take it in quickly.'

Everyone liked Major Buxton. He was the social centre of their lives and also ran a pack of hounds, much to the annoyance of the Geneva police.

'To show what happens, I have attached a copy of each of the documents so far circulated for one meeting of a single sub-committee. The meeting's not till March 19 and there are already about 350 pages of Roneo and 170 pages of print. Documents are still coming in. How can a member of committee cope?

'My proposals are for a new form of agenda which I've designed with short notes on each item. The Secretariat or the rapporteur should also issue summaries of information saying that the original longer documents can be called up if needed.' The meeting accepted Major Buxton's suggestions.

The next item on the agenda was Emergency Procedures. This was Ambrose's big moment at the meeting. Edith and Ambrose had discussed it endlessly over the last month.

Ambrose spoke about the need for the Secretariat to take precautions at least equal to those taken by a Foreign Office, or War Office, to ensure that important communications reached the proper League officials with the least delay at whatever hour they arrived. He reminded the meeting of an incident where a telegram had sat in the Palais over the week-end, unopened.

'If we can be expeditious about the matters of war, surely we can be equally expeditious about matters of peace.' Ambrose had practised that line on her a couple of times and he delivered it well.

There were hear, hears.

Ambrose said that *Agence Télégraphique Suisse* now telephoned through to the League any important news received by them by wireless.

'We have also arranged that if a member of the League sends an emergency communication it is to be marked *Priorité Nations* and governments and foreign offices have been informed that they should mark their cables thus.'

Ambrose went on to propose a duty roster for week-end and nights and the creation of a bedroom at the Palais Wilson for the duty officer.

He paused, went to the door and rapped. The door opened, and to the surprise of the meeting, Jules limpingly wheeled in a model of the bell alarm system. It was mounted on a mobile trolley which Ambrose had borrowed from one of the local street vendors. Jules must have been primed and waiting outside. 'Thank you, Jules.'

Jules audibly muttered, 'For peace, anything.' Everyone was used to Jules' irreverence.

Ambrose stood and went over to his demonstration. 'When the telephonists leave at 8 p.m. they will connect an electric bell running from the telegram tube to the concierge's desk. If a telegram does arrive, the cartridge carrying a telegram will automatically start the bell ringing.'

Ambrose directed their attention to a length of telegram tube he had set up. He took a telegram cartridge loaded with a telegram and dropped it down the neck of the tube. It came out the other end and hit a trigger which rang a bell set up on a tray connected by wires and held by Jules at the other side of the room. The bell continued to ring until Ambrose cut it off.

'To make sure that the cartridges do not become stuck in the tube on their way to the Secretariat, my clever mechanics have arranged that one of the lamps of the tube will remain lighted in the concierge's office until the telegram has arrived safely to the duty officer.'

Ambrose again demonstrated the flashing light. 'And that, gentlemen, is my apparatus.' There was some light clapping.

'Boys will be boys,' Dame Rachel whispered to her. Edith smiled broadly relishing the rapport with Dame Rachel but her smile also carried a private amusement sparked off by Dame Rachel's remark, and a voice in her head said, 'And boys will also be girls.'

There was much approval of Ambrose's memorandum and after discussion of costs and so forth, it was adopted unanimously. A triumph.

'I think the League needs a secret code as well,' Ambrose said in conclusion.

'Oh dear me,' said Dame Rachel under her breath, again sharing it with Edith, smiling at her in collusion, although Edith felt torn between the collusion and her attachment to Ambrose.

Sir Eric ruled that the question of codes should be looked into by the Under Secretary Bartou and a report made to the next meeting.

Following on Ambrose's submission, Sir Eric reminded them of the immense effectiveness of the League when its political workings were combined with the speed of the telegraph.

'Some of you newcomers to the League were not with us during the Bulgarian crisis . . .' He glanced at Edith. 'At one in the afternoon I received an appeal from Bulgaria. Greek troops had crossed the frontier and were battling their way into Bulgaria. Four days earlier there'd been a quarrel over a card game at the border post at Demir-Kapou. A Greek soldier had been killed and a Greek officer coming up to settle the matter under a white flag of truce had been gunned down. I telephoned Monsieur Briand, then President of Council, and urged him to telegraph both sides, asking them to cease hostilities and withdraw their forces, which he did. Both sides immediately complied with our telegraph. Invasion orders were countermanded. This demonstrates the amazing power of the telegraph. After the telegrams arrived the troops on both sides remained frozen in position. We then issued our first League ultimatum — again by telegraph — that both sides must withdraw to their borders within sixty hours. British, French, and Italian military attachés in the Balkans were dispatched by the League to supervise the withdrawal. The war was over in three days.'

There were courteous murmurs of pleasure, and a few said, 'Well done, Sir Eric.' One or two tapped the table in affirmation. 'Well done, Sir Eric,' she said along with the others, in a voice that could hardly be heard.

'Not "Well done, Sir Eric",' Sir Eric said, sternly, 'well done, Sir Telegraph.'

They laughed like school children at the end of class. He closed the meeting.

The complaint from New Zealand and the Stockholm Commission on the Lighting of Coasts had not been reached and were put over to the next meeting. She knew about the New Zealand complaints that the mail always got to them too late and that Sir Eric was paid five times more than their Prime Minister.

As the meeting was breaking up Dame Rachel said, 'Sir

Eric — may I quickly raise a small matter — or what I take to be a small matter?'

Sir Eric looked at the pocket watch which he had on the table in front of him. 'If we can be brief, Dame Rachel.'

'It's about this strange cavalcade which went through Geneva last week.'

People were gathering their papers together and rather eager to go but there were chuckles at the mention of the cavalcade.

Edith coloured and shuffled her papers. Ye gods, please, no.

Dame Rachel said, 'This Captain Strongbow had a military motor-car and a girl dressed I think as a cowboy. Other "girls" were involved. I have no recollection, Sir Eric, that this Captain Strongbow had ever obtained any recognition from us. But his publicity material claims so.'

Under Secretary Bartou gave a comradely glance over at Edith. She wondered whether he was implying that she should say something about the matter. At least he wasn't mad at her for not having sat with him. She tried to avoid Ambrose's eyes, realising that the mention of the cowgirl would have caused a penny to drop. She eventually glanced across. He had a strange expression on his face but it was affectionate and he'd obviously made a connection. He wagged his finger in a gesture which said, 'Just you wait, young lady.' His comradeship didn't help much and she filled with apprehension and fiddled with her notes, eyes down.

'Oh, we mustn't worry ourselves with every exhibitionist who comes to town,' Sir Eric said, himself putting together his papers to leave.

Good. No, we must not.

'I felt that it should be made clear in the *Journal de Genève*?' Dame Rachel continued.

'If you think so, Dame Rachel,' said Sir Eric, agreeing, Edith could tell, only for the sake of avoiding further discussion. He looked over at Comert. 'Could you arrange for a statement to be issued?'

Edith waited to hear if anything else was to be said, whether Dame Rachel was now going to point at her and say, 'Finally, Sir Eric, here in this very room, seated beside me, is the traitor, the person who masqueraded as a silly cowgirl and who besmirched the good name of the League of Nations.' She saw the members of the *haute direction* in unison shouting, 'Off with her head.'

Nothing more was said. The meeting was over.

Dame Rachel said to Edith, 'Did you see this cavalcade?'

Edith was able to answer with technical honesty that no, she had not 'seen' the cavalcade.

'The League could end up attracting every crackpot idea and person in the world to Geneva,' Dame Rachel said crossly.

'I suppose it's our job to assess them.'

'I sincerely hope not.'

Relieved of the apprehension of being implicated in the Strongbow matter, Edith now imagined creating a sensation by defending the ideas of Captain Strongbow. However, she knew that it would be beyond her, and anyhow, the meeting was over.

Sir Eric knocked his pipe on the desk and called for attention. 'Sorry, people, but there is one further matter. Huston has asked that, during the Assembly, dogs should not be brought into the building. Staff should keep their dogs at home for the two weeks of the Assembly, and that includes section mascots. Some of our less stalwart delegates, I am told, have a phobia about dogs.'

More laughter.

Edith felt sweat on her back from her nervousness about the Strongbow matter and she still avoided Under Secretary Bartou's eyes.

142

The meeting broke up at 7.30 p.m, although some of the Directors stayed chatting. Dame Rachel again complimented her on her contribution to the meeting. Although she wasn't looking, she sensed Under Secretary Bartou coming over to her. She forced herself to look up at him, deciding that she wouldn't try to explain why she'd sat with Dame Rachel when she'd said she was going to sit with Ambrose. He congratulated her on her contribution about tendering. 'It is probably uniquely historic.'

'Historic?'

'You got to give an answer on a problem which probably happens once in a lifetime.' He smiled. 'Well done. Good night.'

She walked back to her office with Ambrose. 'Cowgirl scandalises League of Nations,' he said. 'Very, very naughty. I won't ask questions. It was very naughty. You take my breath away, Edith Campbell Berry — or it is E. Campbell Berry now? — you take my breath away.'

'You can be the cowgirl next time,' she said, trying to be self-confident.

'Thank you. So I take it that you were the cowgirl of the cavalcade mentioned?'

'Afraid so.'

'Amazing. I think, in future, we'll keep costumes for the bedroom. Agreed?'

'Agreed.'

The rest of the staff had gone, and she felt a tingle of importance at still being around. She liked it when there were only a few of them working late and she especially loved it when they had to work through the night and came out into quai Woodrow Wilson to see dawn breaking over the lake and all went for a breakfast together in a café. She envied the people in Documents who often worked all night to get the minutes and reports circulated by 9 a.m. and had such wonderful *esprit de corps.*

Ambrose and she decided to go off for a champagne celebration of the acceptance of his memorandum on emergency procedures, and Ambrose graciously in turn added, 'And to celebrate your display of acumen. But not, *not* to celebrate your display of audacity.'

She said she wanted to be known for her diplomacy, not for her commercial acumen.

'You will be. Give it time.'

They collected Florence who was also working late.

On the way out, Edith teased Ambrose about making a distinction between a conference and congress. 'Satow no longer thinks it matters. I nearly corrected you in the meeting.'

Florence, obviously impressed, said, 'Edith! You've been swotting.'

Florence's praise caused her to smirk inwardly.

Ambrose came back, 'Ah, but Sibert does. On these matters of diplomatic distinction, I'm a Sibert man. I think it's good to know what a thing is when you see its name. Really, if one was to be a stickler, which I am, congress should be used only when plenipotentiaries meet to make peace.'

Edith laughed with another, different sensation of gratification. She was glad that Ambrose had made a comeback at her and she was glad to defer to him. She told how as she'd gone into the meeting, Under Secretary Bartou said — Edith mimicked his voice — ' "Remember, Berry, a meeting is a diplomatic endeavour: you pursue interests: you exercise comity." The problem was that I didn't know what comity was. So I couldn't exercise it. I hope he didn't notice.'

They laughed with her.

144

'Comity is courtesy, Edith dear, those courtesies granted among nations. Expressed through protocol.'

'And protocol is formalised goodwill,' Edith said.

'Correct. Ten out of ten. Did he also say that diplomacy is part of a country's arsenal?'

'No, he didn't.' She realised how much she loved to relax in deference to Ambrose. Oh, she did. Though as they walked to the Beau-Rivage, she realised that her deference to Ambrose was, this day, not quite firm. In the beginning of their relationship, it had been there strongly. She realised she was frightened now that Ambrose might fail; she no longer had the same unquestioning confidence in him that she had at the beginning. Perhaps it was Dame Rachel saying 'Boys will be boys' while she'd been quietly cheering him on. Dame Rachel's remark had caused her to see Ambrose slightly differently. She couldn't say exactly how. Maybe today he had gone too much into details over emergency procedures in an almost embarrassing way. The bell business. Jules wheeling in the scale model. No. She worried too much. Today had been a triumph for him.

She moaned to Florence about how she'd been seen as a horse-trader and not a diplomat at the meeting.

Florence said, 'The point is, dear Edith, you were noticed. Now, both of you, tell me what happened. Tell the gossip — is Germany in? Tell all — what exactly did you both do?!'

Edith was about to tell of her contribution in every detail when Ambrose put a finger to his mouth and shook his head. 'Confidential.' He put an arm around Florence, 'Our lips are sealed — you know, it's all hush-hush at Directors' meetings.'

'You can tell me,' Florence said, miffed.

'Surely I can tell Florence about my contribution?'

'No. All's confidential,' Ambrose said, seriously.

She shrugged and grimaced at Florence. 'Sorry.'

'But I was the one who talked you into wrangling your way into the meeting!' Florence was genuinely hurt.

They walked for a little way in uncomfortable silence.

At the Beau-Rivage Florence hesitated about joining them, intending to go off in a sulk. They both grabbed her arms and marched her in and made efforts to jolly her out of it.

With the help of the champagne they were soon giggling and gossiping — but not about the Directors' meeting, although Edith was still hankering to tell all.

The Accepting of Gifts:
Miss Dickinson's Chair

When the Assembly decided, at last, to build the Palais des Nations, Edith cried.

She cried alone in her rooms in the boulevard des Philosophes from an elation which had begun jetting up out of a pool of humble relief. By deciding to build the Palais, the League had affirmed the covenant in an undeniable, durable and irrevocable way. As her father would have said, affirmed it in bricks and mortar. For these, her old father's words, she also cried. And she cried because it happened on St Edith's Day, allowing herself to enjoy a silly congruence.

It also affirmed to Edith that her work for the League would continue, not in the crass sense of having a job, but in the sense that she believed in her vocation and wanted it to go on to fulfil its destiny. Until now the League's only solidity was in its procedures, the making of new files, the enlarging of the staff, and the pumping out of League publications. The Assembly still met in a rented hall and the Palais Wilson was, after all, a renovated hotel.

To get down to the level of the whinge, yes, she would be heartily glad to get out of the Palais Wilson and its foul acoustics and away from office overcrowding. Of course, she would work in a hole in the ground for the League if she had to, but the 'physicals' — again, her father's word; he had always stressed the physicals — were the credence of an enterprise. The League had now to affirm itself and build its Palace as a bulwark against human frailty.

She dried her eyes and put on a gramophone record of *Carmen* and prepared for a night alone, flopping into her big, soft armchair. Though she wouldn't mind if she cried on and off, but it would be the crying of mellow tears from the anticipation of vulnerable, good things.

Although she saw herself as a person who wanted to be with people, she also cherished the aloneness of some of her nights of solitary indulgence. She led a life of ever-changing faces at ever-changing meetings and she didn't bemoan this. Every month at the Secretariat there seemed to be new faces. She had her familiars and her work friends, but sometimes it was a relief to know that nothing was happening or changing in her life that night, or the next morning, and especially if nothing was happening also the following day. She treasured waking up in the morning and realising that she had nothing to do, that no one expected anything of her that day. She was absolutely sure that she was suited for administrative work which required so much dealing with strangers and most of the time she enjoyed the exploration of new faces and meeting someone of a nationality she had not before encountered. She never minded having to tell strangers how the League worked. Every new document which came to her desk she took up with enthusiasm. Nor did she feel strange in Geneva, but there was still some unfamiliarity in the city. She had yet to become fully international but was making progress; she still found her French, while much improved, would occasionally bring corrections from her French friend Jeanne or from those who, unasked, dutifully adopted the role of French tutor at every conversation.

But that she couldn't intensely and tearfully share her jubilation about the new building with anyone was also part of her tears. She cried alone because she thought it would be difficult to share with Ambrose, who was always wanting to live life lightly and sardonically, or with Florence, who was, she now thought, a bit breezy, and who could be seen also as crafty, or with Victoria, who worried, and was not a jubilant type, although they were all committed to the League. If she'd tried to celebrate her joy with Victoria, Victoria would say, 'Prepare yourself to be cheated.' They were all staunch, she knew that, but they did not suffer as much as she did about all this, about designing the future. Florence talked of going to work in Russia for the revolution although she was not a communist. She tried to describe herself as an adventuress but it didn't quite fit. Ambrose still had some arrangement, a bolt-hole he called it, with the British Foreign Office.

For Edith, there was now nothing else in her life. Maybe she had a life back in Australia, but that was fading as time passed — her life back there was rusting away in a paddock. Letters were not as frequent — from her to Australia as well as to her. Except for her family, her friends didn't correspond the way they'd promised they would. She had Ambrose as something of a lover, but she didn't have a husband and family, unlike most of her friends back home, something she kept meaning to think seriously about — because she certainly wanted to be a mother and a wife, it came to her mind every month at the cycle of her womanhood. When? She liked the idea of being a wife and liked the word wife. Those matters had been adjourned in her. Could these things really be adjourned? She didn't have an eligible man and was not conscious of looking for one. Ambrose was too bizarre, and her own behaviour of late with Ambrose had not led her to believe that she was fit to be a bride just yet. She giggled, sniffling from her mellow tears, drying her eyes. Sometimes, in fact, with Ambrose she was more the bridegroom than the bride. Although it was sometimes said that the modern bride, or any bride at any time, had to be something of a courtesan as well as wife and mother to the man. Her behaviour was somewhat different again to that of a courtesan and she didn't have a word for it, if a word existed, and she perhaps didn't want particularly to know the word which applied to her amorous behaviour at this point in her life. The world had changed in that matter, the matter of sexual behaviour. Even her broad-minded mother would die if she could see how people in Europe behaved now. She really believed that sexual behaviour at least had been separated from sin, and then separated from motherhood, and the implications of this were something she meant to learn more about, and that was an advance. Physical love was now also what it should be — a manifestation of the times. The League was not yet concerned with these matters but she imagined that it would get around to it.

All this being the case, she was no longer a girl and maybe the time for her being a Manifestation of the Times was coming to an end and she would have to give some thought to the matter of her amorous behaviour of late. Being in Geneva had permitted her to behave in a way she would never have dreamed back in Australia. This was not only the refashioning of self on which she knew she was embarked. She supposed that it could be seen as a coming out of self, as well as a becoming of self. That is, if she had any 'original self' left. Back home too many people watched her with their own expectations of her, and she'd had to acknowledge this and respond to them as they might want her to respond to them. Now there was the New Edith. The big difference, and the good difference, was that now she had placed herself, rather than finding herself placed, among people whose expectations of her were also her expectations of herself.

The planned Palais des Nations was to be an expression of the grandeur of the League; at the same time, the Palais was to embody the workings of a parliament of the world, or at least act as a business office for the world, and also be a temple of peace. While not herself being exactly what someone might describe as a nun devoted to Holy Orders, she had, she sometimes thought to herself, taken vocational vows. There was a clericature to her life. If there had been a League of Nations vow, she would have taken it. It was more that she was, perhaps, a courtier — maybe a priestess — and needed to live in a Palais, if not a temple. She wished the Secretariat could all *live* in the Palais — not, though, she smiled, as if in a monastery — and she had been disappointed when she learned from the specifications given to the architects for the competition that this was not to be.

They'd been at a meeting where the assistant architect had explained the specifications for the new Palais and Edith had asked where the living quarters were to be.

The assistant architect had been puzzled and had explained that there were no living quarters in the specifications.

Edith had been about to ask 'Why not?' when she realised that the others at the meeting found her question strange and she shut up and sat down. Anyhow, she'd already asked two questions. She'd asked whether the architect had visualised how the building would look in the four seasons, in rain, in snow, in sunlight and how it would look in two hundred years' time. The assistant architect had replied to her that he would ask the head architect the first question, and God the second question.

How grand it would be for all of them to live in such a Palais. It would be like the court of England, when they spoke both French and English, all living in the court, say, about the time of Henry VIII, with ceremonials, jousts, feasting and diplomacy. Under Secretary Bartou said that it was good that the Secretariat and other staff lived out in the city of Geneva with the citizens but she couldn't see much advantage. The Swiss, or the Genevese, seemed fairly indifferent when they were not for having Switzerland out of the League or, in extreme cases, the League out of Switzerland. So why live among them? It really didn't matter what the Swiss or the Genevese thought. She hoped that the League would go ahead with the plans to have its own railway station and airport. There was also talk of the League buying its own train which could speed to a crisis and negotiate.

Edith blew her nose, and with her glass of sherry tried to concentrate on shedding a few more tears of joy or of something like joy, by thinking of the building of the Palais des Nations, her father and mother, her home in Jasper's Brush, sea shells, the swirl and wash of the long curving surf of Seven Mile Beach, and one peaceful world. When no more tears were left, she let herself turn to enjoying her rooms, her own cloister, which were becoming at last a portrayal of herself. The rooms had higher ceilings than she'd ever seen in a private home in Australia. Her curtains were heavy maroon, velvet, velvet being her favourite fabric. They helped to reshape the window. It had seemed out of shape. It also helped exclude from the view some of a building which she didn't like. She argued with herself, on and off, about whether one should 'accept' the view from any given window as being the bona fide and incontestable 'outside' of the room. The windows looked out on a courtyard which she didn't find disagreeable at all. It was a building to the left which she disliked and tried to exclude.

She'd found the low, deep-seated, heavily padded soft arm-chair from the last century, covered in velveteen, a maroon very close to that of the curtains, in which she could sprawl and read — more a sprawling chair than a reading chair. She'd found a low table with two folding side panels, which tended to become a dumping ground for magazines and books, but when she had someone to her room, she could clear it off and serve tea and cakes from it carried up by Madame Didier. For the low table, she had two Viennese bent wood armchairs, which were comfortable enough for sitting up at afternoon tea. If the afternoon tea went well they could retire — the guest to the sprawling chair, and she to the Wilson chair. The American Wilson chair was a much-loved monstrosity with an adjustable back, adjustable body section, adjustable leg panel and an adjustable attached foot stool. She and Florence had found it at the flea market in la plaine de Plainpalais. It could fully recline to become a bed and one night Florence had slept on it, covered by a travelling rug, too lazy from wine to go to her own pension. The chair lent itself to irreverent jokes about President Wilson's Fourteen Points. She tried to tell herself that the jokes gave the chair Historical Lineage but she wasn't convinced. She liked the Wilson chair because it was mechanically ingenious. But she didn't think that mechanical ingenuity was an Aesthetic rule. It was really just a curiosity. She liked it because it allowed her have an unposed attitude, neither demanding that she sit or that she lie. She adjusted it according to mood. She had a few potted plants on her windowsill.

From Australia had arrived the chest containing her few possessions including her much-loved dark-red karri-wood vases, poker-worked with Australian wild flowers. She had three framed lithographs of Sydney, the work of Thea Proctor. Photographs of her family and a class photograph from her last year at school were on the mantel above the fireplace. Her eighteenth-century brass microscope was also there. It was an object which looked bizarre wherever she put it but it had been a gift from her mother. It had to go somewhere. She'd had her mother ship over all her books, including her school books and her science books and all her Everyman's Library books. She'd wanted them all as a way of reminding herself that she did *know things*. It somehow reinforced her as a person to have Porritt's *Chemistry of Rubber* and Marshall's *Frog* in her bookcase. She had a work table with a velvet bag hanging under the table top on slides which meant that it could be pushed away under the table. She had her Smith-Corona typewriter which she thought very attractively shaped, and a wooden clerk's chair on castors. That was also adjustable, and had a sprung back which was supposed to reduce fatigue, but Edith didn't know, having never had fatigue. She was still searching for a pulley lamp for her desk which she could raise and lower with a ceramic weight. She'd found a dressing table with three mirrors, the two side mirrors being on swivels, so one could see nearly all of one's head. It had ten drawers. Then there was her neat single bed in a discreet alcove. The floor rugs were handcrafted. She had five table and standard lamps to allow her to light different spaces of the two rooms for different purposes and moods.

Nearly everything in her two rooms now had been chosen by her, or if not, left there because it pleased her. She savoured her rooms at the Pension Levant and her meagre but irreproachable and agreeable possessions.

The opera played on and she thought to herself, Each of us has a space around us which we could sculpture, and then we could work outwards, each from our gardens, spreading into the world, as in Geneva the League would build a Palais des Nations in the parc l'Ariana, and grandeur and reasoned order would spread outwards. But unless that centre was in good order, no good order could flow out from it.

*

When all the Palais design entries from around the world were in and the competition jury couldn't agree on a winning entry, Edith did not laugh along with the journalists and the rest. That the jury couldn't agree on the winning plan was a joke around Geneva and, of course, at the Bavaria and among the Swiss Germans around the corner at Gambrinus, and among the socialist crowd at the Landolt where, she suspected, all jokes about the League began.

There was a progressive group around the Secretariat and the Bavaria who had wanted Le Corbusier to win. She discovered that she was more of a traditionalist and had wanted someone solid like Nenot from Paris to win. Perhaps she should try to be more modernistic about architecture but she was modern about most things without being wearisomely 'advanced' in her thinking on all matters. About architecture, she thought that maybe she would continue to be an inveterate traditionalist. That would be one of the things that the Refashioned Edith would be traditional about.

'I'm afraid that when it comes to architecture I am an inveterate traditionalist. I prefer the stately,' Edith said out aloud in the Bavaria, for the sound of it, trying it out. The word 'stately' was perfect. 'To be frank, I prefer the august to the angular.' No one seemed to be listening in the babble. She said it to herself and to her wine glass. She thought the League should have some of the grandeur of the world of Roman legations while still acknowledging that the League was trying to break with the diplomacy of the past. That was part of it — she wanted the new building to do something *to her*. To do something for all of them who worked there and who entered there to meet. She wanted to be exalted. 'I want to be exalted by my surroundings,' she said aloud.

Florence heard her this time and glanced at her, and then

looked around the Bavaria, crowded with journalists and the younger set of the Secretariat. 'Exalted?' Florence asked.

'Never mind,' she said to Florence, 'I was somewhere else.'

'To be exalted, you would have to be.'

She hoped that the Building Committee would resolve the impasse and decide for something which acknowledged the past while meeting the future. She did not want Le Corbusier to win and she argued this very well against the progressive set at parties and picnics who said things like, 'The building should be a negotiating machine.'

'I don't want to work in a machine. I want to work in an edifice.' She even argued that negotiation was best done in august surroundings because august surroundings calmed passions and diminished egotism. She wanted to work in a building which spoke to her and touched her every day she went to it. Which daily convoked her ideals as she went up its steps. She did not want to work in a building she failed to notice. Or worse a building which touted the personality of its architect.

When the Australian government was the first nation to offer a gift to the planned Palais of Nations, Edith cried a few tears of pride.

Victoria, who worked in Registry, rang her and said, 'Edith, this will make you happy.' Victoria read out the telegram from the Prime Minister of Australia to the League of Nations.

*

Edith kept an interest in the Palais and its development, and when, in the new file on the Palais furnishing, she came across the letter from Miss Dickinson she was moved to exclaim and went along the corridor to show it to Florence.

Miss Dickinson's letter was handwritten in what seemed to be home-made black ink. The letterhead was from a linocut of her school for war orphans in the Kingdom of the Serbs, Croats and Slovenes and was addressed to Sir Eric.

I am writing direct to you. Ever since the War, I have been in Jugo-slavia where a war orphanage I started in 1919 has developed into a cabinet-making industry. It has always been my wish to make something appropriate for the League of Nations for whose aims I have worked like my brother Sir Willoughby Dickinson since even before the War. My boys have now designed a chair suitable for a chairman's seat, made of Balkan woods and which my boys and I should like to present to the League of Nations. The design represents doves with outstretched wings and is beautifully carried out as regards to workmanship.

Believe me,

Yours faithfully,

Annie J. Dickinson.

They both looked at the photograph of the chair. 'Very nice,' Florence said. 'Who is Sir Willoughby Dickinson? Should we know?'

Edith shrugged.

On reading the letter to Florence, Edith saw the war orphans working industriously on the chair, she saw the public-spirited, practical Annie Dickinson hovering about, caring for them and guiding them. Maybe that was where she, Edith, belonged, working with the orphans. Making things from wood. She'd begun a poem about working with wood. The poem said that the pencil and the paper with which she worked were made from wood. The Secretariat in fact worked with wood.

She went back to her office, glancing through the rest of the file as she walked along the corridor. She came to a minute from Lloyd who was secretary of the Building Committee, to Sir Eric, which read: 'Please see the accompanying letter from Miss Dickinson (sister of Sir Willoughby Dickinson). I suggest this little gift should be informally accepted now and put into use in one of the present committee rooms. It would seem to give it an undue importance if it were left over to be sent in as a gift to the new building.'

Edith lost her calm. 'Little gift', 'undue importance' — what in the world did he know about importance and its size?

Edith's heart hurt. She was about to storm down to Lloyd's office and ask him what he knew about undue importance. She felt that it would be impossible to give the chair too much importance!

She raged about her office, trying to regain a condition of mind which would permit her to speak.

Then she did go to Lloyd's office.

He heard her out.

'I take your point, Berry. You have more of the poet in you than I. See it from my perspective — I have to maintain an overall view on the Palais. I have to see that everything is in proportion. If we started to accept chairs from everyone in the world, where would we be?'

'Everyone in the world does not offer us chairs. If they did, well, maybe that would be a marvellous thing too. We could say that the chairs of the League of Nations were donated by the people of the world.'

'They would not match,' he said and then realising that was an argument not likely to touch her, his voice died off into a cough.

Edith took it that he saw the sadness of his comment and let it pass. She said, 'Furthermore, we have a photograph of this chair. This is a remarkable chair.'

'Remarkable?' He looked again at the photograph in the file. 'I don't know if I'd want to sit in it too long.'

'I agree, Lloyd, that the test of a chair is in the sitting. All things being equal it should be a reasonable sitting chair.'

He agreed to reconsider his advice to Sir Eric.

As she left his office, she thought that it was the nearest thing to a row that she'd had at the League. When she'd first arrived she'd thought rather unrealistically that people mightn't have rows at the League.

Edith kept a watch on the outward file and saw no letter of acceptance to Miss Dickinson. She waited another month and there still wasn't one.

She again went to Lloyd, trying not to fume, and asked him what had happened. He pleaded the burden of the project. This time she waited in his office while he drafted a letter of acceptance, using her female wiles and the force of virtue, speaking for the orphans of the War, there in Jugo-slavia, waiting for their gift to be recognised by the League of Nations in Geneva.

She orated, but mostly she sat on the edge of his desk showing silk-stockinged legs, her ankles, and the cross-straps of her new kid leather shoes.

He worked up a draft of a letter of acceptance which would go to Sir Eric for signing and handed it to her to read.

'Good, that's good. Thank you, Lloyd,' she said, taking the

draft from him and reading it again. 'You say "a chair suitable for a chairman of committee" but I'm sure that Miss Dickinson saw it being the Assembly or Council President's chair. But I'll bow to your judgement.' Like hell she would; she would somehow see to it that the chair was used by one or other of the two presidents.

She left the corner of his desk and stood facing him. 'Know now, Lloyd,' she said, 'that you are a person complete within this day.' He moved papers on his desk, flushed, not looking at her. She went on, 'By writing this to the orphans, you could die tonight and not feel that you have lived badly, or left undone those things which ought to have been done.' She thought that she needed to lay it on thick, he being Welsh.

Lloyd smiled uneasily, looking at her breasts, and then frowned uncomprehendingly as she left the room.

'Maybe a cocktail after work?' he called to her back, in an uncertain voice.

'Maybe a cocktail after work one of these days, by all means. Not tonight. Busy. Thanks, Lloyd.'

She did not trust anyone in Internal Services on this. They did, indeed, lack poetry. She went down and had afternoon tea with Victoria in the Registry and asked her to keep an eye on mail related to the chair and let her know.

'I will not tamper with anything,' Victoria said, defending the honour of her position. Every time Edith looked at Victoria she recalled that one of the first things Victoria had told her about herself was that, back in New Zealand, she'd founded the League of Nations Union in Opotiki.

'Victoria, I wouldn't expect you to tamper with anything. I want only to be alerted to the comings and goings of letters about the chair.'

'Because you feel so strongly about the orphans?' Victoria said, by her tone somehow doubting this.

This surprised Edith, this note of doubt. 'Why? Do you doubt my motives?'

'It's a rather sentimental stand to take, to be interested so much in a chair. Even if made by orphans.'

Edith began to wonder whether she was the only one who saw what the chair meant. 'You don't see me as sentimental?'

Victoria considered her answer and then said, 'You live it up — you don't seem to be sentimental, no.'

Edith realised then that she didn't know whether she'd describe herself as 'sentimental'. Nor had she realised that she 'lived it up', or was seen to be 'living it up'. Then she said, 'Anyhow, I don't consider this as sentimentality.'

She pondered what it was that the chair was about. 'I see it as part of the creating of the new Palais. I think that is how the League should be created — by gift.'

'I suppose so.'

Edith felt inspired. 'We start with just a chair as this — we start with Miss Dickinson's chair. I want the Palais to be layer upon layer of the best of human effort and art, a museum of all the best in human experience.'

'My, my,' said Victoria, 'we are inspired today.'

'I want the new Palais to be an organ of human memory.'

That was all a bit beyond Victoria, although people said she was terribly good at her job.

Victoria wanted to be justified in extending the mail privilege Edith was asking but Edith knew Victoria would do it also because of the little sorority which was emerging in the Secretariat. After all, it wasn't in breach of office rules. 'Victoria, we girls have to stick together,' she threw in, as she left. Victoria didn't respond to this one way or another — the sorority wasn't altogether something that Victoria approved of either. It suggested misty codes of behaviour outside the staff rules.

Victoria, for whatever reason, did keep an eye on the correspondence to do with the chair, and she alerted Edith to the next letter from Miss Dickinson to Sir Eric, which said, 'I am sorry to trouble you again should you have received my first letter, but I fear that is not the case. I am writing again after writing months ago . . .' It was clear that no communication had reached her. Miss Dickinson again described the chair. 'I wrote to Lord Cushendun who is an old friend, asking advice as to how and when to present it but he never received my letter, either. Later I wrote direct to you but I fancy the same fate for my letter. Now this, my third letter, I am sending through England but I have no third photograph to hand. My young craftsman has put his whole heart into this chair . . .'

No one was answering Miss Dickinson's letters! Not Lord Cushendun or the League. Edith felt cheated. Lloyd hadn't sent the letter after all. The so-called draft had been to get her out of his office. Or to get her into his arms.

She stormed down to his office again.

Defensively, he exclaimed that he had been late getting it to Sir Eric but the draft had gone up to him two months ago.

'Can't you see that for these orphans and Miss Dickinson every week is an agony of waiting? They worked for years, well, maybe a year, on this chair and you can't even get a dashed letter written to them in a month!'

'Why don't you yell at Sir Eric?' Lloyd scratched around and found a copy of his reply. 'There,' he said, handing a draft to her. 'That was what I showed you and that was what went to Sir Eric.' She looked at it and then stared at him, uncertain about what was going on. She went back to her office. Of course she

164

couldn't go barging into Sir E's office about Miss Dickinson's chair when he had disarmament, opium, the white slave traffic, and God knows what other world problems on his mind.

Over a gin in the Secretariat lounge, she told Florence about the distressing business.

Florence pondered the problem. Florence drank, then turned to her and said, 'I can solve your problem like that.' She snapped her fingers.

'How, Florence?'

'I'll begin with a tale. I will tell you of Mary McGeachy's last visit to Canada and how she became the Secretary-General. At least for a day or two.'

They were both admirers of Mary McGeachy, a Canadian who worked in Information.

'Tell!'

Florence was renowned for her gossip. 'This is a tale about Girls Taking Their Due. I am sitting in Finance doing expenses claims and in comes one from Mary. I look at it closely and see that she's made an application for annual leave. She's entitled to her paid return trip to Canada. She makes her application as an assistant officer — that's all she is, you know. The leave was approved. Next she proposes to the boys in *haute direction* that while in Canada she extend for a week or so and give talks there, to the YWCA and so on, and they think this is a worthy idea.'

Florence took a drink.

'After she has agreement on this, she then suggests she be given higher subsistence and so on because she will be doing higher duties — talking in public, blah blah. She says she should go to a higher scale of subsistence. Well, we consider this, and agree to give her just a proportion of her time on the higher subsistence.'

'Is that it? I don't see the point.'

'No, more, much more. This is a moral fable, Edith, listen carefully. Comes a third memo. And comes the second drink. It's thirsty work telling moral fables.' Florence held her empty glass to Edith.

Edith ordered her another drink. 'It better be worth two gin fizzes.'

'It is, it is. Thank you, my dear. The third memo asks for . . . ?'

'A *lettre de mission*?' Edith was beginning to see where the story was going.

'Correct. Mary asks for a *lettre de mission* to get her type-writer and "confidential papers" and so forth through customs. She also asks for a League dispatch box.'

'A dispatch box!'

'When I read this, I said to myself there in Finance, three cheers for you, Mary McGeachy. Mary says she needs the official dispatch box because she will be carrying confidential papers and so forth from which to prepare her speeches. About this, they hum and hah. But they give it to her.'

'Good for her. So she starts out on a vacation which ends up being a special mission complete with a *lettre de mission* and dispatch box.'

'Precisely. And at a higher duty scale. And she gets off the boat and walks straight through customs. Dispatch box, ward-robe trunk, tennis racket in a press, and her hatbox, I suppose. There's more. When she comes back, she asks for all sorts of expenses that weren't foreseen in the original applications. So it comes to us again in Finance with newspaper clippings about the great publicity she got for the League in Canada. I read these with interest. What becomes clear is that when she talked in public, she represented the Secretary-General. That is how the *lettre de mission* is worded, anyhow — anyone who talks in

166

public for the League represents the Secretary-General. She arrives in Canada and is interviewed, I guess, by her old buddies from the newspapers, and inflation begins. By the time she reaches Montreal she's reported in the papers as Acting Secretary-General.'

They both laughed. 'I like this story,' Edith said, although she also thought that Mary shouldn't have been underhanded about it.

'There is more. She ends up briefing the Canadian cabinet!'

'No!'

'*So* . . . Mary is Secretary-General, for a few days, at least. By the time she gets back to Geneva, the carriage has changed back into a pumpkin, and she is plain old Mary, a junior assistant, arguing with Finance over her expenses claims. There was one that I liked. We had to query her claims for entertaining because she had no receipts. She haughtily replies that she always entertained "in her clubs" and that we would understand that it was not the practice for clubs to issue receipts.'

'Florence, what's this got to do with the orphan's chair? And I'm not sure you should be telling me confidential things from her file.'

'Pooh to confidentiality. The tale has everything to do with orphans.' Florence paused and said, 'Dear Edith. Just go into Sir E's office and sign the letter to your Miss Dickinson. Sign the letter, if the letter exists, sign it "Sir Eric", and put it in the out-tray. Or if the letter doesn't exist, type it up and sign it and put it in the out-tray.'

Edith looked at her with disbelief.

'If she can become Secretary-General for a few days, you can become Secretary-General for a couple of seconds. The orphans at least deserve that much.'

'I'll have to argue with the police, not with Finance.' It was

167

without one doubt, a dismissable offence. If not a gaolable offence. 'In fact, Florence, I think that what you're suggesting is called forgery.'

Florence laughed and said in a mocking voice, 'You could be dragged before the Committee on Disciplining and Analogous Questions.'

'More likely they'll just throw me out on my ear.'

'Edith, dear, what I'm suggesting is the assumption of command in a situation which requires initiative from a subordinate officer.'

Edith gave a small snort. In the field that may be possible.

Florence said, 'You took initiative when you wanted to go to the Directors' meeting.'

'That was hardly forgery.'

She'd never told Florence about the Strongbow incident. After that fiasco, she'd promised herself that she'd stick to strict and regular conduct.

'I'll think about it.'

'You'll finish that drink, you'll go up there now, and you'll do it. Do it. No one will be around up there now.'

Edith sat at the bar and thought about it. The letter had been drafted; accepting the gift did not conflict with League policy. It was really about delay through pressure of business, she was sure. Of course, she didn't have the authority to sign letters.

She remembered her father telling her about 'overlearning' or learning the wrong lesson from experience. He used to quote the example of a cat which once having sat on a hot stove learned never to sit on any stove again, instead of learning just to avoid hot stoves. Was this plan another hot stove like Strongbow or another sort of stove? She looked at Florence. Florence was more crafty than she, but Edith did not want to be seen as lacking boldness.

'Go on, do it,' Florence said.

And she did. She left Florence in the bar and went upstairs. She went to her own office, armed herself with some papers to give herself the appearance of being on duty and went down again to Sir Eric's sanctum with the movements of someone who belonged in there. She feared his private secretary, Jean 'Tiger' Howard, more than she feared Sir Eric but she knocked and there was no reply. She went in through Tiger's office and into Sir Eric's. Everyone called it the Countess' bedroom, because it was where Countess von Trani always stayed in the old days.

She stood in the large office, immobilised by the magnitude of its role in the world and by her trespass upon it.

She forced herself to continue with her mission.

She then went through papers waiting his signature and found the Dickinson letter, a long way down, the letter drafted by Lloyd. Lloyd had not been lying. Idly she thought that she might owe him something for having done it, and smiled to herself. Virtue is its own reward.

Edith was sickened to see that it was now five months after Miss Dickinson's first letter. That alone, she felt, justified her taking action.

With what would she sign it? Her pen? His pen? The pen in the ivory and gold inkstand? Not brass and glass, nor crystal and silver, but ivory and gold for the Secretary-General. She smiled to herself as she remembered Athena's beautiful ivory and silver pistol. It gave her courage.

With a quick flourish she did a passable imitation of Sir Eric's signature. She then crossed herself in what she thought was the Catholic way, and put the letter under some others in the out-tray. She initialled the corner of the carbon to show that the letter, as drafted, had been signed and sent, and then returned the file to the out-tray.

Did forging Sir Eric's signature make her complete within herself for that day? Not really. Although the action was further justified because, although in the scale of Sir Eric's concerns it was not a great matter, within another scale and the spirit of the League it seemed to Edith that the matter of the chair was momentous.

She knew that the whole world wrote letters to the League but somehow the small, veritable voice had to be responded to and served, as much as the eminent.

Back in the bar, shaking a little, she joined Florence, who was now with Dr Joshi from Health, and Howard Liverright, and she said quietly to Florence across the others, 'I did it.'

'Good for you,' said Florence, in a lowered voice. 'To the orphans.' They drank a private toast.

Then in her social voice, Florence said, 'I was telling Joshi and Liverright about your *coup d'éclat* on the matter of tenders.'

'Very well done,' said Joshi. 'Do you know the Indian answer to the dilemma of identical tenders?'

Edith said she didn't. She was angry at herself for having told Florence and breaking the confidence of the Directors' meeting. Now Florence had broken her confidence. Even if it were a very minor thing. She had to learn discipline.

Joshi went on, 'In India the person handling the tenders would have gone to each of the tenderers and seen which would furnish his house most opulently in return for the granting of the tender. It is he who would then get the contract. That is the Indian way.'

'That is not the Indian way — it's the smart way,' said Florence. 'If you'd used your head, Edith, you could have furnished your rooms.'

Edith said grumpily that the tender system was a fundamental of good administration. She wasn't feeling in a joking mood.

And she was quite happy with the way her rooms were furnished.

'But of course,' said Joshi, 'I was simply making a joke against my countrymen. I do not condone it in any way, shape or form.' At least Liverright hadn't come out with anything bitter.

'Brighten up, Edith,' Florence said. 'You've done your good deed for the day.'

She pushed out a smile and put her arm around Florence and hugged her and Florence hugged back. 'Sorry.'

She couldn't tell Ambrose because it was beyond anything that he would have assented to. Here she was, training to be an international civil servant and here she was bending the rules. No — she was snapping the rules in two.

Of course, it had to be considered also that maybe Annie Dickinson was a pest. The chair, however, existed in all its humble grandeur.

About tardiness, there was nothing much to be done. Within the bureau she became a watchdog for promptness of reply and something of a pain in the neck for everyone.

A few weeks later, Victoria called from Registry. Annie Dickinson had written again. She read out the letter.

'Dear Sir Eric Drummond, I have arranged with the Jugoslavian Foreign Office to dispatch the chair, and I hope it will start on its journey soon.'

That evening she had to again go to his office to head off the letter, which she simply filed.

She dearly wished for the chair to arrive and the matter to be over. Yet another letter came from Miss Dickinson. She groaned when Victoria called her and offered to read it out. 'Yes, Victoria, read it out.' She gritted herself.

Victoria read: 'After much pushing and effort I have got

the chair dispatched but it seems to have been addressed to the International Labor Office and not to you as I had requested because the League of Nations does not accept présents. I am very sorry if you have trouble in this matter but perhaps on arrival somebody will kindly see that it reaches its destination.'

Ye gods. Was there no end to it? Now she had to involve the ILO and pretend other things to other people to find the wretched chair, and deal with this nonsense about the League not accepting gifts.

Edith sometimes felt exhausted from combating the false ideas which circulated concerning the League. Where did they come from? They were not all malicious — it was more as if people liked to sound as if they knew something about the way the League 'worked'. Consequently people just made up things about the League. Sometimes they said things they thought were good for the League; probably this statement was of that nature. How could it possibly work if so much false information was flying around? Should someone write to the Jugo-slavian Foreign Office and tell whoever it was that the League was accepting gifts for the new building on a selective basis? There should be a section for the Correction of Erroneous Ideas.

This time 'Sir Eric' wrote to Miss Dickinson saying he would ensure that the ILO knew that the chair had been addressed by mistake. She rang the ILO's Internal Services and informed them of the matter and that she herself would come and collect the chair when it arrived.

Edith had to go out of her way, up the hill, to call in at the ILO office daily to see if the chair was there. It was no good telephoning because no one knew what it looked like and they might snaffle it for themselves.

She knew they felt she was behaving oddly by calling in every morning and asking about 'Miss Dickinson's chair' and showing them the photograph of the chair, which she had improperly taken from the file.

One afternoon she received a call from the ILO to say that they had the chair.

She went to Lloyd's office and said that the ILO had rung to say that Miss Dickinson's chair was there waiting for them.

'It arrived, did it?' said Lloyd. 'Is it a good sitting chair or not?'

'I haven't sat in it,' she said, thinking that she might not sit in it, superstitiously, that it might be not be proper for her to sit in it — though if she could sign the Secretary-General's name, she might as well sit in the President's throne.

He said he would get it over from the ILO.

'Let me know when it arrives,' she said to him.

He did and they inspected it together. It was a fine chair. They both sat in it and decided it needed a cushion.

'I suppose the Secretary-General would like to see it,' said Lloyd. 'I'll let him know that the chair's arrived. He probably has ideas about where it should go.'

'Couldn't we just take it now and put it in place in the Council room?' She wanted done with it and without involving Sir Eric.

Lloyd said the chair had to be entered in the property register and then numbered and then allocated.

'If it doesn't go into the register of property no one after us would know it existed,' he said. 'I have never understood why you made so much fuss about this chair. We really should only have furniture which is consistent with our needs and the architecture of the premises.'

'That might be the right policy in ninety-nine cases out of a hundred but in this case it would be the wrong policy. That chair has to have a place in our lives or we are living our lives wrongly and running this League wrongly,' she said. 'Heavens above, Lloyd, this chair is a test of us all! Can't you see that!'

'Not really,' Lloyd said, quietly going about his work. 'I suppose we could get the Deputy Secretary-General or an Under Secretary at some point,' he said, 'and have a ceremony. If you feel so strongly.' He was saying this to make her happy.

'*No!* No, don't do that. I don't want a ceremony. It might be a sentimental gift but it is, after all, just a chair.'

He looked up at her, puzzled by her change of direction.

'Sir Eric' wrote saying the chair had arrived safely. Edith hoped that this, her third forgery, would be her last.

A few days later, she went to Internal Service's storeroom in the rented annex and showed them a requisition form.

She signed for the chair and then with Florence's help carried it along the street to the Palais Wilson and installed it in the Glass-room. They took away the President's usual chair and put that in a smaller committee room.

They stood at the door of the Glass-room and looked at Miss Dickinson's chair.

'Mission complete,' Florence said. 'You should feel proud, Edith.'

'I don't, Florence,' she said fervently, 'I feel guilty. This is not the way I want to do things. I worry too much.'

'This time, though, it was the only way really to get the orphans and Miss Dickinson treated right.'

It wasn't all over. Annie Dickinson wrote back.

Thank you for telling me that the chair has arrived safely at its destination. I am waiting to settle on a suitable very short inscription to be put on the plate. Possibly, I might pass through Geneva with my head boy on my way back to Jugo-slavia and I should bring the plate with me and he would fix it in a suitable but not an evident place.

Believe me,

Yrs truly

A. J. Dickinson.

Oh no. Edith went back to her office and wept tears of frustration and self-recrimination.

After a while she pulled herself together, blew her nose, and rang Florence, although she was now beginning to have reservations about Florence's advice and would sort that out later, after she had sorted out this mess.

'Florence, there's an emergency.' She told Florence what was happening.

Florence suggested the restaurant.

'No! This has to be discussed elsewhere. The lounge of the Hôtel de la Paix. Now!'

She grabbed her coat and went to Florence's office and together they went along the street to the Hôtel de la Paix and ordered afternoon tea.

She pointed out to Florence that if Miss Dickinson and boy arrived at the League and wanted to see Sir Eric he would be bewildered and questions would be asked about the chair. The whole thing would unravel, files be called for, signature examined, detectives called in.

Florence said, 'Calm down. We'll receive Miss Dickinson and the orphan. Ambrose will play the part of the Secretary-General.'

'Ambrose would never do anything out of line.'

'He won't know.'

She looked at Florence.

'We'll tell Miss Dickinson and the orphan boy that Ambrose

is an Under Secretary. We won't tell Ambrose that we've told them. We'll tell Ambrose only about the chair and the boy and ask if he would like to meet them. He'll say yes. He'll think he's just coming along — we'll use the Glass-room. He looks like a Secretary-General. They all dress like Sir E. He'll make all the right noises. Without knowing a damn thing.'

This solution filled Edith with further dismay and exasperation. She put her head on her arms on the table. She would leave the League and offer her services to the orphaned children and Annie Dickinson.

Florence put a hand on Edith's arm. 'Sit up, Edith. They'll think something's wrong. It'll work.'

In her own mind, Edith thought of owning up. She thought of getting a letter to Dickinson to prevent her coming to Geneva. But Florence's plan could work.

'When she tells us that she's coming, then we'll go into detail.' Florence made it all sound so easy. Florence stumbled through no slough of despond.

As it turned out, they needed no more plotting and deviousness.

Miss Dickinson wrote that she and the boy couldn't come to Geneva. She enclosed the silver plate, saying that she wanted it fixed under the seat out of sight.

Victoria wouldn't let her have the plate, saying that it had to go with the letter to Sir Eric's office.

Edith sickened every time she went illegally into Sir Eric's office but she went yet again and confiscated the plate and removed the letter from the file. The plate read, 'Beati Pacifici. Cadeau des orphelins de guerre.' Edith was rather annoyed at Miss Dickinson for not including the names of the orphans who had worked on the chair. She wrote what she prayed would be her last forged letter thanking Miss Dickinson for the plate and promising that it would be affixed 'out of sight'.

She watched while the maintenance man put the plate under the chair.

One day Edith passed the Glass-room and saw a black man in robes of national dress, maybe a Liberian, seated in Miss Dickinson's chair presiding at a committee meeting and she smiled a complicated smile to herself, at the centre of which was wistful pleasure, despite all the tribulation to her spirit.

Privately she resolved never again to listen to Florence's advice, no matter how breathtakingly wily. Sadly, she had come to see how Florence's ways were not the ways of a diplomat but the errant ways of a misbehaving student. Mary McGeachy had used wiles as a way to get the League across but Florence was just bucking the system for its own sake. Florence sat in the bar and enjoyed watching others stick their necks out. At some point in the whole thing, Florence had also asked her to take some of Sir Eric's specially embossed notepaper so that she could write to her friends. Edith had said she would but purposefully hadn't taken the paper for Florence.

If she, Edith, were ever to be Secretary-General, she would be Secretary-General actually appointed by the Council and not Secretary-General by studentish subterfuge.

What did interest Edith about the whole business was that she now saw how others might use such stratagems within the organisation of the League, might pursue private policies by stealth, and how dangerous this would be. The League had passed a certain size and was now less and less overseen. That scared her. Or should it please her? Maybe it meant that the organisation itself was now more self-describing, rather than being defined, detail by detail, by Sir Eric, or the Council, or the *haute direction*. However, when she came to a position of authority, she would watch for crafty people like Florence. And she would watch for impetuous, heart-led, young officers like herself with their noble private policies. She would appoint only those officers, who, if they did pursue private policies would by their natures pursue such policies, which, if ever exposed or articulated, would be found by analysis to be perfectly acceptable.

She would strive always to appoint such people, or to delegate in such a way that those people went on, uninstructed, unasked, to fill out the unpremeditated intention of the organisation, even if no one person could ever say what that intention was in all details. They would consummate the organisation, fill it out into an acceptable shape. Again, a shape which could not be foreseen in all detail or planned in all detail. She saw that the secret was in the appointment of people who had this happy implanted latency. One had to recognise this latency and know that it would eventually germinate and that it could be left unattended to elaborate into a flowering. Perhaps there had to be judicious and politic intervention by teaching and leadership, from the interplay of the office. She rated interplay in the office very highly now.

She believed herself to be an officer with happy latency.

She believed that Miss Dickinson's chair also had a happy latency. The Rule of Happy Latency in the choice of belongings. It was not only officers who had it, but objects — objects which could sponsor chains of other detail, chains of consequence which could only later be seen as positive or deleterious. Miss Dickinson's chair was positive and would proliferate into marvellous arrangements not yet imaginable. She now understood that. That the new Palais would grow out of Miss Dickinson's chair.

Edith was also exuberantly gratified that the Palais architectural jury decided in favour of M. Nenot, from Paris, and a M.

Flegenheimer, from Geneva, both reasonably classical in their style. M. Le Corbusier wrote a protest but to no avail.

Edith did not join in the heated discussions about the decision. She felt that for now, she'd done enough for the new Palais des Nations.

International Language:

Scat Singing, its Ramifications,

Magnitude, and Consequences

When Edith said she'd heard 'lots of jazz', she meant on the gramophone and the wireless. She had not been to a performance of jazz, or a rendition, if rendition were the right word.

When Jeanne, her French friend from the office, asked her if she would like to 'attend some jazz' she had thought first of gramophone records.

Jeanne exclaimed, 'No, no — Eddie South is coming — is coming here to play. Really! Eddie South!'

They'd all heard of Eddie South. 'Here to Geneva?'

'No, no, I mean to Paris.' Jeanne, a Parisian, sometimes forgot she was now working in Geneva, which was understandable, given that Jeanne worked for the Intellectual Cooperation section of the League in Geneva although, for all purposes, its central office seemed now to be in Paris. Regardless of the logistics, Jeanne had permanent discord of the head, body and soul though usually, at any one time, part of her was always in Paris. 'Really, you must give me permission to contradict myself,' was one of Jeanne's most frequent sayings.

The jokes about the Intellectual section were unfair. According to Florence, the section's accounting was meticulous and they were good about returning files. It was true that they had more expert committees than any other section, but then, they were the section *for experts*. They had people like Professor Einstein. Although in her work Edith didn't have much to do with the Intellectuals, apart from Jeanne, she had good feelings towards them.

'We could voyage up to Paris. And then go *directement* to the Ad Lib Club,' said Jeanne, with conspiratorial anticipation.

There was no reason why, with a holiday and a week-end coming up, they shouldn't jump on the train up to Paris. Since arriving in Geneva Edith had not left it. It was as if she had to stay on call in case the world needed her. Staying on call, though, had meant that she went dining and to concerts of the Orchestre Romand and to motion pictures with Ambrose or Jeanne or Florence or fox hunting out at Veyrier with Major Buxton — twice — although on most nights she ate at her pension, sometimes reading a book at the table or writing in her journal as a way of keeping the other pension people away, but sometimes chatting with the other residents, and then after dinner if she didn't go into the lounge to chat or listen to the wireless with the other residents — she hated playing cards — she read alone in her room, listened to gramophone records, or got on with work she'd brought home with her. They'd been called back a few nights but never with the urgency or frequency that she'd expected. She was puzzled sometimes by how quickly within the workings of the League all great and urgent questions lost their urgency. It was, of course, that the League was able to subdue and refine crisis — able to turn a crisis into Roneoed pages of data and topics for colloquy, into things which could be unflappably administered, conciliated, the way a surgeon handled mutilation and serious injury.

She had also been straining. She'd been straining to become part of a lofty international community, a world of essentials and high procedure. So often she'd had to pretend to know what she was doing, while still learning, and to make it up as she went along because no one had done it before her, never in the history of the human race. Cooper sometimes forgot that.

As Jeanne talked about going to Paris, she realised she was at last able to relax her grip and go. If the world needed her, it would know where to find her. She would take some leave in Paris. Also, everyone was saying there was not enough iodine in the air of Geneva at present.

'Yes, Jeanne, we will go up to Paris. Let us flee — as the doctors are saying, there is not enough iodine in the air of Geneva.'

Jeanne said, 'You take a long time, Edith, to make up your mind on such a simple matter of going to Paris and going to a club to hear the black men play jazz. Eddie South and his Alabamians.'

She loved the way Jeanne said the word jazz — in Jeanne's mouth it was a word that promised every tantalisation. Edith hardly knew Paris at all, having spent only a couple of days there on her way to join the League. She certainly didn't know Jeanne's Paris. Or Ambrose's Paris of the Club des Cent. She knew the Paris of Flaubert and Balzac.

'I think that the League can now get along without me for a day or so. Should we make up a party?'

Jeanne agreed that a party would be chic.

The Ad Lib Club was hot. Hot in the way that jazz people said hot, and also just hot.

Some of the music was familiar to her from records but the proximity to the musicians and patrons gave the music an almost insufferable closeness. At first she listened too hard and couldn't relax back in her chair. And she wasn't sure which one was Eddie South and had to ask. The jazz records heard in solitude had their own intensity but it could be controlled by tempering the music with a personal mood, or by looking out the window, but here in the Ad Lib Club, she couldn't simply modulate the music with her mood because her mood was being intensified and churned by her friends and the strangers and the champagne and Paris and the hot club and the sight of the black musicians making their music. She could not do anything but allow herself to seethe pleasantly, although for brief moments now and then, she did return to a burning self-consciousness and withdrew and paused, for only a second, an observer of her own perspiring, delightfully nervous body.

Liverright, who was with Caroline Bailey, was joking about the smoke not all being from tobacco cigarettes which she took to mean that people were smoking hashish or whatever.

When he mentioned it they all chorused, 'Stamp it out,' and stamped their feet, a joke their gang had about the League's efforts with vice.

Liverright was from vice-ridden Vienna, and presumably knew about these things. Despite being a League officer, he kept attachments to Bohemia and carried on about 'the cult of the multiple-sensation', talked endlessly about Dada, and always wore red to display his politics, against the unwritten rules of the office. Tonight it was a handkerchief flowing from his dinner jacket pocket. But regardless of that he was very staunchly League. And Edith suspected that it was not so much that he was a socialist but that he chafed against rules.

A Negro woman vocalist was singing and as Edith listened something happened there at the Ad Lib Club which she could not have ever foreseen. All the rest — the atmosphere of the club, her churning aliveness — she could perhaps have imagined. But what she could never have imagined was the way the woman was singing, and how the singing reached into her.

She was hearing something she had never heard before.

Although she must have 'heard' it on records, she now heard for the first time the way the Negro woman used her voice, a rhythmic use of syllables. It was the voice trying to say something which was beyond words. A sort of warbling. The woman was not singing words at all. She was singing sounds in between the music and words of the song.

Edith was transfixed by the singer's way of playing with her voice. Edith felt very certainly that this 'hearing' she was experiencing was revelation. She pulled at Jeanne's arm.

'Jeanne, what is that — the way they sing without words?'

Jeanne shrugged. Jeanne was moving her whole body to the music, away somewhere else. Maybe Jeanne's body was there but her mind wasn't anywhere near by, and even her body looked as if it might be about to leave her too, and writhe away across the club.

Edith asked Ambrose. Ambrose didn't know. 'Humming?' he said.

'It's more than humming!'

She became impatient to know.

In the break, she said, 'It seems to me to be the most interesting thing this whole evening,' more loudly than she expected, 'the way the Negro woman used her voice — like another language.'

The others did not want to talk — they were letting the atmosphere and the champagne overtake them. But she always had trouble getting conversational attention in café groups like this and trouble holding it as well. She thought it had to do with the lightness of her voice, or the Australian accent.

Caroline Bailey had obviously heard what she'd said, and she just rolled her eyes. There had been a long discussion about whether Caroline should ever have been asked to come on this Paris trip. She was rumoured to be writing a novel about the

League. If Florence hadn't been sick with influenza, almost certainly Caroline would not have been asked.

'I need to know,' she said. 'I want to know what it's called.'

'What does it matter?' Ambrose said, touching her hand.

Liverright said, 'Call it bel canto.'

It was not bel canto and she did not want to be calmed by Ambrose. Or have Caroline Bailey roll her eyes.

She wanted to be answered. Though maybe it had to do with bel canto.

'Doesn't anyone know?' she almost shouted, bringing their attention to her. Edith glanced hopefully at Liverright, but he had little attention left to pay.

Victoria wanted to help, but could only say, 'I will admit that it's uncanny, but I'm no use. I don't particularly listen to the music, I watch the musicians more — even in symphony orchestras there's something to see.'

Liverright had another stab at it. 'The cello, you know, has the exact range of the human voice. Basso profundo to soprano. I always think of it as the most human of instruments. And Honegger did do a train in *Pacifique deux cent trente-et-un*.'

'I'll tell you what it is, Edith,' said Caroline in her droll voice, 'it's called voodoo music, that's their word for it.'

'I could use some voodoo in my life,' said Victoria, wistfully.

Liverright pushed the champagne bottle over towards her. 'Have some,' he said.

The orchestra began again.

'Go and ask,' Edith said to Ambrose.

'I can't just go over and talk to them.'

'Why not? I want you to.'

'Well, they look rather unapproachable.'

She looked across at the black musicians in their bow ties and jackets. One wore a bowler hat. She saw what he meant.

'Don't be ridiculous. You're a diplomat. You're supposed to be able to approach anyone.'

'I'm not sure *that's* part of the job. And Negroid musicians aren't, as far as I recall, referred to in Satow.' Ambrose looked apprehensively at the Negro orchestra. 'And if I'm wrong, Edith, don't correct me.'

'Ambrose, please?'

At the conclusion of the next set of music, Ambrose reluctantly stood up, took courage from a draught of champagne and moved towards the orchestra. The orchestra had finished playing for now and were chatting among themselves, blowing out their instruments.

On his way, she saw Ambrose go to the cloakroom girl and buy a packet of cigarettes. As he walked towards the orchestra, he opened the packet and then clambered up on to the stage and offered cigarettes, firstly to the woman singer and then to the others, smiling in his nervous, winning, English way, and gesturing back to their table. The cigarettes were a brilliant move. The orchestra all took cigarettes.

Edith saw then that Ambrose gave Eddie South the whole packet, perhaps to be shared among the orchestra. Edith looked away. That was wrong, wrong, wrong. Giving them the whole packet was colonialist.

When she looked back, she saw that Eddie South was sharing out the remaining cigarettes. Ambrose then talked to one of them — not Eddie South, but the black man in the bowler hat, who listened and then looked across to where she was sitting and looked straight at her, causing her to smile at him in a fuzzy way. The black man put his instrument into its case, stood up, and together with Ambrose, clambered off the stage and began to walk back to the table.

That was not necessary. It wasn't necessary to bring the

black man in the bowler hat to the table but the idea of meeting one of them made her uneasily excited. Ambrose introduced the black musician as Jerome and looked pleased with himself for having captured such a trophy.

Jerome said, 'I am a supporter of you all — deeply in my heart, I support your work at the League of Nations.'

The table became enlivened, and even Liverright rallied, saying that he was both 'honoured and syncopated', before drifting off again into the alcoholic background. They had the waiter bring another glass and gave Jerome some champagne.

There was no spare chair in the club so Ambrose made Jerome sit in his chair next to Edith while he crouched on the other side of her. Ambrose prompted her, 'Ask Jerome your question, Edith.'

Edith stared at the man. It was the closest she had ever been to a Negro. He was different from Arun Joshi. Quite different. She remembered an experiment the physiology class had done with black skin where they tried to extract melanin pigment from it without success. The conclusion was the melanin was stable and insoluble. She guessed that they could have asked a black whether it ever washed off. Edith asked her question but found she had another difficulty; while waiting for him to reply, she realised her eyes had come to rest on the black man's lap. Good Lord, she thought, I'm becoming entranced. But it had also to do with where Ambrose was crouching. That sort of talk among women about jazz men and Negroes was drivel.

'What you have been commenting on is called scat singing,' Jerome said, smiling.

Edith forced her eyes up from below the table. Why hadn't Ambrose brought back the woman singer instead of this formidable man? She felt shaky. It was the Reaction, Negromania, which she considered all bosh. She tried to bring herself together.

'Scat singing?' she said, her voice unreliably off-key.

'Yes, scat singing. Maisy is a fine scat singer.'

Edith couldn't quite believe that it was called scat singing. At university, they'd collected scats on field trips. Why did they call this 'scat singing'? Scats were the droppings of animals. She couldn't quite ask that question, just yet. The situation was becoming an immensely hot confusion, with this talk of scats, and the Negro man's sweaty, sultry smell and smile rolling over to her, lapping her face. The sultry smell she knew was typical of the Negro, and came from a special glandular condition. His fingernails were manicured. She felt entranced by their white moons. She tried to keep her gaze above the table top.

What did singing have to do with faeces? For a moment, she feared that she had asked this. 'It is another language.' Her voice again came out unreliably.

The black man agreed. He said that it was a way of 'saying the feelings'.

Victoria asked him who had invented it and in what year. Caroline and Ambrose broke into giggles. Victoria wasn't being funny, but when people laughed, she always accepted that there could be something funny in what she'd said.

Jerome said he didn't know if it had been invented, as such. He laughed and said that it had been told to him that a singer once lost her word sheets and had invented it to cover up but he didn't really believe that.

She then remembered why she felt it was a revelation, this scat singing, how it all linked to life back at the League, and why she had felt it was pressing to know. She remembered now. It was how it might be used. The work at the League was often a use of language that wasn't argument or even the making of negotiation — it was a way, perhaps, of expressing a presence. Affirmative noise, questing without knowing the questions, hot air. They could turn the hot air to this scat singing.

'Yes!' she burst out, 'of course!'

'Are you all right, Edith?' Jeanne was asking in her over-concerned way.

Edith gestured for a momentary silence, a finger across her mouth. She wanted a minute to think before talking again. She would make a submission to Council. Or to one of Jeanne's expert committees. Esperanto she didn't support. Scat singing was different — maybe this was a language to express things not yet internationally expressible and which would, at the same time, be comprehensible to all people regardless of their language. Maybe a vocabulary of sounds could be compiled. The way the League was an instrument to achieve what had never before been achieved. She raised her eyes from the black man and breathed deeply to bring herself together again. The group, except Caroline, were waiting on her to speak, obeying her edict. For the first time. She couldn't remember what she'd said.

'It's another parlance,' she pronounced. 'Somewhere between language and silence.'

'To say that might be going too far,' said Victoria. 'I wish we could put a date to it.'

'Are you sure you're well?' Jeanne asked again.

Caroline, for all her pose of jadedness, was trying to make conversation with the black musician, being flirtatiously over-attentive.

Ambrose said he thought there was but one way of saying things and that was with words, precisely used. 'Preferably words signed and sealed in a treaty. You may call me limited.'

'I call you Limited,' said Victoria, pleased with herself.

As usual when Victoria tried to be funny, no one laughed at her effort, although Caroline returned to the conversation to try to steal it away from her. 'You can call me Beyond the Limit,' she said, kissing Ambrose on the cheek, probably because she was timid about kissing the black man's cheek, and laughing out her cigarette smoke in an affected way.

Edith was a long way from the joking. Liverright seemed to be falling asleep and trying to light a cigarette at the same time. She thought that Caroline had given up on him, and might now be concentrating her attentions on Jerome. Or Ambrose, even. Edith couldn't worry about that just now.

'My God. It's a new parlance,' Edith said, marvelling, trying both to hold their attention and to hold her thoughts. 'Jerome can come to Geneva and give us evidence about it all.'

Jerome was trying to cope socially with the flirtatious attention of Caroline, with Ambrose's courteous chat, and with her invitation to him to come to Geneva.

'You will scat sing to the Seventh Assembly, Edy?' said Jeanne, with a kind laugh, patting her hand.

The others came back into the conversation with Jeanne's joke and laughed. They laughed, it seemed to Edith, with rather wide mouths, and too loudly. Liverright came awake and said, 'Syncopated, I'm sure,' and returned to struggling with his somnolent state and with his matches and cigarette.

'I well may,' Edith said. They laughed, but she was not joking. 'Will you come to Geneva and tell the Council about this scat singing, Jerome?' she asked. 'Or if not Council, an expert committee?'

She saw now with sparkling clarity where sound became music; where music became jazz; where jazz became poetry; where poetry became scat singing; where scat singing became meaning. Edith heard Liverright say, more to the champagne bottle than to anyone, 'If only the perception could be cleaned — correction, cleansed — all things could then be seen as they are, as they truly are — infinite.'

So he had been paying some attention to what she'd be saying.

'Blake,' he said, smiling sloppily across at her, 'not Liverright. Blake.'

No one seemed to listen to him quoting Blake, they were all talking, but she didn't really care — she saw what Liverright was getting at. For the first time in her life she saw silence clearly too. She saw it. Palpable silence. 'And silence,' she said. 'You must come to Geneva and tell us about silence, also.'

From under his bowler hat, Jerome was considering his answer, tapping off the ash from his cigarette into the ashtray. 'I have not played in Geneva,' he answered, noncommittally.

She felt herself falling a little, falling forward.

She was not, however, falling. She was still decently in her seat. She pulled herself together. 'Then you must come. The mouth is not just for saying words,' she said in a very strange voice indeed. 'Come to Geneva, that is.' She flushed, but again, no one was listening to her or looking at her except this Jerome, who was listening and smiling at her, smiling back at her merrily, she thought, and she smiled merrily at him.

Jerome stood up and thanked them and said he had to play again, and after politely shaking hands with the others he turned, especially to Edith, and said, 'The next occasion we meet, I will talk to you about what the great Erik Satie, God rest his soul, called "furniture music", which he said was the music you listened to without listening, as scat is the sound you speak when you are not speaking.' He then turned to them all and said, 'Enjoy. Keep on with your fine and great works.' And then turning again back to Edith said, 'I may one day come to Geneva.'

Furniture music, another revelation. She wanted to tell him that she understood the music of furniture too. To show him

Miss Dickinson's chair. Then, and then, he kissed Edith's hand.

'You,' she said in her strange voice, her hand still in his, 'you too, keep up your works.'

She wondered as she spoke whether what she said had a double meaning. She couldn't supervise all her words and thoughts — they were streaming through her, and from her.

He shook hands with Ambrose and was gone.

'You made that rather obvious,' Ambrose said in an aside, resuming his chair, trying to be light but she could tell that he was miffed at her establishing a private bond with Jerome. She caught Caroline's eye too, and saw a knowing look.

All of them, then, had been paying some attention to her.

Yes, she and Ambrose were lovers, of a sort, in Geneva, but this was Paris.

She saw that their liaison had now become impossible to wriggle out from, shrug off, duck out of. She was lumbered with it. Though in all fairness to Ambrose, on the train on the way down they had been affectionately nostalgic, she tearfully so, and had felt very close, remembering their first meeting on the train from Paris to Geneva and their grand lunch together.

Ambrose now said, 'In the War, the Boche bugler could bugle out twenty-four different orders, you know, speak to each other in the fog. Sneaky chaps.' Ambrose was trying, she could tell, to diminish the magnetism of the black man but was also, oddly, still competitive with Liverright after all this time.

' "Clever chap, the Boche",' Caroline mimicked Ambrose.

'You could not be more wrong,' Edith said fervently to Ambrose. 'It's the other way around — instruments try to mimic the human voice — that singer was doing something else.' She knew she was becoming confused with instruments, voices, and mouths. Victoria was listening, trying dutifully to understand her. Caroline was trying to rouse Liverright. She lighted on

Caroline. 'Do you have inexpressible emotions in Print-ing, Caroline?'

'In Précis-writing. Yes, we do, Edith. Lots,' Caroline replied without turning her head. She was trying to revive Liverright by pinching his arm rather hard but was getting no useful result.

Edith continued to talk at Caroline, a disguised assault, knowing that Caroline was not in the least interested. 'You see, Caroline, scat singing's more than musical instruments can do because it's the . . .' she stumbled over her words, 'uninterpreted feelings of the person that are coming out. Some things in life, Caroline, cannot be done by the Translating and Interpretation Service.'

'The feelings of the Negroid?' said Caroline with a small snigger of innuendo. 'Tell us, Edith, about these untranslatable feelings of the Negroid.'

The party smiled weakly. It was an attempt at a sophisticated joke in poor taste, she supposed.

'What are these feelings? These feelings of the Negroid? Tell us, Edith,' Caroline persisted.

'Caroline, we heard you the first time,' Ambrose said, using his special superior tone to shut her up although, Edith thought, they were of the same class, but Ambrose outranked her.

Victoria said, 'I think he was perhaps a Bahama Negro — he had aplomb.'

'Victoria seems to know her Negroes,' said Caroline, 'seems to have been around.'

'I read, Caroline,' Victoria said. 'That's a way of being around too.'

'A safer and cleaner way, definitely.'

Liverright aroused himself and said, 'That's what went wrong, you know, between the Greeks and Bulgarians.'

Everyone looked at him, trying to decide whether to bother with his comment.

'How'd you mean?' Ambrose said shortly.

'No bugler. The Greek officer got himself shot with the white flag. Should've had a bugler.'

'You're not making sense,' Caroline said.

'What he means,' said Ambrose without any interest, 'is that a truce party must have a bugler as well as a white flag.'

'That's the point,' said Liverright, pleased with Ambrose's elucidation and pleased with having made what he saw as a contribution to the conversation.

'I should've have tipped him, I suppose,' said Ambrose. 'Should go over and give him something.'

'No, you will not,' Edith said.

The night was almost over, the orchestra had gone from the stage. Edith rose to go to the toilet. Again Jeanne expressed concern and wanted to come with her but she told Jeanne she was all right. She didn't need help to go to the toilet.

She went across the room towards the toilets, guiding herself by the backs of chairs. Drunk but steady. No, unsteady but undrunk. One or the other. On the way, she passed the room *Artiste*.

In the rather dirty, rather smelly toilet she tried to keep herself from contact with anything. She checked her make-up in the cracked mirror and washed her hands, drying them on her own handkerchief because there was no towel. Then she breathed deeply of the smell, liking the smell. She thought of it as a smell of Paris and the smell of women and the smell of animal life, an ancient smell, the smell of ancient sewers, the abyss of the city, the smell of the human beast coming up from

197

the depths of the ancient city. It took her back to the boat trip over, the smell of Port Said.

On the way back from the toilet, she looked into the room *Artiste*.

He was there alone in a cubicle drinking from a flask. Jerome. Bowler hat and all. She smiled. 'Why! Hello?' he said, and held out his flask as a beckoning gesture, and she went into the room, closing the door behind her, over to where he was and took the flask and drank from it, the spirit in it tasting like milk. She handed it back to him and with it the offer of her hand, which he took and gracefully drew her to him, onto his knee. Time and movement then became slippery, as she gracefully slid, seeing for the first time his caramel and cream shoes and without thinking too much at all about things, it seemed his warm dark hands were on her exposed and very alive breasts, which she felt she had delivered up to him; all seemed to happen in flowing fixed steps, something like a waltz, except that they were not moving from where they were adhered together in this strange way, and without any guidance at all and in no time at all, and with no impediment, with no thought at all, warm, fleshly and flowing, it was finishing, and she took her lips, tongue, and gentle teeth away, opened her eyes and looked across the room to an open instrument case. The next thing of which she became mundanely conscious, was a vague worry about the knees of her silk stockings, the only pair she'd brought with her, and her second mundane worry was about the state of her face, and then Ambrose was banging on the door *Artiste* — or had the banging started earlier? His voice saying, 'Edith? Are you there, Edith?' She rested her head on Jerome's knee, unable or unwilling yet to rise, and she let Ambrose's words search for her, and then she heard him say, 'Edith, we're moving on now. Edith?!' She smiled up at Jerome, swallowing, and said softly, '*C'est bon?*' and he smiled down at her, saying, '*Très bon*,' raising her to her feet, she thinking to herself, another life foray, for indeed, she had never done that to any man, let alone a black man. He hadn't taken his bowler hat off.

On her feet, feeling shaky at her knees, helped by his pale-skinned palms, she pulled her corset bodice and dress back over her exposed breasts, shoulder straps back in place, straightening everything that could be straightened, ran her fingers over her damaged stocking knees, and glanced at a mirror, touching at her make-up with her fingers, at her hair, and at her mouth, hoping that she saw all that she needed to see. She turned to Jerome. She smiled at him. He wiped the neck of the flask with a napkin and offered her the flask again. She took a swig, holding the unidentifiable spirit in her mouth, rinsing, and then swallowing and this time coughing on the spirits. She turned and saw Ambrose's head at the door. 'We're moving on, Edith.' She handed the flask back to Jerome. He took her hand and again kissed it. He then screwed on the flask cap and handed the flask to her. 'A memento of your visit. A gift in return for a gift.'

'How kind.' She fondled the flask. 'But you have already given me a gift — your music. But how very kind. Thank you. I accept it.' She thought she sounded like her mother at a Red Cross function.

'*Adieu, belle vamp australienne*,' Jerome said, lifting his hat a little.

'*Au revoir*, Jerome.'

As she joined Ambrose at the door, she was relieved that the scalloped hem of her evening dress covered the damaged knees of her stockings.

In the taxi, Ambrose was at first talkative in a forced, light way, about anything and everything, except about what was, she sensed, on his mind — the room *Artiste*.

199

He let her scat sing, although he was a trifle concerned about what the driver might think, and he refused to drink from the flask. She found she could scat sing quite effortlessly, and knew that she would go on to teach the world to scat sing.

Back at the hotel, Ambrose was still unquestioning about the room *Artiste* but silently and morosely so.

He prevented her placing trunk line telephone calls with the night concierge to Arthur Sweetser in Information, to tell him about her revelation. He said she could book the call in the morning.

She was almost drunk. Unsteady and almost undone. Unsteadily undone, Edith, undone. Absolutely undone. But not dizzy.

Outside his room, she kissed Ambrose, conscious, very conscious of her mouth, and her mouth said to Ambrose that there was nothing for him to worry about. 'It is Paris,' she said into his ear. '*C'est* Paris. No. *C'est-à-dire* — Paris and Edith.'

She awoke in the dark hotel room very alive, full of Paris, her revelations of the night before still clearly in her mind and pleasing to her. She did not know whether it was her room or Ambrose's room. She had on her nightdress. She raised herself and saw her suitcase. It was her room. She tried to recall. She did not know where the WC was. She recalled that Ambrose's room had no bath or WC, but hers did. She did not know the time. She did not know whether there was an electric light switch. There was. She found it. She found her watch. It was 8 a.m. She gave the watch a wind. Her mouth was very dry but she had no headache.

She rolled herself out of the bed and after going to the WC, she opened the windows and the shutters with exhilaration on to a wintry Paris, with only a bare morning light. The rooftops of Montparnasse. She saw a white cat. Behind her the steam-heating in the room made small creaking noises. She heard the building yawning.

She was very thirsty and her mouth savoured the residue and memories of masculinity and champagne and whatever was in the flask of Jerome. She breathed in the baking smells from the hotel kitchen and of Paris.

She stood at the window and exposed herself to the chill air, feeling it in her nipples, and then closed the windows as the cold began to get to her, giggling as she remembered Jeanne suggesting that she should scat sing to the Seventh Assembly of the League.

Since coming to Europe, she experienced winter differently. It tightened her. Although it had to be said that her behaviour the night before had been rather loose. It surely had been. Perhaps she was on her way to being the wickedest woman in Europe. She smiled again.

Turning to the table for water, she saw Jerome's flask standing there and she recalled the gift-giving. She opened it and sniffed it, still unable to identify its contents, but it certainly wasn't milk. She placed it against her cheek and then put it before her on the table, admiring its battered leather and silver. Last night she had not appreciated the animal from which the leather had been made and imagined the silver mines, although she had never been in a silver mine. It also obeyed the Rule of Trophy and Memento as an object which she was admitting into her life. She did not believe that all gifts had to be admitted into one's life. Some gifts were best discreetly stored away or lost.

She poured a glass of water from the carafe on the table.

201

She'd suffered some sort of crash last night. She had, she thought, somehow tumbled off the rails, but had enjoyed rolling down the slopes for a while.

She recalled every teeming detail of the night. She still believed that she'd had a revelation about scat singing and human parlance. But she had no urge this morning to call Arthur Sweetser.

She then permitted herself to face how outrageously she'd behaved but she could not be sure who knew what she'd done. Could it be outrageous if no one knew what she had done? She rushed to apply one of her ways of going from the old days, the Way of All Doors. She had certainly obeyed the Way of All Doors. Cautiously, she examined her inner state and found that she did not feel ashamed. On the contrary, she felt absolutely amazed. Amazed at herself, and at her audacity, and at her carnality. And, furthermore, she said to herself, looking again at her inner state, I think that I am proud of my carnality. She would never do it in Geneva, but she was glad she had been bold enough to do it just this once. With a complete stranger. In Paris. With a black man. Where better to do it than in Paris? With a black man.

She had flexed her own temerity, had taken voluptuous pleasure intuitively and at will. Deep in the situation, her body had known what she wanted to do, and that impressed her. She had been able to confound and ambush herself, confound all her proper feelings.

She recalled that Ambrose had been the first man to talk to her about this form of physical love and had told her that men liked it, although, even as a girl, she recalled that she'd had an inkling of it, and at university there'd been veiled jokes among the girls while eating bananas. She felt unperturbed about it because it seemed a safe and simple thing to do. She did then recall, in a zigzagging way, an incident from her childhood when at about twelve or thirteen, she had been kissing and cuddling her puppy, allowing it to lick her face. Her mother had warned her about microbes but she had disregarded her mother's warning. She could not accept that one should be fearful of the lick of a puppy. Nor, she now felt, should one be fearful of the lick of a man. She recalled how the petting of her puppy back then had sometimes brought on a kind of delirium in her. What she'd done with Jerome was a carnal gesture where she knew clearly the beginning and the end and which she could now confidently begin and carry through. She could see that it was by far the best and safest thing for her to do with a man when her complete pleasure was not likely to be met. After all, the giving of pleasure was itself a pleasure which was not to deny the peculiar pleasure of the experience in itself for her. While not replete in the climactic sense, it was somehow complete. Speaking scientifically, it was a complete oral sensation in its gaminess and tang and corporeality. Without a doubt it vitalised the whole of her.

With her teeming morning-after thoughts, and free of any serious self-recrimination, she flopped into the armchair, cradling the water glass against her lawn nightdress.

Reluctantly, she admitted to herself that she could not see how the League could use scat singing. She said a poignant goodbye to that fanciful idea and the idea, like a genie, smiled at her and vanished into the morning light of Paris, having entertained her, maybe enlightened her, but which had to go.

That day she was lunching with Ambrose and Professor Clérambault at the Club des Cent which was a genteel club for which she would need, she remembered, a new pair of silk stockings. And where she might taste ortolan for the first time.

She toyed with the idea of returning that night to the Ad Lib Club, which was not a genteel club and for which she might not even need stockings, but, really, in the end, she was a girl who belonged at the Club des Cent.

As Edith drank more water in the light of a Paris winter morning, it seemed clear that the jazz word scat had nothing to do with animal scats, but she felt that she'd had a private insight about the animal sense and the jazz sense of scats. That in every conversation there were scats, not all were rhythmical, not all of them were artful. In some conversation the scat was a glimpse of a quandary, or a befuddlement, or in some, a dropping of mystical excrement, something of their soul. True, most conversation was just drapery to make the person conversationally adorable, but the scats were always there, the noises, the rumblings of deeper unspeakable meanings of self, and definitely of quandary and befuddlement. We are all scat singers, Edith declared. She entered some of these thoughts into her personal manual, a beautiful notebook, with its stiff, blue-marbled cover which contained her attempts at poetry and other observations of self and the world. She'd created a special code and she used this to record her encounter with Jerome and to denote the intensity of sensation.

Over a late breakfast, Ambrose referred to Jerome only once. He said to her, 'Did you actually kiss him?'

She looked across, silent, not from evasion, but from surprise at his question.

'I have to know,' he said.

'Kiss him?'

'Did you kiss him?'

She thought back to the night and inwardly smiled, realising from his question that he had not seen anything, but also becoming aware then of the underlying concern in Ambrose's voice. It had to do with Jerome being a Negro. And of course, that had something to do with the whole experience for her. The exotic blackness could not be denied.

Putting down her knife, she reached her hand across to Ambrose's hand, and she said, honestly, 'No, dear, I didn't kiss him.'

They went on with their breakfast and she marvelled that she could do what she had done the night before and yet reappear next morning, back in her ordinary life, washed and carefully dressed, with stocking knees a little damaged perhaps and just barely covered by her day dress, to eat hot rolls and to drink chocolate in a hotel dining room.

'I think I had something of a crack-up last night,' she said. 'I was a bit off the rails.' She didn't explain that she had enjoyed rolling down the slopes.

'You were a little overwrought.'

They discussed their plans for the day. 'I'm to have my hair styled at a place in the Passage de l'Opéra recommended by Jeanne,' she told him, 'and then we'll go to a long Parisian lunch at your Club des Cent with the fascinating Professor Clérambault.'

'Not shorter?'

'The hair or the lunch?'

'Your hair.'

'Yes, shorter. The lunch — longer.'

Although she did not care for strange hairdressers, she looked forward to the touch of a fine hairdresser, to feeling his strong fingers kneading her scalp, to have a strange hairdresser's hands praising her hair, and to be flattered by words and by touch, pampered and cut. To emerge cool and dazzling about the head, to catch sight of her newly shaped hair in shopfront windows.

'If it's any comfort,' he said, 'Liverright was a little more overwrought than you.'

'Yes, even I was aware of that,' she said.

'Truth be said,' Ambrose smiled at last, 'we were all a little buzzed.'

Whatever he'd seen or not seen last night, Ambrose was now brightening; forgiveness was in the air, and the jolly Ambrose was returning. She wanted to go with him to the genteel Club des Cent, *that* Edith was returning also, and *that* Edith had her style and needs as well.

The Question of Germany

It was Edith's job to see that the horseshoe table was correctly positioned in the Glass-room, where the Council met.

She considered herself very good with workmen and with tables.

The workmen made some jokes in French about horses with hooves the size of the table, the resulting manure, and relating this to the business of the League. She understood their jokes, although not all of the Swiss argot, and briefly laughed with them, but not giving herself over fully to their joking, showing by her restraint, she hoped, some mild protest against mindless anti-League humour — and she'd learned how hard it is in politics to argue against a joke. At the same time she tried to show that she did not consider herself above them, showing them Australian mateship while not engaging in that false camaraderie that pretended to deny other differences.

She'd explained to them what the table was for, its importance in the scheme of things, and a little about how the Council worked. She always wanted people to like their work and to understand it.

She was pleasantly aware too, of the constant glint of their male glances off her body, like sun off moving water.

The horseshoe table was on a raised platform at the end of the hall. Edith measured the distance from the walls with a tape to ensure that the table was dead centre. She experimented by coming and going to the table from the door behind it, and ensured sufficient room for chairs to be pushed back, keeping in mind that some subordinate would be perhaps seated or standing behind the member of Council.

When the table was in position, she sent one of the young workmen to get small metal carpet protectors for the table legs.

With her hands on her hips, she then stood way down at the back of the room where the public would be and looked at the table, imagining the Council seated around it. She had positioned Miss Dickinson's chair for the Council President. She was still having trouble understanding quite why Sir Eric thought the horseshoe table overcame protocol problems. She could see that it meant that no member of Council had their back to the room, which would happen with a round table.

She always liked the idea that the Glass-room was formerly the ballroom of the hotel. Momentarily she saw the elegant European couples from the past waltzing on the parquet floor, she heard the murmur of conversation and laughter, the waltzes. The smell of the room always reminded her of the day of her arrival.

She'd had wax polish and a cloth sent up from the cleaning staff and she polished the table and chairs herself. She hummed the Blue Danube.

She then went along the hall to stores and asked for the national place names used by the Council, including the new one for Germany. She arranged them on the Council table, and arranged the chairs. For a finishing touch, she wished that there was a League pennant which she could affix to the table. She gave Miss Dickinson's chair a final polish.

Finally, as her assignment had specified, she called Sir Eric's office and left a message that the table was in place and ready for him to inspect.

He came almost immediately.

He walked around the table, hands clasped behind his back. He tested the moving of a chair back from the table as she had done.

'You know, at Locarno Sir Austen wanted a round table to accent the equality of all present — there was no round table, so he decided on a square one. But no square table either. Sir Austen took a rectangular table, measured it himself and then had them cut it clean in half. Had legs put on the sawn end. Worked well. An historic table.'

He seated himself at the table where the President would be seated. 'Never underestimate the importance of the table.'

'I don't, Sir Eric. I am something of a student of tables.'

'I say, this is a fine chair.' He stood and examined Miss Dickinson's chair more closely. 'Needs a cushion, though, wouldn't you say — or aren't you a student of chairs also?'

Yes, she said, she was a student of chairs and also of rooms. Edith 'reminded' him where the chair had come from. But not how it had got there.

'Can't keep track. As long as someone worries about these things.'

'Yes, Sir Eric.' She suggested he make a reference to Miss Dickinson and the orphans at the next Council meeting.

'Write me a little speech about it. Make sure I get it before the meeting.'

She wrote a note to herself in her notepad, keeping her pad with her for further notes.

'You know,' he said, 'Sir Willoughby — Annie Dickinson's brother — drafted the Covenant. Or had a go at it.'

She said that she hadn't known that.

He asked her to be Germany. 'Go out and come in when I call.'

211

Despite the no-smoking signs, the workmen stood smoking in the corner, catching the ash in the palms of their hands, and watching the play-acting.

She felt a little embarrassed. She stood outside the door of the Glass-room and waited.

'I invite the German delegates to take their places,' called Sir Eric. 'Enter, Germany.'

Edith came in. She stood in the room, not feeling like Germany at all.

'Of course, someone will have to lead them to their seat,' Sir Eric said. 'Make a note of that, will you.'

'We should have a ceremony,' Edith said, surprised at how strong her voice sounded. 'It should be more ceremonial,' she said, this time more tentatively.

He looked at her thoughtfully. 'Could be right. Sweetser said the same thing. First new permanent Council member. Don't get around to thinking about ceremonies. How'd you see it? This ceremony?'

'Oh — well, the huissiers could wear uniforms, for a start.' Was that too Germanic? She stood, thinking. 'A voice could then boom out, "Enter, Germany." There could be a fanfare of trumpets, perhaps?'

'Don't go for fanfares of trumpets myself. Not really a fanfare-of-trumpets man. Or fanfare of anything.'

'I don't mean only for Germany. For each new Council member, in the future.'

'The Americans might like the fanfare of trumpets. They go in for that. Drums for the Germans, perhaps? Do you think the Germans are drum people? Feel somehow we've already done enough for Germany.' Sir Eric glanced over at the workmen as if he had perhaps committed a diplomatic gaffe and that they would immediately communicate it to Berlin. They were watching with curiosity.

Edith warmed to the idea of a ceremony. 'We could have the booming voice read out something grand. "Hear ye, hear ye — it is solemnly declared that the sovereign nation state of Germany . . . is now admitted to the Council of world nations . . . under the sacred Covenant of . . ." and so on, etc.'

'You have something of a feel for this sort of thing?' Sir Eric said, looking at her with interest. 'Didn't think you Australians went in for it.'

'I suppose we don't,' she said. 'But again, this is not Australia.'

'Don't go in for the hear-ye-hear-ye stuff, myself. Too much House of Lords. The Coronation.'

'Oh, I meant something along those lines.'

'Could be right.' Sir Eric looked at her again, recalling her. 'I remember now, you came up with an answer for us on another matter. Tenders for furniture. Something like that. That was you, wasn't it?'

'Yes, Sir Eric.'

'At a Directors' meeting?'

'Yes.'

He looked at her and thought for a second or two. 'Remind me again – what were you doing at the meeting?'

'Filling in. Under Secretary Monnet was away, and Claude Cooper was ill.'

'What grade are you?'

'I'm only class B — I was not filling in so much as reporting back. I was just there to report back anything that our bureau might have to do.'

'Maybe the hear-ye-hear-ye stuff would be better for Assembly.'

She could tell that he wasn't enthusiastic. She decided,

though, that working out a ceremonial procedure might be a way for her to make her mark.

He seemed to remember the Directors' meeting now. 'Edith — that's your name.'

'Yes. Dame Rachel and I were the only women present. I'm Edith Campbell Berry.'

She sat there, still in Germany's place at the Council with Sir Eric sitting in as President of Council. The workmen were now down the end of the hall, lounging in chairs in the public section, being, she supposed, the World.

He pointed to an empty chair. 'America will sit there, of course. When they get around to it.'

'Will they get around to doing it?'

'Difficult to say.'

'I've put up the signs,' she said. She pointed. 'The *Prière de ne pas fumer* signs.'

Sir Eric looked across at one of the signs. 'Very good. No one will take the slightest heed. Don't be hurt.'

She laughed and said she expected that to be the case. She gestured at the smoking workmen.

'Briand won't take any notice either,' he said.

One of the workmen approached the table and asked if they were still needed.

Sir Eric nodded at Edith and said in French, 'She's your boss. Ask her.'

She turned to them and told them that they could go. They gathered their tools.

He leaned across to her. 'Should give them something — a gratuity?'

'I'll offer them something for a glass of Ricard or whatever.'

'Good idea. Could you look after that for me?' He gave her some money and she went over to them and gave the foreman the money and told him to buy his men a drink. As they trooped out, the foreman said something, which she could not catch, about a woman having given them money for it, and they all laughed. She stood, again looking around at the room and at Sir Eric seated at the table.

'Sit down again, Berry,' he called.

She came over and seated herself, this time in the chair in which the United States might one day sit.

Sir Eric seemed in a talkative mood. 'You say you're a student of tables?'

'A student of furniture, to be more accurate, and of rooms.'

'I remember how Lord Curzon always had a personal baize-covered footstool at conferences and meetings — for his gout. You know, he wore a back brace too. People used to say he was very formal — but it was his back brace. Made him seem very stiff.' Sir Eric laughed.

' "A most superior person." '

Sir Eric laughed at the old joke. 'Well, now you see — it was his back brace.'

She was pleased. 'I do know,' she said, 'when the horseshoe table was first used in diplomacy.'

'You know more than I do then.'

She hoped that Sir Eric didn't believe that he'd been the first to think of using a horseshoe table. 'At the Tuileries at the end of the eighteenth century.'

'Interesting.'

'It was for a meeting of the Convention.' As she delivered the information she disliked herself. What a useless fact. She believed in statistical facts but only when made into a worthwhile pattern. She hated smart alecks.

'Tell me, Berry, what would you do if you were me, and you had two member states who want to discuss something or other?

They don't have diplomatic relations — will not talk to each other.'

She was taken off-guard, having had her mind on the lowly matters of tables and chairs, no-smoking notices, and ceremonial procedures.

She wondered whether he was talking about the diplomatic problems between Russia and Switzerland. But Russia was not yet a member. 'Would these countries come into the same room?' she asked.

'I doubt that they would. No.'

Edith began working her way to some sort of answer while fearing that her solution would probably be diplomatically very foolish. Still, she had to have a go. 'You could become a neutral state.'

'Me?'

'I mean your office. The position of Secretary-General could be seen as neutral territory.'

'Where would that get us?'

'If the two countries accepted you as neutral, each could speak to you . . . if not to each other.' She saw then how it might be done. 'One country could tell you what it wanted to say to the other country. You could convey it to that country. They could respond to you and then, you could convey that back. And so on.'

'Where would these envoys be? In their own countries? I would have to go back and forth by train or by aeroplane? It would take months.'

She could see it wouldn't work. 'They could both be here,' she said, suddenly, 'here in Geneva.'

'I would go back and forth to their hotels?'

'I suppose so.' Again, she could see that it would be too undignified perhaps to have the Secretary-General running between hotels acting as a go-between. 'I see that could be undignified for the office of Secretary-General.'

She sensed that he hadn't altogether seriously expected her to come up with a solution. Or maybe he was interested in what a middle-ranks woman might come up with.

He rose and then stopped. 'There's one more thing you might do for me, Berry.'

'Yes, Sir Eric?' She opened her pad.

'You know that this Special Assembly is going to be something of an historic moment?'

'Very historic.'

'After the decision to admit Germany is taken, I think a messenger must go immediately to the German delegation waiting at the Metropole and a telegram must be sent to President Hindenberg in Berlin. Immediately.'

'I think that would be very appropriate.' Thank you, Edith Campbell Berry.

'We must ensure that there's a record of communication with Berlin. Show Berlin that we do things promptly here. I was wondering, would you look after all that? Draft up something like: "Please accept heartfelt congratulations of President and Secretary-General STOP Germany admission unanimous STOP." So on, etc.'

'I'll see to that. And the message to the German delegation?'

'Compose a message and dispatch a messenger. Good lass. See me in my office later, say, tomorrow morning. We'll look at your draft.'

'Yes, Sir Eric.'

That night Edith stayed up very late working on the telegram and the message for the messenger, and also on a plan of ceremonials which she would present to Sir Eric — and, on and off, she worried about an answer to his diplomatic question.

Early the next day, Edith went to see Sir Eric, with three drafted telegrams.

'Tiger' Howard checked with Sir Eric and then took her into the office. With a slightly sick feeling, she recalled the madness of Miss Dickinson's chair.

She handed across the messages. 'I drafted three telegrams, Sir Eric.'

'Three?'

One read congratulations on unanimous acceptance etc. One was the same without the word unanimous, and one told of a deferment. During the night, she'd also drafted a fourth telegram saying 'Germany's entry denied', but this morning had felt that might bring bad luck. She had torn that one up. She'd drafted the deferment telegram only as an act of efficiency.

As he read them, she again imagined his office as the bedroom of the notorious Countess.

'Know something I don't know, Berry?' he joked, looking up from the telegrams and waving them.

'I felt that I had to cover all eventualities, Sir Eric. Nearly all.'

'I see,' he said. 'Red for deferred, green for go, and orange for halfway — is that it?'

'Orange is for not unanimous.'

'I see that you know about telegraphese.'

'A little. I composed telegrams for John Latham back in Australia.'

'I know Latham. Met him at the Peace Conference. Good man. If you're covering all eventualities, hadn't you better compose a telegram saying, "Earthquake Geneva STOP Meeting postponed"?' he continued, enjoying himself. 'Maybe they should be written in the new language.'

She laughed with him, but did not understand his reference to a new language, then she flushed, thinking that somehow he'd heard of her crazy idea on scat singing which she'd babbled on about in Paris. Surely Ambrose hadn't been joking about it in the office? 'New language, Sir Eric?'

'Briand told the Chamber in Paris last week that he and Stresemann were talking a new language. The new language of Europe.'

'I didn't see that, sir. There is certainly a new feeling about.'

'Sit down and I will give you a lesson in statecraft.'

He tore up the 'deferred' and 'not unanimous' telegrams and put them in the wastepaper basket. 'That's your lesson.'

She felt reprimanded. But then he smiled at her. 'In diplomatic matters such as this, there is a rule: "No request is ever made unless it is already granted." '

She pondered this. 'Germany would not have requested admission unless she had ascertained that it was assured?'

'Correct. It is a foregone conclusion by the time that it reaches this stage. Believe me, it has been planned since 1921. All agreed at Locarno. We are at the formalities now. You were conscientious, but unnecessarily so.'

'Thank you for the lesson, Sir Eric.'

He initialled her drafts and gave them back to her. She was pleased enough to be given the job of drafting the telegram and the other message but was not so happy about having to send the telegram. Strictly, that was a messenger's job, but she could see that at a time when there could be excitement, a messenger couldn't perhaps be trusted and, anyhow, the telegraph office was set up at the Salle de la Réformation. It wasn't as if she had to dash up the street.

'I've planned out a new member ceremonial, also,' she said, taking out a plan from her attaché case. 'One for Council and one for Assembly. I thought there also should be a ceremonial just for the opening of the Assembly each year. I haven't got around to that.'

It was quite a massive plan, quite detailed, with floor plans and positioning sketched out, and a sketch of a uniform for the huissiers, with arrows indicating the colours of the uniforms and armbands. She'd abandoned the idea of having different uniforms for different sections and for different levels of authority. She'd remembered Strongbow's uniforms and had taken out the file. Her uniforms were nothing like his.

He was surprised. 'Little late in the day for that, Berry. But well done, maybe next time. Don't give it to me now. You might come to another Directors' meeting. Put it to us.'

'Thank you, Sir Eric.'

'When America joins, yes?' he smiled.

'They seem to be joining in some of our activities,' she said, in a remarkably experienced voice.

'By the way, Berry, you might like to know that the League exhibition in the Düsseldorf World Fair won a gold medal.'

'That's wonderful.'

'I was rather quietly proud.'

At the door she turned back to him, 'Sir Eric?'

'Yes?' He looked up from his work.

'It might be wise not to accept the gold medal.'

He put down his pen, and his fingers touched his moustache. 'Why so?'

'It occurs to me that if we enter Fairs and so on we should not do it competitively. We should stand apart.'

'Stand apart?'

'Be *hors concours*.'

'But in God's name why?'

'It would be bad for the League of Nations ever to be in other than first place.'

'Quite so.' He smiled. 'Thank you, Berry.'

She was conscious that he didn't return to his work but continued to look at her as she left the room and until she had closed the door behind her.

Grinning to herself about her advice on the entering of Fairs, she went up the back stairs to her office. She felt disappointed that her plans hadn't been considered by Sir Eric. She could see that it was too late to do much about ceremonials now, but if the admission of Germany had been planned since 1921, why hadn't the ceremonials as well?

Crowds lined the streets to see the German delegation arrive in Geneva in their special train. They had a large diplomatic contingent accompanied by more than a hundred German journalists, and took nearly all the rooms at the Hôtel Metropole. A fleet of Mercedes motorcars was parked outside for the delegates and attracted the attention of automobile aficionados.

The world press had also arrived in Geneva to witness the admission of Germany along with VIPs from around the world including Wilson's widow, Edith Bolling Wilson.

The Sunday night before the Assembly she was working in her office when Cooper came to the door. 'You too? Working on Sunday night?' he said. He came in and looked at her desk, saw the special folder boldly lettered 'Telegram to Berlin', picked it up and read the telegram.

He looked at her, startled. 'Communicating with President Hindenberg, Berry.' He was unsettled. 'What's this about?'

'Special mission. Directly requested by Sir Eric.'

'You?'

'Yes, Cooper, me.'

'How so?'

She explained how it'd come about.

Cooper digested this. 'Strictly speaking, it should be Legal,' he said, worried about it, but also intrigued. He also seemed to imply that if anyone was going to communicate with President Hindenberg, it should be him.

Still holding the telegram draft, he then noticed the design of the huissiers' uniform which she had pinned to the wall. 'And this?'

'I'm designing a uniform for the huissiers,' she explained.

'You'd be better concentrating on our own work.'

'I think it brings glory to us,' she said lightly, 'redounds to the glory of your section.'

He looked at her, maybe thinking that she had a special connection with Sir Eric. He was cautious. 'I suppose so.'

'I didn't do it in office time.'

'Very well.' He put the telegram down on her desk.

At the door, he turned. 'Might get you to design me a uniform,' he said, smiling. 'Give it plenty of panache, something like our Dictator friend further south might wear. Would please the Marquis Paulucci di Calboli Barone when he arrives, don't you think?' Cooper pronounced the name with an exaggerated comedian's Italian accent. 'Good night, Berry. Get some sleep.'

'Good night, Cooper.'

Cooper's jokes were like badly done icing on a cake but she saw also that he was including her in some mild ganging-up against the Marquis Paulucci di Calboli who was said to be taking over Internal and was a Mussolini appointee. She was, however, determined to be absolutely correct in her conduct about the Marquis regardless of what she privately thought.

She'd also arrived at an answer to Sir Eric's diplomatic problem. She'd decided that the two parties should come to the Palais Wilson but go to different rooms so that they didn't have to meet. Sir Eric would call first on one, and then on the other, and so on, until he had reached some formulation, or had broken the impasse. She decided that when the new Palais des Nations was built, the Secretary-General's office should be constructed with two connecting meeting rooms. She began a sketch plan for that also, and worked on into the night.

Before going home, she removed everything from her desk and laid the telegram out, to be picked up by her the next morning.

The next morning she found a message for her to go to see Sir Eric. She guessed it had to do with the telegram.

'Tiger' wasn't in yet. She knocked on Sir Eric's door. He called out, 'Enter.'

Sir Eric explained to her that the Locarno powers had met last night and were still haggling a little with Brazil. It would delay the admission of Germany for a day or so. She was to hold on to the draft of the telegram until he let her know when the Assembly was to make the decision. He said there was to be another secret meeting that evening in his office.

She stood there, feeling shocked at the idea of a secret meeting in the League. 'I didn't think that we had secret meetings. Here at the League.'

He frowned. 'Sometimes private conversations can, well, "mature" difficult questions before they are exposed. Sometimes needed. Like wine and cheese.'

It was something of an answer.

Each morning that week, she continued to come into work

early. The week dragged on; each day Edith expecting to go to the Assembly and to send the telegram which was now pinned to the inside of her door. But during the week nothing happened except that the Secretariat filled with rumours about difficulties and about more secret meetings of Council. Of meetings without minutes. Of comings and goings from meetings in hotel rooms.

The Assembly, after its sub-committee had formally reported to it that there was no technical objection to the admission of Germany to the League of Nations, also waited out the week with nothing for delegates to do except take trips on the lake and to sightsee.

During the second week she continued to go in at 7.30 each morning. On the Tuesday morning of the second week, she was called again to Sir Eric's office.

On the way to his office, she met Mary McGeachy. 'We're early birds,' she said brightly to Mary. 'I have a feeling that today is to be the big occasion.'

Mary did not smile but said bleakly, 'Haven't you heard?'

'What?'

'It's not going to happen. Germany's been blocked.'

'God, no!' She looked again at Mary and took her hand. Mary tried to sound professional and cool. 'Sweetser and Bartlett are preparing statements. To cover all contingencies. They're frantic.'

'Is it Brazil?'

Mary nodded.

'But they can't,' she said, and then stopped herself from quoting Sir Eric's diplomatic maxim. Of course, Brazil could. Brazil had a veto on Council.

Clutching the telegram and message, she rushed down the stairs to Sir Eric's office, not waiting to hear the rest of what Mary had to say. Although it was so early, she passed quite a few

Information section people running around. 'Tiger' wasn't there and she went straight through into Sir Eric's office.

Sir Eric was at his desk, rigid, tired and worried.

She had never seen him looking so immobilised. She had never seen any man like this. Each hand clutched the other desperately. He hadn't shaved.

He looked at her with some sort of relief. She stood waiting for him to speak.

'Berry. Thank you.' His voice showed him close to tears. He made a cough as if coughing back the tears, trying to cough his voice back to normal.

There were chairs about the room, ashtrays filled with cigarette butts. The room had the appearance of having been used for a meeting and smelled stale.

She wondered whether he'd slept in the chair or in the duty officer's bedroom.

He said there'd been an informal meeting of Council last night and it was a stalemate. Germany's admission would have to be adjourned.

'But the Germans — they're all over there at the Metropole! The Chancellor Herr Luther, and Herr Stresemann and all the others . . .' She died as she imagined their fury.

He sat in rigid silence. She was sure that he was in deep distress. 'An embarrassment of gigantic proportion,' he said. He stared out at the lake. She looked out and could see from his window at least two German flags flying from buildings. The city was bedecked with German flags. She ventured to ask, 'It's just an adjournment? Germany's not going to be rejected?'

He moved his shoulders. 'We call it an adjournment. But Germany may never come back to Geneva. After this. They'll never come back.' Again he looked as if he might be breaking down. 'Never come back.'

She thought of all those people who'd travelled across the world to be in Geneva to see Germany admitted. In their hotels this morning, probably already dressing up, waiting for the celebrations. Good God. It was supposed to be the true end of the War.

'Is there anything I can do, Sir Eric?' She was aware then that she didn't know why she was in his office. If the telegram was not to be sent, she was not needed. 'Do the Germans know?'

He shook his head.

'I could take the message to the Germans.' This was a brave offer and a job she didn't want. Is that why he'd called for her?

He looked at her dully. 'Thank you, Berry. Not your job.'

He was a man in shock. He looked at her in the same frozen way he'd been looking at the lake, unable to break his blank gaze. He made a shrugging gesture. 'Have to go myself. Sir Austen, Briand and I will have to go to the Metropole in person this morning. Tell them face to face.' He sat without moving, hands still gripped.

His voice said that doing this, going to the Metropole, was beyond him.

She was glad that she didn't have to face the Germans sitting at the Metropole dressed in their top hats, with their medals and so on, waiting to attend their admission to the Assembly and Council. Oh God, what a mess. Oh God.

She wondered if there was something she could do — as a woman. Take his head and stroke it.

He made to speak again but couldn't.

The telephone rang, and continued to ring.

She realised he couldn't bring himself to lift it. She put down her folder and went around to his side of the desk and picked it up and said into the mouthpiece, 'One minute, please.' Edith hoped that the call would be someone somehow saying that the crisis had been resolved. As she reached across to take one of his message sheets and a pencil, her shoulder touched his, and she let it go on touching him. She felt his body respond dependently. He was leaning on her. She took down the message which was unimportant. His eyes had turned to her expectantly, also hoping for good news. She shook her head, signalling that it wasn't, looking briefly into his hopeless eyes.

She finished taking the unimportant message and put it before him. He glanced at it.

She stood there now beside him, allowing him the contact with her body, wanting to put an arm around him in a comradely and womanly way.

She saw now quite certainly that there was no 'reason' for her to be there — he had no task for her, but he'd needed some sort of supportive presence. It was a reaching out, but she was unsure quite how to consummate that reaching out.

'If you're going to the Metropole, you will need to shave,' she said in an almost wifely voice.

'Quite so.' He put a hand to his face.

'What time is the meeting?'

'Nine-thirty.'

She kept up the contact between their bodies.

She smelled his exhausted body. 'Is there anyone I should call?' she said in a soft voice.

'No. Thank you, Berry.' He gripped her hand and she gripped his, trying to impart to him her fortitude. They stayed this way for a minute or so. She had to get him moving. She withdrew her hand and left his side, going to the window and opening it, allowed the sun to stream in.

'I'll shave you,' she said, turning back from the window. 'I am an extremely experienced shaver of men. My father and my grandfather will give references.'

She kept chattering as she went to his WC and washbasin recess and found shaving brush, shaving soap, razor and bowl. She ran hot water, prepared the soap, and stropped the razor. She carried it all out and made space on the desk for it.

He sat passively while she took off his tie and collar and helped him out of his coat. She put a towel around his neck and, holding his head with her fingers, began lathering his face. She tried to keep her touch as neutral as a barber's.

The rasp of the razor as she shaved him seemed very loud.

He moved his head obediently as she manipulated it with her hand, relaxing into the sureness of her touch. Shaving was a special nearness to the face of a man and she could see his pores, his lumps, his lines, the hairs of his nose and ears. She could see with intimate clarity the shape of his ears, his balding. She could see with intimate clarity his lips. As she entered this intimacy she did not feel like a barber. She wondered whether she felt like a nurse or a daughter or a wife. Something of all. She hoped and prayed that Tiger wouldn't arrive and come upon this scene. It would be difficult to explain.

She finished the shaving and dabbed his face with the towel and broke the touch.

'That's much better,' he said in a small voice, as if what had happened between them was fairly routine. 'Feel much better.'

He took out his handkerchief, wiped his eyes and blew his nose.

She put the things back and when she returned she reminded him that there was a clean shirt hanging in the recess. She looked at her watch. The restaurant staff would be in. 'And I'll call up some tea.'

She took the telephone and rang the restaurant and asked for tea and toast to be sent up. He began sorting papers on his desk. He looked at her and said with a faint smile, 'The Secretary-

General is not a foreign minister, Berry. He's a postman.'

She helped with his sorting of papers and the taut, self-conscious intimacy faded into a bland usefulness. Presently there was a knock on the door. Edith let in the woman from the restaurant and directed her to put the tea and toast on one of the side tables, which she did and then left.

Edith poured the tea for Sir Eric. 'I'll keep the telegram ready, Sir Eric.'

He managed another small smile. 'Yes, hold on to it, the telegram. Who knows? Save yourself some work.' His voice was still close to exhaustion. 'But you know that it could mean the end?'

'The end of the League?'

'Don't go around talking of it in the corridors.'

'Of course not, Sir Eric.'

She took a wastepaper bin and went around emptying the ashtrays.

'I suppose it'll be in the world press by now. We're a laughing stock. A Special Assembly of the nations of the world with nothing to do. I suspect the United States. I think they're behind Brazil. Berry, I'd appreciate if you'd not mention my — well, the fact that I'm a bit knocked about by all this.'

'Of course not, Sir Eric.'

'Must keep morale up.'

The telephone rang and this time he answered it, his voice close to normal. She stood waiting to hear if it was good news but could tell from Sir Eric's answers that it was not to do with the admission crisis.

She waited. He finished the call.

'Thank you, Berry. Must get on with the day.'

She smiled a very special and spirited smile and left his office taking with her the unsent telegram.

As she walked down the corridor she felt a deep, gaping pit in her stomach, and then felt as if a large flock of black birds were flying out from this pit, through her.

On the way to Ambrose's office, she passed Tiger on her way in and they exchanged formal greetings. She saw that throughout the Palais people were gathered in troubled discussion.

'Is it the end?' she asked Ambrose.

'I don't know about the end. I've talked to Salter. He and I agree that until September the League is immobilised. Absolutely impotent. Let's pray there's no outbreak of war. We couldn't do a thing. No one would listen to us. We're a joke.'

'That's what Sir Eric said.'

'You've been to see the Old Man?'

'Yes. Is it the end, Ambrose?'

'May well be. Tell me, what did the Old Man think?'

'He's holding up. What does Bartou say?'

'As cool as always. Says that in a great experiment such as the League we must learn "that nothing ever quite happens the same way twice". Too much the sage is Bartou. Although, it's true of scrambled eggs.'

It was wiser than the diplomatic maxim Sir Eric had taught her, but she couldn't smile. 'He's probably right.' She remembered her science training — we could not classify by sameness, only by likeness. Resemblance always connoted variation. Of what use was that?

'He also said we'd learned something about Brazil.'

'What have we learned?'

'That Brazil is too small to bully but too big to bend. I believe they threatened to take the Rothschild's loan away from Brazil. Tried everything.'

She wanted Ambrose to reassure her that it wasn't all over. He wasn't reassuring. He went on about Germany. 'Germany made the conditions of entry. Germany's destroying the League. She's the one who wouldn't agree to Brazil having a permanent seat along with her.'

'Will they ever come back to Geneva?'

'I doubt it.'

She wondered what she would do 'if she were Germany'. 'Stresemann must understand what's happened?'

'He will fall — the Reichstag will sack him after this. It was his idea to get Germany into the League. He's lost face. Germany is humiliated.'

She went to her office to find Cooper waiting. 'What's happening?' he asked her impatiently.

She was surprised. Surely he knew. 'You know about Germany?'

'I know the bare facts. But what did Sir Eric say? You seem to have special entrée there.'

As she reported a version of her early morning meeting with Sir Eric, she basked in Cooper's new deference to her.

That afternoon, people gathered gloomily at the Special Assembly to hear the Brazilian delegate, Señor Mello Franco, say that another permanent seat should not be given to Europe if one seat was not at the same time given to South America. He said that they were his instructions. He seemed to be a reluctant convoy for his country. He knew that he was putting the League in jeopardy and seemed sad.

The matter of Germany's entry was adjourned to a special commission with the task of finding a compromise before the September Assembly. But it was considered that the League was in crisis.

In the cafés, even journalists showed distress. Edith saw how much everyone cared for the League. Even Liverright was shaken behind his sardonic humour. He said that he'd seen the Austro-

231

Hungarian Empire collapsing around him and had leapt into the army for security and then the War had broken out around him. He had leapt from the War into the League of Nations and now it was collapsing around him. He didn't know if he were to blame or the world.

Florence, Victoria and Edith — the 'Dominion Sisters' as they were sometimes called — sat up most of the night talking about their future. She had expected Victoria to be shaken, but Florence was no better — she was quite disturbed, her Canadian self-assurance gone. Edith felt she may have been wrong about her, that she too cared deeply for the League.

They drank hot chocolate made on the spirit stove which Edith had in her rooms. Florence lay back in the Wilson chair, Victoria on the velveteen armchair, and Edith on the bed. She lit the room with three candles for a softer, more comforting light. Edith had noticed that, at this time of crisis, League people seemed to draw close to their own national group. The three of them had huddled in the Empire. Or at least among the dominions group. She now saw that New Zealanders and Canadians were the first natural allies of an Australian. Not the British. Ambrose, for whatever reason, for the future of the League or for support and comfort, was spending long nights with his countrymen within the League.

'How can one contemplate working anywhere else after having worked for the League?' Victoria said, which was Edith's reaction as well.

Edith kept trying to imagine packing up her things, booking the return to Australia — and then what? Working with John again? Moving with him to the new parliament house in Canberra? The photographs she'd seen of Canberra showed a dusty paddock. It would be going back to a country town in the middle of New South Wales. Ambrose often said she couldn't ever go back because the Australian climate didn't suit her complexion. She couldn't see it happening yet. She'd somehow stepped outside the borders of herself and did not want to step back — yet. On the footsteps of this thought came another which she hastily pushed away. Had she come to Geneva to escape the 'real world' of her own country? Had she fled to a fantasy, pretending to herself that she was coming to the 'centre of things'?

'I'm going to take the money owed to me and go to Russia,' Florence said. 'Money owed for vacation and for repatriation and allowances for severance, and home leave still owing. It will be a goodly sum.'

The wilful and wild Edith responded to this idea, of having funds, although she also had her mother's money, 'her inheritance' which her mother had sent to her, saying that she and her brother may as well have it now, rather than 'waiting', that it would be of more use to her now in Europe. Her mother's money virtually made her independent. She would not go to Russia. Travelling, maybe — just going away, aimlessly. Maybe Ambrose and she would travel to exotic places. But the responsible Edith was disappointed with Florence's talk of how much the League would pay them if it closed down. She'd also heard two typists talking in the Palais restaurant about how much would be owed to them and she'd almost gone over to them and told them off. That wasn't the correct spirit. 'Why Russia?' asked Victoria. 'It sounds a little too scientific to me. Might suit you, Edith.'

'They might need financial experts.'

'Book-keepers?'

'Why not?'

'Why would a socialist country want book-keepers?'

'Every system has people who cheat on claimed expenses, I'm sure, and who need to be caught.'

Edith listened to this exchange wondering whether anyone wanted her skills. She wasn't truly a scientist. She was half-trained as an international civil servant. Who needed half-trained international civil servants? Victoria was a bit older than both of them and trained in Registry work which was useful anywhere.

Victoria said she couldn't imagine going back to Wellington.

'At least Wellington is a city. Canberra isn't even built yet,' Edith said.

'You haven't seen Wellington,' Victoria said.

They laughed more loudly than the quip deserved and then became sober again.

'I might travel to exotic places,' Edith said.

'But what happens when the money runs out?' Victoria said, as always, looking ahead to the pain of things.

She imagined Ambrose and her sinking into 'decadence' but she didn't quite know what the decadence would be, of what particular kind. She tried to imagine them in Munich or in New York but couldn't. She became frightened then at how much her conception of life existed only in Geneva and at the League.

'Come to Russia,' Florence said. 'Work for the revolution. They will want help from people like us who know about the international world.'

'I don't fancy working for the revolution,' Victoria said. 'I fear that their files are in a mess, despite their claims to be scientific.'

More laughter of a desperate kind.

'I might go back to university,' Edith said. 'Go to Oxford.'

'We could all get married, I suppose,' Victoria said.

'If the worst came to the worst,' Florence said, and again

they all laughed desperately. It was a sensitive subject with them all, each fearing that the other might marry first and go off to bliss, leaving them working. Edith had tried to understand her own feelings about marriage but had only a provisional position, that she wanted to work for the League until she had done all she could. The conversation trailed off eventually. Victoria went home, and Florence slept on the Wilson chair.

Edith tried her best to be positive, and in the Bavaria she argued that the crisis showed that the League was not, in fact, dominated by the Big Powers which everyone always said. That a little nation such as Brazil could force them to think again. Could stop them in their tracks. Not so little. Someone estimated it was the third richest country in the world.

There was talk now of three Leagues evolving. A European League, a Pan-American League, and an Asiatic League. Some said that the US wanted this and had brought about the crisis.

She and the others at the Secretariat went on with their work but it was a time of low confidence. The Secretariat was really to blame. They shouldn't have let anything go ahead until everything was certain. How badly they'd applied the maxim that no request was to be made unless it was granted. And how badly German diplomats had applied it too. Edith kept the unsent telegram in her drawer, thinking that it would be a sad, historic document.

It was not the end of the League.

The most surprising result was a new determination by Germany to gain admission. Germany's interest in the League was spurred on by the rebuff which it saw as evidence of the importance that countries placed on membership of the Council.

As the September Assembly approached, she reminded Sir

Eric about the telegram. She took it to him. He glanced through it again. She changed the date. He made a comment or two about the last time they had been together in the office.

He told her that this time, Germany would not come to Geneva until assured that all formalities were secure and that there was no possibility of loss of face. 'This time when the telegram goes to Berlin, it won't be just to inform the President of the Reich — it will be to summon the German delegation. Do you understand? They'll not move until they get this telegram.' He held it up.

'Understood, Sir Eric.'

'The telegram has to confirm to the Germans that all is right here in Geneva. Signed, sealed, and delivered.'

M. Avenol, the Deputy Secretary-General, was sitting in the room, and said that, given that the Germans would not leave for Geneva until the formal admission had happened, they'd have to accept the consequences, 'Viz, that Germany's official admission to the League will be voted on here on the Wednesday. The Germans will get the telegram in Berlin that day, but given the length of the train trip from Berlin to Geneva, the German delegation cannot possibly be present until the Friday — days after the formalities of their admission have been dealt with.'

He said he thought it would be an anticlimax. 'The first appearance of their delegates will be less glorious than it might otherwise have been.'

'I have sympathy with Germany this time,' Sir Eric said. 'I myself wouldn't budge from Berlin until I knew that admission was concluded.'

She took a breath and said, 'Will I draft an alternate telegram saying that the admission is deferred?'

He looked at her. 'Good God, no. No telegram about defer-ment. I don't want to hear the word.'

She said that she realised there'd been more important con-cerns in recent months, but if the huissiers were not to wear uniforms, could they perhaps wear armbands with the initials 'SdN' and 'LofN'?

Sir Eric said he couldn't see any objection. He looked at Avenol who said that he thought it was a useful idea.

Edith said, 'I know a woman who can make them.'

'Go ahead.'

They went back to looking at some documents on the desk. She hovered about as long as she could. She leaned with them to look at the plans and documents. Eventually it became imposs-ible for her to delay her going any longer. Sir Eric had glanced up once or twice at her, not seeming to mind, but Avenol seemed puzzled by her presence.

Everyone who could get away from the Secretariat was again at the Salle de la Réformation to see Germany finally admitted. Holding the telegram drafts, Edith sat at the front with Cooper and the other Secretariat members who were on duty. She'd heard him mention to others, with some pride, that his office was 'handling that part of things'.

She'd not followed Sir Eric's advice. She followed Bartou's advice 'that nothing ever happened the same way twice', in so far as it was of any use. She'd made a deferment draft, and she had it with her. If deferment did happen for any unforeseen reason, she felt that it was important for her to have a telegram prepared that could be sent without people having to confer over wording while in a confused state. But she'd realised that it was a nonsensical paradox, to talk of planning for the unforeseeable. Life was a series of agile responses. How to modify the response precisely enough was the trick. Life was not technique. It was knack and artistry.

Self-importantly, she waved to Victoria, Florence and the others clustered at the side entrance to the Presidential dais. They were simply there as spectators. Even Caroline Bailey was there looking interested, probably hoping for another disaster to put in her novel. Despite Germany's refusal to attend until the Friday, the Salle was packed to hear the formal admission. Many people had returned, even after the March fiasco. Cooper pointed out to Edith that Mrs Woodrow Wilson and her hat were again seated in the gallery.

She could see the whole Assembly hall, the forty-eight tables for delegates and alternates and Germany's vacant table. Seventeen prime ministers, eighteen foreign ministers, seven former foreign ministers. She waved to John Latham, Freda Bage, and the others of the Australian delegation.

Brazil's table was vacant.

She was proud that the huissiers wore the blue armbands she'd designed and had silk-screened. She hadn't told anyone that she'd also sewn them herself. And chosen the colour.

It fell to the Swiss delegate, Giuseppe Motta, to report to the Assembly the compromise worked out by the Council. There was to be a new category of Council members — semi-permanent — to permit the smaller powers greater representation. Only Germany was to become a new permanent member.

A chill crept into Edith as she heard Loudon, the Dutch delegate, attack the procedure of presenting this new structure of Council without any chance for the Assembly to consider it in advance. 'We are forced to vote today without proper consideration. It forces the Assembly's hand and seriously alters the balance of power between Assembly and Council.'

With growing dismay, Edith heard one delegate after another attack the compromise. It was pointed out that an enlarged Council would have difficulty taking emergency action. All those nations on Council would have to be consulted. Time would be lost.

Even the much-loved Nansen, of Norway, opposed the compromise complaining that most of the Assembly delegates had only heard of the compromise proposal that morning. He would carry weight.

Every time a delegate objected to the compromise, other delegates applauded the objections.

Edith began to feel shaky with trepidation. She realised that the deferment telegram was going to be used. Or worse, a rejection of Germany's application might occur. She had not composed a rejection telegram. She took out her pad from her briefcase and tried to compose a telegram of rejection. Cooper kept trying to see what she was doing.

She read the 'deferred' telegram again to see that it was correct. No words missing. Oh, my God. She could see that Sir Eric was tense.

Lofgren of Sweden took up the objections and supported them.

The President, Mr Nintchitch of Serbia, then called for the vote. The first vote was on the admission of Germany to the Assembly.

Even if Germany were admitted to the Assembly, Germany would still not come unless given a permanent seat on the Council alongside only Italy, Japan, France, and Britain. Germany had made that clear.

He called for the vote count. The tellers stood in the aisles. Edith watched almost too intensely, almost unable to see, but all hands went up. Or was that against the motion? It was for the motion. All states voted yes to Germany's admission.

'I declare Germany a member of the League of Nations Assembly.'

There was applause and some cheering. Edith was confused and realised that the countries who had spoken out in objection had not intended to vote against Germany. That had been more criticism of the Council's presentation of a _fait accompli_, not opposition to Germany. It was all going through.

The President called for a vote on the amendment to the Covenant to permit a restructuring of the Council to admit Germany and to make room for semi-permanent members.

The vote for change in the structure of Council was also unanimous. Germany would sit at the horseshoe table.

It was through. There was sustained applause, with many delegates rising to their feet.

She still could not trust what she had witnessed and turned to Cooper. 'Germany's in?'

'Yes, Berry, Germany's in. Now rush!' He touched her arm. 'Send it off.'

As she rushed, Edith read the two green telegrams — one to Premier Stresemann and one to President Hindenberg — yet again rechecking. She glanced up at Sir Eric who nodded to her.

She moved quickly through the curtains. As she did, she glanced back to see the still applauding Assembly and was bemused to see that the eyes of the men in the hall were on her, giving her the illusion that they were applauding her. Of course their eyes always turned to any woman who came and went through the curtains. She gave them all a quick smile and closed the curtains. As she walked down to the telegraph room she glanced at herself in one of the wall mirrors, seeing what the men had admired in her body, pleased with her appearance.

The clerk stood waiting for the telegram. 'They're in then?' the clerk said. She had positioned a huissier to keep the telegraph available for her and to keep the press away.

'Yes, they're in.'

She again read through the telegrams and decided on one small last-minute change. At the end of the two forms, after the names of Sir Eric and President Nintchitch, she put, 'per ECB'. She wrote herself into history and then handed the forms to him, he signed a receipt, and she in turn signed an authorisation that they were to go priority to Berlin.

The clerk asked her whether the League would pay the supplement for a priority message.

'Of course the League will pay the supplement,' she told him abruptly.

He grinned at her, having had his joke. She managed a tight grin in return.

She watched the clerk sit at the Morse key and tap it out. He then sat for a second or two until a signal came back from Berlin, 'Message received.'

The clerk said, 'They've received it in Berlin.'

'You're sure?'

The clerk looked at her, again grinning. 'Perfectly sure. The German operator sent back "Message received".'

She didn't see how he could be sure but there was nothing she could do about it. She understood Morse and the telegraph but still felt that the message had gone off into a void.

'It's all right,' he said, still grinning at her nervousness, full of his technical conceit. 'They've got it at the Ministry and at the Palace.' She asked for the return of the telegram forms for the archives.

Outside the telegraph office, she leaned against the wall, feeling weak and shaking a little. Newspaper reporters began queueing at the telegraph office.

Robert Dole came over to her. He was a journalist she vaguely knew from the Bavaria and the Club de la Presse. He gestured at the telegrams. 'Are they the telegrams to Germany?'

She nodded.

'May I?' He held out his hand.

She wondered if she could show them. They were diplomatic messages. But they were also happy history. Why not?

She handed them to him and he copied down the messages. She studied him as he wrote. Jeanne was always talking about people's eye colouring: 'Cold and blue like the sea' was a favourite. She said Joshi had 'dreamer's eyes'. Edith couldn't see anything in people's eyes and didn't believe in that sort of thing. She couldn't even tell whether a person was honest or not, nor whether they were a hypocrite. Everyone else claimed to be able to tell by the eyes.

He gave her back the telegrams and smiled. 'The initials ECB — they're yours?'

'Yes.'

'May I ask your middle name?'

'Campbell — Edith Campbell Berry.'

'Thank you, Edith Campbell Berry,' he said, and joined the queue at the telegraph office.

On the Friday, the German delegation arrived in Geneva to another grand welcome by crowds of people at the Gare Cornavin.

Edith was there at the Salle, as a spectator this time, to see the Germans take their place in the Assembly.

As she heard the President of the Assembly call on the Cuban President of the credentials committee to give his report, she went through her proposed ceremonial plan, imagining how it might work. One day maybe they would adopt it.

The President said that the credentials of the German delegates had been examined and found in order.

The President said in a strong voice, 'I invite the German delegates to take their places.'

Superstitiously, she didn't feel sure that her telegram had reached Berlin until she saw Herr Stresemann come through the door of the Salle de la Réformation with his entourage. He had a bull-neck and wore a tight black morning coat, not his special wide-lapelled suit which had become so fashionable. She was aware of a small shock and a special curiosity of seeing Germans. She had, of course, seen them before, had even seen Stresemann back in March drinking beer in the Bavaria, but every time she looked at them, it was as if they were from another world. The word 'Hun' still whispered through her mind.

Clapping accompanied Herr Stresemann and his colleagues down the aisle to their seats. It was dignified but lacked majesty. At Dame Rachel's dinner party for delegates and Secretariat women the night before, Mrs Swanwick, an English woman from the Union for Democratic Control had said loudly and unnecessarily, referring to the admission, that she thought, 'the bloom had gone off it all'.

She decided that in her ceremonials she would have a procession of visiting people who were important to the League such as Mrs Edith Bolling Wilson. And, she supposed, people like Mrs Swanwick.

Maybe next year would see America admitted and that would be the chance to put her ceremonials into action.

She was very unsure about what she'd learned from the

243

episode. She thought that maybe she'd learned that as an officer she was not likely to be immobilised by surprise, panic, or defeat. She thought that somehow she'd always known that — maybe she'd learned thăt already from some childhood situation. Or if immobilised, she should, like Sir Eric, reach out to someone who could break the panic. Curiously, it didn't have to be a close friend. She'd certainly learned about the frailty of Secretaries-General. Furthermore, she'd learned about the frailty of institutions and saw in herself a change of attitude. She had taken the survival of the League for granted and had worked within its security. She now had to watch over the institution and protect it, not only from its enemies, but from the illusion of invulnerable strength.

She had learned something about planning. When planning failed, one worked through the emerging events, making order with agility and intuition. She had, for example, planned to send a telegram but had instead shaved a man.

The Economics of Self

They were all at the Café Landolt after a meeting of the Fourth Committee and they were all down. Brazil and Spain were pulling out and this had seriously reduced the budget, although the effect probably wouldn't show up until 1929, and for the first time, League endeavours were being cut back. Coming after the crisis of Germany's admission, Edith had felt shaken by Sir Eric's confidential circular on finances which she'd seen on Cooper's desk.

Maybe the other member states would not make up the loss of Brazil and Spain, and unbelievably, there were the nations which had become late payers.

For the League, it was the worst year to date financially. She sensed that others were also unnerved.

Edith thought those gathered there in the private room at the Café Landolt were definitely the best and brightest of those now working at the League — well, at least of the younger Secretariat members. Those there in the Café Landolt wouldn't be the first retrenched, if there were ever retrenchments, something else which had been unthinkable until recently, but it seemed to her that it was partly up to them, the younger members of the Secretariat who would one day run the place, to come up with some answers to the League's finances.

Edith was doubly depressed. She had been servicing the meeting of the General Transit Committee on Calendar Reform and was sick to death of arguments about fixing the moveable feasts and the simplification of the Gregorian calendar. Frankly, she didn't care one way or another and was willing to accept that thirteen equal months of four complete weeks each might be best for the world. It was obvious that for the world to work together it had to have one calendar. It was just as obvious that all cars should travel on the same side of the road in every country so that people could use one set of road rules wherever they were. The League could not achieve agreement even on that. Sometimes she despaired. China had its own calendar and was totally opposed to calendar reform and the Pope didn't want to fix Easter. Though if China didn't pay its dues, why should anyone listen to them? Of all the work the League did, why did the calendar reform attract an anonymous donation of $10,000? She knew why, of course. It attracted cranks.

Through the haze of the café and the haze of her tired eyes and the mind haze of the Moselle wine, she saw Cooper expounding. She wondered if she 'liked' Claude. She was having trouble with the word 'like' and 'friend' and 'enemy'. At times, she would find herself thinking that a particular person was foolish but she would make an immediate correction and dismiss this judgement, saying to herself that within all people could be found something of value to any given colloquy.

Maybe she was suppressing her natural reactions to people, no longer permitting herself to say she liked or disliked. It was also in her nature to expect people to perform better than they could, and she expected that all people could rise up to the circumstance. Sometimes she suspected it was a form of sickness in her, this inner tension. It was a sending of telepathic messages to other people, for instance, during a discussion, urging them to be better, or to recognise that they were not qualified to speak, or had not informed themselves sufficiently.

Often at the League, people did behave better. In committees, especially, everyone tried harder and often surpassed themselves, often did better than she would ever have expected. Though when things went badly she felt that it was hurting her to suppress herself so. Sometimes she wanted to yell at a delegate on a committee, or to take over the chair. All that life spirit which she put into connecting and seeing the other persuasion. She wanted the right to express animosity and the atmosphere of the League did not allow it. She had also suppressed her urge to 'apportion blame'. Too often she had had to avoid blaming anyone for what had happened in the world. She felt it was about time blame was apportioned.

She now made herself listen to Cooper, and that itself was an example. 'Making herself listen' to someone. It was a necessary discipline, although when she had time she would dearly love to examine herself to see whether making oneself listen hurt the spirit.

Cooper was talking about investing in the stock market. He was saying that the League could invest, or that one of the funds — say, the provident or building fund — could be invested, or a staff syndicate formed which might channel profit back into the League.

She reflexively opposed this. Maybe it was her dislike or, well, her not being empathetic to Cooper that caused her always to take the opposite position to his. 'We are not an organisation of financial speculation,' she said, taking a drink of Moselle.

'Quite right,' said Joshi, who might be a world authority on malaria but who would certainly change his mind according to the way of the wind.

'On the contrary,' Ambrose quipped, 'as an organisation we are the greatest speculative venture in history. It could be said that we are purely a speculation.'

He won some laughs, and she smiled across at him.

Disregarding the laughter, Cooper said in his boring way

that it would give the League another back-up financially.

'By us — do you mean the League or those of us here?' someone asked.

'Maybe both,' Cooper said. 'We could try to get Council to do it, but if not, we could set up our own fund to safeguard us, the staff, from financial disaster if everything crashes. After all, some of us gave up good jobs to come halfway around the world to work here.'

Sitting beside Edith, Florence was reading the *Continental Daily Mail*, ostentatiously expressing abstention from the proceedings while still hearing what was being said. She worked in Finance but said she knew nothing of 'shocks and snares'. Nor would she do anything that Cooper proposed.

It was not alien to Edith to consider investing, although her father and mother had only a small investment in the stock exchange. She could remember her father being opposed to simply gambling on the stock market but not to investing in it. Gambling, he said, produced neither goods nor services and therefore must be taking from the labour and intellect of the economy without giving anything in return. 'I like to make things,' he would say, 'or I like to make things happen — one or the other. There is nothing else worth doing.' Consequently, as far as she remembered, he invested mostly in new companies and didn't make much money from it.

She sat there and changed her position slightly about Cooper's scheme, although not about Cooper. What came to her was that she found herself warming to the idea of being 'a woman who owned shares'. She imagined herself talking at dinner parties about her share-holding and she imagined having wonderfully printed share certificates in a bank strongroom box which she could examine, which said Amalgamated Oil, Trans-Pacific Railroads, Brazilian Gold Mines, and Consolidated East Africa

Coffee. Maybe not Brazilian Gold Mines, given their behaviour at the League.

She and those there at the Landolt were supposed to be experts at organising the work of committees, yet tonight they were breaking all the rules by not having a position paper, an agenda, or anything. She suspected that even Cooper was not an expert on the stock market. They shouldn't be meeting in the Landolt either. It was the wrong atmosphere in which to inaugurate serious projects. The meeting was a professional shambles.

She looked over at Ambrose who had borrowed Florence's paper. He and Joshi were looking at the financial pages.

Ambrose owed her six hundred francs.

'You seem to have views on the stock exchange, Berry,' Cooper came back, friendly mockery in his voice. 'Maybe you'd like to say something?'

Cooper was guessing that she wouldn't know anything about the stock exchange, which was correct, despite her background.

She needed a Way, one of those Ways from days past when she had such things. She decided to go the Way of the Fool, to seek the protection of conceded ignorance. 'As a matter of fact, Cooper,' she said, pausing to take a drink of Moselle, 'I know bugger-all about the stock market.' She just stopped herself saying, 'And so do you.'

This caused laughter of relief which told her that some of the others knew bugger-all about the stock market. She hadn't sworn in public since university days.

Joshi slapped his hand on the table with appreciation. 'I also know bugger-all about the stock market,' he said laughing, wiping his forehead with his handkerchief. 'I know bugger-all about motor-cars. I know bugger-all about Persian carpets. I know bugger-all about the game of bridge. My professors at

Oxford said I know bugger-all about medicine.'

He roared with laughter at his own joking confessions. He kept on going. 'However, I do know a bloody lot about tennis,' he said, 'and I know too bloody much about mosquitoes.'

More laughter.

Amid the laughter, she continued with her private reflections and it crossed her mind that owning shares might make her 'independent'. What was the idea of independence about? Apart from earning her living, why did she feel she needed more? She had her mother's inheritance, the gift of money her mother had sent her some months back. It then occurred to her that the 'inheritance' showed that her mother had been almost financially independent of her father. She returned herself to the conversation.

'Where, then, should I begin to explain the stock market?' said Cooper, savouring the chance to lecture, addressing them as he might a school class. He explained the stock market to them.

'The secret to my plan,' said Cooper, seeming to swell with his sense of himself, 'is that we are well placed to hear — not about individual companies, but we have a bigger ear. We see all those statistics before anyone else, about crop production and the assessment of ore potentials and so on. Predictions of the future of things, of wars and the talk of wars,' he said. 'Even the weather affects the stock market and we at the League hear lots about weather prediction.' He explained about the business people and delegates and experts from the countries of the world who came in and out of Geneva. 'They're the people we have to pump.'

Edith did not like the idea of pumping people. She felt uneasy about the use of the League's information, even if it wasn't confidential. This was not the use for which it had been gathered. She felt the conversation was getting close to breaching the proper conduct of officers.

There was definitely another inner voice speaking to her about this stock market business. She thought it might be the voice of avarice. She was always pleased to find some inkling of vice in herself. Sometimes she felt too saintly working at the League. Which was probably why she sometimes let herself be decadent with Ambrose.

Although she was not being won over to the plan of involving the League, she was curious to know about the stock market. Her friend from back home, George McDowell, would probably know and he had said he would visit her in Geneva as part of his world trip. John Latham was in Geneva with the Australian delegation to the Assembly. Maybe he could advise her.

Assembly time was a fifth season for Geneva. The city overflowed with delegates, journalists, and visitors from all over the world. A new social season at least. It disturbed and changed Geneva just as much as the climatic seasons.

The meeting broke up with an understanding that those present would 'think about it'.

As she and Ambrose walked home from the Landolt, she listened to Ambrose enthuse about the idea of the syndicate. 'I must say that I rather like the idea of "playing the market",' he said.

She found herself annoyed by his enthusiasm, and by the way he was ignoring his debt to her. He made no mention of it.

They reached his apartment.

'Coming up?' he asked. 'It's Friday.'

She again noted how much she made the decisions within

their love affair. 'Not tonight, dear Ambrose. No.'

He walked on with her to her pension and there they kissed, and he went away without demur.

Slowly rubbing the night cream into her face, she pondered the motley feelings she had about Ambrose owing her money. At first she'd been happy to be needed by him. It had been a tangible expression of their bond, and yet now it dissatisfied another part of her.

That 'borrowing dulled the edge of husbandry', came to her at the dressing table. Also something, she supposed, her father had said. She liked the play on the idea of husband. Ambrose — no husband he. She should look for more, though, from life than an adventurous lover. She was, deep down, more emotionally ambitious than that, but it would have to wait. She had other things to do. A world to set right. And now, perhaps, she had the stock market to 'play'.

She sat for some moments then in lascivious wanderings, her fantasy settling on recollections of Jerome in Paris. The fantasy led her hand which held her bone-handled hairbrush down between her legs, and with the cool handle of the brush, and with her eyes shut, she pleasured herself.

The meaning of Ambrose's debt to her persisted even after this dalliance with fantasy. As she went on to brush her hair, she observed that the problem with lending money to a friend was that a strange burden fell onto the lender.

Were you a good enough friend to lend money? In asking for the money back, the lender then ran the danger of impugning the honour of the friend who had borrowed it, of suggesting a fearfulness about the money being repaid.

But to avoid asking for the money caused the debt to become

something that the friends couldn't talk about. It created a perilous spot in the friendship.

The repayment was not only in money, it involved the borrowing friend's 'gratitude' which could unbalance things, too. Too much gratitude was uncomfortable for both people. Gratitude represented an unspecified and unagreed 'emotional interest' on the loan and with the limits of gratitude being so poorly defined it was difficult to ever get it out of the system of the friendship.

She massaged cream into her feet, the final act of the day, and tried, as always, to get to the bed without her feet touching the floor. Since she'd been about fifteen and conscious of her body and its care she had done this, trying to fly from the dressing table to her bed without touching the floor. She'd told herself repeatedly over the years to use her bedroom slippers, to break the childish habit of hopping barefoot to the bed, but she never had.

In bed, before sleep came to her, she enjoyed the idea of becoming a modern woman who knew about stocks and shares.

She took time off to go to the Assembly meeting in the Salle de la Réformation, to hear John speak. She went to hear him at the Assembly as an Australian, to 'support the home team', and for an hour or so she allowed herself patriotic feelings, silently barracking for the Australians to acquit themselves well. She was proud that Australia was an international presence in its own right.

She was glad that the three hundred seats in the press gallery were almost full to hear John speak.

John had argued well against the French delegate M. Loucheur, who wanted blank votes included in the count when deciding whether a majority had voted for the candidate nation. M. Loucheur called blank voting '*inertie courtoise*'. He said that some Assembly members cast blank votes to avoid the discourtesy of voting *against* the candidate country, which perhaps national foreign policy might in other circumstances require, but allowing them at the same time to indicate that they had no opposition to the candidate.

John said that courteous inertia was an inconclusive argument and that nations should show the courage of their convictions. There should be more plain talking. People should vote yes or no.

Proudly, she liked his style and she agreed with his defence of plain speaking.

She caught up with him after the meeting and they went for tea at the Hôtel de la Paix where the Australians were staying. She had talked with them on the day they arrived and had helped them book into the hotel. She congratulated him on his call for plain speaking.

He said that as a politician, or as a diplomat, he hoped that he never had to engage in double talk or to wear his underpants the wrong way round. She laughed and asked him why he would wear his underpants the wrong way round.

He said, with a small smile, that some diplomats claimed it was a way of avoiding divine punishment when telling a justifiable diplomatic lie. 'It is another way of crossing your fingers,' he said, tickled by sharing it with her.

For John, it was probably a risqué thing to say. She said that she could never think of him as a double-talker.

'Remember though that evil men will always pretend to be frank,' he said. 'I think there's an argument to be made for "delaying the truth". I remember at the Peace Conference I wanted to release something to the press — I was a secretary to the Committee on Czech-Slovak affairs. I forget the substance of the communiqué. The Chairman, Paul Cambon, said to me, "Your communiqué is quite precise. And if it is published tomorrow, hundreds of men will die in fighting." '

'How could he be so sure that it would result in fighting?'

'It is judgement. In fact when the final draft of those provisions was released, fighting broke out in Czecho-Slovakia.'

'Delaying the communiqué only delayed the bloodshed.'

'Any delay offers hope of avoidance. By all means, publicise the agreements — no more secret arrangements — but deliberate in confidence.'

She thought then about how she would describe to herself her 'secret arrangement' with Ambrose, often thinking that if she ever had to face a judge in the Court of Proper Life Conduct she would say, 'What we did together was part of my coming to understand life, and as a caring for another human being in his confusion. I didn't do it as an act of simple carnal pleasure.' The judge would then say, 'How then do you explain your carnal pleasure?' She would say that her carnal pleasure was 'after' she had entered into the situation for other more virtuous reasons.

Edith?

Yes, she had done it *as a vice* — out of carnal curiosity and arousal. There, that was out — admitted to herself, at least.

She attended to their discussion.

'I heard an argument about what the different armies of the world mean by "surrendering",' she said. 'Some soldiers hoist a white flag. Some throw down their arms. The Prussians raise their rifles butt end up. The French required them also to kneel.' She laughed. 'And the Russians embrace those to whom they are surrendering.'

He laughed. 'Beware the embrace of the Russian bear.'

She told him that there was really no international agreement on even this matter. She was trying to impress him by showing the sort of things she heard and talked about here in Geneva.

She said that confusions such as this made her sympathise with those who tried to govern. She said she was more and more amazed that government was possible. She said she was impatient with those people who scorned politicians.

'I am amused by the League talk of electing "semi-permanent" members of Council. It all sounds very much like our talk about a "temporary permanent" parliament house at Canberra, don't you think?'

She told him Ambrose's joke about semi-virgins. He liked that.

'I worry about the League speeches sometimes,' he said. 'I was talking with one of the British delegates, Mrs Swanwick, after Count Apponyi's speech . . .'

Edith made a gesture of dislike at the mention of Mrs Swanwick's name.

'Mrs Swanwick not to your taste?'

'Not at all. I agree with her on most things but I can't abide the woman.'

'I think I know what you mean. Anyhow, I said that in his speech Apponyi had been brave by withholding nothing and Mrs Swanwick came back at me saying how sad it was that to tell the truth in Geneva was considered "brave".'

A typical Swanwick remark. She leapt to find a position away from that of Mrs Swanwick. She no longer believed that 'empty rhetoric' was empty. She had come around to seeing that rhetoric was useful, even if unfelt by the speaker, because it contained within it the expression of what was 'acknowledged' as being desirable. That a hypocrite was affirming virtue by paying 'lip service'. Next time the virtue might be harder to disregard.

Rhetoric contributed to the formation of a future consensus.

He kept talking and she listened as she went over her thoughts, wondering whether she should say them to John. She decided she might as well speak and see what he thought.

She said, 'Even if the speaker doesn't believe it, and even if the country has no intention of doing it, the important thing is that they feel compelled to *say it* and to *say it in those words* to the international community.'

She felt she was perhaps overstating her position and she threw in something light. 'I do admit that I've heard too many speeches which begin with the words, "When mankind first emerged from the primeval mud . . ." '

He laughed. 'But that's quite an observation,' he said. 'Doesn't it reduce the weight of your praise for my plain speaking? Aren't you saying that there is more than one way to "speak" diplomatically? Arc you becoming a diplomat, Edith?'

She detected in his voice a tone which began as teasing and then turned into bemusement as he realised that he'd been pulled up.

She was unprepared for the impact of his interest. She was flummoxed too, by his observation of the contradiction and her devaluation of her earlier praise of him.

Suddenly she saw that maybe John was wrong about courteous inertia. The French were perhaps wiser on this. There was nuance and that was what she had to learn. The blank ballot was a courtesy containing a comment, a nuance. A yes vote which was cast without conviction was perhaps the true hypocrisy. The courteous inertia created a third type of vote.

It crossed her mind then that there were perhaps other ways of voting than yes and no. The League needed more ways of voting than yes, no and abstention. *Inertie courtoise* was already one. She remembered now that at a League conference she'd attended, someone had wanted to be counted as absent when they were present in the hall. They wanted to be listed as absent during the vote. They did not want to abstain, nor vote yes or no, nor put in a blank vote. Being technically absent was more than avoiding making a decision at that time — it was saying that you were not ready even to confront or acknowledge the issue at that time. Intellectual absence.

There was also the French use of the word '*voeu*' — an expression of a wish rather than a decision.

Within conversation, too, she realised there were many ways of 'voting'.

She felt this was a personal breakthrough in her thinking, *une prise de conscience*. She felt she had to digest it before putting it out into conversation, especially with John who was now in her mind clearly wrong. Simple plain speaking was not always the scrupulous way. It tried to pretend that everything could be expressed. But the greater fault in politics and discussion was careless imprecision. Diplomacy was closer to the truth because by creating honest silence it tried to avoid saying things which were untrue through imprecision. Diplomacy could create the 'semi-silence'.

Or it avoided saying things *at that time*, before anyone was ready to say something. It was a way of maintaining verbal relationships while at the same time holding off superfluous statement and unneeded position-taking. The raisings of unnecessary disagreement. Which, she guessed, was also the value of card-playing.

As she registered her thinking, she realised that she was changing her position on something rather important. She felt nicely nervous.

'I liked what Briand once said about it all,' John went on. 'He said that at the end of all diplomatic proceedings, all tedious speeches, and all the consecutive and simultaneous translations of dusty communiqués there are people in anguish.'

She could agree with that wholeheartedly. 'Briand is my hero,' she said.

'Oh?' He gave a wry smile.

'After you, of course.'

'You don't have to place me ahead of Briand.'

She did not want to be a challenge to John. Deference and affection, nicely blended, stepped between them. Disagreement, if it existed between friends, did not always have to be expressed or pursued. It could be left forever peripheral to the friendship or even in silence. Everything didn't have to be said. She turned the conversation and sought his advice on the stock market but he seemed to be unacquainted with its workings. He said that some of his friends were making large amounts of money on the share market. He advised her to buy property. He said that owning property was good for the personality 'simply by the span and variety of responsibilities which it brought' — legal questions, maintenance, improvements of it. He said that owning property also involved you in a community, questions of governance at a local level, belonging in a neighbourhood. 'Money-making isn't bad for the character,' he said. 'It's perhaps the most harmless employment there is. Compared with politics.'

He did tell her to beware, though, of stock market 'pools' and so on. When she questioned him further about these stock market pools he retreated and was uncomfortable, having been caught going conversationally slightly too far on too little knowledge. He was usually cautious about stepping too far from the path of his certitudes.

She again changed the subject to avoid discomforting him. She realised that she was manipulating the conversation to protect his pride. For the first time she was having trouble achieving a conversational ease with him. She thought of something soft and unthreatening to say. 'Do you remember your advice to me about ordering soup on trains?' she said smiling, her voice turning back through the years to that of the girl she had been then when he had given her this advice in Australia. Her voice again had a girlish lightness.

'I do remember. Never order soup on trains,' he said with mock judicial certitude.

'I broke your rule. On the PLM train from Paris to Geneva, I ordered soup.'

'And you spilled your soup?'

'No! There was no spilling. I think trains have improved.'

'Perhaps the soup is thicker?'

'The suspension of the trains is smoother, I think. Or the tracks are more even.'

Ye gods, here she was contradicting him again. She was finding it difficult to play the younger person. 'I learned a new rule for eating on trains which I will pass on to you. In return for your advice to me, even though I disregarded it.'

'What's your advice to me?'

'When dining on a train, order all courses.'

'Why so?'

She summoned up her girlish voice. 'As an antidote to boredom!'

'I am rarely bored,' he said, somewhat ponderously.

She told John about her first meal on a train coming up from Paris with Ambrose Westwood.

John smiled. 'I can see you are learning the rules of a more opulent world than mine. You've left behind my sober colonial precautions about eating soup.'

Oh dear. She glanced at him to be sure that he was joking but sensed that maybe there was vulnerability there, maybe he regretted not being part of the cosmopolitan world. He was part of it, of course, though not as fully as she was, perhaps, living in Geneva.

'Geneva is hardly opulent,' she said. 'It can be rather cheerless.'

'It's opulent compared with dusty Canberra, I can assure you.'

'When do you move there?'

'Next year, it seems.'

She wanted to flatter him. 'Please, John, don't get me wrong. You gave me much good advice and not only on the eating of soup. And you could never be described as colonial.' She took his hand and smiled at him. 'Maybe a little out of date in your knowledge of the suspension of trains.'

Here she was bringing him up to date on trains. She wanted him to be the wiser one. She wanted to be girl to his man. She then found herself asking how much older he was than she, and whether she should be taking his hand. She let it go. He was a married man and there had never been any suggestion of impropriety. Until now, though, he had seemed to be almost of another genus to her, a mentor, not a man as such. He had become a man as such.

He asked her to do the ordering — 'My French is rusty' — and complimented her on her French and her 'aplomb' and also on her accented English. She said it was because her mouth had to make French sounds every day. They drank their tea and ate their cakes and talked of the health and fortunes, of the births, deaths, and marriages of mutual acquaintances back home.

He asked her whether she read much in French. She said she tried to.

He told her that when he was in Paris for the Peace Conference one of his jobs had been to read the Paris newspapers each day.

'Not a bad job,' she said.

'There were forty-three daily newspapers in Paris then,' he said wryly.

The Australian substitute delegate, Freda Bage, came into the salon then and joined them.

Two days later a message came to her to telephone John at the Hôtel de la Paix. She did and he said he wanted her to meet James Jackson Forstall, an American who could answer all her questions about the stock market.

She went again to the Hôtel de la Paix for tea, this time in the suite of James Jackson Forstall, a hearty American in his forties.

'You will probably not know this,' John said, smiling in the direction of Forstall but talking to Edith. 'This man is buying La Pelouse for the Secretary-General's residence. As a gift to the League.'

She didn't know that. La Pelouse was a fine mansion in which Sir Eric lived and she'd been there for League receptions. It impressed and warmed her that this American should be buying La Pelouse for the League.

John said that he sometimes believed that the United States had two foreign policies. 'The one that comes from Washington and the one that comes from people like James and Rockefeller and Carnegie.'

Mr Forstall liked that.

John told Forstall that he'd mentioned the skulduggery of pools. 'But I'm afraid I don't really know the ins and outs of it all. I said you could enlighten us, Jim.'

'I hope, young lady, you're not contemplating setting up a stock market pool?' Forstall smiled at her. She said it was about time she understood something about the stock market. Everyone else seemed to be talking about it these days.

Forstall said, 'If you do set up a pool, you must include me. That's all I ask.'

'I will when I know what one is and if I like the sound of it.'

The men laughed.

Forstall said that people could manipulate the stock market by forming a pool — which was really a group of share buyers getting together to distort things.

'They buy and sell shares in a company with no apparent pattern — for no reason, you see. Their pattern of selling is based on nothing. What it does is that it makes that particular stock "active and higher" and so makes people interested in the stock. Speculators outside the pool then begin to buy up the stock because of this activity. They believe that someone somewhere knows something about this stock that they don't. The stock continues to attract more speculators and the price continues to rise. Then comes "pulling the plug".'

Edith wrote down in her notebook the expression 'pulling the plug'.

'At a carefully judged moment, the pool manager feeds the stock held by the pool back onto the market. They unload their shares in that company at a profit and then the price collapses. That's called pulling the plug.'

'Isn't there a law against it?' she asked. 'This pulling the plug?'

'If the Democrats ever get their way, there will be.'

'How could you tell whether a stock was being manipulated?' John asked.

'You can't. Unless you knew the company being manipulated, and knew that any active trading in their shares was without reason.'

'Or unless I were part of the pool.' She smiled at him.

Mr Forstall chuckled. 'I like this girl, John.'

At this point John excused himself. 'I want to chase up an Assembly medallion for myself. You stay on, Edith.'

She did not particularly like the idea of staying on alone in the suite with Forstall and said she must go as well. It was more that she felt a little intimidated by him; he was not from her milieu. It was easier to appear bright in a threesome than in a couple. Forstall looked at his watch and suggested that they move down to the lounge.

She agreed to that.

In the lift he said to her, 'Put your notebook away. Learn to let the mind take notes. Don't try so hard to remember. The mind will retain what it needs to remember to survive. Never took a note in my life. Never wrote down a damned thing.'

He placed her hand under his arm in a friendly way as they walked into the bar.

Over drinks — Mr Forstall having a Coca-Cola, she having a gin fizz — he told her not to be scared about pools and other talk of traps and pitfalls. He said that they were excuses for the faint-hearted. 'The reality of it all is that people invent things, people still get companies going, people want to make things and do things, and to do this they need money. In the end, as haphazard as it may seem, people with money exercise judgement to find people with good ideas. Good things are made and people find reward.' He said that most money was still to be made by venturing in small companies.

Stocks, he said, were influenced by rises in the interest rates charged by banks on money, by foreign wars, by domestic upheaval, by apprehension in a country and by rumour. 'Remember that Nathan Rothschild said that the time to buy is when blood is running in the streets.'

'How then do you get to the stock exchange?' she quipped.

'By telephone,' he replied, joining her playfulness. 'Stay off the streets. The great mystery is judgement — something which I seem to have.'

He told her that if everyone knew as much as everyone else and was equally smart, you could never have a chance of making money on the market. 'Everyone would invest only in those shares which would yield the greatest return, that is, the same shares. But people are not equally informed or equally wise. So it is always in a state of play. The secret is to be able to identify the overvalued share and the undervalued share.'

He had given her too many 'secrets' to keep in her mind. She tried to follow his advice about memory, but every time he mentioned the word 'secret', she tried too hard to remember it. She realised Mr Forstall had a love of secrets and mysteries.

'Any analysis of stocks is always incomplete. Except mine.' He laughed. 'No, I too have taken some whippings. What I mean is that you can never know all there is to be known. And there is never an equality of knowledge.' He told her that it came down to two rules which were mutually contradictory.

He was also, she noticed, fond of reducing the world to one or two rules.

He said she could choose either of these rules. 'I give you these with my blessing. May you prosper whichever path you ride along. The first fork is this: take more trouble than the other investors in gathering information. This is one approach. It means working like the devil day and night to find out. You listen, you read, you prowl around and you poke about. It then becomes a vocation. It means you study the world and all its madness every waking moment.'

She thought that maybe she did that already.

He took a sip of his Coca-Cola. 'Or you can do another

thing, you can ride along another trail. You can put together a collection of shares bought pretty much unaimed, you understand? You close your eyes and fire. Then open and see what you hit. Sit back and see how they go. You'll probably make money just as well this way. Maybe never as much as the first way.'

'My father favoured new companies.'

'Is he rich?'

She thought about this and was fazed by the question. She didn't really know. 'He isn't poor.'

Forstall enjoyed the answer. 'He isn't poor. I like it! We call that "venture capital". Did you know that?'

'No, I didn't know that.'

'Sure you can get big returns on that. But you meet some fancy talkers, some big dreamers, some impractical asses. Brilliant but hopeless people. But you can also meet the young geniuses. My advice: if venture capital is your inclination — mix them. That's James Forstall's advice: mix them. Old and new, big and small, north and south, dreamers and mechanics.'

Edith decided there and then to buy an unaimed bunch but she didn't know whether or not to wait for blood to be running in the streets.

'Should I wait for blood to be running in the streets?'

He chuckled and then his face clouded for a second or two. 'If you wish to become a Nathan Rothschild, you can, sadly, always find some place in this unhappy world where blood is running in the streets. But at times the stock market bears no relationship to the economy or to the real world. Sometimes it becomes a world unto itself.'

He looked deeply into her eyes, a look she was coming to know in men. 'You could let me invest for you.'

She thought this attractive and easy. But no, it was her mother's money — she would have to play a part in its manage-

ment. She would have to have stewardship. 'If I am to understand this business,' she said, 'I'll have to learn by venturing.'

'So be it. Now tell me — which trail will you take?'

'A random bunch.'

He smiled but she didn't know whether it was in approval.
'Tell me all about yourself,' he said, ordering another drink for
her. 'How'd you meet Latham?'

'He is a friend of my father's, through the Rationalist Society.
I did science at university but decided I was not really a scientist. I liked insects and flowers but not science. I was good at
birds too, owls especially. I had an interest in politics through
my father and uncle — my uncle once stood for a state seat but
lost. I helped him put leaflets in letter boxes, went to rallies,
worked as a helper. John offered me a job as his assistant when
he was elected — if I would learn to type. So I went to Melbourne — federal parliament is there. I learned to type, but
working with John was not all typing. He's been arguing for
Australia to have its own Department of Foreign Affairs.'

'And you ended up in Geneva?'

'Thanks to John.'

'Where did you get your French?'

'School, university — but really I learned it from the family
who lived next door when I was growing up. They were French.
I grew up with their daughters. That is where I really learned it.
And my parents knew the French writer Paul Wenz who lives in
Australia and we always spoke French with him.' She silently
supposed that he wouldn't have heard of Paul Wenz and that
she was talking too much.

'The League is the future. You know that?' Forstall said.

'I believe it to be.'

'My country has to join the League — hell, we should
be running the League.'

'No country should run it.'

'There will always be a leader in any herd. You just have to be sure that leader is benign — not out to hurt anyone — and wise — that is, knows what it's doing. Or if not, at least controllable. My country can become wise, if it works at it.'

As they parted, he said, 'I'll give you another piece of advice about the buying of stocks and about life. It's Gypsy wisdom. The Gypsy tells his son to get up on a horse and ride it so that he can see how it looks. The Gypsy's son says to his father, "Should I ride to buy or ride to sell?" Do you follow that?'

'I think I do.'

'You probably already know that people who are trying to gain influence ride the truth differently than those who are trying to hold influence. There are different ways of riding the truth.'

As she walked home, she made another leap in her thinking. Given that she were to invest her mother's gift, she would use any earnings from the shares for eccentric causes. Or if she made pots of money, she would, like James Forstall, give something to the League. A library or a radio station. Her investment of her mother's legacy would be a memorial to her mother. That was what she thought. This decision seemed to nicely complete her musing about the money she had and the stock market. As a first step she would place her mother's gift at the disposal of the Landolt syndicate for now, invest it in Cooper's scheme. Although the financial situation of the League looked better as the Assembly adopted the budget for the coming year.

That week-end, in bed with Ambrose, she talked to him about the stock market.

'The question is,' she said, 'do I wish to lead a humble but decorous life or do I wish to lead a life of dash and of risk?'

'Dash! With dash, Edith! With pure caprice.' Ambrose was always championing caprice in her life. In everyone's life. He often quoted Emerson: 'I would write on the lintels of my doorpost: whim.'

Perhaps that was why she liked James Forstall's idea of buying some shares 'unaimed' — maybe this would give expression to caprice in her life.

She said to him, 'And I dare say that you are for me a caprice.'

'I like the idea of being your caprice,' said Ambrose, and then, 'I am going to play the market, too.'

'What with?'

'With whatever boodle I can scrape together.'

He must have sensed that at that moment his debt to her entered both their minds, because he said, 'I will repay that loan, you know.'

She raised herself in the bed and looked at him. 'I know you will repay, my sweet.' She did not know this at all and was surprised to hear iron in her voice, as much commanding the repayment as assuring him of her trust.

'I'll repay you from my stock market winnings,' he said.

This tipped her from feeling generous to feeling that he was trying to fool with her in an unpleasant way.

'I do not think, temperamentally, you're the person to play the market, darling. I really don't.' Her voice had hardened.

The atmosphere in the room had lost its playfulness.

She was about to say to him that he lacked 'the nerve' to play the market. More, that he had a predisposition, she thought, to lose. To say this to him, though, would not just be being candid with Ambrose, it would be nasty, and she tried to stop it coming out, but out it came. 'You lack the nerve.'

He sat up, his voice changed a little, back towards being fully masculine. 'Oh, I think I have nerve.'

That was true. 'Perhaps the stock market requires a different nerve. Needs a different sort of courage to the battlefield.'

'The nerve to play with money isn't what I call nerve,' he said.

She couldn't stop herself. 'There's no nerve required if you play the stock market with someone else's money.'

A silence came between and around them.

He pulled to the other side of the bed, his back towards her. 'For God's sake, if it's the four hundred francs I owe you . . .' he said, more to the wall than to to her.

She sensed in herself a pause, during which she considered whether to say that the amount was, in fact, six hundred francs. She did.

'Whatever.'

'And you lack the judgement. You would lose.' She didn't say, and you will always lose. It was good for him to hear the truth at last, to know what he was.

'I accept that I am not particularly clever about money.'

'Oh, stop simpering,' she said. 'Be a man.' This statement caused a cold silence.

'It hasn't bothered you before,' he said, again his voice wavering towards the masculine. 'You seem to like someone who isn't a man. Maybe I am something more than a man. Maybe you wouldn't care for a man who was only a man.'

His insult did not land home.

'I know what I am. And I know what you are.' As she heard herself say it, she realised that it was a serious insult, and that it could very well have been cruel.

They'd never said things like this to each other before.

He pulled back the covers and got out of the bed. 'You

should've spoken sooner. It would have been more honest for you to have spoken up. Much earlier.'

He sat at the dressing table in his nightdress. She let him burn in his humiliation.

She began to get a glimmer of understanding about why the outburst had happened. It was not all aimed at him — she had wanted to be cruel to the world.

It had not come out as pure cruelty. It had posed as fake principled behaviour. It was also said to relieve herself of what she felt about Ambrose — about his deficiencies. But he would not grow strong from knowing his weakness. Or what she thought were his weaknesses. Having been callous released her from her irritation and she didn't feel a need to go further with her cruelty.

Nor could you insult someone into awareness of their faults.

She thought about 'imperfect friends'. Maybe that was all she had. Maybe that was what she was. Was anyone ever a 'perfect friend'? As a child she'd believed that all insects were perfect, ladybirds for example, but under the microscope she found that even insects are flawed, crippled.

'I'm sorry,' she said.

'For what?' he asked in a small, defeated voice.

'For the suggestion that you lacked nerve.'

'Others decide if we are brave. I don't think I have it.' His voice was self-pitying.

She had no antagonism now. She wanted things to be calm and intimate again, not only for his sake, but for her own peace. 'I said I'm sorry. Come back to bed.'

He did so.

As he entered the bed she pulled him toward her and kissed him as he began to sob. She stretched out a hand and turned off the bedside lamp.

'It's all right, darling,' she said to him, feeling contained and clear-seeing and controlled. 'I'll be the one who worries about money.'

Through his crying, he said, 'I'm really hopeless about living — living outside some institution, some organisation.'

'You're not. In so many ways you're a remarkable person.' That was true. 'Maybe not so good with practical living.' She did not really think that she'd go on worrying about money for him as well as for herself, not through life. She made that silent reservation.

What was she to do with Ambrose?

'You do good things for the world,' she said. 'Now hush.'

On the day he left, John sent her a note containing a warning which he'd meant to give her before. He said that in his experience, successful people rarely knew the reasons for their success. When they contribute their success to these or those factors, they were often wrong.

'This is simply a gentle warning against the well-meaning wisdom of successful people like James Forstall. Good luck.'

But then who could explain what they did and why?

On the day it had been decided that the Landolt crowd would make up its mind about investing in the stock market, Edith was the only one who came to Cooper's office.

'Where are the others?'

'Not interested,' said Cooper abruptly, eating an oatcake biscuit.

'None of the others are interested!?' she said.

'You're the only one.'

Cooper said not one of the others had been interested at all and he himself had lost interest. 'Have a biscuit.' He pushed the plate of biscuits to her.

Oh.

She sat there in his office, looking at him. She realised that although he'd put up the scheme, deep down he too lacked nerve. He had never had the nerve to carry it through.

For want of something to say, she asked, 'Are you waiting until blood is running in the streets?'

'I'm sorry, I don't follow.'

'Never mind.'

How odd.

This made her different from the others in the crowd.

How odd.

How different? Different how?

'You can have the name of my brother's broker in London,' Cooper said, reaching for his address book, 'if you want to go ahead yourself.'

'It's all right. Mr Forstall has given me the name of a broker.'

Cooper was piqued and surprised. 'Oh,' he said, restraining himself from asking further about her knowing Forstall.

She found she was relieved that they weren't setting up a syndicate. She would manage it herself and for her mother. She would do it with caprice. At least for her first splash. After that she would take advice. She did not have the time in her life to study both the stock market and the troubles of the world.

That is how she came to invest her mother's gift in the stock market. Her first investment was in Firestone Rubber because they were investing in Liberia, the nation run by former Negro slaves from America. She wanted to help Liberia but she also wanted to commemorate another caprice — her night in Paris with Jerome.

The Receiving of Envoys:
George McDowell Comes to Town

When she'd left home to go to Sydney University, George McDowell had been the most promising young man in her district, although sometimes laughed at for his schemes. He'd gone on with the blind expectation that people *should* take him seriously, and as long as he paid his bills, she supposed they *would* take him seriously, and she presumed that George made money, although he never seemed to boast about it and did not live in a flashy way. Though she remembered that he always sought to be treated preferentially with expressions such as, 'I know this is not the usual way things are done but I want you to do it for me as a favour', or 'I am going to ask you to do a rather difficult thing for me.' Older men called him 'Mr McDowell', even when he was barely twenty-one. He had a rapid manner, reminding her, in recollection, of some of the earlier, jerky motion pictures.

While at university she had been his 'agent and technical adviser' in one of his schemes for marketing a water clarifier and had made, she recalled, about fifteen guineas out of it. He was the only man she had ever seen wear overalls over a suit and tie but it expressed him perfectly. He was always ready to muck in on a job but underneath it, he was always the manager.

Although he was a few years younger, she'd flirted with him at balls when she had been home on vacation. As a suitor, he had been a possibility, but she had other roads to travel. George was a man with big ideas in a small town, and she could not see herself back there, living on the coast with George.

The letter from George said he was coming to Geneva. To 'inspect' the League for himself.

She remembered that George, as a young man, had been the first person in their circle to go overseas. He had gone not to Europe, but to the States, where he believed the future lay. There'd been Scribner, an older man of no particular age, who'd earlier been to Oxford, or at least that was what people said, but if he had been to Oxford and gained a degree, what was he doing back in the town?

Scribner existed without a job, although he was always in the street first thing in the morning in collar and tie, involved in undertakings of a mysterious personal kind which seemed to fill his days, and from time to time he worked with George on schemes, writing brochures, cranking handles, driving George about in George's Studebaker tourer, both of them dressed in white dust jackets, goggles and suits.

As much as she had affectionate memories of George and of those days, Edith really didn't want George McDowell in Geneva and around in her life now. She wasn't the flirtatious girl from the town balls any more, doing the hokey pokey and the progressive barn dance. She certainly was not 'Edy', as George had addressed her in the letter.

There was something unnerving about the idea of a visit from someone she had left behind. John had been different — he belonged half in her world anyhow. George's visit would mean facing the self she'd left behind. The discarded self, even. Did the visiting person seek to find the person they'd known? Or did they hope to find a new person who'd surprise and dazzle them? Or did they fear meeting some formidable new person who would dismay them? Whatever, it was an unwanted reunion with no definable purpose.

Typically, he talked in his letter of her helping him to make 'the best use of his time in Geneva'. George led a relentless life.

George would want to meet Sir Eric. Oh, she saw it now. George believed in 'going straight to the top'. Just when she'd begun to be noticed by Sir Eric and had the very special bond with him, along came George to muddle it. Admittedly, she hadn't been back in that office since the crisis about Germany and the shaving of Sir Eric. It was as if that special morning were something holding them at arm's length in their work, that Sir Eric did not dare allow her to be too close again.

She couldn't arrange for George to meet Sir Eric, anyhow, but deep in her heart she knew that, by one means or another, George would get to see Sir Eric. As long as he didn't drag her into it. The more she thought about it, the better it was that he do it himself, and she would beg him not to mention their connection back in Australia. At all. In any way.

It then crossed her mind that George might propose to her if he wasn't yet married to Thelma, the belle of most of the balls, who came from one of the older families. One of her mother's letters had mentioned Thelma.

It wasn't that Australia was not a 'real' place, full of real people doing real things, finding happiness, making families, practising the arts of friendship, practising the arts of politics, and practising, albeit in a youthful way, the arts and scholarship — doing all the things she knew mattered in life. It was that she needed now in her life to put herself in a position which made her productively *nervous*. Even if it was a bit uncomfortable at times. She had to be where she didn't know quite what was happening next, to be living precipitously. She wanted to be in the presence of people who made her a little nervous. She wanted to be among objects, buildings and art works which made her mindful and sentient, which could cause her, now and then, to be in awe.

She wanted to feel that she was *absorbing* from her world, she wanted to feel as if these buildings and objects were entering her spirit. She knew that French culture, or at least Genevan French culture, would shape her, not into a French person, but into another sort of person.

There was a loss from living in Europe, she acknowledged. For instance, on the day she first visited Mont Blanc, she had lost the mythical 'Alps' of her childhood with all their fables and fantasy. They were no longer 'the Alps' in quite the way they'd been before when she had seen only photographic postcards or just heard the words 'the Alps'. They were mountains now.

She had also lost mythical 'Europe'. The mythical Europe of her childhood picture books and the many hearings of the word spoken so longingly and with such aching and worried significance by the adult world around her as a child. She lived in a real Europe now — and in some minor ways, regretfully. A Europe of visible and touchable places to walk, to ride, to shop, to eat and drink — and of dull and ugly places as well.

Still, sometimes on a mountain road driving around a bend to face a vista of farms and churches and fields she became breathless, or when driving through the dark, narrow, winding cobble-stoned streets of a village. The word Dubonnet on a sign above some tables and chairs could still thrill her.

She was willing to forgo such things as family and friends for now, to have placed herself where these European sensations might become part of her, because she felt at times that she might not be able to have her own family, could not yet see how that could be in her life. It was also true that she was not sure how much she was prepared to forfeit to be able to have these sensations of Europe and the work of the League. She prayed that what she was pursuing was more than just sensations. Or more, that they were consequential sensations. And, as time moved on, she was aware of the dire bargain she was making with her life, and with her womanhood.

Sir Eric wanted them to be representatives of their nations within the Secretariat, in the sense that they should be able to guide the League in its dealings with their own countries, although no one had officially asked her anything about Australia since she'd been at the League. Nothing whatsoever.

For good or for ill, she now lived in Geneva. The capital of intellectual life, as Flaubert said. Her life was assemblies, congresses, receptions, banquets, and she had a lover. That was her life and that was how she wanted her life for now. She did not see how a visit from George fitted in.

Would she introduce Ambrose to George? She groaned. Not likely.

She sat in her office and ashamedly cursed George McDowell away from Geneva and her life.

The curse did not work. George came. George paced about her office, examining the pneumatic tubes, the window-opening devices, holding the League notepaper to the light to look at the watermark, and standing on a chair to look at the electric light. She wished her office wasn't so small, was more impressive for George to report on back home.

He glanced through the files on her desk.

'Those files are confidential, George. Secrets of the nation states of the world.'

' "Have no secrets",' he stated to no one in particular, but he respected the files, and closed them. He took the glass from over the water flask, and poured himself a drink. He appeared to 'taste' the water. He was cultivating his taste, he'd told her. He went to look at one of Mantoux's jokes pinned to the wall.

'It's an office joke, George.'

She was frightened that he'd take it seriously and write it down in his notebook. The joke was a 'formula' for disarmament.

PROBLEM: Find out on the basis of what principles it would be possible to establish the proportion of armaments to be attributed to each country, taking into consideration especially:

the number of inhabitants. . . . . . a

the resources of the country. . . . . . r

the geographical situation. . . . . s

the length and the nature of the maritime
communications. . . . . . . *cos. m*

the density and the extent of the railways. . . F

the vulnerable frontiers and the vital centres near these same
frontiers. . . . . fr

the time necessary (varying according to the different countries)
to transform armaments on a peace footing to armaments
on a war footing. C

the degree of international security, etc. . . . S

SOLUTION:

$$\frac{(h \times r.cos.m.S.F}{\sqrt{fr.} + C \times \infty \text{ (infinite)}} \quad \text{log.} \quad \frac{d}{\sqrt[3]{S}} = \frac{x^2 y}{z^2} T \quad \pi R^2$$

$$\frac{y^3 + z^3}{69} = Q.$$

'Has anyone tried it? It might work.' He next looked at the Punch cartoon of the 'League of Nations Hotel' and laughed.

Edith saw it afresh after all this time and decided to take it down. It was something she no longer saw on her wall.

Turning back to her he said, 'On this trip I've picked up five new ideas. I came from the United States to here. You know I've been to the United States twice now? Do I sound American?

You can't help picking up some of the American way of talking. I'm not going to England because England has nothing to teach Australia.'

That was typical of the breathtaking ideas that George came up with — to travel the world and to avoid England.

'But I came here because Geneva's more important than London. That's one reason why I looked you up. I am admiring of you, Edy. You were the first internationalist from the south coast. Maybe the first from New South Wales.'

'What about Scribner?'

'Scribner?' George chuckled. 'Scribner. You know what he asked me to bring him back?'

She shook her head. 'I'd imagine it would be a book or a musical score.'

'Wrong. He wanted me to get him a honey spoon.'

She allowed herself to laugh. Suddenly it was nice to hear about Scribner, Doctor Teddy Trenbow and the others from her younger days. These people lived on in her life now only in dreams and recollections; they would never reappear in her life. Except for George. 'A honey spoon!'

'A wooden Alpine honey spoon. I'll admit I'd never heard of such a thing. It exists, all right. It's made of wood and doesn't look like a spoon. It has this grooved end. You push the thing into the honey pot and twist it. It winds up the honey. You hold it over the bread and unwind the honey onto the bread. Scribner explained it to me. In fact, he made a drawing of it. I've got it back at the hotel.'

'We'll have a look for one.' She was beginning to relax with George.

George said there could be a market for it, Australians being big honey-eaters. Then he said, 'Scribner is not an internationalist

285

or a citizen of the world.' George stood at the window presumably thinking of Scribner and at the same time examining the geraniums in her window box.

He laughed. 'I remember you lecturing me about gardens. You told me that gardens were nature in a prison.'

She had once said that. She smiled, flattered that he'd remembered something she'd said. 'Yes, that is my little prison. Those are my Swiss geranium prisoners.'

George turned to her. 'Seriously, you were the first from our district to know what it was all about. About being international.'

He waved his monogrammed leather-bound notebook at her. 'I don't mean inventions. I mean ideas in the realm of the philosophical.'

She leaned back in her chair and smiled at him with the protective superiority of an older sister indulging the enthusiasms of a younger brother.

'An example: take this key.' He went to the door and removed the key. 'The teeth of this key might be the same as in other countries; the shank is the same; but in every country I have visited the finger-turning part is different. Why is that?'

'I've really never thought about it, George.'

'It has to do with different countries' ideas of what looks good. Beauty.'

She'd never heard him talk of beauty.

'I have another example not related to beauty. Back home when travelling I always carry a strong electric light bulb because the bulbs in hotels are too weak. But the world has foiled me. Each darned country has a different sort of socket and different voltage. I've turned it into a lesson. I will put that light bulb on my desk back home to remind me.'

He didn't sound at all like an American but he wanted to, so she let him think he did. He had pep and she liked that.

'Do you know what that badge is?' He leaned over to her and held his lapel towards her.

'No, George, I don't.'

'That, Edith, is the badge of Rotary.'

He explained that Rotary was a world organisation of businessmen. Not just any businessmen. An organisation of the most motivated of men, those with the esteem of their fellow businessmen. Those businessmen with respect for life. Membership was, he said, by invitation.

'It is not the differences in locks and key and taps and switches that worries me. What gets me down, from time to time, is that people love their differences too much,' he said ruefully. 'And, believe it or not, I think the world could learn something from Australia.'

'One day we will all be one,' she said.

George burst into a song from the musical *Belle of New York*, ' "Of course, you could never be like us, But be as like us as you're able to be".'

She laughed. George seemed to have attained a much better balance between the serious and playful parts of his nature than she remembered.

'What do you think the world has to learn from Australia, George?'

He thought before he spoke. 'No bombast. No showy politics.'

She said jokingly that she'd learned new approaches to tendering since coming to the League. She told George of her advice to the Directors' meetings. 'My friend Florence said that I could've furnished my rooms by taking gifts from the tendering companies.'

'Don't ever do that, Edy,' George said with concern. 'It's better to be hard up than to have to live your life feeling bad about yourself.' He leaned over to her across her desk. 'Bribery is death to a good country.' Then he grinned. 'If you're short of a chair, I think I could make a contribution.'

'No, George, I'm not short of a chair — but thanks. And I don't take bribes.'

'I never thought for one minute that a girl from the south coast ever would.'

She winced as she recalled the gift of a pistol in her first days at the League.

In the Jardin Anglais, he had coffee and she a glass of wine. George still didn't drink alcohol, although he did taste her wine. George tasted everything. Apart from having a passion for wine, she realised with a frivolous, faint embarrassment, that she was also having the glass of rosé to show George that she was a woman of the world now, who could drink alcohol and who knew her wines.

'For the French, George, wine is food.'

'For a young man like myself it's a mighty powerful food,' was all he said.

He said he was impressed with her French but that he believed that all people understood one language. Did she know what language that was?

She told him that Briand had said that he and Herr Stresemann were now speaking a new language — the language of Europe.

'I don't know about the language of Europe. The one language I do know about that all peoples understand is the language of Usefulness,' George said, smiling. 'I can get across to people as long as they know I am a man of use to them. What is my letter of introduction?'

She shook her head.

He held out his hand, 'My handshake is my letter of introduction.'

His face showed that he was about to change the subject, and that the subject was important, delicate. 'Edy — about your speaking of French.'

' "Edith",' she corrected. 'Yes, George?'

He seemed to leave what he had been about to say, and now seemed to ponder her shift from her girlhood name to her full legal name. He seemed to come to a private conclusion about that, and then returned to what he had been about to say. ' "Edith" — sorry. I want to say something to you straight from the shoulder.'

'Go ahead, George.' She took up her glass of rosé as if it would shield her, a chalice of magic fluid. 'You were always one for straight talking, George.'

'I want to say that I find that you sound different. Very different.'

'I *sound* different?'

'When you speak English, you don't sound like the Edy I know.' He looked her straight in the eye, his jaw firm, then remembered. 'Sorry, "Edith".'

She coloured because she knew what he was talking about: her intonation had perhaps changed. Sometimes she wondered whether hidden parts of herself came to express themselves through her use of another language, especially when that language *encouraged*, well, certain mores, traits and peculiarities. She thought briefly of her carnal behaviour with Jerome, and with Ambrose, whether that had to do with her being impelled to speak French and to live a French way of life. The 'French' coming out in her? She was sure she ate differently, with more attention to her food and with more pleasure — that came from the French. What of the sinister, nastier traits which might sneak out through the speaking of another language? What if she were speaking one of the less cultivated languages — what would come out then?

Then he said, 'The Japanese believe that when you learn another language you lose part of your Japanese self. They think it's a bad thing.'

Where did George pick that up? 'We should all have another self or part of our self perhaps which isn't tied to one nationality,' she said.

He said that he thought that learning another language might be a way of disguising oneself.

'It's perhaps a way of slipping across the border,' she said.

'Do you know what I think about learning another language?'

'No, George.'

'I think it means having to learn two words for the same thing.'

'It's a key to the door of another culture,' she said. 'You get let into another people's secrets.' She hoped he didn't ask her to give him an example.

'Maybe one day I will learn. I want to be a cultivated man, Edy, but it'll just have to wait. I'm in too much of a hurry.' He showed regret and then pulled himself into another mood. 'I see why you don't want to be called Edy. I know about wanting to get away from childhood.'

'You were called Georgie.'

'And Pudden. And Pie. And King.' He smiled quickly. 'Rather liked King as a name. Billie Fowler still calls me Pudden. I've asked him to stop. He won't.'

She was still holding herself defensively, but knew she'd

better face it somehow. It had to do with mouthing French sounds, day in and day out. She had let her voice change and maybe even pushed it in that direction because she was glad of a new voice.

'I'm an internationalist now,' she laughed. 'I had to change, George. What would be the point of being an internationalist and not changing?'

George didn't laugh. 'No, Edy, it's more than that. I see myself as a Rotarian and a Rotarian is a citizen of the world. I don't speak differently. Except for the American style of speech which is because I was there for a few weeks and I admire them. I picked up American because I wanted to be like them a little. That's different. Americans have a way of speaking to convince themselves of what they've just said. They stimulate themselves with themselves. In business, that's good.'

'In politics, that's bad.'

'In politics, that's bad, I agree. With me, it's mostly playing around. I fear for Edith, the person.' He reached out to hold her hand. 'I am talking, Edith, about you, the Australian.'

She was shaken slightly because he made it sound grave. She was facing the representative of all that she'd left back home. She didn't think she'd changed as much as that. Still, she had not been back to Australia to hear herself — if you could ever hear yourself. George made it sound like a treason, punishable by ominous penalty.

'Have you been homesick?' he asked.

'Not really.'

'I see.'

Was the opposite to homesickness — desertion, disaffection?

'May I talk to you about your card?' From his wallet he took the business card she'd given him when he'd first arrived. He placed it on the table squarely between them. 'I want to say something about your business card.' He studied it while finding his words.

'I think using an initial in your name is a natty manoeuvre. Very American. I might do it one day myself but I'd be laughed at back home. Not that being laughed at has ever stopped me. When my firm's a bit bigger, I might add a letter to my name. To stop me being confused with my father.'

'I didn't see it as American. I saw it as making my name memorable.'

'Precisely. Good move.'

'What else?' She swigged her glass of rosé.

'The card gave me my first clue.'

'To what?'

'To your metamorphosis. To your personality predicament.'

'George — I may've picked up an accent and I may've played about with my name but I don't see that I have a predicament.'

'I'm not so sure about that.'

She became aware that her defensiveness had within it a suppressed real fear, which was wriggling up from her soul, a fear of being exposed as a cheat. 'We all have to grow up.'

'Definitely. I don't say that. What I say is that we have to keep on growing "upward" and I say that it's a lifelong science. That's not what I'm talking about. I'm talking about being out of shape.' He made it sound ugly, as well as grave.

'You mentioned a clue?' she asked, now quite defensive.

'Your card has too many names on it.' He dramatised the counting of the names. 'One — *Edith*. Two — *the initial A*. That counts as a name in this situation. Alison, isn't it? Three — *Campbell*. Four — *Berry*. You know what it said to me, what the card said to me?'

'No, George.'

'It made me think you were four people trying to crowd together on one card — to come together as one.'

He was breathtaking. She now remembered why he was the most surprising man in the district. He had not gone to university but he was a man who ruminated. He was spirited.

'That's fairly psychological, George.'

'I understand psychology.'

She suspected he meant not the science but psychology as the 'methodology of life'. Oh God, perhaps he was right about the four names. She'd sensed it when she'd had the new cards printed. It was Florence's influence; Florence had decided that she would champion Edith to the top and this was part of her plan.

She glanced across at him. Could she admit to this country town go-getter that he was right?

'We shouldn't be secretive about our middle names,' she said, trying to be conversational. 'I don't know why we're all frightened of our middle names. Do we want to keep one name for our secret self?'

George seemed to be remembering. 'At school we always tried to keep our middle name secret but I ended up being called by my middle name.' He laughed.

'It was usually a very old-fashioned name, the name of a grandparent, and we were embarrassed by it,' she said. 'Maybe it is our name from our former life — the life before we were born. That might frighten us as children.'

'That could be right.'

The meandering didn't get her out of George's analysis of her card, her life. He had taken up the card again.

'I'm still finding out how to make my way. That's the problem, George.' Her voice sounded almost discouraged. She felt a gust of deep, deep, fatigue, a feeling new to her.

The confession seemed to deflect his investigation. He raised his eyes to the sky, lifted his right hand as if conducting an orchestra. 'I suppose, though, that truly we are a Federation of Selves. There's the person within us who goes about the daily affairs and there's the person who goes in to sleep at night alone.'

She thought to herself that there was also the 3 a.m. person. She felt tired and tearful.

Ambrose had a persona which was in acute and total disarray but it didn't matter that much to him. He seemed positively to delight in it.

'Should we trust the three a.m. person any more than the other selves, George?' she said. She knew he would know what she meant.

His face seemed to cloud, and he said with defiance, 'The three a.m. person is the least brave self.'

She thought the 3 a.m. self was the frightened child within. Should it ever have a voice? She saw from George's reaction that the 3 a.m. self frightened him too.

'Sometimes it might be the most realistic voice?'

'No,' he said, slapping the table, 'never take counsel of your fears.' He then left the platitudes and said quietly, 'I'm wrong. All our inner voices must be listened to, paid their due. The final action of the whole must be decided after listening to all.' Then with an effort he said, 'Even the small nasty voices.'

There was silence.

Then in a loud, different tone of voice he said, 'We have a birthright but we have to honour it and, if required, we have to forgive it in ourselves. I'm thinking of some of the bad things we've done as a nation.'

She was glad and relieved that George was a person who could not stay in one chair, or one room, or one place for long, nor on one subject, and that they'd moved away from talking about her. She ran to catch up to his thinking, and said, 'But, George, isn't the possibility of regeneration part of our birthright as Australians — the privilege of being able to fashion ourselves?'

George nodded; he liked that idea. He smiled shrewdly. He knew she was mustering herself and beginning to meet his earlier case against her. He conveyed by his smile that he knew his limitations in arguments of this sort. 'We need you to help make the country, Edith. We need people like you. We're short of people like you.'

They walked across the garden towards his hotel which was on the other side of the lake. She let herself take his arm.

'I know, Edy — I know. I too am a man refashioning himself. In that refashioning, we take risks. You take your life, and you work on it with your hands.' He held out his hands, palms upward. 'It's as dangerous as self-surgery.'

George said this as they were opposite Rousseau's statue. She pointed this out. He insisted on going to view the statue. He looked at it closely, as if examining it for cracks. No one she knew looked at things with quite the scrutiny that George did. 'Should I read this man's book?' he asked her, looking up at Rousseau.

'I don't think you need to do that, George. I think you're a Voltairian. We'll go to Voltaire's house if you've time tomorrow.'

He was tickled that she tied his name to that of Voltaire. 'You think so? You see me as a Voltairian? Scribner often mentions the name Voltaire.'

He asked her for a quote from Voltaire but she didn't know one.

'I'll read that man's books then,' he said, 'I'll need something for the ship. Write down some titles for me.'

That night, as she removed her make-up, sitting at her

three-mirrored dressing table, she saw too clearly three selves at least in the cross reflection of the mirrors. She smiled at each, helplessly.

Although George said he wasn't one for sightseeing, she took him up Salève by cable car. She thought he should do at least that. He paid tribute to the view of Geneva, to Mont Blanc, and the Jura. The view did not stop him talking. 'I want to raise another of the reasons I'm here in Geneva.'

She wondered when he would get around to talking about his mission. He'd hinted at it, and, in a way, she had not wanted to know about it. She had a foreboding that it might be a proposal of marriage. She knew her answer and had ready an affectionate and careful reply. Obviously, being high above the world on Salève was an appropriately 'romantic' locale for a proposal of marriage. She did not want to hurt him. Anyhow, she could never live with a man who didn't love wine. She braced herself and asked quietly, 'What's your mission, George?'

He gripped the railing with both hands, and spoke out to all of Switzerland, to the whole world. 'To get the United States into the League.'

She broke out grinning and only just controlled her laughter, chastising herself for her vanity, but with relief. 'George — Woodrow Wilson and many others —' again laughter caught her throat ' — sorry, George, but a great many people have tried to get the Americans into the League. How in God's name do you think you can?'

He leaned towards her and held his lapel Rotary badge to her. 'My secret weapon.'

*

Over dinner at the Beau-Rivage, George tried both snails and frogs' legs for the first time, pronouncing them more ordinary than he'd expected, and saying he wasn't sure that he could taste the snails at all because of the garlic. She said that when you did taste them they tasted of the dankest part of the forest floor.

He chewed one in silence.

Then he said, 'I think I see what you mean.'

She said, 'You know, George, apart from my family, you're the only person from Australia who really writes to me still.'

He looked away from her and down at his plate.

'Why is that?' she asked.

He looked directly at her. 'People probably think that you've become high and mighty. That you no longer need them. Or that you're silently criticising them by choosing to live away. You aren't part of their lives any more, Edy. Edith.' He looked at her sheepishly. 'To tell the truth, I was a little scared of meeting you myself. Didn't know what you might have become.'

She realised that George was frightened of 'losing her'.

'I don't want Australia to lose you, Edith, and I don't want to lose you.'

'It won't lose me, George; I'll always be Australian. And you won't lose me either.'

He then took his wallet from his jacket pocket, opened it, and brought out an envelope.

She found herself always worried by his moves. She expected that they would make defeating demands upon her.

He took from the envelope a eucalyptus leaf from Australia and he handed it across to her for her to smell. She did so but found only the slightest whiff of home.

'It is time for the leaf burning,' he said.

He put the leaf in the ashtray, took matches from his pocket, and lit it.

She glanced around, feeling slightly embarrassed by the performance.

He pushed the burning leaf over to her. 'Home,' he said.

She leaned over and smelled deeply and, yes, it was home. It was the cooking of chops over the open fire, it was Girl Guide campfires, it was the bush on a hot summer's day, it was the smell of the bush in pain during bushfires. Most of all it reminded her of a balm used by her mother to relieve congestion of the chest when she was little. She was still embarrassed.

'Thank you, George. You brought that all this way?'

'I brought it for this purpose.' He was pleased with himself. 'About the way you talk . . .' he said earnestly, preparing, she could see, to make a pronouncement.

'I'll do something about that, George, when I come back. I'll make myself speak Australian.'

'That's not what I was going to say, Edith. I was going to say that I find the way you talk is pretty damned foxy.'

'Why, thank you, George.'

On the third afternoon, she sat in George's room at the Angleterre and drank tea while George, in white shorts and white singlet, did his callisthenics with dumbbells and Indian clubs. It had impressed her that he would ask the hotel to get him dumbbells and Indian clubs. She had been impressed, too, that the hotel could find some for him, although there was something of an exercise craze sweeping Switzerland.

When she asked him why he did the exercises he'd replied, 'For stamina.'

She suggested that exercise should also be a way of developing bodily grace. She herself did not care much for exercise. It seemed an artificial use of the body. A straining of the body in

directions it did not wish, naturally, to go. She tried not to look
at his male member bouncing around in his shorts.

With his breathing broken by exertion, he said that his life
did not have time for grace — just yet — but it did have a need
for stamina. Stamina was his objective.

'You, Edith, you can afford the time here in Europe for
grace. Australia is a country in a hurry — and for hurrying you
need stamina.

'After we get things straightened out,' he puffed, 'we'll go
in for grace. And believe me, I need the strength,' he said, 'to
wrestle down my shyness — or it'll be death of me.'

'If you don't take it more slowly, George, those dumbbells
will be the death of you.'

Shy? She didn't think of him that way at all. It was a very
personal thing for him to say. She didn't want to know about
George's weaknesses. She had a picture of him which she wanted
to keep and it was not of a shy man. It was of a go-getter. He
was the man in a panama hat sitting in the Studebaker, driven
dangerously fast by Scribner in dust coat and goggles.

'I've never seen you as shy.'

He stopped exercising. He said to her, dumbbells in his
hands, 'Edith, sometimes I fall exhausted onto the bed when I
get home after a day of running about. It's a dreadful drain on
me, going out in public — going about my business. I'm a
dreadfully shy person.'

'I never knew.' But she had nothing to say either.

She glanced down again at the documents stamped 'Confidential' which George had shown her. They came from the
League of Nations Non-Partisan Association Incorporated in
New York. There was a letter of introduction to Sir Eric written
for George by Charles C. Bauer, executive director. Edith knew
of this organisation and knew it was sound. George obviously

believed he needed more than a handshake to get to see Sir Eric.

'You know Bauer?' she asked.

'Bauer and I got along,' said George, still short of breath.

She studied the documents to see whether they contained difficulties for her or the League.

'You can see,' he said, 'the plan is to get Rotary International to meet here — organised by the League. Once the businessmen of America see that the League is a well-run outfit we can sell those Americans the whole conception.'

She'd been impressed that George had been guest speaker the night before at the new Rotary Club of Geneva. For a shy man he certainly was a man who made himself known.

She wondered whether bringing businessmen to Geneva and convincing them might work, so that they, in turn, could convince America. She'd told George that she couldn't arrange for him to meet Sir Eric — she'd told him she didn't have that sort of influence in the Secretariat. But the truth was she hadn't wanted the embarrassment of the meeting between Sir Eric and George. Although she had to admit that George was quite presentable and she'd come to see that he was a smart man. But there was the other indeterminate bond between herself and Sir Eric which she wanted to keep untangled and untarnished, which one day might be of professional significance to her. Or even personal significance but she didn't know what she meant by that.

As George washed his face in the room basin, he said, through the splashing, 'You don't seem to be put out by being in a hotel room with a man doing his exercises, Edith?'

'You're someone from home, George. And we *are* old friends.'

Privately, though, she assessed George also as being a *real man*.

*

Seated in Sir Eric's office with George she felt very nervous, but not in the way that she wanted to feel nervous. This was pure dread of what George would come out with.

She knew that Sir Eric and she were going through that morning again in their memories while listening to George.

George had brought about the meeting through the good offices of Bauer and the Rotary Club of Geneva and he had *invited her* to join them at the meeting. She stared out of the window as George propounded his scheme.

Sir Eric said that the League Council had invited Rotary to send a representative to the Economic Conference and they had. 'I know that Rotary represents men of the highest standing in their communities. I, and the League, am aware that it stands for some of the same things as the League, and we're aware also that it's a growing organisation.'

'Three thousand, two hundred and thirty-nine clubs with 151,574 members worldwide,' George said.

'Quite so,' said Sir Eric. 'Impressive numbers.'

'Sir, it is not the number of men in Rotary which counts but the amount of Rotary in men.'

'Quite so.'

She supposed George got these sayings from some central bureau of Rotary.

'Here, then, is my first manoeuvre,' said George, and pulled from his briefcase a single sheet of paper.

To her discomfort, George then got up and went around to Sir Eric's side of his desk and, leaning in, began to explain. She hardly listened. She wanted to be out of there.

He said he believed that all sound propositions could be reduced to a single sheet of paper.

She'd joked to him that some people at the League believed

every sound proposition could be extended indefinitely to an infinite number of sheets of paper.

After the meeting, outside the Palais Wilson, walking towards his hotel, George turned to her, grinned, and said, 'See what a shy Australian can do if he dedicates his mind to it?' and then he added, 'As long as that shy Australian keeps up his callisthenics.'

On the night before he left they had another grand dinner, and at a point in the meal George said that he had something very serious to say to her.

He was going to propose. She waited while he stacked his finished dishes to one side in a way that had constantly embarrassed her at restaurant meals during his visit.

He put his hand over to cover hers and looking into her eyes, he told her that her mother was not well.

'Ill?'

'Very ill, Edith. Your father told me that he believes your mother will not live much longer.'

His hand held on to her and she gripped his. She was thrown off-balance by the news. Letters came regularly from her mother and father and nothing had been mentioned. 'No one told me!'

George had not mentioned or hinted at it when they had talked about her family.

The money. Her mother had sent the gift of money. She must have been ordering her affairs.

'I think they felt you shouldn't be worried. In this new job and living so far away and all.'

She didn't know what to say.

'I'm sorry to be the bearer of such news but your father asked me to break it to you. I kept it till the end of my visit because I didn't want a pall to be cast. That was their idea as

well. That was your mother's wish. That I should mention it
only when I was at the end of my visit.'

'How ill — how soon?'

'It's a tumour, Edith. The doctors think she's dying. Maybe
a few more months. She's been to Macquarie Street doctors.
She's been treated by the best.'

Edith put down her spoon and put both her hands into
George's. He held them tightly.

'In his letters my father said nothing.'

'They were being careful about worrying you. You being so
far away. There was nothing you could do.'

In her mind she began to plan a return to Australia, although
it couldn't have come at a worse time for her.

'I guess you'll be coming home,' George said.

'Of course.'

'Do you want me to see if there is a passage on my ship?
You could come back with me.'

'Thank you, George — no, I'll have to arrange things here.'

'I could wait.'

'You must go about your business, George.'

George left Geneva with his new ideas and his honey spoons on
the lake paddle-steamer *Italie* for Lausanne where he was to join
a train for Marseille and home.

Edith's last view of him was in the Captain's cabin, having
the controls explained to him, and then waving to her. It seemed
to her that he captained the boat out.

She smiled away a tear of affection for him and for *patrie*,
for her dying mother.

'Let me know your ship,' George had said as he left. 'I'll
drive up to Sydney and collect you.'

Crying, she waved sadly to him. She blew him a kiss.

That same week, in her office back at the Palais Wilson, Edith happened to see a circular to Under Secretaries-General, Directors and Chiefs of Section. The circular outlined much of what George had told Sir Eric and suggested that members of Secretariat when visiting another country should inform Rotary of their willingness to speak at Rotary meetings, especially in the United States. It said that 'one of the characteristics of Rotary being the weekly lunch or dinner'.

George had been taken seriously in his own right although perhaps the secret bond between herself and Sir Eric had helped.

She smiled back tears again, this time pleased by the memory of George's energy, so much of which, she now knew, he used to 'wrestle down' his shyness. She didn't know whether this was a sad knowledge or not. In George there was no aggressive energy. It was an authority which tried to Get Things Done Properly.

Edith grappled with her dilemma about returning to Australia. She could take a home-leave back to Australia. She wrote to her mother and father and said that George had broken the sad news of her mother's illness to her and she would come home just as soon as she could.

After George's return to Australia she received an invitation to the wedding of Thelma and George.

She wondered if he'd come to Geneva to 'look her over' before deciding. If things had been a little different, she thought that perhaps she might have considered George as a husband. He hadn't asked and as Florence said, one did, at least, like to be asked.

She observed to herself, pointedly, that during George's visit she'd kept Ambrose mostly out of sight, except for a few polite drinks, and George, on the other hand, had barely mentioned

Thelma. Confused reactions rose in her heart. What was it that he'd found lacking, or was it just that they were headed along different roads? Had she found him lacking and, if so, how? She feared to look, dreading that what it was she saw lacking in him was unworthy of her consideration and that to value those things meant she was becoming condescending or creating a superiority based on spurious values. Was her sense of self causing her to disqualify people? She sent a cable of congratulations and resolved to search for a gift. If, as George had suggested, they'd gone back together, would this have led to a courtship? A shipboard romance?

She was just not ready to go back home yet. Furthermore, she couldn't afford to leave the League for the twelve weeks travelling there and back together with time away. Too many things were happening.

Her mother wrote a long letter which absolved her from the dilemma and the moral disquiet of her decision not to return home. In her letter her mother said, 'I would rather think of you going on with your fine work in this one chance that the world has to set things aright than to have you moping at my bedside and fetching lemonade. I would feel proud and happy to know that you were going about your destiny and if you were here, I would fret that you were not in Geneva.'

Her mother said in the letter that she wanted Edith to do great things for which the family would be remembered.

Edith sadly doubted that parents were ever remembered for the greatness of one their children.

She'd known that as Rationalists her father and mother would argue that her life was in Geneva and that her work was more important than, well, customs and rituals of death. They were those sort of people although her mother was far less of a Rationalist than her father.

She wanted to see her mother but she had to take that course which furthered her own life, rather than that which served to comfort the end of her mother's life.

She hoped that her mother was being truthful when she said that she would be comforted more by her being a good daughter out in the world doing good works.

She cancelled the appointment with Nancy Williams in personnel which she had made to arrange for her leave. She wrote to her mother in these terms and, as she expected, her mother wrote back again affirming her decision and her father did as well.

A few months later her mother died.

She took a week in the Jura on her own but then returned to work. She repeatedly told herself that by staying at work she was affirming life and not doing what the conventions of grief expected and that this would please her mother.

But she was still filled with guilt for not having tried to get home and all her mother's assurances before she died did not help, and Edith knew she would have to live with her regret for a long time.

Not having seen her mother at her deathbed was unattended-to business and now no way existed for her ever to attend to it and it would remain for ever unattended-to business.

Public Life (1):

Cry Me a River

Over drinks in his apartment one winter's evening, Ambrose tried to prepare her for the Molly Club by explaining that it was frequented by those in Geneva who 'do not quite like being the way God had made them'. At least, did not like it all the time.

She understood what he referred to and yet again inwardly uttered something like, 'Ye gods, what am I doing with this man?'

She said something about he being one who liked to go in the opposite direction to the way God intended.

He said that he didn't see it as a matter of willpower. Or a quarrel with God. 'But it is fun.'

He said that he would need her guidance on what to wear, but he would be honoured, 'Is "honoured" the correct word? Honoured if you would accompany me to the club.'

Was 'honoured' indeed the correct word? She replied, 'I am trying to imagine this club.'

'It is a decent sort of place. Spotless.'

'Spotless.'

'Spotless but not blameless.' He was joking to win her participation.

'You've been there already?'

'I entered it, so to speak, in mufti. I had a poke about. Looked around. Sniffed it out, so to speak.'

The nature and practice of her and Ambrose's affiliation was still something she could not describe to anyone she knew.

Perhaps not even to herself, not precisely. It was assumed, she supposed, that they were a romantic duet, but she was sure that it was gossiped about because they had not, for instance, talked of engagement. The people at her pension well knew that she did not spend the week-ends in her own bed although she had now forgotten what explanation she'd originally given to Madame Didier. In their moments of secret-sharing and personal confidences, Florence sometimes made discreet forays into the matter but Edith was aware that she had to conceal Ambrose's behaviour from even the closest of her friends for the sake of his career and for the sake of her own appearances and her self-regard. Really, though, apart from his penchant for dressing up in women's clothing, he was terribly correct. She was, in fact, sometimes quietly proud of being associated with such a typical Englishman and even his vice seemed somehow part of it all. Perhaps that was being unfair. That they slept together, unmarried, was no longer such a remarkable thing, especially in Geneva — the times certainly seemed to wink at it, if not condone it. M. Avenol, the Deputy Secretary-General, had a liaison which was not actually conventional: a wife in a clinic and a mistress in his residence. So she and Ambrose dined, they danced, they were occasionally invited semiofficially as a couple. But try as she might, she still found herself baffled at times by Ambrose's feminine posturing, though it never displeased her.

For a while after the bad quarrel they'd had about this matter of character, he had not practised his dressing-up or introduced it back into their love life. Their physical love life had, in fact, faltered for a time. But gradually it had come back and with it their old ways, and again she had found herself helping him buy women's underwear and other things so that he could dress up.

Her reactions to his dressing up were not predictable. She was attracted to their long embracing and the feel of his lips and hands, and his private parts. She enjoyed the intimate privilege of knowing about his clandestine self. He told her that she was the only woman he had ever told about it. But sometimes it did nothing to encourage her desire. At those times, that he was dressed in satin underwear was of no consequence. At other times, she became aroused by the whispering of depravity and she could feel sexually entranced, perhaps when tipsy with champagne, and then she found his coming to her bed dressed as a woman something of a mysterious arousal. He was then another person, perhaps a stranger, and that person resembled her, and while it was not quite a mirror of herself, it was a sexual gyration which could intensify her. He was nearly always properly aroused as a man but sometimes he became unmanned and soft and they fondled until she had been satisfied and she liked that too, and he seemed also to like it, even though afterwards she saw only traces of male staining. But this dressing up had until now all taken place in his apartment. Had not gone out into the streets of Geneva.

To go to this club which he'd found, and mix, she imagined, with other men dressed as women did not appeal to her as such, apart from intriguing her curiosity.

'Surely you don't plan to walk through the streets and so on to this club!'

'It's only two streets from here.'

'It's not the fatigue of walking, darling; that is not what I am worrying about.'

'Do you think I look so unfeminine? Would they know?'

'The Genevese?'

She considered this. He was quite presentable as a woman, with his slender build and smooth complexion. He was not naturally hairy. His feet and hands were not mannish. In the streets the Swiss never looked at one, at least, not detectably.

She believed, however, that they had a way of looking without being seen to look. Hence their world-famous interest in the science of optics.

'Isn't it against the law? Don't we risk a scandal?' she asked. 'What about the League?'

'I don't believe it to be against the law. Nothing in office rules either.'

'Is it formal evening wear?'

'Oh — anything goes, really.'

She did not like the sound of that. 'Do you mean a costume party?'

'You could say that. But not fancy dress in the sense of a fancy-dress ball.'

She was having difficulty imagining what it would be 'like'. Her last fancy-dress ball had been as a child in the School of Arts at Nowra. She'd gone as a grasshopper. Maybe she would go to this club as a grasshopper.

'You could wear the muslin,' she said, as some sort of an answer. She was thinking of something rather simple for him to wear. She realised that she was drinking from an empty glass. The conversation was making her tense.

'It's too folkloric.'

'You can have my tulle evening gown — the one with the gold and silver sequins.'

'I hoped you'd say that.'

'I knew you would. But what does it leave me to wear?'

'You look stunning in the black lace. And I could hardly wear a V-neckline.' He was right, the tulle had a square neckline.

'How do you know about these places?'

He looked at her vulnerably. 'One just hears, I suppose.'

'Are there such places everywhere?'

'I suppose there are. I haven't been everywhere.' He stared out of the window. 'Yes, I suppose there are.'

'I am sure there is no such place in Sydney. Definitely not in Melbourne.' She rose and poured herself another sherry.

'Maybe not Sydney or Melbourne. I wouldn't be so sure though. About Sydney. Or Melbourne.'

'Oh, I'm sure. And I'm sure that if there'd been such a place, the men I knew would not have been habitués.'

He became silent, and she saw how he could be taking her remark as a reproach, as implying that Australian men had a more dependable masculinity. She saw that it had drifted them closer to the unpleasant shoals of their quarrel a few months before.

'I don't mean it in any derogatory way,' she said. 'I just mean Australian men aren't like that. The ones I know, I mean.'

'Maybe Australian men are different; perhaps they don't care for lace and silk. Suppose it could be so. Pioneers and so on. Living rough.'

'I'm sure they like lace and silk on their women.'

'Not on their men, you think?'

She leafed through *L'Illustration*. 'Not on their men.'

'I wouldn't be an attraction down there, you think?' He was lightening it up, rowing away from the shoals.

'I think you'd be better appreciated here in Geneva. Or Munich, frankly. You're more a Weimar person.' She smiled at him, feeling her patriotic moralism receding. Uncharacteristically, he worried away at the implied admonishment.

'You think I'm a little . . . disordered . . . as a person?'

That might very well have been the word she would have used. 'I think you're a little feminine and I don't think femininity is a disorder. No, you're not "disordered", dear.'

'If it's not in the right body, femininity is a disorder.'

She moved to sit near him and to touch him, to reassure him, regardless of what conflicting notions moved in her about this matter — she was too tired to fight. 'We have to live with it, if it's in the wrong body. If we find we are the one with that body,' she said, trying to ease him.

'Some of us have to live with it.'

'And some of us have to live with those who have to live with it. The secret is, I suppose, for all those involved, one way or another, to enjoy it.'

'I like your answers,' he said, returning the affection.

'I'm sometimes too good at making answers,' she said. She thought about her wider life. Was she glib? Was she too good at self-justification? 'I think Cooper believes I'm too good at finding clever answers.'

'Will I wear a flower on my shoulder? Or is that out of fashion?'

At least when they reached the club entrance Ambrose behaved like a 'gentleman', despite his female attire. At the club stairway he went ahead of her, down the stairs into the menacing, dark cellar and its door with a peephole, wearing her new fur-trimmed double-breasted coat, while she wore her second best overcoat. There was no street sign announcing the presence of the club.

Even with her assistance, he had taken hours to get himself ready. He looked quite stunning, she thought, with fashionably flat breasts. He'd insisted on wearing her violet corset, 'for the nice tightness of it'. His wig was a good fit. She had convinced him to reduce the amount of lipstick. 'Let them find out you're a siren — don't advertise it,' she'd told him. He had applied *philtres d'effarement* to his eyes to make them more striking.

'I thought a siren was just that — someone who advertised it,' he'd replied.

In the low, kind lighting of the surprisingly large club, which had a small orchestra playing Negro music, she saw every possible combination: there were men dancing with men, women with women, and men dressed as women dancing with men, and dancing with women. And inclinations, about which she was not sure.

She ran her eyes over the musicians. The atmosphere caused her to think, unreasonably, that Jerome might be there. But of course he wasn't.

Edith sat at a table waiting for Ambrose to return from looking around for another 'couple' whom he had planned to meet at the club. She felt insecure, because once in the club, he'd begun relinquishing the male role of looking after things, and she'd had to find a table. She wasn't going to look after things. Not in a club like this, where everything was inverted. It was his club, not her club. What happened at the toilet door? Who went where? She supposed they didn't care. She suspected that when the time came, she would care. She would care dreadfully.

She found that she kept averting her eyes from the surroundings, but she ventured to look around her again. She was relieved to see that some of the clientele appeared normal, in dress at least, although God knew what was occurring in their minds and hearts. Most of the 'men' were in tuxedos or dinner suits. But then, so were some of the 'women'. The more she looked, the more she realised that it was a very mixed club indeed, and perhaps more normal, not as confused as she'd first thought. Surely there could not be too many confused people in Geneva?

Ambrose, quite adept in his ankle-strapped high-heels, returned without his two friends and without her fur coat.

315

'Where is the coat?'

'I put it in the cloakroom.'

'I hope their honesty is more reliable than their sexual character.'

'How witty, Edith.'

A waiter put down the cocktails which she'd had to order for them.

Ambrose asked, 'Do you want me to put your coat in the cloakroom?'

'You may put it in the cloakroom when I am sure I'm staying.'

She drank deeply from the cocktail. She might as well lose herself in drink.

'You must stay.'

'Can I have the cloakroom ticket?' She held out her hand to him. Ambrose took the ticket from his handbag, on loan from her, and handed it to her. 'In case you decide to disappear with a man in a dinner suit, never to be seen again,' she said. 'I don't want to lose my fur coat. I can afford to lose you, but not the fur coat.' She hoped he didn't take that as a reference to the money he owed her.

He was looking around, as if searching for attention.

She went on, 'I suppose — if you did disappear — that I might eventually see you again years later, say, one night at Monte Carlo, in the casino — but I couldn't bear it if you were there in my fur coat.'

He chuckled.

As she and Ambrose joked, it occurred to her that she did not quite know how the evening was meant to turn out and she thought she'd better ask. She had difficulty phrasing it. 'Do you intend to be approached by these . . . men?' she asked.

'Asked to dance, you mean?'

She meant that and more than that.

'Asked to . . . whatever.'

He looked at her, perhaps surprised at her implication. 'I don't know, I suppose I want to be admired.'

'Don't we all.'

'I admire you, Edith.'

'You look far better than I do tonight.'

'Not true — you're being charitable.' His voice implying that he would love it to be true.

'You look better, darling, because I got second-best choice of my clothing and jewellery. And handbags. And coats.'

'Touché,' he said, then went on, awkwardly, 'In reply to your first question — you know that I don't care for men. I prefer to be with women. As a rule.'

'As a rule?'

'Yes, as a rule.'

Once someone used that expression it meant that there were no rules. She wondered if there were rules at all in this place.

By the time they'd finished their first drink, Ambrose was asked to dance by a man. He was nervously delighted, and he beamed at her over the man's shoulder.

Shortly afterwards, she was asked to dance by a man. She put her coat in the cloakroom, and they danced. She found that dancing relaxed her.

As she danced past Ambrose and his man, she remained comically impassive, pretending not to acknowledge him.

After the dance she was escorted back to their corner table where Ambrose was already seated, thankfully without partner. He was sitting elegantly, remembering to keep his knees together.

After thanking her partner, who then went off, and sitting down, she said, 'In our discussion about Australia the other day, about what Australian men might or might not wish to wear, I think I was being a little naïve.'

'Oh.'

'I mean, there must be men in Australia who dress as women. Australia isn't that different.'

'I think that's probably closer to the truth.'

'You do?'

'I think so. A little closer to the truth. Simmel or someone said there were not enough sexes.'

'Oh, did he? Of all things, I hate being naïve, or maybe patriotic. Just as bad.'

'It's youth. Savour it. You're given bonuses to compensate for being naïve.'

'And I think two sexes are quite enough. Make quite enough problems. Well, two sexes and a half.'

Ambrose laughed. 'Very good, Edith. A little slow, but first class.'

'And what are the bonuses of youth?'

'Youth.'

'That's circular.'

He thought. 'Oh, litheness. That's one.'

'Litheness is little better than agility. It's a rather gymnastic bonus. And in my case, it goes with red hair and freckles.'

'Freckles are a rustic form of beauty, Edith. And I would describe your hair as *rousse*.'

'Agility and freckles. Topnotch. And I'm hardly a youth. And giving the colour of my hair a French word no longer impresses, nor does it change a thing: its colour is fading. I would gladly give up my agility if I could also lose my naïvity.' Thankfully her freckles were fading too; the Lord giveth and the Lord taketh away.

He looked at her. 'You're allowed to be naïve — for one

more year. I think those are the rules. After that, you are just considered wrong-headed, not naïve.' He smiled across at her. 'Edith, I think you're a handsome woman. A graceful woman. And I like your freckles.'

'Thanks. So are you.'

'I wish you meant it.'

She did mean it. 'I do. You are among the most beautiful here tonight.'

'Thanks.' Ambrose sighed, and looked around. 'Among the men? Or both men and women?'

'Don't push for too much, darling.'

She still didn't know what was supposed to happen at the club that evening, between them. His earlier answers were not complete. She knew she should ask him, while there was time, although she wished she'd had it out with him before coming to the rotten club. 'Ambrose, I'm confused,' she said. 'Are you looking for another lover tonight . . . a man lover?'

She felt boorish, but it had to be asked. Anyhow this club was well on the other side of refinement. Boorish behaviour could hardly matter.

'I want to be with you,' he said.

She sensed that he was being honourable. She coaxed him to answer honestly. 'Come clean, Ambrose.'

'Well, if I really did attract a man, and that is unlikely . . .' Modestly, he made a woebegone face.

She made a motherly, tell-the-truth-now face back to him. 'Go on,' she said, 'tell me.'

'Oh — it might be fun to be with a man for the night. I suppose.'

She thought about this. What did 'be with a man for a night' mean to Ambrose? 'Maybe you'd better elaborate,' she said, fiddling with her drink.

319

He gathered himself, made his voice confident. 'Yes, I might like to have a sexual act with a man.'

His answer seemed to somersault onto her lap like an angry cat.

'Oh,' she said, 'I see.' She didn't see at all, really, although she did see that his wish excluded her. They rested there in a conversational crater. She was not sure how much further she wanted to go with her questions.

But he went on, sounding as if he was wanting to spill it all out. 'No, not by a man. I think that most of all I want to have a sexual act with a man dressed as a woman.'

She was still excluded.

'I think that's what I want,' he said, now satisfied with his reply.

She made herself imagine the difference, the difference between him in a sexual act with a woman, and in a sexual act with a man dressed as a woman. They would be both responding sexually to the feminine image. She was still not sure, though, what Ambrose meant — did he mean that he and his lover-dressed-as-a-woman would both pretend to be women? Or that they both behaved like men, or what? What did they do with their male parts? So many quandaries. Instead, she said, timidly, 'I see. At least, I think I do.'

What was really foremost in her mind was that she did not want to be abandoned by Ambrose in this club. As she stared across at his made-up face, the cut of the wig hugging his head, the long pearl *rivière* necklace, the pretty shoulders framed in the square neck of the evening dress, she felt lost. Lost in the passageways of his sexuality, its turnings and its corridors and its doors — leading to where? Here in the club it was different from being back in his apartment when they played with clothes and make-up, sexually. She was part of it then — indeed, in control of it. In the apartment, she felt that wherever he went in his fantasies, ultimately she was with him and she knew that it all came to be focused on her and in the service of her bodily pleasure.

'Can I be really straightforward with you?' he said, drinking from his second cocktail.

There in the smoke of the club with its low lights, its glitter-ball, its bizzareness, and the Negro music, she felt she had no way to restrain him, that the whole atmosphere extended the right to absolute, and even flammable, self-revelation and conduct and, anyhow, what was there about him that she did not already know. Probably too much. 'Tell me. I thought I'd heard it all. Tell me the rest.'

'Are you sure you want to know?'

'How can I be sure I want to know? Stop being so coy.' Her toughness was false. Her breathing was not quite right.

He leaned a little towards her, which emphasised the innermost nature of what he was about to say. 'I feel a definite need sometimes — I feel a real physical need sometimes, in my rectum.'

She took this in. The low lights of the club concealed her blushing. For an instant, she thought he meant to go to the toilet but then the intended meaning swiftly arrived.

'Rectum?' She said the word. She wondered whether she had used this word before — maybe she'd used it to a doctor, maybe in science at university; had written it, maybe in a physiology examination. The word did not seem at all clinical there, then, in this club, with Ambrose dressed so appealingly, even voluptuously, the word coming from his pretty red lips, altered in midair to sound brightly lurid. She honestly didn't know what to say next.

He went on, 'Desire — I feel desire in my rectum. Sometimes. A passionate desire for a man.'

She felt herself mentally staggering back from this revelation. Obviously she hadn't heard all. Where was the end to 'all'? With what she thought was admirable calm, she said, 'It's all right if you do, if it happens. If a man wants to escort you home.' She was astonished to hear herself saying conventional phrases such as 'escort you home'. Who was going to see her home? She supposed Ambrose would be gentlemanly enough to call the depot for a taxi. 'Or, a man dressed as a lady.' But then who did the escorting?

'You don't mind . . . if it happens?'

'As long as you let me know what's happening. I suppose. As long as everything is decorous.' The word quailed in the atmosphere of the club. She was hesitant now, not being at all sure how far she wanted to go with the conversation, but an insensible, prurient curiosity pushed her along. 'I suppose that a man dressed as a woman might be able to give you something that I couldn't. Some stimulation that I couldn't give you.' She regained composure and altered her voice to a bantering toughness. 'Heavens, darling, I wouldn't want you to miss out on any of life's pleasures. Who would wish that on anyone!' But her tone hid her dismay, as Ambrose and some strange companion dimly acted it out in her imagination, despite the fact that some of the pieces of the puzzle were missing.

'You're very magnanimous,' Ambrose said very seriously, reaching over and taking both her hands. 'You are a very magnanimous person, Edith. Very.'

'I am your friend, Ambrose.' She strove towards a joking tone. 'I suppose I am entitled to give the bride away.'

She knew then as she made the joke that they would never marry, not that it had ever been discussed.

'I don't always yearn for it,' he rushed to say, 'that sort of thing. I don't lie about every day yearning for a man dressed as a woman, or wanting you to be a man dressed as a woman. I don't always want those sort of thrills.'

'Good.'

'I want you, just as Edith, most of the time, nearly all of the time.'

'That's good.' She was still struggling to comprehend all this and not to show any dismay. She'd heard of physical sex via the rectum as a birth control measure. She and Ambrose had never done it. When men had physical sex with other men, she had thought that they probably fondled each other and used their mouths. But the rectum, now that she thought about it, seemed obvious.

At this moment, Ambrose's two friends arrived. Ye gods. They were men dressed as women — one very young and one not so young. They were British and on holidays, old friends of Ambrose from London.

'We're travelling as two sisters,' the older one said, as if it were an especially clever thing to do.

The younger one seemed sulky. He went by the French name of Laure. Edith gave him marks for his choice of name.

Edith found it difficult to talk to them 'as girls', yet they probably didn't want to talk about themselves as men. It was all very difficult. She sensed they did not wish to talk about their occupations, for instance. From some of their cryptic remarks, she thought they might be British Foreign Office. She let Ambrose talk to them. Their chat sounded to her like a feminine burlesque. They talked about the places where they'd be able to pass themselves off as girls. They seemed to enjoy talking about make-up, hair, and the pumicing of legs. She speculated about how they might have come to know Ambrose, how they came to share the same predilection. She would ask later. She wondered about Ambrose's feminine voice, now heightened by their company — from his mother, his sister?

She was relieved when a man came to her and asked her, in French, to dance.

The three men dressed as women pretended to be put out that she had been asked and not them. There was much giggling.

The man was swarthy, maybe even dark, but in the low lights of the club it was hard to tell.

As she danced with him, he seemed morose, maybe slightly drunk.

She asked him, in French, where he was from.

He replied, 'Azerbaijan.'

She guessed he was an émigré. Geneva was a home for these émigré people, in flight from fallen countries like Azerbaijan. She tried to recall what she'd read about Azerbaijan. It had been refused membership of the League because its boundaries were obscure.

'You're an émigré?' she asked.

'I am a castaway.'

'I am sorry about your country. You will return to it one day.'

'I do not have hope.'

She wondered why he was at this club. Maybe his masculinity was also castaway.

He asked her before she could ask him. 'Why do you come here?'

'Oh?' She looked around as if she had just found herself there in the club by mishap. 'Oh, I have a friend — a friend who comes here.'

'You are not a lover of women?'

'No.' She nearly answered that her friend was a man but it was tripped up by a new thought — when she coupled with

Ambrose which sex was she loving? Where was she in all this ambiguity? Did she make love to his ambiguities? 'No, not at all,' she said, wanting to have this man's approval and attention.

He said, 'I relax in this place because here all is lost too.'

'I suppose so. How, though, do you mean, "lost"?'

'These people are outside of it all, lost from the ordained paths.'

She was having trouble with his accent and his French but she followed his thinking.

'I am lost from the soil of my nation. But these people,' he nodded his head at the club crowd, 'they are lost from the natural world. This is a netherworld.'

She too, glanced around, seeing it through his eyes, and yes, it was a netherworld. She changed the subject. 'It is difficult here in Geneva — being an émigré?'

'I am more than an émigré — I am also government in exile. With me, the government of my country resides.'

He said he wanted to drink — would she join him? He did not dance well and she was glad to leave the dance floor. They went to his table where he had a bottle of cognac. He said that here in this club he was doubly exiled. 'I am a man of normal feelings. And here, here I feel double exile and that takes me beyond the pain of the first exile. I am a normal man in pain.'

She saw how he was using the bizarre atmosphere to dilute his pain but she still did not trust his normality. Was she looking for a normal friend, here in this club?

She looked across at Ambrose who was dancing with the younger *travesti*. The older *travesti* now looked sullen.

Edith felt the evening was slipping the reins of her personal order, and she felt she might very well fall, fall down some trap door into a dark, sensual chamber. Maybe a silken chamber in Azerbaijan. Did they have silk? She tried again to recall what she'd read about Azerbaijan. Nothing much was coming up. She knew that after the Soviets had taken them over, they had applied as a government in exile to be accepted by the League but had been refused because of the border problem.

Ambrose and his young dance partner stopped where she and Mr Huneeus were sitting.

'Introduce us, Edith,' Ambrose said, in a jealous falsetto voice, standing there holding the hand of the younger man.

She stumblingly introduced Ambrose by his female name of Carla and the young Englishman also by his *nom déguisée*.

'Mr Huneeus is an émigré from Azerbaijan,' she said, thus recklessly granting him his claim, she observed.

It turned out that the younger one knew much about Azerbaijan and displayed his knowledge. This pleased Mr Huneeus.

After some small talk, Ambrose and the young man danced on.

When they'd finished their drink she felt it was safe to invite Mr Huneeus to join the others. He gathered up his bottle of cognac and the glasses. She was uncertain whether Mr Huneeus was now attached to her for the evening, and what he might construct on their remaining together after the dance. But what did she care? Here in this club her own etiquette seemed inapplicable, rules of behaviour were either nonexistent or they were 'unspoken'. What, she asked herself, are 'unspoken rules', and from where do they come? No, she was sure that even in this inverted world, there were rules. She knew that you couldn't always see the rules simply by looking at people mixing together, but she suspected that strict rules always commissioned social life even when there was a claim to social illicitness. She had no intention of bothering to learn them.

Ambrose exchanged inquisitive glances at her, curious and maybe unsettled by Mr Huneeus's presence. It wasn't possible to answer him, and she then realised that she couldn't answer herself — what was she at the club for? Why was she in the company of this Mr Huneeus? Was she also laying herself open to the turn of events? Was Mr Huneeus a 'turn of events'?

She hadn't had quite enough to drink, nor was she yet quite relaxed about the nature of her surroundings, to be free to throw herself into the turn of events. She knew about a timidity within herself when it came to allowing things to just happen. A threshold over which she had to be led, preferably blindfolded, or which she had to make herself jump like a shy horse. She landed well, though, she thought, on the other side. When and if she made the jump. On those two or three occasions in her life that she had made that jump.

During a toilet absence of Mr Huneeus, Ambrose, in a lapse back to his everyday self, leaned across to ask her if she'd told Mr Huneeus about their being League officers.

She said she hadn't.

Ambrose said that it might be wiser to avoid the subject, and then said, 'But if it comes up, so be it.'

Edith wasn't sure that so be it at all. Émigrés always had problems to be solved and always looked to the League to do the solving. Problems of constitutional legitimacy. Problems of missing treasury gold. She did not wish to be used as an intercessor for the forsaken Republic of Azerbaijan.

'And has he become your escort for the evening?' Ambrose asked, in a quite different voice from that which had talked about their being officers of the League; he had returned to the effeminate voice belonging to his role that evening. It carried a suggestion of jealousy, but it lacked sharpness. His was a played-out jealousy, some sort of obligatory courtesy. As well it should be, given his own early musings and declarations of desire.

Before she could answer, there was a commotion at the

bottom of the stairs, where the foyer opened into the club.

About ten youths with black armbands entered the club, most wearing black leather caps, black leather gaiters, and many carrying batons, pushing aside the doorman, and causing a scared lull in the exhilarated noise of the club. The lull was immediately followed by a louder nervous resumption of the noisy chatter, competing with the music — as if the club guests were pretending that nothing was happening.

But as the youths pushed and shoved their way deeper into the club, the noisy chatter and laughter died down. Soon the sounds of conversation had died away, leaving only the music of the orchestra playing on bravely, but ignored, with the dancers slowing to a shuffle, then stopping, and then standing, holding their poses while the music went over and around them, but unable to move.

Edith recognised the uniformed youths as Action Civique, a Swiss youth group friendly to Italy and the Mussolini government.

'Action Civique,' Ambrose said to his two friends. 'Not nice.'

Mr Huneeus returned from the toilet and looked at the youths with distaste. He seemed to know the Action Civique too. 'A bad lot,' he said to Edith.

Some of the youths were speaking Italian in a bombastic, showy way, as part of their political exhibition.

The orchestra continued to play but at a faltering volume.

The Action Civique went around the room, stopping in front of some of the *travesti* and using their batons to lift the front of their low-waisted skirts and dresses like theatre curtains, running their batons lewdly up the stockinged legs to their groins, but not going as far as violence, interested only in embarrassment and the parading of the power which flowed from their uniforms, their batons, and their political arrogance. Some of the *travesti* pretended, with bravado, to like the attention of the young men and bravely played up to it. Weirdly, this play-acting in the face of threat seemed, then, almost natural to the atmosphere of the club, almost part of the evening. The frightened behaviour of the *travesti* with their exposed stockings and knickers unveiled the threatening nature of it all.

The owner of the club came through the crowd and approached the youths. He offered to provide the youths with tables and with drinks but they roughly pushed him away. As the owner reeled back from the shove and fell against the some of the standing couples, the music from the orchestra trailed off and the club became quiet under the revolving glitter-ball.

Of all things, Edith feared first for her fur coat but decided then that the youths were not thieves, and reminded herself that despite their Italianate political posing, they were, after all, Swiss, which she found vaguely reassuring. And that they belonged also to some political organisation and, presumably, had some sort of discipline.

Edith and Mr Huneeus and the others sat down and tried to resume an imitation of conversation but the youths reached their table and stared down at them, especially at Mr Huneeus.

For some reason, Mr Huneeus stood up, not respectfully, but as an assertion of himself. The leader of the group moved very close to Mr Huneeus and said, in Italian and then in French, 'Your papers!'

Mr Huneeus seemed now quite dark and foreign in his heavy-weave double-breasted suit.

'I am here as guest of the Swiss federal government and you have no right.'

'Your papers.' The leader pushed Mr Huneeus's stomach

with the baton. 'In here, we are the government.' One or two others stood behind their leader, their batons resting in the palms of their hands in a practised way.

'I am the Deputy President and the Ambassador-at-large for the Republic of Azerbaijan. I request that you honour that.'

Edith was impressed by this information from Mr Huneeus, and wondered whether the Action Civique would respect his position.

'You have no place in this country,' the leader pronounced, and hit Mr Huneeus across the mouth with the baton, hard enough for a hard cracking sound to be heard. Blood came from his broken lips and he tried to stand his ground, staggering, ignoring the bleeding.

'Now look here!' Ambrose said, rising to his feet and stepping forward. 'Easy on.'

His English male voice came through the lipstick and make-up ludicrously and ineffectually. Edith felt embarrassed for him.

The leader lifted Ambrose's dress to reveal his lace underwear and then jabbed at his genitals with the baton. Ambrose instinctively recoiled and pushed his dress down, his hands covering his genitals. One of the youths gave a cry of triumph at the unmasking. In a diminished voice, Ambrose said, 'Please stop!'

She saw that Ambrose had lost his male authority, his English authority. She felt that even she might have more authority as a woman than he did now as a man dressed as a woman. But she felt that her limited authority could not save Mr Huneeus. Nothing could be done by speaking or appealing to them, and instead she stood up and moved in front of Mr Huneeus, shielding him, and said to the leader, 'Stop this. Ambassador Huneeus is with me,' hoping still that the use of his title might help.

The leader looked her over and then took hold of her dress

on both sides of her body and pulled her skirt fully up, revealing her underwear, and put a hand on her crotch.

She pushed his hand away, and pulled her skirt down, in a firm movement which was something she realised that the *travesti* had not done. The leader stood perplexed, having touched her enough to know that she was a woman, feeling maybe that to touch her further would be not so much an abuse of power but an impropriety, something of which his mother would not approve. Or perhaps it entered his mind that he might have committed a criminal offence.

Another of the crowd of young thugs, however, seemed not to be so restrained and came forward saying, 'Is she a woman?'

The leader said yes, trying to push her away now, to get around her to Mr Huneeus, but she stayed protectively interfering with his efforts, but weakly, defencelessly.

The second man pulled Edith away, and said, 'Let me carry out a search.'

She struggled with him but another youth moved in to hold her arms. Another two grappled with Mr Huneeus who was trying to come, now, to her rescue, and Ambrose and his two friends were also grappling with youths. As the scuffling began to spread, the second man put his hand up inside her skirt and she felt his hand inside her knickers, felt a finger probing, trying to find her opening.

Mr Huneeus cried out in rage and lunged free from those holding him. In trying to protect her, he was again struck on the head with baton blows.

She kicked out a foot and screamed, and felt her kicks connecting with the youth's legs who simply grunted from the kicks and moved off, resuming an uneasy laughter, smelling his fingers, offering his fingers to his colleagues — 'Pure woman.' Now some of them acted as if the smell was repugnant. All this

331

happening under the glitter-ball and in the bizarre decor of the club made it seem even more nightmarish.

Had they really dared to touch her there? She heard herself cry out again.

The leader said to the others to leave her alone but she saw that he now had little command.

The club seemed to erupt, with scuffling breaking out at the other end of the club as well and with others going to their assistance, attention turned from Mr Huneeus and from her.

She caught Ambrose's eye, and cried out in English, 'Let's run for it!' She reached down and took off her shoes and Ambrose followed her example and took off his shoes also. Ambrose took her hand, she took the dazed, bleeding Mr Huneeus by the arm and pulled him with her. The other two came good and acted as a sort of running guard as they pushed their way towards the door through which other people were also beginning to flee the enveloping mêlée.

The scuffling spread through the club with the Action Civique using their batons and clubgoers using chairs and other objects which came to hand. Glass was being smashed. The black musicians had taken their instruments and disappeared from the stage.

At the bottom of the stairs, before running for the street, Edith thought momentarily of her fur coat but kept on going.

She, Mr Huneeus, and the three men dressed as women rushed up the stairs, burst into the chilly air of the street, and ran.

With her arm around Mr Huneeus, he holding on to her and to Ambrose, they ran for it, along rue de la Cité and down towards the lake and Ambrose's apartment.

They all paused on a corner about a block or so from the club, all holding on to each other, breathless. Ambrose had both his shoes and wig in his hand, Mr Huneeus, more breathless because of age and weight and maybe his injuries, was coughing. The soles of Edith's stockings were holed, her feet were hurt.

They limped up the stairs to Ambrose's apartment, and once inside, fell into chairs, heavy with exhaustion from their fear and running, safe behind the locked door.

Ambrose changed out of his dress into a silk house robe and took up his doctor role, attending to Mr Huneeus's smashed lips and cut head, and to the older of his English friends, who was beginning an asthma attack.

The younger friend went to the kitchen and prepared cocoa which Edith found an incongruously practical thing for the young man in a women's evening dress to be doing.

After regaining her breath, Edith went to the bathroom, and, alone, began to sob from the indignity of the molestation and from the panic of it all. She was burningly aware that her indignity had happened in front of these unknown Englishmen and Mr Huneeus. She kept splashing cold water on to herself. She doubted that she could go back out to the others in the drawing room.

After a while, Ambrose came looking for her. 'Edith? Are you all right in there?'

She thought for a moment that she did not have the will to open the door, but he remained outside, calling to her, and she did open it and he came in looking worried. She held on to him.

'Should we call the police?' he said, but without conviction. She saw that he was caught in their private predicament as well as in the urge for justice. She saw instantly too, that the police would be too much for her to take at this time or for any of them to take.

Mr Huneeus was lying down on a couch, covered with a blanket, suffering from shock. He kept saying that a bodyguard usually accompanied him. That he would, tomorrow, instruct his bodyguard to track down these thugs. They would be dealt with. Dealt with.

She wanted to believe him; she thought it probable that someone like Mr Huneeus would have a bodyguard. She believed it and felt good about it and she wanted him to track down the thugs and beat them.

While Mr Huneeus rested, the four of them sat around, the English couple in their women's clothing without wigs, the older one inhaling from a preparation, all retelling, cursing, and sharing observations now in their fully male voices — as survivors from a shipwreck, all solicitous of Edith. They were all made very close from what they had been through. She no longer felt any antipathy towards the two Englishmen. She kept shivering and Ambrose fetched a rug which she draped around her shoulders. The couple asked if they might stay, and Ambrose fixed a bed for them in the guest room and they said good night, kissing Edith and holding her in a strong embrace.

After dozing for a short time, Mr Huneeus awakened and said a formal good night. Ambrose, who had a telephone, called the taxi depot. As Mr Huneeus prepared to go, he handed her his card. She fumbled in her handbag and found her card which she gave him, without any thought of protocol or the League or any of that. He read it, bowed formally to her and to Ambrose.

In bed she began to cry. As Ambrose comforted her and they talked there in the dark, she realised that Ambrose had not seen, or had not registered, what had happened to her. He spoke of the brutish behaviour towards Huneeus but did not mention the behaviour of the youth to her.

'And there was what they did to me.'

'Are you hurt too?' He half sat up in the bed.

'Not bodily.'

'You were very brave.'

She wondered if she should tell him. 'I mean the other thing, the thing they did to me.'

He was silent, as if trying to recall. 'I don't follow.'

For a flashing second, she thought that she might have imagined it all, that it was her mind enacting a primeval terror. 'They molested me.'

Ambrose turned on the bedside light and looked at her. She could tell that he was disturbed, was perhaps worried that she was hysterical, that she was caught in frenzied fantasies of womankind. Or that she was using the language loosely.

'You were molested?' His voice now had the protective concern of a doctor. She began crying. 'I didn't see this. Was it at the time you tried to protect Huneeus?'

As she cried she suffered a peculiar opposition of feeling — relief that he hadn't seen and that maybe others hadn't seen, and yet also a yearning for pity.

'How were you molested? I mean, talk to me as a doctor.'

'I'm all right. In a way I'm glad you didn't see it. Maybe others didn't see it either. I don't want to describe it. My head aches, but it's more from humiliation.'

He held her. 'I didn't see what happened in the confusion. I don't want to sound disregarding.'

She liked that he was a doctor, and she relished a sense of protection. 'It's all right. Turn off the light. Let's sleep. I need to sleep.'

'I'll get you a sleeping draught.'

'No, don't bother. Thank you.'

He ignored her, and left the room, returning with a mixture in a glass. He held her head as he would a child, and helped her drink it and she felt comforted by him there in his regimental striped pyjamas, and as a doctor.

For the first time since coming to Geneva, she wanted to go home to Australia.

She did not go to the office on the Monday but by Wednesday her spirits had returned, her agitation had settled somewhat, and, though still deeply sombre and occasionally shaking, she went into work.

In her office, there was a formal note from His Excellency, Mr Huneeus, and flowers from him which had been put in water by one of the women in the bureau, but they were wilting. The note invited her to come to his embassy on the Tuesday of the following week. She wondered tiredly if the invitation implied amorous interest by Mr Huneeus. She felt affection for him from their having shared a horror and survived, but she did not want to encourage any amorous affection. She pushed the matter aside for now.

Ambrose had gone back to the club and retrieved their coats and hers was on a hanger behind the door of her office.

She decided to have Ambrose accompany her to the Embassy of Azerbaijan. They discussed whether Mr Huneeus would recognise Ambrose as a man, and decided that, given Mr Huneeus's condition on the night, he probably would not, and that if he did, he would choose not to refer to the strange circumstances under which they'd met.

It was a rambling, clean office in Servette, and she surmised that Mr Huneeus and others lived in the upper apartments. On the wall was a framed portrait of the President, a group photograph of his cabinet, a framed copy of the constitution of the Republic of Azerbaijan, and a national coat-of-arms.

Mr Huneeus sat at a green-covered desk. His lips were still swollen. There were three other men and one woman in the room. A map was spread on the desk. A rubber stamp and inking pad. A document. An ink well. A wooden rocking-blotter.

He rose and, as a traditional greeting, hugged them both. If he recognised Ambrose, he did not indicate it by any word or gesture.

Speaking with some distress and further distortion because of his lips, he said that it was to be a formal occasion after which they would retire to a less formal reception.

He handed a sheet of paper to one of the other men who read from it in French, as if reading a proclamation, using a deep, loud voice: 'I wish to announce to the world that the Deputy President of Azerbaijan, with the powers vested in him, in gratitude for the efforts of Edith Campbell Berry to save the Ambassador-at-large and Deputy President of Azerbaijan from bodily harm, in recognition of her gallant and courageous efforts to extricate all from a situation of certain danger, the Republic of Azerbaijan hereby declares and irrevocably assigns, the name of Edith to the River Akara in the sovereign republic of Azerbaijan and that henceforth this river will be known as the River Edith.'

Edith was suffused with emotion and began to shake. From where he'd been standing in the background, Ambrose came up behind her and she felt his arm supporting her, as tears rose to her eyes.

Mr Huneeus took up the rubber stamp, inked it, stamped the proclamation, signed it and blotted the signature.

He rolled up the proclamation, tied it with blue silk ribbon, and handed it to Edith, again formally hugging her and kissing her on both cheeks.

'I am overwhelmed,' she said, feeling truly overwhelmed,

tears now coming to her eyes and flowing. 'I cannot say how moved I am.'

One by one, the other men and the woman came to her and hugged her, and kissed her on both cheeks.

Ambrose said softly, 'Well earned, Edith,' and gave her a hug and kiss.

'Come.' Mr Huneeus gestured to her to look at the map, and he traced with his finger, the river. 'This is the River Edith. It is a fine, clear river, it flows through forests and snow-covered mountains to the Caspian Sea. It is untouched and unspoiled.'

Edith had another burst of crying then, briefly, but dried her eyes and pulled herself together like a good diplomat, though remaining on the brink of tears. She realised that it was not her courage alone that was being attended to. She knew from his words that Mr Huneeus was also attending to her hurt.

He said, taking her arm, 'Come, now we will feast,' and he led her to a drawing room where traditional Azerbaijan food was laid out. Champagne was served by a member of staff dressed as a waiter, but who did not move as deftly as a waiter.

She was toasted. The champagne seemed to her to be from the waters of the river. She felt cleansed by its clean taste, and cleansed by the image in her mind of the clear, fine river flowing through forests and snow-covered mountains, and she felt herself healing, felt the sullying being taken from her by the river and by the sincere and serious honour which these people had bestowed, even if, as she suspected, their authority was doubtful.

'I hope,' she said, tightly holding her champagne glass, tears again in her eyes and her voice, 'I hope one day to visit my river, in the free Republic of Azerbaijan. I toast the free Republic of Azerbaijan.'

They all toasted the free Republic of Azerbaijan.

Public Life (2):

Return to the Molly

Leaning back in her office chair, Edith said that she would not, not, not go back to the Molly Club. Standing against the filing cabinet, hands in the pockets of his tweed suit, without his jacket, his waistcoat affecting fob watch and chain, his regimental cuff links visible, Ambrose stared out at the snow slush in the Palais courtyard.

'That I appreciate. And consequently, you're "parade exempt", Edith. Attendance not expected. I thought that you should know about the meeting, that's all.'

'How did they contact you? How did they get your name!?'

He shrugged. 'When I went back for the coats there was a notice. And Follett, the owner, talked with me.'

For no good reason, Edith felt that what Ambrose said sounded like an evasion. She had no reason to think it was evasion. He had no reason to be evasive. What did she care if he had been back every night? But when it came to this matter he always sounded evasive. He had explained the two 'sisters' from England as having been part of his old gang from London which meant that he had indulged his predilection before her. Perhaps she considered Ambrose inherently dubious, in the deepest sense. If his sexual rudiments were unstable, did not all of him become questionable? No, that was unfair. It was because of the loathsome incident which made the Molly Club and anything about it seem to her so murky. She felt that much more was going on than she was being told or that she understood. The loathsome incident had stirred up a nest of spiders in her mind.

341

Anyhow, it was his peculiar mania. She simply shared his secret and participated in it in their private life. She did not really belong in his darker covert life outside the bedroom. If, indeed, he had one. If it wasn't all in her distraught head. But she continued to wonder whether he'd been back there without her, and if so, what he'd got up to there.

It was that she was jittery and moody about it all. Nothing sat well with her at present. Her work was scrappy.

He went on, 'We — those who have been to the club — we, they, feel we should stand up to them.'

'Stand up? We? I thought you had been to the club only that once.'

'Oh, you know, go on as usual, I mean, but with a little more precaution.'

'It doesn't need me.'

'Quite right. They feel that to bow down to them would be giving up too easily.'

She nearly said, harshly, that the Action Civique were just trying to clean up the town, to keep Geneva decent. Not that it needed to be much cleaner. And it probably needed a little indecency. With effort, she curbed her antagonism and reversed her first sentiments and forced out a joke. 'I suppose Geneva needs all the indecency it can get.'

Ambrose gave a short laugh, but coloured. 'Indecency?' he said, as though he'd never thought of his behaviour as indecent. He glanced at her to see if she might not also have been sarcastic. 'I suppose it does.' He regained his humour. 'And we're just the people to maintain Geneva's sense of indecency.' He also forced out a laugh.

'Indeed you are.'

The thing she found sticky and displeasing was that all this had nothing to do with the League. She wanted no outside untidiness or demand in her life. The League was too urgent. She had no time for other things, let alone messy and murky things.

'It's a matter of standing up to them,' Ambrose repeated, trying to sound righteously firm, 'to go peacefully about our business.'

She sensed then, that for all his releasing of her from the matter, he was still trying to persuade her to be involved.

'One day you must explain to me what precisely that business is — that the Molly Club goes about.'

'If only I knew, dear. Words fail.'

He looked at his watch, came over and kissed her, and said he would be off. 'Don't you worry.'

After he left, she went to the window wondering if it would snow again. A snow-covered European city was still a wonder to her and it made her feel she was living inside a toy village. She watched the smoke tumbling lazily from the apartment chimneys. But the snow denied what happened in the buildings that it covered with the false white innocence of snow. The snow was oblivious of her hurt.

She found it bewildering that she shared the indignity of that night only with the shadowy incognito people of the Molly Club who she would never see in daylight. Or see again. Or maybe she did see them. Maybe they worked here at the Palais, maybe she saw them in the mornings stamping the snow from their shoes, brushing it from their shoulders. Maybe she passed them daily in the streets and byways of Geneva because, truth be known, she would not recognise them without their costumes, the cloak of inversion, and heavy make-up. She paused, but they must recognise her, she had not been disguised on that evening. She didn't know what to make of that thought.

She saw how a few natural women, like her, were permitted, chosen maybe, to be a court to their behaviour, to be an affectionate, indulgent audience of natural womanhood, to sanction them in their play.

Approached from another position, maybe she had a democratic obligation to go to the club and stand up to Action Civique. The Molly Club was not part of the toy town. It could be argued that it was all very well for her to be fighting for world order and peace with letters and memos. What about the threats of disorder now, here and now, in her own life or at least, in Ambrose's, her friend's life? In the town in which she lived. But which was the disorder? The *travesti* who contradicted their nature? Or the Action Civique? If Ambrose were there she would have made a joke about it. The difference, she forced herself to note, was that there was no violence in what Ambrose and his effeminate pals did. It was the arrogant young men in uniforms with clubs. The other night at the Bavaria, Herr Stresemann had told her that duelling in student corps was fashionable again in Germany in the Borussia Corps and so on. Getting their cheeks slashed to prove their aristocratic manhood. Stresemann himself had slashed cheeks but he was a man from another century. Even Bernard Shaw, whom she usually admired, had seen something impressive in Mussolini and his uniformed youths.

She saw that if she continued to think like this she would have to go to the meeting. Didn't she already give enough to the bloody world? She again felt close to tears as waves of recall from that night at the club passed through her.

Throughout the day she felt she was dodging the moral dilemma of attending the Molly Club meeting by hiding behind her personal hurt. She was then more annoyed that she should be troubled at all by it as some sort of moral dilemma.

What would it be, this meeting? Would the meeting be businesslike or would they all dress up again and carry on? But for the first time since the dreadful night she recalled the other ungruesome parts of the occasion. Her fears about her fur coat. The two Englishmen dressed as sisters, preening and giggling, and saying some very funny things. She remembered the younger one getting the cocoa at Ambrose's apartment when they were safely home, and how close they had all felt that night. And then the naming of the river. She became tearful again.

Curse it. She would call Ambrose and say she would go to his stupid meeting.

And again she helped Ambrose with his costume and make-up at the dressing table in his apartment. He sitting there in stockings, suspender belt, knickers, and chemise, enlivened by the clothing, delighting in the application of powder, lipstick, and mascara. The painting of his nails.

She had groaned out aloud when he timorously told her that he was going to the meeting dressed as a woman. He explained defensively that it was considered essential that they go to the club as they usually would go, and not to bow down in any way by dressing in everyday clothes.

She had again questioned his use of 'usual', but without pursuing a reply.

'I take it that they don't know about the meeting — the Action Civique?'

'I doubt that they would. I don't see how. It's a private meeting. It's hardly likely to be written up in the *Journal de Genève*. At least, I hope not.'

'Ambrose, I can't go if they are going to turn up and all that is going to happen again. I just can't.'

'I cannot see how they could possibly know. And there will be precautions.'

'What precautions?'

'Doormen and so on.'

'Why are you dressing up, then? Won't that be provocative?'

'I am not going to parade through the streets. Nor, I doubt, are any of the others. We are dressing up as an act of self-respect.'

She refused to allow herself to see that it had to do with self-respect. The contradictions defeated her.

He turned away from the mirror and took her hands. 'I speak as a doctor and I think that going to the club again might be good for you. It might be what is known in psychology as cathartic.'

'What is "cathartic"?'

'It might help banish your phantoms from that horrible night. By challenging them, they go away.'

She wasn't so sure. Couldn't it also revive the phantoms?

He went on, 'I don't mean confronting the Action Civique — I mean confronting the place where it all happened.'

She could see that he was being brave. She knew that she should also be brave. 'It's all right — I'm coming with you.'

'Thank you, Edith. I mean that. Thank you.' He stood and kissed her cheek.

He sat down and turned back to his face, back to plucking his eyebrows. 'Back to the important things,' he joked.

She managed a smile. 'I agree with the amber bracelets, rings and earrings. They will work well.'

'I think so — with the green dress.'

When he dressed as a woman he wore a reddish wig so that he could take advantage of her wardrobe and jewellery.

'I'm curious about something, Ambrose,' she said, as she stood behind him, fitting his wig.

'Yes?'

'Do you really feel desire in your rectum?' she said good-humouredly.

He smiled back at her through his reflection in the mirror. 'As a matter of truth, Edith, I do. Just here.' He touched his rear. They both spluttered with laughter.

'What do you really feel?' she said.

'Oh, it's rather nice. I would rather like to think it is what you feel.'

'I suppose we will never know if it is like what I feel.'

'We do know one thing. We know it's satisfied by the same shape of thing.'

They both laughed.

'Only very occasionally though,' he added, seriously, 'do I feel this.'

'By "very occasionally" do you mean occasionally every day? Or every month?'

He made eyes at her in the mirror. 'Or occasionally every waking minute. No, seriously, every few months or so.' He took her hand and squeezed it reassuringly. 'But best of all, I want you, Edith. That's the best.'

She also wondered to herself if she ever wanted to have physical love his way.

At the door of the club, the shuddering recollection of the dreadful night went through her and she had to will herself down the steps. Entry was more supervised this time. They knocked, the peephole opened and they were scrutinised. Ambrose said something about the meeting and gave his name to the face at the peephole. This time he did not wear her fur-trimmed coat but wore his own everyday coat and hat over his dress, and they came in a taxi. Ambrose, discreetly, did not talk during the ride in the taxi. The bolt was drawn and the door opened to admit them. In the club the manager-owner, Mr

Follett, dressed in women's clothing and wig, recognised Edith and came over to her. He took both her hands and thanked her for returning and said something about her courage on the night.

Dressed as a woman, he was rather flamboyant.

'I took what seemed the only course of action. At the time,' she said to him. And for my distress, she thought, I now have a river named after me, which is one of the nicest things which has ever happened to me. The worst and the best that had happened to her in life so far had sprung from the same sordid source.

'You did more than that,' Mr Follett said sincerely.

The club was set up for a meeting with chairs in rows, rather than as a nightclub. Mr Follett seated them and brought them drinks.

She wondered how many of those in the club had witnessed her indignity that night. She knew Ambrose hadn't seen it and therefore it was likely that others hadn't seen it, but she would never know who knew and who did not know. Looking around, she saw others in the club who still bore signs of their injuries. Two had arms in slings.

The weirdness of the evening was heightened because of the formal seriousness of the discussion by men dressed as women and a couple of women dressed as men. Again, a few natural women like herself were there as themselves. Mr Huneeus was not present. She found that she was relieved to be in a meeting where, for once, she had no duties, and was almost invisible. Pity it was that she was not fully invisible.

'We appreciate your presence,' Mr Follett said, addressing the meeting, speaking with a normal male voice. It was all too bizarre.

'We made every endeavour to contact those who come to the club. As you would have seen at the door now, we are using the peephole more strictly — in future all guests to the club will have to be identified — and we have a mirror to view the street from the club. And we will have, not one, but two doormen, who will be armed with stout clubs.'

There were noises of approval. Everyone looked to the door and to the two unsmiling doormen who looked powerful and competent in bow ties and dinner suits.

One of the *travestis* said, 'I lay claim to the one on the left.'

Another said, 'I lay claim to both.'

There was some laughter, but the doormen didn't smile.

'Please, this is a serious meeting. Some amongst us are in the position to try discreetly to make sure that such a thing does not happen again. And to punish, in various unseen ways, those responsible for what happened that night.' Mr Follett then gave a malevolent smile, and added, 'Those so punished may never know they have been punished.'

There were knowing noises from members of the audience, and a light clapping of approval.

Edith was fascinated by this statement. It made graphic the fact that, in life, there were people who made decisions for or against us, who might be acting from punitive or other concealed reasons, about which we would never know. There were hidden gods. There were perhaps many such gods in any one person's life. 'For obvious reasons, we do not wish to bring police attention to the club.'

'I, myself, would be glad to invite any attention I can get,' said the *travesti* who had claimed both the doormen, in a stage falsetto voice. He was becoming the meeting comedian. Lessening tension. A few laughed. Mr Follett smiled, and said, 'Olivia, you get too much attention,' and then went on seriously: 'To put it another way, we do not wish to become a police file.'

He suggested that in future people leave the club in groups.

Ambrose asked if he could speak. He rose to his feet and said in his normal male voice that it was important the club members show they were not intimidated. They should go on with the activities of the club. However, it was also important that club members not provoke the Action Civique by flaunting their behaviour. Comings and goings, for instance, should be discreet, and he suggested with respect, that patrons leaving the club wear regular overcoats and hats, and so on.

'Darling, I wouldn't know how to be discreet,' Olivia said, drawing laughter, 'it goes against my nature.' Edith sensed that the audience felt Olivia was overtaxing its willingness to joke about the matter.

For the first time that evening, Edith also smiled. She realised that the sense of bizarreness which she'd felt up to now had dissipated and what was around her, and where she was, had become unexceptional, almost prosaic.

Mr Follett said he noted and he hoped others noted, and he hoped that Olivia noted, Carla's point, which he endorsed. Edith was surprised that Mr Follett knew Ambrose's *nom déguisée* and it awakened the feelings she'd had about Ambrose's evasiveness. That Ambrose had more to do with the club and everything about it than he'd told her. But she also decided to cease worrying about the club and Ambrose's murky connections. This was to be definitely her last visit.

Those who had been injured would be compensated from a members' fund which the club was starting with a donation of 1,000 francs. There were other details.

Free drinks and hors d'oeuvres were then handed around and Mr Follett's assistant manager announced that a diverting spectacle had been devised and would be performed.

Those club members who were to perform left the meeting

to prepare themselves. The chairs were pushed into clusters, tables brought out, and the meeting dissolved into a social evening. The Negro orchestra appeared and took their places. Other people were arriving now, perhaps having chosen to miss the meeting.

'Can we go now?' she asked Ambrose.

'Let's see the show.'

'I'm not sure I want to see the show.' She wanted to leave but remembered the menace which still hung about the club. Irritated, she realised she would have to wait for Ambrose as an escort.

The lights went down and the orchestra began to play. The curtain rose on the small stage.

There were uneasy giggles and appreciative gasps, as three of the cast danced on stage, costumed as Action Civique.

A voice in the audience shouted out in mock horror, 'Oh no. Who asked for an encore?'

Edith felt a clutching of her stomach as she saw the armbands, the black leather caps and the batons again. Ambrose gave a small sideways glance at her, as if checking to see that she was all right, and he took her hand.

Then on stage danced three pretty *travestis* who joined with the Action Civique actors in singing popular songs. After the singing, the female performers went into a salacious cabaret routine of grappling, resisting and dancing with the Action Civique, and then baring themselves, offering themselves. Edith was both riveted and chilled. She watched as those dressed as Action Civique went through a re-enactment of the lifting of dresses with the batons and the touching of the genitals with the batons, much, much play with batons, but with the *travestis* circumspectly keeping their backs turned to the audience.

351

They played out a funny sketch full of sexual innuendo where the Action Civique were vanquished with a repeated chorus line about 'men who needed batons'.

Edith thought that the spectacle had been well rehearsed. There were cries of 'show us' and eventually, as the finale, the girls did turn around, lifting their skirts and dresses to show their underwear and glimpses of their tucked away bulges.

Edith was glad the lights were down, because she had never seen anything as salacious as this. Taking another drink from the waiter, she drank deeply, seeking calm from the alcohol. She had heard of shows in Berlin and Paris. The atmosphere in the club was no longer prosaic. It was, she thought, very much an atmosphere of the times. During other events, she had felt that she was of the times. Being in Geneva she sometimes felt that, too. And now, in this cabaret, she felt it. The darker side of the times.

There was excessive applause from the audience, and the cast came back and took a bow, the Action Civique and the 'girls' of the cast linking arms. The lights came on.

Mr Follett thanked the audience again but said that as it was not a regular night for the club, the club would be closing now and he wished them all good night. He reminded any club patron who had suffered injury and medical expenses to give details to himself or to the assistant-manager.

She was relieved that the night was over.

As she and Ambrose stood up, Mr Follett came to them and said quietly that he would like to invite them upstairs to his apartment, for a nightcap drink and a chat, when the others had gone.

Edith rushed to say that really they had to go, and found that her voice wobbled from the drinks she'd had.

Mr Follett said, 'You are a heroine of mine, you were very

brave. I insist you honour me with your presence.'

Edith managed to say graciously, 'We were all heroines on that night.'

But she again felt an embarrassed worry about how much he had seen on the dreadful night. She now worried too about compromising the League by any closer involvement with the Molly Club. She glanced at Ambrose, hoping that he would extricate them from the invitation by saying that they had to go. He didn't. Instead, he enthusiastically accepted.

They waited, drinking, while the last few patrons, reluctant to leave, clinging to the evening, were eventually ushered out by the doormen, good-naturedly protesting as they went. Mr Follett went about putting out lights and collecting ashtrays. She and Ambrose finished their drinks in the emptied club and she felt, standing there, how the empty nightclub seemed to rebuff the presence of only one couple, as if one couple alone did not belong in a nightclub.

His duties finished, Mr Follett came to them and led them by an interior stairway at the back of the club up two flights to his apartment. He knocked on the door in a way that announced his arrival to whoever was inside the apartment. The door was opened by one of the young men who had acted as Action Civique in the show, and who was still in costume, and they went in. She and Ambrose were introduced and she was again praised for her courage. She said she would prefer now for that to be put behind them all.

'Agreed,' said Bernard Follett. 'Bernard Follett says that to laugh is to demolish.'

She thought, but did not say, that sometimes humour simply dodges.

It was a luxurious place, with well-chosen furniture and *objets d'art*. While Mr Follett fussed about drinks, she occupied herself by examining a bright blue screen which divided the room and which was decorated with golden peacocks whose tails reached from the top of the six-foot-high screen down to the floor in an oriental style.

She turned from the screens and screwed herself up to being sociable. The company of the smiling boy dressed as Action Civique caused an unsteady apprehension, an entwining of the pleasant and the unpleasant. He was a living sculpture of a threat and of her dread, now turned to a matter of play-acting, to a social ornament — for when she allowed her gaze to focus on him as a person, she could see that he was muscular and very handsome.

Music came from a gramophone. *The Firebird*. Bernard Follett began dancing with Ambrose, and she, by pressure of circumstance, danced with the Action Civique boy, who called himself Patrice.

The pairing into dancing couples seemed to happen so easily, so inescapably, although it became obvious to her that Ambrose was an attraction to both Bernard Follett and to Patrice. This at first surprised her but she had to remind herself that Ambrose, well, was very familiar to her, but that to them he was 'fresh', and when she looked at him through their eyes, she could see that he made a very attractive *travesti*. She also reminded herself that these men were not necessarily interested in a woman as a woman.

Patrice took something of a polite interest in her, although she felt she had to share it with his over-the-shoulder interest in Ambrose, but this interest was sufficient for her, for that night, and for the circumstances. She did not want, in any way, the burden of amorous attention.

The record on the gramophone came to an end and she

considered that she might let herself become drunk. Or she might not. She might get up from the sofa where she had now flopped, find her coat, and take her leave. Or she might not. But if she was simply contemplating 'getting up' while remaining seated, she was almost lost — that was a sure indication that her will was oozing away.

She might let herself be kissed by Patrice. Their eyes kept meeting each other's lips as they talked. Or she might not.

She would go now. Rising to her feet she asked Mr Follett to telephone the taxi depot and arrange for a taxi to be sent to the club.

'Of course.' He offered no argument.

Ambrose said he would go with her.

'Stay,' she said. 'Have a night out.'

'You don't mind?'

She smiled and shook her head. Their eyes met and registered that she was 'resigning' from the club. She was backing away from the club and all its works.

'I'll see you at the office,' she said. This told him that she was going to her own rooms.

He took her hand. 'Thank you, Edith. Again.'

Follett helped her into her coat and walked down the stairs with her to wait for the taxi.

The doormen were still putting things away.

'It is all right,' she said to Follett, 'I will wait here on my own.'

Follett told the doorman to see her to the taxi and he said good night and left her.

Shortly after, her taxi driver came to the door of the club and the doorman called to her.

In the taxi she wondered whether such things as the Molly

Club had happened in her parents' times. Her mind attempted to visualise what Ambrose might be doing back in Follett's apartment.

As she lay back in a late-night bath she thought to herself that she wouldn't be surprised if the night had indeed been, in Ambrose's word, cathartic. However she did not think that she would go back to the Molly Club.

Next day at lunch she asked Ambrose whether he'd had 'a good time'.

He smiled diffidently. 'Oh yes. Nothing wrong with a little Greek revelry. Once in a while.' She smiled, but without the confidence of knowing fully what she was smiling about. Nor did she wish to know more.

'As long as it's without moderation,' he added.

She asked him if he thought that there had been such clubs as the Molly in their parents' time.

Ambrose looked at her with his frown of amusement. 'As shocking as it may be, dear Edith, I believe that it happened also in our parents' time.'

'You think they were as wicked as us?'

'I do believe they were. Some of them.'

'How do you know?'

'Oh? I've seen the forbidden books of their time. And I hear tell.' Ambrose prattled on. 'We could die of etiquette. In fact, I knew a chap who died of etiquette. Death from good form, the coroner said. Need to break out now and then.'

She could tell that he was trying to be sure that she felt 'right' about it all.

What she felt glad of was that she had ventured into that dark world not as a place to live, but as a locale she had now visited and where she'd been able to glimpse more of the nature of things. Or perhaps, the de-naturing of things.

*

About three weeks after this strange night, Edith was walking along the rue de Berne when she saw the young man who had assaulted her. He was unloading boxes from a truck outside a store. He looked hot and miserable. She took off the glove of her right hand, walked over to him, and slapped his face.

His hand went to the slapped cheek and his eyes were dully uncomprehending, stunned.

She walked on, her knees a little shaky, but quite coolly replacing her glove. She thought that a few people had seen it. Not that it mattered.

The young man and she were not, in playground parlance, 'even' but it was something of a retribution.

It was said that revenge should be undertaken unemotionally if it is to be successful. She was not sure what her emotions had been at that moment of small revenge.

Confidence and the Giving

of Confidences

Sophie Langer, from the ILO, let the Drama Club use the big front room in her apartment for rehearsals, 'As long as I don't, as honorary President, have to sit through them.'

She'd also added, 'I will adjudicate tantrums only among nation states but never among theatrical types.'

But this night there were no rehearsals. Caroline Bailey was to read from her novel set at the League, and the drama club cast and supporters and a few outsiders were crammed into the big room. Rumours about the novel had been going around for months.

Caroline was a South African in her twenties, who tried to pass as English. She was only a filing clerk but was well educated and proud of her English accent, which Edith acknowledged was very good.

Caroline had masses of self-assurance and said she wasn't at all nervous about reading to an audience. She said she believed that stories were really meant to be read or recited and that she would do what Dickens did and, one day, tour, reading her work.

Edith sat on the floor of Sophie's big room next to Florence and Victoria, jammed in with the others, nearly all women. Ambrose would have nothing to do with it and some of the other men had been scared off from what they'd heard about the book. Perhaps everyone there secretly hoped to be in the book. Favourably. The lights went out and the audience sat in darkness for a minute or so. Then a reading light came on, revealing in half-light the face of Caroline who sat on a high-backed oak chair next to a table on which there was a vase containing a single red tulip, a water jug, a glass, the reading lamp, and her manuscript in a leather folder. She wore a shirt-blouse buttoned down the front, a large floppy bow tie, and a long jacket almost to her knees. Her hat was a striking stylised turban. It was all very theatrical but passed Edith's tests except for the tulip. Edith was still fascinated by seeing tulips and thought that they seemed to be made of wax.

Caroline opened her manuscript with studied care.

She looked up and around at her audience before speaking, as if she'd been told to do it. 'In this rendition, I intend to jump around a little in the story. It deals with my male character, Humphrey Hume — described in the opening pages of the novel as a "lanky young man who no rain could dismay and, despite his enthusiasm for work, was liked by everyone".' Caroline made herself pause here to collect laughter from the audience, which she did receive. She continued, 'Some of his colleagues are discussing him in the Office.' She cleared her throat, took a sip of water, and looked up from her manuscript.

For all her boasting about going on tour like Dickens, Caroline was shaking a little as she held the leather-bound manuscript.

She added to her introduction by saying, 'First, we learn something of Humphrey Hume from his colleague Barlow, less well loved.' She began reading. ' "Barlow was a Jew with a dolorous face. Long ago he had done something wrong, no one knew what, but everyone knew it was something dreadful, which had ruined a brilliant career and made him glad enough to use his trick of languages to earn his keep as a translator in the Office. His life had stopped when he did this dreadful thing, whatever it was, and now he led a posthumous existence, drinking a spectacular amount, and from time to time, just in time, in fact, doing a month's work in a night." '

There was uneasy laughter as people recognised, or thought they recognised, this character as Liverright. Some looked around in case he was there. Edith thought it a cruel portrayal. He and Caroline were friends although something might have gone wrong there.

Caroline continued, ' "It was odd to picture him eating, getting into his pyjamas, or shaving in the morning. It was as horrible as imagining a dead man doing these things. In the Office he appeared in character as 'that disgusting beast, Barlow', frightening the typists by talking innuendo to them in whatever might be their own tongue and rolling half-drunk about the corridors. Some of the men, especially Mr Whibley, used to drop in to see him, lured by the malevolent charm of his conversation, and his appalling comments on the lives of their colleagues. Sometimes he described alleged vices and practices among their colleagues so unnatural and far-fetched that if the Office had, in fact, held one single specimen who practised them, it would have been an unique organisation indeed." '

While many might have guessed that Barlow was Liverright, Edith alone thought she knew, perhaps along with Liverright, that some of the unnatural practices alluded to were not as far from the Office as Caroline thought. It was amusing that Caroline thought the unnatural practices existed only in Barlow's imagination. And Edith recalled meeting Liverright's malevolence on her first day.

' "Mr Whibley, monologist by nature, in Barlow's company humbly took the part of feeder. Now this name, now that, he placed the lamb or the goat in the jaws of his lion and sat back to hear the bones cracking. This time, he asked Barlow about Humphrey Hume. Barlow replied, 'He went to the War. A medical man. I don't somehow see him grinning behind a bayonet, but he was there, and no one, on either side, put a bullet into him. But it smashed him just the same, smashed his little soul. When it was over, there was nothing left and he dared not feel about in the dark for bits which might have been worth sticking together — he dared not. If you can imagine a dying man who thinks he can be cured by telling himself and his friends that he is quite well. Then, in the very nick, as I said, the politicians made this place, the Office, and he sprang to it, and pulled it round him, warm and comfortable, clerks and typewriters and committees and minutes and resolutions, and he lifted up his shaking voice and cried, "There shall be no more war!" Everyone said, "What an excellent young man!" They are still saying it; he looks fine, talks fine, feels fine, but *n'y touchez pas, il est brisé!*' " '

Victoria said to Edith in a whisper, 'Is Humphrey Hume Ambrose?'

She whispered back, 'I don't know. Could be.' The description of Hume could fit a few of the men who were in the Secretariat, especially the men who'd fought in the War. His being a medical doctor narrowed it somewhat.

Caroline went on. ' " 'And when will his crash come?' Mr Whibley asked Barlow.

' " 'Never,' said Barlow. 'He's saved. Got religion. The Office is his religion.'

' "Barlow sat smoking, a great bulk, staring with dull eyes at the patch of sky outside the window, surrounded by his own peculiar atmosphere of idleness, and defeat, and emptiness." '

Caroline looked up from her manuscript and said, 'We next meet Humphrey who has just returned from a disappointing interview with the Chief Secretary . . . "The moment had appeared to him ripe for intervention by the Office in a peculiarly abominable situation in the Near East. He had pressed his point with fervour. The Chief Secretary, of necessity, had listened with attention, since the ultimate responsibility for Humphrey's actions rested with him. He had been very kind, had agreed with Humphrey down to the last detail, and then, blandly, genially, almost as if he were continuing to agree, he had vetoed any action in the affair.

' " 'Too expensive,' he said. 'I'm sorry — as sorry as you are. We might do something' — by 'we' this time, he meant the British Government, not the Office — 'but any action on the Office's part would be resented by the French: not a hope of cooperation from them; and if they did not cooperate, none of the little fellows on the spot, who all look to the French, would do anything, and then where would we be? — but you've had your head too close to it these last weeks; you see it a little out of proportion.'

' " 'They've appealed to us for help,' urged Humphrey." '

There were titters at hearing Sir Eric and the procedures of the League presented so critically.

' " 'If you like, we can circulate these telegrams to the member governments without comment. I think we had better, and in acknowledging the telegrams, say they have been circulated.'

' " 'I should so much prefer — '

' " 'To do something, and explain later. Of course you would, it's perfectly natural; but I'm sorry, it's also perfectly impossible.'

' "Humphrey returned to his room and threw the pile of telegrams on the table and went and stood in the bay window overlooking the courtyard, and stared at the insipid lake with its transparent summer blue. It was the pale blue which little girls couple with pale pink as their favourite colours. He shifted his gaze to Captain Creighton-Downes's bull-terrier chained up in the courtyard." '

Again at the mention of the bull terrier, there were titters of recognition; everyone knew whose dog this was. Caroline looked out and smiled at the shared recognition, enjoying all signs of appreciation for whatever reason.

' "Humphrey tried patiently to accommodate himself to his disappointment, seeking with his agile mind for some sidelight of action. He yearned for the life of action. Instead he circulated telegrams." '

Edith smiled to herself as she recognised her own urges to a life of action but she didn't share Caroline's sneer at Sir Eric's decision. Caroline's was the typical view of someone who had no feel for political reality.

Caroline then turned pages. 'We move on now. Humphrey's in love with a woman named June who dies tragically in a mysterious operation.' Caroline paused, waiting for signs of recognition at the mention of this office scandal. There was a rustle of recognition — one of the girls from typing had died just before Edith'd come to the League. At the time, everyone said she had been trying to terminate her pregnancy. She'd been considered morally loose.

Caroline continued. 'This part is before she dies. It is set at a dance at Maxim's. I think we've all been there.' Chuckles of acknowledgement. 'Perhaps too often,' she added, again winning appreciative laughs.

' " ' You've come?' cried June, as Humphrey arrived at the dance. Among the heightened complexions and brutally emphasised prettiness of the other women, June looked, at first sight, almost plain. Her hair was not even tidy, and her dress was not suitable and was badly put on; she was careless. Then she tilted her head casually, and it was immediately obvious that beauty was the simplest thing in the world for her, and that her beauty was unlike anyone else's in the room. She laid her hand on the lapel of Humphrey's coat.

' " 'Dance the next with me,' she said.

' "The orchestra began to play a waltz, the 'Clair de lune', and the manager, according to his custom, obliterated the lights, all except the green ones.

' " 'Dance this with me,' repeated June in her alluring voice.

' "Humphrey, with a dazed smile, put his arm around her. She laid her head on his breast, and they moved away to the heaving tune.

' "Heaving, throbbing, almost breaking with emotion, the tune reverberated with a brazen laughter, and heaved and throbbed and almost broke again; under the green light, eyes gleamed out of the pools of darkness, lips were black and heavy, joined to the shadow they cast on the chin, and the arms of the women looked unearthly against the black sleeves of the men. The couples moved with close-pressed thighs and swooning looks and clung together as if they were united in the last intimacy of love." '

There were chuckles of embarrassed recognition at the dance hall behaviour. Caroline threw the room a quick smile.

' "The room grew very hot, but the music was merciless: forty francs per couple, and they got their money's worth. The manager appeared during one of the brief intervals followed by waiters carrying paper caps and toys and balloons on trays. Everyone shrieked with joy and the men fought to get toys for the women, and the women made the men put on paper caps." '

Caroline looked up and said that the romance between Humphrey Hume and June took off from here and ended tragically in the mysterious operation. She was enjoying saying the words 'mysterious operation'. She went on to read other sections about the allure of June, the office vamp, and its havoc on other men in the Office but most of all on Humphrey.

'After her death in the mysterious operation, Humphrey is devastated. The other men who had been involved with her all distance themselves and try to avoid being implicated. Humphrey, already a man broken by the War, cannot avoid showing his feelings when faced with this second catastrophe in his life. He alone publicly acknowledges his involvement with the girl by going to visit her in hospital at her final hour. Captain Downes, an old colleague from the War, also working at the Office, tries to look after Humphrey in the only way he knows, and takes him out on the lake in his boat.'

Again, titters of recognition.

'Finally, we meet Barlow again: " 'Downes thinks fresh air will cure anything,' said Barlow. 'Even a broken heart. And so it would; fresh air would cure Downes of anything. May I shut the window?' " '

There were peals of laughter at the mention of windows and fresh air as the audience willingly turned away from the unhappy part of the story. A struggle went on in the League offices between the those who wanted the windows open, usually the British and colonials, and the Continentals who wanted the windows closed. These tussles were called 'international incidents'. Last year one of the drama club sketches had shown a French man committing suicide by standing in a draught.

' " 'You may shut the window,' said Whibley. 'If you will take that red handkerchief off your throat.'

' " 'It isn't a handkerchief; it's a fine-quality scarf, worn for two reasons.'

' " 'What are they?' Mr Whibley had the curiosity to ask.

' " 'Loyalty to my political party, and loyalty to my body which I protect from draughts, and which I place above elegance.' Barlow looked down at his bulging waistcoat.

' " 'Ugh,' said Captain Downes. 'You don't really believe in that socialist stuff?'

' " 'Believe in it!' said Barlow. 'My dear man, you don't know our family. My elder brother is working with Lenin now. We are very proud of him. Mother says — '

' " 'Do you mean to tell me — ?' began Captain Downes.

' " 'Yes, we all played our little part in the business of 1917, but only Morris stayed on. Russian Jews, you know.'

' " 'I don't believe you,' said Captain Downes, red and flurried. 'You speak English as well as I do and Barlow isn't a Russian name.'

' " 'Nor a Jewish one and you'll hardly deny I'm a Jew, I suppose?' Barlow laid his forefinger pointedly against his nose. 'It's all right, Downes. I went to Oxford like the rest of us.' " '

Apart from allusions to the office scandal of the mysterious operation, the audience was enjoying the reading because it was, for some of them, a look into the world of the men of the League and some of the identifiable people from the *haute direction*.

' " 'Well, well, poor Hume!' Barlow said. 'He's going mad, cracking up. Of course, the fact is, we are all going mad here — some quickly, some slowly, but all going the same way; it's the departmental work, which is known to lead to insanity, and this appalling town where even the ordinary citizens are constantly going out of their minds.' " '

Again the audience broke into knowing laughter. Cursing Geneva was a favourite pastime.

' " 'Some of us take a drink, and some to women . . .' " '

'And some to men,' a woman's voice called out from the darkness, getting a few laughs. Everyone looked around to see who had called out, and Victoria whispered to Edith, 'Who said that?!'

Caroline ignored the interjecter. ' " ' . . . and others turn
to — but we won't go into that — and even Hume, even
he has stopped serving the cause and now runs after strange
gods.'

' "Barlow turned his opaque eyes on them questioningly.
'You don't know if we are all mad? Neither do I. Give my love
to Hume and tell him when he is over the worst, if he does get
over it, I know just the little girl for him, not mixed up with the
Office, *completement dévouée a son métier*, you know. There is
quite as much purchasable vice here as in Paris, whatever people
say. Only it's more expensive.'

' "Captain Downes sighed. This was what he hated most,
picking over and slandering a man who wasn't there, like a pack
of gossiping women." '

There was scornful laughter from the women in the
audience.

' "After Barlow had left the room, Mr Whibley said, 'I never
knew that Barlow minded about being Jew.'

' " ' Minded? Why the fellow was bragging about it,' Captain
Downes said, 'positively shoving it down our throats. And, pray
tell, who or what are these strange gods, to which he so know-
ingly refers?' " '

Caroline finished her reading, looked up and said, 'I thank
you for your kind attention. Good evening.' She closed the
manuscript, and theatrically turned off the light, leaving all in
darkness.

The audience applauded enthusiastically. Edith had never
realised that Liverright was Jewish. Apart from Liverright, she
had never met a Jew.

*

370

Later, over coffee in the Café du Siècle, Victoria, Florence and Edith discussed the reading. Florence and Victoria smoked cigarettes.

They were all stunned at the unsympathetic portrayal of Liverright.

'He'll be devastated,' Victoria said. 'Someone should warn him.' Victoria, who was stuck down in Registry and didn't see as much of office life as Edith and Florence did, felt it wasn't true to the life of the Secretariat. 'I mean, how could a woman know what men say when there're no women present? Unless she eavesdropped.' Victoria, who in her job spent all day reading other people's mail, would not condone eavesdropping, even for the sake of art.

Florence thought it was true to life, and liked the sniping at the Secretariat men. Florence was also sure that Humphrey was Ambrose — 'except his heart isn't broken,' she laughed, turning to Edith, 'and you didn't die "in a mysterious operation" .' She looked hard at Edith. 'Was Ambrose tangled up with her — June, the one who died? Before you, I mean.'

In reply, Edith simply shrugged. Ambrose had never mentioned any involvement with the typist. She was a little embarrassed at Florence's careless assumptions about her real life and the fiction of the book. She supposed that she hadn't really told all to Florence either, but she had tried hard to describe her feelings about Ambrose to her, of how it resembled love, but probably wasn't love. Florence had said that it was important to describe a thing correctly to oneself. If you described it as true love and it fell apart then you had a tragedy and had to act out a tragedy. If you described it as an affair and it fell apart, you could then simply describe it as an 'interesting chapter' in your life.

Victoria thought it was a picture of Ambrose to a point and she repeated her criticism that she couldn't see how a woman

371

like Caroline could know what men said when women weren't around.

Edith said that at the League the filing clerks and typists were invisible and the men didn't see them and talked as if they weren't there. 'As we become more important we become more visible.' She was also, in another part of her mind, wondering if Caroline knew more about Ambrose than she did, whether Ambrose had yet another secret life, and had been connected to the typist who died in the 'mysterious operation', although she knew that Ambrose was infertile and couldn't have caused the pregnancy which brought about her death. That would make his public identification with the dying girl more chivalrous.

Florence said, 'They're not invisible when they're pretty filing clerks and typists. Then they suffer from always being looked at.' They all laughed. 'Especially coming down the stairs.'

Victoria said she wished she wasn't so invisible and could 'suffer' being looked at. They laughed.

Florence broke in with more gossip. 'But it's Caroline who has the broken heart — surely you've heard that?' she said. 'That part of her is in Humphrey Hume. She came here to get away from her lover in England who jilted her. Jilted her very publicly.'

Victoria answered herself. 'I suppose she could ask men what they say to each other when we aren't there. But would she get an honest answer?' Victoria then turned to the gossip. 'You say her heart is broken? In Registry we miss all this. Even the messengers know more. Tell.'

'She was left standing at the altar. A church full of guests. Her work still suffers after all this time. She's been close to the sack too, for sloppy work. She writes away in this book in office time and mopes about her lost love. And makes mistakes in the office, as well as in life, it seems. She is the one suffering *brisée*. She can't get over it. Probably never will.'

They sat for a moment trying to contemplate the idea of a broken heart that never healed.

Edith said, 'I don't think calling it the Office instead of the League and referring to the Chief Secretary instead of Secretary-General, is going to fool anyone or get her off the hook if there are legal problems with the book.'

'She might have legal problems with Liverright,' Victoria said.

Edith also thought that Caroline showed no understanding of the subtleties of diplomacy. It was clear that Caroline was on the side of 'why can't we just get on and do it', the 'to hell with the stupid politicans' school of thinking. Edith had left that behind, although she still puzzled over how and where room could be made for initiative and drive and individualistic schemes and solutions within the League.

Victoria kept on, 'Humphrey wouldn't know what colours little girls like — that's a woman talking. And what does she mean when the character talks about unnatural acts and vices and so on? Harlots, I suppose,' she said, again answering herself.

Edith and Florence snorted. They were always laughing at Victoria, who expected it and played up to it.

'A little more than that, Victoria,' Florence said, in a worldly voice, husky from too much smoking.

'I suppose so.' But Victoria was obviously unable to imagine what additional unnatural acts there might be.

'I do wonder what strange gods Humphrey Hume could find in Geneva,' said Florence.

Edith was interested in Florence's remark. For all her so-called worldliness, Florence wasn't that far ahead of Victoria when it came to knowing about strange gods. The Molly Club, for instance. If that were a church of strange gods. Did Caroline Bailey know about the Molly Club?

'I will say that I think her book is better than *Ulysses*,' said Victoria, backhandedly.

They had all been reading James Joyce's *Ulysses* which someone had brought back from Paris, but Victoria had given up.

Edith was finding it hard going too but she was certainly going to push on and finish it, and defend it. Florence, of course, claimed to have read it all and to have loved it, which Edith found doubtful.

'Come off it, Victoria, *Ulysses* is a masterpiece,' Florence said.

'You've only read the scandalous bits,' Victoria said to Florence.

'Victoria, you reveal yourself. I thought you hadn't read it — how do you know about the scandalous bits?'

Victoria coloured. 'I can see why it's banned in England.'

'But not in France?'

'The French are too far gone,' Victoria said.

They all laughed.

Victoria said that she still felt that Caroline's book wasn't true to life. 'Life is much duller,' she said, really meaning it, but winning unintended laughter from Edith and Florence, which Victoria happily accepted. 'Well, life really is — much duller. My life is, at least. You two aren't in Registry.'

'You get to read everyone else's mail,' said Florence.

'Not the personal mail,' she said regretfully. 'Unless "opened in error".'

They laughed.

After a while, Victoria went home. She was always frightened, above all else, of 'not getting enough sleep'. Her daily anxiety centred on this — her conversations were often elaborate calculations of her nightly and weekly hours of sleep and of sleep 'lost'.

Although she liked Victoria, Edith was relieved to be alone with Florence, to be able to slacken from work talk to personal talk. Every person in a conversation changed the nature of that conversation.

'What did you really think of it?' Florence asked Edith after Victoria left.

'Oh, quite good. Weak on the science of politics. I wonder if she'll ever get it published?'

'She says that the Hogarth Press will publish it. That's the story she's put around.'

'Do you believe that?'

'That's what she's been saying. I think the book's trying to embellish life at the League with all those references to unnatural acts and strange gods. And the mysterious operation.' Edith felt troubled about keeping back from Florence her private knowledge of the Molly Club and also her secret life with Ambrose. She wanted also to talk about Jerome and what had happened in Paris. Keeping secrets made her feel dishonest with her friend. Secrets separated you from people. She no longer wanted secrets from Florence. It occurred to her also, that maybe Caroline hadn't been explicit about these things because she didn't really know of these things. Not in any detail. But Edith wanted to find out if others were finding the carnal life as strange as she was finding it and perhaps she wanted to boast a little.

'Geneva has its secrets, Florence.' It came out a little smugly.

'Oh really, Edith. You have a secret life?' Florence was teasing.

'As a matter of fact, Florence, I do know about one secret world. Here in Geneva.'

Florence blew a smoke ring towards her in playful disbelief.

'All right, I won't tell you.'

Florence stared at her and then said, 'Out with it, then. Tell me about Geneva's secret life.' Florence looked at her as if expecting an anticlimax.

'It's difficult because it involves others.' And that was a real problem — how much of Ambrose's secrets should she reveal? How to tell it without hurting him.

'Pooh to confidences. Tell me.'

'All right, but let's order some more coffee.'

'If you don't tell me everything I'll certainly not tell you any of my secrets. Best friends aren't supposed to have secrets.'

Edith's heart warmed at Florence's indirect declaration of deeper friendship. She sometimes felt inferior to Florence because of her self-assured ways and she'd noticed herself becoming somewhat jealous when Florence had outings and meals with others without her. She felt very happy that Florence now declared her as 'best friend'. Or 'a best friend' though maybe she was doing it only to get her to open up. 'I suppose we are best friends now,' Edith said, angling for further confirmation.

'Of course we are.'

'I'm truly glad, Florence.'

'Now get on with it — tell me that dark, secret story.'

Edith wanted to linger and savour their declaration of friendship. Wanted to give it time to set, to celebrate it, but Florence wanted to gallop on to the confidences. Edith now found herself frightened to tell because it might alter everything. It might blow up in her face. If she had Florence as a best friend, she did not need to win her by further confidences of an outlandish kind.

She'd gone too far to retreat. 'It's bizarre . . . I warn you.'

'Better still. God knows we need some of the bizarre in our lives. Caroline Bailey should have had more of the bizarre instead of all that coy hinting at strange gods and unnatural practices.' She snorted. 'If Caroline Bailey knows, she should tell. She's a milksop.'

'What I have to tell, Florence, is truly bizarre.'

'Edith! Tell it! For Heaven's sake, tell!'

'It's in strictest confidence.'

'Cross my heart and hope to die, stick a needle in my eye.' She went through this childhood ritual.

'Do Canadians say that? In Australia we say, cross my heart and spit my blood and hope to die.'

'All very interesting, but get on with it.'

'A male friend, who will remain nameless, from the Secretariat, took me to a club called the Molly Club.'

'Never heard of it. And you mean Ambrose took you.'

'I said I wasn't going to use names. This club doesn't advertise.'

Florence gave a knowing smile. 'What sort of club?'

'Be patient, Florence. Do you want to hear the story or not? This is a club for those who do not like being the way God made them.'

'Say that again?'

'*Travestis* — you know about those? Men who want to be women and women who want to be men. Actually it's not that simple, I've discovered.'

'Of course I know about *those* — but a club for them?'

Florence's voice betrayed that she was now outside her experience. 'Where is this club — what street?' She could tell that Florence was slowing the revelation to allow herself to digest it. 'So we have one in our Secretariat? A transvestite?' Edith realised that she hadn't quite been sure there was a word in English to describe them. But the way Florence said the word further told Edith that this was an unknown realm for her. 'How high up? And why you? Why did you go with him?'

Edith also realised that Florence thought that was the end of the story — that it ended there. 'I said that I wouldn't name any names. He likes to dress in women's clothes but I don't think he's a . . . transvestite? Is that the word?'

'But why you?'

Why her, indeed. 'Just say, I share his secret.'

'The secret being that he likes dressing up disguised as a woman?'

Ambrose would say it was the opposite of disguise. 'Because of this, he asked me to go.'

'Fancy dress?'

'Not quite.' She smilingly remembered herself having used that expression with Ambrose.

'Were other members of the Secretariat there?'

'I wouldn't know. You see, it's bizarre: everyone — everyone except me that is — nearly everyone was dressed as the opposite sex. It's a bit like a masked ball.'

'That's what it was then — a fancy-dress masked ball?'

'Nothing like a ball. There are two parts to my confession.'

'I want everything.' Florence's voice was both ravenous for the secrets, and at the same time beginning to sound resisting, as if she couldn't bear to be 'told' about something, couldn't bear being the one who didn't have prior knowledge of all things.

Edith could tell also that there was something resentful in Florence's voice which was a warning. A part of Florence did not want to hear any more. She saw that she wouldn't be able to tell all. 'The ugly bit is that while I was there at this club, the Action Civique came in and pushed people around, including me. They were very threatening and ugly and we had to flee. I was, in fact, assaulted.'

'They assaulted you? They always seem rather dashing to me when I've seen them on parade at the Place behind my pension.'

She could tell Florence was not quite believing her. 'They hit one of our party with a club — a Mr Huneeus, a former cabinet minister from Azerbaijan.'

Florence looked at Edith with some disbelief. 'You're making all this up.'

'When things became very dangerous, we ran for it.'

'It all sounds very far-fetched.'

'If you find that far-fetched, listen to this. Last month I was invited to the embassy of Azerbaijan — it's up in Servette. They named a river after me.'

'Edith! There's no such embassy.'

'It's a government-in-exile.'

'You're making this up! Why would they do that?' Florence was becoming almost grouchy now.

Edith ploughed on — what else could she do? — but she resolved to make it short. 'I missed a bit: when the Action Civique were pushing people around, they picked on Mr Huneeus, the Ambassador, and I stood in front of him to protect him. That's why they named the river after me.'

She flashingly recalled to herself the real ugliness of that evening, and a deep shudder passed through her. She saw that she couldn't bring herself to tell Florence about that particular ugliness yet. Maybe later in the night. 'He named the river after me because of that.'

'He doesn't have the authority. It's a Soviet republic.'

'It could one day be restored to independence.'

'And the League doesn't recognise them. They have been trying for years to get us to recognise them.'

'Florence, I don't care. I don't care whether Mr Huneeus is the King of Azerbaijan or whether he's an impostor or whether he's a waiter at the Bavaria — the point is that he made this gesture.'

'It's not the legitimate government.'

Florence had a leaning towards the Soviets. They did not share that.

'Do you want to hear the rest?' she smiled at Florence, trying to mollify her.

'There's more? I take it that you help your friend dress as a lady?'

'Yes. On this particular night he wore a tulle evening dress.'

'Your tulle evening dress with the sequins?'

'Yes,' Edith hesitated, 'my tulle evening dress.' Which perhaps would never seem the same again to her. She might give it to Ambrose.

This could be too much for Florence; she realised quite distinctly that she'd moved a great distance from Florence's experience. She doubted also whether she had the aplomb to tell it. But it would be a test, too, of the friendship. She had to share it. It was something she needed to tell another woman. She knew also, perversely, that she was boasting as well as sharing, boasting of her sophisticated other life. But she was hearing a caution bell ringing, that it was too bizarre and might cast her for ever in a bad light with Florence. Or the other possibility was that Florence would want to come to the club. That was a possible reaction. Yet if she could not predict Florence's reactions, then she did not know Florence that well yet. She did have difficulty seeing Florence at the Molly Club, but then she'd had difficulty seeing herself there. Florence had male escorts, and had confided a sexual experience. They had shared in a guarded and hinted way a curiosity about sexual matters, and when talking about herself, Florence always claimed to have been 'wild' back to Canada.

Florence then blurted out, 'Did you have an affair with this man in the dress?'

'Yes.'

'When he was dressed like that!'

'Yes.'

Florence stared at her. Edith could not read her expression.
Edith decided to leave the story at that. 'That's the story.
About the darker side of Geneva.' She laughed to bring the
confession to a close.

'I don't believe this. You're making it up. To compete with
Bailey's book.' An almost relieved smile came to Florence's face,
as she grasped at this idea.

'I'm not making it up.'

The smile went. 'Then you're becoming a neurasthenic.'

'It has been the strangest experience in my life and I told it
to you, to share it with you as a friend. As a gift. And to show
that bizarre things can happen here. Here in Geneva. Even to
me. I didn't go looking for it. Isn't that something of what
we're here for? On the Continent? To experience life?'

'Not that sort of experience and I don't want to share it.
You could hardly call me a Dismal Jane but I find it sordid.'

'I didn't find it sordid. I suppose it sounds sordid. Perhaps I
told it rather badly.'

Florence was certainly sounding like a Dismal Jane.

'Edith, I can't accept this. And your mother's only been dead
a matter of months. You are doing dirt on your womanhood.'

Edith didn't know what her mother's death had to do with
it. Edith was frightened at Florence's vehement recoil from her.
For a second, she considered saying that she'd made it all up.
Too late for that. 'Florence — it was just an escapade.' She was
now trying desperately to find a word to describe it that would
blow away the abhorrence which had leapt to Florence's mind.

'It's debasing. I'm a free thinker, Edith, but really, this is
going too far. What about your womanhood?'

Their voices were rising. 'My *womanhood*? Florence, this was
an escapade. I told you about it as experience of this strange

world.' Edith hated hearing herself disowning her life with Ambrose this way.

'I find it objectionable. You have besmirched your womanhood.'

'You don't have to worry about my womanhood, Florence. I'll look after my own womanhood.'

Florence's comment about womanhood struck her hard. It was just what she had not faced. What it meant, the incident about her sense of her own sex, being among those people. Perhaps she had gone beyond the pale. She felt herself tightening with tension. She wanted to get back to their warm friendship. She had tried to move from friendship to intimacy too fast and she'd offered the wrong confidences.

'Florence — it was an escapade.'

'You have humiliated yourself.'

Florence fished some money out of her purse and dumped it on the table.

'What are you doing!' she asked Florence, seeing only too well what Florence was doing. Her voice sounded assertive but inside she was plunging.

'I'm going,' Florence said coldly. 'I've heard more than I wanted to hear.'

'Stay, Florence, let me explain more . . .' She held up her hand to Florence but Florence walked away.

Edith found herself alone with smoke curling from a half-stubbed-out cigarette in the ashtray. At first she did not let herself understand what had happened. She sat there as if the departure of Florence had been as ordinary as the departure of Victoria. How odd. Good night, Florence.

She then let herself realise that she was sitting there rigidly alone, had not moved. Her mind tentatively opened again to the light of what had happened and she felt shock, social shock. She couldn't accept that Florence had walked out on her. After their avowal of friendship. She then looked to the door, expecting Florence to return any minute, having had second thoughts, to have realised that walking out was hurtful, to have begun to worry about their friendship.

Minutes went by and Florence did not return. The waiter came and asked if she wanted anything and she said no. What sort of friendship, then, was it? Worse, a second shock came rushing at her, a panic about the correctness of what Florence had said. Florence's words about the besmirching of her womanhood now ricocheted. She had been all too aware of the violation of the Action Civique. But what of the club itself? To be audience to nature debauched, and thus be, herself, debauched as a woman? She had trouble recalling the justifying pleasure of it now, sitting there in the Café du Siècle. She tried to find her way back to the legitimatising pleasure of it when she was with Ambrose. She felt she might cry. She had not told her secrets at all well. Nor fully. She had not told of Paris and Jerome which was what she had really wanted to tell. Yet on the other hand, nor had Florence waited to hear it out. Florence's manner had been against hearing the truth, had warded away the truth. She hadn't had the chance to tell Florence that she might never again listen to this siren song. Or was she trying to remake the situation and her true feelings in a way which would win Florence back? She had to state that, yes, that on that strange night with Jerome something within her had sung. The fault was that Florence by her tone, even before she left, had blocked her full confidences. She felt her hurt turning to resentment. How could Florence ride a high horse when she was herself so crafty? At the notion of 'defect of character', her spirit rebelled: she was not telling Florence about her 'defects of character' — she had been about to tell of a remarkable episode, sharing it. My God, she remembered giggling with Florence every time they ate spaghetti, because Florence once told her what the sound of cooked spaghetti and olive oil reminded her of. Florence was a hypocrite, a person who pretended to modern views but was really censoriously unchanging. Being 'wild' back in Canada was probably as innocent as being wild in Sydney. Had probably meant drinking beer from a bottle. Not wearing gloves.

She hoped that whatever her anger and whatever offence Florence had taken that she would still respect the confidence.

'May I join you? Are you alone?'

Edith looked up hoping to see Florence back, smiling, apologetic, but instead saw Caroline Bailey still in her striking turban and outfit.

'Yes.' Edith gestured at the chairs ungraciously.

Caroline Bailey, too, looked unhappy.

She forced herself to smile at Caroline. 'Congratulations, Caroline. It was a fine evening — your book is marvellous. We were all just saying it.' Edith gestured to indicate that there had been others.

'Would you mind if I ordered a drink? I feel wretched.'

'I'll have one with you. Whatever you're having.'

Caroline ordered three Scotches; two, evidently, for herself. Unless she expected someone else. She lit up a cigarette, offering one to Edith who declined. 'But, Caroline, you were marvellous — it was a first-rate show. You should be chuffed.'

'Everyone just went off. Left me. Sophie made me some tea and I had to sit with her and make dreary conversation about the dreary ILO, when I wanted to be with real people and have a drink. You're alone?'

'Yes, the others took an early night.' Edith realised that the drama club audience back at Sophie's might have snubbed

384

Caroline because of the book's revelations. Or more likely, no one thought to ask her to go with them to a café or wherever. 'People are probably shy of you, now that you're a novelist.'

'Do you think so? I think they're snubbing me. I think they were all put off by the book and think I went too far.'

'Robert Dole told me that the other journalists began behaving strangely to him when they knew he was writing a novel.'

'He's writing a novel too! The bookshops'll be flooded.'

'I doubt it.'

'A hundred novels about the League of Nations. Ugh. At least I have a publisher. The Hogarth Press are going to take it. I sent them a few chapters.'

'That's marvellous.'

'Don't tell anyone.'

'I'll keep your secret.'

'Don't tell Robert Dole — he'll send his book there and they'll take his rather than mine.'

'He wouldn't do that.'

'Yes, he would. Newspaper people.'

Edith saw dourly that she had been socially switched from tending to her own distress about Florence's behaviour to listening to the moaning of this temperamental, rather jumped-up young woman. Part of her mind continued to fret about whether she had truly lost Florence or whether it would all be healed in the morning.

'Did you really like my book?'

'I really did. I liked the way you showed the men finding out about each other's secret self. And the problem of the League itself taking a lead,' Edith added, scratching for something more to say.

Caroline lapped it up. 'Ambrose is your *friend*, isn't he?'

385

The implication was obvious. Why lie? 'Yes.'

'I suppose you recognised something of him in Humphrey Hume?'

'A little.'

'I don't draw exactly from life in my work. I am more an impressionist. You don't think he'll be angry?'

'I shouldn't think so. But how well do you know Ambrose?'

If it were Ambrose depicted in the book, Edith wondered, what had been his connection with the typist who died in the mysterious operation? More, what was his relationship to Caroline Bailey? He had mentioned her and her book once or twice. There was the trip to Paris together. Caroline was on the edge of the Bavaria crowd, but had never become a friend. Surely she hadn't gone to the Molly Club with Ambrose? Ambrose had said in some general way that he had not lived the life of a monk before she'd arrived in Geneva.

Caroline burbled on, 'I see him around the office, at the Bavaria. I move about, I see things. God, I hate this town. Did you like the bit about the insipid blue of the dreadful lake? I must be the first writer in history to criticise their sacred lake.'

Edith loved the lake. She knew all about the mysteries of the origins of lakes, springs, and artesian wells. 'Someone said that it was perfectly described, but maybe a man wouldn't describe it like that. It's more the way a woman might see it.' Was Caroline secretly observing her and Ambrose? Was their life, her life, revealed in the book, and about to come tumbling out for all to see?

Caroline was immediately defensive. 'The bit about pale blue and little girls coupling it with pale pink? Men have little sisters. Men know about these things.'

'I suppose that's right.'

Caroline seemed hurt. 'Little boys grow up with their sisters.'

'I didn't mean it as a serious criticism.'

'I think that it's perfectly all right for a man to think that. The lake reminded him of, say, the way his little sister would see it.'

'Of course.'

'Heavens, most of Chaucer's tales are about women or told by women. Have you read Chaucer? Anyhow, who cares. I'm going to live in Paris. When we were all down in Paris that time I went to the Café Certa. Where the surrealist crowd goes. I don't know what you were all doing.'

'Nothing much.' Edith enjoyed, in a joyless way, having her secret to herself. She half-listened to Caroline's frenzied talk, knowing that Caroline didn't want answers to the questions she threw out.

'Ambrose wasn't mixed up with the typist — the one who died?' Edith wanted answers.

'Wasn't he?' Caroline was being enigmatic.

'I'm asking you the question,' Edith said, keeping an over-friendly smile on her face.

'Every man in the section was mixed up with her.' Caroline kept glancing about her at the strangers in the café as if waiting for them to come over and congratulate her. 'I hate this city. And I hate this café.'

Edith decided to let it pass. Caroline was temperamental and restive and, for a writer, was not a person who seemed to care much about the precision of things.

Edith had to defend the League. 'You shouldn't be so hard on everyone.'

'The Secretariat is a toy shop of broken dolls. Everyone here is busted up somehow. That's what the book is about.'

Edith held back a sharp answer, remembering what Florence had said about Caroline's broken heart, which explained other things. And I, for one, she thought, am not a broken doll.

The Scotches came and Caroline threw both hers down, one-two, like a Boer, Edith thought. She watched to see how they affected her. They appeared not to affect her at all, yet.

'I have no faith,' Caroline said, and called to the waiter, 'Monsieur! *Encore, s'il vous plait.*' Edith said she didn't want another.

' "The road of excess leads to the Palace of Wisdom",' Caroline said. 'Let's hope Blake's right — but anyhow, at least you get the excess even if you don't get to the wisdom.'

Edith stored away this quote from Blake, smiling inwardly as she recognised it as part of Liverright's repertoire of quotations. Although she didn't believe excess led to wisdom, she might say it to Florence when she attempted a reconciliation tomorrow. She was finding Caroline objectionable. 'I think we have to learn to work with perplexity,' she said to her, wanting to say something much harsher.

'You think I don't understand?'

'I don't believe we should throw up our hands in horror. I think there are better things to do than that.'

'It's about time someone threw up their hands in horror. It's about time we all threw up our hands in horror. But my book's about more than that.'

'I wasn't thinking of your book so much. We were wondering what you meant by "strange gods"?'

'Nothing. I just like the expression — "strange gods" — I like the mystery of it. "Strange gods". Everyone is going to hate me when the book comes out.'

Edith struggled to be civil. 'You'll be the toast of quai Woodrow Wilson, although you were hard on Liverright. Don't you care what he feels?'

She giggled like a bad schoolgirl. 'I've read it out to him

and he doesn't give a damn. He's not that sort. Anyhow, by the time it comes out, I'll be back in Bloomsbury, I hope. Or Paris. Out of this bloody place. We must have a talk one day about "older men".'

Edith doubted that they would. 'Leonard Woolf owns the publishing company?'

'Leonard Woolf owns the Hogarth Press. He liked the book because he's interested in international matters. Don't know what Virginia thinks of it. Don't particularly care.'

Apart from Robert Dole, who hadn't yet published a book either, Caroline Bailey was the first author Edith had known. Though Caroline hadn't published anything she seemed closer to it than Robert Dole. Yet Robert Dole seemed more 'like' a writer. She wondered whether she was a 'writer' herself, having written eleven poems. None ever submitted for publication. She hadn't told anyone except Florence and hadn't shown anyone, including Florence, and now probably wouldn't.

'I'm cynical through and through,' Caroline said. 'To the core.'

'I'm not,' Edith said, stubbornly. 'In fact, I'm rather engrossed by it all.'

'Bully for you.'

'That's a little rude.'

'You said something earlier about me not using my intelligence. I found that rather rude. I think anyone who's not cynical isn't using their intelligence.'

Caroline Bailey looked around her in disgust at the café, Geneva, the League, the world. 'The most boring place on earth. And this café! Why do you all come to this wretched place?'

Edith kept herself in control. She wanted to find out what Caroline knew and didn't know. 'You made Geneva sound rather glamorous, with mentions of vice and dark practices and so on.'

'Oh, every town has *maisons closes* but this bloody city has them discreetly out of the city on the French border. Did you know that?' Caroline blew smoke out at Geneva, and said in a voice which sounded full of regret, as if talking about art museums or street markets, 'This town really doesn't have any true vice.'

'Your characters aren't being truthful then.'

Caroline looked at her with derision. 'You're a rather naïve woman for your age. About novels.'

Edith didn't respond, allowing a formal silence to settle. She did not know whether it was the reference to her age or to her naïvety which nettled her most but still, Caroline's rudeness was unsuccessful.

Caroline said dismissively, 'I thought, after the Paris trip, that you might be different from the rest of them. I thought your carry-on about the black woman singer was very astute.'

This came as a surprise to Edith, but she didn't want to talk with Caroline. 'I'm rather tired. I think I'll say good night.'

'Say good night then. Go along with all the rest. Bye bye.' Caroline rudely waved her hand in front of her face.

As Edith stood up, Caroline added offensively, 'Oh, by the way, you should be careful — they say you're becoming the office vamp, now that June-alias-Rose is dead.'

'Good night, Caroline.'

Edith gathered her things.

Caroline went on. 'I observe things. I see you vamping around those people at the top.' It was as if she would say anything to keep her there as company, did not want to be alone.

What Caroline was saying was astonishing to her but she wasn't going to stay to hear it.

Aware that she was, in a way, repeating Florence's behaviour, Edith worked out from the waiter's tickets how much she owed, took money from her purse, placed it on the table, and left.

At the door she glanced back to see the beturbanned Caroline looking about for the waiter, for another Scotch, no doubt. Edith wondered whether it was true that the road of excess led to the Palace of Wisdom. She hoped, for Caroline's sake, that it was.

As she walked home through the night, still cold although winter was almost gone, Edith felt miserable and alone. How could she possibly be a vamp? What exactly was a vamp? Is that how people saw her? She vaguely remembered Jerome calling her *belle vamp australienne*. But that had been friendly. Within the League she hadn't had intimate relations with anyone but Ambrose and considered that in the office she conducted herself with men in a pally, but correct, manner. Too pally, maybe? What she'd done for Sir Eric during the crisis wasn't vamping. That was comradeship. But Caroline's perception couldn't be trusted.

Together with this disconcerting idea, recklessly thrown at her by Caroline, there was still the earlier alarm from the unreconciled sense of herself, the sense of herself as daring, as having had a strange adventure in human passion, against the sense of her proper womanhood, about which Florence had so strongly reminded her. Somehow those had to be reconciled. Maybe her sense of womanhood was changing. Maybe some episodes which occurred in one's life could, in fact, be put aside from one's life, had no bearing on what one really was. Or were we the sum total of all that we allowed to happen to us? Were we made from everything that happened to us?

She arrived at another troubling thought. If her experiences were in fact 'untellable' to her friends, she was doomed to being a liar and a sneak with them, having those parts of her which she could not show. Or was there no obligation to tell all? What about if she married? When and how should she explain these things then? She realised that Ambrose was the only person on earth who truly knew her. And, of course, now Florence. Although Florence now 'knew' things about her, she didn't feel that Florence knew her — fairly.

That made her feel very much alone.

She thought of calling in on Ambrose and worming her way into his bed. But she saw herself, once there, beginning a cross-examination in the middle of the night about his connections with the typist who had the mysterious operation and died. That would be a nice way to end the night and anyhow she had the Disarmanent Preparatory Commission beginning tomorrow. At least she would not have to face Florence for a few days.

She used self-control and went home, having lost a friend, although deep in her heart she believed there would be reconciliation in the morning, a friend who had called her a neurasthenic, and on top of that, a silly young writer had called her naïve and also branded her as the office vamp. A top night, a real top night. She tried to smile away her fears with this flippant Ambrose-style expression, but she was, she saw suddenly, at risk in the world.

Pact of Peace

At the preparatory commission, Edith had changed the way the conference papers were placed. Instead of the conference papers being placed on the table blotters, she had them placed in specially carpentered stationery stands made from beech wood of the Jura.

She also instructed that bottled water *plat*, together with a crown seal bottle-opener, should be placed at each of the delegate seatings along with the usual carafes of water and glasses. As she gave the instructions to the catering officer she observed to herself that it was an instruction she would not have been able to even conjecture back home, where she had grown up knowing only of tap water and soda water. And, at times, safe water and unsafe water. And times of water shortage when the water became muddy. And the clear icy water in the winter creeks of the Pigeon House Range. Now that she thought about it, she smiled, even in Australia she had known of *assorted* waters. She stood in the winter gloom of the conference room, there in the Salle de la Réformation, her eyes running along the national designations, sure, once again, that little national flags would have been too much like a fête, unbusinesslike. She was pleased with her conference-table livery. Not pleased: triumphant.

'Why the bottled water? Everyone trusts the water here in Geneva,' Cooper asked as he came to her side and then quickly said, 'No, I withdraw that — no, I didn't ask that,' showing that he realised too late that Edith would have an answer.

She didn't look directly at Cooper but decided to give her

reasoning to him for the pleasure of hearing it for herself and for the pleasure of rubbing Cooper's nose in her method.

'Because, Cooper,' she said deliberately, 'some people do have a preference.'

She thought that was the least part of her rationale, though basic to it. So she went on, 'I want bottled water because it contributes to the gravity of the work.'

She turned to him with a poised smile. Cooper was again, she could see, wary and also admiring of her because he knew she marshalled herself well, although she could see that the relationship of bottled water to the gravity of an agenda required something of a leap in reasoning.

'And that, dear Cooper, also explains why we have the leather blotters instead of say, leatherette,' she continued, 'because the objects that people handle determine how they treat themselves, how they treat each other, and treat the things they are treating. The appropriate objects can cause people to be more contemplative.' Edith thought that didn't explain it fully either. 'Make people more fertile — ' wrong word; she didn't falter — 'more resourceful in themselves than they might otherwise be. To elevate their political emotions, Cooper. Some rooms, some chairs, even, I believe, coarsen political emotion.'

He held up his hands to say stop. 'All right, Berry, all right. I knew I shouldn't have asked. Thank you.'

Alcohol came to mind as something that coarsened politics. Especially in smoky hotel rooms. It did not always coarsen other situations. And her silk underwear came to mind, and champagne, champagne spilled onto her silk underwear, the dampness of the champagne showing up the skin of her body at that place, showing fleshly through the champagne dampened silk. She lingered on the effects of alcohol and how it heightened elegance at other times, at other more intimate places but how the drinking of alcohol always needed to be 'managed'. Then, businesslike, she hurried those thoughts on. It was that time of the month for her, when desire was heightened.

'It is the "crystal and silver or the brass and glass" principle,' she said, turning to Cooper, who was going about distributing papers, and who had indeed heard all this argument from her before.

'Remind me of that principle,' he called to her with a smile, as he moved away.

She repeated a story told to her by Ambrose of Lord Curzon who, when made Secretary of State, had told Ambrose that he wanted silver and crystal inkstands, not brass and glass. 'You see,' she said, reciting lightly to Cooper, 'for the commission, "My name is George Nathaniel Curzon, I am a most superior person". And "My name is Edith Campbell Berry, superior but capable also of being rather merry".'

'Very amusing,' he called from across the hall.

'Do you know what sort of inkstand Sir Eric has?'

'No.'

'Ivory and silver.' And I once used it.

'Well, of course, you and Sir Eric are special pals.'

This quip flooded her with connections and implications. She assumed he was simply referring to the special work she'd done for him during the admission of Germany. He wasn't the sort of person who would make a snide implication.

She'd opposed leatherette at the commission *pourparlers*. She had initiated, and sketched out for the carpenters, the upright stationery stands for each delegate so that a private screen and a working domain, was formed on the table immediately in front of each delegate. The conference papers she ranged within the stands, so that the heading of each document was visible. She put blank stationery there also. She had argued that delegates not only talked at a conference table, they wrote notes to themselves, to others, and sometimes they needed to be able to go on with other work when something was happening which did not occupy them — 'To write to loved ones, to write to mistresses, and other *notes diplomatiques*,' she had said, winning easy laughter from the men at the planning meeting. She had further proposed that the stationery holders also be designed, by her, to act as a temporary filing device for documents not under consideration.

Major Buxton said in opposition that the holders would create a partition between the delegates on each side of the table.

'Sometimes,' she had argued, thinking quickly, 'relief from the meeting of eyes is needed in conference rooms.' Again she was interested by how in argument her mind came up with an answer to questions which she had not before confronted. As a girl, she had also learned while helping her mother and the maid arrange for dinner parties that if you wished to discourage general conversation at a dinner table among people who may intensely disagree, you placed large flower arrangements in the centre of the table, which confined people to talk in twos and threes to those judiciously seated alongside each other, and not across the table. She believed that she had a surpassing grasp of the psychology of meetings. Why this should be so she could not say, except that her family had been a family of public life — all members of the family had been forever going to meetings, including the children from an early age. She had a surpassing grasp too of the tone of meetings and the gradations of those tones. She knew when and when *not* to have bottled water or a plain carafe of water. Cooper, unfortunately, might have learned that it was important sometimes to have bottled water. But he would never know when to have both.

'Finesse, Cooper, is the word. Finesse,' she called to him

across the hall to where he was distributing papers. That, indeed, was the word. And the Rule of Happy Latency applied. She also had finesse of touch, but you, Cooper, will never discover that of me. Or would he? She looked again at Cooper from this point of view, and confirmed yet again to herself that she would never be touched by him. They got along all right now at work, but no, he would never touch her. How immediately one knew that of another person. Although a vamp wouldn't know it. The whole world touched, and was touched, by a vamp. Maybe that proved she wasn't a vamp.

She turned to look afresh at the layout of the commission table and was elated. It was perhaps a masterwork. She had transferred her arts and ceremonies of home life to the League now that she had no real home life.

It was, after all, a preparatory meeting on the long march to disarmament. The import of it was that the preparatory commission involved the United States and also that the United States was now about to ratify the Kellogg–Briand Pact of Peace even though it had not joined the League. If the United States could be yoked by treaty to France it was, de facto, yoked to the League. Anyhow, all nations, League or not, would, she and the others predicted, sign the pact. And thus war as an instrument of international policy would be outlawed, if not ended. She now knew that it had been unsophisticated to believe that the Great War was the War to End All Wars, and this pact also corrected, to an extent, the grave errors of the Treaty of Versailles.

From a possessive loyalty to the League, she was disappointed that everything was not happening *within* the League but she was now learning to enjoy the craft of political solution: how for any given political predicament a political design and form of words could be found to meet it. She accepted now that the League was a working model for these things, a machine energising the good forces of the world, an example of how the craft could be practised at its highest level. If the Secretariat had no real power, it still had the power of example. Of settting standards. Standards contained values. She loved also the way new idiom evolved for each political situation and for each conference. So now the vogue word was 'outlaw' — to put war beyond the law. Even the term 'preparatory commission' had been invented. She loved it all and, standing there in the Salle de la Réformation, she prayed that her work would not ever be taken away from her. She feared, in the way she imagined someone in love might fear, that their loved one might be taken away by cruel fate.

She remained at the commission for an hour to watch her table livery at work. The delegates did use it as she predicted and no delegate changed the arrangements. All delegates drank from the bottled water. Some read the label of the bottle. She did wonder if they drank from it simply because it was 'there'?

As she walked to the Bavaria she felt pleasantly stateless. She thought that Geneva with its medley of languages helped people feel stateless. Someone had said that being in Geneva was being nowhere. Whatever she had shed of her nationality had been replaced with a sense of the momentousness which she drew from her work at the League. Though she was annoyed sometimes because people granted you the mystique of your nationality but couldn't see how you were international. And although opinion in the Secretariat was against the idea of the League being a super-state, she liked the idea. She now liked the idea of the League having its own flag and stamps and passports. Its diplomatic status. It was not going to adopt Esperanto or find its own language, but it did have its own vocabulary and it was making its own customs.

Harold Nicolson had said to her that being internationalist for him meant that he would have to stop using the word 'wogs'. She did not like the man. There was something deficient in his oh-so-civilised self.

Sometimes, too, she was left with the lonely feeling of being part of a new organisation which didn't yet have itself very well known. She yearned for the League to be stronger. Although when she showed the American millionaire James Forstall through the Secretariat at the Palais Wilson he'd said, 'You have taken over the biggest and best hotel in Geneva. That shows that the League means serious business. An organisation with a plant like this cannot fail. And back home we've outlawed slavery and we've outlawed the saloon — now let's outlaw war.'

She agreed that it was difficult to understand why it hadn't been thought of before.

Ambrose was waiting in the Bavaria. 'Sherry?' he asked.

She felt thirsty. 'Beer.'

'Beer! How queer to want beer. Local or what?'

'I suppose it's now permissible to order a German beer?'

'I suppose it is,' Ambrose said with mild surprise, and with a slight grumpiness, 'it may even become fashionable again.'

He called Maurice, the waiter.

'Pilsen or Munich?' Maurice asked, order pad and napkin so correctly held. German beer seemed never to have disappeared from the Bavaria. 'You come from thirsty work?'

She agreed with Maurice that she had indeed come from thirsty work. 'Munich, please — for the taste of Weimar.'

'Your best Munich *lager bier* for madam and a sherry for me,' Ambrose said. 'Remember, Edith, I am a child of the War. They cut down the oaks, remember.'

'The oaks?'

'In 1870 — the Germans cut down the oaks of France.'

She laughed at him.

He flared with irritation. 'Hell, Edith! There were atrocities. They did happen. The Germans did commit them — and within the first month of war. Dreadful things. Believe it or not, they are not like us at all.'

'Sorry.' She still sometimes forgot the consternation that Germany always caused in him.

He forced himself to recover immediately. He gave his wicked smile. 'Although, as you well know, I am very much a Weimar girl.'

'Indeed you are.'

The drinks arrived.

'A drink to — what?' Ambrose asked. 'The triumph of stationery stands?'

They touched glasses and drank.

He said to her, 'Did you get your bottled water?'

'Yes.'

'Good for you. You know the stationery stands and bottled water controversy resurfaced at the Directors' meeting today.'

'Ye gods!'

Ambrose mimicked McKinnon Wood: 'Is this proper *professional* concern with the work of the conference or is it an *excessive* womanly concern with unimportant detail?'

'He worries about women taking authority.'

'Sir Eric approved. On the basis of defending "delegation of duties". The Marquis Paulucci defended your good taste. It wasn't a big issue, Edith.'

'It's more than good taste,' she said, her voice rising. She also wondered testily what she and the Marquis had in common when it came to good taste.

'I know, I know. Be calm.'

'It's a question of *sense of occasion*. There's a case for pomp and circumstance. Bottled water isn't exactly pomp.'

'Sir Eric liked your stationery holder.'

'He did?'

'He wants one. You had better send one up first thing, And I want one.'

Since the morning of the shaving, she'd had peculiar sensations when Sir Eric showed any interest in her. She didn't know what to do with these sensations. It wasn't infatuation or anything like that, it was more a deep binding which had occurred but for which there were no real protocols of expression or progression. He hadn't come to her with any special tasks since then. It was as if he didn't know how to handle it either. She was thrilled that he wanted a stationery holder and that something of her would perhaps be on his desk. She wondered if this were a message for her from Sir Eric?

'Cooper tried to start the argument again today but gave up before combat.'

'He is a man who, in his mind, prepares constantly for engagement but refuses the engagement.'

'He was just being pally.'

Ambrose told her that Jacklin had opposed bottled water at conference tables in the future — 'might give the impression that the League is profligate'.

This did not deflate her too much.

During their drinks Robert Dole, the prickly English correspondent, came over and forced himself onto them. Dole was known as something of a naysayer. For Dole nothing could ever be innocent. When things were really as innocent as they seemed, people like Dole went badly wrong. He had no understanding of the cunning of integrity in human affairs, which had ways of escaping from the hands of those who tried to manipulate it.

As Dole arrived at their table, Edith noticed the way that

the ever-genial Ambrose avoided making a sitting space for Dole.

Dole leaned over their table. 'You know that the pact is really France trying to marry America,' he said. He went on to say that the Kellogg–Briand Pact, if signed, was simply France manipulating America into a military alliance disguised as a peace treaty. Dole was going about at present arguing that France was the real threat to the peace of the world.

They were trapped into chatter about the preparatory commission and Edith, as usual, started coolly enough but lost diplomatic restraint and became defensive, arguing in what she called her ill-behaved voice, which rose unpleasantly to just below a shrill. She said that even when countries pretended to obey international law they were, at the same time, inescapably recognising international law.

Ambrose placed a cautioning hand on her and she strove to get back her reserve and swallow down her shrillness.

After this unavailing exchange, she and Ambrose had a light meal and then went to his apartment even though it wasn't yet the week-end. She needed comforting. The falling out with Florence worried her. Dole unsettled her.

Ambrose took her head in his hands and spoke calmly to her. 'You must not be so visionary when talking with tipsy journalists. Even the smart ones like Dole — or especially the smart ones like Dole.'

'Even if Dole is right about the French motive, the French may find themselves captives of their pretence. Captives of the Pact.'

'Enough, Edith,' he said. 'Enough.'

She noticed that these days he tired easily of the business of the League.

He went to the Scotch bottle which stood on a butler's table with the soda siphon and poured them both a large one. She heard the hiss of the soda siphon and his deeply tired voice say, as he had so often, 'Edith, you give it all too much heart.'

She went over to him. 'Please — before we change the subject — you agree, don't you?' she said. 'Everyone agrees that since Locarno, and since the proven power of the League to settle conflicts — Germany in the League, and so on — you agree that things have never looked better?'

He smiled. 'I agree. It is a historical fact. Things have never looked better. But you must also keep a realpolitik view of things, Edith.'

'But that's my point!' she shouted at him. 'International accord is realpolitik! Why is it that only disagreement and secret treaties are seen as the realpolitik!'

'Yes, yes.' He pushed the drink at her.

'Mr Stresemann said it is now Sunday in the life of nations. If the German Minister of Foreign Affairs can say that, surely something has changed?'

'Drink your Scotch, Edith.'

Later, after the Scotch, lying in the dim pink-shaded light of his room, she did relax and she pulled Ambrose to her and ran her hand through his hair, undressing him in the manner that he liked, and she responded to his liking it, undressed him as she would a child, he standing arms raised as she pulled off his shirt, he surrendering to her ministrations, she marvelling once again that although Ambrose was older than she, both in years and worldliness, that age was dissolved and reversed and shifted by the elixir of sexuality. She began to undress, holding out her foot so that he could kneel and take off her shoes as he always did, kissing her feet. She put on her most sensual nightgown while he lay on the bed and watched, as a child might love to watch his mother change, although she, like a mother, revealed little of her body during the changing into the nightgown, she

405

held away discreetly the secret parts of her body he dearly loved to glimpse, if he could, but the peeping and not seeing was, she knew, what also aroused him, and then she came to the bed and sat on the bed, releasing her breast from her nightdress, cradling his head, raising him to her breast, and feeling him so naturally taking the nipple into his mouth, loving to surrender, loving to be released from all the roles of her working day, which she experienced with an intensity that, at times, was almost unendurable, and he also was released from the load of his work, and from himself. She felt the joy of their being able, as grown woman and grown man, to play the games they played, to be unashamed with lascivious words and with their hidden sexual games. She fondled him, pleasured his anus the way she had found he liked, felt herself moisten, and together they became calmly aroused, to the state where she would lie back and spread her legs wide, edging up her nightdress, welcoming him with her hands, guiding him into her, his mother. He calling to her as his mother. Then he would thrust himself into her in what was probably a fairly manly way. And he would sigh and she would peak, and he would flow into her in boyish spurts. In her clouded consciousness, she sensed that he was alive to the sequence and progression of her finishing, now that they knew each other so well, but it did not seem that he did it consciously, it did not seem that it was at all calculated; there was a charming physical harmony between them in their strange, uncommon coupling.

Next day at the Salle de la Réformation she was met by Cooper, whose face warned her to prepare for complications. His face said that Something Had Gone Wrong. She was annoyed that she hadn't been the first at the Salle that morning.

He followed her into the temporary administration office which they shared there at the Salle. She pulled off her gloves and leafed through the daily memoranda, waiting for him to speak. There was a note from Caroline Bailey which she opened and read while Cooper talked.

'You'll never guess what's happened.'

She abhorred that way of beginning a conversation.

'Tell me,' she said, without looking up from Caroline's note.

'Your stationery holders.'

Caroline Bailey had written apologising for her 'hysterical behaviour' in the Café du Siècle. Caroline asked her to forgive 'a very nervous and insecure young writer who was making her debut'. There was a postscript which said, 'I believe in the League.' Edith was touched and put the note in her handbag. She would go out of her way to make a friendly approach to Caroline. There was no apology from Florence.

She turned her attention fully to Cooper. 'What about my stationery holders?'

'Firstly, they're empty.'

'Empty? Why so?'

She sat down and looked at him, preparing herself for what he obviously felt was bad news for her.

'Empty. People took the stationery.'

'People? Took it? Locally employed staff? Who?'

She could see that Cooper was experiencing a confusion of feelings, maybe taking pleasure from her discomfort, but he was also being her superior and trying to show the concern of a senior for a junior in trouble.

'The delegates!' he said, with a small flourish.

This did not so much disconcert her as it won her interest. She looked at him. 'Tell me what happened.'

407

'The delegates took the stationery. At the conclusion of business last night. They took the stationery. Stuffed it in their bags.'

'All of it?'

'Pretty much all of it. But that's not all.'

He stood there, tight from having restrained himself enough to allow for another revelation. She could see he was intrigued too by the strangeness of what had happened as much as he was with trying to surprise her.

She said, 'We have more stationery. I'll replace it,' knowing, as she said it, that she'd talked too soon, that this was not an answer to what he was about to reveal to her.

'But other things have happened.'

'What else?' she asked, flatly. 'Tell it all, Cooper, what are you waiting for — a roll of drums?'

'Some took the blotters.'

She was genuinely intrigued. 'They took the leather blotters?'

'Some did. I won't say which nations. You can guess. But more . . .' He again paused, maybe trying to protect her, she thought, more than disconcert her. But he was always so ill-timed in his delivery of even the most surprising information, he usually managed to spill the amusement before it reached the table.

'Cooper, go on.'

'Some took the stationery holders!'

This more than confounded her. She did not want to show him that she was in any way unprepared for anything that could happen within the jurisdiction of her preparations. But this. This was confounding. Senior diplomats and members of parliament of some of the great nations had taken — stolen — League property? Or maybe it was more likely to be the advisers and aides and so on. She restrained herself from dashing to the meeting room to see for herself.

She now realised that she felt quite cold. I'm *shocked*, she thought. She looked back at Cooper who was watching her. This was not *his* problem, this was her part of things. I piss on you, Cooper, she thought to herself, wondering where that expression had sprung from. The Bavaria, no doubt. She used it not against Cooper, really, but against the world.

'I'll take a look, in due time. Thank you for telling me.'

'I say, Berry, I am sorry — but when you look at it another way it is a bit of a joke, isn't it? I mean, do we call the gendarmes or agents from Securitas? And then, you couldn't very well arrest the Latin chappies, could you?'

I piss on you, Cooper, she said to herself as incantation, I piss on you, piss on you, while acknowledging that in his clumsy way, he was trying to ease things. She got up. 'Thank you, Cooper.' She left the office to go to the main hall. He made to follow her. 'I won't need any help, thanks, Cooper. I'll work something out.'

The hall was empty save for a man in a dust coat working on a microphone. She was conscious that Cooper while not having accompanied her was now standing over at the far door, watching, concerned. Many of the blotters had gone, twelve of the stationery stands, nearly all the stationery. Even ashtrays were missing here and there. All the inkwells remained. At least they had not spilled the ink on the floor and taken those.

She could simply remove those stationery stands which were left and pretend that they'd never existed.

She *would not* pretend that they had never existed.

Edith felt weak.

It was true that most of the delegates to this preparatory commission were politicians and their assistants and military experts — not diplomats. She did not know if that made a difference. Still, only twelve of the stationery stands were missing.

She sent a messenger to stationery supplies and had the spare blotters sent across urgently. She had the replenishment stationery in the office there at the Salle de la Réformation but had not planned on them taking it all or using it all on the first day.

She tried to come up with a plan. I would imagine, she thought, that they will souvenir only one of each thing. She hated the aesthetic shallowness that 'souveniring' represented: a collection of things stolen — worse, usually things easily stolen. It was about as aesthetically discriminating as plunder. Well, those who took the stationery stands did show some taste. But the stationery stands she could not replace.

At the morning meeting of staff she could see that her conference table livery and the aftermath were a joke. They were mainly Disarmament section people, not Internal.

'You invited theft,' said Rosting, who was in charge of premises and house staff, 'you give people things so good, of course they steal. I will ask the President of today's session to request their return by 0900 Wednesday. I will be personally present to witness their return.'

Mustering what she hoped looked like *hauteur*, she said that it was perhaps, yes, almost certainly, the importance of this commission that had led to the incident. Yes. The delegates had taken memorials, commemorating the conference, because the objects taken were destined to be historic. She listened to herself with wonder.

'I anticipated that there would be, on such an historic occasion, the need for memorabilia. On all adventures, we instinctively seek trophies from strange or dangerous places. We have them around us to create a sense of life lived. These mementoes will go back to the countries of these people, to sit on desks in the offices of Ministers of State or in display cases of fine homes, and will speak the message not only of world disarmament but of the League.'

She marvelled at her facility — not to lie, but to articulate what had been thought somewhere in her head, but not consciously reasoned. She did not believe this to be duplicitous — more that some thinking went on in an unpremeditated way. Or, at least, had been meditated in some other part of the mind, well before the question ever came, and that this sort of reasoning did not necessarily pass across the front of the mind until needed. That was her explanation of it.

She marvelled that it contradicted her first wave of thinking of only an hour earlier and now replaced it. She now believed what she had just said about souvenirs being trophies of experience.

'I would ask that you not officially request the return of these objects — it is more important that they go to the countries of the delegates as part of our propaganda.'

She'd held their attention but she had something of a reputation now for this sort of speech. She was expected to come out with something novel.

'You have more of the elegant stands then?' Rosting asked, perhaps amused now, or careful not to take her on — because he had on other occasions and been trounced. 'You can replace them?'

She held her breath. 'Yes,' she lied.

'If you replace all without difficulty so that we are not embarrassed, so that the appearance of the hall is correct and complete, there is no problem — let's move on then. But another thing . . .' Rosting added, 'these stands — may I have one of those stands for my office? I also like mementoes.'

The others laughed.

'Of course, Rosting.' She smiled.

She was, she realised, also protecting the honour of the nations which had taken the things. She did not want scorn against those particular national delegates who came from countries not as rich or as sophisticated as others. And anyhow, there were European nations also incriminated. Although as far as she could see no English-speaking nation.

She excused herself and left. I am not only a liar, she thought, I lie myself into impossible situations.

She went around the Salle de la Réformation and noted down the countries which had taken the stationery stands. She then tried telephoning the personal secretaries and liaison officers in the guilty delegations, one by one, and explaining that there'd been a dreadful misunderstanding about the stationery stands. She got on to some of them. She said that of course the stationery stands could be taken as mementoes at the conclusion of the conference, but should remain in place in the Salle until then. She managed to get the cooperation of some of the culprits. She then took a taxi — for which she knew she would personally have to pay — and called at the hotels of those delegations and retrieved the stands.

Five of the delegates who had taken the stands were staying at the Hôtel Metropole, but she'd been unable to contact their secretaries.

Leaving the taxi waiting, she asked to see the hotel *chef de Securité* at the Metropole, a M. Dupont.

When he came to the lobby she recognised him from the Richemond and from Captain Strongbow's party. He looked at her as if trying to place her. She couldn't see that there was anything to be gained by reminding him of it.

She explained to M. Dupont that she well understood the

irregularity of her request but that she had to get into their rooms on League business. 'They have League property which I have to collect.'

She made vamp eyes at him. Yes, Caroline, there is a vamp in me somewhere.

He said that it was not proper to let her into the rooms.

She then showed him her League *carte de légitimation* from the Political Department of the Swiss government in Bern which was an important-looking thing.

He examined it.

'This is a matter of diplomatic urgency,' she said desperately. She watched his face and could see that the peace of the world being in balance made little impact on M. Dupont.

'They have madames running the League of Nations?'

'There are a few women,' she said, feeling that this might weaken matters in his eyes, 'but only a few.'

Then he grinned at her. 'They have cowgirls running the League of Nations too.'

She smiled and they were immediately old friends.

'A detective never forgets,' he said, pleased with himself.

He looked back to her *carte de légitimation*. He read all the writing on the card.

She added, in an unhappy voice, 'I could lose my position.'

At these words he did look at her with concern. He drew on his cigar, then said, 'You could recommend me for a job at the League of Nations? Yes?'

'A job! What sort of job, M. Dupont?'

'A job in the police of the League of Nations.'

'We don't have any police. Yet.' There had been talk of a League international police force.

'I hear they will make a police for the League of Nations.'

'There will be an international police force, yes, soon. I will

413

see that your name goes before the Secretary-General. Yes. Definitely.'

He looked at the burning end of his cigar, blew on it, and fiddled with the sodden mouth end. He had saliva at the corners of his mouth. She could tell he was a man who had trouble managing his saliva.

She looked away. Now she was appointing people to the League police force.

He took out a bunch of keys and they went to the rooms where he stood and watched while she retrieved the stationery holders herself. In one instance, from the valise of the delegate, where it had been guiltily hidden. She felt confident, reasoning that none of them were in a position officially to complain.

He asked if she'd heard of Captain Strongbow but she said she hadn't. 'I was at the party to see he paid his bill,' he said. 'He swore me in as a World Sheriff. I have a certificate somewhere. All nonsense.'

M. Dupont then realised something of what had happened with the stands. 'These great men steal these things?'

She looked at him ruefully, and nodded.

He laughed, coughing on his cigar. 'On these men, the future of the world rests?' He laughed for the rest of the time they were together, and repeated this a couple of times. She also recovered two blotters.

He helped her carry the things and found a floor bag in the kitchen into which she placed the holders.

At the hotel door, she smiled at him with immense gratitude and then, regardless of his saliva problem, she impulsively kissed him on the mouth.

He smiled at her for the first time.

He carried the bag of stationery stands to the waiting taxi

for her. She thanked M. Dupont again, realising that she had thanked him too many times already.

She returned to the Salle de la Réformation and placed them in position. Some of the delegation leaders would be surprised at the magical reappearance of the stationery holders. Perhaps the guilty ones would experience that delicious relief felt upon waking from a dream in which one had committed a criminal act.

She had it all in place for the afternoon plenary session and sat in her office trying not to crow; for some perverse reason she did not want to be in the hall when they saw the stands. She did not wish in any way to betray her concern.

She was sitting there when Jules brought a note to her.

It was from Robert Dole.

'Dole?' she looked at Jules.

'Dole is a true intellectual. He has the correct amount of melancholy and the correct amount of the ridiculous.'

She didn't need a character portrait from a messenger.

The note requested they meet in the Club de la Presse that day. He had, the note said, something to show her.

Jules stood there waiting for a return message.

'You aren't at the beck and call of reporters, Jules.'

Jules shrugged. She scribbled a note, reluctantly accepting the invitation. Though she was not a spokesman for the Disarmament section or the preparatory commission, she felt honourbound to face up to difficult thinkers such as Dole. She would be guarded but 'assisting and cooperative', as M. Avenol had advised them.

Then she thought, Oh God, Dole knows about the disappearance of the stationery stands. But surely that wasn't international news?

When they met she made the usual references to the rules

415

of their meeting, how she was not able to speak for the League.

'I know how correct you are, Edith Campbell Berry. But we must study statistics if you are to survive in this diplomatic business.'

He was a little drunk and trying to be playful, even courtly. She looked at him, at what Jeanne called his liquid brown eyes which she said denoted a 'seeking person'. 'I have already survived, Mr Dole, and the League has survived. And I value statistics above all things. Persuasive statistics.'

'Good.'

She had sherry. He had Scotch.

He took out some tables and showed them to her. They were French population figures.

'Let me explain.' He pointed at the charts. 'By 1933, France will begin a five-year period of sterility because the mothers born in the War years did not find husbands — those possible husbands are rotting dead in military cemeteries.'

Edith had a queer reaction to Dole's charts on the sterility of the French. She felt a clutch of concern for her own fertility, for her maternity. She had quite a strong private reaction to the words. She returned her attention to what Dole was saying.

So, he continued, following on this period of sterility the number of French boys at military age would drop by half. France was desperate to either disarm the world or to find a strong ally with lots of young boys — that was to be the United States. 'This so-called Kellogg–Briand pact to outlaw war is France's desperate effort to get itself a family of young boys. She is buying flesh.'

'Who is to say that a France which feels safe will not mean a world which feels safe?'

'It is a disguised military alliance with the United States against Germany — against whoever.'

'If that is true, it doesn't worry me. I think that non-aggression treaties between any two nations amount to renunci-ation of wars — one at a time,' she said.

This time with Dole she was not passionately shrill. She remained calmly conversational. She found her words coming to her, she kept breathing evenly. 'And surely you trust Briand?'

Dole said that Briand was the only Frenchman he trusted. 'It's the Quai d'Orsay that I do not trust.'

She concluded the discussion with Dole, thanked him for his lecture on the sterility of France.

He took her wrist. Her first reaction was what the waiters at the club would think. Pointedly, she looked down at his hand on her wrist.

He said, 'May I tell you a joke which is going around about the disarmament talks? You may have heard it.'

He kept holding her wrist and did not wait for her agreement to the telling of the joke. 'The lion looks sideways at the eagle and says wings must be abolished. The eagle looks at the bull and declares horns must be abolished. The bull looks at the tiger and says claws must be abolished. The Russian bear in his turn says, all claws, wings, and horns must be abolished. All that is necessary, says the Russian bear, is a universal embrace of fraternity.'

She had heard the joke before, but she paid the necessary polite smile and pulled her wrist out of his grip.

'What say another drink and dinner?' he said.

'No, thank you, Mr Dole.'

He took hold of her wrist again. This time she could not pull her arm free from his grip so she unbent his fingers from her wrist and with what she felt was a suitably diplomatic bow of her head, left.

He followed behind her to the door and caught up with her,

again taking her wrist. This time it raised her temper and she roughly prised away his fingers. 'Please, stop it, Mr Dole.'

Oddly, he said, 'Why do you recoil?' sounding surprised that she should remove his hand from her wrist.

As she went off she looked back from the footpath to where he stood in the doorway with his sheaf of documents. 'It's France we have to fear!' he cried to her.

As she walked away from the Club de la Presse, she paused and allowed herself to be calmed and refreshed by the swift flowing waters under the bridge. She again worried about the question of what was 'politically feasible', 'politically realistic'. The politically feasible often depended for its feasibility on those involved throwing their political weight. If enough people behaved as if it were feasible — threw their weight, so to speak — it became so. If they had the weight.

Something else occurred to her then, which interested her more, although she did not know what to do with it — Mr Dole wanted to convince her, to win her, and she found this pleased her vanity. She was being treated seriously by Mr Dole. It more than pleased her vanity, it caressed it. Staring down into the river waters, she realised a second thing. She realised how close she had been to succumbing to his physical approach. How could that be? The man was compelling. He had been trying to 'hold her' with all that wrist business, to stop her going away. And she had been on the edge of being dragged to his arms. He had not realised just how close. Nor had she, until now, staring down at the swift waters. Oh my God, she thought. In that regard, I know nothing about myself. Memories of Jerome, of the Molly Club swirled in the waters.

She continued walking back to the Palais Wilson, her face

burning with fright at her self-blindness and the turbulence of her day.

At the Secretariat lounge in the Palais Wilson, Ambrose, good old comfortable Ambrose, welcomed her.

She had another sherry. As she drank the sherry, she was able to tell Ambrose about the turbulence of her day. 'I stole back my stationery stands.'

'Bravo!'

'I won't name names. Not only the South Americans. As it turns out a few European diplomats of distinction had taken mementoes.'

'Really? Give me the names!'

'No names. And I took back two blotters as well.'

Ambrose broke into laughter and his laughter instantly freed her from the earnest agonies of her working day concerns. She told him of her magnificent defence of the souveniring. He was so good like this. No matter how much of a personal disaster a situation was Ambrose would say, 'What a romp', or 'How delicious', and it would dissolve.

She did not tell him of the infertility of France and the obvious potency of Mr Dole.

'Oh, and another thing,' she said.

'Yes?'

'M. Dupont, the Chef de Securité of the Metropole — I said I would get him a position in the League of Nation's police force.'

'Police force?' He laughed.

'I promised. It was an agreement.'

'For having done such a service to world peace, he deserves a position.'

'Will you write to him and say something encouraging?'

'I will write to him and say that if we ever form a police force, he shall be Commissioner in Chief.'

'I don't think he wants to be chief. Just detective will be enough.'

She told him how Captain Strongbow had sworn in M. Dupont as a world sheriff.

'Did he believe it?'

'Apparently not,' and then added, laughing, 'At the time I almost did.'

She again went back to his apartment and to bed.

After, as they lay still, she chattered about the Pact of Peace. Ambrose listened and then rose on an elbow to interrupt her.

'Edith, there is something of which you should be aware.' The boy-girl lover had gone and he was now diplomat and man. How extraordinary that the transformation could seem so natural.

'Yes?'

'I don't wish to quell your spirit — I admire your spirit — but there is a doctrine in international law which you should know. It is known as *rebus sic stantibus*.' Ambrose changed his tone of voice to pronounce the Latin.

She had done Latin at school but she did not know this expression. 'Which means?'

'Which means that the circumstances surrounding the treaty must continue to exist if that treaty is to continue to exist. You should always remember this.'

She said nothing, allowing the lesson to wander in her mind, searching for companionship among her many ideas. It was a more severe idea than the others she had stored away.

'Doesn't that mean that any pact can be abandoned whenever a nation has a whim?'

'Well, yes. Germany created the doctrine when she invaded

Belgium in 1914 after having pledged to respect the borders. She used the existence of a treaty as a military tactic. Put them off-guard.'

She found this idea disconcerting and she was not ready to talk about it.

On the third day of the commission she found Mr David Hunter Miller, one of the American team from the United States State Department, and had coffee with him at the kiosk across from the Salle de la Réformation. He was said to be an expert on treaties and said to be pro-League.

'You see,' the very scholarly American said, 'it is impossible to imagine a breach of this new pact which was not also a breach of the League Covenant. Consequence: like it or not, the United States is involved with the League and the League is involved with the United States.'

'Tell me how the Pact of Peace will work?'

He smiled gently. 'A crisis occurs. The United States is consulted by telegraphic exchange. Every one of the pact signatories, except the United States, is a member of the League. So at the same time that the pact is involved, the League becomes involved. Only a very rash and uncontrolled government would resist the United States and the Council of the League in combination. The pact is a psychological obstruction to war planning and then an obstruction to war itself.'

'Mr Dole is saying that it is really a military alliance between France and the United States.'

'I've read his pieces. He's wrong. The pact links the United States not to France but to the League and therefore to the world. It involves sanctions as well and it's accepted wisdom that the *fear* of sanctions, rather than sanctions themselves, will make

421

this work. Really, I see the great contribution of the League and this pact as being *delay*. The dragging out of a dispute without settlement.'

Edith expressed surprise.

He said, 'I know it sounds odd. To call this "peace". But peace is inactivity. There is little difference between a dispute without settlement and "settlement", as long as nothing is done about that dispute. The delay can become the status quo. The dispute often disappears.'

'An example?'

'An example: the dispute between Great Britain and the Argentine over the islands.'

Edith didn't know about this dispute.

Miller warmed to it, having obviously used it many times in his classrooms and elsewhere. 'The dispute has existed on paper since 1833. It remains an unsettled dispute. What characterises this dispute which should interest us?'

As if a bad student, Edith was without an answer.

He did not let her hang there in ignorance for long. 'Answer: it is a dispute which the lapse of time has neutralised. Nothing has happened.'

He paused, drinking from his iced tea, which he was having instead of coffee, to which he said he was opposed because he felt coffee was an addictive drug, which one day when other things were put aside the League might like to examine — the coffee trade, that is. With enthusiasm, he continued his exposition. 'The most significant change in international relations since the War has been . . . ?'

Edith shook her head, not wishing to guess.

'The substitution of the "conference" for diplomatic letters and notes.'

Edith's mind went to her stationery holders which had not disappeared again.

'It has introduced common sense into negotiation because a conference is a face-to-face affair. In any face-to-face situation, common sense will be present. If the Pact of Peace is signed, it will be perpetual. The parties are bound for ever. That is the big difference with this treaty. It is perpetual.'

She sat there with this idea, the perpetual treaty in collision with what Ambrose had taught her about *rebus sic stantibus*, not knowing what to do with this collision. She assumed Professor Miller and the State Department had taken it into consideration. She felt that it wasn't up to her to tell the Professor or the American State Department about *rebus sic stantibus*. She feared it might quell his ardour. The world needed American ardour and she didn't want to be responsible for quelling it when they seemed to be edging closer to the world community.

She wanted to believe Mr David Hunter Miller but *rebus sic stantibus* and Dole were haunting her. Dole remained in her mind, in his long-faced melancholy way.

Later that day in the Salle de la Réformation, she heard informally that the news from Paris was that the Kellogg–Briand Pact of Peace to outlaw war was assured of all signatories. Although this was not the business of her commission there in the Salle, it was of intense concern.

There was also a note of apology from Robert Dole on her desk. It had been a week of written apologies. Never had so many people desired her forgiveness. But no apology or acceptance had come from Florence.

In formal session she heard the President mention the Kellogg–Briand Pact but he warned the delegates that there was a danger in empty demonstrations of good intention. But he went on to say that according to information received by him personally that day the time of empty words was finished. 'It is now obvious,' he said, 'that the principal nations are persuaded at last that a frank renunciation of war as an instrument of national policy should be made.' He indicated that he had been informed that the final document would be drawn up and signatures affixed in Paris following ratification by the Congress of the United States.

There were hear, hears. Bravos. An outburst of clapping.

Disarmament would come next.

Edith was jubilant. And you can take the stationery stands, take home whatever you want, Edith cried out in herself, take the furniture. She remembered that she had to secure one stationery stand for Sir Eric and one for Ambrose. Rosting, she'd noticed, had taken one already.

Afterwards, clutching two stationery stands, she went to the Bavaria to find Ambrose and instead found Dole who was writing at a corner table.

'It is going to happen, Mr Dole,' she called to him as she pushed through the crowd.

'What is going to happen?' He was deep in self-preoccupation and, for whatever perverse reason, obviously had not been at the concluding meeting of the talks. 'What, Edith Campbell Berry, is going to happen?'

She tried to bring her voice to a level of diplomatic calm.

Unpredictably, she felt protective of the worried Mr Dole. She saw him as a person who was concerned, despite his strange thinking; she sensed her protective feelings had to do with her upbringing as a woman more than they had to do with Edith, the international diplomat. She felt sorry that she had to break the news to him and spoil his fearful view of things. 'There is going to be a renunciation of war, Mr Dole.'

He smiled at her. 'Ambrose Bierce said peace is a period of cheating between wars.'

'I see you are a follower of *rebus sic stantibus*,' she said, feeling that having said it for the first time, she had taken away its mightiness as a diplomatic dictum, and she felt that by saying it to Mr Dole she had neutralised him. She also saw, but pushed aside, that she was displaying it, seeking Mr Dole's approval. She must not sit with him. His gaze was transfixing and his manner always reached out at her.

'*Rebus sic stantibus*,' Dole repeated, looked up at her again, focusing on her, smiling with approval, 'I am relieved that you know *rebus sic stantibus*, Edith Berry, very much relieved.' He returned to his drink. 'Very much relieved.'

'Mr Dole, you miss the importance of all this. For the first time, nations are *talking* like this. Don't you see? And the circumstances surrounding this pact will continue to exist. A change has happened in the psychology of the world. That is what has happened, Mr Dole.'

He did not seem convinced.

'And here — here is a memento of this historic occasion,' and she gave him one of the stationery stands.

He took it, surprised and pleased. He turned it around, admiringly.

'I thank you, Edith Berry. And once again I apologise, not for my position, but for my ungentlemanly behaviour. I trust you got my note?'

She nodded.

'I was trying to make someone listen,' he mumbled, obviously finding it hard to say.

'I listened, Mr Dole.'

She broke away from his gaze and left him to find Ambrose.

'They are going to do it,' she said.

425

'I heard. It was buzzing all over the Palais an hour ago.'

'Buy some champagne.'

'I will.'

Edith reminded herself that history was 'being made' and she was where it was being made. She laughed wryly at her contribution to history — stationery stands and bottled waters.

That night even the Bavaria was ebullient, even the journalists. Except for poor Robert Dole.

Holding the Fort:

The Night Sacco and Vanzetti Died

On the day that Sacco and Vanzetti were executed in Boston, Edith suffered an intermittent discomforting anxiety, which was weakly opposed by a barely enjoyable probity. She had refused to sign a petition protesting their conviction, which she still believed to be a correct stand, but now, as the day of their execution arrived, the atmosphere of publicly expressed outrage, even in Geneva, had disturbed her, making her feel distantly, but morally, implicated in their execution.

All along she'd had none of the emotional involvement in the American anarchists' fate — she was too conservative — but she was against capital punishment and felt for the men. But frankly, her moral calendar was full and she'd had all the human tribulation she could handle in the day to day life of the League. More than that, for her the anarchist and communist attitudes were, like those of the Action Civique, out of step with the spirit of Locarno and the negotiating spirit of the League — out of step with history. And they seemed to hate the League. She felt they were a creation of impatience. The politics of impatient outrage. She could sympathise with those emotions but they were driven by a belief that for every problem there was a dramatic and violent solution. Or any sort of solution. She had a deeper conviction that procedures and attitudes could be evolved that extracted the poison from disagreement. She had a fantasy that there was always a formulation which could give painless compromise, if one only had the time.

Individuals were defeated and gave up, but the League went

on. Always adjourn, never give up. She wanted things to be arranged in such a way as to bring about those political conditions which avoided intolerable and brutal choices.

She couldn't find anything very civilised in the reports she had about Russia.

She'd been at a lunch at the Expatriates' Club where they'd had one of the drivers from the Russian Auto Trial as guest speaker. The auto trial had been run by the Soviet government to test cars for Russian conditions and went through St Petersburg–Moscow–Tiflis and back — 5,000 kms. More than any foreigners had seen of Russia recently. He said that after nearly ten years of Communist rule the country was primitive and the people badly treated, which contradicted the propaganda put out by the Soviet government. Eight nationalities were represented among the drivers and those who survived were unanimous about the wretched treatment of the Soviet people. One of the jokes that the driver had heard from the Russian people was: 'We had 200 bad years under the Ivans, then 300 bad years under the Romanovs — now we shall have 400 bad years under the Soviets.'

She dismissed the desire to abolish all government; what was needed was more people involved in more kinds of government — not the absence of government. Governing and arranging our lives, from the art of the domestic to the universal, was what life was all about. That was the truly Great Experiment. She had been in a conversation with Sir Arthur Salter, Director of Financial Section, one of the best financial brains that the League had, and he'd pointed out that since the Great War, prosperity had been regained and parliamentary government was spreading and everything seemed to point to the emerging of a civilisation much richer than anything the world had known.

Nor was she a pacifist. She knew there was a time for taking up arms against evil. She knew that there were times for citizens to go into armed rebellion against grossly unjust government. But she was against the use of political violence within a properly working country.

A month earlier, when Caroline and Liverright had approached her to sign the petition at lunch in the office restaurant, wine glasses and *pichet* in hand, it caused her great discomfort to resist their social pressures. In the office restaurant at a busy lunchtime was not the way to handle political matters.

'Put your name on this,' Caroline said with a smile, pushing the petition across to her.

'One day, come the revolution, the names on this petition will be hallowed,' Liverright said with mock solemnity, 'and those who are not on it will be . . .' He made a throat-cutting gesture, and poured out what must have been his third glass of lunchtime wine.

'Ah, the revolutionaries of the League,' she joked back at them. 'Let me see what you're up to.'

She read through the petition and then pushed it back to them, smiling. 'Petitions are not my cup of tea.'

'This is a very special petition. Two men's lives depend on this petition,' Caroline said determinedly, out of character with her usual flippancy about life.

Liverright said half-seriously, 'If you don't, you'll be vilified by history.' He could never say anything with much conviction.

'How could I possibly know whether they're innocent?'

'The American system is politically prejudiced against the radical . . .' said Liverright, repeating it as a formula, again without conviction, drinking from his wine glass as if to wash down the words.

She liked them both now. From her first day, Liverright had attracted her and had, in a diffident way, courted her for a short time. She felt that his political posturing came from some Viennese despair. With Caroline, it was a personal anger which came, perhaps, from her broken heart. Her anger came and went. Some days she was against all politics and called herself whatever was the fashionable artistic label, surrealist or whatever. Edith couldn't understand why they were still going around together after what Caroline had written about Liverright in her novel.

Edith glanced around to see who was listening to the conversation, and was relieved that it was not being attended to by the whole table. On the other hand, across the room sat Florence. Usually she would be eating lunch with Florence but they still hadn't made up after the night of the reading. It looked as though they might never make up. They were avoiding each other.

'I am afraid I can't sign.'

'Because of your neutrality and all that?' Caroline said at her.

That was in her mind, but to hide behind it would be cowardly too. 'Not only that,' she said. 'If I felt strongly about it, I would disregard that.'

'You don't want to protest about two simple people like this being put to death?'

'I would sign something against the electric chair. I would sign something against a corrupt legal system, if I knew it were corrupt.'

'Sign it because you're against electric chairs,' said Liverright.

'The petition says "we protest the innocence" of these people. I don't know if they're innocent.'

'Come on,' Caroline said to Liverright, 'Edith's not with us.'

There was something intimidating in the situation, an implication that her refusing to sign would cut her out of their lives altogether for ever more. Just when she and Caroline were beginning to become friends. She had even shown Caroline some of her poems. The first person to ever read them. Not even Ambrose had seen them.

'Let me see it again,' she said weakly, and took the petition and read it again. It said that the people who signed the petition 'knew' that the two men were innocent and that they had not been given a fair trial. She didn't know either of these things and had no way of finding out. She really wished she could sign and be part of the emotional flow of things, or be sociable, which was a silly way of looking at it. They were part of her crowd. She looked through the list of others who'd signed, nearly everyone at their level. Florence. Even Ambrose, who was at a higher level, had signed it. She felt weakened by the loss of her friendship with Florence. She couldn't see Victoria's name on it.

'Jeanne has signed twice.' She pointed this out to them.

'We'll cross out one,' said Caroline.

'Jeanne feels twice as strongly as most people,' said Liverright.

'No, I can't sign this.'

'Even if they're guilty,' Liverright said, 'it's an economic crime — not a crime against people.'

'They're accused of killing people.'

'Come on,' Caroline said to Liverright, 'we can't torture her into signing.' They moved off, Liverright carrying the petition and the wine glass and the *pichet*, marching behind Caroline. He turned and gave her a smile behind Caroline's back. She watched them go over to Florence's table and sit down, laughing. What had Florence told people about the night of the reading? She doubted that Florence could get the words out to tell and then wouldn't be believed. It would sound like maliciousness. She hoped.

*

The refusal to sign the petition had been a month ago. Now she was suffering remorse and that wasn't just. Why should she suffer because she'd been sensible? It wasn't that she lacked compassion. She felt sickened by the executions. For the last month, Caroline had worn a black armband, although Liverright had not gone along with that. He was reported as saying that if he began wearing a black armband every day he felt grief, he might as well wear one all the time.

On the day of the execution she avoided Caroline and avoided going to the restaurant for lunch. She was skulking in her office when Miss Figgis, Dame Rachel's secretary, came in and asked her if she would like to attend a slide talk at the International Students' Union that night because they'd heard an Australian student would be at the meeting. Australian students were so rare in Geneva and they were usually lonely. She eagerly said, yes, for the company.

At the meeting, she introduced herself to the student but he wasn't that lonely. His family were in Geneva, his father was attached to a bank there, and consequently, she had no patriotic duties to perform with him. She was rather disappointed that he wasn't lonely, although he was a little young to drag along to the Bavaria or Maxim's.

A few of the students wanted to talk about the Sacco and Vanzetti case but, as the matter came up, Dame Rachel said firmly that she had been invited there to talk about Traffic in Women and Children. Those who wanted to talk about other matters should go elsewhere. No students left the meeting, probably for mixed reasons — Traffic in Women and Children being a rather notorious subject because of its titillating references. The students, all men except for two women, had probably heard that Dame Rachel's talk included lantern slides of girls who'd been sold into Baghdad licensed houses. The talk went well.

They were driving back to the League garage when they came across a crowd blocking the road at the Hôtel Beau-Rivage. Coolly without a word, Miss Figgis swung into the rue Plantamour to avoid it.

'What's it all about?' Dame Rachel asked.

Edith knew immediately — Sacco and Vanzetti. They were probably after her for not having signed the petition.

'It's probably to do with the wretched Sacco thing.' Miss Figgis said the word 'wretched' in such a British way you weren't sure whether she was annoyed at Sacco and Vanzetti or the American legal system or the Issue or the crowd or what. Just annoyed at being inconvenienced, at being diverted from her own mission.

'Poor devils,' said Dame Rachel.

Again, Edith didn't know whether she meant Sacco and Vanzetti or the crowd in the street.

'I think it's me they want,' she tried to joke. 'I didn't sign the petition.' Maybe they'd both signed it.

'It was poorly worded,' Miss Figgis said. 'Nor did I.'

That cheered her. Dame Rachel didn't comment.

They encountered another angry crowd further along rue Plantamour. The crowd was shouting slogans against America and the capitalists.

'Oh dear,' said Dame Rachel. 'They *are* angry.'

Miss Figgis turned again, into the rue des Paquis. A few decently dressed men flagged them down.

'Shall I stop?' asked Miss Figgis. 'They don't seem to be part of the rabble.'

'See what they can tell us,' said Dame Rachel. 'Yes, they seem not to be part of the mob.'

Miss Figgis pulled up without stopping the engine and wound the window halfway down. The men were agitated, and

435

warned them to get out of Geneva because the rioters were burning down all things American. The American garage where the motor-car was usually housed was on fire. The men said that the rioters were attacking any American manufactured motor-car, which theirs was.

Dame Rachel leaned forward and thanked the men. 'Wind up the window,' she said to Miss Figgis. 'We shall not retreat to the countryside simply because we drive a Ford motor-car.'

It sounded a very attractive idea on a summer's night. Edith had to stop herself saying, 'Why not?'

'Figgis, drive to the Palais Wilson. We'll put the car there.'

Miss Figgis was driving very well under the strain. Even relishing it, it seemed to Edith. Maybe it reminded her of driving ambulances during the War. Edith was not relishing it.

They got to rue Butini and drove in through the open gates and Miss Figgis parked the motor-car.

'Park over there in the dark corner,' Dame Rachel instructed. Miss Figgis started up the motor-car again and moved it.

The concierge came out with a man from Securitas and the concierge's dog, a St Bernard named Volkerbund, who would be useless as protection.

'What is his name?' Dame Rachel said to Miss Figgis, sotto voce.

'Volkerbund,' Miss Figgis replied, sotto voce.

'I know the name of the dog. What is the name of the concierge?'

'I don't remember.'

She looked at Edith. Edith shook her head. Edith patted the dog.

Dame Rachel turned to the concierge. 'Close the gates, man. There are rioters about in the streets.'

'I don't think the gates can be closed,' the concierge said. 'There's a problem with the hinges.'

Of course the gates couldn't be closed, thought Edith. Fate will hound me to my very last refuge, to my very own office.

'Well, get inside and bolt the doors.' The man from Securitas and the concierge moved off to do this. Dame Rachel suggested that they make their way to her and Miss Figgis' apartment in rue Plantamour. Before they could go, they heard the smashing of glass from the other side of the building near the lake-side door, and moving quickly, they followed the concierge and the Securitas man into the Palais, bolting the door behind them. The smashing was coming from the library and they ran along the corridor to see what damage was being done. The noise sounded fearful and the dog hid under a table.

The crowd had gathered out in quai Woodrow Wilson and was throwing stones through the Glass-room and the library windows.

'I think we'd better stay here in the building, Dame Rachel,' Edith said, saying to herself, 'and accept our fate.'

'I think so, too,' said Dame Rachel quietly. 'This is no *manifestation* — this is full-blown riot.' She spoke as if she'd experienced everything in the way of angry crowds.

'I have a pistol,' the concierge said.

Edith thought of her pistol back in her room, now more an ornament and memento than a weapon. This was perhaps the very occasion Captain Strongbow had given it to her for. And she didn't have it.

'Maybe it will come to that,' Dame Rachel said, as the concierge went to get his pistol.

'I should've signed the petition,' Edith said as a kind of gallows humour.

'What?' asked Dame Rachel urgently. 'What did you say?'

'Nothing, Dame Rachel. Just thinking aloud,' said Edith. 'Praying.'

'Where are the police?' Miss Figgis said.

'Obviously not outside our building,' Dame Rachel said.

Edith looked out. 'The rioters have entered the courtyard.'

'Get down the fire hose,' Miss Figgis ordered the Securitas man. 'If they set fire to things or if they come in — flush them out.' The Securitas man seemed to be considering his position. Miss Figgis said impatiently, 'No matter. I'll do it. Leave it to me.' Miss Figgis took the fire hose nozzle, and began unreeling the hose. 'I'll take some of the fire out of them.'

Edith peered again. 'They're not all men — there are women throwing stones too.' A thousand angry eyes. She wondered if Liverright and Caroline were out there. Surely not. Whatever their posturing, they wouldn't stone the League.

Without fear, Miss Figgis went to the window, dragging the hose by its nozzle. 'Men or women — I'll hose them all.'

The concierge kept pointing his small pistol out at the crowd but it seemed ineffectual.

The crowd swarmed in the grounds of the Secretariat.

Stones broke the glass of the front door, a flying splinter catching Edith's thumb.

'I've been hit.' She said it more to herself. She backed away towards the interior light and bent down, trying to see how badly she was cut.

Miss Figgis dropped the hose and came across to her, gripped her wrist and examined it. 'Move inside and sit down. I'll get the first-aid box.'

'Why us?' Edith asked, holding her wrist tightly to staunch the bleeding.

Miss Figgis returned with the first-aid box from the infirmary and began to swab and bind her wound with the proficiency of a nurse.

'From minute to minute, a crowd has no reliable information; they're rife with rumour,' Dame Rachel said coolly, again speaking as if she had had much to do with such crowds and civic disturbances. 'And they are rarely sensibly led. Have the police been rung on the telephone?'

The man from Securitas said that he had tried but the gendarme post did not answer. Dame Rachel looked at him with some disbelief. 'Call the fire brigade. Call *les pompiers*, man.'

'Or the military,' Miss Figgis added. Miss Figgis seemed ready for a fight.

Dame Rachel looked out at the crowd through an unbroken window, her hands cupped at her eyes. 'They harm their cause,' she said, sadly. 'Put furniture against the door.'

The Securitas man came back and said the fire brigade were not answering either.

'They are probably fighting the fire at the American garage,' Dame Rachel said, 'or they've bolted to the countryside.'

She and Miss Figgis began to move a desk against the door.

A fearful sense of being abandoned and in danger came over the five of them. The stones were smashing in. They huddled back from the splintering glass, yet staying where they could keep the rioters partly in view.

'Upstairs,' ordered Dame Rachel.

The damage was now quite bad. The candelabra in the lobby were being smashed by stones.

'Call Huston,' Dame Rachel said. 'You people watch the doors. Where are the police? Where are any of the authorities? Figgis, turn the hose on them if they come in.'

'I have every intention,' said Miss Figgis who had again taken up the hose.

'Should we put on the lights?' Edith suggested. 'Maybe indicate that people are here. Get the dog out?'

'Show our flag?' said Dame Rachel.

'Yes. Show the flag.'

'Wouldn't that give them a target? Defiance might incite,' Dame Rachel said, looking at her with full attention. She then looked at the two men but realised that they were not offering opinions. She turned again to Edith, 'No. You are right. We should reveal ourselves and take the consequences. They might be more careful if they knew we were here. Or they might turn and run. Put on the lights. Show yourselves.' Turning to the concierge she said, 'Don't call Huston. Call Monsieur Munier. Huston is an American and it would be unwise for him to arrive here.'

Edith recalled an incident from a novel by Mrs Gaskell, *North and South*, where the heroine threw herself between the crowd and Thornton the hero during an angry riot in the industrial town of Milton. They had no Mr Thornton who could go and address the crowd. But they had Dame Rachel.

She recalled her father telling her how Colonel Ingersoll had thrown himself in front of President Garfield to stop Guiteau's bullet. It had shown that Rationalists could be both patriotic and brave.

Maybe Dame Rachel would go out and address the crowd. Edith would throw herself between Dame Rachel and the crowd. That was the least she could do for not having signed the wretched petition. She could place herself between the crowd and Dame Rachel and take the stoning and the blows that fell upon her. Obeying Dame Rachel, Edith went about turning on lights. Figgis dragged out the dog, strengthening it with encouraging words and references to duty.

The concierge returned to say that M. Munier did not reply.

440

Dame Rachel swore. 'I'll call Sir Eric.' She went off, and, after a while, returned. 'He will try to raise the police through higher channels.'

Edith said to her, 'I'll show myself on the front balcony.'

'We'll all show ourselves,' said Dame Rachel.

'I'm the tallest and the youngest,' Edith said, and before they could stop her, she opened the smashed glass door and stepped out onto the balcony.

She heard both Dame Rachel and Figgis call to her to come back in. Peering out at the crowd again, Edith said in a reporting-back voice, 'They seem to be moving down towards the Paquis.'

Dame Rachel and Figgis then joined her on the balcony with Dame Rachel saying, 'We will face them together.'

Figgis dragged the dog with her. 'Teamwork,' said Figgis, 'face them as a unit.'

Edith wondered what they would do if the rioters turned on them or stones began to stike them. Stand until they fell bleeding to the ground? She thought about what she might say to the rioters; the only words that came to her were a forfeit from childhood play: 'Bow to the wittiest, kneel to the prettiest, kiss the one you love the most.' Or maybe 'stone the one you hate the most'. She thought it might work simply by being so dumbfounding. She began to put it into French.

The rioters, however, had turned away and were streaming down quai Woodrow Wilson.

'Bravo. It worked,' said Dame Rachel. 'Well done. Good move, Berry.'

Edith's own observation was that the rioters had not seen them and had been moving before she'd stepped out. Dame Rachel and she stood on the front steps, resolutely in the military 'at ease' stance, hands behind their backs, feet apart, side by side, facing out at the enemy. Figgis held the dog by the collar. The dog looked the part but she could see that it was quivering.

Quiet settled about the building and the night. The two men now joined them.

They all stood in the sudden silence for a few minutes.

'All's quiet,' announced Dame Rachel. 'Everyone inside.'

They went back in and secured the door by pushing the table against it.

Edith helped Miss Figgis to begin cleaning away some of the glass.

'No, leave it,' Dame Rachel said, 'leave it for the repair men.'

'I'll make tea,' said Miss Figgis, putting down the broom. 'I think we could all do with a cup.'

They sat around drinking their tea with the concierge, M. Bochut, and the Securitas man, M. Louis. The five of them felt great camaraderie, an emotion which Edith found strengthening. Dame Rachel sent Figgis up to their office to get a bottle of cognac and they each had a glass. Dame Rachel had two glasses. Every now and then, Miss Figgis went to the window and inspected the outside darkness.

At about eleven-thirty, they decided the League was not threatened and left, with the Securitas man seeing them home, 'or vice versa', as Dame Rachel muttered.

At home in her rooms, Edith locked the door and began to shake for the first time since the riot. It was her first violent crowd. She had a sherry which made her feel queasy after the cognac. She lay on the Wilson chair, not yet ready to go to bed. She wished they had turned the hose on the rioters. Drenched them. Done something. That had been the problem. They had not retaliated. If only they had fought back, she might have felt less uncomfortably charged up.

Soon she drifted towards sleep and fell into her bed.

Next day, they each wrote an account of what had happened for Sir Eric, who said that a report would have to go to Council and to all member states.

As she was writing her account, Dame Rachel came to her office. 'Morning, Berry, how's that thumb?'

'Fine. No pain.' She held it up. It still had Miss Figgis' bandage on it.

'Take the day off and get that dressing changed. Or go down and show it to Joshi or Westwood. I am saying in my report that you behaved with bravery and presence of mind. You did. And I thank you. Do you wish to take the rest of the day off?'

Edith shook her head.

'Good woman.' With that, Dame Rachel departed.

She thought about the night of the Molly Club riot. Maybe she was courageous. Audacity was better. Although General Pétain said that the art of audacity was knowing when not to be. Sir Eric telephoned her and thanked her for defending the Palais. He, too, suggested she take the day off. She declined again. When talking to her, his voice began as that of the Secretary-General but changed as he spoke and became quieter and more personal as, she supposed, they both remembered their special morning together. Whenever they spoke now, she thought, that morning would pass silently through their minds.

Ambrose came to see her, and as the word of the riot got around the building, a couple of others rang to see how she was. Cooper brought Joshi along and fussed about while Joshi redressed the thumb.

'I do my best work on mosquito bites,' said Joshi, 'but I'll see what I can do.'

Victoria came up with flowers from the Registry staff.

She had a minute then to think about what Dame Rachel had said about bravery. She did feel that she had perhaps been

443

brave at the Molly Club but she didn't see how she had shown any virtue at the riot — it didn't feel like 'virtue'. It was, she saw, in her nature to be cool in the face of disorder. It seemed wrong to accept praise for what was in one's nature rather than an act requiring one to surmount one's nature. She went around to see Dame Rachel. And she had seen the crowd moving away before she'd stepped out on to the balcony.

'I don't think what you said about me being "courageous" is accurate. One does not take credit for good upbringing.'

Dame Rachel was taken aback. 'It was, I suppose,' she said, 'platitudinous, it could be more fully described. I can see that, now. I respect you for raising it, Berry, you are quite unusual. But I have to say you did not panic, you kept your post, you came up with a plan, and you carried it through. You accept that?'

Edith considered this. 'Yes.'

'Now, what else? I could say that you made observations of the riot and you reported coolly on the state of play?'

That seemed accurate. 'Yes. Thank you.'

'I do think all that could be called "bravery".'

Edith stood there and then said, 'Not quite.'

Edith went back to her office.

Robert Dole called her on the telephone and wanted to come and talk. She didn't feel that she could handle Mr Dole today. She said that she couldn't issue statements, he should know that. He said he would get the official statement but Sir Eric had suggested he talk with her as an 'eye' witness.

Sir Eric. She relented. 'As long as you don't put my name in the story.'

Later that morning in her office, she talked with Dole. He commented on her thumb and she shrugged it off.

'You're a very correct person, Miss Berry.'

'I try to be a good officer.'

'Are you "correct" outside the office?'

'Oh, definitely.' How could she say that so readily and with such conviction? She wasn't that 'incorrect' either.

'I heard that, in future, there will be a permanent police guard placed in the League building,' he said.

'I haven't heard that.'

'It would be breaching the League's diplomatic status.'

'I suppose it would.'

'The Swiss would put a spy in, of course.'

'I suppose so.' She couldn't see why they'd bother. 'Why?'

'Everyone believes that something is being hidden from them.'

Mr Dole had a reporter's view of the world.

She said, 'I suppose that because something is hidden from you doesn't mean that it is important to you.'

'I would like to decide for myself what is important to me.'

'No more secrets?'

'I'd be against letting in the Swiss if I were Secretary-General.'

Edith said, 'My position would be that if Dame Rachel, Miss Figgis, and I can keep an angry crowd at bay, why do we need police?'

He laughed. 'Let me quote you in my story.' She'd made the melancholy Mr Dole laugh. She flushed with pleasure. 'I don't know you well,' he said, 'but if I were in a crowd I wouldn't tangle with Miss Figgis or Dame Rachel. But especially Miss Figgis.' He laughed again. 'But what about the twenty police who helped you?'

'Twenty police?'

'I was told there were twenty police defending the quai Woodrow Wilson.'

'Not while we were there. Who said that?'

445

'No?' He wrote in his book.

'They must have arrived after it was all over. After Sir Eric called them. When we were stoned we had no police. Just ourselves. And a St Bernard dog.'

'You know they wrecked Maxim's?'

'Maxim's! But why?'

'Because of the sign saying American Bar. They burned that too. They struck wherever they saw the word American. Even American Express.'

'Ye gods. Still, the League doesn't have anything to do with America and they attacked us.'

'I think the crowd probably thought of it as President Wilson's summer place. Quai Woodrow Wilson and so on. They looted the bar at Maxim's.'

'Drank it dry?'

'In my story, I said "looted". But yes, they drank it dry. Regardless of the nationality of the liquor. A few of your people were there and had to be rescued by the police.'

'Anyone I might know?'

He looked up his notebooks. 'James Gibson?'

She shook her head.

'Caroline Bailey and Howard Liverright — you know them — and a couple from the ILO.'

'Caroline Bailey and Liverright were at Maxim's last night?'

'Yes. Liverright in his usual state.'

'Were they rioting or roistering?'

'They were among those rescued.'

'How delicious.' She laughed this time.

'Let me in on your joke.'

She shook her head. 'Tell me, did people try to stop them looting Maxim's or any of the places? Did anyone appeal to the crowd?'

'People were injured at Maxim's. Bernard the maître d' came out and tried to stop them. He was hit with something. Anyhow, we'll all sleep more soundly tonight — the Federal Government has called in three battalions of Swiss Infantry.'

'Is it that serious?'

'There's rioting in every capital of Europe, maybe every capital of the world.'

She was stunned. She had not realised that it was such an issue.

'Did you see Vanzetti's final statement?' he asked.

'No.'

He took a cable from his briefcase and read from it: ' "Never in our full life could we hope to do such work for tolerance, for justice, for man's understanding of man as now we do by accident. Our words . . ." '

She stopped him. 'I don't want to hear it.' She felt sick again.

He folded up the cable and put it away. He wanted to talk more about Sacco and Vanzetti. 'Did you people sign the petition which went around?'

'How do you mean, "you people"?'

'League people. Officers like you.'

She pondered whether she could answer that. 'I can't really answer for everyone.'

'Did you sign it?'

'No.'

'Why not?'

'Isn't that a matter of personal conscience?'

'Yes. But may I ask — as a matter of personal curiosity?'

She told him her reasons.

'I agree with you.'

'That's a comfort.' It came out more drily than she meant. Was she learning from Caroline? He took it that way and blushed, which interested her. 'Why is it such a big issue?' she asked him.

'Sometimes cases like this seem to get through all the glitter and frivolity of the times. Express all our political frustrations, I suppose. Cases like the Dreyfus affair. They come to stand for things. It's difficult to guess what case will excite the political imagination. Sacco and Vanzetti, though, like Giordano Bruno and Francisco Ferrer, will never be forgotten.'

'It doesn't mean that what people choose to take up is correct?'

'I think not.'

He offered to buy her lunch. She declined. Although they had both made each other laugh, he was still a man with whom she couldn't yet feel at ease. Although while talking with him now she'd realised for the first time that he was only a few years older than she. She'd always thought of him as much older. As he was leaving, she asked him if Ambrose had been at Maxim's. He shook his head.

'What about Florence Travers?'

He looked into his book. 'No.'

She didn't know why, but she was relieved that Florence wasn't with Caroline and Howard. She didn't want to feel ganged-up on. 'There were a couple of diplomatic chaps. A Mr Huneeus claiming to be from the Azerbaijan Embassy.'

'Really?'

'You know him?'

'Professionally. Was he hurt?'

'He was. He was hit by something.'

Poor Mr Huneeus. Maybe he was destined to be hit. She couldn't be everywhere at once.

As he made ready to go, she said, 'You'd better read out their statement to me. I should hear it all, I suppose.

'If you wish.' He got it out again. ' "Never in our full life could we hope to do such work for tolerance, for justice, for man's understanding of man as now we do by accident. Our words, our lives, lives of a good shoemaker and a poor fish peddler — all. This last moment belongs to us — this agony is our triumph." '

They sat in silence.

'Vanzetti said that,' he added.

Edith was moved but did not let go of her sense that she was still fundamentally correct in her behaviour.

'It's a cruel world,' she said.

'Yes. For good shoemakers and poor fish peddlers especially.'

'Do you think they're innocent?'

He smiled darkly. 'That we will never know.'

After he left, Edith sat in sadness for a while. Then she did some work and her mood lifted.

Just before lunch she strolled around to Caroline's office in Précis-writing to razz her about Maxim's. She looked into her office. 'Well, Caroline, how was Maxim's last night? The dance orchestra in good form?'

Caroline grinned wryly. She said she'd heard that Edith had had an adventure as well. 'How's your thumb? I was going to call you.'

'All right. Miss Figgis took care of it.'

'It will probably fall off. Seeing that you're the heroine of the hour, let me buy you lunch.'

'Why, thank you. I'm meeting Ambrose down there, is that all right?'

'Of course.' Caroline got her handbag. 'You must tell me your story. I don't agree with rioting. Bad form.' She was a more subdued Caroline. The experience at Maxim's must have been ugly for her. There was some sort of apology in Caroline's manner and offer.

In response, Edith relinquished her slightly gloating tone, and said soberly, 'You must tell me your story. I hear Maxim's was wrecked.'

'When they start smashing bars and dance halls, I'm against it,' Caroline said, trying for her more usual sardonic tone, linking her arm with Edith's. 'And when they hurt my friend's thumb.'

Edith found she was pleased to be claimed by Caroline as a friend.

They looked at the damage on the way to the restaurant and Edith pointed things out. As they entered the basement restaurant, Edith heard Joshi call for three cheers and she was given a small cheer from the tables of eaters. Even the usually very reserved Swiss waitresses clapped.

Florence got up from her place and came over and they hugged. 'I'm sorry about your thumb and everything. Eat with us.'

'Sorry, Florence, I'm Caroline and Ambrose's guest. It seems for once in my life I'm besieged with invitations. Sorry.'

'So you should be. You're a heroine. We'll have a dinner later this week.'

Edith and Caroline went to where Ambrose had kept a place. Her thoughts were about Florence. Florence could care about a cut thumb but not about her risks and tumbles of other kinds, the more complicated risks and tumbles of her psyche. She saw now that Florence would not ever return to being a proper friend.

The Tenets of Civilisation

and Various Wonders Not to Be Talked Of

Following the Sacco and Vanzetti riot and the realisation that her deep rift with Florence was to remain, even though they were talking again, Edith felt she must go to some place quiet to think. Her thumb wasn't healing quickly either. She asked for a week of her leave but Nancy Williams suggested she take all her annual leave which was anyhow overdue, and she agreed.

She'd been shaken by the stone throwing at the Palais Wilson more than she thought she should be. It was as if all the transgressions and the foolish daring of her life since coming to Geneva had goaded the angry crowd. The stone-throwing crowd had become oddly fused with the molestation at the Molly Club, as if she herself were somehow to blame for it. And it was true that by going out of bounds she was partly to blame. She'd gone out of bounds in other ways and places too. All these things had come together with a wobbly underlying logic which she couldn't interpret but which had made the stone-throwing riot into a storm against her as a person. As mad as it sounded, it was as if on that night she'd been stoned as a witch or as a scarlet woman.

For a time, perhaps since the time of the Molly Club incident, she'd had a numb indifference to her psyche and to her body. She'd fostered an optimism in herself that it all didn't matter, that it was 'the Continent', that everything would feel familiar and normal in the morning, or by next month. There'd been too much drinking going on in her life too, which, perhaps, she'd needed to sustain her numb indifference, or her waiting for the return to 'normal'. She was frightened now that she could not return to normal or that, for her, there was now no normal.

She'd also noticed that her drinking sometimes allowed her to enjoy a despair about the world and herself. The relief of desperation. She was frightened of this enjoyment.

Florence had made overtures, but Edith felt that a decision was required on her part as to whether there was value in her returning to friendship with Florence, and she'd decided there was not. She remained amiable towards Florence but politely evaded her invitations and did not return invitations, allowing the friendship to wither away. And this winter, she'd been disgusted to see Florence wipe her nose on her glove.

It was time to attend to herself. To mull on her life. To perhaps find her standards again.

It was time to think out how she felt on consequential matters, to take time away from the daily procedures and office panics of the League, to turn away from her overfull days. Maybe to consider going home. And what to do with Ambrose. Was he getting in the way of something more serious with a man? Or did she want to use it that way? Was a man like Ambrose best for her? Even Caroline had said to her recently that she must stop concerning herself only with the tactics of life and design for herself a life plan.

Recently she'd felt on the brink of being over-challenged by all things. Most days she felt no justifiable method for doing whatever it was she was doing from one moment to another. Mary McGeachy had reminded her that she did have inherent capacities and that her judgements in League affairs were based on her dining-table education in mercantile life from her father, and in public life from her mother and father, and from her

454

uncle. Yet so many situations at the League seemed to lack practices. They spent so much time making the rules. It was more what McGeachy called 'the hunch', which determined what Edith did. Unless someone told her, she rarely had a confident idea of whether she had done well or badly. Oh yes, she was good then at vindication. She never faltered in finding the reasons for what she'd done — although you only needed reasons for having done something when what you had done turned out to be a failure. If it worked, everyone could see the reasons for it. Sometimes it was as if she were inventing the theory after the event, tidying up her behaviour behind her with methodical explanation and with words of good order.

Maybe it was time to go back to Australia. To visit her mother's grave. And what about being, herself, a mother? And other Questions.

She went to Chamonix for a week, in the footsteps of Shelley and Ruskin, to the supposedly healthy 'gentian zone', where the gentian flowers grew. Where Ruskin wanted to go when, 'Lost in various wonder and sorrow not to be talked of'. Although he seemed to be mainly worried about his liver and his teeth: 'If those would keep right, I could fight the rest of it all', she'd read on the way down in the train. She thought she knew what he meant. She had a problem with a recurring hand rash. Some days she thought if that could be cured, then she could cope with the rest. Or maybe when she could cope with the rest, it would then be cured? Perhaps she should apply the gentian lotion of her childhood.

It was her first vacation without Ambrose, but on the following week-end, Ambrose, Jeanne and some of the others were coming down. Per Jacobbson from the Scandinavian Club was going to teach them all to ski. If her thumb had healed. She imagined that she might be more a cross-country skier although she suspected that if a sport had not entered her life by now, it was not likely to enter it.

She resolutely brought only one book, Ruskin's *The Stones of Venice*. She had reserved a deluxe room at the Hôtel Mont Blanc. After settling in, she moved the writing table to under the window and opened her day book, her personal journal. She'd filled three such books in her time in Geneva. She poured herself a Scotch from Jerome's flask. She always held the flask for a second against her face in recollection of that aberrant night. She drank from the silver travelling cup which she also carried in her luggage, carefully packed in a specially made leather pouch, and she said to herself, glancing at the mirror, 'Now Edith, mull.'

She went to the mirror to look more closely at her face but stopped that and returned to her desk.

She dated the page with her fountain pen.

Firstly, she copied her last poem into the book from the sheet of office paper on which it had been composed.

The Pirouette of Knowing

Look into the eye of the eye
to the egg of the eye
look until you reach the pirouetting ego
of the egg
and its staggering dance
leaden-footed dance
made so by a politic not yet known
engaged in a cause for those
who know not their cause
the unknowns and the know-nots
pirouetting inside a Palais

> proposed to be
> within reach
> of the wretched
> but which, itself, has no reach
> no-ledge for the grasping.
> Knowledge without reach
> is a no-ing, not a knowing
> is a retching not a reaching.
>
> (unsubmitted)

It was a little stern and needed more work but was not so bad. Maybe she would try to have it published in something like *The Nation*, which Caroline had shown her.

She decided to begin the mulling with a list of civilised tenets because of what she'd heard herself say in the Club de la Presse. She worried about mixing with journalists. They were so often damaged by their way of life, maybe from living so close to world anxiety and then having to make the anxiety into sense, into words, knowing always that they had got something wrong, yet never knowing until the next day what it was they'd got wrong. But as Ambrose said, it was diplomacy *inter pocula*.

Recently, she'd said in front of some of them that surely at the bedrock of everything — what the League stood for and what it pursued — were 'the civilised tenets'. No one had disagreed. But no one had taken it up either. The journalists hated talking like that because whatever good they believed in on that night would be proved false by morning.

After she'd said whatever it was she'd said in the Club de la Presse about 'civilised tenets', she'd looked across at Robert Dole. He had the look of a man who liked her, maybe more than that even, was an admirer. But he had the look also of a man who had thought his way through to another wiser place. To a wiser but not a happier place.

Exactly. That was how Robert Dole always looked. And his look said he was waiting for her to join him there, at this wiser but not happier place. Since the unsettling encounters they'd had back during the preparatory commission, his behaviour towards her had changed. After the Sacco and Vanzetti night, he'd been considerate with her during his interview and had agreed with her about the petition, and had moved her when he read Vanzetti's statement. Now when he disagreed with her, he did not do so in front of people as he had in the past. In fact, he now shielded her. As he'd left the club that night, Robert Dole came across to her and said with a smile, 'Trietschke said, "Civilisation is soap". Good night,' causing her to smile.

She was being coy with herself. Robert Dole was, in truth, preoccupied with her. She'd been surprised at times to hear him come to her defence. Sometimes he came to her help and gave her position more lustre than she ever could. Maybe he agreed with her?

And, she knew, without her permitting anything to happen about it, that he desired her carnally. She feared that if she allowed herself to desire him, it would mean that she would be induced by him to go through a black curtain to the wiser but not happier place where he seemed to dwell. He came from a different ilk of men to those she knew.

What further restrained her, one way or another, was that she'd found herself in enough strange, intimate places with men, and needed a pause, perhaps, in that part of her life. Before it got totally out of hand. She again counted up the men with whom she'd had some carnal association, fearing that somehow, unobserved by her, the total had crept up. She'd now had three carnal experiences in life — or maybe two and a half — including one lover — Ambrose — and not counting her ballgowned skirmishes back at university, the outcome of which seemed at times in recollection difficult to appraise, experiences which were lost somehow in the layers of the fabric and studs and buttons of those nights. There had been one serious and fairly correct young man in Melbourne but they had parted ways as it became clear to her that she would go to Europe and to the League and not to live in a house in South Yarra. And she did not know whether to count Jerome or to simply to see it as a 'Paris escapade'.

She had no intention of becoming a loose woman, and she considered that perhaps carnal experiences with three men before marriage was the boundary line between a modern woman and a loose woman.

She wrote down on a fresh page the word 'Intimacy' and then '(i) bizarre (ii) decorous'. Maybe these bizarre places she'd visited were good to visit but could not be encompassed as part of, or within, an orderly and natural life. She'd tried to tell Florence that was why they were on the Continent, to go off the rails a couple of times. But truth be known, she could not really account for that tumble into the outlandish in Paris or the nature of her carnal life with Ambrose.

But anyhow, it all belonged to her youth which was rapidly passing.

She decided to add 'Youth' to the heading 'Intimacy (i) bizarre (ii) decorous'. She inserted the names of 'the men so far' in the section called Youth and then ruled a line. She then added '(iii) married'.

She stopped then, realising that she had no rules for the handling or classifying of carnal experience. Proceeding from the mild to the stronger? As with the eating of cheese? It certainly had not happened that way. What, indeed, were the 'stronger' experiences? Nor did she have a life plan about what she expected from carnality. Indeed, she did not have the knowledge with which to make such a plan, although she certainly had more knowledge now than when she'd arrived on the Continent.

Thinking of Robert Dole and about finding herself in bizarre carnal places was not, though, why she was in Chamonix. Or not entirely. That was an altogether different question to mull, requiring, she reckoned, its own week-end. A week.

She turned the page, deciding that 'Intimacy (i) bizarre (ii) decorous (iii) married', was a subject for another time.

She wrote: 'How should we live?'

Robert Dole both unnerved her and heartened her — heartened her by his persistent interest in her but that same interest unnerved her, so that sometimes she wished he were not in the same room, be it committee room, conference hall, or café. That he was not there watching her from a distance. She hadn't spoken directly to Robert Dole about civilised tenets but his bent, private smile to her when she had mentioned civilised tenets in the club that night, and his parting comment, meant that she'd better work out what she meant by civilised tenets before she raised it again in front of him.

Edith decided that she saw the word as 'civil-ised' and wrote it down that way. She recalled her Latin — *civicus, civilis, civis, civilitas* — civilian, civility. The relations between the state and its citizens and the way citizens behaved towards each other. Especially the way strangers behaved to each other.

Urbanity. The real test, though, of our political urbanity might be how we handled those who *disliked* us. How we could continue to work with, and be sociable with, people we knew disliked us. That was the test.

In talking of civilised tenets, she had not meant simply what the League was 'for and against'. She'd been caught out before on that. War, yes, but what if it were a League of Nations militia which waged the war? Opium, yes, but some of them dabbled with the smoking of opium. Liverright was fond of saying that because a thing was bad on a large scale it was not necessarily bad on a personal scale and that one's personal conduct didn't change a thing in these matters. That one could enjoy what one believed should eventually be forbidden or erased from human conduct. Obscene publications were an example — Ambrose with his strange collection which she'd found alluring when she'd dipped into them. Traffic in women and children — oh yes, they were all against that, but she knew some took advantage of the situation as it was at Geneva's *ceinture de chasteté*. And how could one explain the remarkable demand for the reports of that committee which had sold better than any other reports of the League? What about the Molly Club? She supposed that was a private matter and hurt no one, even if indecency of behaviour was involved.

It was time to stop going to the Molly with Ambrose, even if, against her better judgement, she'd been back only a couple of times since the incident.

What are the values to be pursued?

Are some choices, some values, not available at some times?

Maybe the difference between a brutish and a civilised person was that a civilised person in times of strife or war might take an uncivilised action but it would be with reluctance. The civilised person would be aware that they were crossing a border. She knew from League reports and from accounts of history, that all people had the potential for villainous behaviour. She was not certain within herself whether she knew yet how to discern *inherent* evil. Working for the League had not given her the experience in discerning evil that she might have had in other places.

461

The best political arrangements were those which did not place ordinary people in situations in which they had to make difficult choices, because often they would choose badly and behave badly. She was also sure that people needed to be given time to study and think about politics.

Formalities and procedures were the wisdom of human organisation and were in themselves civilising instruments. She knew that now. When she was younger she'd opposed all red tape. Not any more. Red tape was often just a way of causing a pause in the impatience of things so that everything could be properly checked and considered. She realised that when enthusiasm and dedication had been expended, an organisation had to leave in their place a bureaucracy. She'd also come to know, sadly, that idealism did not ensure that things were done well or efficiently.

The League had the task of making the manners of the world. To create the conditions which allowed people to behave well. To remove those conditions which coarsened people, making it *easier to be civilised*. She wrote that down.

She remembered a picnic back home, beside the Clyde River, on her first vacation from university in Sydney when her friend George McDowell had said that most of the formalities of life were there to overcome the problem of human nervousness, that people were shy of each other. 'Remember,' he'd said, 'that at most times, nearly always, everyone is nervous. In crisis, doubly so.'

She confessed then that she was addressing herself to Robert Dole. Not writing *to him* but 'addressing' herself to him, using him as a hypothetical opponent. He wasn't much use as a hypothetical opponent because he'd changed to being this new something-else, smiling at her privately from across rooms. She pushed him aside.

After her second Scotch, finding herself staring at the page, Edith decided to leave the loftier categories and think of the more everyday civilised tenets. She suspected that others had done the work of the loftier tenets and that she would come to their thinking in the reading and learning which still lay ahead of her. She doubted that it was her destiny to elucidate these things.

She was then conscious of a distinctive sadness which she had not experienced or identified before. It was the sadness of knowing that one would never be 'a great thinker'. She thought she might have liked to be that but deep in her heart she knew she wasn't. She felt she had a chance still to become 'great' in other ways but not as a thinker. She saw around her at the League how the unrealistic striving for greatness of this philosophical sort when one did not have the capacity, developed into a hell of self-deception, posturing and ridicule. She prayed she would never fall into that delusion. Which didn't mean that she couldn't find her own pattern of connections and insights, for her own pleasure, and perhaps for the enlightenment of others. But erudition either made itself known in conduct and action or it gave to one's life private meanings. An erudite person wasn't someone who could 'quote' or who could pass examinations.

The first of her civilising tenets was the competence to be able to — she was going to write 'to make colloquy', but it was more than that. It was to be able to discourse without guile and without rancour. It was not only avoiding what Dr Johnson called 'talking to win'. She was talking about discourse which was conducted with a generous capacity for concession. She knew that some argued that advancement in thinking could only be through conflict — the holding of position followed by the conflict and then, the moving on to a third position. Well, there were times when she forgot her tenet of conversational calmness and became heated. Or as Ambrose would say, 'a trifle shrill'.

But conversation should be as quiet and as calm as a library.

As George had pointed out to her, making generous allowance for nervousness and the mistakes of nervousness — even in statesmanship — was part of being civilised. She knew very well that nervousness made some very clever people seem awkwardly voiceless and she knew that the very eloquent did not always truly know, but were simply very plausible. Some people caused her to talk stupidly, even when she agreed with them. Mrs Swanwick, an English delegate, was one of those sorts of people. She knew now to avoid them, or if she couldn't avoid them, how to remain silent. Mrs Swanwick caused her to talk against herself.

Yes, conversation and the conduct of conversation was the pivotal part of all civilised life. Conversation had ultimately to do with politics. She believed that the League of Nations would bring about a new way of people talking to each other. David Hunter Miller said that already the conference had replaced the diplomatic note. That the League was a continuous conference. She was learning, though, that a political negotiation was different from a conversation.

Conversation was sometimes an 'event'. Like going to the theatre. Wine was good because it contributed to people being decent in conversation. Up to a point. Of course, conversation could be just a way of touching someone, of being with someone, and content didn't matter then. Somehow she felt that gossip was good, despite its sometimes scandalous and political purposes. She thought she knew when it was being used as secret mail to circulate political and professional mischief and when it was simply a harmless revelling in human imperfection, a revelling in the relief that no one was perfect. Gossip showed that life was not the way that formality, convention and manners pretended. Truth — telling about the world, if not about the person under discussion, occurred in gossip but it was also to be found in the obverse of gossip — in the exchange of confidences. The exchange of confidences was sometimes a form of courage. Florence would never experience that courage and its rewards, although maybe she was the sort of person who inflicted its punishments.

How did you avoid the errors that came from being young? She supposed you could avoid some by imitation of older models, by having wise mentors, and through reading — borrowed, but provisional, wisdom. She wanted to know what it meant to be forty or sixty or whatever. Ambrose said the only advantage he could find in being older was that he was better at guessing the time and the temperature. She talked with older people. She would like to talk more with Under Secretary Bartou and get to know him. She was talking more with Dame Rachel too. Or Dame Rachel was going out of her way to talk more to her. Why weren't the wise things of life self-evident?

She needed to manage her ignorance with more flair, to conduct her ignorance gracefully in conversation. She needed to be able to talk well on a subject in which she was ignorant, to be able to turn her ignorance into a graceful accessory to conversation, not by make-believing that one knew, not by pretence, but by revealing her ignorance in an interesting way. She tried to talk about the philosophical difficulties and the working difficulties of finding information and of testing it — the whole difficulty of 'confidently knowing'. She was a believer in statistical investigation to reduce the bumph and the theoretical waffle of life. She had nothing but scorn for those who dismissed statistics as another way of lying. They were people overprotective of their theoretically dressed-up prejudices. Dole believed in statistics. He said statistics would be the news of the future.

She was learning that curiosity was a great resource and one of the higher traits of character, although she was still aware in

465

herself of the unwillingness of the mind to move from where it was secure out into the darker waters and to enter, with happy curiosity, into its ignorance. Especially when she was engaged in public conversations.

In her case, being graceful also meant learning to make grace from her unfinished self, from her provincial inexperience with life, from the gaps in her sensibilities.

Edith turned to a new page of the creamy paper.

She would leave 'colloquy' for now. She would like to join a Society for the Study of Conversation if one existed. Maybe she'd start one.

The detail of one's life.

To be able to shape the detail of life, if not into a work of art, then at least to make of one's life a work of conscious arrangement. As William Morris said, 'Have nothing in your home you do not know to be useful and believe to be beautiful.' Although she would have to say to William Morris that she had a few things in her rooms which were just curiosities. And one monstrosity — the Wilson chair with its fourteen adjustable positions, well, eight, really; she said fourteen as a joke. That may have to go. She found some hotel stationery in the desk drawer and began a list of mundane things to do when she went back to her rooms in Geneva. She wrote down a reminder to have all her clothing thoroughly cleaned. She found that how one's clothes smelled to oneself was important.

The French had taught the world that the arrangement and design of food was important. The arrangement of appetite, the ordering of competing appetites. She supposed the English middle classes had also introduced the notion of disciplining and withholding the appetites, of withholding the lesser appetite for the enjoyment of the greater. She supposed arranging the appetites was connoisseurship. Too often, though, some of her friends just withheld, postponed indefinitely whatever challenge of appetite they feared, and hence the challenge of some of life's pleasures. Or did some of the challenges of life and of appetite have to be let pass?

On the question of good taste, she had dilemmas. Somehow good taste in Australia was so much easier because the choice, say, of tea, was so much more limited. She even thought that in Europe there were more colours to choose from, but that couldn't be correct. She had discovered that Europe had not only more options but also more ways of deciding which options to take. She no longer thought that good taste was intuitive.

Maybe good taste and good living were about making good choices within what was materially available to you, within your assets and within your learning to date. She believed that it had to be an act of personal 'creation', a fashioning of self. You had to make choices, too, which combined with other earlier choices and choices to come. Although, maybe you didn't know the pattern in advance, more that it shaped up as the result of all the decisions you made. It was both. It was a matter of interacting parts. You began with a vague blueprint from your mother and father and then life presented you with options. You made choices which reshaped the blueprint and so on and on. But that could hardly be called a 'plan'.

She firmly believed that what you surrounded yourself with and exposed yourself to helped to make you, although it didn't always seem obvious how it made you or into what.

She hadn't yet got straight in her head where people fitted into the blueprint. Did one 'collect' friends as one did objects? Were those you gathered around you really 'gathered' or did they just happen? Did you make the best of what was available?

Friendship was trickier to make than gardens or a collection of *objets d'art*. She supposed that in the case of her rejection of Florence, she was beginning to make choices.

She felt that you had to have friends and family in your life to be truly fulfilled, or if you did not have family you could have vocation and friends, or if you did not have vocation she supposed you could have a cause, or public life, or maybe even a recreation or hobby would do. She wondered whether Robert Dole was interested in these lines of talk, the knowing of one's preferences about tea? She thought she could argue the importance of this with him.

If only she could get her preferences straight. She had to be able to see where those preferences came from. Oh, of course, as Liverright or Caroline would be quick to point out, they came from her 'class'. Where had her class got them? From the heightened life experience that good income offered? From the education which her class had offered to her? And how to explain differences of opinion and taste within her class?

Edith wished the dinner chime would sound.

She began to draw up a list of the tendencies in her taste.

The Aesthetic of Happy Latency. She believed that Miss Dickinson's chair had a happy latency which would sponsor a chain of other cheerful and assertive details. Likewise, those things she had gathered around herself in her rooms and, to a degree, in Ambrose's apartment. A central object which suggested others which might join it.

The Aesthetic of the Elemental Surface: say, in the choice of stone against concrete — she brought to mind the rage for concrete and a house in Paris which she'd been shown, decorated on the outside by concrete in the shape of tree branches. She had been appalled by the use of concrete to imitate nature. Why not grow a vine? She did not believe that concrete trees were the future. The natural spoke of connections directly with the lair and the hunt, the earlier days of the race. For these reasons she liked leather and fur and burning wood fires which reminded her of the days when the race lived closer to the animal kingdom. She liked a city to have places where animals and birds and plants could exist as a reminder of nature. She believed that more animals should be allowed to roam the streets. Not savage animals, but certainly wild ones. Deer, for example. She opposed those who argued that trees had no place in the streets of a city. She liked to eat dishes which were made from animals and birds and to wear clothing made from the fur and the leather of animals. She felt that a person should know the skills to catch the living things that they ate, even if it were no longer practicable for all people to exercise these skills. She had only ever shot one rabbit.

She was, however, against the use of natural objects such as sea shells and stones as decoration, feeling that they should be appreciated only in their natural location, although she enjoyed the temporary arrangements of fruit and vegetables in kitchens and flowers on tables. The rage for dwarf plants was also a deforming of nature. She wasn't interested in *les jardins de salon*.

The Aesthetic of Dress was too complicated for this list. She had known since she was a young woman that her underwear was meant to be seen at some time in one's life by a man and should be chosen with that in mind and be very fine but that it should first please her. She should every day be pleased and pleasured as she put her underwear against her body. Much of her taste in jewellery, clothing, and cosmetics had, though, come unquestioned from her mother, changed here and there by the demands of fashion.

The Aesthetic of Play Within Unequivocal Boundaries. She believed in the formal occasion, where all the rules were known to all. The casual was too demanding, the rules too ambiguous for relaxed pleasure. The casual required blatant behaviour to ensure that understanding had occurred. The formal allowed subtlety to play within its firm boundaries.

The Aesthetic of Ancestry. The old contained within itself a history and was, thus, another connection with the life of one's personal lineage or the lineage of the race. She found also that design and buildings and things from other times calmed her in these days of change. She liked to be surrounded with objects from other times — maybe they reminded her that the world had survived crisis and upheaval before, parts of it, at least. Although she had much reservation about cathedrals, about which so much was made. She had never said it, but she believed as a Rationalist that they were a wicked waste of human effort and she always avoided entering them.

The Aesthetic of Many Shapes and Spaces. She was for large rooms with high ceilings, as well as for nooks, for alcoves, attics, terraces, balconies, pergolas, and cellars.

The Aesthetic of Proper Reticence. The work of one's hand — objects knitted, sewn, carved or written — had to be left to speak for itself and should not be paraded, although there was a special pleasure in showing what one had made at fairs and so on.

The Aesthetic of Touch Within an Object. She was for the craft-made against the factory-made because, in the handmade, you could find the touch of the person who made it. To touch the object was to touch another person, not a machine, and each thing was different.

The Aesthetic of Rarity. She was for the rare rather than the readily available in all things. That might be snobbish but it was more that the possession of the rare object was an *accomplishment*. It could be achieved by identifying what it was you wanted and then having the money to buy it, or by searching for it, or by having it made. And rare possessions were a way of expressing one's sense of specialness but not superiority. Of reminding oneself that one was different in some ways from other people, even if only in minor ways.

The Aesthetic of Insignia and Bonds. She supposed, also, that some things that one had around one were to express bonding with others of the tribe. Chosen and collected things did both — expressed one's difference and one's sameness. She liked badges, medals, decorations, emblems, regimental ties, and even regimental pyjamas. This was related to the Aesthetic of Ancestry.

The Aesthetic of the Earned Memento and Trophy. Jerome's flask. She laughed aloud about that. Oh dear. She laughed again when she remembered the stationery stands.

The Aesthetic of the Outside of the Inside. She liked sometimes in a restaurant to be seated at the window at night and to see the reflection of the restaurant in the window 'outside' as it were. She had not resolved, though, in her own mind whether, in choosing a place to live, you had to 'accept' the view from the window or whether you searched for a 'good view'. She believed that if you thought about it there was a relationship between outside and inside. It should be harmonious although she had doubts about the value of looking out on a major scenic attraction such as Mont Blanc. She feared that people who dwelt on major scenic attractions were either searching for the sensational or engaged in private worship of the Lord's work. Neither of these motives served her.

She thought that one should be able to look at an *objet d'art* and know the material from which it was made, and something of the properties of that material, be it brass or bronze or copper or whatever. If wood, which wood and the properties of different woods. She thought that one should be able to identify and know the history of its decorative motifs. Should be able to determine at least which century, if not which half-century, it came from. Whether it was a replica or an original. Which culture produced it. Who, in some cases, designed it.

With a quiet, comic despair, she acknowledged that she could rarely do all of these things. Finding the time for attention to detail was her difficulty.

She heard Robert Dole's voice in her head. Of course, while in general, her list was, she acknowledged to him, the more expensive path in life to follow, her preferences were not to do with expense. She could see that some people who made choices to buy something delightful 'that cost next to nothing' mentioned price to show that they had taste enough to buy for reasons other than price.

She put all that aside and turned the page and wrote 'The Unconsidered Particulars of Life'.

'You should read Erasmus. Read Swift on ordure, that is where you should start,' Robert Dole had once shouted at her, in the days when he had still been inclined to shout at her. 'Read about the unconsidered particulars of life, the way we eat and the other unmentionable personal functions.' She remembered that he'd left that particular conversation in an alcoholic despair. In those days he'd behaved as if he thought that he could break through to her by saying severe things and that once he had 'broken through to her', everything would be all right and they would both go to heaven. He had not been attacking her as such, she had come to realise, rather that he'd been trying to reach her on another more intense axis, to take her mentally by the hand and drag her through the curtain, down other passageways. He wanted to win her over. To win her?

She would not let him break through the hedges of her temperament just yet, but she knew why he wanted to break through and why he believed it mattered to both of them. Maybe one day she'd be strong enough to do that. To go to his wiser but not happier place. In the meantime, it was important for her to have restrictions or she would lose her poise. She then recalled, with a smile, that she had once shouted back — only once? — at Robert Dole after he had gone on about 'what she should read'. She'd had enough of being told what she should read. She had shouted at him that while he was reading Aristotle or whoever, she had been doing 'something else' maybe just as valuable to her. Maybe looking at an insect under a microscope. Or helping her uncle with his electioneering on muddy roads, listening to disgruntled farmers. Or sitting on a stump in the hot bush, eating a sandwich of corned meat, looking at the ants and lizards which gathered, as if from nowhere, to eat with them. Every use of time required a forgoing of something else.

Anyhow, she'd also told him that she found that people who'd read Aristotle didn't seem to behave any more wisely than those who hadn't. He'd said, 'How do you know who's read Aristotle?' She'd said that she had a pretty good idea. They had both laughed.

She remembered also at Caroline's farewell party. She'd been the last to leave and had sat with Caroline until sunrise to watch what Caroline called 'the embarrassing dawn'. Edith had said to Caroline that she often felt that Caroline sounded as if she'd 'read everything'.

Caroline had replied, 'I read too fast, as if I am trying to catch up. But catch up with whom?'

Edith said she believed the ghosts of philosophers past moved in all conversations and attitudes and also in novels; even if we cannot name the philosophers and even if we have not read them, they are transmitted through the atmosphere of our times.

'But Bartou says that only the reading of history can save us from political hysteria.'

'Did he say what would save us from people who haven't read history but who gain power?'

'As a matter of fact, he did say something once about that.'

'And?'

'He said that only superior political cunning and dexterity would save us from dangerous leaders. If you are not interested in making history it is sometimes best to get out of the way of history.'

'Typically Swiss.'

They had fondly held on to each other and watched the embarrassing dawn and Edith had wished that Caroline was not leaving the League.

After the exchange with Robert Dole about the unconsidered particulars of life, she'd gone to the American Library and had begun to read Erasmus. He'd lent her his copy of Swift. She'd understood then why he'd shouted that at her and what it was that he wanted everyone to face up to. Robert Dole wanted people to regain their humanity by facing themselves as they were in all their frailty, dirtiness, and primitiveness.

At some point, she'd told him how she wanted her life, her personality, to be a big house with towers, attics, a conservatory, a gazebo, garden mazes, and yes, of course, a cellar, and to have secret passageways and hide-outs.

'And a WC?' he'd joked.

'Yes, and a WC,' she'd replied impatiently.

He'd said that he'd be interested in visiting the secret passageways and so on, implying that he doubted they existed yet. She couldn't tell him that she had, indeed, begun such construction in her life.

But in compliance with his challenge, she began her list of

the Unconsidered Particulars of Life. She could see it was a concession to him in her imaginary conversation. What was there to say about her monthly cycle? Or about the business of the morning lavatory, her fleshly blemishes and excrescences? She pondered the morning lavatory, those days when she saw that it floated and on other days that it didn't float. What did this mean? There were days when it seemed to take a long time for her body to finish, when she was impatient to get on with life and the affairs of the day and simply broke off, as it were, before it was properly finished. She did not like doing this, fearing it would damage her health, but she was sometimes an impatient woman. And when she strained to get it done, she worried about this. Were these the things which Robert Dole wanted her to note in her manual of life? To 'face up to'? There were the days when, after some effort, she looked in the bowl and saw next to nothing. Why did it sometimes smear the side of the bowl and have to be cleaned off, yet on other days it did not? Was it better to have one long solid piece and if so, how did one accomplish that? What about many scrappy pieces which were not as satisfying or, she felt, as healthy, as the long, solid, single pieces? Did men do it differently? There were days when she was almost shocked at the size of it, when it hurt coming out of her, as childbirth might. When the pleasure of the pain of the size of it would cause her to recall the one time when Ambrose had put his member in there fully, that pleasure and that pain. She had let him do it so that she might know what he felt when such things happened to him. She supposed that she might also do it again, for pleasure. Those mornings when she enjoyed the movement and feel of it coming out of her body — was that perverse? She always washed her anus before the sexual act but that was for fear of bad odours, not as a preparation for any sexual act involving it. How she hated someone knocking on the

475

door of the WC in the pension while she was there. At the toilets at the Palais, she always hoped that she was alone when she had to do it and always wondered who the person was in the next cubicle and whether they were listening and, at the same time, telling herself that, at her age, she shouldn't worry about these things, but still, it was true, she did wish to be unheard. What about enjoying the bidet's spray of hot water? What did enjoying that mean? As a little girl, Edith's mother had taught her to wipe from front to the back away from her other opening. She'd read with interest that in the fourteenth century people did it in any dark corner. That it was thought unacceptable to talk to a person who was so engaged. Only gradually did the examining and discussion of other people's dung become unacceptable as well.

Enough. Enough of considering the unconsidered particulars.

She looked at the page and worried that one day someone might read it. Would Robert Dole be proud of her if he ever read her appraisal of the unconsidered particulars? Was there an aesthetic to be applied to the unconsidered particulars of life? She wasn't up to doing that.

Looking back over the pages she saw that she had not gone very far with her list of civilised tenets which she might use to respond to Robert Dole. She reread her poem. It was a failure — a grappling with an idea rather than the charming portrait of an idea.

But there, thank goodness, was the dinner chime. She could go down and be self-indulgent.

She washed her hands and did her face. Maybe civilisation was soap. Maybe it was also self-indulgence.

To hell with Robert Dole.

Somehow the self-scrutiny had not been the dark night of

the soul which she'd felt she needed. Yet she sensed that she'd begun to expel toxins.

On the stairs she noted that it was snowing, that she was now on holidays, and that she had a good appetite. She would order the *menu gastronomique*. Wine would dissolve what was left of her anxiety. She would stop making lists and stop making agendas for herself. She would not spend a week harassing herself and her soul. Instead she would give over to sloth and indulgence. She wished that she had brought more books. Light and silly books. The hotel would probably have some in its guests' library.

She observed that she was glad to be alone.

The Nature of Spies

'We're going as Australians,' Ambrose said to her in the Secretariat lounge. 'Edith, you will be my mask. He hates the British — even circulated a fraudulent document claiming the British want to bring America back to the Empire. Fairly amazing, you must admit, seeing we can't get them into the League.'

Edith looked Ambrose over, as if 'going as an Australian' was somehow a matter of looks. 'There is a respectable body of opinion that believes the Americans should be back in the Empire.'

'Lord Strabolgi!'

'And Bernard Shaw.'

'Hardly that respectable a body of opinion. Well, I can tell you now, it's not going to happen.' He smiled. 'Of all the diplomatic predictions I might make, this is the one of which I am most sure.'

Jeanne, sipping her drink, asked the barman for more gin. 'Too much vermouth.' She also looked at Ambrose as if to appraise his passing as an Australian. 'As an Australian, you'll not do,' Jeanne said to him. 'Even for Edith, passing as an Australian is a difficulty these days.'

Edith made a face at Jeanne.

'I can but try,' Ambrose said, putting on what he considered an Australian outback accent.

'And if you don't pass, we'll all be thrown into Lac Léman by Mr Shearer's bodyguards,' Edith said.

481

'Could say I was a British newspaperman. Could say I was Robert Doleful.' He looked at her. Ambrose seemed now openly jealous of her and Robert Dole, although nothing romantic had happened between them. Well, she was discussing more with Robert Dole, which could be seen as a 'romance of the intellect', she supposed. There was nothing on the horizon and she was still very unsure of Robert Dole. 'You might find that intriguing,' he said, looking at Edith.

Jeanne also looked sideways at Edith to see how she reacted. Jeanne herself was obviously curious about what was developing there.

She was about to let Ambrose's innuendo pass, but instead said to him, 'For you to act as a Robert Dole type of man might be even more intriguing.' She didn't know exactly what she meant but it was an unkind wave in the direction of Dole's obviously surer masculinity. Characteristically, Ambrose ran away from this needling. 'Whatever the subterfuge, we must get into the party — Sir E. wants a report on this odd American chap and his efforts to make trouble at the conference.' He tasted Jeanne's drink. 'That drink really bucks. What is it?'

'A Gin Turin — gin and vermouth.'

'I think it's what back in London we used to call a Gin and It.'

'I had it for the first time here in Genève. Not in Turin. Never visited Turin.'

Ambrose savoured it, closing his eyes, focusing his attention on his taste. 'A multifarious combination — what flavours have we got here? In the gin we have the juniper berry, coriander, maybe licorice, and in the vermouth, I can detect the dried grapes. Have I missed anything?'

'Herbs in the vermouth,' Edith said.

'Yes, the herbs — *plantes aromatiques* galore. Very nice. A multifarious combination.'

Edith enjoyed Ambrose when he talked food and drink. He analysed all the flavours of his meal while she argued for experiencing the whole, in the mouth, unanalysed, although she tried to hold each mouthful until she had captured it as an experience of the palate. But often she forgot to do this.

There was no problem getting to the party in Shearer's apartment in Champel, up among the decent dwellings of the better-off part of Geneva. The party was crowded with hangers-on from the Naval Conference and a few press, but naturally no League staff.

And Edith danced with a woman for the first time.

A rather beautiful American woman in a green beaded dress with bare shoulders asked Edith to dance. The woman's invitation was so natural that Edith wondered if women dancing with women was becoming the done thing. The woman then danced very close to her. Body against body. All the more iniquitous because the woman had introduced herself as 'a merchant of death'. Edith felt her neck at last relaxing, from the gin and the rhythmic movement of her body.

'And you're an Australian journalist?' the American woman asked. 'Would an Australian newspaper send you all the way here to cover this Naval Conference? A woman reporter?'

'We're sent over from London, not from Australia.'

'How interesting.' The American woman weighed this lie and stowed it. 'You don't seem to mind dancing with a woman?'

'I did it a lot back in Australia,' Edith said, with a foxy smile.

'You have such clubs — in Australia?'

Edith doubted it, but thought of her experiences with the Molly Club. She laughed. 'Those sorts of clubs in Australia are called "boarding schools". I danced with other girls at dancing classes at boarding school.'

'How charming.'

'We had to take either the man's part and lead or the woman's part and follow. Actually, never with a woman before.' She was aware that the American woman was 'leading'.

She smiled at Edith's playful answer. 'You don't mind me taking the man's part then?'

Edith caught the innuendo in this question.

'Not at all,' she said softly, not sure, as she made her pliable reply, whether it was the real her or the spying Edith who was accepting the misty invitation, feeling safe from it at that moment in a crowded party in an apartment in Champel. 'Tell me about Mr Shearer,' Edith urged the attractive American woman. 'Mr Shearer is the talk of the town this week.'

'As a reporter, I thought you might know all about Mr Shearer.'

'Never enough is known about someone like Mr Shearer.'

The American was amused by this reply. Edith was pleased with it.

Edith said, 'I heard he'd run a nightclub in London before he became spokesman for the arms-makers.'

'You think he's a spokesman for the armaments people?'

'For the American naval interests, yes.'

'Mr Shearer did — "promote", I think might be the right word — the first nightclub in London and I worked there — the Lotus Club.'

'How interesting.' Edith was pleased that she had turned that phrase back on the woman. 'You say you "worked" at the nightclub?'

'I was an entertainer.'

' "Entertainer"?'

'I can be very entertaining,' the attractive American woman said. Having said that, she led Edith by the hand away from the dancing couples into another room and out to the balcony among the geraniums. Edith had not expected to be led away like that.

The American sat Edith on a balcony settee in the summer air and sat beside her, still holding Edith's hand. Edith felt that it was all right for this familiarity to develop because, she reminded herself, she was there as a spy and was licensed to pretend to be anything which she needed to pretend. It would perhaps lead to her finding out a thing or two about this man Shearer to give to Ambrose to give to Sir Eric to give to the man who lived in the house that Jack built. 'All in a good cause' were the words that formed in Edith's mind, in case she needed them. She thought also of the owl and the colourful ruff of its neck. The ruff, she recalled, was for acoustics, and increased the ability of the owl to hear by ten times. Tonight her body was serving as her ruff.

The woman had taken Edith's other hand and placed it on her breast. Edith allowed her fingers to move a little and felt the fullness of the woman's breast and the breathing of the woman through the beaded satin. The fullness was unexpected because it was fashionably disguised by the dress. She felt then the woman's hand on her breast and felt her own breathing quicken.

'Is Mr Shearer your lover?' By asking this, Edith surprised herself but felt that the woman's fondling of her breasts earned her the right to boldness, earned her one searching question in return.

'Oh no,' the woman said.

'Are you then, perhaps, a lover of women?' Edith impressed herself with her audacity.

'I have loved women and I have loved men,' the attractive American woman said, nonchalantly.

Edith had a mental compendium now on ways of loving which she'd observed, one way or another, in Europe. But she had never experienced such a woman. I could, she thought to herself, also put this down to Continental experience as well as to the good of the cause. Edith felt she might need an additional moral justification for what she felt was happening, or what she vaguely felt was on the way to happening. Although she also reminded herself that she had decreed that such irregular 'experiencing' was now over for her. That she had done enough experiencing to last a lifetime.

The attractive American woman was fondling her breast and had leaned towards her, her lips approaching Edith's. Their lips met and they kissed, Edith being reminded momentarily of kissing Ambrose's lips when he wore lipstick. They kissed lightly and then the American woman urged the kiss towards intensity, towards passion. The touching of their velvet headbands was also sensuous; their pearls swung out from their necks and clicked together like dice. The meeting of their lips, the smoothness of the lipstick on their lips and the powdered smoothness of their faces was calming to Edith, although without thrill, and mild in sentiment. But although mild, there was a strong proposal in the kissing, a proposal of an alien voluptuousness. I now know what that feels like, Edith thought, to kiss a woman fully, trying to use her mental notetaking as a way of remaining composed. But she found she could not hold herself in complete indifference, and her breathing was hurried.

As their lips parted, the woman said, 'Mr Shearer is a happily married man who is devoted to his ships,' as if the words were formed during the kiss and could only come out when the kiss ceased and her mouth was free.

'Warships?'

'All ships.'

The woman continued to fondle her, and Edith gave herself to snuggling up to the other woman, indulging in small kisses.

'Why does he want to wreck the Naval Conference?'

'Does he want to wreck the Naval Conference?'

'It would seem so.'

Edith found her hand was making play with the woman's breast as some cover or consideration for being rudely inquisitive and Edith was surprised by the knowingness of her hand which seemed to know what it was that it wanted to do, and to enjoy the doing of it.

'Because, my darling nosy Australian,' she said, moving again to kiss, maybe feeling that Edith's pointed question had earned her another, 'he wants to build ships and wholesale disarmament would be bad for that business. Very bad.'

They kissed and Edith met the American woman almost halfway this time, moving her breasts against the American woman's breasts, meeting her lips and encountering again a proposal to voluptuousness. From perhaps a truly evil woman.

When they came out of the kiss it was Edith who spoke first. 'He's a shipbuilder?'

'He is a friend of those who build ships.'

'And they pay him to come to Geneva to make this trouble?'

'They pay him well and he pays me well,' she laughed, 'and that is a secret. And does he make trouble?'

Edith was aware that she was going further and faster than a careful spy should and that she would have to pay for this information, now so readily dangled before her by the attractive American woman in the beaded dress, although maybe it was the American woman who was being extravagant with her information as a way to hurry what Edith assumed was her seduction.

She was aware that the American woman had put her hand into her dress and freed one of Edith's breasts from the brassière of her corset and was moving her tongue languidly around her nipple, and suckling, then nibbling with her teeth to give the nipple exquisite twinges which she felt all the way through her body to her crotch.

It felt exotic and off-course but Edith stroked the American woman's hair, breathing her perfume, cradling her head.

Edith was aware that she was becoming aroused throughout her entire body but that she had no idea of how and where this arousal, this playing each with the other, was leading nor what to do about it.

It was then that she heard shouting from the next room.

The American woman's head moved away from her nipple, leaving it wetly cold to the air, as she turned towards the shouting. They were both abruptly returned to the wider reality. And Edith used this distraction to put her breast back inside its brassière cup in the dress, turning things back to normal.

They heard Ambrose's voice and another voice that was almost certainly that of Shearer.

The music stopped. Someone had stopped the gramophone.

Edith registered that Ambrose's voice had given up any pretence at being 'Australian' and that he was being his indignant British self. Surprisingly, it sounded as if the argument was about Boy Scouts and Girl Guides but she decided that she must have missed some of the exchange.

'I think we'd better go back,' Edith said to the attractive American woman, using the shouting as an excuse for running away. 'My friend seems to be in trouble with your Mr Shearer.'

The American woman, although seemingly disappointed,

rose also, perhaps feeling the pull of the situation and perhaps also a duty to the party and to Mr Shearer. But scared of decadence, no, she did not seem at all scared of decadence. 'Promise that we will see each other again — soon?' the American whispered, taking her hands and kissing Edith's ear.

'Yes,' said Edith knowing that when she left the party, she would dissolve into the night and slip back into her identity and be gone from this woman's reach, although at the same time she secreted away the option of seeing the woman again, if the urge should ever come to her.

'Check my face,' the woman said to Edith, doing the same for her, cleaning off some lipstick with a handkerchief she moistened with her mouth. They then returned to the party.

In the diffuse purple light of the party, Ambrose and Mr Shearer were indeed in dispute, standing aggressively close to each other, surrounded by spectators.

Edith was relieved that no one paid attention to her return or her absence.

'I am saying,' Mr Shearer said, his finger pointing his remarks into Ambrose, 'that you British have enrolled one million of our American boys in this British Boy Scout thing and nearly sixty thousand of our girls in the Girl Scout thing. And who's the head of these movements? I will tell you who is the head of these movements. A Lord and a Lady from England. We have put the cream of our youth in the hands of the British.'

'What arrant nonsense,' was all that Ambrose came out with, as Edith reached his side.

Mr Shearer turned on her. 'And you, I suppose, are also British. I will not have the British here in this house — you are in conspiracy to weaken our navy, our youth, our nation. Furthermore, I can prove that the YMCA and the YWCA have Directors who are also in the British Scout movement. What other country would permit the forming of a foreign legion of the young, pledged to a British Lord and Lady?!'

'What nonsense,' said Ambrose.

Edith was bemused, having never heard of anyone fearing the Boy Scouts and Girl Guides but then she saw them the way that Shearer saw them, as something like the Action Civique, or like Mussolini's youth squads.

'They are being turned into colonists for England and, as a patriotic American, I have, sir, to ask you to leave, for having abused my hospitality by posing as something you were not. Australians you are clearly not.'

The attractive American woman hadn't gone to Shearer's side but was over at the drinks cabinet pouring drinks. Edith thought that she would bring a drink to her and wondered how she could distance herself from the woman, but instead, to Edith's relief, the woman took the drink to Mr Shearer, linking her arm and his, maybe in a move meant to calm him but by doing so, placing herself clearly apart from Edith, and then she smiled at her surreptitiously. Edith flashed a quick surreptitious smile back, wondering what tangled allegiance she was accepting by the exchange of smiles.

Edith then went to find her and Ambrose's coats.

As they left, watched by the intrigued crowd, the attractive American woman blew a small quick kiss to her but did not come to her to say goodbye, clearly having to stay clear of the Britishers. Edith realised that she'd been searching for the woman's eyes, to have one last exchanged glance.

Out in chemin de Miremont she and Ambrose walked for a while, arm-in-arm.

'We weren't very good spies,' she said to Ambrose.

'How do you mean good spies?' Ambrose said crossly, still disconcerted by it all.

'Spies for Sir Eric — we were unmasked.'

'Oh yes, that business. I have enough from the newspaper people to put something together.'

'I found out things.'

'You did?' He looked at her.

'I had to trade with my body to get the information.'

'You did what with your body?'

'Traded with my body.'

'With *Shearer*?'

'With a woman friend of Shearer.'

Ambrose turned to her with closer attention. 'Go on!'

She told him what had happened and gave him her scraps of information.

They walked for a while and then Ambrose burst out, 'The fool — it's not only about how many sixteen-inch guns and fourteen-inch guns each country has. We're quite happy to ban submarines. The others say, of course, that would leave England master of the seas.'

'I traded my body with a merchant of death and you don't even thank me?' And, Edith thought, it would indeed leave England master of the seas, even though she was for the banning of submarines.

'Sorry.' He gave her a small hug. 'Bad manners. Thank you, Edith. I hope it was pleasurable, this trading with your body.'

Edith thought that, yes, she'd found small unusual pleasures with the female voluptuary, the merchant of death, that she would like to follow the woman's overtures into further voluptuousness. If she had another life to lead. If she were still 'seeking experience on the Continent'. But really she was also relieved that there were so many obstacles to her following the woman into voluptuousness, and was glad of the barriers.

'I was not sure how pleasurable it was,' she told him. 'Boy

Scouts and Girl Guides interrupted my Sapphic adventure.'

'Again, thank you, Edith — how very Weimar of you.' He squeezed her arm with his. 'You are a wizard spy.'

That Sunday, Edith was at Ambrose's apartment and she happened to glance at what he'd been writing in his typewriter. She saw that it was about the man Shearer. The word 'Sapphist' attracted her eye, standing out on the page, and reading it, she was alarmed to find that the happenings at the party, while without naming her, made it obvious to those in the Secretariat that she was Ambrose's woman 'sub-agent'. She had begun to read the whole document when Ambrose came into the room and, joking about 'matters of state', rolled the page out of the typewriter, gathered the other pages and put the document away.

She was astonished by his action. Earlier that day, they'd spent time together while she recounted in detail what she'd learned from the attractive American woman and consequently she felt she knew already much of what was in the document — had herself contributed to it. 'Come on, Ambrose, we've never concealed things!' she said, her sense of offence growing.

'It is a confidential report to the Old Man.'

'So? Can't you see that it pretty much identifies me? And can't a fellow member of the Secretariat be trusted?' She felt she had stumbled on an echelon of secrecy within the League of which she had not been aware and it unsettled her.

'You aren't in the *haute direction*,' he said.

'But I'm mentioned in the report!'

'I'll remove anything that could identify you. I promise.'

'You link me to that Sapphist!'

'You told me that he employed one. You seemed to be happy in her company that night.'

On that night, she had not been herself — she'd been acting someone else. 'I didn't quite say that. And anyhow, what are *you*? The League employs you and you're hardly a paragon of purity.'

It was a harsh thing to say. They stood in heated silence. She had obviously hurt him.

He said in an injured voice, 'I said I would delete anything which could identify you.'

'Good.' Her anger was still high.

'I can't let you read it.'

'That's your business,' she said.

'I'm afraid that it is.'

'I don't care.'

They looked away from each other and moved about the room in high tension.

She decided to trust that he would delete the references and not to pursue it. She left the room to sit out on the balcony until she'd regained her composure. She later apologised for her ugly personal retort. Of course she was not in the *haute direction* of the League and she supposed the League had to have confidentiality on some matters.

In her office the following Monday, her curiosity and her fear about the report drove her to call Registry and ask Victoria if she could see Ambrose's report on Shearer. Victoria hated these irregular requests but always gave in.

She called Edith back later on the inter-office telephone. 'There is no such report.'

Edith pondered this. 'Thank you, Victoria.'

Maybe the report had gone straight to Sir Eric and had not been filed. But that would be irregular.

After thinking about it, something about the report occurred to her and she rang Victoria again. 'Victoria, as a Registry person, what do the letters "MI-c Attn: NO" mean to you?'

'It is not a League file number.'

'I know that.'

Victoria asked her to repeat it and then said, 'MI would mean, to me, Military Intelligence.'

'Whose military intelligence?' Edith was confused, although the League did have a permanent miltary commission. Maybe that was where the report had gone. 'You mean the military commission?'

'No, I don't mean the military commission, not unless they are playing soldiers or doing something against regulations. I would say English intelligence. And it's directed for attention of the Naval Office — the letters NO.'

Edith was sure they were the letters which had headed up the document in Ambrose's typewriter. She thanked Victoria and hung up the telephone. Edith felt a wave of shock move through her mind. She sat there in her office feeling cold and lost. The document in Ambrose's typewriter had been definitely headed MI. This must mean that Ambrose was making a report to the British intelligence service — that he was working for the British.

She called Victoria again. 'And the League — we don't use those file references ever? You're absolutely sure?' Edith noticed that her hands were trembling.

'You know full well what filing system we use.'

It was absolutely wrong conduct. She sat trying to think. Very, very wrong.

'Why do you ask? What are you doing with military intelligence?' It was the voice of Victoria still on the line, a voice which had changed from impatience at the request to curiosity.

'Sorry, Victoria. I'm not doing anything with military intelligence, nothing at all. Thank you.'

'You sound queer.'

'I'm all right, thank you, Victoria.' She put down the telephone.

Plainly something had now to happen. Either she confronted Ambrose, and then what? He would admit or deny it. If admitted, then what? And if denied, then what? Should she induce him to stop or to resign? Or she could go to Sir Eric and alert him to Ambrose. What kind of loyalty did she owe to Ambrose as a friend — her lover — or to the League? And could he be a friend if he secretly worked against the League and concealed this from her? Maybe he used things he'd heard from her. How was this part of friendship? What would she do if the matter required her to inform the Swiss police? She could not see herself doing that. Her ethic was clear there. Friendship was a sanctuary and a protection. A source of counsel. A friend lent herself to advocacy for a friend, lent herself to giving the best possible defence of her friend, if defence were feasible — although not complicity — a friend was not required to deny guilt when there was guilt. A friend should make all efforts at the best vindication and mitigation of consequences. The immunity of the life and welfare of the friend, that was the obligation of a friend. About this, she was clear. There was no obligation to do the work of the police or government in making a case against a friend. A friend's obligation was to look to her friend's welfare. Others would impersonally do the work of prosecution.

But the League was different — the League was not a police force. The League was her very life and the hope of the world and she had always believed it to be Ambrose's very life. The League was not a government, nor an employer as such. It was a unique entity and of a distinctively higher order than anything else in the world.

Was not an enemy of the League an enemy of hers?

That was, perhaps, too dramatic.

Yet it was clearly understood that League officers would regulate their conduct with only the interests of the League in mind. And that they should never receive instruction from any government or other authority. Including the Pope. True, no oath of allegiance was taken. But Edith felt that everything she said at the League was a statement under oath.

A huge painful emptiness opened in her heart about Ambrose and his deception of her and of the League. She couldn't consult with Jeanne who seemed to have a different cultural ethic from her. They had never quite found common ground. Victoria was too much a woman of practical matters, not a person to consult on complicated ethical behaviour. She certainly couldn't consult with Robert Dole who was a competitor with Ambrose for her affections, and a reporter. Caroline was erratic in her judgements, occasionally wise, sometimes just cranky and wayward. They had become close since the stoning business but Caroline had left the League and was leaving Geneva that week to make her life as a writer or a 'surrealist' in Paris, London or Vienna. Another loss. Liverright, too. Sometimes she was frightened that the old gang was going.

She did go to talk with Caroline.

Over tea at the Hôtel de la Paix she told a simple version of events and tried to be hypothetical and not to mention Ambrose.

Caroline saw through the hypothetical camouflage. 'You mean Ambrose is a rotten spy.'

She nodded to Caroline.

Caroline played with the sugar bowl, obviously taking in both the sensation of the information and the seriousness of the advice she'd been asked for.

'You have to decide whether you are A Person Who Has Spies as Friends or whether you are not.'

The answer *was* simple. It was dazzlingly simple. 'And I am not.'

'No, Edith. You are not.'

'As my mother would have said, "The forks shouldn't be in with the spoons." '

'And especially not with the knives.'

'Are you, Caroline, someone who has spies for friends?'

'I have every sort as friends. I even have Liverright.'

Edith managed a cheerless laugh. Then she asked, 'Do you also have earnest members of the Secretariat as your friends?'

'I do indeed, if that earnest but very interesting officer is named Edith Berry.'

They held hands.

'Thank you,' Edith said, feeling the turmoil of having gained a friend who was about to leave her life.

'I also think that while you are definitely not A Person Who Has Spies as Friends, you could very well be A Person Who Has Writers as Friends.'

'If that writer is named Caroline Bailey,' she said, thinking also of Robert Dole.

They held hands tightly, looking directly into each other's eyes, confirming all that they were saying.

'I have observed you, Edith Berry, and although I know you are an earnest officer, you are more, much more. Remember that. Not a vamp — I've already told you I was wrong about all that. That was just Caroline having an hysterical night and that was long, long ago. No. You are uncommon.'

Her spirits were lifted by Caroline's praise. She hadn't heard praise for a while. Everyone went on with their work, no one really had much time for praising each other. At any other time, she would have been wildly elated by this character analysis and praise but now she could only store it like a squirrel, to savour at some other time when, if ever, her personal crisis had lost its distress, had stopped spoiling all her feelings.

Caroline empathised with her. She said it was a nasty dilemma which tainted all. It was important, she said, that Edith came through it as well as possible, and safely.

Caroline said, 'One promise? When this dreadful thing is all over, write to me and tell me all.'

'A promise.'

'I ask for your sake as well as out of my writer's need to know all.'

She also sensed that she could tell Caroline about her darker experiences. She wanted one day to show Caroline that she wasn't just an earnest officer. Not a vamp, but nor was she a woman who hid from the strangeness of life.

What sort of person would she be after this mess?

In one simple sentence, Caroline had made the next move clear. Heavy-hearted, she decided to consult with Under Secretary Bartou although such an action came perilously close to making it an official matter. He'd been good to her in the past. She remembered him speaking encouragingly to her at her first, and only, Directors' meeting, way back in the early days.

In arranging the appointment with Under Secretary Bartou she tried to make it clear to him that it was not an official report she was about to make, more an '*échange de vues*'.

He said that he understood. 'An exchange of notes which precedes the opening of a file. Is that it?'

'No file may be required.' Deep in her heart, she knew that there would eventually be a file and that the matter was grave, that she was delaying the moment of crisis.

He'd suggested then, an informal meeting place, the parc

l'Ariana, where they were unlikely to be observed.

In the park, seated at a park table, he gestured around them. 'Can you imagine the new Palais des Nations built here?'

That wasn't really on her mind but she looked about her. 'Oh, yes — yes I can.'

He turned back to her. 'Well?'

She outlined what she knew of Ambrose's spying activity with Shearer and possibly other things. 'That is, I think he's spying on the League.' She frowned at a tone of self-importance she detected in herself. It was not the most actively present of her broiling sentiments but it was lurking there dishonourably, like the nasty child in the playground. She hoped Under Secretary Bartou couldn't detect it.

As Under Secretary Bartou sat listening and thinking, he took out two oranges from a paper bag and from his pocket he took out a folding fruit knife. He offered an orange to Edith which she refused, feeling that she could not, that afternoon, handle the matter of Ambrose and an orange.

He told her that Robespierre had a passion for oranges, adding, 'I do not compare myself in any way with Robespierre. If anything, I am a Mirabeau.'

She smiled nervously, although not having enough of a command of history to understand the reference. Would there come a day when she would understand all the references and allusions?

On the park table, he peeled the orange in a way that Edith had never seen before. He cut off a lid of skin from around the top of the orange and then with a sharp knife cut down the orange peel, top to bottom, cutting only into the skin, making four or five incisions into the skin from top to bottom. He then peeled away the skin segments like the petals of a flower to reveal the orange. The peel formed a sort of plate for the orange.

She watched him eat his orange, impatient for him to

comment. Under Secretary Bartou carefully removed the core
and all rind and membrane, and ate first the juicy reservoir from
the crown, and then delicately broke away each segment. No
juice ran down *his* arm. She observed to herself then, strangely,
that she wanted him to wish it all away, for it to be resolved
somehow by him, so that she need do nothing more, to have
the burden of it taken from her. But she also saw that there was
no way he could do that — that no one could do that — and
she began to feel the impending wound to herself — the wound
of the breach looming between her and Ambrose and the ruin of
Ambrose. She could not be released from doing something and
yet whatever she did, she would suffer for it. She felt like crying
out that she did not deserve another wound. She had been
wounded at the Molly Club and she had been wounded by
Florence, and somehow also wounded by the stone-throwing.
These wounds had healed and become scars. She did not think
she could take another. She then saw herself, her spirit, as being
scarred and said to herself, I am becoming a scarred person. She
remembered then, her father once saying to her as a little girl
that the world judged people not by their medals and diplomas
but by their scars. Back then, she'd thought of scarred knees and
only now did she understand that he'd used the word scars to
mean the marks of a courageously led life, but she felt she had
no courage left to open herself to another wound.

He then said that he was not sure that it was so serious.

She was taken aback. It seemed to her the most serious thing
in her world.

He then said, 'You are a close friend of Major Westwood?'

'I am.' Or was the friendship in suspension?

'I will rephrase. Seeing that we are dealing with what could
become a serious matter, but which, on closer examination, may
not be so serious, may I be frank?'

'Certainly.'

'I have been told by friends more experienced than I with diplomacy in eastern cultures, that eunuchs make good diplomats. They do not waste their time chasing the pleasures of the flesh, they sharpen their wits so as to be ready to retaliate against insult, they pose as the confidants of all, and they have a sceptical advantage of living between the world of men and the world of women. As well, they possess a feminine intuition.'

Edith felt that eunuchs were outside her world and her specifications of human conduct and, in so far as it was a reference to Ambrose, she was uncertain how it applied. She showed that she was uncertain.

'There is talk about Major Westwood's nature. Yet, on the other hand, talk that he is your lover.'

She took his meaning, wondered how they — who? — were talking about him. 'Do I have to answer?'

'You could — if you take what I say as a question.'

'I would rather not take it as a question.'

Under Secretary Bartou didn't say anything, waiting to see whether she would speak. She knew that stratagem, the Way of the Silent Void, although she had not consciously used her Ways for some time now. She, too, knew the defence, and remained silent.

Under Secretary Bartou broke first. 'They sometimes simulate masculinity,' he said.

Edith blushed at this; her blushing had returned after she'd thought that it'd gone from her life. Maybe her blushes were telling him what he needed to know.

He left that subject and went on, 'Don't judge too harshly, or too quickly, about this spying business,' he said, touching her hand briefly and lightly, signalling the end of the other line of questions. 'Remember the words of Taine: "for a young person the world always seems a scandalous place". Later in life, the world seems only to be an imperfect place which can be worked on here and there. I'm told that finally, in old age, the world becomes either infinitely amusing or infinitely annoying — according to one's temperament.'

'I am over thirty,' she said, putting her age up a little, sensing at the same time that one didn't say 'over thirty'. It occurred to her that maybe she knew more about the ambivalence of masculinity than Under Secretary Bartou.

He went on, 'Despite what we say in the League, we cannot build a Republic of Virtue,' and again changing direction, he said, 'The League is your vocation?'

She couldn't see where he was headed in his thinking. 'I see it that way,' she said, although Under Secretary Bartou did not need to reinforce her loyalty.

He went on to say that as long as British foreign policy was not in conflict with the League's policies and Britain was a pre-eminent supporter of the League, both in concept and spirit, he could not see a great danger to the interests of the League in the conduct of Major Westwood. However, that could always change, he supposed.

She was amazed to hear him so unperturbed about the spying which she felt to be self-evidently alarming.

Secondly, he said, it could well be that Major Westwood did not spy on the League as such but could be seen as reporting on those matters which were of interest to the British Foreign Office in Genevan life. 'What you describe — this report on Mr Shearer — that is not League business, not directly. Although we all wish Mr Shearer would go home.'

Thirdly, he said, it could be that he was bringing to the attention of the Foreign Office only those things which, while being in the public domain, were buried under the weight of documents which the League begat. This may be to everyone's advantage.

He let this sink in before he said, 'It could be argued that we should leave things be and let him go on with his work.'

She had trouble comprehending this.

'Even assist him in his work without his knowledge,' Under Secretary Bartou said, watching her closely.

'That would mean that I would not mention all this to him?'

'And you would go on as if nothing had happened.'

She was stunned by this proposal. She couldn't imagine how that could ever be.

'After all, he has gone on as if everything between you were as you thought it to be.'

'But that I couldn't contemplate doing it means that I am different from him.'

'It means you are not good spy material, yes.'

Under Secretary Bartou spoke no more about this possibility and went on with his analysis. Fourthly, Major Westwood may be aggrandising himself in the eyes of the British Foreign Office by pretending to them that what he sends is very secret. Unintentionally — intentionally? — he could be doing nothing more than being a publicist for the League within the British Foreign Office. 'In that sense, he may be working to our advantage,' Under Secretary Bartou said, again confounding her.

'Are you telling me that perhaps he's working for the League in this underhand way?' For a mad minute, Edith thought that she had been relieved of the burden, that in some twisted way Under Secretary Bartou was saying that Ambrose was innocent, was working for the League, that therefore nothing need be done. She even felt the beginnings of a crazy elation.

'I am not telling you that. And I doubt it as a hypothesis.'

She ventured then to ask directly whether perhaps there was nothing to be done.

'Something has to be done,' he replied. 'It would be a disaster if we did nothing and a member state discovered this. What we have to do is determine how bad that danger is, how harmful to our interests, and how much alarm should be taken.'

She took this in.

'It's up to you to determine this,' he said.

'How can I do that!'

'By looking into what he has been doing — by spying on the spy.'

The interview had not gone the way she had foreseen it. Not at all.

'Me on him?'

'Yes.'

'I'm afraid that I couldn't do that,' she said.

'To spy on a spy is no crime,' Under Secretary Bartou said.

She was against spying. She supposed. Edith told Under Secretary Bartou this. 'It goes against my nature.'

'Spying is best justified simply as a way of knowing what other secret agents are doing against you,' he said. 'In our case, we want to know so that we can protect ourselves. Secrecy and publicity — both do their own kinds of harm. But remember, secrecy is not a badge of fraud or evidence of conspiracy.'

'It goes against my sense of what is right. We are supposed to be bringing to the world the rules of fair play in international affairs.'

'That may be. We haven't achieved that yet. We can't really function by pretending that the world is already humane. You forget one thing. You've made an allegation against Major Westwood. I have no evidence which would establish that allegation in my eyes.' His voice hardened somewhat.

She blushed again, this time with embarrassment at her innocence and the warmth of the blush quickly turned to a chill. She had assumed that she would be believed, that she was above doubt.

'From all I know of you and have heard of you,' he said, 'you are a sound officer. But I think, on reflection, you might see why others would doubt you, suspect personal motives — that perhaps he has in some way injured you, wronged you.'

She sat in silence, confounded by this shift in the course of the matter. Then she nodded; she understood. 'Could I perhaps drop the whole thing then?'

'You could. How would you be then in relationship to him?'

'An accomplice by default.'

'Precisely. And even though this is not yet a formal matter, I would have to personally adopt some precautions on behalf of the League, without Major Westwood knowing, and perhaps precaution against you unwittingly serving Major Westwood, and we would all find ourselves in some unspoken conspiracy against each other. It is best that we know just what it is that he's doing.'

'I agree,' she said, reluctantly.

'You are probably, at times, alone in his apartment. You will perhaps find what he has sent. It will almost surely be in a locked place and you might need a locksmith who is friendly to the cause. I will help you there.'

Talk of locksmiths and talk of distinctions between secrecy and conspiracy was new to her and she would have to digest it. But anyhow, the whole thing had shifted to her. Now she was in the position of having to establish that she was not driven by a personal malice.

Shaking Under Secretary Bartou's hand, she went away from the interview — she in one direction, he in another, like conspirators. She was suffering a second kind of shock and with no one to whom she could turn to ease it. Under Secretary Bartou, while counselling her on her initial moral quandary, had left her with a second quandary. She was really alone with both.

Later, sitting in her rooms, she felt influenced by Under Secretary Bartou's hard wisdom and by a need to rest upon his guidance as an escape from her own moral confusion. Yet by so doing she would have to suffer the wound of Ambrose's betrayal of her. She had been avoiding this wound. It was a friend betraying friendship. Or was he just an 'imperfect friend'? Where did imperfect friends fit in one's life? They could become an obstacle to one's life. There was a borderline between the imperfect friend and the bad friend and between the bad friend and the enemy.

Yet during the evening she was gradually overtaken by another mood, if not a position, a dishonourable mood — it was a swelling, morbid need to know what it was that Ambrose had been doing, not only with the League but with her, with his life, to know what else it was that he concealed from her. Her thoughts had returned to the Molly Club and the suspicions she'd had about the depth of his involvement in it. This morbid mood was followed closely by an incitement to strike back at Ambrose — not a very nice urge, but an insistent one. The morbid desire to know and the desire to strike at him, both overwhelmed her moral dilemmas and swept them away, anaesthetised her. She found herself burning to be at his apartment and to be searching his things. It was the morbid need of a wounded and suspicious lover. It was the desperate need to be sure, or to know the worst about a lover. It was a demented feeling. It was a need to know everything. Regardless of what sort of lovers they were and even though their love had never been pledged, she was driven by a lover's rampaging need to know all about the desired one. That alone was sufficient to justify her. She could now see how a stronger love than the love she felt for Ambrose could disorder all judgement, all ethics. And his behaviour justified her in whatever she might decide to do against him. That was a new dispensation — the dispensation of being a fevered lover, the single-minded drive of jealous suspicion. Perhaps love was also a form of spying. 'Everyone believes that something is being hidden from them,' as Robert Dole would say.

This morbid torment of suspicion and the need to know was with her still in the morning, and she went to Under Secretary Bartou's office, wondering if by going to his office she was changing the status of the situation to 'official'. She told him that she would search Ambrose's apartment and report what she found. He gave her the telephone number of a 'friendly' locksmith should she need one.

She saw that Under Secretary Bartou had Ambrose's personnel file on his desk and then she saw her own.

He saw her looking at the files. 'Would you like to know more about Major Ambrose Westwood?'

She said she would. Was he whetting her?

He opened the file. 'Schooled at Exeter. Medical studies, Universities of Glasgow and Edinburgh. Won the Parkes Memorial Prize. Practised medicine for a few years, gave it up to go into the FO. Was there for a few years, a spell in the embassy in Durban. In 1915 went into the RAMC, thus back to medicine. Divisional Sanitary section in the War. Commended for effective measures against trench fever and cerebro-spinal fever. Five mentions in dispatches. Seems he did see some fighting. Brevet of majority. Came out of the War briefly back to the FO and then to the Peace Conference where he worked with Sir Eric and then joined the League. Major Westwood has a good record.'

She nodded. She knew most of this. 'How old is Major Westwood?'

He glanced at the file. 'Forty.'

Ambrose seemed at times much younger and, at other times, much older. She couldn't remember what age he'd given her.

She had a question. 'You say that he may have copied only those things which are available to member states. What would he be able to copy in the League that the public shouldn't know?' She hoped the question wasn't naïve.

He raised his eyebrows with interest at her question. 'Even an organisation pledged to open diplomacy has its secrets.' He paused, seeking an example, then held up Ambrose's personal file. 'This is an example of a confidential document, the files of personnel. Armament statistics sent by member states which are available only to those nations which themselves supplied statistics. The advantage which could be gained by spying on the League would only be to know something in advance of other countries. You are correct — ultimately, nearly all we know becomes public knowledge. Except minutes of secret meetings of Council.'

She nodded, letting the question of secret meetings of Council problem pass by. At the door to his office, she turned and said, 'Will he be dismissed from the Secretariat?'

'You are now assuming that this is an official matter?'

She saw that she was but tried to hold off the moment of crisis a little longer. 'Not until we know how guilty. If he is guilty, will he be dismissed?'

'Sir Eric will decide that. Not necessarily dismissed. Oh, and another thing — I would be very glad if you would copy for me the report on this American, Shearer. That might interest Sir Eric and the Supervisory Commission. Perhaps the Council.'

She recalled the mention of Sapphists. 'I'll try.'

They arranged that she should call on the telephone if she found tangible evidence which he should see.

It occurred to her that she could go to the apartment, satisfy her own burning need 'to know all' but report back that she'd found nothing. It was possible that she *would* find nothing. However, she felt a need to establish herself in the eyes of Under Secretary Bartou and not leave any suspicion that her allegation grew from some silly personal malice. And if she did lie to protect him, she would still have to face the fact that their friendship was deeply injured.

She gave herself the whole day to systematically search his things while he was at the office. Once inside the apartment, she detected a rather pleasant agitated part of herself, a Girl Guide self with an important adventure unfolding, but she found she couldn't run away from the moral and other discomforts of this matter by seeing it as a Girl Guide 'adventure'. That picture of it dissolved away almost immediately, and she was left with the pain of it and the compulsion of her morbid needs.

The morbid and suspicious part of herself charged on. She wanted to read all his personal letters, his diary, to know his income, to see his childhood mementoes, anything. She wondered if she would find things to shock her, evidence of another lover, say, but she knew so much of his private life, that had been the delight of their affair, but she also saw that their shared candour had been a delimited candour, confined to the carnal appetites, especially. Although the passion which drove her carried with it a willingness to imagine and to believe that anything was possible, that monstrous secrets might lay hidden.

She began with the drawing room, systematically looking in

all the drawers, behind paintings for a safe, under carpets. She riffled through every one of his books. She found that his sexology books now bore a gummed label saying 'From the personal library of Dr Ambrose Westwood', and that in case of death, the books should not be opened but should be sent to the medical school in Edinburgh. He hadn't told her of this eccentric label. Then to his bedroom, under the mattress. In one drawer she found copies of a German magazine, *Transvestismus*, which he'd shown her from time to time. Again, the magazines now bore the same queer gummed label. She shook her head. There was one drawer of women's underwear, some of which she had bought for him. There were some of her things permanently there. She pondered whether to take them now, but to do that would alert him to what was happening. She kept seeing in her mind the horrible parting of the ways which was almost certainly ahead of them.

Having looked for his private papers as well as for the evidence of his spying, she found nothing. In his desk she found the name of his solicitor, Allen and Overy, 3 Finch Lane, EC3. His London bank, Lloyds of St James' Street, SW1 and his accountant, Allan Charlesworth and Co., 17 Helen's Place, EC3. His Swiss bank account was overdrawn and in the three-monthly statement she saw no income from any source other than the League. His English account contained hardly anything and showed no recent deposits. A few bills. A letter from Professor Clérambault thanking him for the 'costume' photographs. What photographs were they? She had found Professor Clérambault an unsettling person on that one meeting in Paris. But no private letters. A letter from White's telling him about changes to the club's constitution. A notice of a meeting of the Saintsbury Club. Nothing personal at all. Either they were hidden or they did not exist. Why would he hide them? He'd talked of his family but most of them were dead. A brother somewhere in the colonies. Was it possible that she alone constituted his private life? She felt a creeping sickness arising within her; it would make the break with him even more wounding for him and therefore for her. She put the meagre things back as she'd found them and got up to continue her search for his spy papers.

In the kitchen she searched in the pots and pans cupboard and then the cleaning cupboard and poked in the potted plants on the balcony with a knife blade.

Having found nothing, she stood in the apartment and looked slowly about her.

She had an intuition. Ambrose was a fine cook and the vegetable bin was always freshly full. She went to the vegetable bin and pulled out the vegetables. Under them she discovered a sheet of frosted glass sitting on four corks, and under the glass a dossier. She experienced a sense of empty-hearted cleverness but her morbid drive was waning.

She took out the dossier and went through it. It contained reports all headed 'MI-c' with 'Attn'. Only the Shearer file was directed to the NO. There was a code book. Not all the documents were from the League; a few were from foreign legations. She saw a report on Mr Huneeus and Azerbaijan. She saw the armaments statistics mentioned by Under Secretary Bartou. There was an address of an agency which she also noted down. She read the Shearer report and to her dismay saw that Ambrose had not altered it as he'd promised. It still mentioned a sub-agent and Sapphists, but then it hadn't gone to the Secretariat and her identity was surely not known at Whitehall. Worry descended on her as she considered this possibility. She sat down and copied out the report on Shearer for Under Secretary Bartou, deleting the references to Sapphists or to any woman 'sub-agent'. She didn't consider that the deletion of these references constituted hiding things from Under Secretary Bartou. They were an aberration within an aberration.

As arranged, she called Under Secretary Bartou on the telephone and described what she'd found. He said that it sounded as if it were important enough for him to sight the material with his own eyes and that he would drive straight over to the apartment.

As she put down the telephone handpiece she wondered if she should place a coin in the telephone money box which Ambrose kept by the telephone for payments from his neighbours when they used it.

She rehearsed how she might bring her version of the Shearer report to the attention of Under Secretary Bartou and steer him away from examining the original report in any detail.

He arrived and she handed him her list and gave him her version of the Shearer report. He glanced at the report and grunted. He leafed through the other material in the cache and made notes.

She watched with relief as he turned away from the cache without looking closely at the original Shearer report. He said that the matter was now reasonably serious.

After she'd replaced it all the way she'd found it, she pointed out to him Ambrose's bank account statements which showed no income other than from the League.

'Maybe he's an honorary spy,' he said.

She let them out of the apartment, but before closing the door, she looked back sadly. Under Secretary Bartou went on down the stairs, discreetly leaving her standing there. She and Ambrose had made the apartment together, had found the furnishings with such laughter and with hours of discussion and searching for the right pieces, the right colours, the right shapes. They had held joint dinner parties there. It had almost been domestic, almost. She thought of what she would like to take from the apartment into her own life and decided that there was nothing she would now wish to include into her life. It would possibly be the last time she saw it. Except to get her things. She wished she could take them now and for it all to be over. An ignoble exit. She closed the door.

They returned to Under Secretary Bartou's office where he went through the notes he'd taken, pipe in mouth, grunting. 'Much of this is available to the public or to member states. It's simply drawing the British attention to some documents. But some of the statistics — there he has made an infraction.'

'What will happen now?'

'I still don't consider it so much a deeply alarming problem — more an unfortunate one. We all like Major Westwood.' He smiled at her as a doctor might smile at a worried patient.

'He'll be dismissed?'

'It is not for me to say.' Under Secretary Bartou looked at her closely. 'Are you not suffering? Remorse perhaps?'

'It's mostly anger and disappointment now.'

'How do you fortify yourself? To defeat your remorse?'

' "To spy on a spy is no crime",' she replied, and they both smiled without the zest of humour.

'If it will help, I can contribute another maxim: to lie to a spy is no crime.'

Had Ambrose within this hour ceased to be a lover and become simply 'a spy'?

She then said something which she had been saying to herself to justify her actions: 'I believed that he and I shared that higher allegiance to the League. He betrayed it — and me — by having, in fact, a concealed allegiance.'

Under Secretary Bartou nodded, making a gesture of understanding. 'This secret allegiance which Major Westwood has is sometimes not fully understood by the person who has sworn it. It begins often as a patriotic virtue but it can lead that person into very savage and grim decisions in times of conflict of interest. The secret allegiance can ask of its servant that he turn against all around him.'

'It's a clear case of *rebus sic stantibus*,' she said, thinking that it was such a case where the conditions of the original treaty of love and friendship between Ambrose and she had changed, had been nullified, adding, 'both in my relationship to him and his to the League.'

Under Secretary Bartou thought for a moment and said, 'There is a strict view of *rebus sic stantibus* which says that no party can ever liberate itself from a treaty without the consent of the other party.'

'But what if conditions have changed?' She didn't want a diplomatic argument. She wanted comfort.

'*You* say conditions have changed. But you are right, the strict view is untenable. But so, too, is the lax view which would allow any party to disregard a treaty on any pretext.'

Her hold on *rebus sic stantibus* began to collapse in her mind. This must have showed.

'A nation has to be very skilful sometimes in deciding whether conditions have changed. Or whether the dishonouring of a treaty is going to carry penalties unforeseen.'

She didn't know if Under Secretary Bartou was warning her about treaties and penalties. 'Are you warning me? Is there something that I do not understand which I should fear?' she asked, fearing his answer.

'More a lesson than a warning.' He said that for him the sad part of the matter was that Ambrose was 'a spy with nothing upon which to spy', playing at espionage at great professional and personal risk. A spy without value. 'I suspect that he wanted to keep a special relationship with his FO. I also suspect that they didn't treat it all that seriously.'

He stared out the window and she prepared to leave although she felt unable to return to her everyday work, too pent up with diverse feelings, most of which were disturbing.

'Why are treaties ever made if they are so fragile?' she asked.

'Because they are sometimes respected.' He began cleaning his pipe. 'And to use a treaty as a trick works only once.'

'Will we ever need spies? The League?' she asked, trying to extend the discussion of the whole matter and to have the afternoon exhaust itself, and so as not to be alone. Looking afresh at what she had always thought of as the abominable custom of espionage.

'Maybe. Maybe we will have need of other people's spies to inform ourselves at times of crisis. Yes, I can see that.' He looked at her. 'I have a question for you — about something which intrigues me,' he said. He seemed to want to spend the afternoon mulling over the matter also.

'Yes?' She tensed herself against more probing into her intimate life with Ambrose.

'The pain of turning against a friend I can understand, but as an Australian, your soul began where Major Westwood's soul began — in the heartlands of England, with some Nordic blood perhaps. You are of the same stock — do you not feel allegiance? Loyalty? Can you so easily turn against him? I suppose I ask as a former Swiss diplomat with a very great curiosity about the English and their empire.'

Sitting there, she thought about it as best she could. She'd had too many other complications concerning standards of self and friendship to have had time to think of grander notions. She had not thought of the allegiance of British blood. 'It did not come to me in those terms at all,' she concluded, wondering if this was another dagger which would come sooner or later to cut her in the dead of night.

'Interesting. Your soul came from the same place but it has been altered. Altered by the sun and by the pioneering and by the distance in under a hundred and fifty years. I am interested in what happens to the national soul when it's transplanted.'

'What happens to our souls when we are transplanted to Geneva?' She gestured at the unseen thousand people working away in the Palais Wilson and the other buildings. 'Or what about you? Seemingly still on the soil of your own country but legally in a diplomatic nether region.'

'The discovery of our international soul?' He smiled. 'You're right. Those of us who come to work at the League are all immigrants.'

'You return home though when you step outside the door, back onto Swiss soil.'

'True. But I can never be Swiss again in the same way. Another question: is there an Australian way of handling a friend who turns out to be a spy?'

She thought of the romanticising of the bushrangers in Australia, which she didn't like. She said that a spy might stand a chance of becoming a popular legend like a bushranger — if he or she spied for the right country at the right time.

'But I grew up in a family which believed in polity — my father's word: that we were involved in the making of the polity, the making of our new culture. Openly doing this. People secretly serving foreign masters — even spies serving English masters — were considered to be something of a danger.' She smiled. 'Especially those serving the Pope.'

'What was your father's occupation that led him to use words such as "polity"?'

'My father was in business but he was also something of a

private scholar. He had a large library. He read a lot.'

'What business?'

'He had a small factory which made water tanks. And other things. He sold anything to do with water — piping, pumps. He said that Australia was always going to worry about water and that's the business he went into.'

'Tell me of your upbringing.'

'My mother put everything into the Red Cross. That was her life. After being a mother. She was State President and held all sorts of positions. Although now it's a bit inactive in the town.' She was away a lot, Edith thought. Perhaps a good mother should not be around too much. Edith found herself at last on prepared ground, having thought much about her upbringing while in Chamonix. 'I was raised on Six Ethics. The Ethic of Rationalism which kept me away from religion and pushed me towards science although as it turns out, I am not a very good scientist. My father's mother was a follower of Ingersoll.' She looked at him to see if he knew Ingersoll. 'The great American agnostic,' she said, in case he didn't know. 'He believed in what he called the "enfranchisement of the human mind". He liked good wine and good food, too.' She tried to be light. 'I follow him on that as well.' That was perhaps enough about Colonel Ingersoll. 'That's how my family came to know the Lathams. John Latham worked for the Rationalist Society for a while.

'The Work Ethic — which as a Swiss you understand — pride in work, thoroughness, the making of things.

'The Study Ethic. I grew up in a house of books and talk of books and of magazines; we had Ingersoll's magazine in the house for as long as I remember — my father still sends me issues — and we were Democrats who believed we were responsible for our domain.

517

'The Obligation to Participate. The citizen had to participate — my father would say, "Those who expect to reap the
blessings of freedom must undergo the fatigue of fighting for
it." That sort of thing. Both my mother and father talked of
democratic voting as "the ceremony of the whole". The family
were forever at meetings and the family itself was a continuous
meeting. They would quote Ingersoll: "every family a republic,
every fireside a democracy".

'And my mother taught me the Ethic of the Domestic, how
to make a beautiful life around oneself, the ceremonies and
graces of domesticity. There were codes of conduct which followed from these ethics. That's how I understand being
Australian.'

She sat there with a satisfied smile. He sat there with a
surprised and interested smile.

'My father also drilled wells. He searched for water but he
wasn't a water diviner. He used geology.'

'To me it sounds like Calvinism sans Calvin. I see why you
are at the League of Nations.' He said he thought she had
mentioned only five ethics.

She ran through them again in her head, cursing herself.
Was there something deficient in someone who couldn't hold
six points in their head? 'I missed the Bush Ethic. Self-reliance
yet willingness to give help to others and to combine to do
things together as a community — mutual aid. We liked to go
out into the bush as a way of exploring the country and nature.'
She decided she'd said enough. She hoped it didn't sound as
though her family was dreadfully serious. But she supposed it
was a serious family.

'One day you might explain to me further about what you
call the Bush Ethic? Do you know the bush?'

'I know how to find water.'

He seemed very pleased with her answer. 'I believe you would know.'

'When I say that I was not a very good scientist, I should say that I passed well. At university my herbarium was much praised. I think I had more species than required. I remember I had more fungi than required.' She stopped herself, sensing how she was babbling on.

He took his pipe from his mouth and held it at arm's length as if studying it. She had once been told that the distance he took his pipe from his mouth was a measure of the importance of what he was about to say.

He then asked her if she would like to work with him.

She hesitated. Was this a reward for her informing on her lover? She wanted no reward which would be tarnished, which would carry with it a load of remorse, and be an enduring reminder of this affair. And people were right about the pipe.

'Why are you offering me this?'

'I have asked people about you. I know something of your flair. I remember very well the day you instructed the Directors on how to run the business side of the League. I have followed your files which begin with the visit of an American showman. You've handled well what you've been given. It's time you were given more.'

Strongbow. That was so far back and she often felt that others knew what she had really done. Of course, they couldn't know.

'Would you have offered me this position if I hadn't — exposed Ambrose Westwood?'

He thought about it. 'This matter has brought you into my focus. I like the way you handled it. There was no "clean" way of handling it. You rolled up your sleeves and did the job. I imagine that's an Australian characteristic. And a Swiss characteristic also.'

Dirty work. He was right, she had done some dirty work.

'You did not come to me as an informer. You came to me as a concerned colleague.'

She did not want to go on working for the Marquis Paulucci. Her realistic expectations had been eventually to transfer into Social Questions with Dame Rachel to work with *La Commission Sentimentale*. 'At what level would my appointment be?'

'You would be, in British parliamentary rank, my Private Secretary, as it were. However, because of the accommodation problems you'd not have your own office, you'd work in here with me.'

'Would I be able to attend Directors' meetings? That'd be good training for me.'

He looked at her, smiling. 'The League of Nations was not created for you to complete your education, Berry.' He continued to smile at her. 'Although the new countries, I notice, treat us as a college in international affairs.'

She said she would like a short time to think about it.

'Remember that ill-defined appointments suit ambitious personalities — you can expand the appointment to suit your aspirations.'

As she got up to leave, he said to her, 'Do you know what this agency is — the address that was in Westwood's secret papers?'

She could guess at some licentious possibilities. She shook her head.

'It's strange. It's an agency which, for a fee, will post your letters from any part of the world.'

'So that you can pretend to be where you are not?'

'Precisely.'

'How odd.' As she walked down the corridor, she wondered how Under Secretary Bartou knew the function of such an agency. She remembered how she had originally seen Ambrose as a proper English civil servant with endearing vices, and had been rather proud at having him as an escort. But this sort of Englishness held no appeal for her now.

She was unsure how she would like Under Secretary Bartou, but it was not a question of friendship — it was vocation. Under Secretary Bartou seemed to have become her ally. She smiled grimly at something Ambrose had once said about allies — the surest ally is one with whom you share the spoils. This made her uncomfortable. She assumed that Under Secretary Bartou would earn some commendation from presenting the discovery to Sir Eric and presumably to Council.

After she left his office, she sat in the parc Mon Repos over from the Palais Wilson but felt no repose. Edith saw now that she'd arrived at yet another position in life. She was going deeper into the hierarchy of the League and closer to it. Ambrose was going further away from it, if not totally away from it, and she from him. She wondered whether, for all his perfidy, she could continue to accept Ambrose as a colleague — if, that is, they permitted him to remain. She now believed that the situation as it had developed excluded Ambrose from any protection from the consequences of breaching that allegiance, and she would not extend sanctuary to Ambrose, nor protection from the repercussions of her actions upon him. He had negated, within the friendship, one of its highest requirements and was entitled now to only a lesser relationship of, say, acquaintanceship. She would have to confront Ambrose with this. Another dreadful deed ahead of her.

She was learning that to attend to one's own interests

required, at times, the making of hard decisions against others. It was far easier to serve the interests of others.

She would also consider it a relief to be free of Internal Administration under the Marquis Paulucci di Calboli Barone. He wore a Fascist party badge in the office and was not her style of man. While she had nothing very much against the Fascists or Mussolini, she was against the wearing of badges in the office. Liverright had stopped wearing red in reaction against the Marquis' example. She'd had less to do with him even than with Under Secretary Monnet.

She consulted with Dame Rachel who told her to take the position with Bartou. 'Enough women are shunted into Social Questions. They think we're best dealing with "miseries and forlorn hopes", as Mrs Swanwick calls the work of the Fifth Committee. Take it.'

She went back to Under Secretary Bartou and accepted the position. Under Secretary Bartou agreed that she should talk with Ambrose before any official reaction was communicated to him.

Her only other thought at this point was that she would, from now on, sit with different people at lunch in the office restaurant. A long way from Florence and her crowd. That didn't bother her at all.

She suggested to Ambrose dinner at the Lyrique, one of their familiar places. As soon as they entered the restaurant, she knew the choice of meeting place was wrong and that they should have gone to a neutral place or perhaps to his office. She was embarrassed by M. l'Hôte, the owner, who had known them both for some time now, who presented them with a complimentary *apéritif* of port wine, treating them not only as favoured customers, but as a favourite couple. Ambrose made one of their old jokes about 'having a port' when for most people 'a sailor or two would suffice'.

She observed how well she maintained the pretence of normality with M. l'Hôte and Ambrose while they ordered. Another petty deceit in a chain of deceit.

After they had settled their orders, with Ambrose ordering with gusto and she ordering apathetically, and had their second *apéritif* of port in their hands, the first having been hastily drunk, she confronted him with her discovery of his secret work for military intelligence. Her hands were not shaking but they felt as if they were. She did not tell him just yet that she'd been to see Under Secretary Bartou or that she had searched his apartment. Maybe she still hoped that it could all be understood in a dazzling new light and that she could then tell Under Secretary Bartou that the matter should be forgotten. She observed that in the early days she would have told everything at once.

At first his face showed a coldness and hardness which she had never seen in all the years she'd known him, as if all masks had fallen to show this hardness. He was disturbed and for a few seconds did not look at her. She in turn, seeing the look of hardness, hardened herself.

Then, in his fashion, he switched to the manner which presumed that the serious things of life were best taken lightly. 'The game's up, then. I'm unmasked. And you occupy a new position *uti possidetis*.' The jocular pose had replaced the hard face.

She knew it but couldn't be sure that she had it right, so she played along and indicated that she didn't know that diplomatic term, concealing her irritation with his forced jocularity and this game-playing, allowing Ambrose, for the last time, to take his old role as diplomatic teacher.

'It refers to possession of territory. The two parties making a truce at the end of hostilities remain in possession of what they have conquered from each other — in your case, the moral high ground and information about me and my government; you have that by right of conquest. I retain my intelligence work, for what it was worth. But what each of us has conquered must be precisely defined — that is, if we're to make a treaty of peace between us.'

He lost jocularity towards the end of this speech and a nervousness began to show. 'If we are making a peace treaty?' he repeated.

He was trying to bargain with her. She wondered if there could be a peace between them. She asked Ambrose how he justified himself.

'Oh, you know old Ambrose — right hand doesn't know what my left is doing — Ambrose in the daytime is one thing: in the evening she is something else. Life's rich tapestry and all that.'

Ambrose then abruptly abandoned the bantering form of life-lightly-taken. He said that coming out of the bloodiness of the War, he'd determined to do everything to secure the peace. 'And in my view of things that meant both working at the League and also working for my government which I believe also wants to avoid further war. I was helping both parties, dear Edith, because I believed they were as one.'

She was dissatisfied with this. 'And if they subsequently became not one with each other — who then was your master?' She went on with her eating without appetite.

Ambrose said that sometimes people turned into revolutionaries or zealots before your very eyes. One's duty then, he said, was to collaborate with those who opposed the zealots. Especially to oppose those zealots who thought they were your friends but who had unwittingly become your enemies. He said it wasn't required by the rules of the game that you told them you were working against them.

She saw the worrying convolution of his mind which over the years she'd seen surface now and then.

'You see us in the League as dangerous to you? As dangerous idealists? You see me that way?'

'Some in the League are. I am saying that it's conceivable that the League could be captured one day by zealots. I don't only mean Paulluci. It could be said that I was helping the League in a way — guarding it. Keeping an eye on it. Helping others to keep an eye on it.'

This rang hollow or barmy. It was the spies who were the zealots. Conspirators were the real zealots.

'No — you were serving the British government. But the important thing is that this particular higher allegiance was never in the preamble of our friendship. The important thing is that you deceived me.'

'To reveal myself would have defeated my mission. Deception is in the nature of spying. It's not like other deception. Not like personal lying or anything like that.' He waved his fork. 'And I wasn't a dastardly spy every minute of the day — I could also give my very best to the League at the same time. I was a dutiful servant of the League.'

She realised she yearned still to be his friend, for things to be as they once were. She wanted to believe him, to be logically convinced of his innocence, even a form of innocence, and to have the pain of the breach and the suspicions and the deception talked away, turned to mischievous joking. But his words were not doing that and she was still left with his massive breach of friendship, as well as a breach of his contract with the League. An ugly blight had settled over the table.

'I want to be your friend, Ambrose.' She touched his

hand. 'I do want a treaty of peace.' She regretted using the word friend — it was too imprecise a word, too strong for what she saw for their future. She avoided his hand which reached out. He turned the gesture into the taking of a piece of bread.

'I consider that very, very generous, dear Edith.' He seemed tearfully grateful, and he reached out for her hand again, in a clumsy way, but again she avoided his hand. 'Have me as your "rotten friend".'

Could she do that? Put him in the peculiar category of rotten friend? Did you need some category like that in life? No, she couldn't see that. What she needed was to make herself absolutely clear without being unduly cruel.

'I want a peace with you, is what I mean. But there is a preamble to the peace — my allegiance is to the League. Any friendships I form must never conflict with or harass that allegiance.'

'How binding is a preamble?' he said lightly, referring back to some old discussion, using their old conversational style.

She replied in a dull voice, obedient to the call of the old days but no longer part of them in spirit. 'A preamble has no binding force. It simply states the purpose and spirit of the treaty.' She saw how he was clinging to the rituals of their old friendship, trying to keep them both bound together in the old ways.

'You always learned well, Edith.'

'You were a good teacher. Ambrose — ' her voice becoming firm and neutral, stripped of intimacy and of warmth, she wanting no misunderstanding, 'whatever we are to each other in the future, it will never, can never, be the same as it was. It can be a peace between us but not a friendship.'

'Not a friendship?' he said in a voice as hard as his face during his first reaction to her announcement.

She paused while the main course was served and the waiter had gone.

'A peace between us,' she repeated, 'but not a friendship.'

The situation had shuffled itself and it became starkly obvious to her that she could not again be seen to be associated with him. That he could jeopardise her integrity, her career, her standing. She hoped he would resign and go out of her life.

He did not touch his food. He spoke in a low pained voice, 'Remember, Edith, *surtout pas trop de zèle.*'

He was hiding also, hiding behind this diplomatic talk, inveigling her into it as well. It seemed so ridiculous. She felt, though, the point of this remark. She did tend to be zealous and she sensed she was becoming more so. Time was so short to remake the world. She was impatient. This led her to zeal, or was she just sedulous?

'I take your advice,' she lied — maybe zeal was what might be needed — 'I see myself, though, as sedulous, not zealous.'

He managed to capture her hands in his and said with a friendly voice, oddly inappropriate to the words he seemed to be uttering, 'Let us cease to be friends and lovers then.'

She was surprised to have him take her hands at the same time as he'd relinquished her and their friendship.

He then said, 'Let us, dear Edith, instead, marry, and be man and wife.'

The idea cuffed her. She looked to see if he were jesting and he clearly was not. She removed her hands from his, as her first reaction. 'And who will be the wife?' she managed to get out, making it as a joke, but it was a biting statement, containing her refusal.

He smiled seriously and said, very seriously, 'We know all the worst things about each other — or at least you know my worst tricks.'

'Ambrose, it is simply not conceivable.'

'I would give up my bad habits. Some at least.'

'Which, dear Ambrose, which of your multitude of bad habits?' She hated now his way of reducing the gravity of things by college flippancy which again infected her way of responding.

'The spying habit, for one. I'll retire hurt.' He was regaining his airy style, his life-lightly-lived form.

She was not playing with him any more. They were no longer playmates in life.

Perhaps it was a chance to save a spy, to reform a spy. She smiled inwardly, with a sad severity. That was what a spy would say to save himself. And that observation established simply the impediment now in any relationship with him: from this whole dirty incident onwards, she could never again believe what he said. That was the gist of it for ever more. She supposed that he would realise this too, sooner or later.

He was, unbelievably, waiting for her to answer his proposal of marriage. She almost said she was married to the League, but simply said, 'I'm afraid, Ambrose, that I couldn't.'

He nodded, small tears came to his eyes and he pretended to rub his face while his fingers wiped them away. She thought that the pretence was in the transparent act of concealment, that she was meant to see him trying to conceal his tears. She did not reach across to him.

He did not urge his suit of marriage. 'But at peace then.' His voice was forced back to the businesslike, if not the flippant. 'You won't tell. I will retire as a spy.'

She looked at him again with disbelief. 'How could I believe you?'

'Because we are dear friends.'

She felt the beginnings of disgust with him. 'I have already told them.'

'Why didn't you come to me first?' His voice was toneless.

'Why didn't you?'

He didn't answer.

She told him then of spying on him. She also brought up the fact that he had said to her that he would reword the report about herself and the Sapphist, but hadn't. She didn't mention Under Secretary Bartou's role.

He listened without speaking or eating. He seemed to accept that he was fully exposed and that she was deeply hurt.

She said, rather bluntly, 'Why don't you leave — resign — go home?'

'What has Under Secretary Bartou in mind for me? I suppose he knows all?'

'He knows all. I don't know that it's up to him.'

'I think I will wait and see — *attentisme*. Take my chances.'

She said, 'And I see that as a master spy you know to whom I have been speaking. How did you know that I'd talked about this with Bartou?'

'When you were at lunch yesterday in the restaurant with Victoria, I saw the way you ate your orange. I know about the Old Swiss Fox and his passion for oranges.'

He was obviously pleased in a minor way with himself about the orange observation, again slipping into his frivolous tone. He chuckled, 'You're impressed.'

She let him have his petty pleasure. Regardless of his outward act, Ambrose was increasingly distracted and neither of them did justice to their dish. She wished to end the dinner now but it had to run its course and it continued in a strained way, as he returned once or twice to his attempts at justifying himself, still arguing that to serve two compatible masters was no crime.

He then came up with the defence that he was not so much a spy as an observer in a balloon. 'I was really carrying dispatches by observation balloon from one part of the army to another. That's how it should be seen.' He mumbled something about the status of an observer in a balloon being left as an open question by the Brussels Declaration.

'But you weren't in a balloon.'

'Not strictly speaking. No. True.'

For one odd moment, he appeared to have seen himself in a balloon. He seemed to have actually entertained the idea, literally.

'Or even more pointedly,' she said, attempting a lighter tone herself, 'if you were in a balloon, then that was something else you forgot to tell me.'

He was grateful for her lightness of tone, and seized on it, laughing too much at her small joke and prattling on about the 'balloon defence' as if that might be his exculpation.

On and off, she entertained the idea that his conduct could be mitigated by explanation, but no, for all his twisting rationale, the breach had been made and she was distanced from him and she stopped listening with the hope that something might be said which would erase everything, which would, by some verbal alchemy, return things to the jolly way they'd once been. As the meal laboured on she was still able to enjoy his refinement, his attempts not to succumb to the unhappiness of the evening, his banter, now a little half-hearted but still there, and his possession of exotic information now all brought to the service of perhaps gaining her complicity, her forgetfulness, or her forgiveness. How painful it was to try to eat fine food when you felt such unhappy tension. She was tormented, too, by the memory of fine dinners they'd shared there in the past. She felt a sad, shedding feeling and it left her standing alone on a new windy plateau in life, yet as he prattled, he seemed to be determined not to acknowledge that he had wrecked their friendship. His refusal to face it served to keep her dry-eyed, at least for now, and prevented her from falling into grief.

Only once during the meal did he approach self-pity or the maudlin and it was while throwing out some of his typically exotic information.

He told her that he'd heard of despairing African soldiers doing it during the War — using an incantation to commit suicide. By uttering a long combination of sounds and words and, at the same time, manipulating the breathing, this self-cursing, this incantation caused sufficient psychological and neurological pressure to come to bear against the human system that it literally stopped the person breathing and caused a nervous seizure, resulting in collapse and immediate death. He said that it probably inhibited the vagus nerve. 'I wish I knew it,' he said. 'I believe it could be taught only in sections — taking over a year. The witch doctor charged a very large fee for teaching it. I suppose by the end of the year you'd forgotten why it was you wanted to die.'

She'd said that it sounded fanciful and added that whatever the outcome of all this was, he would survive. 'The Foreign Office will always have you back,' she said both to continue to bring home to him that something very serious had happened in his career and between them, and to lessen the horror of it for her.

'Of course,' he said, replacing his mask of self-possession, 'always a bolt-hole there.'

She wondered if this was a situation where she should practise the skill of knowing how to make someone resign.

He made only one mildly unkind remark: 'We always spend third term at college getting rid of those people we befriended too quickly in first term.' She did not take it up, except to say, that in their case, it had been a long first term.

It allowed her one intimate criticism of him. 'You've never bought me a gift as long as I've known you,' she said. She'd always thought it was more of a confirmation of the limits of their former love and, at the same time, said something about his selfishness. Now it was an idle remark of curiosity, given the circumstances.

His reply bewildered her. 'I never had the courage to buy you anything,' he said, his voice humble. 'I thought I might get it all wrong. Might buy you something which damned me in your eyes.'

She had no reply to this. She saw that her power had been unfelt and therefore unexercised, at least consciously. It was the unfelt power of the young and of the beautiful.

After uncomfortable excuses to the proprietor about their not fully consuming the main course, they managed some cheese for the sake of appearances but did not have dessert, and there was no lingering over after-dinner drinks.

There was the final act of severance to be gone through, that of collecting her things from his apartment. As they took a taxi, she explained that she would do it tonight.

'Of course. Best thing,' he said.

The taxi reached his apartment and she had the taxi wait for her, feeling as she did, that it made her intentions about the visit severely clear.

She was surprised that Ambrose made a gesture, without much ardour, towards continuing the carnal part of their life, propelled perhaps by some insistent male urge, or maybe by deviousness. 'The comforts of the bed — one last time?' he said, as they went up the stairs, and although his voice was without any confidence in her reply, it did carry some right of assumption. 'Shall you and I play the dally? What do you say, Edith?' As if this could continue without friendship.

She shook her head and perfunctorily squeezed his hand. 'I will collect my things and say good night.' She wanted for it to be over quickly and to be gone. Her sexual desire for him had been waning, and she found no desire within her this night. She hoped that it stayed this way and that she would not have to live with any sexual torment, as well as whatever other torments of spirit lay ahead for having been involved in this mess of his downfall.

As they went into the flat, she felt the pull of another bond that had been in his proposal, another allegiance, but she'd let it pass without listening to its demands. It was the bond of petty decadence: their sexual practices had been a secret bond. She glimpsed the outlines of another web of allegiances spreading from this — it was the midnight intrigue and involvement which surrounded his minor vices and her indulgence of them, and her tolerance of the Molly Club people, that small, strange nation of the night, and she saw that, yes, it too had its allegiances and made its demands. But she could walk away from that web because it had never truly enfolded her. She'd been simply audience to his petty decadence. She thought that Ambrose, in a way, had also disgraced their secret life because there had been a courageous truthfulness that had sprung from their petty decadence which, it was now revealed, he had not fully honoured.

While she gathered her things from the apartment, he stood by abjectly with a large Scotch. She put her things in one of his suitcases.

He prattled bravely to cover his nervous unhappiness. 'The business in bed — the girl's clothing and all that — tell me, you were put off a bit by that?'

'No, I rather liked that from time to time — our love in costume. You looked good in the clothing.' That sexual play had touched something in her. He was simply seeking to recover something of their intimacy; he was desperately holding on.

'Thank you.' He said only one serious thing: 'Admit that I battled for the whimsy in your soul, Edith. I was a friend to the caprice in you.'

Her soul was receiving some scrutiny these days. 'I know,' she said, 'I always appreciated that.'

'I hope it stays alive.'

'It will. I'll see to that.'

'Don't let sedulity, or whatever, destroy your caprice, Edith.'

'I won't. I will return the suitcase to you at the office tomorrow.'

'Here — let me.' He put down the glass, and carried the case down to the waiting taxi.

'Cheerio and toodle pip,' he said, tears in his eyes, his merriment, again, abject. Tears came to her eyes too, but she did not show them. As the taxi began to pull away, he was still moving alongside and he tapped on the window. She told the driver to wait, and wound down the window.

Ambrose whispered to her, 'Without you to help with my clothes buying, I will go out of fashion.'

She smiled. 'You'll find another lady buyer, I'm sure.'

She wound up the window, telling the driver to proceed.

She felt a cold, lifeless relief from having parted from him. As the taxi passed through the night, Edith thought briefly of the American woman, the voluptuary upon whom she had spied and from whom the whole sad matter had arisen. She found it impossible to believe that she had ever contemplated going back to dally — using Ambrose's word — with that woman. That she had entertained that idea at the time was to do with the atmosphere of petty decadence created by Ambrose around them both. But she summoned up the voluptuous feeling of being with the woman that night, savoured it, and then let it fade.

*

The following month, having agreed to sever his connections with the British Foreign Office, Ambrose was moved to the part of the section where he would be concerned with building maintenance, furniture, and cleaning. Even this, she saw as evidence of the British at the top looking after their own. Or maybe it was the other club — of those men who had served in the War. She had begun to sense that within the organisation many 'clubs' had formed. Even she belonged in one or two. Had he been a spy for the Bulgarians or a Balkan state he would not have kept his job. Later when she queried this with Under Secretary Bartou, he had replied in a mock British accent, ' "You don't ruin a good fellow because he's been a silly ass." ' She didn't know if it was Sir Eric he was quoting.

Ambrose's acceptance of this demotion and that he did not bolt back to the Foreign Office showed her that he was determined to go on working for the League in whatever capacity and that he did have an allegiance of a kind. Or was it that, in reality, he had no other place to go? A few months after his demotion, he sent her a cheque for the money he owed her, although it was for a lesser amount than her records showed. It contained a note which cried out for some reconciliation but she couldn't grant that. She wished he'd gone back to England.

She formally received an invitation to work with Under Secretary Bartou, and on the day that she went to see him to formally accept, she made clear one thing which had been worrying her.

She reminded Under Secretary Bartou of an earlier conversation about eunuchs.

Under Secretary Bartou nodded.

'I feel honour-bound to make a statement,' she said.

'Please do.'

'Ambrose Westwood is not a eunuch. Or anything resembling a eunuch,' she said.

She felt she owed Ambrose that. She didn't want to dislodge by her silence any avalanche of rumour and innuendo which might begin to further fall on him with his demotion. Maybe Under Secretary Bartou might be able to check some of that avalanche. Although Ambrose may not have been an altogether conventional man, they had, for a time, been true lovers, as a man and a woman. She saw that she was also protecting the reputation of her womanhood. She did not want to be known as Someone Who Had Eunuchs as Friends. Not, at least, until she knew more about eunuchs.

'I note that,' Under Secretary Bartou said, and with a smile added, 'in my head.'

Leaving Under Secretary Bartou's office, she was now sure that she walked the corridors in a different way. It was a self-assurance but it did not come so much from her rise within her vocation, but rather from the dark, maybe grim, wisdom which increasingly seemed to come from the daily practice of the idealism of her vocation. Her body in her new suit felt vigorous, but her heart had been scarred again. She did recall Edward Trenbow, a friend who had been for a while a doctor in her home town, once saying to her that a scar was the strongest part of the skin. She fervently hoped that he and her father were both right about scars.

The Weight of the Stone

As she let go from Ambrose, Edith began to see that what they'd shared as a couple was a covert dependency but that their initial meeting could probably still be seen as an auspicious encounter, regardless of what had happened. She recalled how inflexible her personality had been then as she faced the ordeal of proving herself at the League and yet, for all the rules of the League and all her own rules of inner management, she recalled also how unguided she'd been. But, looking back, she'd quickly learned how to turn her gullibility into an unclosed approach to the world. How to turn her naïvety in the direction of original reflection. At first, she'd tried to make Going Against the Rules a personal rule until she'd realised that it was just inflexibility wearing a different uniform.

She also saw that in her initial isolation she had been too quick to befriend Ambrose, or as it turned out, perhaps he'd been forcing the relationship along for his private reasons as a mask for all kinds of concealments. Yet she tried not to believe that of him. He himself had quite early in their friendship told her of the advice of Lord Malmesbury to be cautious of those who, on your first arrival, appear the most eager to make your acquaintance. But then, someone contriving a relationship would say that. It was not knowable. She was learning to clear her mind both of those things which were unknowable and of those things which were unchangeable. Anyhow, she had gripped on to him as a companion and because, with his Foreign Office background, he'd been able to tutor her, so that from another point of view it could be seen as a contriving on her part. To a degree, perhaps both of them had been contriving a relationship.

One's first friends usually showed you how you saw yourself at the time. Perhaps how others saw you. Or was friendship more accidental than that? A surrounding of haphazardly formed contracts. And was life always too short to allow you to ever sort them out?

No. There had been real attraction between them, and in that first year it was only when in bed with Ambrose or when making banter over drinks with him that she had ever been able to slacken from her rule-bound self. She saw now how unthreatening he'd been because of his illusive maleness and how this had been a respite for her, both from the burdens of work and from the claims of womanhood. He himself had been escaping from the worldly part of himself into his silken fantasies of Woman and resting in, and relishing, the feminine aura which she could provide. He had never seriously offered himself as husband. His last-minute declaration had been more of an attempt to hold on to her as a comfortable friend — or maybe simply to turn her into an accomplice — than to win her as wife, and he had, over the years, made only the most diffident claims as a lover. She, for her part, had never offered herself as a wife. But had she succeeded in being an accomplished mistress? Perhaps she too had been pretending and hiding — pretending to the world that she had a proper man and pretending to her friends that she was a proper mistress. No, she believed that it had been an authentic coupling with its own character, but still, authentic.

While being a safe and temporary man, Ambrose had, at the same time, opened her to 'experience' in the most graphic meaning of the word. He had emboldened her, had been an exuberant leader and companion in escapade. She suspected that she would have become a grey person sequestered in her pension and her work had it not been for his leading her on excursions into his own and Geneva's few dark secrets. This companionship had also been a meeting with some peculiar traits within herself, although nothing, that she could yet discern, which caused her to question or deviate in any dire way from the natural drives of womanhood. Despite what Florence had once said.

From Ambrose she had also learned about the codes men lived by, of avocation and protocol and also about the hidden rules, known as good form and bad form, by which men also lived. She'd learned about the aptitude some people had for concealing parts of themselves in sovereign compartments, so that at any given time you were never seeing a reliably complete person at all.

And he'd taught her yet another lesson: the presence of the third level of existence. This was not the existence of the institutional self which often involved a precautionary conceal-ment of one's true opinion, an understanding that there was no social obligation to always express disagreement when one disagreed. Nor was it casual duplicity, which she knew about now only too well. Nor was it the contradictory nature of the murkier self which appeared sometimes in the passions of the night. This third level was the life of methodical subterfuge — which meant that apparently good men like Ambrose could be spies. It was by this unintended and final lesson that he had tutored himself out of true friendship with her.

She suspected that Ambrose and she would have only a pale professional acquaintanceship. This gave her pain of loss. They had lost the friendship in which everything was possible, without the constraint of righteousness or self-regard. She was learning that this was a rare thing, of the highest value, and she was fearful that she would not find it again with anyone. But she could see another lesson in this which she hadn't quite seen before. That candour could be divisible.

She sometimes wondered whether if she hadn't been an officer of the League, and knowing that he spied, she could have gone on being Ambrose's intimate friend. She thought it feasible, but then, if she did not work for the League she would perhaps be a different person. We become what we do. She would have become, in Caroline's words, Someone Who Had Spies as Friends, whatever that sort of person was.

She hoped that his final lesson to her hadn't been to teach her permanent and universal mistrust.

Her working with Bartou was a tutoring too, a form of higher study. Bartou practised wisdom, including what she called dark wisdom. Ambrose had a good background in diplomacy from the FO but she wouldn't say that he had wisdom. To know the doorways of minor decadence was perhaps a fascinating lore, and a knowledge of the mysterious self and its pleasure, but it was not really a wisdom.

One other thing had to be faced. Although she now had a Wise Man as her superior in her professional life — her own *chef du protocole* — she had no Lover, both in its carnal sense and in its other meanings. Having had a Lover, she felt its absence more tangibly than the way she might have felt it as a girl, when it had been a romantic abstract. It was, she found, another conscious incompleteness about her life. It was something she saw clearly and unhappily expressed in Victoria. Victoria had dreams of being with a man but could not seem to form a crossing of the boundary between men and women. Victoria caused men to be uncomfortable about passion yet they liked her as a pal, as if refusing to see her as a woman. Edith's private theory was that Victoria was a victim of her name. Her name came from another generation and another time and from royalty. Men perhaps thought she was from the world of their mothers.

Was she now destined, like Victoria, to give herself more and more to the League?

During her breakdown over it all, she'd kept up the practice of disappearing from the pension at the week-ends. It had served as an opportunity to go away by herself into the countryside for solitary walks, to stay by herself and read in country inns. But finally, on the advice of worried friends, she had begun a round of social activities as a way of overcoming not only the loss of Ambrose from her life but the shock which had come from the nature of that parting. So had been the new clothes, the new style of hair — not quite Louise Brooks, but similar — and even a change of cosmetics. She found that she could not tolerate the thought that some of her toiletry had been used by her and Ambrose in their weird former affair. She had gone about removing any object in her life that had come out of that companionship while, curiously, still having erotically charged recollections about their time together.

She had a sense of loss but she did not have a broken heart. She had talked with Caroline about it before she'd left. She'd asked Caroline about her own heart. Caroline had become immediately tearful — the only time she'd seen Caroline cry. Caroline said that once your heart had been broken you could never again believe in a merciful God. She said that once your heart was broken all the fine and happy times spent with that person were brutally effaced. Every time you saw the lover's name or something triggered a recollection of your time together it scratched your heart. She said she feared that people with broken hearts went on to break other hearts because, emotionally, they were blinded and were simply stumbling through life bumping into people. If you did not withdraw from life, you could hurt others in your ruthless search for solace.

She'd asked Caroline about Liverright. Caroline said that Liverright did not have a broken heart but that life had taken away from under him the ground on which he'd stood. 'The secure ground disappeared from under his feet. It seems to give a similar result to having your heart broken. He and I are both broken dolls.'

She'd held Caroline in an embrace while she sobbed.

Edith had never heard Caroline speak with such bitter fervency. At least Caroline had had the experience of great love. And at the time that she'd had it, those hours and days could not be taken from her. Surely only the memories were effaced? But she could not ask this.

Edith was spending more time dancing at the Restaurant des Eaux Vives or Maxim's and going to every new motion picture. She even went to see *The Sunny Side of the War*. She usually went as an invited companion of one or other of the polite young men about the place, invitations which she accepted almost without discrimination, as a personal tenet — yet another personal tenet! — because she felt, and Joshi and Jeanne also advised, that she should expose herself more to men in more customary ways. At the same time, she was watching for a sign of that relaxing candour she had lost when she broke from Ambrose — although she sometimes despaired that she would ever find it in these polite promenades, suspecting that it might flourish only in the irregular byways. None of these companions became lovers in the carnal sense. As she'd said to herself a few times now, she had no intention of becoming a loose woman, and she considered that perhaps a few experiences before marriage was modern but that there was a boundary line and she was approaching it. She had no intention of becoming like Iris in *The Green Hat*.

Without regret, she was spending less time in the Bavaria,

the place where she was more likely to run into Ambrose.

She somehow hoped that the laying of the foundation stone for the new Palais des Nations might mark all manner of things both for the League and for herself. And she so decreed that the occasion of the laying of the stone would mark the end of her time of sadness and deadness.

She accepted a minor task there as Bartou's consort.

She was standing near the canvas awning erected for the dignitaries, after having made sure that all the dignitaries were properly acknowledged and seated. She was, she thought, almost the hostess of the occasion, certainly more so than Lady Drummond. She couldn't see Ambrose anywhere in the crowd. Nor Florence and her crowd. Robert Dole was there with the press and she could see McGeachy fussing around them. Victoria was there with some of the Registry people. A group of children from the League school, led by the exuberant Zilliacus girl, was barely behaving itself.

The President of Council, M. Foroughi of Persia, stood in the parc de l'Ariana, and tapped the foundation stone of the Palais des Nations with the silver trowel and began to speak, but the loudspeaker still wasn't working and it was difficult to hear his words unless you were as close as Edith. She finally went over to the man working the loudspeaker and, while not shaking him, told him what it was that he was doing wrong. He didn't take kindly to her advice but the sound did improve.

She waved and smiled to Victoria. She had nearly lost that friendship too. Victoria had come to her after the crisis with Ambrose and said that she wanted to know what had happened between her and Ambrose and why Ambrose had been demoted. She said that she felt she had a right to know. She'd heard all sorts of gossip. She realised then that Victoria saw herself as a closer friend to her than she had seen herself to Victoria. This had saddened her and she wished that she could be a close friend to Victoria. It had been easier when there'd been the three of them but now that Florence was no longer her friend it had become harder being just with Victoria. The 'Dominion Sisters' no longer existed. She acknowledged Victoria's right to know and told Victoria most of it, although not the carnally irregular parts of her and Ambrose's story. She told of Ambrose misusing League documents, showing them to people outside the League and how she felt Ambrose had used her.

Surprisingly, Victoria had said that she felt she, too, had been used — by Edith. Edith had been stunned by this. Victoria said that often over the years, Edith had requested things of her, sometimes asking her to bend the rules, yet had rarely ever explained the reason. Had rarely brought her into the secret. More surprisingly, Victoria said she'd suspected Edith of perhaps betraying the League by misusing documents. Edith had spent time assuring Victoria of her loyalty as a friend and colleague and to the League and apologising for her thoughtlessness. Against her personal inclination, she had gone out of her way then to invite Victoria places. She couldn't bear the loss of someone else, however meagre that friendship might be.

In the special cavity in the foundation stone, the President placed the casket containing a document describing the event in thirty languages and including coins from all member states. Well, nearly all — South Africa had missed out. And as for languages, Sir Eric had said no to Esperanto, and for India they'd had to settle on English. New Zealand nearly missed out with their coins because the letter asking for it, as usual, got to New Zealand too late. Poor old New Zealand. Sir James Parr had saved the day and sent some New Zealand coins over from England.

The President sealed the cavity with the silver trowel but his words were still distorted. The wretched loudspeaker man.

Edith was watching so intently that she had trouble realising that it was done and over. She was striving to exact something emotional and historical from the placing of the casket, from the foundation stone, from the occasion. To make herself feel something, to stir her deadness. And now it was over.

This strange, so immediate vanishing of 'the occasion' reminded her of a day from her childhood when the first aeroplane had landed in the town, in a paddock, and she, together with the whole town, had been there to watch. She had strained to watch as the plane circled and then approached, and then bumped down and across the grass and stopped. She'd been as close as was allowed and as close also to Uncle Fred, the Shire President, closer than any of the other children, even back then, intent on approaching the experience as closely as possible. But after the plane had bumped to a halt, and its engine had died and its propeller had stopped, the leather-clad pilot had hoisted himself out of the cockpit and had a cup of tea from a Thermos flask. And that was it. Nothing more 'happened'. The shock she recalled was in realising that the experience was over and done. The aeroplane had landed and stopped.

She'd expected so much more from her first landing of an aeroplane.

Here in Geneva, she felt she was back in the paddock watching the plane land. There were even a few dogs, as there had been back then. The men all wore frock coats which helped. She'd heard that during the planning Lloyd had argued for having a brass band but Sir Eric had opposed it. A band might have helped. If she'd been back in Internal, she would've convinced Sir Eric to have a band.

Now it was over. Just like that.

And she had wanted a sign that she was over the loss of her Lover and his betrayal. There was no sign.

Oh well, the fact was that the stone was laid and that the Palais would be built. Miss Dickinson's chair would be in it, though the drama of the chair all seemed a long time ago. When she passed it in the Council room now, the chair didn't look as glorious as it once had. It was beginning to be, well, part of the furniture.

In his speech, the President of the Swiss Confederation had said that the League had become for all mankind a definite path, a meeting place, a common workshop, a bond, a way of life. She had felt almost moved by this. However he had gone on to say too much, and the power of these words was smothered out.

She'd liked best President Foroughi saying that in monuments and buildings the lessons of civilisation were preserved. They were the common patrimony of mankind. He said that while some famous buildings and magical towns seemed to belong to all of us in our minds, the Palais des Nations, for the first time in history, was to be a building erected as the common property of all peoples united in brotherhood. That was a new idea in the world — that the world should construct buildings.

But when she looked at the event, apart from these sentiments and this new thought, she was left with very little.

After some uncertain clapping, the crowd broke up, unsure whether that was all there was and without having a sense of much having happened, or a sense of conclusion. She wiped away a small tear of disappointment about the ceremony. She saw that Mr Zumeta from Venezuela, whose idea it had been to have a grand ceremony, was not happy either. His country had also missed out on having a coin in the capsule. She wanted to go over to him and say something kind but she had nothing to say.

She watched Robert Dole go over and touch the foundation stone, as if testing that it was truly stone and not a fake. She resisted going over and talking to him.

After checking with Bartou that she wasn't needed, she too strolled away across the park, and fell in with some of the British delegation as they walked over to the motor-cars. Not that she felt that much at home with them. Over the years she'd had trouble with Mrs Swanwick, especially.

'That was one of the worst managed and dullest functions I have ever attended,' Mrs Swanwick was saying.

'Oh no,' Edith said loudly, involuntarily, pained, 'it wasn't like that.'

'Oh?' said Mrs Swanwick in an encouraging conversational tone used for gals from the colonies. 'And how then should I see it?'

'Well, nothing like this has ever happened — it could never be said to be dull. Surely?' Edith tried to bring in a note of self-doubt to modify the strength of her reply to Mrs Swanwick. She tried to sound not so defensive. 'It is to be the first building built and owned by the entire world.'

'But my dear, I felt there should have been pageantry, flags and flowers and singing, didn't you?'

'The appropriate pageantry hasn't been thought of yet. No pageantry would be suitable. Any pageantry would just be borrowed from some lesser activity. There just isn't any pageantry suitable yet,' Edith struggled to say. 'For me, it was a simple event of the most magnificent order,' and then added, rather pompously, 'and we were invited by history to witness it.'

That wasn't really quite what she felt.

Mrs Swanwick said she would've liked some Swiss choral singing and 'people from the countryside in peasant clothing'.

That was the last thing Edith wanted. It would then have been nothing more than a Swiss fête. But in general, if she didn't grate so much with Mrs Swanwick, she would have allowed herself to agree with her more. She would have agreed that the event had needed something else.

Although she had a lot of time for the other people from the Union for Democratic Control, Mrs Swanwick had always put her teeth on edge. At any banquet, she always made a point of never taking all the courses, as if to say, Look at all you gluttons, look at how frugal and sensible I am, why can't you all be as frugal and as sensible as me?

At other Assemblies where Mrs Swanwick had been a delegate, or a supplementary delegate, she was always going bemoaning the banquets and balls and the lavishness of the social life around the League. She didn't realise that people with less puritanical ardour than she came to the League and supported the League and they needed refreshment and reward to keep their spirits up. Edith felt banquets and so on kept up people's confidence. And celebrated their labours. Ye gods, what were a few glasses of champagne? People had to feel valued.

And as for herself, she wanted to take from life as generously as she gave to life.

She had to admit that Mrs Swanwick was good about always refusing to speak 'on behalf of women' because a man never spoke 'on behalf of men'.

Edith declined an invitation to dine with Mrs Swanwick and the others.

*

'It was a new type of History,' she expounded to Jeanne over tea at Jeanne's apartment. Jeanne couldn't come to the laying of the stone because of a sprained ankle.

Edith felt pressingly that she had to get Jeanne to agree with her about the solemn symbolism of the laying of the stone — and to make herself feel something. 'Even if it was like a shire council function. It will be the first time a building will belong to the whole world.' She was still struggling to feel right about the day.

'You make it sound dull, Edith. Oh so dull. I hate to agree with Mrs Swanwick. But certainly not Swiss peasants in costumes.'

Jeanne asked her to explain what a shire council function was, which, impatiently, she did. 'But, Jeanne, for the first time, the world is creating a building. And I was there. I was one of the handful of people in the world who saw it happen! Jeanne?'

'It was one way to look at it.'

'The grandeur was inherent. It couldn't be expressed by a brass band. Or by ceremonials.'

'Edith! But I thought you were for ceremonials? I hear you at other times carrying on about the need for ceremonials.' She laughed.

'I was. I am. But no one else is — except for Mrs Swanwick who gets it all wrong and wants peasants in Swiss national costume, and anyhow, she's usually the one who wants less pomp and ceremony. The trouble was that all the ceremonials anyone could think of were from some other time and place and not made for our historical time and place which has never before existed. That was where I was wrong.' She heard herself declaiming. 'Maybe I ask too much of the world.'

'That is probably a truth, Edith. But why not ask too much of the world, I say.'

Edith sometimes worried that the world did not know how to live properly, and that she did. Ye gods, she had often said that the League existed to teach the world manners. Did she, in turn, have to teach the League how to live?

Really her mood had to do with the leftover feelings of the break with Ambrose. She suspected that Jeanne knew that.

'I wouldn't mind a glass of something,' she said to Jeanne.

'Look in the cabinet — some port maybe, some pastis?'

'*Et pour toi?*'

'*Une goutte de porto, peût-etre.*'

These drinks didn't appeal. Edith got up and poured Jeanne a port. From Jerome's flask in her handbag, she poured herself a Scotch.

'That flask? You hint at the history of the flask but I have never heard the history of that flask.'

Edith smiled. She wasn't going to risk another confidence. She stared at her Scotch, ate another madeleine. Her sixth. Her father would frown at her for eating cake and drinking good Scotch. 'One day, over lunch. It's a long story. A romantic story.' Romantic?

What of ceremonials? Weren't they part of the complete picture of an institution? The Catholic Church, for example. Ceremonials were the theatre of the institution. The periodical display of the institution's inner self. Ceremonials were a commitment in a dignified form. Did the paltryness of the League's ceremonials mean that the League was sober, determined to be about more important matters of substance and that it had no time for the trappings and the pomp of a Church?

She was grumpy with herself too because of the strength of the remarks she'd made to Mrs Swanwick. In a way she had been put against herself by Mrs Swanwick.

Last week Mrs Swanwick had talked some of them into

going to the Armenian restaurant and eating a peasant's meal or something of that sort as a political stunt. They all paid what they would have for a five-course French dinner and the money went to some Armenian fund or other. Those people couldn't enjoy themselves unless it was for a good cause.

She tried to explain to Jeanne how her exchange with Mrs Swanwick had unintentionally led her to see the stone-laying as 'simple magnificent history', quite properly stripped of all commonplace pageantry. She wouldn't have been forced to see it that way if she hadn't disliked Mrs Swanwick.

That raised other terrors. What if there was a whole false way of seeing things which she and other people customarily had, and which she would have gone on having had she not been tripped or trapped into seeing another way by chance encounters such as this?

It was not because the person you disagreed with saw the world correctly, but that you were forced to see it in an altogether different way, both from how you had seen it and from how the other person had seen it. Through the collision with that person, you were deflected into another third trajectory by the impact. By wanting to distance yourself from that person, you ended up in a new place entirely. But that was hardly a way to find one's position in life.

It had been a laying of a simple stone in an empty field, with a casket of languages and money. With words said over the stone.

But upon that stone would be built the first building owned by the world.

'You know, Jeanne,' she said, wondering if she was going to weep, 'I thought it was going to be the most wonderful day of my life. And it wasn't.'

'Oh, Edith.' Jeanne awkwardly leaned out of her chaise longue and gave Edith a clumsy half-hug in sympathy, and they remained in this awkward but comforting embrace. 'What about if you marry — your wedding day! That will be the most wonderful day of your life, will it not?'

'You are a true *romantique*, Jeanne.'

'And you, Edith?'

She smiled at Jeanne. 'If I marry. Well, that would be something else. But historically the most wonderful day of my life should've been today.'

'Maybe you watch for history too hard, Edith. And me, I search for the *romantique* too hard?'

'I think you're right about me, Jeanne.'

'Wedding night might be more likely the most important day, if you can say that in English,' Jeanne said.

'We aren't the sort of people who wait, are we? For the wedding night?'

They both smiled. She knew Jeanne understood what was still disheartening her.

Jeanne said, 'It would be nice to wait, I think, sometimes. But — too late.' Jeanne gave the impression of having had many lovers.

'Yes, too late for girls like us.'

Something grand should have happened tonight after the laying of the stone. There should have been a banquet in every village, town and city, the whole world should have been banqueting, watching fireworks. Something should have happened on this day of all days, some celebration not yet imagined. Everyone remembered where they were on Armistice Day — no one would remember where they were on the day of the laying of the foundation stone of the new Palais of the League of Nations.

'Showmanship' was what had been needed. Just that week she'd been saddened by the news that Captain Strongbow had been murdered in China. She'd been touched that Athena had written to her. Athena thought that perhaps the 'Grand Assembly' of the League could observe a minute's silence for Captain Strongbow because of his work for internationalism. Athena had also asked whether the League of Nations had a burial fund to pay for the expense of the return of Captain Strongbow's body to California.

Instead of great celebrations, the silly Mrs Swanwick wanted to have tea at an inexpensive place called the le Creux de Gentot.

Edith thought that maybe she should be appointed Master of Ceremonies for the World. But she instantly plummeted from this grand notion and crashed down amid her own life. She saw that she had lost the domestic ceremonies from her life, she had no true home, she had tried to make the world her dinner table, her fête.

She couldn't even choose true and trustworthy friends.

She poured herself another Scotch and began to weep.

Arbitrarily appointed Days of Healing did not work.

The Key to All Predicaments

At first, Edith was perturbed that Ambrose had been invited to the next Directors' meeting and had been given permission to make a statement on Agriculture. Apart from it not being his field of expertise, she supposed that she felt that he should have been denied access to the Directors' meeting totally and for ever more, as part of his punishment, but more than that, she didn't like the idea of being in the room while he made his statement, though she wasn't going to miss a meeting because of him. Since their parting of the ways, now over a year ago, she'd barely seen him, except to say hello while passing in the corridor, and consequently no etiquette had evolved to allow them to exist socially or professionally in close proximity. Bluntly, her opposition to him attending the meeting came from a selfish reasoning. She had an equivocal status at the Directors' meetings, as a stand-in for Bartou. She wanted eventually to be seen as a bona fide part of the meeting and she certainly didn't want to have to cope with a disgraced former lover at a Directors' meeting when she had enough to struggle with already.

Ambrose didn't seem in any way to hold her actions against her and in the corridor he always tried to ensnare her, while she, on the other hand, always kept going, waving and smiling, but not stopping. She felt she had nothing to say to him. When she'd seen him around the Palais or, very occasionally, at the Bavaria he appeared to her to be going off somewhat. His smile seemed to be overanxious to find a smile in return; his clothes, while still well-made, were not properly cared for. She was also irritated that his going off was still being interpreted by those who didn't know the full story as being a result of a broken heart.

Sitting at his large desk, smoking his pipe, Bartou said that Ambrose had been given leave to address the meeting because everyone had a special respect for those officers who'd been there from the beginning.

'Even if that long service was somewhat disloyal?' she said, grumpily, standing at the window looking at the first snow of winter. 'Even if it isn't his field of expertise?'

Bartou shrugged. 'Maybe it's his attempt to find grace again. He can't be punished for ever.'

She still felt much more strongly about this matter than he did. Perhaps she didn't accept that one could regain grace once having fallen from it the way he had. She said she couldn't see why Ambrose wasn't asked to put his statement or whatever in writing.

'He said he couldn't put it in writing — it was philosophically too involved.'

She could tell there was amusement in Bartou's tone.

Bartou added, 'I suspect that the Latins think that he might be about to tell them a *British* secret — as penance.'

'It's a big mystery then?'

'It is, I suspect, a small mystery. And over a fine lunch some time this week, perhaps, I expect you to tell it to me as a good mystery story should be told.'

'You won't be going to the meeting?'

'This is one for you, Edith.'

The fine lunches were too common now, and although she described them as luncheon 'tutorials', he was teaching her more about lunching than the League. In the old days, Ambrose had taught her about the importance of dinner as a gastronomic expedition whose course was plotted by wine, and a conversational event where wine was the master of ceremonies. Now Bartou expounded the value of the lunch. Back in the office after these lunches, Bartou tended to doze. He was growing old and had earned easy afternoons. And in her case, the guilt of a good lunch made her work even harder and longer. She'd begun also to take telephone calls and answer letters on his behalf, making his decisions.

Bartou had taken to sending her along to the Directors' meetings more often than not, unless he had something very pressing to say at a meeting. She felt he was pushing her forward, although at the same time, he was withdrawing somewhat from the internal life of the League to get on with preparing the ground for the world disarmament conference which had become his overriding mission. And by devolvement and choice, it was also becoming her overriding mission. The third leg of the tripod — arbitration was in place with the court of international justice, economic sanctions had replaced war, and now followed disarmament.

He returned to the subject of Ambrose saying, 'Diplomacy sometimes requires the capacity to forget. Or, more precisely, it requires some officers who remember and some who forget. Those who can forget are free to get on with making things afresh with optimism, while those who can't forget issue warnings. If everyone remembered everything in politics, we would all stand eternally condemned and frozen. I think that is why the world forgives and forgets its liars, cheats and other villains. I know we pretend that people in public life who make a serious error are finished. They seldom are if they stay alive and stay in the game. There but for the grace of God, go I.' He said he thought that knowing 'when to forget' was a diplomatic art. And a social art.

'Not I. In this particular case,' she said. She didn't care if it sounded priggish.

But by the time the meeting came around, she'd softened her position a little about Ambrose, and felt that maybe it was time for him to be given a chance to redeem himself, although she would oppose any permanent return to the *haute direction*. She was also curious to hear what he'd been thinking about and what he'd come up with.

Her arrival at the meeting room was always carefully timed so that she was not the first there, not wanting to appear an eager beaver, nor the last, fearing that either way she would draw attention to herself, and perhaps bring into question the legitimacy of her presence there. Entering the room, she said hello and sat, as usual, beside Dame Rachel.

She looked down the agenda. She saw that Ambrose was to be called to the meeting first.

He entered the room rather loudly with photographs clumsily pinned to a board and Jules coming behind him carrying an easel. Jules wasn't a messenger in Ambrose's section and must have been there as a favour to Ambrose. The photographs seemed to be of a tractor and farming implements. She recalled with a smile her first ever Directors' meeting and Ambrose's successful arguments for emergency procedures, with working models. She mentioned it to Dame Rachel who said, 'Oh yes, I remember very well.'

After Jules had put the easel in place, he said, 'Is that all, Major?' and Ambrose, in a brisk voice, said, 'Thank you, Jules,' and Jules left the room.

Ambrose came across to Dame Rachel and her, saying hello to Dame Rachel and then turning to her and taking her hand, 'Edith, it's so good to see you up here with the gods. And good to have a friend in court,' he said warmly. 'How's tricks?'

'We're all agog about your mysterious presentation,' she said, in a restrained but sociable tone, uncomfortable with his assumption that she was unquestionably a friend in court. He seemed to have made an effort with his appearance. She glanced at his polished shoes with private unhappy amusement. He had once showed her how he tied his shoes with a double cross in the laces, saying, 'Things like that are important to me.'

He narrowed his eyes mysteriously. 'I think you'll all be somewhat bowled over.'

She hoped they would, and that he'd be back in favour again, something of his old self, and that she would be relieved of the guilt she occasionally, and unjustly, felt for his downfall.

The meeting was opened by Sir Eric and he invited Ambrose to talk to them.

In his best English accent, as if also polished for the occasion, Ambrose thanked the Directors and other heads of section for permitting him to speak. He said it was good to be back in such exalted altitudes again, since his own 'change of circumstances'.

There were supportive chuckles. Edith tried not to chuckle but did, pulled in by the laughter of the others.

'I want to begin philosophically. In my banishment, I have been able to give much time to thinking philosophically. What has come home to me is that we, in the League, have been dealing with all things in isolation, in compartments, when we should've been looking at them as a whole, as a planetary system, with the planets revolving in fixed axes to each other. We have not been thinking universally. I blame myself as much as I blame anyone. Believe me, it was how I thought until recently. More anon.

'I see all international predicaments as linked one with the other, all in cause and effect. If we are to wallop these predicaments, I would now argue that we must begin at one correct and vital place. Not at all places at once. And it is at this one point that we must apply all our coffers. That somewhere, that beginning point, is the key to all our endeavours.

'For having once found this point, and then having changed this one cardinal part of our universe in an absolute and productive way, it will follow that all other parts will therefore change in an absolute and productive way. There will be a cause-and-effect repercussion through to all the other predicaments — an explosive chain of consequence — through the whole of the universe of predicaments which bedevil us. In medicine we once called it the reflex arc, the theory that one organ can sicken another.'

This was a tantalising, if fanciful, beginning and Ambrose had the attention of the meeting.

'Down in my place of banishment, my Siberia, I asked myself which predicament it was to which all others are linked.

'I knew that if I could determine this, then I would have the key to all predicaments. Time went by and no answer came to me.'

He went on with a tense enthusiasm. 'While on leave, I saw an invention and was struck by the whole philosophical and organic connection to this one invention and I said to myself, "Why, here it is!" We look to conferences and assemblies and parliaments to solve the calamities of the human condition when here before our very eyes — my very eyes in this case — ' he smiled, but went on without waiting for any responsive laughter, 'here then was the answer, in a field of hay. It is not political theory which will save us, but one simple useful invention. How obvious it now looks!

'It came to me that all predicaments of the world are linked to a very rudimentary thing — they are all linked to hunger. That if we solved the predicament of hunger then all others would be resolved, as it were, overnight: war and so on, good health — here I speak as a doctor.'

There were some glances one to the other now as Ambrose talked. He was sounding not like a doctor at all, and less and less like a League official — more like someone at Hyde Park Corner. Or one of the many crank correspondents who wrote to the League.

'If people are well fed, nourished correctly, they will resist all illness. I believe this. That correct diet will armour people against all illness. I see your first objection. That surely it also matters what persuasions and beliefs these people have to life, that also determines their health mentally. I argue that persuasions and beliefs flow from good diet — good politics comes from good diet.'

Everyone in the room now seemed to know that it was going wrong and that Ambrose was not well, but they were immobilised by courtesy.

He was oblivious to the change in the mood of the meeting. 'With my haversack and birch staff — very English — ' he smiled at the non-English members, 'here I was, on a walking trip through Wiltshire in the sunshine, listening to the birds, smelling the flowers, smelling the hay, and I stopped to watch the haymakers at work. For anyone wanting to refresh their spirits, I would recommend Wiltshire at the end of summer — I have some inns, some addresses if anyone is interested — it was here in Wiltshire and in a field of hay that I saw the answer to all to which we have dedicated our lives: the simple invention which will revolutionise all our lives — trust the British to come up with it, I thought — gentlemen, ladies, this invention is called the New Century Hay Sweep.'

He paused for dramatic effect.

For a single minute, as he stood there expectantly with his

pointer, she was able to look at him dispassionately and she saw that he was unbalanced — perhaps the shock of being demoted and the continuing mental strains from the War had now unbalanced him seriously. There was a desperate tension oozing through his affable manner. She could see now that the affable manner was, in fact, an imitation of an affable manner. There were some nervous clearings of throats, some shuffling. Oh my God, thought Edith, and she looked at Dame Rachel who had closed her eyes.

'I know what some of you are thinking.' Ambrose tried for a joke, sensing for the first time, perhaps, that the audience was not altogether with him. 'You are thinking, some of you, that I have a financial interest in the New Century Hay Sweep or that I am connected by family or something like that to the inventor. Not true. Not true at all. No fiduciary connection exists at all. None whatsoever, I assure you.

'I saw the New Century Hay Sweep being used both with horses and with tractor and the farmers and men using it have nothing but praise for it.

'It is an absurdly simple contrivance and until you see it in use it looks quite unpractical, quite ungainly — clumsy even.

'The hay is left in long rough lines on the field and the sweep is drawn either by two horses or a tractor.

'The machine consists of long wooden prongs which can be raised or lowered by a lever in the hand of a single driver. The prongs are lowered until they just scrape the ground when picking up the hay and raised when the sweep is empty or has a load.

'The sweep takes the hay right up to the stack or barn. I saw it at work on a hot day and the horse hardly lathered at all. I touched the rump of the horse to test if it was straining. I can assure you gentlemen, ladies, that it was not.' He said this with inappropriate intensity.

'If the sweep, as often occurs, drops or fails to pick up a lump of hay, it merely stops, backs at once out of its load which remains on the ground, and then picks up the bit it has left together with the main load and goes forward again. Do you all follow?

'Now for the revolutionary fact: I am told that the sweep does the work of four men and eight horses.'

Edith looked around. Dame Rachel was now trying to catch Sir Eric's eye to stop the embarrassment. But Sir Eric was looking fixedly at the papers in front of him, as if frozen. He'd worked so closely with Ambrose as far back as the Peace Conference and then in the early days of the League. For Edith, it was an agony of empathy together with personal mortification. She had never been in a meeting caught in such a paralysing tension of embarrassment.

Ambrose, unaware of the mood of the meeting, went on with his speech. 'With a tractor, the result is even more striking. The sweep is fixed at the front of the tractor and the lever for raising and lowering it is at the driver's right hand. The man at the wheel said he could do a steady eight miles an hour. He said he had not broken a single prong during the season. I confess that the machine looks as if it would perpetually be dropping part of its load and as if the prongs would always be catching in the ground and breaking off, but these things do not occur.

'There is one problem, and I rush to admit this. The sweep is wider than most gates. But in countries with no fences this should not be a problem — that is, in the poorer countries which desperately need such an invention.

'What I am saying is this: if we can speed up agricultural production worldwide by eight times, we can feed eight times more people, roughly speaking. Hence, banishing hunger for all time.

'So, in conclusion, with your permission Sir Eric, I would ask the meeting, with respect, to consider urgently putting information about this sweep before our new Subcommittee of Agricultural Experts and before all governments across the world.

'I have since sought out the man who patented it and he would be happy to arrange for a demonstration in Geneva for all interested governments.'

He beamed out a smile which begged for applause and for compliments. Maybe for a standing ovation. Ambrose must have sensed at this point that there was considerable unease in the meeting and that he had not convinced them, had been somehow off the mark. No one was looking at him directly; no eye would meet his eye.

She forced herself to look across at him and smile, but it was a pained smile. He mouthed something back to her — maybe something like 'Am I going well?' — but she looked away.

After an agony of silence he started up again, 'I suppose the meeting is worried about the sweep being too wide for farm gates. I knew that this would worry some people and it worried me. One of the answers is that the widening of gates could be subsidised by the better-off farmers and governments . . .' he began to scramble, ' . . . or if that proves impracticable then the farmers themselves might consider widening their gates. Not a big job. After all, what originally back in the mists of time determined the width of a gate? The width of a gate is not God-given.' He stared into space as if wondering whether to go on further into the history of gates and then turned away from that direction.

'Surely no one could say that this is an expensive item. It costs about twenty-four pounds sterling.'

He faltered again as some of those at the meeting began now to frown at him while others began leafing through their papers. Someone should have thanked him and let him go, but no one moved. Sir Eric was still staring at his papers and consequently Ambrose stood in the room with his notes in his hand beside the photographs on the display board. These now caught his eye.

He tapped the board. 'You can study the photographs which I took personally. Not too brilliant in terms of focus, but the points I have mentioned are illustrated by them well enough . . . to recap: the New Century Hay Sweep is the answer to hay-gathering. Hay-gathering and preservation is the secret to the feeding of animals through winter. Maybe I forgot to mention that. Oh yes, that is important. Keep that in mind. Hay is the secret to good husbandry, good husbandry is the secret of good farming, good farming is the secret to famine, the elimination of famine is the secret to the ending of disease and war.'

He stood before the Directors, now sensing that something had gone wrong but clearly unable to make any assessment of what it was that had gone wrong. He groped through his notes, maybe thinking that it was some piece of information which he'd missed out that would make everything more convincingly complete and sway the meeting.

Edith felt a squirming discomfort in her muscles, wanting for the situation to stop but not knowing how to stop it.

'Oh — yes!' He seemed to think that he'd found a solution to his dilemma. 'Questions — of course! Are there any questions? How silly — of course you must have questions. I am no farmer, but bowl them up.' And then, speaking to himself, said the word 'questions' as a reprimand, as if to say, how silly of me to forget to call for questions, that of course everyone was waiting to be invited to ask questions — that was what was wrong. 'You must be bursting with questions. Don't worry — I don't expect you to know about agriculture.'

Nearly everyone was looking now at Sir Eric, their gaze almost demanding him to bring the embarrassment to a close. He looked up slowly. 'Thank you, Ambrose. Very informative. We must, you understand, get on with our agenda, and I'll be in touch in due course.' She had never heard Sir Eric refer to anyone by their first name.

Ambrose was nonplussed that there were no questions, no applause, and perhaps at hearing his first name.

'But . . . ? Of course, I am glad, Sir Eric, that you found it so informative — when I was there in the field, in Wiltshire, in the sunshine, I found it remarkable — dazzling — that I should've come across the answer there in a field of hay in Wiltshire. I am so glad that you all see what I mean . . .'

He was struggling to find conviction now, hoping that soon he would hear the right words of acclamation spoken by Sir Eric or by someone in the group, the words which would recognise his discovery and applaud it.

'Yes, well, good man, keep on with your philosophising, and now we must be on with our work here.' Sir Eric sounded as if he were talking to the man driving the tractor, not to a former close colleague.

It was as though one of the cranks had climbed over the Palais walls and into the very heart of the League.

'Perhaps, Sir Eric, if there are questions which occur to anyone, they could contact me down in Siberia?' He beamed out his entreating smile. 'Glad that all is now forgiven and so on and so forth.' He still stood there, unable to break away from the place where he so desperately wanted to be and where he wished to belong.

Edith could stand it no longer and she got to her feet, feeling that she had to take responsibility for Ambrose as he stood at the edge of his chasm. She went over to him, taking his arm, saying quietly, 'Thank you, Ambrose, that was useful,' and led him to the door.

'You're convinced then?' he said grasping at her words, then looked behind him. 'My photographs . . .' He made to go back into the room. She stopped him, saying that she'd get Jules to bring them down to him, adding, 'People might like to study them.' She wanted him out of the room.

At the door, he looked across again at Sir Eric and the others and waved. She guided him out, closing the door behind them.

'Of course,' he said, 'they'll want to study them. It's a delightfully simple idea, isn't it?'

'It is, indeed.'

'One second — something else to tell.'

Before she could stop him, he ducked back in the room. She called, 'Ambrose — no.' But he poked his head into the room and said, 'One point — forgot it — to convert the horse sweep to a tractor sweep costs only ten guineas. Sorry. Forgot. Thanks again, chaps.'

She was about to go after him and tug him out of the room, but he came back to her. He still had an ingratiating, boyish smile.

He was now optimistically insensible to what had happened. 'I think they liked the idea of the hay sweep but they may need time to understand the philosophical point — that all is related — like the planets — and that all is soluble — all is . . . well, all is whatever.' He laughed. 'That's *it*: "All is whatever".'

It was almost a glimpse of the old self-teasing Ambrose laughing at himself, but it wasn't really the old Ambrose. It was not the laughter of someone confident in the uncertainty of life. His laughter and his expression were different; they expressed the forlorn hope that what he'd said was not something about which to laugh, but was indeed a remarkable expression of genius.

Out in the corridor, he still kept on. 'In Australia it would be fine. No gates there.'

'I expect that it would be.' She smelled his breath for the first time, and detected no alcohol. She wished he'd been drunk and that it could all be explained by that.

She almost steered him down the corridor, standing until she was sure he was going. He turned twice to wave.

She stood until he had turned the corridor corner. She was struck by an unworthy feeling, that she'd been embarrassed by the idea that the others might still associate him with her, and that she'd made a mistaken move by getting up and seeing him out. Still, what mattered was that her decent self had got to its feet and helped him. And surely long ago gossip had made sure that everyone knew that they were no longer in any way a couple. She went back into the room. She heard someone say, 'Yes, with Curzon for a time . . .'

Sir Eric looked at her and said, 'Thank you, Berry, nicely done. Now let's get on.'

After work, she talked with Claude, who was now Ambrose's superior. Claude knew what she was talking about. He agreed that Ambrose needed help.

'His work is no longer really good enough. I've talked to him — gently — but he's declining.'

'Why don't you do something!'

'Me? I can hardly go to someone like Westwood and tell him that he's shell-shocked or whatever. It's hard enough being his superior. In other circumstances, he'd be *my* superior.'

She asked about Ambrose's friends.

'He's become something of a recluse. I can't think who I would designate as his close friend.'

She recalled seeing him drinking alone in the Bavaria. Sometimes someone would drift over to him to say hello.

'Anyone who talks to him simply stands at his table and chats but they never sit,' Claude said.

'You and I do that to him.'

'Precisely,' Claude said.

Immediately after his demotion he'd still drop into the Bavaria as if nothing had changed, as a way of keeping up appearances. At first she'd thought he was coming there to be pathetic, to indict her, but Edith realised that she had no idea who knew or who didn't know about the reasons for his fall.

Claude said nervously, 'Have a talk to him, Berry. I know it's hard to do. Might have to pack him off back to England. Let the FO have him back. His relatives, maybe.'

'He has no relatives that I know of.'

'I can't manufacture relatives or friends for a chap.' Claude tried to be light but she could see that he was feeling the sadness of it.

In her rooms at the pension, she collapsed in her armchair, her eyes closed, reliving the nausea of the meeting.

It was growing on her that she was obliged to do something about Ambrose and this agitated her. But too often people one knew at work, or socially — or worse, former lovers — were observed to be breaking down but no one talked with the person about it; everyone pretended everything was all right, acquaintances just let the person slide into catastrophe until they were taken seriously ill. She'd wondered about herself at times. After the stoning of the Palais Wilson, when she'd gone to Chamonix — she had hidden the fact that she was a bit odd. In those cases a holiday, or the passing of time, had cured her.

There was the added difficulty of taking such an action with a former lover. She searched her mind for another person she could ask to intercede, to go to him and help, but she couldn't think of anyone on whom she could off-load the responsibility. Claude had dodged it and, as he'd confirmed, Ambrose had become somewhat isolated. She imagined that his old associates were probably steering clear of him. She would have to go to him.

What could one do to help a person in decline? She could lead him to seek help from a physician or a clinic. One could offer solace — if the person was a friend. One could amuse and keep the person cheerful for an hour or so. One could participate in the person's illusion that everything was unexceptional. Drink with them while they died in drunkenness night after night.

She had to get it off her mind now, and heavily she forced herself up, put on her coat and went out again, dog-tired. She would take him to dinner.

She rang the bell and Ambrose came to the door and let her in, obviously delighted by her visit. She hadn't been there since the night they'd parted ways.

He was welcoming and seemingly in good spirits.

'How good of you to call — what a pleasant surprise. During the afternoon I was expecting some of the others to drop down and talk about the hay sweep. No one came by.'

The apartment was dusty but tidy, still very much the way they'd done it together back in the mad, giggling days. There was a smell of cooking, well, of toast burning, and under that, a smell which she would describe as the smell of a man, a man alone, of self-neglect.

He wore a dressing robe over his work clothes. He still had on his tie. He had an open bottle of Scotch on the glass-topped round table, drink in hand. He had changed his shoes and had on his tasselled loafers.

He hugged her, she offered her cheek for a kiss but he kissed her lips, still holding his glass. 'I was drowning my indigestion,' he said, waving the Scotch glass.

'You always said that if you had indigestion Scotch only stirred up the frogs in the swamp,' she said for want of something to say, taking off her coat.

'The first one does but then the others knock them on the head. But, oh, this calls for champagne.'

'No — a Scotch will be fine.'

'Not good enough,' and he went off to the kitchen, calling out to her, 'A champagne day. My lecturette. Return of a long lost friend.' He returned with the bottle of Lanson, labouring with the cork.

'Please, Ambrose, no champagne.'

Ambrose ignored her, and the cork popped. He went to the glasses cabinet and took out two cut-glass champagne goblets, pouring the foaming champagne until it overflowed onto the carpet, which was not like him at all. 'I was just about to have something to eat — not much really, but you're welcome,' he said.

She took the glass of champagne with sad reluctance.

'It's early for dinner,' she said. 'But thank you, if you have enough.'

'I was just having something eggy on a tray.'

Somehow his saying that confirmed her apprehensions about Ambrose, Ambrose who'd always been a fastidious eater. 'Something eggy on a tray and something horrid on toast,' he said.

'I don't believe it! You abhor people who eat like that!' She found she was thinking before she spoke, and she said this, hoping that he could be perhaps teased or shamed into pulling himself together, and she decided then to say, 'Remember, we both swore to each other than we'd never end up living like that, that we would always eat the French way, come what may?'

'Oh, standards have slipped a bit around here. Back to trench food. Cheers. What a grand day!' He touched glasses with her. 'To the return of a friend.'

She then suspected that his description of his evening meal was intended to sound pathetic, especially to her, that he was twisting her sympathies, although she noticed that he didn't renew the invitation to eat with him nor did he go near the kitchen. Thankfully, he let pass the idea of their having something eggy on a tray or something horrid on toast.

And she, in turn, decided not to invite him out to dinner, recalling their last trying meal together. She couldn't face sitting through dinner with him.

'I think I know why you've come,' he said, propelling her to the lounge, sitting her down and sitting himself too closely beside her, assuming a manly command which teetered a little.

'What's your guess?' Without having touched it, she put down the glass of champagne on the dusty glass-topped table. It left a ring. She felt, given her inner thoughts, that it would be perfidious of her to let the champagne touch her lips.

'Sir E. has sent you. I'm again *persona grata*? You and Bartou put your heads together? Had me reinstated? Am I correct? I know you are a Power in the Land these days. More so than I — even in my heyday. Hay-day today? Like the play on words? You liked all my games,' he said with empty flirtation.

He was speaking quickly, rambling on, perhaps not wanting to face her reply just yet, in case it was other than he wished.

She smiled, wishing that the momentum of his chatter would

carry him far enough away from his hopeful questions, so that she wouldn't have to answer.

But eventually he asked, 'Well, what did Sir E. say? Am I back in?'

'Too soon for that, I'm afraid — for now . . .' She hated herself for sugaring her reply.

'I knew the meeting had a long agenda. Sir E. told me that I really could only ask for ten minutes or so. I tried to keep it short. That wasn't the problem, was it? Too long? I timed it. I may've gone over a minute or so — they aren't holding that against me, are they? It was, after all, rather top-line stuff. Couldn't expect that the reinstatement of old Ambrose would pop up on the agenda. You know, don't you, that my lecturette was an attempt to resuscitate my fortunes? Save the world: save Ambrose. Get back to form. I tried to keep it short but telling at the same time. Did you think it went over?'

He stood up, with slight agitation, and poured himself a second glass of champagne, having quickly, burpingly, drunk the first.

There was no easy way to do it. 'Ambrose, sit down and let me talk with you.'

'Oh — right!' He sat down again, like an obedient school-boy. 'You have Something to Say. I can tell. I've become rather good at picking when someone has Something to Say.'

Looking into his eyes she said, quietly, 'I am worried about you. We are all worried about you.'

'You did talk about me then, the meeting?'

'I mean generally. Your friends.'

'My friends?' He seemed to be searching his mind to remember who his friends could be.

'I am worried about you, Ambrose,' she took his hands in hers, 'dear Ambrose.'

'Oh, come on — I might be a bit . . . well, I am a bit absent-minded one way or another . . . but not too bad. I was in good form today, wasn't I? Forgot to call for questions, but they didn't hold that against me, did they?'

She had to plough on and get it over with. 'No, Ambrose, you were not in good form. Not at all.'

He started to show indignation. 'Comert seemed to be won over. He was taking notes and so on. Sir E. said that it was all "highly informative".'

'Ambrose, look at me.' She took his hands and held them firmly. 'It was something of a disaster. They weren't impressed. It's a misguided idea you have about this hay sweep. You sounded very fatigued, you sounded worn down by things, you've been pushed beyond your limit. It's time for you to stop for a while — to take care of yourself.'

'But I'm just back from leave.'

That was right. She'd forgotten Wiltshire. He was, then, truly ill — it was more than a holiday that he needed. Before she could find the words to bring home to him his condition, he jumped in with another rally. 'I agree with you now, I can see that it was my mention of the British — when I said "trust the British to come up with the answer", that line — that was what put their backs up. The non-English-speaking chaps don't like that. Error of judgement on my part.' Ambrose released one of his hands from hers and slapped his wrist. He looked at her conspiratorially. 'Obviously the British were with me. Even if they couldn't come out with it at the meeting.'

'Ambrose, it wasn't anything like that. It was that the whole thing, the idea of the hay sweeper solving the problems of the world — Ambrose, it's fanciful, it's not aligned to reality.'

This registered with him. 'You think I'm going potty?'

'I think you need a long rest, a break from this sort of work, and a little loving care.'

He seemed to brighten at her saying this. 'I did it for you, you know — trying to impress. Say it did. Today was all for you. Are you offering?'

She didn't quite understand. 'Offering?'

'Loving care.'

Oh, God. 'No, Ambrose, it was not for me. Today was something else. I don't think it's me you need to help you.'

'You think I'm potty!' He huffed.

'I think you're under strain. Maybe it's something left over from the War, as well.'

'You don't see that you might be a bit to blame?'

'Me? How?' she said, tiredly.

'Turning a chap down.'

'Ambrose . . .' She felt expended and ineffective. 'We were never going to marry — that wasn't why we were together back then. And there was the spy thing.'

'Fuss over nothing. I was on the right side. In a balloon with a telescope. Just doing my bit.'

She saw now that she really couldn't help him, that he saw her as part of the blizzard blowing against him and blowing deep inside him. She also saw that he had no repentance about the spying business.

He became self-defensive and haughty. 'I don't see you for almost a year, then you show up to tell me I'm potty — trying to blame it all on the War.'

'I came to tell you to get help — if you don't you'll be left to rot where you are and never rehabilitated. You might even be let go.'

'You don't understand. You don't really understand, do you? They can't do that.'

'I'll make an appointment with someone you can talk to about what's worrying you, and then when you're well again we can talk to Sir Eric about getting things back to normal.' She was trying to use the possibility of reinstatement as a carrot. She turned it into a rule, something like, 'Promises made to sick people to help them get better are not binding.'

'I think you've misunderstood everything,' he said, with a patronising tone. 'I would expect Sir Eric to be talking to me before too long. He said he would be in touch. It will mean exports for the British, you see. I should've emphasised that. We like that, we British, doing good and selling a few machines at the same time. Especially now we have this economic silliness.'

He went to a drawer and took out pencil and paper and began making a calculation on the scrap of paper.

She stood up. 'You're not well, Ambrose. Think about it. I am going to call to see you again tomorrow at the Palais. I'll bring Joshi.'

'If you haven't anything funnier to say, don't bother. Don't bother to bring Joshi either. I haven't got malaria and anyhow, I'm a doctor myself. Can look after myself. You lack caprice, Edith. Always said that.'

He was very nervous and went on scribbling figures on the sheet of paper.

How did you help? Did you let them go completely mad? Did they have to start wearing pyjamas in the street before anyone took notice? She remembered a Mrs Cobb from back home who'd lost a son in the War and who had gone to the corner of their street each day expecting his return. She sometimes argued that those people close to someone who suicided should be held responsible, should be questioned about their negligence. She would talk to Joshi about it.

She was letting herself out of the apartment when he looked up, realising that she was leaving, and came to the door. He took her arm. 'Don't go yet.' His voice sounded normal and was so pleading that it hurt her heart.

She leaned to him and kissed his cheek. 'I must, Ambrose, I'll call in to see you at the office. Think about what I've said.' She thought that his body had changed its smell.

'If you came back — if we could get together and make things work — promise no more dresses. Scout's honour.' He made a Boy Scout salute. 'Will be a regular chap. What do you say? We might make a go of things? I'd be much improved. I think you'd set me right. I'll become a gastropath instead.'

'Ambrose, I can't help you. You have to go to a physician.'

He frowned and then smiled in an exaggerated way. 'Oh well, can't blame a chap for trying with a girl, can you? Fare thee well, pleasant evening, all that.' Without looking at her, he went back inside the apartment, and closed the door behind him.

Bartou agreed with her. He'd heard the painful story of the meeting from others and he, too, was worried about Ambrose. 'Some of us have seen it happening over the years.'

'Over the *years*?' This perturbed her. Did he mean that others could see that Ambrose was ill when she'd been with him? That she hadn't been able to see this? 'What exactly?'

'There was his overconcern with detail below his rank. I remember him worrying about the soap. The soap the cleaners used. Matters like that. He said the soap was too strong. Would eat into the soil.'

She remembered the business about the soap but she hadn't

listened to him. She now remembered other things. She realised how little one actually saw of one's lover. Even when they worked in the same building. 'What is to be done?'

'There is,' he said, 'the Swiss way of handling it and the British way.' He said that if Ambrose went back to England, he might be looked upon as a lovable eccentric. ' "Tis no great matter there." '

'Or an unlovable eccentric.'

'Quite so. Here they would place him in a beautiful Alpine clinic and treat him with machines and long walks and keep him there until he recovered. I hear they eat well.' He said something about the Fogel clinic at Montreux where Zelda Fitzgerald, the author's wife, had gone — and a couple of League people.

'*Machines?*'

'Oh, exercise machines, I think. Nothing from the Inquisition.'

'There is also the Viennese way.'

'For that you have to get him onto the couch. Can you get him onto the couch?'

'I can't see him going onto a couch. No. How could we get him into a clinic?'

The ugly word 'commit' leapt at her, from its use in Australia, from the grim world of lunatic asylums. 'It wouldn't be a lunatic asylum? He's not a lunatic.' She wondered if he were. Was he going mad?

'The Swiss word is kinder,' he said. 'When we say "asylum" we mean it. As in political asylum. A refuge from trouble.'

'But are the Swiss? Kinder?'

He shrugged.

At least if he went to a Swiss clinic, she could visit. Would she visit? Would anyone visit? There was no pretty way of doing it.

'I'll talk with Joshi.'

'I have doctor friends here in Geneva who will help.'

'Thank you.'

She talked with Joshi, telling him everything except to mention Ambrose's sexual predilection. She did not want to be the one to mention that to anyone. Nor was she sure that it was a part of the illness. Maybe it was part of his health.

Joshi said he would visit Ambrose himself, examine him, and then talk with Bartou's doctor friends.

A day later, Joshi called to see her and to report on his visit. He agreed that Ambrose should be given help. 'He seemed to realise why I was there but tried to suggest that you had your reasons for going about telling people he was mad.'

She felt cold at the unthinkable possibility that Joshi or anyone else might possibly believe that of her. 'How unjust.'

'It's clear to me that the man is sick.' Joshi knew of the Directors' meeting, had talked to others. Joshi looked at her and said, 'Well?'

'Well what?'

'Are you going to put him in the clinic?'

'Me?'

'Someone has to initiate it. Someone has to say it.'

'Say what?'

'That he is a danger to the public — or to himself.'

Was he a danger to anyone? He was certainly in danger of hurting his professional standing. His health?

She looked hopefully at Joshi. 'Can't you?'

'If I were licensed to practise here and if he were running amok.'

She saw that Joshi was putting the responsibility onto her.

He said, 'Usually it would be next of kin.'

She stared at the wall. 'I suppose I am the nearest to him. But I am not "next of kin".'

He nodded. 'Legally you could pass as wife, de facto. Stretching it a bit.'

'But I'm not. I shouldn't be responsible for him. That's hardly right. It certainly *is* stretching it a bit.'

'I accept that it's stretching it a bit. Not fair at all. But someone known to be close to him has to sign.'

'The clinic? This clinic will make him well again?'

Joshi's face showed sad scepticism. 'It is his best chance. Though some might prescribe love and the passing of time.'

She wondered whether she had the time or the love to give Ambrose. No, she couldn't give Ambrose the type of love that he needed.

She looked at the Laurencin lithograph of *Les deux soeurs* on the wall of her corner. She and Ambrose? Her selves? The sisters she didn't have and wanted? A postcard of The Three Sisters, three huge rock projections in the Blue Mountains. Until that moment she hadn't seen the connection between the painting and the postcard.

She looked back to Joshi. 'I will do it.'

He said he would arrange for Ambrose's admission to a good clinic, probably the one at Montreux.

On the following Saturday, she and Joshi went to Ambrose's apartment and explained to Ambrose what was happening.

Her glass of undrunk champagne was where she had left it, flat and untouched. The bottle had not been finished.

He tried to laugh them off. They had to wrestle a bottle of Scotch away from him and then he broke down. Joshi talked him into allowing him to inject him with a calming drug.

The ambulance arrived while she was packing some clothing

for him. They went with him to the ambulance. He was unsteady on his feet from the drug and was helped into the ambulance by two attendants.

She had no urge to stop them taking him.

Joshi and she stood together on the pavement as the ambulance drew away.

'And about you, how is it with you, then?' Joshi said, turning to her. 'Are you bearing up?' He held her face in both hands, looking at her closely, kindly.

'I am not all right at all.'

'I'll walk with you back to your pension.'

'Thank you. Please walk with me.' She took his arm, feeling absolutely blighted by Ambrose's crash.

The Dance of Negotiation

It was a grim observation, but as the weeks passed she felt now that Ambrose was truly out of her life. At least she did not see him scurrying around corridors at the Palais. Somehow it helped that he was considered scientifically 'ill'.

Sir Eric, and some of those who'd served in the War, had visited him at the clinic. They said he still seemed to be lost in delusion. The most encouraging sign, Major Buxton said, was that Ambrose had claimed to have become 'rather keen' on one of the machines.

She didn't have the fortitude to ask them if he was saying anything against her or whether he blamed her.

She'd offered to go to read to him but his doctor believed that ex-lovers could not heal those they'd spurned. She had not been able to clarify this as well as she wanted and let it go, assuming that it was probably part of Ambrose's story to his doctor.

She paid the rent on his apartment and wrote to him each week, although he never replied.

She didn't suffer as much from this second episode which was more an emphasising of their breach, more a confirmation that they would not be falling back together again from habit or from forgiveness or from the blurring of time. That she had moved on. Now, more than a year after the breach, her own disheartened state at last began to lift.

As she danced at Maxim's and walked in the Jura, going about her own healing, she became increasingly alive to the idea of having something romantically to do with Robert Dole, despite all the friction that had existed between them and her times of resistance to him over the last couple of years. The irony of her situation was that despite her holding him at bay, he had only recently given up asking her to join him for social activities and consequently he wasn't among the young men who had become her social escorts. But nor could she have coped with a strong contender for her emotions during this last year of the breach and of Ambrose's collapse. She hadn't been ready. She barely coped with her polite dancing and concert escorts. Had the breach, though, not occurred the way it had, she saw now that her relationship with Ambrose would have had to change.

She wanted only to associate with people who were robust and undefeated. That was another of her New Tenets of Self. She hoped that as she took on new tenets, she discarded others — if not, she laughed, she would have a very crowded personal creed.

She would have to determine whether Robert Dole was going to be victorious in life, and perhaps, distinguished. Although when she came to consider it, he was somewhere in his thirties and maybe he should have been distinguished by now if he was going to be distinguished. Perhaps being League correspondent for an important London newspaper *was* distinguished? She thought that might be prominence, not distinction. She thought that Robert Dole might have wisdom too, wisdom of a knarled kind rather than a dark wisdom. She knew to make a distinction between wisdom and the instinctive scepticism of some of the newspaper people. Variations of cynicism were perhaps youthful standbys until one of the wisdoms was reached. But she found these varieties of cynicism unsatisfying. In men she wanted intricacy of mind. She found this alluring and becoming. And manly. Manly. Yes, she wanted something substantially *manly* in her lover now. For a time Ambrose had suited and she'd been content during that time to carry on her life with him within the semilight of the glitter-ball.

After making discreet enquiries as to his past she discovered that he'd been an officer in the War and had been discharged as a captain, but she could not discover which regiment. She'd already observed that for some reason or other he still used khaki handkerchiefs. That would have to change if a romance ever developed between them. She also found out that he was five years older than she and was not known to have a wife hidden back in England. Having observed that he didn't seem to have a regular escort here in Geneva — although she knew that there'd been 'women in his life', and as far as she could decently enquire, assuring herself that there had been no men in his life — she turned from her enquiries to take action, that is, to write a note to Robert Dole.

To open her further analysis of Robert Dole, she would invite him to a luncheon at the Expatriates' Club of Geneva — called by some of its members the Homesick Club. The luncheon was to celebrate the ratification, at last, of the Pact of Peace by the United States Senate.

For her, it would be something of a debut, coming out from the twilight, coming out from being a person in rehearsal and stepping, she hoped, onto the lighted stage.

For one thing, deep in her heart she knew she could not be a lover with him until she was sure he shared an affirmative sentiment about the League. It had sometimes crossed her mind when talking with him that he wanted her to convince him about the League, that he was a man hungry for conversation, yearning to be given a deep conviction in life. Maybe Jeanne's reading of his eyes had been right.

'I know that you have had reservations about the Pact,' she

wrote in her note of invitation to him, enclosing the luncheon programme, 'but I'd like you to be my guest.' She recalled the strange occurrences between them when the Pact was first being discussed. She left the note in his slot in the pressroom.

A reply came back that afternoon by messenger: 'I accept your delightfully unexpected invitation to the luncheon, if you will be my guest for an *apéritif* this evening and then dinner.'

How excessive — lunch and dinner on the same day. How *driving* of him. He was still strong on her, despite her discouragement. She scribbled back a reply: 'Must you make an invitation into a negotiation?' She felt her reply had a clever strength to it.

As she wrote the word 'negotiation', she remembered precepts that she had heard from Bartou: know what you want for an outcome; be sure you know the negotiating customs; and have a plan of concessions, in which you know well the limits, both up and down, beyond which you will not negotiate.

Without being sure, in any way, of any of these things, she said to herself, staring at his note, Yes, perhaps I will join you for an *apéritif* and dinner if I am satisfied with your conduct at lunch. She did not answer his proposal in writing, giving in her reply only the arrangements for the luncheon.

Some people created a beguilement which caused you to believe that you had approached them, but in fact they brought you to them, caused you to come. Over the years, she had always felt this about Robert Dole and it had been only her philosophical frustration with him, her preoccupations with work, and the convenient obstacle of Ambrose, which had weakened the powers of his beguilement. She'd felt until now that she did not have the time or strength to deal with someone like Robert Dole. Because the city was small and the social life of those around the League so in-turned, the friction between them had not stopped their coming together at the same League social occasions, and also, it was the resilience of his interest in her that had kept her preoccupied with him. There was something flattering about this resilience of interest which he had displayed virtually up to the last six months. She had remained vividly conscious of him whenever they'd been in the same room. Thoughts about him had come in a flurry after she and Ambrose had parted. She found herself relieved that, in the period when she had discouraged him or had been emotionally numb, no other woman had entered his life.

His manner marked him off from the rest of the press. He sometimes sat alone in the bars or cafés reading, or writing his book. He had been a friend of Stresemann, for instance, and knew Sir Eric.

She saw that if, perhaps, she'd been flirting into the net of beguilement spun by Robert Dole, she had this time, not so unconsciously, chosen a meeting ground which was securely hers. The Expatriates' Club was predominantly feminine, and at this luncheon a woman would be guest speaker, Madame Weiss. Edith would have her friends about her, it was her table and it was by her invitation.

That she needed such a background showed her, though, that she was still apprehensive of him. She thought now that the friction she'd sometimes felt with him might have been, in fact, apprehension. And now the possibility of entering into the embrace of this apprehension, and of dissolving the apprehension into something else — into passion? — tantalised her. Robert Dole was not thin soup.

With the American Christina Merridale chairing the luncheon and because of a sprinkling of other Americans, including Arthur Sweetser, Mary's boss from Information, there were opening jokes about the Yale–Harvard football game, which, she gathered from the remarks, was being played that very day in Boston.

At her table there were Jeanne, Victoria and some of the women from the Registry, some of the women from Social Questions, and Robert Dole. She had been unable to convince Bartou to come. She went out of her way to smile across at Victoria.

Florence was at another table with her bunch and had openly stared at her when she'd come in with Robert Dole. She no longer acknowledged Florence. It had been reported to her that one night in the bar someone had asked Florence what had happened between Edith and Ambrose. Florence had replied, 'Didn't you hear? He went mad and she called the police and had him shot.'

She enjoyed Florence's boggling.

The only members of the press gallery who were there were Rachel Chaies, Gertrude Dixon, the editor of the Official Journal, Robert Dole — and he only as a guest — and Emery Kelen, a caricaturist, who went anywhere that he might find a subject for a caricature which he could sell to a newspaper.

'I hope you don't mind being the only man at a table of women?' Jeanne asked Robert Dole.

'My male friends would find it an enviable situation,' he replied charmingly. Edith had not heard him being charming.

He urged an *apéritif* on her. She said that she drank *apéritifs* only after seven.

As she agreed to a sherry, she said, 'You see, I am making a concession.' She didn't know why she said it.

'Must I now make a concession in return?'

'Not immediately.' She then heard herself say, so naturally, 'It is not clear yet what it is we are negotiating. Or, whether we are negotiating.'

He smiled at her with his astute smile, indicating that he thought that a negotiation *was* taking place and that they both knew what it was that was being negotiated.

She smiled back, but not in full complicity with his smile. No, Mr Dole, you do not know quite what is being negotiated here between us, apart from lust. She realised that it was perhaps nice, when personal things were being negotiated, for some of them to remain unlisted, vaporous even to both parties.

In her opening remarks, quavering a little, Christina Merridale said that mankind was once more on the move: 'The very foundations have been shaken and loosened.' She said the League of Nations provided that regulating influence to give practical and benign shape to this progress. She then introduced Mme Weiss, a French expert on world affairs.

They applauded as Mme Weiss took the rostrum. She announced that because of the composition of the club, she would speak in English.

'I remember back to when I was at Locarno,' Mme Weiss said. 'On the day the treaty was initialled, people of the countryside crowded to the Town Hall to see the treaty held up at the window. The sound of bells rang from the church of the Madonna del Sasso across the lake. Women of the village knelt and crossed themselves when they saw the treaty, and fathers held children high to see it. Most of the homes burned a candle in the window to commemorate the signing. There was dancing in the village of Locarno square that night, danced by young men and women who will never have to know war. Today I want to quote only one statesman, my most dear compatriot, Aristide Briand, now sadly ill. He told me of one letter he received after the Locarno agreement which made a lifetime in politics worthwhile. It was from a French mother who wrote to him saying, "May a mother congratulate you . . . Now I will be able to look at my children and love them without fear of losing them to war." '

There was appreciative applause.

As she clapped, Edith leaned over to Robert Dole, conscious that her body just touched his, enjoying the odour of his body and clothes, and said, 'Personally, I'm not one of those people who believes *all* things can be negotiated. I don't believe, as Arthur Sweetser is fond of saying, that there can always be a "deal". I agree more with Salisbury: "If one country wants to eat another, no accommodation is possible." ' She sometimes worried too, about what was a 'principle' and what was 'negotiable', especially for a moral woman in matters of intimacy. A tolerably moral woman.

Robert Dole smiled as he listened to her but made no reply, instead, raising his glass, he made a sotto voce toast around their table to Aristide Briand, and to the recovery of his health. He directed his glass to her. 'To Aristide Briand,' Robert Dole said quietly, raising his glass. 'Aristide Briand,' Edith and the others said quietly. Robert Dole and Edith touched glasses first and she felt that, for them, it carried a personal implication, an echo from an earlier argument they'd had, and then they clinked glasses with the others, but Robert Dole returned his gaze to her. Jeanne had tears in her eyes from Mme Weiss's mention of Briand and Locarno, and joined the toast fervently. Although Edith thought that Jeanne might also have been aligning herself with Robert Dole, perhaps a little too strongly. They had all known Aristide Briand when he'd been around the League.

Edith felt confirmed in her feeling that Robert Dole was not as ironclad as he sometimes pretended.

Mme Weiss continued, saying that the Locarno Non-aggression Pact and the Kellogg–Briand Pact of Peace were not pacts as pacts were once known — they were the crystallisation of deep changes that had occurred in the human condition. She said they were not pacts between nations or governments but pacts on behalf of people in perpetuity.

'I hear,' Robert Dole said to her in a whisper, leaning towards her, his body quite unmistakably leaning into her, 'that there has been a change in your human condition in the last year.'

He waited for her to reply but she simply smiled and raised an eyebrow.

He then said, 'I know that sometimes to change one's attitude is an uncomfortable inner negotiation.'

While hearing him clearly, Edith did not look at Robert Dole, and again made no comment. She paid studious attention to Mme Weiss, while Mme Weiss went on to trace the agrarian reform which had 'changed the face of Europe'.

Edith sensed Robert Dole watching her face for a response.

Mme Weiss said that millions of peasants had now become small owners of land and were looking to the preservation of their property. They were now hostile to military ventures which threatened their property. 'There is a deep change in the human background of the world.'

Edith realised that a whispered personal negotiation in public, at a luncheon talk like this, allowed time for the parties to manoeuvre, delayed the parries and the replies of the conversation quite nicely. Their whispering reminded her, too, of classroom whispering back at the one-roomed school of her childhood at Jasper's Brush. The intimacy of whispering gave an excuse to lean closer together.

Mme Weiss said that most people not only now had property — they also had an alphabet in their heads. This was the truly invisible revolution. Before this time in history, many people had lived in huts and had only religion. They had hoped for a better life after death. Now people wanted a better life here and now.

'It is true that there has been a change,' Edith whispered, 'and it is true that my attitude to you is being reviewed. And you, Robert Dole, as a man used to these things, you must at least be aware that negotiation, for both parties, involves the use of a crystal ball. It is a game of wishes.'

She had made Robert Dole smile, and she smiled too, so as not to appear to be too restrained.

Mme Weiss said that the new democratic administrations were another sign of the times of which President Mazaryk in Czechoslovakia was the best symbol. Another sign of the times was the League, a conception which was being taught in every school. The idea of international collaboration with the central guidance of the League was being understood by children who would, tomorrow, become the leaders. A new understanding also existing among the labouring classes, the intellectual class and the peasants. They were closer together than at any time in history.

'I sense a new understanding between the fourth estate and the Secretariat class. And it is true that I am wishing,' Robert Dole whispered, 'but I am also reading the signs.'

Edith smiled, a smile which didn't mean much, was simply further kindling for the warmth between them.

Mme Weiss said that Geneva was a town all people had learned to cherish, but that Geneva was not just a town — it stood for a method and a hope. 'A method, because we have a crowd of young administrators and international diplomats working for the League. They understand the psychology of international interchange. In the League we have a large, well-financed organisation which is making a new expertise with the know-how to influence the press, and which will shortly have its own radio station.' Wireless offered the hope of instant communication among peoples, allowing for the dispelling of rumour and false information. And, she said, for the first time in history, the opinion of the public mattered in international affairs.

Robert Dole whispered to her that he believed they now shared both 'a position and an intention'.

It seemed to Edith that Robert Dole was trying to be sure that she was offering more to him than just being pals. He wanted to be sure that she was no longer dismissing him as a possible swain. She sensed that this had become for him a point of anxiety.

'I understand,' he whispered, 'that to give up something can be painful but it can also free the spirit.'

If he were referring to Ambrose, she wondered what he knew about their life together and their parting.

'When to compromise, or when to abandon a position, or when to fight to the finish — these are three subtle judgements,' she whispered in reply.

'Indeed, and judgements upon which lives often depend. My very own in this case.'

'Come, Mr Dole,' she smiled, 'to exaggerate the extent of a concession is a crude manoeuvre.'

He smiled and they again turned to Mme Weiss. Edith was conscious that Jeanne was paying more attention to their whispered negotiation than to the talk.

Mme Weiss said, 'We once heard the cry that war is the health of a nation. This is plainly contradicted because the world is becoming habituated to using international negotiation.'

Robert Dole leaned over to her, bringing their bodies warmly back into touch. 'This exaggerating of concession gives room for manoeuvre.'

'I don't like that approach,' she whispered in reply. 'Negotiations which involve asking too much, so that something may be painlessly given away, or cleverly offering too little, so that something can later appear to be generously added — these are not sincere compromises. I do not call that genuine negotiation.'

'It is a leisurely way to reach a real position,' he persisted. 'Perhaps over-asking or under-offering could be seen as a dance?'

'Are we dancing?' she asked.

'Are we?'

Mme Weiss said there had been a 'moral relaxation of tension' in the world. There were some titters. Maybe Mme Weiss should have chosen different wording. 'Too much so in Geneva,' someone from another table interjected playfully. There was a festive spirit in the room.

Mme Weiss joined in the smiling herself but without yet seeming to comprehend what the tittering was about, and she went on to say that Locarno and the Pact of Peace were not just the inventions of brilliant minds. They were the result of laborious effort by many people over the last ten years — the logical development of mankind's thinking.

'It helps too,' Edith whispered to Robert Dole, 'in the case of concession, if your adversary in negotiation smooths the way for that change in position — if your opponent allows that change to happen gracefully.'

'*Apéritifs* this evening at the Hôtel des Bergues at seven o'clock — is that graceful enough?'

He was choosing a very manly locale, and an expensive one. Her first day at the League and her great dinner there with Ambrose crossed her mind, but she found no troubling associations. She found the Hôtel des Bergues quite acceptable.

'Agreed,' she said to him. 'The choice of locale — is it to honour Aristide Briand?' Modifying, perhaps, what she sensed was the single-mindedness of Robert Dole's invitation, making the purpose of the invitation a little more diffused.

'I had that in mind also,' he said, readily accepting her

addendum, or perhaps he had truly had that in mind.

They smiled at each other.

Under the cover of the table, he clasped her hand. She squeezed his. Sealing what? Maybe losing, instantly, the diffusion of meanings she had tried to bring to the evening's invitation. She smiled to herself.

They turned back to Mme Weiss, who was saying, 'Our madam chair pushes my elbow.'

Christina had indeed touched Mme Weiss's elbow, much to Edith's admiration. It was Christina's first time in the chair and she had touched Mme Weiss because her time was up. Bravo, Christina.

'The push on the elbow — a forthright American way of saying, stop now with your long-winded European speech,' Mme Weiss said, smiling generously.

Christina was flustered and said something about not having meant to touch her quite so hard. Mme Weiss was not put off. 'I will end by saying we are not the same Europeans as we were before these Pacts — thanks to Aristide Briand, the first true European. And, madam chair, I will finish with one brief story of Aristide Briand. I visited him in his apartment in Paris recently — three rooms, a few paintings given by friends, a few books. His bodyguard said to me, "How is it that a man many times premier of France and responsible for the secret funds of France could be so poor?" ' She turned to Christina. 'He was an honest man.'

During the applause, Edith's attention was taken away from Mme Weiss by the arrival of a sheet of sketching paper with a blank sheet of paper pinned at the top to cover it, which had been passed to her, hand-to-hand. She lifted the cover sheet to reveal a sketch of her and Robert Dole done by Emery Kelen. He had drawn their table as a bed, a bed set in the luncheon hall, surrounded by people attending to a speaker but with Edith and Robert Dole, both in night attire, gesturing to the other to enter the bed. Both had cartoon words coming from their mouths, and both were saying, 'After you.'

Edith was taken aback. Robert Dole held out his hand for it, but she momentarily withheld the caricature, covering it. Pausing to absorb her embarrassment. They had been observed not only by Jeanne, but by Kelen. Maybe by all in the room. She stole another look at the sketch. I must react like a modern woman, she said to herself, and then passed it to Robert Dole who looked at it and smiled to himself, and then smiled at her, warmly and merrily. He handed it back to her, touching her hand as he did, and she again quicky covered the caricature with the top sheet and turned it over on the table, her hand holding it there. Both Jeanne and Victoria signalled to her and at the covered caricature, unable to contain themselves, dying to see what it was that had been passed to her. She shook her head in a very definite, if mysterious 'No.'

Robert Dole turned and gestured 'thank you' to Kelen and then touched her hand again. 'Emery sees everything,' he said.

She was no longer abashed and she, too, could now turn and wave to Kelen, and she blew him a kiss in the way of a modern woman.

They had been observed in their emotional diplomacy by Kelen, who'd hung around the Bavaria and the League for centuries. Ye gods, she and Robert Dole's flirtation had entered history.

After work that day, she went back to her pension, spending enough time on her make-up for it to be clear to herself that she was taking this dinner seriously. She dressed in her velvet evening dress. She took out her long pearl necklace which, when she put it on the glass top of her dressing table, sounded wonderfully arctic and chilling. White pearls on the glass top echoed back to when she was a little girl watching her mother dress to go out, the dressing room filled with smells only smelled on the nights when her mother went to a ball or dinner, of rare perfume brought out for that night, and the sound, that chilling sound, of pearls on glass.

She pulled on her long kid gloves and momentarily crossed her fingers for luck. She thought, fleetingly, about birth control, her mind dodging away from it — it was all too soon for that. She was not going to be Bohemian any more in life. She wanted to have a decorous life.

He came for her in a taxi. He had changed too, and was in black tie, including pale grey gloves and hat, and looked spiffing. Well, well, even the hard-bitten Mr Dole was taking this dinner seriously. He had not brought flowers, but then maybe it was not yet quite right to bring flowers. She remembered to bring the caricature which Robert Dole wanted to see again.

They were shown to their table whch was not the table she and Ambrose had eaten at those years before. 'Briand's table.'

'That table over there is where Briand sits when the French delegation are staying here,' she said.

He looked over to where she was pointing.

'They always eat in a private room,' he said. 'Although Briand sometimes takes tea with a mixed bunch out in the lounge.'

Ambrose. She laughed to herself.

They studied the sketch over champagne, giving them something to talk about during the first stilted minutes. He explained his dinner suit and the champagne as being to mark an announcement he intended to make, as well as to celebrate and mark the change in their 'respective alignment'. Surely, he wasn't intending to propose to her? This unlikely notion caused her to quickly

603

compose a speech which would be courtly, not off-putting, and yet would not require her to give an answer that night. Even if she suspected that she already knew her answer.

'Now my announcement,' he said. He announced that Longmans, Green, and Co. had accepted his novel and that it would be out in June. 'Mr Longman and Mr Green and Mr Co are all very complimentary about my poor long-time-coming book,' he said. And they had paid a decent advance on royalties.

She toasted him and his imminent fame.

It had not been a proposal of marriage but it answered one of her questions about his prospects. He could become a distinguished author. She argued to herself that to be interested in success was not uncouth. Her father, had he been there, might have asked Robert Dole about his prospects. It was the same thing. If and when, of course, a proposal of marriage were made. The other thing that made it consequential was that as a woman dedicated to the affairs of the world, she wanted a man who was able to proceed with her in the affairs of the world, who would not be a Dull Freddy or an impediment to her life. She wanted the exhilaration of accomplishment and the access to life which it brought — both for herself and for any man she was bound to. She felt her professional and private life had nearly suffered a complete disaster through her association with Ambrose.

She asked him what it was about. He said it was a detective novel but with literary pretensions. 'I sneak in some philosophy.'

'May I read it?'

'You will be its first genuine reader, yes. You are also the first to know of its acceptance.'

She saw that it was not just a celebration of his news. He was using his news to embrace her.

At dinner in the gleaming dining room he asked about the place of Ambrose in her life. 'Some time back we heard of a change of fortune for Major Westwood and in your affections also. Now we hear sad news of him.'

Edith considered this an acceptable enquiry but wondered how to talk about it. She did not want the change in Ambrose's fortunes and the change in her affections to be directly related.

'Ambrose Westwood and I parted ways over a year ago.'

Robert Dole absorbed this. He said, 'My analysis of his position in the Secretariat before his recent breakdown was that he'd slipped a number of rungs on the ladder. My analysis of your position is that you had gone up — at least more than two jumps.'

'You know I can't talk about Ambrose's personal affairs.'

'I respect that. Allow me to think aloud. It seems to me that it was punishment, but for what? Not incompetence, because incompetence would have been revealed earlier.' He watched her face.

'Please,' she said, realising as she said it, that serious limits surrounded their relationship because of his work as a reporter, and further, she felt a pang of guilt on hearing Ambrose's fall and her rise twined together.

'I am thinking aloud,' he said, pursuing the subject over her objections. 'He did something wrong and you did something right. It is unlikely that he got caught with the family silver. He didn't seem to have a drinking predicament — any more than any of us, that is. He was not lazy. I found him at times a little daft, but how would that make him stand out in this town? He had an acid wit. But that wouldn't be sufficient to warrant demotion. What, then? I say that it was probably some very serious gaffe he had made in a very important place. Maybe he annoyed one of the Council members? Offended the pride of some nation?'

Bartou also had seen Ambrose as a bit daft. She'd never thought of him that way and it startled her. Perhaps she'd been too close to him. And if he had an 'acid wit', he had never used

605

it against her. Had what she'd taken as his fun-loving self really been a form of madness?

She did not want Robert Dole to be a correspondent. She wanted to be free to talk about all things with him.

On he went, 'Or did he seriously annoy Sir Eric? And for you to be rewarded with promotion? As always, there's much spy talk. Was Major Westwood spying for the Russians?'

She was impressed that in his meandering way he had unknowingly reached close to the truth, but she was not made in any way comfortable by seeing the bared truth, ghostlike in the conversation, even if she alone could see the ghost.

'Please, Robert, I don't like this talk. We have to change the subject. What's happened to Ambrose is sad but recent reports about his health are encouraging.'

'I apologise. He isn't the first to have broken down. The League is hard on people, it seems.'

To enforce the change of subject she asked him whether a member of the Secretariat and a member of the press gallery could ever be true friends.

'Good question,' he said earnestly. 'But as from tonight I may not be a member of the press gallery — I am from tonight an *author.*'

She dearly hoped that was correct.

He then spoiled it all while they were eating their *canard à l'orange*, by being flippant about the League.

He repeated a rather old joke about the League of Nations being the wastepaper basket of the world. But the joke caused her constraint with him to return, and her willingness to follow her desire for him to weaken.

He made it even worse by saying that, no, the League was not a wastepaper basket, that he would withdraw that remark. Instead, he agreed with Stresemann's remark. The League was more a marketplace where nations were bought and sold.

She further withdrew into herself and held back from the conversation. He noticed it and commented.

She said that defeatist jokes about the League pained her.

He said that she should develop a sense of humour.

She said that he should develop a sensitivity of humour.

There was a momentary silence between them. Then he laughed in appreciation of her retort. She smiled to herself but was still distanced from him.

'I am really a little tired of these old jokes about the League,' she said. 'It is not that I lack humour or that I cannot joke about the League.'

'But remember what Stresemann went on to say. He said that he wanted to be there *because* it was a marketplace. If there were dealings going on, he wanted a seat on the stock exchange.'

'I still don't like to talk about the League that way,' she said, and thinking that it sounded priggish, 'I like jokes that sharpen points, not jokes that dismiss thinking.' In truth, she still had a lot of trouble with joking about serious matters.

'Hence, you enjoy the Kelen caricature,' he said craftily, touching the rolled-up sketch on the table.

'Yes,' she said, looking at it again.

The conversation did pick up but she was still resistant to him and he had again lost her concurrence in any ventures of a romantic kind which he might have had in his head for this evening, although she doubted that he knew he'd lost this concurrence.

They were choosing cheese from the chariot when the head waiter came to the table and said that Mr Dole was needed at the telephone.

While he was away, she worked half-heartedly on her speech of non-acceptance of any amorous invitation which might follow dinner. She smiled as she remembered Jeanne's joke about the women in Secretariat spending all day saying, 'Yes, monsieur,' and all night saying, 'No, monsieur.' Especially when the Assembly was in session or during a large conference. This would be her no-monsieur speech. She wished with her whole heart she could have given a yes instead.

He returned in a mood of nervous aliveness.

'My office is looking for me. That was Miriam.'

'Do you have to go?'

This would be an easy way for her to escape the claims and inducements of the night. Or was he, perhaps, escaping the night, fleeing from her? That idea made her feel alarmed — that this call from his secretary might have been prearranged for him to get out of a dinner if he felt it had gone badly. She heard of people who made such pre-arrangements. But why was she thinking like that? Was suspicion now branded into her soul?

'I should. Tonight, at least, I am still a newspaper man.' He looked at her meaningfully. 'However, I do not plan to go just yet.'

'That's nice,' she said, relieved by his wish to stay, seeing it as evidence that he wasn't fleeing her, regardless of her own plans for flight, and confused that she should have cared whether or not he was fleeing her.

'Regardless of the calls of duty I can assure you that I intend to remain with you as long as it pleases you. To hell with London and Berlin.'

'I am honoured.'

'Given that we are, among other things, honouring Aristide Briand, I recall that he once said, "There will be no war as long as I am alive." He could very well have meant that when he died, there was sure to be war. He is not far from death. Stresemann's gone — not only from a broken heart and too much

608

work either. I once saw him eat half a pound of caviare.'

He referred again to his humour, as a way of apology. 'Edith, you shouldn't misread my humour. I know that I am sometimes brutish.'

Was he really brutish? If so, what would she make of a man who was so? Was he capable of white anger with her? What underself would she find in him? She recalled the wrist-grabbing incident. How scintillating we all are, she thought, when we are simply curious creatures in the distance, before we come close and search the other, find the underselves and the blemished nature.

He looked serious, and then grimaced. 'I have too many painful feelings about too many things about which I can do nothing. I use joking to avoid being hounded by them.'

He was giving her an insight into his nature, which did not seem to her to be brutish at all, and she could see that it was hard for him to say it, and her tenderness towards him returned and went out to him. 'My jokes are pain,' he said, grimacing.

Edith suspended her speech of non-acceptance of romantic proposals, and again thought fleetingly about birth control.

He seemed bent on continuing with confession. 'You'll be curious to know, Edith, that I have now, these recent minutes, concluded a negotiation within myself, a change of position. A not altogether painless change of position.'

She looked at him, indeed with curiosity. 'I hope,' she said smiling, picking up the reference to the negotiations at lunch earlier in the day, 'that I can make it easy for you to negotiate this change, whatever it might be — as long as it is, of course,' smiling encouragingly at him, 'a change of stance which I favour.'

'I do not see — if I ever did see — the League as a wastepaper basket.' He looked down at the table in thought.

'That pleases me.'

'To change the metaphor, I see the League as our fire station.'

Edith had never heard the League referred to as a fire station.

He went on, 'I have this feeling, new to me, and it came to me tonight — I'll explain — that the League will need all the firemen it can get.'

On hearing Robert Dole commit himself to the League, she said, 'Surely it hasn't been the pleasure of my company that has changed you? My company could've been had for a lesser concession.' Not true.

He shook his head. 'You haven't told me what changed your attitude to me,' he said, parrying her question, 'your reappraisal of me?'

'I have reappraised my attitudes to you, Robert Dole,' she said lightly, 'but I should warn you that the reappraisal continues.'

She hoped her tone was emotionally reassuring to him.

He said that the telephone call from Miriam was about news from Berlin. In the elections the National Socialist party had 107 deputies elected. 'They'd only twelve in the old Reischstag.'

'And this has changed your stand on the League?'

She did not quite see the connection.

Robert Dole said he was opting for the bureaucratic wizardry of the League, however lumbering it was, against the diseased magic which he saw happening in Germany and Austria. 'I sense magicians at work to summon up the dark forces. Democracy is no safeguard. It can allow civilised behaviour but it does not guarantee it. Democracy can endorse evil. Only a guardian of the ethos can save us. The League. If only it can make a powerful military combination to defend the Covenant.'

She thought he was probably over-alarmed by the Berlin

election result. The British ambassador in Berlin, Lord d'Abernon, had told Bartou and her privately that the National Socialists were not the problem. She wouldn't say anything about Lord d'Abernon just now. She'd tell him at some other more useful time. Maybe she'd tell him 'in the morning' — she savoured the expression and all it meant.

She thought of the night when he had argued that France was an enemy of peace, and a danger, and she hadn't understood. 'I feel embarrassed.'

'About what?'

'About that time you argued with me about the danger of France. I was naïve. I've been embarrassed ever since. France is a danger. I know that now. I was bewitched by Briand.'

'I don't really remember. I know that for a while I went on about France. I was frightened by France.'

'You don't remember the night we . . . tussled . . . we argued? You wrote me a note of apology?'

'We've had a few disagreements, Edith. I remember the note but not the argument.'

He said her name in a way she had not heard him say it before and it warmly alerted her to the changes happening between them.

It was mollifying to realise that events which we recalled in embarrassment were often forgotten by those who witnessed them. Of course — those who witnessed such embarrassment never felt the embarrassment.

She sat there enjoying the release from that embarrassing night when she'd argued against him. She was released from her naïvety. He remembered nothing of it.

'And to think I nearly wrote you a note apologising for my naïvety,' she laughed.

He smiled back. 'Naïve is the last thing I would see you as.'

How extraordinary.

He then said, 'Why don't we stay here at the Bergues?'

'Stay?' The proposal, of a kind, had arrived, perhaps more decisively than she had fantasised. 'Book into the hotel, you mean?'

'Yes.'

'Without bags, without being married, without a reservation?' Was she now about to reveal her naïvety?

'Without all those things.'

'With the staff knowing?'

'I am afraid I can't arrange for us to stay without the staff knowing,' he said smiling at her, taking her hand. 'Of course, if you prefer . . . I realise that it is rather impulsive. Inconsiderate?'

She had vowed to cease being Bohemian. Prefer what? What had she expected to happen? She supposed they might have gone to his apartment. If anything was going to happen. She'd never taken a man to her rooms, which would be embarrassing, facing the inquisitive eyes of the other residents the next morning. She had managed to avoid that so far in her life and had kept, at least, her rooms chaste. His place? She had no idea where he lived. He seemed to be forever in bars and cafés.

'I hadn't anticipated staying, well, staying here at the Bergues,' she said, and as she listened to herself, she realised that it implied that she had intended staying somewhere else, with him. 'It is difficult. The arrangements.' She had trouble imagining the 'staying' without luggage, without proper attention to her personal details.

'You remain here at the table and I will arrange everything.'

'Isn't it scandalous?' she said half-seriously, and wondering how he would take care of everything which included her personal necessities.

'I don't think that we can do anything that the Hôtel des

Bergues hasn't seen before. And we are, for the present time of our lives, in the rank just below where our behaviour becomes public scandal. And it is, after all, the hotel of the French delegations and we know about the conduct of the French.'

She looked directly at him. 'I know this sounds unmodern — but I really haven't done this sort of thing before.' There was Ambrose but that was another sort of thing, too. She remembered Ambrose in her first week and the Alpine inn.

'I haven't done this sort of thing very often either. In fact, I have never done this sort of thing,' he said.

She wondered whether he was also making exceptions and special exclusions.

'I want things between us to be — serious,' she said.

'They are serious.'

'Good.'

'Will I make arrangements then?'

She took a breath. 'Yes, make arrangements.'

He stood and came around to her, taking her hand. 'I am very serious, Edith.'

She lightly, and quickly, kissed his hand.

'We are, after all, part of *l'aristocratie internationale*. We can do as we wish,' he said.

She then managed to sound lightly accepting by saying, 'Perhaps we could stay in Briand's suite.'

He laughed. 'I'll see.'

She realised that she was making a private joke back to her beginnings at the League and therefore the Time of Ambrose. She didn't seem to feel any guilt.

He then excused himself and went to arrange things with that authority which she'd seen before in men who'd been at the War. They behaved as if they'd earned the right to ask anything, to break any rule. He'd earned this while she'd been working with her mother in the Red Cross to preserve $327\frac{1}{2}$ dozen eggs to send to Number Four hospital and making 1,194 pounds of jam—what privileges had that earned her? She realised curiously that she envied the men their war. She sat at the table nervously avoiding the eyes of the waiters who, she felt, must know what was going on, as Emery Kelen had known at the luncheon, as the whole of the luncheon must have known. As the whole of Geneva would ultimately know. Probably, eventually, also the *Journal de Genève*.

And tomorrow morning? Tomorrow they would have to leave the hotel in daylight, go into the street in evening clothes, clearly from the night before. She didn't have to go to the office but still, they did have to go out into the daylight of the street. She had no toiletries with her. In the morning, she would have to face him, and face the staff of the hotel. It all seemed too much. To say no now would also require a huge exertion of will. As Machiavelli would say, regard all courses of action as risky. Never imagine there was such a thing as a safe course. When one tried to avoid one danger, one encountered others. The danger in saying no at this point would be to upset his planning and his desires, and her desires too, perhaps, and to present herself as some other sort of woman. No, they were embarked but it would be her farewell to Bohemia.

Robert Dole returned and sat down. She looked at him. He gave her an embracing smile the like of which she had never had from him. She returned the smile in kind and looked down, thinking, this is ridiculous, I am nearly thirty, and my knees should not have turned to jelly.

'They are very willing to have us as guests. I talked with the night manager, not with the desk clerk. At first, I said something about "lost luggage and missed trains". It was all unnecessary.

He is a man of the world, he seemed to know who I was, remembered from some event.'

'They'll want to see our passports?'

'I think the formalities will be overlooked. But not the niceties.'

She felt he was securely in charge of the evening and she was quietly happy for that. She would just let it all happen.

'Good,' she said, not feeling it yet. 'Bad. Really, I'm nervous.'

'That will pass.'

She was relieved to find that they were not expected to leave the table that minute and go to The Room. They went on, in an urbane manner, to have their desserts, with the nervous, but beckoning, thought of The Room sitting, somehow, on the table with them, like an oversized gift box. With further urbanity, they then had their cognacs and coffee in the lounge and were just finishing when a porter came to their table in his smart brass-buttoned uniform and said, in a discreet, whispered announcement, 'Your room is prepared, Monsieur, Madame, when you are ready.'

Robert Dole thanked him, and turned to her: 'Shall we go up?'

Just like that? 'I suppose so.'

'You've finished? Do you want anything else?'

'I would like a glass of something.'

'There will be a glass of something in the room. Courtesy of our *bon* host.'

She could think of nothing further to arrest the moment, although it was not delay that she wanted really, what she wanted was to be magically whisked from the comfortable seat in the calm lounge to The Room, without any intervening movements.

Avoiding any other eyes, she stood, took Robert's arm and they went from the lounge and its calm, murmuring conversation and its ordered service, and, clutching the rolled caricature, she was led by him and the silent, uniformed porter to the lift and its too noisy door, and staring liftboy, up the three floors, along the wide corridor, to The Room, a journey taking at least a month. To The Room, where nothing would be methodical or calm and nothing quite certain.

The porter fumbled with the key and took another week to unlock the door.

'How very Weimar,' she whispered to Robert Dole, striving for urbanity.

He chuckled. 'Very.'

How ruthless new love was. Yet she decided not to do it again. She decided that new love had to have its own language and its own sayings.

There was, indeed, a bottle of champagne. Champagne, at least, was a certainty in life. So were their hats, gloves, and coats, also there in the room.

'Shall I open the champagne for you, sir?' the porter said.

'Thank you, porter, no. I will do it myself.'

He was a man who opened his own champagne. After glancing around, but not taking in much of the luxury of the room, seeing at first only the large turned-down bed, she went to what she took to be the door of a bathroom, and, seeing from the corner of her eye Robert tip the porter, she went in to the bathroom for temporary respite more than for any bodily need.

She refreshed her make-up and tried to garner strength from the coolness of the tiled bathroom and its new efficient taps and sumptuous towels, leaning her cheek momentarily against the cool tiles. Should she bathe? She did not want to go to him with the light but inescapable dampness of body. Nor did she have the boldness to do such a definitive thing even if it would give her more time. But she used the bidet to make sure that her private parts were fresh and clean.

When she came back into the bedroom, he was opening the champagne.

They drank to their future, and to authorship, and to the League, linking arms for the toast in the European way.

As if to take command of the room, she turned on the bedside lamp and turned off the overhead light. She checked that the blinds were drawn. She unrolled the caricature and held it to the wall, then went to the bathroom and returned with a wet cake of soap and used the soap to fix the caricature to the mirror in the room.

'Where did you learn that?' he asked.

'Boarding school.'

He reached out to her, and stopped her nervous busyness about the room, pulling her to him. They kissed for the first time, champagne glasses in hand.

Coming out of the kiss, their faces close together, she saw closely his male skin, smelled his shaving soap. Her heart was excited.

'Still nervous?' he asked.

'Yes. In a different way now.'

'What way now?'

'The happy kind. Not the anxious kind.'

They kissed again, following that timing which kissing sets in motion, where all is naturally urged and fashioned by the body's impetuosity, advancing but without haste. And so, amid the kissing, they gradually undressed. She liked the gradual inevitability of their undressing, and relaxed. She liked both the gradualness of it and the inevitability of it, the way he watched while she removed her evening dress, leaving on her white pearls, to stand before him in her underwear.

The way he removed his studs and bow tie and shirt and singlet, showing eventually his naked, almost hairless, chest. The muscles of his stomach, the way he removed his trousers and hung them over a chair, then she almost gasped. His back had a single bad scar. She knew that it must have been from the War. Were all the men scarred? He turned to her in his undershorts and took her into an embrace, kissing again, their bodies clothed only in their underwear. The underwear no longer a barrier as such, but an enticing setting of their bodies, a display of their physical differences and their allures as a man and a woman. She was at first frightened to let her fingers come to rest on the scar, but then she did, and she caressed it.

She knew he was aware of her cognisance of the scar but he didn't say anything. They parted and she was pleased by the way he watched her release her stockings from her suspenders, the way she eased down her lace-edged corset, as she wriggled out of it, to reveal her favourite short petticoat with lace inserts and edging, shrugging it off to show to him, at last, her breasts. And then she took down her satin knickers and stepped out of them. Showing him at last, her full nakedness, fully pleased by the way she had done it, by the artfulness of her revealing of herself. She always dressed carefully for sleep, always with her appearance in mind, her appearance to herself as much as to anyone. Now, intuitively, she left on only her earrings and her necklace. Her apprehension of him was of a different kind now, it was the apprehensive anticipation of the marvel of their bodies meeting, naked, although she found she had no doubts that what she was and how she was, would please him.

She glanced quickly at his crotch and saw that he was stiffening.

And then they were lying on the turned-down bed and she felt that it had happened by wishing, rather than by effort or decision, again, a flowing inevitability.

He quietly asked her about the hazard of her falling pregnant. She remained silent as if having not heard his query, thinking now that the wonderful flow of it all had halted, was lost now.

He again said quietly, 'Edith?'

He was waiting for an answer, bending over her. He kissed her lightly. 'Well?' He smiled at her. 'You have a personal method?'

'Not exactly.'

He laughed at her. Not his hard laugh, a soft and caressing laugh. 'You either have a method, Edith, or you do not. There really isn't any halfway.'

She was shamed and she felt foolish. She said in a small defensive voice, 'I really didn't think that tonight was a night when I should be prepared for such eventualities.' What made it all worse was that she had studied science, that she did know about it vaguely but had never quite got around to facing it. As a science student she'd been considered by the other students as 'worldly' in the way that medical students and nurses were thought of as worldly. Reproduction, asexual and sexual — although at this very moment her mind seemed to recall more about asexual reproduction of cells and such. And before, because of Ambrose's infertility, there'd been no need. She told him this in a small voice.

He said, his voice soft and reassuring, 'I have to worry — the male line in my family are all perfectly potent.'

She liked him saying the word potent, it was fleshly and forthright. It was then that she realised that she didn't give a heck about birth control, this night, with him, but knew that was not correct either and should not be said. That it was romantically delinquent to feel that way. Or was it an observance of a higher order of biological being?

Then she said it. 'I really don't care.' Without looking at him. 'I am happy for you to take me.'

He kissed her and said quietly, 'That's a beautiful thing for a woman to say to a man. Thank you, Edith. But we have to be careful, for now.' She detected in his voice and body an urging to accept her submission to him, that he was struggling with control.

They then joined under the bedclothes in a flow of kissing and caressing, their passion forgiving them for the interruption, for being sensible. She went into his arms, enjoying the muscularity of his body, her breasts firm against his chest, her nipples sensitive to the light hair of his chest, her pearls excitingly hard between them.

She could feel that he was hard and moistening against her body and that they were moving inexorably to his entering her and she wanted it fiercely.

But he held back, tantalisingly, delightfully, returning in a natural way to a whispered, loving conversation, their hands moving about each other's body, arousing and coming to know. She sensed it was also his way to keep his passion from bursting too soon.

'And what changed your mind about me?' he asked, softly. 'How did I finally after all this time, find favour with you?'

'The last glass of champagne,' she said, into his ear. 'No, I'm wrong, it was the cognac.' She lay there thinking, I must be honest. 'It was your toast to Aristide Briand, at lunch — I knew then you would be on my side.' This was, perhaps, closer to the truth. As a quick answer. 'And that you would be *by* my side, one day soon,' she said with an easy boldness.

She whisperingly asked him if this was the bed that Briand

had slept in. He whisperingly replied that he had asked for just that bed, and yes, this was the bed that Briand slept in. They were playfully joined in their jesting.

He then revealed to her, with a hint of self-congratulation, that he'd arranged the caricature with Kelen before the luncheon.

She became nervously tight. She lay there, dismayed. She pulled slightly away from him, 'You didn't!'

She remained in his arms, but unresponsively. The amorousness of their joining and the mood had fled to the corner of the room.

'Edith?' He was startled.

Whether now to leave this bed; or whether to laugh and pretend to amusement. To then pretend the night away in the interests of a makeshift harmony, in the interests of a makeshift love? No. It would not be in the interest of their love to begin with a sham. She would not pretend laughter, she did not want to misuse urbanity, she would not put down her disquiet. She was never again going to pretend to laughter. She did not want to be swindled any more by the connivances men and women used with each other. And she with herself.

'What are you doing! For Heaven's sake, where are you going, Edith?' he said, as she pulled away out of his embrace and left the bed.

She got out of bed, holding her breasts with her cupped hands to take them from his gaze, and stood in front of her underwear which was lying on the dressing bench.

He sat up in bed with surprise. 'What has offended you?' He seemed genuinely surprised. 'Edith — what is it? What have I said?'

'I don't like secret dealings and slyness.' She paused in her ineffectual efforts to dress. She decided to remove the caricature from the wall. She might even tear it up. She did not have any idea how she could graciously leave the hotel. Down in the lift, down the foyer stairs, past the staff. Out into the night. She was, frankly, defeated by it all.

'Secret dealings? The *caricature*? I thought it was a tribute to you, to us — it was a gift to you. I thought you'd like to have a Kelen caricature.'

A gift had to pass many tests before it got into her life. He would have to learn that. 'You got together and planned a bawdy joke!'

'I asked him to draw us and to send it over during the lunch. I gave him a bottle of champagne this afternoon in payment. Where's the offence?'

'The offence is that you asked him to draw that before we went to the luncheon! Before anything had been said, agreed, or pledged. You told him to draw us going to bed! You told him what you intended to happen intimately between us before any intimate agreement had been arrived at. You said all this to Kelen. A third party. A stranger.'

'Hold up.' He came from the bed and took her in his arms. 'Hold up. Hold your horses, Edith.'

He was still erect and she thought him long and big. She did not remove her hands from her breasts. Ambrose had always described his own as 'a Cupid's cock'. She would definitely say that Robert's was long. She'd been taught in art classes by Julian Ashton that Christ was given small male parts in statuary as a way of showing his renunciation of carnality. Robert showed no signs of such renunciation.

'You'd already decided the whole outcome for yourself,' she said, trying to keep to her grievance.

Her attempts at dressing were not getting very far. She supposed she could sleep on the floor of the room. Or huddled in the armchair.

He said, 'I didn't tell him *what* to draw. I simply wanted a memento of the luncheon because I felt it was going to be important — for us. I asked him if he would mind doing us a caricature. I didn't ask him to draw the bed and so on. I sensed that things had changed between us and that we were destined to, well, find each other now.'

'You didn't ask him to draw the bed and so on?'

'No.'

'The subject theme was his idea? The bed?'

'Entirely. I asked simply that he make us, make you, a drawing to celebrate the occasion. Nothing more.'

She stared at his face to be sure he was being truthful and she saw in his eyes the fear of losing her and of losing the night.

He said that he had been surprised by the bawdiness of it.

'That's all right, then,' she said, going to his arms, relieved that her grievance had evaporated. 'I will accept crassness from a court jester like Kelen,' she managed to say, feeling that it sounded adult enough, while her behaviour now seemed less than adult, and then she added laughing, 'but I will not accept crassness from a wooing lover.'

He took her back into his arms and they kissed, naked, standing in the room at the Hôtel des Bergues. Their skins felt so right against each other. She was aware he was wet and hard.

'I'm a nervous pony,' she said, 'forgive me.'

'I am wooing you,' he said, 'and I ask you to marry me.'

He'd said it.

Without hesitation, she said, 'And I'm happy to be wooed, although — strictly speaking — shouldn't wooing precede the proposal?' Her voice was breathless.

'I have wooed you for years, and I think you knew it.'

'I think I knew that I would eventually know it.'

'What is your reply?'

'Yes is my reply. Yes, I will marry you.'

'Thank you, dear Edith.'

They kissed and then returned to the bed and she closed with him freely and fully, again marvelling how patient the sensual mood of the evening had been with her antics, how readily forgiving, how eager it was to return from its temporary banishment, how eagerly it flowed over them and covered them with its heated urgings. She went into his arms and opened herself, freely and fully.

She had never felt a man so hard and so penetrating nor herself so wet and yielding. It was so rigid at its core, yet, in its fullness, so compliant and smooth to her flesh, the elasticity of solids, filling her tightly and then untightening her. The pleasure was mostly in the urgent ardour of their first physical enfolding and his deep penetration of her, more than any completeness of the act.

They rocked together for some time and then with regret she felt him withdraw from her at the peaking of his excitation and then experienced the corporeal excitement of his hot fluid throbbing out onto her belly and she smelled its earthy odour.

They lay in silence, glued by it, sealed together.

She used the sheet to wipe them both.

Then in whispers they returned to each other and to the room. They whispered that their relationship was 'ratified', and went on together to weave it into a joke. They talked intimately, close together, and warm in the bed.

He said: Within the limitations of my talents and my writing, I am committed to truthful explanation of the world. I am willing to respect your calling, your not telling me things and I will not ask. If you will respect me seeking what I have to seek, the explanation of things.

She said: If I commit myself to you I commit myself to your

career insofar as I am honestly able to aid it without injury to my own.

He said: And I to yours.

She said: And could you never be my full and perfect confidant?

He said: I would not want to take from you that which I could not apply to my work. I would happily be your confidant on all the matters of your soul but, perhaps, I cannot be your confidant in matters of state. If you wish, I can be your full and perfect confidant on matters of the heart and soul.

Yes, be the confidant of my heart and soul.

And you, mine.

She said then something that she had to say. 'Will you take me regardless of what I have to reveal to you of myself?' Yet knowing, as she asked, that no one could give that undertaking, and fearing that she would not have the courage to tell, that some of her had become untellable. But he said, 'Yes, if you will accept me regardless of what I have to reveal.' She thought fleetingly of Ambrose's revelations but said, with faith, 'Yes, I will accept you.' And would he read her poems? He was happily surprised. 'Yes, I will even read your poems.'

She asked him to prevent her becoming a zealot. He said that maybe it was a time when we might need to be zealots. She said, no, zealots could not negotiate, zealots could not see with clarity. He said, what if we have to deal with zealots? She said that a non-zealot could always defeat a zealot in the end. He said only if the non-zealot was well armed and cunning.

They said to each other that together they would think and write, make sense of the world together, make the peace together, and have adventures together.

They coupled again and this time she gained full pleasure. She realised how physical love with Ambrose had become in the last period when they'd been together much more a touching, an easing, sometimes a kindness, but not so much a releasing, and rarely with passion.

Before they finally slept, she began to tell him a story which she prayed she would remember and get right.

There is an Austrian story, she told him, about a blind beggar who was walking through the country led by a little boy. The blind beggar complained that he was thirsty. The little boy said, 'Uncle, we are in the country. Perhaps I can get you a glass of milk.'

The blind beggar said, 'Milk. I have never tasted milk and I am blind. I have never seen milk. What is it like?'

'Milk is white.'

'What is white?'

'Uncle,' said the little boy, 'there is a goose over there in the field. The goose is white.'

'What is a goose?'

'A goose,' said the little boy, 'is a bird with a crooked neck.'

'Oh,' said the beggar, 'but what is crooked?'

Then the little boy crooked his arm and said, 'Uncle, take your hand and run it along my arm. That is crooked.'

The beggar ran his hand along the boy's arm and said, 'Now I understand. Now I know what milk is.'

She felt strongly compelled to tell the story to him. Since she'd heard it the story had returned to her from time to time, resonated with her. She told Robert how it charmed her with its twisted meaning. We desire to know, she said, we go much of the time in blindness, we use strange logics in our striving for assurance, we so readily accept any meaning which brings to us a coherence, an order to our mess of mind.

You told it well. It is a good parable. It sounded, he murmured, dropping towards sleep, much like the business of reporting the world. She felt his body twitching, and heard his night noises, as he drifted towards sleep, his mind leaving the waking world.

She did not sleep at once. She felt his warm fluid between her legs and realised that during the second time he hadn't withdrawn. She was unperturbed. Their mutual, unspoken romantic delinquency enchanted her.

It was 1930 and she had a new lover, and, she was sure, was also *in love*, sleeping in the Hôtel des Bergues and now, maybe, even a woman of the world. But for all the pleasure of the romantic delinquency she knew they were not ready yet for that, she would grit her teeth and go to her Swiss doctor. She was helping to make the future of the world. She had not lost money on the stock exchange like so many others. Most of her stocks had been wiped out but she had made money from her Firestone shares. She had put her earnings from her mother's money into the League International School. Since coming to Geneva, she had refashioned herself much to her own satisfaction. She smiled as she recalled Jeanne and she changing their handwriting, learning a new calligraphy, entirely different from that she had been taught at school. Jeanne believed that how you wrote not only had an impression on those who read it, but on you, the person who wrote that way. If you changed your handwriting you would change yourself. She had pointed out to Jeanne that if you set about to change your handwriting, you had already set about changing yourself and, therefore, could not be sure that it was the handwriting that was doing the changing. When she had first come to the League she had been decent and proficient, but somehow unadorned. She felt now more accomplished. Australia taught me *civitas*, but it would not give me the wherewithal to become accomplished. I had to find that and do that for myself.

If she were scared, it was because she was sometimes too

aware of the million of unseen, unruly things going on about her in the world and within her, in the inner world, beyond her consciousness not only in the way the Freudians meant, but in another way — the unruly world which could not yet be confined to a statistical size. Sometimes her heart became aghast at the realisation of the million of unseen and unruly things yet, at other times, these unmeasured and disordered things caused her heart to beat with the exhilarated anticipation that these things could be harnessed to give a pattern of meaning and to serve order. Another realisation then stole into her mind. If Robert were no longer a correspondent, she could talk to him of the secrets of the League and her fears there: though if he were now a novelist he would be interested perhaps, not in the secrets of the League but in the secrets of her heart. Would he steal those secrets from her, as Ambrose had stolen League secrets? She lay there and appreciated, in a nervous way, the symmetry of her life.

She decided that she was not afraid of giving the secrets of her heart to Robert for his books, and those secrets would come to inform the spirit of the world.

In Robert's arms, Edith began to weep from the fear of the million unseen and unruly things, over which she had no supervision. She wept also for the trembling chance that the world now had to become safe and just, and she for the trembling chance she had to love and be loved, and she entreated the million unseen and unruly things to help her become wise and brilliant and loved. Then she willed for Ambrose to find peace within himself and to be healed.

Robert came awake at her crying and said, 'It's all right, Edith, it is all right — we can be true to each other, and true to our callings — it can happen.' He was partly right in thinking that was what was making her weep; she was crying about that too.

She would tell him in the morning about the million unruly and unseen things going on in mysterious ways, about which she was crying. She suspected that he already knew about these things and knew the feeling that they engendered, and maybe that he also knew ways of calming the beating of her heart and the discord and clatter of her mind, which at times felt like a thousand birds taking flight from a lake.

In the morning they would order a grand breakfast to their room and celebrate the start of their decade, and she would not be intimidated by the waiters of the Bergues. After the breakfast they would go down, not by the lift, but by the elegant wide stairs which she had liked the look of, and they would step out into the Saturday sunlight of Geneva in their evening clothes, without qualm, emboldened by love. It had been her farewell to Bohemia. The magnificent two-backed beast of passion was to become the magnificient two-headed animal of marriage. She would also be stepping from the hotel into the nineteen-thirties. Her debut.

Tramcar terminus Palais des Nations

Edith had never in her life before needed to talk to a doctor about procreative matters. Although she'd studied science at university, as Robert had reminded her at least fifty times, she was still reluctant to interrogate and unveil her body. She supposed that despite all her study, what she desired from her body was grace and health, not physiological understanding. Preferably, this grace and health should be present without her having to do too much about it. In fact, not having to think too much about it was, to her mind, the essence of grace. It should be effortless grace — apart, that is, from hygiene and cosmetic care of the body. Fitness was another thing one shouldn't have to worry about too much.

After the grand night of passion at the Bergues — her 'farewell to Bohemia', as she described it in a letter to Caroline — she was happily convinced that she would fall pregnant. Her body seemed to say to her that she had conceived. She'd even confirmed confidentially with Nancy Williams that she could keep her job if she had a child and married.

'Depends which comes first,' Williams had said with amusement.

Edith had laughed with a private pride, pleased that all this was happening to her.

Williams had said, 'Just make sure they're in the right order and you'll have your position, and you'll get special leave.'

But she hadn't conceived. Her body hadn't been bringing her news, although it may have been talking things over with her.

She was also inexplicably resistant to the notion of birth control. Robert's withdrawing was not giving either of them the sentiment of intimacy. She wanted to feel his fluid inside her. She wanted them to bodily close together without impediment. However, in conversation with Robert, it was commonsensically agreed that she shouldn't fall pregnant. So for this reason and to improve the pleasure of their physical love, she made an appointment with her Swiss doctor to get the question fixed up once and for all, and also, she reluctantly conceded, in the interests of scientific self-knowledge. She did not want to appear to be a blockhead about all of this.

The doctor was close to Robert's age. He glanced at her left hand for an engagement ring. She inferred that perhaps Swiss law required her to be married, or engaged to be married, and she rushed to tell him she was to be married soon. She liked the sound of it and reminded herself again that it was true.

The doctor, practising his English, took a polite interest and asked whether the wedding would be at the English church.

She told him that it would be. The minister there was a friend of her fiancé. She used the word fiancé confidently, although she and Robert didn't really believe in the 'engagement' and certainly not in long engagements, although it could be said that they practised long courtships. The minister at the church was also a friend of the League and had agreed to say 'love, honour and trust' instead of 'love, honour and obey' in the wedding service. She didn't tell the doctor that both Robert and she were non-believers. She wanted to be free from the deceptions that being unmarried lovers involved. Yet, to reach the state of declared and loudly proclaimed love, she would have to go through the deceptions of the Church service and the hypocrisy of that, although she rather liked the ceremonial of the wedding service. Her father would shake his head sadly but would understand. She didn't know what John would think, but he'd married Ella in a Methodist church. Colonel Ingersoll believed in marriage. If the hypocrisy of it worried her, she supposed that she could always wear her panties back to front during the ceremony. George would simply ask if it was the biggest church in town.

The doctor said, 'Why come to a doctor about birth control?'

Flustered, she said that she was sorry but she didn't follow his line of thinking.

'The medical profession thinks that birth control has nothing whatsoever to do with medicine.'

She said that she assumed that a doctor would know more about the body than anyone else and how to safely guide her in — she was about to say 'physical love' — but changed it to 'the planning of her fertility'.

'Thinking in the medical profession is that it's not a medical problem. It may be a theological question. It may be a question of methodology, in the realm, say, of the principles of mechanics, but doctors mostly say that it is not a medical question.'

Irritated and flustered, she began to rise, pulling on her gloves, saying to herself in her head, 'And the properties of matter, sound, heat, and light.'

'I'm sorry, Doctor, there has been a misunderstanding.' She even held out her hand to say goodbye. She couldn't see why she'd ever considered it to be a 'medical problem'.

'Sit down, please.' He now seemed mildly distressed that he'd disconcerted her. 'I do not express myself clearly — I say this only to show you the stupidity, sometimes, of my profession. Of course, birth control has to do with the health of women. I believe that.'

She sat down.

'More, it has to do with the pleasure of men and women. That interests me just as much.'

She must have looked at him, this time, with a different reservation, for he rushed to say, 'Happy people are healthier people, is what I believe.' He said, 'You must know this English nursery rhyme — "There was an old woman who lived in a shoe"?'

Edith nodded, feeling a little tossed about.

'A colleague tells me that in England the birth control reformers have a poster now that says — please forgive my English — "There was an old woman who lived in a shoe, She had so many children she didn't know what to do. Don't be like her. Ask the doctor for birth control advice." '

This obviously tickled the doctor and he laughed heartily. She smiled, to show she appreciated his efforts to put her at ease, but she wished he would get on with giving her the advice she needed so that she could be out of this situation. He was, she thought, relishing the opportunity of doing this service.

To show she was not totally ignorant, she said that she knew that there were now heavy penalties in France for people who gave advice on evasion of pregnancy. She believed that was not the case in Switzerland.

'Oh no, not here. The French need children.' His voice then became impersonal as he began his professional advice. He explained the Dutch cap, the Waldenberg loop, and the pessary, and other methods, all of which caused her inwardly to groan. He told her of the latest development from Germany, a silver ring invented by Doctor Graefenberg. She had only a vague idea where the silver ring went and no idea of what it did and she did not ask. She contemplated a joke about having shunned an engagement ring she was now to wear a Graefenberg ring but it was beyond her. *I am a blockhead*, she thought. She was overwhelmed by the idea of making a choice.

He advised against the sheath. 'It is now believed that the condom deprives the woman of the benefits of true coitus,' he said. 'It biologically starves her of the seminal secretions of the man absorbed through the walls of the vagina.' He wasn't quite able to look at her as he told her this.

She forced herself to look at him.

She appreciated very well what he meant but she hadn't realised that it was also 'good for her'.

'Like vitamins?'

'In a way, yes.'

He relieved her of choice by advising a Dutch cap, made of rubber, and she nodded, being able to somehow conjecture how a rubber cap might work and where it might go and liking the sound of rubber rather than the sound of the silver ring. 'I am a rubber cap sort of person rather than a silver ring person,' she joked aloud, more to herself.

He laughed heartily, probably suspecting an English language joke that he should have understood. He suggested that an X-ray impression be made. He would also 'take measurements' for a sketch and order a personalised cap from a laboratory in Germany. He then made a joke about Dutch and German hats — about helmets and tulips — which she didn't listen to attentively enough to understand but at which she laughed heartily in return.

She was not at all clear about the taking of measurements and she had never had an X-ray impression. She inwardly whimpered at the idea of the taking of measurements.

The doctor began to explain what the cervix was and she was pleased to find that she remembered where the cervix was and was able to display some scientific knowledge.

'Good, you know the cervix, then,' he said. He asked her to sign a form releasing the X-ray impression, after use, to the University of Munich for scientific purposes. 'Or you can have it returned to you.'

Damnation. 'Can I simply have it destroyed?' Even this idea went against her spirit.

'Of course, but I thought that as an official at the *Société des Nations* — scientific research, and so on.'

Was there no end to it?

'All right — give it to Science, give it to the university.' No greater love hath any woman . . .

She undressed behind a screen, which seemed purely a gesture to modesty given what she assumed would next be happening to her. A nurse helped her into an open-fronted, starched white robe which she found inexplicably reassuring, and guided her to a reclining stirrup chair.

She closed her eyes and thought of the township of Jasper's Brush and Australian wild flowers growing in profusion on sweeping, sunlit plains.

'It's coming from Germany,' she told Robert at his apartment that weekend. 'In a laboratory in Germany they are, at this very moment, looking at my most intimate part on an X-ray photograph and the doctor's sketch.'

'A sketch?' Her description of what had happened was making him uncomfortable.

'Doctors do have to touch me,' she said.

'Yes.'

'Let me explain the alternative methods of birth control,' she said teasingly. Having come through it, and knowing now about Graefenberg rings and such, she wanted a chance to display, in some way, her newly won expert knowledge.

He stopped her. 'I don't wish to know.'

At first she was surprised by his shying away from this. She could appreciate his possessiveness about her intimate body, but she had difficulty understanding his masculine discomfort. She couldn't see why he should be behaving as if he'd been, well, subjected to it. Still, if he wanted to avoid the subject, so did she. 'Let's then not talk about it any more. Evermore. It's done,' she said.

She began to sense why they should not talk about it but it was difficult when both of them avowed that the Health of Being came from the ability to talk of everything, freely and without shame. Yet she sensed that contraception as a subject was *sui generis*. It certainly did not belong in the romance of all that was happening to them and was best excluded by silence unless it could somehow become part of the erotic play of love which was something she could not see happening.

He mumbled apologetically about his squeamishness, smiling ruefully.

At dinner, the wine lifted her spirits and she even ventured a joke about it all, violating their prohibition, 'I suppose I could have the X-ray photograph and the sketch returned and we could frame them along with the Kelen sketch. An illustrated history of modern love.'

'You're out of order,' he said. 'We agreed not to talk about it.'

She again accepted the prohibition as being correct and inscribed it on her mind. 'I'm sorry,' she said, 'I do agree with you about it.'

The agreement 'not to talk about a subject' caused her to return to a qualm which had been with her since the night at the Bergues. She had wanted to tell Robert of all the things which had made her. Not just her Rationalist childhood and her electoral work with John Latham. She wanted especially to tell of those things which might cause him to think again. She wanted to rid herself of her secrets.

Until now she had been excusing her failure to 'tell all' by using John's advice about the diplomatic delaying of truth. The need to consider the timing of the telling of truth so that it was not damaging or ill-placed. She also saw that the truth had to be told in the right tone and with the vocabulary appropriate to the situation. And other items in their life had to be encountered before she could make her dramatic life confessions. But now the confessions had been over-delayed. Some confessions should obviously come before the sending out of invitations to the wedding. She smiled, recalling a similar joke she'd had with herself about Ambrose.

Yet she was still aware of the repercussions of her revelations to Florence and she winced at the delicate demands involved in the telling.

Her father would remind her of the lesson of the hot stove and the cat. She had to decide whether the telling of the episode was another hot stove that she was about to sit on or whether she was the stupid cat who avoided all stoves and thus forfeited the warmth of stoves. She decided that telling Robert was not another hot stove. And she winced again, this time at the very idea that her father would ever have to be appraised of her secrets so as to give such advice on the telling of those secrets! For all the family's Rationalism, sexual matters had always been heavily wrapped in the broadest of progressive theory and had thus been denuded of any useful detail.

She momentarily considered whether the telling of her past might be similar to talking about birth control. That it might do damage to the erotic romance of their life. It could, on the other hand, enhance this — could bring tang to their life. She would keep that in mind when telling. She would not be impersonal or clinical in the telling. She closed her eyes and leapt into the dark.

But what was the right language in which to tell a new lover of her former carnality?

She poured herself another glass of wine. 'Robert.'

'Edith?'

'Robert, I want to tell all. I want you to know the woman you're taking as a wife.' She tried to make it sound light-hearted.

'Do I have to tell you my sins in reply?'

She hadn't thought too much about that. If his vices were as off-course as Ambrose's had been, maybe she should know before the wedding day. But she couldn't conceive of breaking it off now, regardless of what he told her. Not even, she decided, if he admitted to Ambrose's vice, although she considered that unthinkable. At least if it were that, she would be experienced in dealing with it. 'I can't conceive of anything which you could tell me which would cause me to reconsider,' she said, wondering whether that was true. How much about the world did she still not know? 'I did make enquiries — we have observed each other's conduct over a few years.' Yet this too was a foolish thing to say. People had observed her and Ambrose when they'd been together and suspected nothing. Or had they suspected? Bartou had talked of eunuchs. Obviously there'd been talk of *something* fishy. She was again startled at how she must have looked to others after having been Ambrose's escort for so long. 'I withdraw that statement,' she said, wanting to be at her intelligent best with Robert, 'at least the part about having observed each other. I realise that what we see of other people in public is not the full story.'

'Quite.'

'What I am about to say concerns Ambrose, inescapably. It is therefore in strictest confidence.'

His interest was clearly aroused yet he was struggling with a question of propriety. 'I'm not at all sure we need to do this confessing. I already know that when you awaken in the morning you like to discuss your night of sleep as if you have been on a long journey. I know that you once shaved Eric Drummond although I still find that difficult to believe.'

She smiled at him, seeing that he was implying that they not pursue it. Should she take the dispensation? 'As for the matter of sleep,' she said, 'I consider that if someone has been absent for eight hours in an interesting place, it should be talked about. As for my confessions, you, as a writer, should be curious.'

'But I write mysteries.'

'With serious intentions.'

Or did writers make our secrets more frightening?

He didn't comment.

'From you,' she said, 'I ask only that you tell me that which you consider could affect our love or marriage.'

'Why don't you apply that test to your own confessions?'

Should she say that she was also using her confessions to discover what sort of person he was? Was he someone like Florence who might recoil from her? She also wanted to *share* her experiences, to be able to scrutinise them with another human being, and to be told by another human being that what she had done to herself was not contemptible or ruinous. To have someone else answer Florence's question about what she might have done to her womanhood.

'I am applying that test,' she said, allowing fear to trickle through her.

'Then I await this revelation with wonder,' he said, rather cockily.

Did he think that her life had been such that she could not shock him? That she was a person who could not possibly have led a life within which bizarre experience occurred? She gazed at him speculatively and nervously. Or did he want her to be the sort of woman who'd led a correct and suitable life? He had not expected a virgin, she knew that. Or did he? 'You were not disappointed that I wasn't virginal?'

'I would've thought less of you if you had been. I would have then found myself with an inappropriate person, a person who would have been an unsuitable match to my own misspent life. We are both people of our times. We are both *voyageurs*.'

'Yes, we are.' That was right. That was how she saw them both.

She then told him of Ambrose's predilection and how she had happily indulged him in it and how she had enjoyed the perversity of it and she told a little about the Molly Club.

He listened without speaking but he widened his eyes theatrically and put on a small accepting smile, all intended to reassure her that he was not recoiling. 'I have never had an inclination to dress as a woman — that is my first reaction to your confession,' he said, 'but I did have a friend who preferred men. My second reaction is that if I were to find such an inclination in myself, I have the right companion.'

She considered whether the second part of his answer constituted a foreshadowing of something but decided that it did not. 'I don't think that Ambrose really wants men. He wants to be a womanly man among women,' she said. Robert had not said anything about what it had meant about her womanhood. 'You do not think that my having indulged in this degrades me as a woman?'

He seemed to consider this. 'To me, it makes you a woman who has seen something of the world. Who knows about

643

the deviance of human beings. I've heard of this club but have never been there. You must take me there.' He seemed openly curious.

'Maybe.'

Now for the harder part. Jerome.

Before she could begin, he added some more information, perhaps trying to show that he was also knowledgeable about this part of life. 'I know of Follett. I hadn't quite connected him with the club. I know him in another role.'

'How?' She asked as a conversational courtesy, overriding her impatience to get her story told.

'As a patron of the arts. He gives money to the Museum of Geneva and makes other such gestures. Some say he spies for one or other of the non-member governments. We live in a nest of spies.'

'I suppose so.' She would eventually have to tell that she had also been the lover of a spy. She wondered whether Ambrose and Follett were spying confederates. She stored that away for another time.

'Is there more?' he asked.

'There is a further confession,' she said. She wanted to be quickly and absolutely reassured that he was not recoiling or would not recoil at some other time in the future. She fervently hoped that he would be able to so convince her.

She told of what she'd done in Paris with Jerome, an unknown Negro man. As she told it, she remembered Ambrose's reaction. He had never been able to joke about it, but nor had she ever known quite what he saw that night. It was the one thing which he had never turned into banter. She realised as she told of that night that it was not only about a lasciviousness in her nature but also about a man who was black. That was something she had not really ever been able to think about. It

644

was a psychological nerve centre. The blackness and her subordination. And nor could she focus on it, nor deal with it. But if she could not explain it, she could at least tell it.

She tried to tell it with lascivious detail.

'I remember it as being very rigid, yet it was not hard, and it was hot and became wet quickly, not only from the wetness of my mouth.'

'In the room *Artiste*?' His voice told her that he was responding well to her telling, but his question was a way of maintaining his balance in the conversation.

'Yes.'

'Where were the others?'

'Ambrose came looking for me. He came to the door of the room *Artiste* but I don't know what he saw.'

'You think he saw you?'

'I don't know what he saw.'

She sat silently, not wanting to prejudice or falsify his responses by making insecure requests for assurance.

'He didn't say anything?'

She tried to give out a nervous giggle. 'He said: "*Adieu, belle vamp australienne.*" '

'I really meant Ambrose — what did he say?'

'About this? Nothing.'

'It is true that I am amazed,' he said. 'Truly amazed.'

She chilled and rushed to say, 'As difficult as it may be to understand, at the time it did not feel unnatural that this should happen.'

'I think I can understand the urgings towards the exotic.' She watched as he found things to do with his hands. He blew his nose.

It was Jerome's blackness that unsettled him as it had allured her. Then he looked back to her eyes and said, 'We shouldn't regret our experiences.' She did not regret them at all. He had gone to a platitude.

It was not a fully personal response. But he had not exploded, flared, or shattered. She still needed more assurance. It was a different Robert Dole she was meeting. Not the Robert Dole who had told her to go read Erasmus and to consider the unconsidered particulars of life. He was being something of a man of the world but he was not quite a man of repose who could take with nonchalance all that the world could parade before him.

She said, 'It was such wayward conduct. It was going out of bounds but I was exhilarated.'

He sat pondering it all. She watched his face.

She became apprehensive again and rushed to say, 'I am not *that sort of person*. But I am a woman who has done that thing. That's all. Done it with a stranger.'

She wanted to make it absolutely clear to him. 'I am the sort of woman who has done that with a black man.'

He did not hesitate in his reply. 'It's all right, Edith. Nothing in your "confession" causes me to shrink from you. For me, colour does matter dreadfully even if I believe that we must sometimes pretend, anyhow, that it doesn't matter.'

'Do you fear it?'

'I can never really get around it to the person. It is so . . .' he struggled for his words, 'it is a very visible difference. It demands that I see the person as different.'

'But we mustn't let it affect judgements?'

'No. To pretend that it doesn't matter to us is an honourable pretence.'

'So, in my confession, it is that which bothers you?'

'It astounds me. But he was a musician. It was jazz music. It was Paris. But I am astounded that you could overcome so much

646

in yourself to be able to do that. It is the leap in conduct which astounds and impresses me.'

It was honest of him to admit to being astounded. She could see that he was not going to be disgusted. 'Yes, it was Paris. He was a musician. It was the only time in my life that anything remotely like that has happened.'

He said quietly, his composure returning, 'There is another thing about it.'

'Yes?'

'I found your description and the way you enjoyed it, I found that exciting me. And perhaps sometime,' he smiled handsomely, 'perhaps you will do it for me?'

She was now reassured. She smiled assent and compliance. 'It will come to happen and you must know now that my body is for you only. For you in whatever way will arouse pleasure in you.'

'Thank you.'

'Thank you for hearing me and for accepting what you heard.'

He said, 'I have been with other women. But I have never loved before, properly.' He paused, as if about to tell her some appalling secret, as if it were hard for him to say. He coughed and said, 'I have only truly been with one other woman, in a loving way. Back in England when I was young.'

She realised then that in these matters she might be more experienced than he. In panic she sensed that this was not good for a man.

She had rarely been *more experienced* than others in anything. She didn't want to overwhelm him with her knowingness. 'I have had only one lover, really — Ambrose,' she said, 'and as you see, he was not fully of ease as a man. I really am something of an innocent.' She wanted him to feel secure.

'Experienced enough.'

She glanced at him to be sure in what tone he had said that. It was affectionate.

'I think we are both experienced enough,' she said.

'But I do have a confession,' he said. He began his confession in return. 'On leave during the War some unusual things happened. I have, for instance, been in the same room as my friend while we were with women. Paid women.'

'You were each with women? In the same room?' This interested her.

She asked whether they had done it because of the lack of another room.

'We did it because it seemed appealing to drunken soldiers.'

'You found it appealing?'

'Oh yes, very.'

'You liked the noises? The sounds of it?'

'Yes.'

'You watched your friend and the woman?'

'Yes.'

'You liked seeing your friend enter the woman?'

'Yes, I did.'

Tentatively, she queried whether he wanted to repeat the experience.

'Not involving you,' he laughed. 'Some of the bizarre things of life come to us when we are wandering lost. There is no one more lost than a soldier on leave in a strange city. When we aren't lost, these out of character experiences don't occur.'

She saw that he might be right. But she struggled to say that she felt the experiences she'd had represented another part of her which was also her true self. But she could see that all the selves within one could not be fully lived out, were not all compatible.

'I was not out of character,' she said. 'It was me.'

He grinned. 'Then nor was I "out of character".'

Their conversation became a low, happy collusion, and they questioned their way back over their experiences openly but carefully. They delighted in the cautious liberty of their conversation. It was a different liberty to that which she'd had with Ambrose. With Ambrose life had always to be fitted to banter. With him, matters which could not be made into humour could not be talked of. With Robert, an erotic precision of wording and feeling mattered most.

As they talked, she marvelled that two people who'd known each other for so long could have combusted into love and found a new, vivid awareness of each other.

Negotiated positions were often disappointing: less shining than the hoped-for outcome, less shining than the preliminary rhetoric of hopes and dreams which came before negotiations began. But their love was a negotiated position which didn't fail the shining vision of either of the negotiators.

Despite their confessions, they laughingly agreed to keep to their injunction never to mention the subject of contraception again, but the subject arrogantly and disobediently entered her life that week at the office.

She was discussing with Bartou a speech she'd written for him when Dame Rachel came to the door with a letter in her hand and interrupted.

'Bartou, could I have a word with you? And you too, Berry; this might interest you.' Dame Rachel was always including her, as a way of coaching her. 'It's this World Population Conference. I think I'll go along. I think we should be there. I've been talking to Mrs Sanger — or is it Doctor Sanger? — and I now

649

have an invitation to the conference from Sir Bernard Mallet.'

Bartou said, 'Sensitive invitations usually go through Sir Eric.'

'Sir Bernard says an invitation is on its way to Sir Eric.'

They exchanged a glance which Edith could not understand. Bartou spoke. 'You know he won't have anything to do with it. Especially if Sanger is involved.'

'What should I do — just go without clearing it with him? But I can hardly just sit discreetly up the back. They all know me and I'll be dragged into the spotlight a little. It has to be raised with Sir Eric.'

'Do nothing. Wait and see if it goes through his office unobstructed. See whether "the first nail will drive",' he said.

Dame Rachel stood in thought, staring out of the window. Then said, '*Très sage*,' and left.

'What,' Edith asked Bartou, 'is a world population conference?'

'I understand it's a gathering of scientific men to work out the best size of population for each country. To worry about the mental and moral hygiene of the race.' Bartou laughed, and added, 'They want to take over some of God's load.'

'How can a country control the size of its population?' Her mind partly answered the question with a clang. 'Yes, I think I know something of the answer,' she hurried to say, and then steered the subject by saying, 'It does sound like League-type business. The size of a population in one country could affect its neighbour.'

She began to recall her study of genetics. She had read Pearson on eugenics but had never given it much thought, had just accepted that it was a move in the right direction, as long as the weak were sheltered and not 'driven to the wall'.

'It does.'

She thought about it and then said, 'I suppose it's only sensible to be concerned with racial hygiene.'

'But we don't know what the implications are for the race if we encourage people to control their fertility. Which family may or may not have this or that number of children. Difficult. It will not get on Sir Eric's agenda.'

She mentioned the conversations to Robert. He found it curious as well. 'I suppose it could be linked with our proscribed topic.'

'The proscribed topic. Yes.' She thought and then asked, 'How would it all work? Racial hygiene?'

'I know that it's about preventing undesirable elements in the population from breeding — the insane, the crippled, the criminal and so on.'

'Well, we can't go on spoiling the human race.'

She found that on all this her mind maddeningly refused to think, but she didn't want to show this reticence, this dimwittedness. She wanted to clarify it all but her mind seemed to be going at its own pace, happily dithering with other matters, refusing to logically engage with the subject. It was as if her reticence were acting as something of a protector for the time, though how, she did not know. This protective reticence would have to go, sooner or later. But she saw how reluctant her mind was to leave the village of her womanly instinct, as unprogressive as it may be. She had a suspicion that her intention of becoming a married woman, a wife, had caused these primordial instincts to try to reclaim her. She was being called back to the womanly village and its unscientific ways.

*

651

It came up yet again at work the following Monday. It was as if birth control were following her around like a lurking stranger.

A memorandum passed across her desk from Dame Rachel to Sir Eric in which Dame Rachel reported that she'd warned Mrs Sanger against trying to link the World Population Conference with the League and against trying to have formal recommendations made to the next League Assembly on birth control. But the memorandum at the end implied, at the same time, that she, Dame Rachel, would be attending the conference. Attached to the memorandum was material about the conference which Edith read with interest. Both Dame Rachel and Sir Eric were marking the correspondence for the attention of Bartou.

'Dame Rachel is trying to drive the nail,' she said to Bartou, 'with a few heavy blows of her hammer.' She read him the memorandum.

'Interesting. She's almost disowning this Sanger woman. Even if it is as a tactic.'

Edith noted to herself that she was able to read out the memorandum mentioning birth control to Bartou without being rattled.

Next came a copy of a letter from Sir Eric to the conference organisers apologising to the conference and saying that it was impossible for the League to be represented in any way because the conference coincided with the meetings of Council and Assembly. But this wasn't strictly true.

Edith read his letter and Dame Rachel's memorandum through again. Something was eluding her. She knew now, only too well, that birth control was a difficult subject for private discussion and still not a matter for newspaper discussion. The Church of England and the Catholics were both against birth control. But surely it could be discussed among modern people, League people?

She made a comment about the letter and the minute, to draw Bartou into saying something which might dispel her confusion about it all. She said, 'But the conference doesn't overlap with Assembly.'

'A ruse. For a good Catholic like Sir Eric it's a subject whose name cannot be spoken.'

She then looked away. Her mind became giddy from the uncanny linkage between the business of the office and her personal life, an abrupt linking of her most intimate life with this business of Sir Eric and birth control. That afternoon she had the 'fitting and practice' with the doctor. She realised, too, that she'd never thought of Sir Eric as 'Catholic'. She had seen him as being above religion and nationality. And she had grown up feeling that all religious people lived by superstition but that, with education, they would eventually disregard it.

'Is population control an "inadmissible idea"?' she asked.

Bartou thought about it. 'Yes, it is at this point in civilisation, an inadmissible idea.'

Later, Sir Eric came into their office and stood where Dame Rachel had stood, and also talked with Bartou about the conference. She could see that he was uneasy about discussing it in her presence and he kept his eyes away from her and talked in a voice specially directed in tone towards Bartou. 'Behind the scenes I have chatted with Sir Bernard. I told him that the things which his conference was going to discuss arouse the strongest national feeling and are of a highly delicate character.'

Bartou said, 'True.'

'Regulation of the population excites religious feelings. It would be extremely dangerous for the Secretariat to have any official cognisance of the conference.'

'You think so?'

'Anything whatsoever to do with it, is what I mean. It would

653

lay us open to attack. Italy would be very unhappy.'

Edith sensed that Sir Eric wanted Bartou's support for his action.

Bartou said nothing.

She realised that she was not certain where, in all this, Bartou's opinion lay. She was curious and waited to hear.

When Bartou failed to answer, Sir Eric said, 'I suppose there's no way I can object to individual members of the Secretariat attending privately. Is there?'

Again, he seemed to want Bartou to come up with a justification for stopping Dame Rachel going along privately.

Bartou moved himself in his chair, leaning back, and busied himself with lighting a cigar, but said nothing which would give Sir Eric reassurance. 'It would be difficult.'

'Sir Bernard asked that I treat the conference with "benevolent neutrality". I said I would show neither benevolence nor malevolence. Do you agree?'

'I really don't see any problem with the Secretariat sending a technical observer. Sooner or later, these things will come to us. Whether we like it or not.'

'I would prefer to wait and see if these things ever come to us. Or whether, as I suspect, they will simply go away. After I raised the issue of the Sanger woman and her movement, Sir Bernard said he would ensure that the subject was not raised in any way at the conference. Unofficially, Sir Bernard is very much on my side about this. Which is something achieved.'

Bartou spoke again, 'Which subject is that, Sir Eric?'

'Birth control, of course. The wretched Sanger woman and her incessant shouting in public about contraceptives.'

'My advice is to send technical people. Send Joshi. Or send Berry. People not seen as too political.'

Sir Eric glanced at her, as if she had suddenly appeared in

the room, conjured up by Bartou from the teapot spout. She didn't respond to the proposal, could think of nothing to say. Her fitting that afternoon was on her mind and so was her new awareness that Sir Eric would be bitterly opposed to it, if he were to know.

Regardless of her Rationalism, she felt she didn't want to have much to do with this 'Sanger woman' shouting about birth control, even if Sanger was an apostle of scientific enlightenment. Even if she, herself, was now an expert on the subject. But she was for forthright contention and therefore not clearly on Sir Eric's side and that troubled her. Well, she was for open discussion in the arena, if not in the bedroom.

Bartou pointed out that to ignore the conference was itself a political statement, and then added, 'Berry has a scientific background.'

She wished that would be forgotten.

'I want no official presence at this conference,' Sir Eric said, 'with all respect to Berry, and to your advice. And to Dame Rachel.'

Bartou gently exhaled the smoke of his cigar. Sir Eric left the office, without saying anything more, and not in a very good mood.

She and Bartou exchanged glances like school children amused at the teacher's discomfort.

'How can he keep it out of the League?' she asked.

'Sir Eric argues that most of the member states are Catholic. But remember that even your Church of England is against it.'

It was not 'her' Church of England. Curiously, she had never before seen her positions as being those of the minority within the League. On this it seemed she was very much in the minority.

They both went back to their respective daily tasks. Bartou, without looking up, said, 'I have never heard the expression "benevolent neutrality". Nor can I conceive of the diplomatic condition of malevolent neutrality or of benevolent neutrality. Neutrality is either impartial, blind to good and to evil, or it is not neutrality. Sir Eric is correct on that.'

At dinner in the Lyrique, she raised the subject again with Robert, telling him of the further developments.

'I can't believe it,' she told him. 'In and out they come, talking about nothing else. It's a nightmare come true.'

'And, consequently, now we seem to talk about nothing else,' he said. 'Exactly — it seems that what was for us a personal bother has become a matter concerning the whole world. I feel plagued by it.'

She asked if he was going to write up the conference. He said that no newspaper would touch birth control. He thought that he could perhaps write about it for one of the quarterlies. She went on to say, 'I've been to see Doctor Monet. That's all done.' She wondered if he would ask to see it. Should she take it out and put it on the table? Would he suggest they go to his apartment and 'try it out' even though it wasn't yet the week-end? She was keeping strictly to the week-end only rule — to make their coming to live together as man and wife more exceptional.

'What are your thoughts then?' he asked.

'My thoughts?' Her thoughts? She'd had to practise in front of Monet but she wouldn't talk of that. From Monet, she'd also learned something interesting about using her vaginal muscles to increase the pleasure of physical love. But that could wait.

He said, 'Put it out of your mind.'

He was dodging the fact of its arrival from Germany. Fine —

so would she. 'I was wondering whether it was really proper for Sir Eric to be trying to stop discussion and so on. Some scientific control of population seems sensible. For some classes, at least.'

'Some classes? You mean because the rich have few children and live in the largest houses and the poor have the most children and live in the smallest houses?'

'Something like that,' she said. 'And I think there's a conspiracy.'

'A conspiracy?' He teased her. 'Sir Eric?'

'It could be a Catholic conspiracy.'

'It could just be fear of talking about it. We have enough trouble ourselves.'

'I suppose it could be seen as dysgenic if women in large numbers begin using it to escape from having children, from lactation and from the care of children. But I don't think Bartou is frightened of the subject reaching the Council.'

She tried not to bring Bartou up too often, because Robert felt a foolish rivalry with him.

He said, 'It's about working with nature.'

'You know what I mean.' She looked at him seriously. 'I think it's probably not a laughing matter. I don't think Sir Eric is behaving correctly.'

'He probably isn't.'

'I should raise it with Dame Rachel.'

'From what you say, she has her own difficulties. And she's leaving soon.'

She felt a miserable loss when she thought of the Palais Wilson without Dame Rachel. 'Someone should raise it. I could get Bartou to raise it.'

'With whom?'

'With members of Council. Or at a Directors' meeting.'

'Would Bartou take on Sir Eric — head-on?'

'I don't know. He's so much the Swiss diplomat, the house expert on neutrality. I might do it. I see now why neutrality is an ugly position. You have to be impartial to evil. I will raise it at the Directors' meeting — drag it screaming into the light of day.'

'Edith, I can't see you talking about this subject at a Directors' meeting. You're there by Sir Eric's grace and favour and this isn't a matter which concerns your bureau.'

Robert was right. And she had a rule that even over drinks, one should never take strong positions which, if one had power, one would not have the stomach to implement. Only argue for things which one would have the stomach to carry through. 'I'll get someone else to do it. A man.'

'Is that what Mrs Swanwick would do — ask a man to do it?'

'I'm not Mrs Swanwick.' She realised then that the controversy was, for her, very grave. 'To put it more strongly, if I can't get this matter raised, I might resign.'

'You're not serious?'

'I don't like it. I think Sir Eric is serving another master. Betraying the Covenant.'

'You mean he's serving God.'

'Serving the Vatican. And I don't believe that the Vatican is God's secretariat on earth. There's a battle going on. I see it now. They come to Bartou for advice to win him to their side. But I think Dame Rachel feels too demoralised to fight it through.'

As she let her temper run, she again found an unfamiliar inner discord. She saw that her primordial, or whatever, feelings were not impressed by her talk of scientific progress and betrayal of the Covenant. The primordial feelings were more in tune with the old woman who lived in the shoe. But she wasn't going to listen to primordial feelings.

She reached over and took his hands. At one side of her

feelings, too, was a fear of losing her respect for Sir Eric. 'I'm tired, Robert — the unruly things are eating me.' She also wished that it were Friday night and they could go to his apartment and go to bed and have done with this strange device sitting in her handbag.

He held her hands warmly and firmly.

She went on, 'Whatever else the League fails at, we should be a shining example of good social practices. A model of how to do things. How to discuss things. I'm afraid, Robert,' she said. 'I will have to take a stand and I don't want to.' She looked over at him with the look that he knew. 'This is a question of the integrity of the Covenant.'

He then suggested that maybe it was *her* soul that Dame Rachel and Sir Eric were fighting for. Maybe they were talking to her through their visits to Bartou.

She'd never thought of it that way. 'Why would they do that?'

'Because you're young. You're the future. They are coming to the end of their time. They want you to be there after they've gone, as their progeny.'

Robert could be correct, that she was being indirectly enlisted. She was Bartou's protégée. But perhaps he was immobilised by neutrality. She had spent much more time with Dame Rachel since the night of the riot and she was deeply unhappy that Dame Rachel was leaving. 'I either speak or I fail myself.'

'Resign? What would we do then?'

Until this day she'd never really considered resigning. 'Go back to Australia,' she said. 'Live in a shoe.'

'This is serious, then?'

'Very serious.'

'Just one thing.'

'Yes?'

'Australia is not my country. I'm not an Australian. And after we marry, nor will you be. You'll be British, legally speaking.'

'In the eyes of the League I will always be Australian.' As she said this, she thought of how she'd once hoped to become an Internationalist and to shed her nationality. She'd had some notion that one day the Council would call her up and declare her International and relieve her of being Australian. Now she was assuming the burden of two nationalities. 'And, anyhow, you were at Gallipoli — that makes you something of an Australian,' she said to him.

He grunted. 'I was at the Dardanelles.'

At present, she didn't have time to think about marriage or the changing of her nationality when, truthfully, she wanted to think about nothing else but the promises and fears of marriage and the changing of her status. She was being distracted by this office issue. She hadn't time to think about marriage in all its meanings, nor the wedding in all its details.

She glimpsed a smiling village woman within her who welcomed the idea of resignation. It was the primordial self which would welcome that. She would then be fully a wife, able to live with Robert in equanimity, collaboration, and quiet passion. To go on and make a family.

She first raised it with Dame Rachel. As they discussed it, she found herself doing much of the talking and then found that Dame Rachel was looking at her with solicitude.

'Resign?' said Dame Rachel. 'But we have so much work to do!'

'I can't go on with my work.'

'You're agitated.' Dame Rachel then placed a hand on Edith's forehead. 'Are you unwell?'

'I don't believe I am. Why do you ask?' What were the meanings of unwell? Pregnant?

'You are putting more passion into this than it's probably worth.'

'Oh?' Edith felt then that maybe no one else was giving it proper importance.

'This place is a railway station of issues and debates. They arrive. They depart. You know that.'

'Yes.' She was very unwilling to be relieved of the propulsion of the issue, increasingly conscious that the conflict could lead to her resignation and that resignation would lead to her release.

'Get away for a few days. Take some leave. You're getting married. Take some time off beforehand. And thank you for the invitation to the wedding. Figgis and I will be there with bells on.'

'I want to take up the matter at the highest level or resign.'

Dame Rachel became concerned and asked Figgis to get out the brandy bottle and to call Bartou. 'But you can't go,' Dame Rachel said, 'we defended the Palais together on that dreadful night.' Dame Rachel's concern brought Edith close to tears.

Figgis poured them both a drink.

'Figgis, tell her she can't go. We need her.'

'We need all the good soldiers we can get,' said Figgis obligingly but sincerely. 'Especially someone who can confront an angry crowd and not flinch.'

Figgis called Bartou through the switchboard and he arrived shortly after. Figgis poured Bartou and herself a drink.

Bartou turned to her and said, 'Is it this population conference?' She heard that his voice was softer than his normal office voice.

661

She nodded.

In a fatherly way, he said that a young diplomat must be on guard against the notion that her own post was the centre of affairs. 'This applies to all of us sitting in our offices preening our own sectional concerns.'

'That's true,' Dame Rachel said. 'The S-G and Council have the job of estimating the urgency of issues. The League has to choose its fights carefully.'

She found this hard to take. She sipped the brandy. She suspected that Dame Rachel and Bartou between them had decided to evade this particular issue.

Dame Rachel took up the argument. 'We have to trust them on questions of priority. Even if it's galling at times.' She said that the issues which were temporarily disregarded, maybe wrongly disregarded, would, if they were of enduring concern, arise again.

Meanwhile, Bartou said, they must concentrate effort. 'Let's go on with disarming the world. You must be here for that, Edith. The world has begun to disarm and now we have to keep on, "we band of brothers". We must not sink the boat to catch a fish.' He had never called her Edith before. Sir Eric had called Ambrose by his first name on the day he'd gone mad at the Directors' meeting. Maybe she was crazy too.

'Or even to catch a whale,' Dame Rachel added.

Figgis began firmly to massage her shoulders.

Bartou said that the work of the League, like diplomacy, was not a hurried endeavour, or a single episode, but ceaseless activity, a never-ending engagement. 'You have heard it said many times, Edith, that the League always adjourns, it never gives up. It never walks out of a meeting. It never loses patience. It never tires. Individuals do those things. The League persists.'

She again felt close to tears. Her efforts to gain release were being thwarted by them. She saw how much she wanted to get out, to find a way out. And they wouldn't let her.

Bartou finally said, 'Everything in life is *pis aller*, Edith — you know that — we take a course of action because there is no better one. Rarely are we able to follow the ideal course. We are forced always to follow some imperfect way. The style of our character is made by how we involve ourselves in the imperfection of the world and how we handle the imperfection of ourselves. How favourably we exploit and conduct the imperfections of our life.'

They had blocked her in with advice.

Bartou had a little more. 'And how we solace them — our imperfections.'

Drying her eyes, she said she thought she might take the afternoon off. They all agreed that would be a good idea. The Way of Imperfection. She was sick of wise advice.

She wandered, unseeingly, through the art museum. She sat and looked at the few other people in the museum. She often felt that those in an art museum were members of a club. She liked to think that they were all potential friends and shared a love of the same world. But it was a club in which the members did not speak.

She realised that what had been gnawing at her was an immense personal confusion of grand matters, of trivial matters, of the intimate and the public, of the primeval and the ethical — a noisy mêlée of all her sundry selves. Clouding her mind was Sir Eric's falling from respect in her eyes. Also, tonight was Friday and the start of another week-end with Robert. They would certainly have physical love, and for the first time with the new device. It was too much in her mind, the whole thing. And also with clarity, she acknowledged her wish to, one day soon, or even now, have a child with Robert. Instead, they were engaged so much in not having a child and, in all this, the talk of controlling birth in all the world.

She left the museum and walked to Robert's office. She went in past the sloping bench where the back issues of the newspapers were kept, hacked apart by scissors. Miriam said, 'Hello,' looking up from typing but continuing to bang away at the typewriter. Edith lifted the flap of the counter and went into where Robert worked.

Standing next to him, Edith told Robert that she was on her way to confront Sir Eric.

Robert, in shirtsleeves and bow tie, leaned back in his spring-backed chair, hands behind his head. 'What do you expect to happen?'

'I want to clear it from my mind. I don't care what happens,' she said. Then, half-smiling, 'I may send a telegram to a President: or I may shave a man.'

He smiled. He put an arm around her waist and held her. 'Do what you have to do. I am quite flexible myself.'

She leaned into him and then reached out to use Robert's telephone to call Sir Eric's office, sitting on his desk, a hand on his shoulder. As she waited for the exchange to answer, she looked at the stationery stand which she had once presented to him in the Bavaria.

She got through to Tiger and asked for an appointment. Tiger asked her to hold on, saying efficiently, 'Apologies, Berry — placing telephone on desk,' and Edith heard the telephone receiver clatter on the wooden desk while Tiger went to check. She imagined the little scene. Tiger came back on the telephone. 'Resuming the call: Sir Eric is free to see you this afternoon at 4.40. He has about fifteen minutes free. Will that do?'

Edith thanked her and said that she would be there. She replaced the telephone.

'Call me as soon as you're finished,' he said. She nodded and they exchanged an affectionate glance. As she left, Miriam said, 'Bye,' without looking up from her typing.

Back in Sir Eric's office again, she and Sir Eric exchanged a smile and a meeting of eyes which indicated that each was recalling the morning of the shaving. She saw her stationery stand still in use on one of his side tables.

'Nice to see you again. Thank you for the invitation to your wedding,' he said. 'Dole's a good man.'

'It was good of you and Lady Drummond to accept.'

'Will your parents be able to come from Australia?'

'My mother's dead but my father will come. He sails this week.'

'Good. I look forward to meeting him. Tell me, that Australian Rotarian chap who called on me — some time back?'

'George McDowell.'

'George McDowell. Full of verve. Do you hear from him?'

'He's married now. Battling through the Depression. He's in the aerated waters business.'

'You won't be leaving us right away? You'll stay on for a while?'

This was the time to tell him. 'Robert and I will not be having a family straight away.' She watched to see how Sir Eric would react.

'Good. We'll need you. But you know that you can stay on after you have a child?'

'Yes. Williams explained that to me.'

Within a minute of being in his office she had told him she

was practising birth control. Within minutes they were talking about her most private bodily processes.

It again linked everything together in a confusion. What if she had a row with Sir Eric and then had to face him at the wedding? Well, too bad.

She spoke out, but her voice was not as firm as she would have liked. 'I'm unhappy with what's been happening about the World Population Conference.'

Sir Eric was surprised. 'How so?'

She said that she considered it to be League business but she feared that he was blocking debate.

Sir Eric was cautious. 'What in particular do you see as League business?'

'Well, the world is rapidly filling up. Except for France. More importantly, we should be concerned with the quality of the people being born into the world.'

'You support that line of thinking?' He seemed surprised that she did. 'You support the thinking of the eugenicists and all that?'

'People say, that is, people who should know, say that the national stock is deteriorating. That more people with mental and physical defects are being born.'

'Berry, you are a first-rate officer. I admire you and so do others. I don't see how this concerns your work now with Bartou. I was simply seeking Bartou's personal advice.'

She nearly said that all the problems of the world were related. But it echoed Ambrose's pathetic presentation on famine. That way lies madness. There be monsters.

'Bartou suggested that I be sent along and you vetoed that.'

'Only to keep this out of the League.'

'Because of the Catholic members?'

'I think that we should let this matter mature outside the

League first. I don't believe that the debate is at a point where it could be successfully considered by the League.' He didn't respond to her mention of his religion.

She could no longer find her indignation. She realised that in confronting Sir Eric, she was carrying through some sort of personal formality. She could no longer see what she wanted as an outcome. She was no longer sure that she wanted to be put in a position of resigning. She thought that she might simply want to be able to say to herself that she had registered her position. She went on with her case but her voice became that of a junior officer seeking guidance, not that of a birth control reformer. 'Don't you think, Sir Eric, that controlling the quality of the human stock is important? If you had a magic wand, wouldn't you remove the suffering of deformity and insanity from the world?'

He thought for a second or so. 'I believe that we can feed all the children of the world if we become less wasteful. Surplus population could be allotted to the new countries and to Japan. I would rather we rely on compassion for those who enter life regardless of their "quality".' He then added, uncomfortably, 'In extreme cases, I would rather rely on the humanity and compassion of doctors and nurses exercised with wisdom. Not on broad laws.'

She said, 'I really wanted to say that we should be listening to what scientific people are saying on this.'

'I was about to give you advice,' he said, a wry smile coming to his face, 'but I then recalled an embarrassing piece of advice I once gave you which proved not to be wisdom at all. I think about that day very often.'

She smiled. 'I too. But I would still like to hear your maxim.'

'I was going to say to you that even the supreme values of mankind are not necessarily always compatible. Rain may be good for the farmer and bad for the cricketer. Serious discussion may be good in one arena and dangerous in another. Listening to scientists on eugenics or racial purity may be intriguing for individuals such as yourself and Dame Rachel but bad for the League at this point in history. The Secretariat should not introduce onto an agenda those things which will disrupt our other work. But what do you advise?' he asked.

'That officers go in a private capacity.'

'You know that while the League invites "observers" to our activities, it is impossible for the League to ever be simply an "observer". Our presence is always a form of recognition.'

She nodded. 'We could send technical people. Or junior officers. That would temper the League's presence?'

'Do you wish to go?'

Suddenly she did not. 'No.'

He seemed pleased. 'May I ask if you have a position on the matters at the conference?'

'I suppose I'm swayed by scientific thinking on racial hygiene but I still have trouble seeing how governments could do it.'

'Forced sterilisation has begun in South Dakota in the United States. Sterilisation clinics for people who are considered not capable of parenthood,' he said with obvious disapproval. 'I don't like the idea.'

Edith said, 'Perhaps colonies could be set up for the unfit. With segregation of men and women. Only to prevent genetic contamination and racial pollution. Or maybe financial incentives should be offered.'

'Or penalties? Regardless of my Catholicism, I believe that some questions should be for ever put out of the reach of scientific experiment and government officials. And of the League.'

They sat in silence for a moment or so. Her mind was blank.

The issue had for her closed. Tiger knocked and put her head around the door. 'Sorry, Sir Eric, sorry, Berry, but Monsieur Avenol is here.'

She stood up. Sir Eric stood up. 'Thank you for giving me your views, Berry. You're always welcome in this office.'

She looked about the office. She had first entered this office as a thief in the night, illicitly signing letters in the name of the Secretary-General. She had then been here on that remarkable morning when she had become a daughter. Or was it that she had become almost a wife? She was here now as an officer making her point with a confused heart.

They shook hands and he held her hand that second longer which said that he and she had a compact and were above being separated by disagreement on policy. And that her personal practices would not change anything between them.

As she went up to her office to call Robert, she realised that there had been an even deeper purpose behind her confrontation with Sir Eric. It had been to reconnect with him, to discover if her special tie with Sir Eric still existed and to silently reconcile her own controlling of birth with what she knew to be Sir Eric's view. She had gone to his office to seek his blessing. How petty and personal her behaviour seemed. And would she have behaved differently if that blessing had not been offered and if the compact had not been reaffirmed?

She reminded herself that she had not betrayed Dame Rachel or Rationalism.

She stood on the landing and rested her forehead on the glass of the window looking out on Geneva. She loved both Sir Eric and Dame Rachel. And Bartou. It was essentially subaltern love, the gratification of giving loyalty. Yet over the years it had become more that distinctive love which grew among 'a band of brothers'. Perhaps it was both of these forms of love. She saw that she was reluctant to let go of her subaltern status. But soon age would not allow her to serve and shelter there.

She went to her office and called Robert on the telephone. 'I'm not resigning.'

'Good. I think that's the right thing to do. Did you have a row?'

'No.'

In bed that night she felt close to screaming. It was all so contrived and extraneous. 'I will get up and try again,' she said.

'It's all right. It isn't worrying me.'

It plainly was worrying him. She stopped herself talking about it but thought, I must get it right. From the very start.

She eased him away and he withdrew from her gently and rolled on to his back, sweating, a hand on her stomach, still aroused. He leaned over and kissed her, perhaps to keep the mood of concupiscence alive. She pulled down her satin night-dress and left the bed and went to the bathroom. The nightdress had been meant for their wedding night but she had decided that this night would need something of powerful feminity and voluptuousness to see them through. She had been right. For a moment she thought about removing the cap and leaving it, forgetting about the whole business, but knew that would be spineless. She crouched and went through the procedure again. She applied a little of the oil which had been supplied, washed her hands, and returned to the bed, still on the edge of tears.

They coupled again, she wanting to have done with it, and to put behind them the first time with the device. She didn't expect to be able to surrender to it but he whispered that he felt nothing, and then went on to whisper strange lascivious things, caressing her with provocative words about the hot suck of

670

her opening and its tightening, and soon, contrary to all her expectations, she was deep in waves of sensation which rolled through her and without straining, she used the lessons given to her by Dr Monet. Soon nothing much was in her mind and she relaxed away, knowing that it would be all right, and their physical love was complete.

They sat there at breakfast, Robert reading the day-old London *Times*, she reading the *Journal de Genève*. He was dressed in his dressing gown and regimental pyjamas. The pyjamas were the only thing he and Ambrose had in common, although of different regiments — that is, on the occasions when Ambrose had worn pyjamas.

'About last night,' he said.

'Yes?'

'One thing,' he said.

'Yes?'

'I liked what you did, while we were together in bed. Was I enjoying the proceeds of your worldly experience?'

She smiled and said, 'No. Womanly arcana.' She pulled a tantalising screen across it all. She was, perhaps, learning when not to speak.

A feeling warmed and encompassed her like a cloak, the feeling that her personal life and bodily person, were in order and were safe. There over coffee, in the chilly sunlight, with the newly baked rolls, the blackberry jam and the good white salty butter from the market, she could see now that things were in order.

She told him that Caroline Bailey had written from London congratulating them and saying she and Liverright would be coming to the wedding although she 'didn't believe in marriage'.

John had sent congratulations on the letterhead of Leader of the Opposition. Her father had written, saying that if the good Rationalist Bernard Shaw could be a pallbearer at Thomas Hardy's funeral in Westminster Abbey, he could attend to give his daughter away in the English church of Geneva. Her father was thrilled and envious that she'd met Bernard Shaw at the last Assembly. The invitation to her brother, not unexpectedly, was returned 'not known at this address'.

She said that Ambrose had not replied to their invitation.

He made a consoling face. She experienced the bewildered sadness which came to her now and then about Ambrose. Some nights she awoke and lay in bed in alarm, fearing that her conduct about the spying and about Ambrose's illness had been misjudged. What if his spying had been harmless and of no consequence? Done for foolish but well-meaning motives? What if she had been ignoring his love for her over the years for her own purposes? What if she had broken his heart? Before she could return to sleep she would have to go over every detail of it again to assure herself that she had behaved honourably and compassionately, to convince herself yet again that it was not in her power to heal him.

On the Monday morning they always had a hurried breakfast.

'I must catch the tram and go to work,' she said, looking at her watch.

'And you're not resigning,' he confirmed.

'I am not resigning. I promised Bartou I would stay until the disarmament conference.'

'If you stay until the world is disarmed, we will be here in Geneva for quite a while,' he said without looking up from his newspaper.

'We shall see. I intend to disarm the world only "to the lowest point consistent with national safety and the enforcement by common action of international obligations".'

He laughed. 'Good.'

She stood behind his chair, her arms around him. He kissed her hands. She said, 'Can you think of a better way for us to spend this time of our life?'

She knew that part of her still wanted him to say, yes, that he could think of another way for them to spend their time and their life. He looked up and back at her from his newspaper, and seemed to be seriously considering this question and to be preparing an unexpected answer. After a few seconds, he said, 'We could just go off. We could let the world look after itself.' But his voice said that he was not seriously offering this, yet he was *saying* it.

Her heart beat hard. She nearly said, yes, let's go. Let's go now. 'Off to where?' she said, using the same unserious tone that he had used, yet also *saying* it.

'We could go to Australia. Buy a sheep station. You talked once about going back and helping to "make the ethos". We could have a large family. And lots of sheep. Write books.'

She forced down the impulse to say yes. She said instead, 'That'll have to wait. The sheep will have to wait.'

She kissed his hair and let go of him. She gathered up her files and papers. 'And I am not from sheep country. I come from milk, butter and cheese country.'

Maybe if he now said, let us have a dairy with many cows and goats and make cheese, she would say yes.

He didn't say anything.

She let the fantasy of a farm and children tarry in her mind before sending it away. As she was leaving, he called to her at the door.

'Edith?'

'Yes?'

'Were you a cowgirl?'

She laughed. 'Yes, I was a cowgirl once.'

'See you at the Bavaria this evening?'

'Indubitably,' she said.

As she walked to the tram stop, she heard the fluttering of the unruly and unseen things going on in mysterious dangerous ways about her. Robert knew how to calm the beating of her heart and the discord and clatter of her mind. One of the ethics of her upbringing had been the stewardship and care of her domain but she had tried to make the whole world into her domain. In this domain she was doomed to choose one direction and to turn away from other directions with full awareness that every choice could entail an irreparable loss. She felt the terror of having again turned away from the more primordial womanly course. But it was just for now. Just for now.

The tramcar, 'Terminus Palais des Nations', came along, stopped, and Edith, with her files and papers, got on board.

THE YEARS WHICH FOLLOWED

The 1932–4 World Disarmament Conferences which the League had been planning for six years were a total failure.

Dame Rachel resigned in 1930, after not having been granted full status as Director of her section. Sir Eric retired in 1933.

In 1936, the new Palais des Nations was finished and the League moved in.

Three years later, at the outbreak of the Second World War, some of the League Secretariat went to safe havens in other parts of the world but most of the staff were placed on indefinite suspension.

The Deputy Secretary-General, Sean Lester, an Irishman, and about forty staff wrested control of the League from the defeatist French Secretary-General Avenol, and stayed on in the newly built Palais des Nations, waiting and ready to negotiate the end of the war.

They were never asked.

The League of Nations ceased to exist on 18 April 1946, when the Assembly meeting in Geneva formally dissolved the League of Nations and the Permanent Court of International Justice. Its property was handed over to the United Nations which had been established in San Francisco the year before.

POSTSCRIPT

Recently I talked to Vernon Bartlett, a British MP, and veteran of the League. He told me he had visited Geneva and lunched in the Brasserie Bavaria, whose walls are decorated with some hundred and fifty of our caricatures. Directly above his head was a drawing of Briand.

Some young American tourists were there, a boy and a girl of that generation for which we can afford every gift except the gift of the tranquillity Briand wished them to have. The boy came to study the drawing.

'Bryand,' he called to his companion, 'Bryand? Who is Bryand?'

And Bartlett said, 'I could have cried.'

FROM THE MEMOIRS OF EMERY KELEN,
Peace in Their Time (1964)

Emery Kelen is dead. Kelen, with his collaborator, Derso, was an internationally renowned caricaturist in the days of the League of Nations.

Aristide Briand as Foreign Minister of France received the Nobel Prize for Peace in 1926, together with the then German Minister for Foreign Affairs, Gustav Stresemann. Briand died in 1932 and Stresemann in 1930.

Vernon Bartlett is dead. He worked with the League of Nations before becoming a British MP.

The Brasserie Bavaria no longer exists. There is a restaurant on its site called Le Relais de l'Entrecôte.

The caricatures are gone.

HISTORICAL NOTES

Rationalism

The Rationalists were established in 1889 in the United Kingdom and spread to the United States and throughout the English-speaking world. They stated their position as the adoption of 'those mental attitudes which unreservedly accept the supremacy of reason and aim at establishing a system of philosophy and ethics verifiable by experience and independent of all arbitrary assumptions or authority'. It had no doctrinal tests for membership and included as members Julian Huxley, Somerset Maugham, George Bernard Shaw, Bertrand Russell, Arnold Bennett, Georges Clemenceau, Clarence Darrow, Sigmund Freud, J. B. S. Haldane, H. G. Wells, Aldous Huxley, Albert Einstein, Professor L. Susan Stebbing, Havelock Ellis, and Professor V. Gordon Childe. They saw religion as their main opponent. The movement declined after the Second World War.

Eugenics

The study and advocacy of eugenics, or population engineering, was internationally active from the late nineteenth century, originating in the genetic research and ideas of Sir Francis Galton and, to some degree, from the thinking of Florence Nightingale.

It combined an interest in genetics and demographics to formulate social policy aimed at eliminating hereditary suffering. Firstly, it set out to measure and describe the population, looking especially at crime, poverty and hereditary disease. It was interested in whether criminal behaviour and poverty were 'genetic'.

The Eugenics Society of Britain in the 1920s described itself this way: 'Eugenics is the study of those agencies which are under social control that may improve or impair the racial qualities of future generations either physically or mentally.' Many prominent members of the scientific community and progressive intellectuals of the times belonged to the international movement until the 'thirties, when it fell into disarray and became intellectually disreputable mostly because of the German Nazi party's misuse of the science of genetics to justify its policies.

Union for Democratic Control

A British society which campaigned to have foreign policy treated as a matter of public debate. It was opposed to all 'secret diplomacy'.

The World Population Conference

As a point of historical accuracy, this conference took place in Geneva slightly earlier than when it occurs in the book.

Under Secretaries-General

In practice, the Secretary-General, Deputy Secretary-General and the Under Secretary-Generals of the League together reflected the nationalities of the permanent members of the Council. Consequently there was never a Swiss Under Secretary-General.

HOW A REGISTRY WORKS — AN OVERVIEW*

One of the tests of an organisation such as the League was whether its officials could quickly put their hands on all relevant papers.

The system to ensure this was called the Registry. The League used an adaptation of the classification system of the British Foreign Office.

All official papers (letters, notes, drafts, etc.), confidential or non-confidential, were filed and kept in the Registry. That is, everything on paper produced or received by the League.

The material was arranged in files, cardboard folders containing all the papers relevant to a particular question.

All documents were held in the folder by a metal-tipped cord drawn through holes punched in the left upper corner of the file and documents.

The last letter received was the top letter of the file.

No correspondence could be removed from the file unless the Registry was notified by the section concerned.

No document was circulated without being fixed into a file.

The files were kept in steel cabinets in the Registry, classified by the names of the sections of the League.

There were eight messengers in the Registry who took the files to the offices of those officials who needed them and then replaced them when the officials had finished with the files.

* This description is based on the work of Catherine Pastuhova, in the book *The International Secretariat* by Egon F. Ranshofen-Wertheimer, and draws from the book *Yes, and Albert Thomas* by E. J. Phelan, from *The Guide to the Archives of the League of Nations (1919–1946)* and on my personal experience with the archives of the League.

There existed only a few secret files, one of which contained the minutes of the secret meetings of the Council of the League. These files were kept by the Registrar himself, in his office, under lock and key, and the schedules and the numbering of the documents were made in his office.

These secret files could be consulted only by the Secretary-General or the Under Secretaries-General, and were brought to them in sealed envelopes by a responsible official of the Registry, not by messenger.

Only Directors or heads of services could, in exceptional cases, take a file home, and the Registry had to be notified.

The Registry consisted of three branches: classification, registration, and index.

The correspondence coming to the League was received by the League of Nations post office, which delivered it to the Registry.

Some sections, such as the Library, received their mail direct, but in principle the Registry received all mail and only letters marked 'personal' or 'private' were delivered directly to the addressee.

Each League section had a classification number under which was filed all the correspondence concerning that section.

The sections were (with some changes of name and structure over the years): Political, Administrative Commissions (e.g., the Saar, Danzig), Legal, Minorities, Intellectual Cooperation, Mandates, Disarmament, Health, Communications and Transit, Economic and Financial, Social Questions, Opium, Information, Council, Assembly, Library, Treasury, Internal Administration, Publications and Refugees.

Each file had three numbers: the first indicated the section to which it belonged; the second indicated the incoming number of the first letter or document in the file; the third indicated the number of the file series.

Mail arrived at the Registry from the post office in the morning and was sorted at once by the classification branch. All new correspondence received on a given day was numbered in its sequence (the middle number).

The classification branch placed the letters in their cardboard folders and sent them to the registration branch.

The registration branch entered the number of the folder in the appropriate section register, wrote the title and the subtitle on the folder, and numbered and classified the correspondence in each folder.

The index branch entered on the index cards all new correspondence included that day in the file.

If the contents of the file were confidential, notation of the fact was made in two places only: the front page of the file was stamped with Confidential, in large red letters, and the classification card was stamped Confidential.

The file so stamped was always sent in a sealed envelope.

If a section asked for the confidential files of another section, the Registry asked the permission of that section.

Once the new communication was classified and registered in the Registry and put in a file, it was taken then by messenger to the 'action section', that is, the section which needed to respond to the incoming letter.

It took about fifteen minutes to start a new file and five to ten minutes to take the file to its action section.

When the messenger arrived at the section with the file it was handed to the secretary of the section who was responsible for the record of files received by the section and for the circulation of them within the section.

Each official of the Secretariat had In and Out trays in which the secretary of the section would place files and from which the messengers collected files.

The sections could not forward files from one section to another without notifying the Registry which marked on the outgoing card 'Passed to . . .' But the normal procedure was to send the file back to the Registry first.

If a file was needed urgently for a meeting, it was directly dispatched by messenger.

Letters written by the sections were called the out-letter files and sections were responsible for placing in the files two copies on heavy paper of each outgoing letter. One was placed in the file on top of the letter it answered, and other was inserted, in chronological order, in a special out-letter file.

Drafts of large reports and minutes were called Bulky Enclosures and were kept in special envelope files called Bulky Enclosures. They were not usually circulated because of their volume. A note was placed in the file mentioning the existence of the relevant Bulky Enclosure.

A fireproof room with a special lock was built in the basement to hold the Bulky Enclosures and the confidential files.

Within a section, at the end of each day, the secretary had to place under lock and key all confidential files currently in that section.

When the Registry received a communication which needed to be added to a file which was not at that moment in the Registry — that is, a file that was circulating — a messenger would be sent to fetch the file. If the messenger found the file on the desk of an official when the official was out of the room, the messenger left a slip stating that the file had been taken back to Registry and would be sent back as soon as possible.

Files could be requested by telephone by the secretary of the section or by officials.

After 7.30 p.m. there was a Registry official on night duty.

Some of the correspondence was summarised daily by an official of the Registry. This was called the Daily Synopsis. It could consist of letters from well-known individuals, important proposals, discoveries, appointments, appeals, decisions of important character, frontier incidents, circumstances which might disturb the international peace, and so on.

It was sent to the Information section before 9.30 a.m. This was considered to be a confidential document and was intended for circulation only within the Secretariat.

While the correspondence and files of the sections of the Secretariat were, in theory, handled, established, and kept by the Registry, for practical reasons, some sections established duplicate files independently of the Registry. They did this either because they were authorised to function autonomously, or because they kept parallel files close at hand for their own use.

THE IMPORTANCE OF THE DUPLICATING MACHINE

By the end of the 'twenties, the League staff had duplicated more than ten million sheets of paper — about a million pages a year.

It is doubtful whether the League of Nations could have functioned without the invention of the duplicating machine which came to be commonly known by the company name of Roneo or Gestetner.

It was introduced into office work in 1899. It was a rotary duplicating machine using a wax stencil cut on a typewriter without the ribbon, or by hand, using a pointed steel stylus.

The stencil was stretched over a perforated drum and ink was supplied by a roller inside the drum as it was rotated.

As a sheet of paper was fed through in contact with the drum, an impression of the work cut onto the stencil was transferred to the paper.

The turn of the handle produced one copy.

This process was necessary to allow the circulation of multiple copies in an organisation. To print the copies using a printing press would have been too expensive and would have taken too long.

Before the duplicating machine, the original document from which copies were to be made was produced by ink to which had been added sugar or gum. A wet tissue was pressed onto the original.

From this developed the letterpress, where a strong aniline ink was used and the impression transferred by hand pressure to a tray of gelatine. Again, impressions could be made of the original by pressing damp paper onto the gelatine.

Carbon paper was then developed, which allowed up to six copies.

But the duplicating machine was perfect for an organisation the size of the League because a wax stencil could give up to 1,000 copies in a couple of hours.

Later heavy-duty stencils were developed which could give up to 5,000 copies without wearing out.

THE COVENANT OF THE LEAGUE OF NATIONS —
WITH COMMENTARY

President Woodrow Wilson described the Covenant as ' . . . a practical and humane document. There is a pulse of sympathy in it, and yet it is intended to purify, to rectify, to elevate.' He saw the first biblical covenant as being between Man and God. The world now needed a covenant between Man and Man.

On the ship from Australia to London on her way to take up her appointment, Edith read *A Handbook to the League of Nations* written in 1919 by Sir Geoffrey Butler KBE, MA, Fellow, Librarian and Lecturer in International Law and Diplomacy of Corpus Christi College, Cambridge. This book contains a copy of the Covenant.

Australia made a small contribution to the format of the Covenant. At the meeting of the 7th Assembly in September 1926, the Delegate from Australia, Mr John Latham, moved: 'The Assembly instructs the Secretary-General to cause the paragraphs of the articles of the Covenant to be numbered in all future editions published by the Secretariat.'

He said that he thought his proposal did not require an elaborate defence. Few documents were so often discussed and dealt with in many publications as the Covenant of the League of Nations; unfortunately it was somewhat difficult to refer to the Covenant owing to the length of certain of its articles. He argued that it was not an amendment to the Covenant, as such.

The motion was adopted without opposition.

The following is the original League of Nations Covenant as adopted in 1919 together with Sir Geoffrey Butler's commentary. The

Covenant was amended, from time to time, during the life of the League.

(Million upon million of lives had been lost in the five years of the War. Million upon million had been wounded. Horrors innumerable, experienced and apprehended ... A new spirit of freedom and of independence was the heritage left to mankind by those who had fallen in the War: the common sense of their legatees seemed to resolve that the best war memorial that could be erected to them was an instrument for the perpetuation of this spirit. Mankind was prepared to give the League of Nations its chance.

The document that has emerged is not the constitution of a super-State, but, as the title explains, a solemn agreement between sovereign states, which consent to limit their complete freedom of action on certain points for the great good of themselves and the world at large. It is no more derogatory to their sovereign independence so to do than for a Rugby football club to bind its action, permanently in effect, by the regulations of the Rugby Union. Such sacrifice on its part is a necessary condition of each club performing its own functions without producing chaos in the world of Rugby football, as those who remember the game half a century ago will bear full witness.)

THE COVENANT

The High Contracting Parties, in order to promote international co-operation and to achieve international peace and security by the acceptance of the obligation not to resort to war, by the prescription of open, just, and honourable relations between nations, by the firm establishment of the understandings of international law as the actual rule of conduct among Governments, and by the maintenance of justice and a scrupulous respect for all treaty obligations in the dealings of organised peoples with one another, agree to this Covenant of the League of Nations.

ARTICLE I

The original Members of the League shall be those of the Signatories which are named in the Annex to this Covenant and also such of those other States named in the Annex as shall accede without reservation to this Covenant. Such accession shall be effected by a Declaration deposited with the Secretariat within two months of the coming into force of the Covenant. Notice thereof shall be sent to all other Members of the League.

Any fully self-governing State, Dominion, or Colony not named in the Annex, may become a Member of the League if its admission is agreed to by two-thirds of the Assembly, provided that it shall give effective guarantees of its sincere intention to observe its international obligations, and shall accept such regulations as may be prescribed by the League in regard to its military, naval and air forces and armaments.

> *(It is arguable that this article is the Covenant's most significant single measure. By it the British Dominions, namely, New Zealand, Australia, South Africa, and Canada, have their independent nationhood established for the first time. There may be friction over small matters in giving effect to this internationally acknowledged fact, but the Dominions will always look to the League of Nations Covenant, as their Declaration of Independence. That the change has come silently about, and has been welcomed in all quarters through the British Empire, is a final vindication of men like the United Empire Loyalists.)*

Any Member of the League may, after two years' notice of its intention so to do, withdraw from the League, provided that all its international obligations and all its obligations under this Covenant shall have been fulfilled at the time of its withdrawal.

ARTICLE II

The action of the League under this Covenant shall be effected through the instrumentality of an Assembly and of a Council, with a permanent Secretariat.

(The Secretariat has immense possibilities of usefulness and a very wide field will be open for the energy and initiative of the first Secretary-General. A reliable supply of facts and statistics will in itself be a powerful aid to peace.)

ARTICLE III

The Assembly shall consist of Representatives of the Members of the League.

The Assembly shall meet at stated intervals and from time to time as occasion may require, at the Seat of the League or at such other places as may be decided upon.

The Assembly may deal at its meetings with any matter within the sphere of action of the League or affecting the peace of the world.

At meetings of the Assembly each Member of the League shall have one vote, and may not have more than three representatives.

ARTICLE IV

(A smaller body is required to deal with emergencies; such a body is found in the Council, the central organ of the League, and a political instrument endowed with greater authority than any the world has hitherto seen. Its unanimous recommendations are likely to be irresistible.)

The Council shall consist of Representatives of the Principal Allied and Associated Powers, together with Representatives of four other Members of the League. These four Members of the League shall be selected by the Assembly from time to time in its discretion. Until the appointment of the Representatives of the four Members of the League first selected by the Assembly, Representatives of Belgium, Brazil, Greece, and Spain shall be members of the Council.

With the approval of the majority of the Assembly, the Council may name additional Members of the League whose Representatives shall always be members of the Council; the Council with like approval may increase the number of Members of the League to be selected by the Assembly for representation on the Council.

(It is through the machinery provided in this clause that the members of the late hostile alliance may hope to regain their position among the family of nations. It allows for admission of both Germany and Russia to the Council when they have established themselves as Great Powers that can be trusted to honour their obligations.)

The Council shall meet from time to time as occasion may require, and at least once a year, at the Seat of the League, or at such other places as may be decided upon.

The Council may deal at its meetings with any matter within the sphere of action of the League or affecting the peace of the world.

Any Member of the League not represented on the Council shall be invited to send a Representative to sit as a member at any meeting of the Council during the consideration of matters specially affecting the interests of that Member of the League.

At meetings of the Council each Member of the League represented on the Council shall have one vote, and may have not more than one Representative.

ARTICLE V

Except where otherwise expressly provided in this Covenant or by the terms of the present Treaty, decisions at any meeting of the Assembly or of the Council shall require the agreement of all the Members of the League represented at the meeting.

All matters of procedure at meetings of the Assembly or of the Council, including the appointment of committees to investigate particular matters, shall be regulated by the Assembly or by the Council, and may be decided by a majority of the Members of the League represented at the meeting.

The first meeting of the Assembly and the first meeting of the Council shall be summoned by the President of the United States of America.

ARTICLE VI

The permanent Secretariat shall be established at the Seat of the League. The Secretariat shall comprise a Secretary-General and such secretaries and staff as may be required.

The first Secretary-General shall be the person named in the Annex; thereafter the Secretary-General shall be appointed by the Council with the approval of the majority of the Assembly.

The secretaries and staff of the Secretariat shall be appointed by the Secretary-General with the approval of the Council.

The Secretary-General shall act in that capacity at all meetings of the Assembly and of the Council.

The expenses of the Secretariat shall be borne by the Members of the League in accordance with the apportionment of the expenses of the International Bureau of the Universal Post Union.

ARTICLE VII

The Seat of the League is established at Geneva.

The Council may at any time decide that the Seat of the League shall be established elsewhere.

All positions under or in connection with the League, including the Secretariat, shall be open equally to men and women.

Representatives of the Members of the League and officials of the League when engaged on the business of the League shall enjoy diplomatic privileges and immunities.

(While resident in Foreign Courts, diplomats are exempt in a very great degree from the operation of the local law. Their persona are inviolable, unless they are actually plotting against the security of the state to which they are accredited, in which case they may be arrested and sent out of the country. They are free from legal processes directed against the person, unless they voluntarily consent to waive their privilege and appear in court. Their wives, families, and servants share the same immunities to a very considerable, but ill-defined, extent. Their property, too,

has many immunities, especially the official residence and except in extreme cases it may not be entered by the local authorities.)

The buildings and other property occupied by the League or its officials or by Representatives attending its meetings shall be inviolable.

ARTICLE VIII

The Members of the League recognise that the maintenance of the peace requires the reduction of national armaments to the lowest point consistent with national safety and the enforcement by common action of international obligations.

The Council, taking account of the geographical situation and circumstances of each State, shall formulate plans for such reduction for the consideration and action of the several Governments.

Such plans shall be subject to reconsideration and revision at least every ten years.

After these plans shall have been adopted by the several Governments, the limits of armaments therein fixed shall not be exceeded without the concurrence of the Council.

The Members of the League agree that the manufacture by private enterprise of munitions and implements of war is open to grave objections. The Council shall advise how the evil effects attendant upon such manufacture can be prevented, due regard being had to the necessities of those Members of the League which are not able to manufacture the munitions and implements of war necessary for their safety.

The Members of the League undertake to interchange full and frank information as to the scale of their armaments, their military, naval, and air programmes, and the condition of such of their industries as are adaptable to warlike purposes.

(This article makes it plain that here is to be no dictation by the Council or anyone else as to the size of national forces. There was a suggestion that a Commission be given a general power of inspection and supervision of armaments. It was rejected because such a power would not be tolerated by many national states and would cause friction and hostility to the idea of the League.

Preparation for war on a large scale cannot be concealed, while no inspection could hope to discover such really important secrets as new gases and explosives and other inventions of war.)

ARTICLE IX

A Permanent Commission shall be constituted to advise the Council on the execution of the provision of Articles I and VIII, and on military, naval and air questions generally.

ARTICLE X

The Members of the League undertake to respect and preserve against external aggression the territorial integrity and existing political independence of all Members of the League. In case of any such aggression or in case of any threat or danger of such aggression the Council shall advise upon the means by which this obligation shall be fulfilled.

(Here there would seem to be difficulty. Modern democracies are not easily worked up to the point of hostilities, particularly when the issue at stake is remote and to the public unfamiliar. Again, the incidence of the burden of declaring and conducting war is not uniform. The only way out seems to be in postulating of the 'new order' a desire to avoid and not provoke disputes, and in a thorough ventilation by all means known to experts of publicity of the points at issue.)

ARTICLE XI

Any war or threat of war, whether immediately affecting any of the Members of the League or not, is hereby declared a matter of concern to the whole League, and the League shall take any action that may be deemed wise and effectual to safeguard the peace of nations. In case any such emergency should arise, the Secretary-General shall on the request of any Member of the League forthwith summon a meeting of the Council.

It is also declared to be the friendly right of each Member of the League to bring to the attention of the Assembly or of the Council any circumstance whatever affecting international relations which threatens to disturb international peace or the good understanding between nations upon which peace depends.

(This international encouragement of the 'candid friend' is not without its importance. A similar provision in the 1st Hague Peace Conference (1899) enabled President Roosevelt to hasten peace between Russia and Japan.)

ARTICLE XII

The Members of the League agree that if there should arise between them any dispute likely to lead to a rupture, they will submit the matter either to arbitration or to inquiry by the Council, and they agree in no case to resort to war until three months after the award by the arbitrators or the report by the Council.

(Indulgence in hostilities without waiting for arbitration or inquiry is the only international crime bringing immediate outlawry by the mechanical severance of relations between the guilty party and all the remaining Powers. It is, accordingly, the kernel of this whole agreement.)

In any case under this Article the award of the arbitrators shall be made within a reasonable time, and the report of the Council shall be made within six months of the submission of the dispute.

ARTICLE XIII

The Members of the League agree that whenever any dispute shall arise between them which they recognize to be suitable for submission to arbitration and which cannot be satisfactorily settled by diplomacy, they will submit the whole subject-matter to arbitration.

Disputes as to the interpretation of a treaty, as to a question of international law, as to the existence of any fact which if established would constitute a breach of any international obligations, or as to the extent and nature of the reparations to be made for any such breach, are declared to be among those which are generally suitable for submission to arbitration.

For the consideration of any such dispute the court of arbitration to which the case is referred shall be the court agreed on by the parties to the dispute or stipulated in any convention existing between them.

The Members of the League agree that they will carry out in full good faith any award that may be rendered and that they will not resort to war against a Member of the League which complies therewith. In the event of any failure to carry out such an award, the Council shall propose what steps should be taken to give effect thereto.

ARTICLE XIV

The Council shall formulate and submit to the Members of the League for adoption plans for the establishment of a Permanent Court of International Justice. The Court shall be competent to hear and determine any dispute of an international character which the parties thereto submit to it. The Court may also give an advisory opinion upon any dispute or question referred to it by the Council or by the Assembly.

> *(Ultimately, and in the long run, the only alternative to war is law, and for the enthronement of law there is required such a continuous development of international jurisprudence, at present in its infancy, as can only be supplied by the progressive judgements of a Permanent Court working out its own traditions.)*

ARTICLE XV

If there should arise between Members of the League any dispute likely to lead to a rupture, which is not submitted to arbitration as above, the Members of the League agree that they will submit the matter to the Council. Any party to the dispute may effect such submission by giving notice of the existence of the dispute to the Secretary-General who will make all necessary arrangements for a full investigation and consideration thereof.

For this purpose the parties to the dispute will communicate to the Secretary-General, as promptly as possible, statements of their case with all the relevant facts and papers, and the Council may forthwith direct the publication thereof.

The Council shall endeavour to effect a settlement of the dispute, and if such efforts are successful, a statement shall be made public giving such facts and explanations regarding the dispute and the terms of settlement thereof as the Council may deem appropriate.

If the dispute is not then settled, the Council, either unanimously or by a majority vote, shall make and publish a report containing a statement of the facts of the dispute and the recommendations which are deemed just and proper in regard thereto.

Any Members of the League represented on the Council may make public a statement of the facts to the dispute and of its conclusions regarding the same.

If a report by the Council is unanimously agreed to by the members thereof other than the Representatives of one or more of the parties to the dispute, the Members of the League agree that they will not go to war with any party to the dispute which complies with the recommendations of the report.

If the Council fails to reach a report which is unanimously agreed to by the members thereof, other than the Representatives of one or more of the parties to the dispute, the Members of the League reserve to themselves the right to take such action as they shall consider necessary for the maintenance of right and justice.

If the dispute between the parties is claimed by one of them, and is found by the Council to arise out of a matter which by international law is solely within the domestic jurisdiction of that party, the Council shall so report, and shall make no recommendation as to its settlement.

The Council may in any case under this Article refer the dispute to the Assembly. The dispute shall be so referred at the request of either party to the dispute, provided that such a request be made within fourteen days after the submission of the dispute to the Council.

In any case referred to the Assembly, all the provisions of this Article and of Article XII relating to the action and powers of the Council shall apply to the actions and powers of the Assembly, provided that a report made by the Assembly, if concurred in by the Representatives of those Members of the League represented on the Council and of a majority of the other Members of the League, exclusive in each case of the Representatives of the parties to the dispute, shall have the same force as a report by the Council concurred in by all the members thereof other than the Representatives of one or more of the parties to the dispute.

ARTICLE XVI

(It is true that, in default of a strong international striking force, ready for instant action in all parts of the World, the Members of the League must make their own arrangements for immediate self-defence against any force that could suddenly be concentrated against them.

But where the aggression is not sudden, it is certain that those Powers which suspect a breach of the Covenant will have consulted together unofficially to decide on precautionary measures. These meetings will develop into the Supreme War Council of the League, advised by a military joint staff.)

Should any Member of the League resort to war in disregard of its covenants under Articles XII, XIII, XV, it shall ipso facto be deemed to have committed an act of war against all other Members of the League, which hereby undertake immediately to subject it to the severance of all trade or financial relations, the prohibition of all intercourse between their nations and the nationals of the covenant-breaking States, and the prevention of all financial, commercial, or personal intercourse between the nationals of the Covenant-breaking State and the nationals of any other state, whether a Member of the League or not.

It shall be the duty of the Council in such cases to recommend to the several Governments concerned what effective military, naval, or air force the Members of the League shall severally contribute to the armed forces to be used to protect the covenants of the League.

The Members of the League agree, further, that they will mutually support one another in the financial and economic measures which are taken under this article, in order to minimise the loss and inconvenience resulting from the above measures, and that they will mutually support one another in resisting any special measures aimed at one of their number by the Covenant-breaking State, and that they will take the necessary steps to afford passage through their territory to the forces of any of the Members of the League which are co-operating to protect the covenants of the League.

Any Member of the League which has violated any Covenant of the League may be declared to be no longer a Member of the League by a vote of the Council concurred in by the Representatives of all the other Members of the League represented thereon.

ARTICLE XVII

In the event of a dispute between a Member of the League and a State which is not a Member of the League, or between States not Members of the League, the State or States not Members of the League shall be invited to accept the obligations of membership of the League for the purposes of such dispute, upon such conditions as the Council may deem just. If such invitation is accepted the provisions of Articles XII to XVI inclusive shall be applied with such modifications as may be deemed necessary by the Council.

Upon such invitation being given the Council shall immediately institute an inquiry into the circumstances of the dispute and recommend such action as may seem best and most effectual in the circumstances.

If a state so invited shall refuse to accept the obligations of membership in the League for the purpose of such dispute, and shall resort to war against a Member of the League, the provisions of Article XVI shall be applicable as against the State taking such action.

If both parties to the dispute when so invited refuse to accept the obligations of membership in the League for the purposes of such dispute, the Council may take such measures and make such recommendations as will prevent hostilities and will result in the settlement of the dispute.

(All these provisions are new, and together they mark an enormously important advance in international relations.)

ARTICLE XVIII

Every treaty or international engagement entered into hereafter by any Member of the League shall be forthwith registered with the Secretariat and shall as soon as possible be published by it. No such treaty or international engagement shall be binding until so registered.

(This clause is aimed at securing so-called 'open diplomacy'. It was the custom before the War for Governments to accompany treaties concluded by them and actually published, with secret understandings which did not see the light of day. This will henceforth be impossible. It is particularly encouraging to realise that the use of publicity in international affairs at last seems realised. The obscure issues from which international quarrels arise will be dragged out into the light of day, and the creation of an informed public opinion made possible. It is a subject upon which much might be written.)

ARTICLE XIX

The Assembly may from time to time advise the reconsideration by Members of the League of treaties which have become inapplicable and the consideration of international conditions whose continuance might endanger the peace of the world.

ARTICLE XX

The Members of the League severally agree that this Covenant is accepted as abrogating all obligations or understanding *inter se* which are inconsistent with the terms thereof, and solemnly undertake that they will not hereafter enter into any engagements inconsistent with the terms thereof.

In case any Members of the League shall, before becoming Members of the League, have undertaken any obligations inconsistent with the terms of this Covenant, it shall be the duty of such a Member to take immediate steps to procure its release from such obligations.

ARTICLE XXI

Nothing in this Covenant shall be deemed to affect the validity of international engagements such as treaties of arbitration or regional understandings like the Monroe Doctrine for securing the maintenance of peace.

(This is aimed at reassuring American sensitiveness with regard to the inviolability of their Monroe Doctrine whereby European powers were warned off transatlantic territory and transatlantic politics by the then President of the United States, James Monroe (1817–1825), who did not want America becoming a theatre for the intrigues of European absolutism, and of their 'gentlemen's agreement' with Japan as to immigration of yellow labour into the Pacific states.)

ARTICLE XXII

To those colonies and territories which as a consequence of the late War have ceased to be under the sovereignty of the States which formerly governed them and which are inhabited by peoples not yet able to stand by themselves under the strenuous conditions of the modern world, there should be applied the principle that the well-being and development of such peoples form a sacred trust of civilisation and that securities for the performance of this trust should be embodied in this Covenant.

The best method of giving practical effect to this principle is that the tutelage of such peoples should be entrusted to advanced nations who by reason of their resources, their experience, or their geographical position, can best undertake this responsibility, and who are willing to accept, and that this tutelage should be exercised by them as Mandatories on behalf of the League.

The character of the mandate must differ according to the stage of the development of the people, the geographical situation of the territory, its economic conditions, and other similar circumstances.

Certain communities formerly belonging to the Turkish Empire have reached a stage of development where their existence as independent nations can be provisionally recognised subject to the rendering of administrative advice and assistance by a Mandatory until such time as they are able to stand alone. The wishes of these communities must be a principal consideration in the selection of the Mandatory.

Other peoples, especially those of Central Africa, are at such a stage that the Mandatory must be responsible for the administration of the territory under conditions which will guarantee freedom of conscience or religion, subject only to the maintenance of public order and morals, the prohibition of abuses such as the slave trade, the arms traffic, and the liquor traffic, and the prevention of the establishmennt of fortifications or military and naval bases and of military training of the natives for other than police purposes and the defence of territory, and will also secure equal opportunities for the trade and commerce of other Members of the League.

There are territories, such as South-West Africa and certain of the South Pacific Islands, which, owing to the sparseness of their population, or their small size, or their remoteness from the centres of civilisation, or their geographical contiguity to the territory of the Mandatory, and other circumstances, can be best administered under the laws of the Mandatory as integral portions of its territory, subject to the safeguards above mentioned in the interests of the indigenous population.

In every case of mandate, the Mandatory shall render to the Council an annual report in reference to the territory committed to its charge.

The degree of authority, control, or administration to be exercised by the Mandatory shall, if not previously agreed upon by the Members of the League, be explicitly defined in each case by the Council.

A permanent Commission shall be constituted to receive and examine the annual reports of the Mandatories and to advise the Council on all matters relating to the observance of the mandates.

(The collapse of the Central Powers and Russia, together with the strain throughout the War, led in 1919 to something like a European debacle. Sections of old empires and kingdoms had shot off and floated pilotless. Were all these to be regarded as booty for the victors, to be the objects of a scramble now and a constant cause for wrangle through the ages? To a thoughtful student of the centuries-old growth of the British Empire, to a Briton or a man from the Dominions, of strong imperial views, it would seem but a concrete recognition of a commonplace of our imperial doctrine, in that it took from us the theory that our power was but a trust administered in the interest of those we have been called to rule.)

ARTICLE XXIII

Subject to and in accordance with the provisions of international conventions existing or hereafter to be agreed upon, the Members of the League

(*a*) will endeavour to secure and maintain fair and humane conditions of labour for men, women, and children, both in their own countries and in all countries to which their commercial and industrial relations extend, and for that purpose will establish and maintain the necessary international organisations;

(*b*) will undertake to secure just treatment of the native inhabitants of territories under their control;

(*c*) will entrust the League with the general supervision over the execution of agreements with regard to the traffic in women and children, and the traffic in opium and other dangerous drugs;

(*d*) will entrust the League with the general supervision of the trade in arms and ammunitions with the countries in which the control of this traffic is necessary in the common interests;

(*e*) will make provision to secure and maintain freedom of communications and of transit and equitable treatment for the commerce of all Members of the League. In this connection, the special necessities of the regions devastated during the War of 1914–18 shall be borne in mind;

(*f*) will endeavour to take steps in matters of international concern for the prevention and control of disease.

ARTICLE XXIV

There shall be placed under the direction of the League all international bureaux already established by general treaties if the parties to such treaties consent. All such international bureaux and all commissions for the regulation of matters of international interest hereafter constituted shall be placed under the direction of the League.

In all matters of international interest which are regulated by general conventions but which are not placed under the control of international bureaux or commissions, the Secretariat of the League shall, subject to the consent of the Council and if desired by the parties, collect and distribute all relevant information and shall render any other assistance which may be necessary or desirable.

The Council may include as part of the expenses of the Secretariat the expenses of any bureau or commission which is placed under the direction of the League.

ARTICLE XXV

The Members of the League agree to encourage and promote the establishment and cooperation of duly authorised voluntary national Red Cross organisations having as purposes the improvement of health, the prevention of disease, and the mitigation of suffering throughout the world.

ARTICLE XXVI

Amendments to this Covenant will take effect when ratified by the Members of the League whose Representatives compose the Council and by a majority of the Members of the League whose Representatives compose the Assembly.

No such amendment shall bind any Member of the League which signifies its dissent therefrom, but in that case it shall cease to be a Member of the League.

> *(There is a chance that the mass of men may rally to a constructive Internationalism which preserves and not destroys the tradition of the nation State. It is wise neither to talk, nor to pitch our hopes, too high. The new diplomacy is bounded with the same limits as the old. The men who will serve the new diplomacy are certainly not wiser than the men who served the old; they certainly have less experience of international affairs. Capitalist greed and mob ignorance have at times informed the foreign policy of states ever since man gave way to his gregarious instinct. The old Chancelleries were, in the last resort, the servants of the state, alike in monarchies and in republics. The Geneva delegates will find themselves the same. They will only have rather better instruments to work with. To sum up in a sentence, the nations have pledged themselves not to go to war without waiting for reason to have its chance.)*

ORIGINAL MEMBERS OF THE LEAGUE OF NATIONS

Belgium, Bolivia, Brazil, British Empire (Australia, Canada, India, New Zealand, South Africa), China, Cuba, Czecho-Slovakia, Ecuador, France, Greece, Guatemala, Haiti, Hedjaz, Honduras, Italy, Japan, Liberia, Nicaragua, Panama, Peru, Poland, Portugal, Rumania, Serb-Croat-Slovene State, Siam, United States of America (signatory of the Treaty of Peace but never formally seated in the League), Uruguay.

STATES INVITED TO ACCEDE TO THE COVENANT

Argentine Republic, Chile, Colombia, Denmark, Netherlands, Norway, Paraguay, Persia, Salvador, Spain, Sweden, Switzerland, Venezuela.

WHO IS WHO IN THE BOOK

ATTOLICO*, PROFESSOR BERNARDO, Italian, Political section.

AVENOL*, JOSEPH, French, Deputy Secretary-General (1920–32), Secretary-General (1932–40).

BAGE*, FREDA (1883–1970), lecturer in biology at University of Queensland and then Principal of Women's College, Australian delegate to League of Nations Assembly 1926 and 1938.

BAILEY, CAROLINE, South African, clerk in Précis-writing, and would-be author.

BARTOU, Swiss, Under Secretary-General.

BAUER*, GEORGE, American, executive officer of the League of Nations. Non-Partisan Association which campaigned to get the US into the League.

BENES*, DR EDUARD, President of Czecho-Slovakia at the time of the Munich agreement and highly respected delegate to the League.

BERRY, EDITH CAMPBELL, Australian, member of Secretariat.

BOCHUT*, night watchman of the Palais Wilson.

BRIAND*, ARISTIDE, Prime Minister and Foreign Minister of France, great supporter of the League of Nations, received the Nobel Prize for Peace in 1926. Died in 1932.

BUTLER*, SIR GEOFFREY KBE, MA Fellow, Librarian and Lecturer in International Law and Diplomacy of Corpus Christi College, Cambridge.

BUXTON*, ANTHONY, English, personal assistant to Sir Eric.

CECIL*, LORD ROBERT, member of House of Commons, sometime member of cabinet, dedicated British proponent of the idea of a League of Nations, frequent member of British delegation, helped draft the Covenant.

CHAIES*, RACHEL, Rumanian, journalist for Rador press agency.

* Actual person

CLÉRAMBAULT*, G. G., French psychiatrist famous for his lectures on drapery and clothing at the École des Beaux-Arts, and for his collection of 40,000 photographs of draped costumes.

COLBAN* ERIC, Norwegian, Minorities section.

COLUM*, MARY, US journalist and friend of James Joyce.

COMERT*, PIERRE, French, Director of Information section.

COOPER, CLAUDE, South African, Edith's immediate superior.

CROWDY*, DAME RACHEL (1884–1964), English, Head of Social Questions section from 1919 to 1930 (this section changed its name a few times over the years). Dame Rachel was one of the first professional social workers and had a distinguished record during the First World War behind the front lines as Commandant of the Volunteer Aid Detachment (VAD) for which she was made a Dame of the British Empire. She was never officially made Director of the section but she was the only woman who headed a section during the history of the League, although for a time Florence Wilson was in charge of the library and Nancy Williams was in charge of personnel.

CURZON*, GEORGE NATHANIEL (1859–1925), Foreign Minister of UK, and Viceroy of India. He represented the UK at the first meeting of the League Council.

CUSHENDEN*, LORD, British member of Cabinet, led 1928 delegation to the League.

DICKINSON*, ANNIE, English, ran a workshop-school in Yugoslavia for war orphans.

DICKINSON*, SIR WILLOUGHBY, British campaigner for League of Nations.

DIXON*, GERTRUDE, Irish, editor of the *Official Journal* of the League.

DOLE, ROBERT, English, journalist for the London *Telegraph*.

DRUMMOND*, SIR ERIC, English, Secretary-General (1919–22) was born in 1876, a member of a prominent Catholic family, educated at Eton, entered the Foreign Office. Was successively private secretary to Asquith as Prime Minister, and to Lord Grey and Balfour as Foreign Secretaries. He accompanied Balfour on his American visit in 1917 and was Lord Grey's secretary at the 1920 Peace Conference. After retiring from the League he became British ambassador to Italy.

DUFOUR-FERONCE*, F.A., German, Director of the International Cooperation section.

DUPONT, Swiss, Chef de Securité at the Hôtel Richemond and later at the Hôtel Metropole.

FIGGIS*, MISS P., MBE, Irish, assistant to Dame Rachel Crowdy.

FOLLETT, BERNARD, Swiss, owner-manager of the Molly Club, Geneva.

FORSTALL*, JAMES JACKSON, investor, friend of the League.

GALTON*, FRANCIS, British founder of science of genetics who together with Florence Nightingale created the eugenicist movement.

HOWARD*, MISS J. 'TIGER', English, private secretary to Sir Eric Drummond.

HUNEEUS, Deputy President in the Azerbaijani government-in-exile.

HUSTON*, H. R., American, Internal Services.

INGERSOLL*, COLONEL ROBERT GREEN (1833–99), lawyer, Attorney-General Illinois, friend of Mark Twain and Walt Whitman, campaigner against religion and for liberal causes.

JACKLIN*, S., South African, Financial Section.

JEANNE, French, Intellectual Cooperation section.

JEROME, US, horn player with Eddie South's Alabamians.

JOSHI, ARUN, Indian, doctor in Health section.

JULES, Russian, Internal Administration, messenger.

KELEN*, EMERY, Hungarian, caricaturist world famous in the 1920s and '30s for his cartoons of the League.

KENNEDY, MR, American, associate of Captain Strongbow.

LANGER, SOPHIE, English, International Labour Organisation.

LATHAM*, JOHN, Australian (1877–1964) one-time deputy Prime Minister, Minister for External Affairs, Federal Attorney General, several times delegate to League of Nations Assembly, became Chief Justice of the High Court 1935. First President of the League of Nations Union in Australia.

LIVERRIGHT, HOWARD, Austrian, Translating Section.

LLOYD*, F. I., English, Building Services.

MALLET*, SIR BERNARD, former Registrar-General for England and Wales, active in the Eugenics Society.

MANTOUX*, PAUL, French, Political section.

MASARYK*, JAN, Czech, diplomat, one of the founders of Czechoslovakia.

McDOWELL, GEORGE, Australian, businessman.

McGEACHY*, MARY, Canadian, Information section. Became the first woman appointed to the British diplomatic service. Served with UNRRA following World War II. Executive of International Council of Women.

McKINNON WOOD*, H., English, Legal section.

MERRIDALE, CHRISTINA, American community Geneva.

MILLER*, DAVID HUNTER, American, adviser to US delegation, co-author of the discussion draft of the Covenant used at the 1920 Peace Conference.

MONNET*, JEAN, French Under Secretary in charge of Internal Administration until the appointment of Marquis Paulucci.

NANSEN*, DR FRIDTJOF, Norwegian, famous Arctic explorer, first Commissioner of Refugees, created the Nansen passport for stateless people.

NICOLSON*, HAROLD, British diplomat and writer, attended Paris Peace Conference, participated in early days of the League.

PAULUCCI*, MARQUIS DI CALBOLI BARONE, Italian, Under Secretary-General, first appointment from Mussolini's regime.

PEARSON*, KARL (1857–1936), mathematician, first Galton Professor of National Eugenics (1911) at the University of London and at University College. In his book *The Grammar of Science*, he attempted to apply scientific training to social questions. Considered 'the father of statistics'.

RAPPARD*, WILLIAM, Swiss, Director Mandates section (1920–25), delegate, diplomat.

RICHIE*, ALISON, South African, typist, author of *The Peacemakers*, Hogarth Press (1928).

ROSTING, Italian, Internal Services.

SAINTSBURY*, GEORGE (1845–1933), in his day a very well-known newspaper book reviewer, held Chair of English Literature at Edinburgh, known as the 'king of critics'.

SANGER*, MARGARET (1883–1966), American birth-control reformer, teacher, nurse, argued for women's right to control the size of their families. Opened first birth control clinic in US.

SATOW*, SIR ERIC, British barrister and diplomat, author of *A Guide to Diplomatic Practice* (1917).

SHEARER*, WILLIAM B., American, arms lobbyist, Geneva.

SOUTH*, EDDIE (1904–62), American, jazz musician, toured Europe with the Alabamians in the '20s, child prodigy on violin, educated Illinois College of Music.

STRESEMANN*, GUSTAV, German Minister for Foreign Affairs, and Chancellor, who negotiated the entry of Germany into the League of Nations. He shared the Nobel Peace Prize in 1926 with Briand. He died in 1930.

STRONGBOW, ATHENA, wife of Captain Strongbow.

STRONGBOW, CAPTAIN, US, adventurer, internationalist.

SWANWICK*, HELENA MARIA, English, several times UK delegate to Assembly, editor of *Foreign Affairs*, activist in the Union for Democratic Control.

SWEETSER*, ARTHUR, American, Information section, informally responsible for League relations with the United States.

TRAVERS, FLORENCE, Canadian, book-keeper Finance.

TREITSCHKE*, HENRICK VON, German historian, advocated power politics.

VICTORIA, New Zealander, Registry section.

VOLKERBUND*, (German for League of Nations) dog belonging to the night watchman of the Palais Wilson, M. Bochut.

WALLACE*, THEODOSIA ADA, Australian author of *The Etiquette of Australia*.

WEISS*, MME, French, international affairs expert.

WENZ*, PAUL, French author who lived in Australia and worked as farmer.

WESTWOOD, AMBROSE, English, personal staff of Sir Eric Drummond, later in Internal Services.

WILLIAMS*, MISS NANCY, English, head of Personnel.

ZILLIACUS*, STELLA, British, daughter of Konni Zilliacus, Information section.

ZIMMERN*, SIR ALFRED, Wilson Professor of International Politics,

University College of Wales, Aberystwyth, Deputy Director of the Intellectual Cooperation Organisation, Director of the Geneva School of International Studies, played a role in the formation of Unesco.

ACKNOWLEDGEMENTS

Of all the curious things which happen to an author during the writing of a book, my meeting with Mary McGeachy, a member of the early Secretariat of the League, was one of the most memorable and unexpected.

For the foundations of my fiction, I had been using material in Geneva from the League of Nations archive at the Rockefeller Library. I worked under the guidance of the remarkable Swedish archivist, Sven Welander, to whom I owe a very special debt. He directed my attention to the career of a young Canadian woman, Mary McGeachy, who joined the Information section in the twenties. As I read the files, mostly unopened for fifty years or more, her life in the Secretariat began to fill my mind and to inform my book as I wrote it. Although I did not use her directly as a main character and the book is not her life story, Mary McGeachy did become a guiding spirit for the book.

My preoccupation with her life led me to make enquiries about whether she had deposited her personal papers with another library. The papers weren't in the National Library of Canada and two Canadian historians with an interest both in the period and in women's studies couldn't help me.

While I was working at the archives in Geneva, I began visiting the French town of Besançon. On my second visit to Besançon I met, by chance, a Canadian couple, Donald and Flora Harris, of London, Ontario, who were on vacation in France. Naturally, I talked about my project and mentioned my preoccupation with Mary McGeachy.

They became curious and said that they had lived next door to a Don McGeachy in London, Ontario, about twenty years before. We agreed that it was possible that this was the same family. Eventually the address of Don McGeachy was passed on to me and I wrote to him about my project. Almost a year after my chance meeting with the

Canadians at the dinner party in Besançon, a letter came from him saying that he had discovered that Mary McGeachy was, in fact, alive, and was living in upstate New York, aged ninety-two.

She was, as far as I could ascertain, the only living survivor of the Secretariat from those earlier days of the League, from among the band of officers, who came to Geneva for this great experiment. Mary McGeachy was living with her adopted daughter, Janet Holmes, and her son-in-law, David, in upstate New York. I went to Keene Valley where they lived, and I spent days talking with Mary McGeachy. Mary McGeachy died on 1 November 1991.

I came across some lines from a poem by Stephen Spender which I think are a just description of Mary McGeachy and her fellow officers:

> . . . they travelled a short while toward the sun
> And left the vivid air signed with their honour.

I thank Jacqueline McNaughton who led me to her relative in Paris, Marceau Hautrive, aged ninety-four who worked as an interpreter with the League in 1920.

I refer readers who would like to know more of Edith to my book *Forty-Seventeen* which deals with her much later in her life. George McDowell features in *The Electrical Experience* (Angus and Robertson).

The title of the episode 'Cry Me a River' is taken from the title of a song written by Arthur Hamilton.

The episode 'Confidence and the Giving of Confidences' loosely adapts sections from the book, *The Peacemakers*, by Alice Ritchie, Hogarth Press (1928) — the most interesting English language novel to have come out of the League period that I have come across. I would like to pay tribute to her. I am grateful to her sister Trekkie Parsons for other valuable information.

I want to thank the following people for help with research and other matters related to the book: Senator Patricia Giles who gave me accommodation and assistance in Canberra during my research there; Tim and Julie Baker; Brian and Suzanne Kiernan; Meredith Sime; Judy Rymer; Annie Hollander; Rob Crooks, for accommodation in Washington; John McManus and Professor Bruce Johnson who helped as music consultants; Norma King, Nowra Red Cross; Richard Hall, whose background in politics and whose fine library and memory assisted me; Don Anderson, one of my kitchen critics who looked after the home front; Jenny Carleton, who carried my computer 20,000 kilometres; the editor of the *Sydney Review*, Michael Vanstone and the editor of the *Adelaide Review*, Christopher Pearson who were, in their own inestimable way, honourable patrons of the project; Errol Sullivan, of Southern Star Films who showed faith; Gilles and Carla Brepsant of Geneva who helped me in those first few weeks in Geneva with accommodation and guidance, along with Shelagh Rogers who helped with curses, French, and companionship; Kasia Koralewska-Skibinska and Leshek Skibinsky, of Geneva for advice and friendship; Simone and Jean-Pierre Rosset, who helped with accommodation; Bernard Zumthor, Conseiller en conservation du patrimoine architectural pour la Ville de Genève; and Bernard Erbeia and his wife Miriam, of Geneva, for arranging for me to see the Palais Wilson.

To Besançon I owe a special debt. I spent two years in this beautiful Renaissance city writing my book and while there I was warmly welcomed and helped by many people who opened their libraries and homes to me. I especially wish to thank Roslyn Young who was not only one of my French teachers, but whose personal generosity helped me and the book in many ways. I also thank my other French teachers, John Olsen, Suzette Lachaise, and Christiane Rozet. I thank Dr Danièle Olsen (who occasionally looked after my health), Donna and Alain L'Hôte, Dr Pierre-André Peuteuil (who was my consultant on psychiatric matters) and his wife Nancy, and Lois Rose, Debbi Hicks, Glenys Hanson and Christian Bastian. I thank Isabelle and Philippe Dubois at La Chamade, my favourite restaurateurs, in whose restaurant I wrote some of the book and who put up with my poor French and who saw me in many moods.

I wish to acknowledge assistance and encouragement, in many forms, from the Australia Council, especially Max Bourke, the Literature Board, the Australian Film Commission, the Department of Foreign Affairs, the Department of Army, and Qantas.

I appreciated the advice and work of Professor Martin Dubin of Northern Illinois University and of Anique H. M. van Ginneken, both specialists in the League of Nations. I am grateful for the information and courtesies extended me by fellow writer and child of the League days, Lady Wallinger (formerly Stella Zilliacus).

I wish to acknowledge the valued support and guidance of my editor at Pan Macmillan Australia, Jane Palfreyman, and to thank the managing director of Pan Macmillan Publishers Australia, James Fraser, who showed faith and came to the rescue a number of times during the writing of the book. I want to also thank my editor at Pan Macmillan UK, Georgia Garrett, for her commitment and editorial advice.

I appreciate the special commitment brought to the book by my UK agent Derek Johns.

In 1986 I was awarded the Sir Harold White Fellowship at the Australian National Library to study the library's holdings of documents and personal papers connected with the League, especially the papers of John Latham. This was of immense value to me and as the first fiction writer to receive the Fellowship I am especially grateful to the trustees of the Fellowship and to the Library. The Library assisted me in finding my way into the project and in planning its future directions. I especially wish to thank John Thompson, Indulus Kepars, Pam Ray, William Thorn, and the Director-General, Warren Horton. A number of other libraries and librarians helped me with the book. They are the Rockefeller Library in Geneva; the library of the Institute for the Study of International Relations in Geneva; the Fisher Library at the University of Sydney; Wolfson College Library, Oxford; Rhodes Library, Oxford; the American Library in Paris; and the Université de Franche-Comté library in Besançon, France.

Military and diplomatic officers also helped me. To inform myself on matters of international organisation, I visited the multinational peace keeping force in the Sinai Desert in 1982. There I was helped by troops from the Australian, Fijian and Swedish contingents especially Lieutenant-General Fredrik Bull-Hansen, Lieutenant-Colonel Jim Sanday, and Captain Steve Meekin. I went to Lebanon during the siege of Beirut and owe special debt to members of the Israeli Defence Forces and the Christian Militia Forces Lebanese. As an accredited writer, I observed the dramatic 1986 renegotiation of the nuclear nonproliferation treaty in Geneva, mixing then with the various delegations, and I also observed the General Conference of the International Atomic

Energy Agency in Vienna again with contacts with the delegations. Captain Peter Bartu of UNTAC in Cambodia also helped. During the development and writing of the book I was the guest at a number of embassies and thank the following ambassadors, spouses and staff for their hospitality and advice: Owen Harries and his wife Dorothy, Gough Whitlam and his wife Margaret, Peter Curtis and his wife Chantal, Kim Jones and his wife Elizabeth, John Rowland and his wife Moira, Richard Butler, Mark Pierce in Israel, and Gregson and his wife Maria Edwards in Vienna.

Two people generously offered to read the book in manuscript as specialist readers and gave very valuable advice: Carol Miller, St Hilda's College, Oxford, who also shared her work on Dame Rachel Crowdy and the League of Nations with me, and Owen Harries, editor of *National Interest* and a former ambassador to Unesco.

I thank my lawyer Nick Dettmann, and his wife, Carol Dettmann (who in 1969 edited my first book, *Futility and Other Animals*), and who have been friends, patrons and advisers. I owe much to my agent, and friend of many years, Rosemary Creswell, and her associate Linda Funnell, who both gave a high level of personal, technical and creative help above and beyond the role of their office. I thank Murray Sime who has been my friend and exasperated financial adviser over a number of years. He was steadfast during the writing of this book. I thank Susie Carleton, faithful patron and friend.

I pay tribute to Jean-Paul and Monique Delamotte of Paris, who facilitated, encouraged, accommodated, and tolerated me during the different European parts of the making of this book, and who, when I was younger, gave me my first deep introduction to France and who have continued over the years to guide me in my enjoyment of France.

I pay tribute to my mother and father who lived through the historical period of this book and who have helped me with their recollections and by just being, inescapably, representatives of that time.

Finally, and especially, I would like to pay tribute to Christine Allsopp who shared with me the experience and difficulties of writing this book, in Geneva and Besançon, and who helped and supported me in many, many ways.

FRANK MOORHOUSE
April 1993